More Praise for *Damascus Gate*

"Here is our masterpiece writer, Robert Stone, writing his book of books, his millennial novel of the millennial place. . . . Here are Stone's most magnified, vivid, lunatic, and tender characters. Christopher Lucas engages us profoundly: a modest wit, who keeps faith in a faithless world. . . . *Damascus Gate* is a narrative of good and evil written in letters of fire."
—Annie Dillard

"A major work in every aspect . . . bold and bracing, ambitious and inspired, *Damascus Gate* is . . . an astonishment."
—*Publishers Weekly*

"Robert Stone is an explorer who takes his readers to the fractured edges of the known world. *Damascus Gate* is a triumph. Stone at the height of his powers."
—Ward Just

"Complex, brilliant . . . *Damascus Gate* keeps our attention riveted . . . fiction that combines the pleasure of a thriller with those of a novel of ideas."
—Francine Prose, *The New York Observer*

"A superb thriller."
—Amazon.com

"Erudite eschatological noir. A marvelous novel. Never has the 'Holy Land' appeared so diabolical, beckoning, and strange."
—Joy Williams

"Robert Stone remains Robert Stone, America's most astonishing novelist. And *Damascus Gate* is his finest novel to date."
—David Bowman, author of *Bunny Modern,* writing for BandN.com

"Page-turner of the week."
—J. D. Reed, *People*

als who yearn for more. . . . This ambitious, exhilarating novel is a major work that is as rewarding as any book I have read in a long while."
—James A. Schiff, *Cincinnati Enquirer*

"In his sprawling new novel, *Damascus Gate,* Stone . . . offers up a feverish visions of what spiritual faith means at the end of the twentieth century."
—Jennifer Howard, *Civilization*

"If you were planning to write a millennial thriller, don't bother. Robert Stone, whose work has always had an apocalyptic tinge, has made the newborn genre redundant with one grand, sweeping, multidimensional novel."
—*Booklist*

"His meticulous research and descriptive flourishes perform well together in this literary thriller. But it certainly should delight the Stone faithful and intrigue readers of Middle Eastern fiction."
—Stan Abbott, *Des Moines Register*

"An astonishing and thrilling novel. By turns scary, funny, and deeply moving. Prose at such a high pitch it sometimes seems hallucinatory. Stone is a genius."
—Frank Conroy

"The soul of this amazing book is the perennial human quest for the ultimate high. It's worth a little work to take this thrilling ride through *Damascus Gate.*"
—David Crumm, *Detroit Free Press*

"The best suspense writing Stone's done."
—Bob Hoover, *Pittsburgh Post-Gazette*

"A master of the urgent action scene, Stone is at his finest here when he's inside the dramatic volatility of Jerusalem and Gaza."
—Gail Caldwell, *The Boston Globe*

"Combining the intrigue and pacing of a thriller with the moral and spiritual investigation of serious literature."
—Lloyd Sachs, *Chicago Sun-Times*

"The writing, often dense with metaphor and landscape, is powerful and the result is a pulsing, profound novel about the treacheries of absolute conviction. A."
—L. S. Klepp, *Entertainment Weekly*

"*Damascus Gate* looks at the clash and tangle of faiths in the Middle East. Robert Stone had to face up to his own beliefs to write it."
—Josh Getlin, *Los Angeles Times*

"A culmination of Stone's recurring themes."
—Joan Smith, *San Francisco Examiner*

"Everyone in this novel is compelled—toward love, sex, drugs, faith, power, or revenge—in a profoundly moving story of religion and warfare set in the perilous boil of contemporary Jerusalem. Robert Stone takes us, as ever, into the dark dangerous, unmapped places."
—Frederick Busch

"At the heart of Robert Stone's books is the quest for something to believe in."
—Dan Cryer, *Newsday*

"*Damascus Gate* is an ambitious and powerful novel."
—James Shapiro, *Fortune*

"*Damascus Gate* is about a plot to blow up the holy places of Jerusalem by an assortment of religious maniacs, international psychopaths, and political manipulators. It is also a fierce take on the mysteries of the spirit. I know of no other contemporary novelist who has Stone's gift for combining intellectual depth and unrelenting narrative drive."
—A. Alvarez

ROBERT STONE

DAMASCUS GATE

Scribner Paperback Fiction
Published by Simon & Schuster

SCRIBNER PAPERBACK FICTION
Simon & Schuster Inc.
Rockefeller Center
1230 Avenue of the Americas
New York, NY 10020

First Scribner Paperback Fiction edition 1999
Reprinted by special arrangement with Houghton Mifflin Company.

SCRIBNER PAPERBACK FICTION and design are trademarks of Jossey-Bass, Inc.,
used under license by Simon & Schuster, the publisher of this work.

Designed by Robert Overholtzer

Maps by Jacques Chazaud

Manufactured in the United States of America

1 3 5 7 9 10 8 6 4 2

Library of Congress Catalogin-in-Publication Data
Stone, Robert, 1937?–
Damascus Gate / Robert Stone.
—1st Scribner Paperback Fiction ed.
p. cm.
1. Jerusalem—Politics and government—Fiction.
2. Terrorism—Jerusalem—Fiction.
3. Journalists—Israel—Fiction. I. Title.
[PS3569.T6418D36   1999]
813'.54—dc21   99-12233
CIP

ISBN 0-684-85911-4

The author is grateful for permission to quote lines from the following:
"V. Cape Ann" from *Collected Poems 1909–1962* by T. S. Eliot,
copyright 1936 by Harcourt Brace & Company, copyright © 1964, 1963
by T. S. Eliot, reprinted by permission of the publisher. "Rillons, Rillettes"
from *The Mind-Reader*, copyright © 1966 and renewed 1994 by
Richard Wilbur, reprinted by permission of Harcourt Brace & Company.

FOR CANDIDA

Enigma and evasion grow;
And shall we never find Thee out?

— HERMAN MELVILLE, *Clarel*

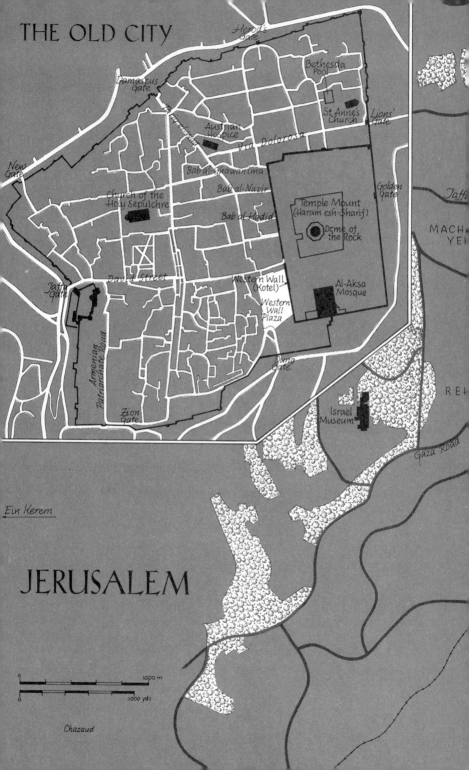

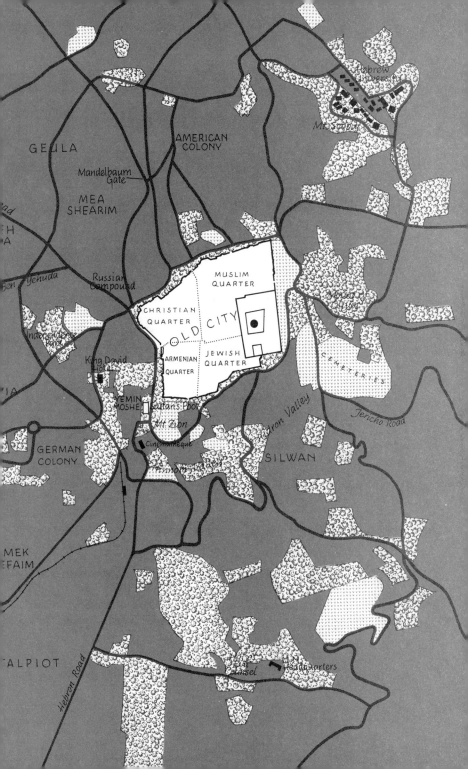

NORTHERN
AND CENTRAL
ISRAEL

S Y R I A

Mt. Hermon

GOLAN
HEIGHTS

Katzrin

Hula Valley

Sea of Galilee
(Kinneret)

Mt. Meron

Safed

G A L I L E E

Capernaum

Tiberias

Yarmuk River

Bet She'an

Nazareth

Jezreel Valley

Megiddo

Mt. Carmel

Mt. Gerezim

S A M A R I A

Haifa

Caesarea

Herzliya

M e d i t e r r a n e a n   S e a

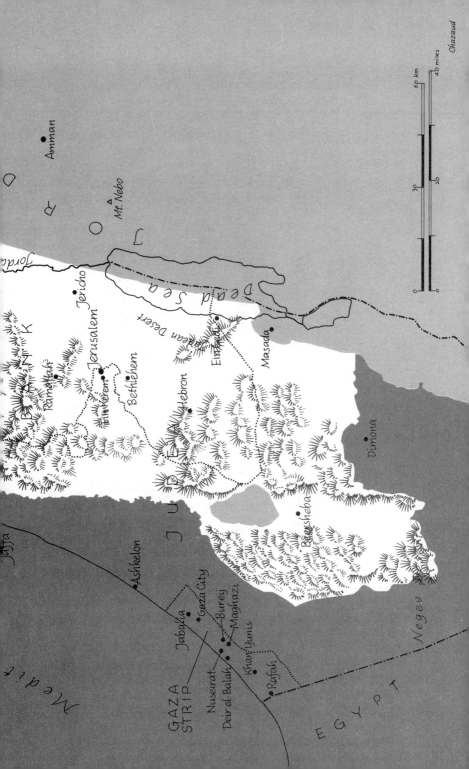

PART ONE

1

T HAT MORNING Lucas was awakened by bells, sounding
across the Shoulder of Hinnom from the Church of the Dormition. At first light there had been a muezzin's call in Silwan,
insisting that prayer was better than sleep. The city was well sup-
plied with divine services.

He climbed out of bed and went into the kitchen to brew Turkish
coffee. As he stood at the window drinking it, the first train of the
day rattled past, bound over the hills for Tel Aviv. It was a slow,
decorous colonial train, five cars of nearly empty coaches with dusty
windows. Its diminishing rhythms made him aware of his own solitude.

When the train was gone, he saw the old man who lived in one of
the Ottoman houses beside the tracks watering a crop of kale in the
early morning shade. The kale was deep green and fleshy against the
limestone rubble from which it somehow grew. The old man wore a
black peaked cap. He had high cheekbones and a ruddy face like a
Slavic peasant's. The sight of him made Lucas imagine vast summer
fields along which trains ran, long lines of gray boxcars against a far
horizon. Once Lucas dreamed of him.

He had grapefruit and toast for breakfast and read the morning's
Jerusalem Post. A border policeman had been stabbed in the Nuseirat camp in the Gaza Strip but was expected to recover. Three Palestinians had been shot to death by Shin Bet hit squads, one in Rafah,
two in Gaza City. *Haredim* in Jerusalem had demonstrated against
the Hebrew University's archeological dig near the Dung Gate; ancient Jewish burial sites were being uncovered. Jesse Jackson was
threatening to organize a boycott against major league baseball. In

India, Hindus and Muslims were fighting over a shrine that probably predated both of their religions. And, in a story from Yugoslavia, he saw again the phrase "ethnic cleansing." He had come across the evocative expression once or twice during the winter.

There was also a full-page story on the number of foreign pilgrims visiting the country for Passover and Western Holy Week. Lucas was surprised to find himself overtaken by the holidays.

He dressed and took a second cup of coffee out on his tiny balcony. The day was innocently glorious; spring sunlight scented the pines and sparkled on the stone walls of Emek Refaim. For weeks he had been postponing work on an article about the Sinai he had contracted to write for Condé Nast. The deadline had passed the previous Friday, and before long they would be phoning him for it. Still, the fine weather inclined him to truancy. When at last he went to his desk, his open appointment book confirmed the date: Easter Sunday in the Latin church and also the sixteenth of Nisan. Passover had arrived the day before. On a sudden impulse Lucas decided to go over to the Church of the Holy Sepulchre.

Bethlehem Road was nearly free of traffic. In spite of its elderly population, Lucas's neighborhood in the German Colony was the most secular in the city and its atmosphere was never one of piety. Old couples strolled in the spring sunshine. The day before, he had seen a few young families loading their Volvos for camping trips in the desert or the Galilee. But walking up the nearly deserted avenue, past the terraces of the Cinematheque, under the ramparts of the Church of Scotland Hospice adorned with its bonny blue flag, he could feel the gravity of the ancient city across the canyon. A hundred tour buses were parked in the streets under the Old City walls. At the distant Jaffa Gate, he could see the swaying forms of mounted policemen herding a pressing crowd of bright pilgrims. At the other end of the fortress, a line of devotees toiled single file up the slope to the Zion Gate.

He walked down into the shadow of the valley, over the bridge by the Sultan's Pool and past the Koranic verse carved in the shell of the Ottoman fountain. "All that is created comes of water," it read. Then, humbled by the looming walls, he trudged up the ascent to Zion.

On the path to Zion Gate, he walked mainly among Orthodox Jewish men in black, bound for the Western Wall. Some of the Jews tried to converse with each other as they climbed, scrambling along the shoulder to keep pace. Besides the *haredim,* there were a few German Catholics on the path because the Dormition Abbey above them was a German church. These pilgrims were of the era before Germans had become once again thin and handsome; many were florid and overweight, too bulkily dressed and perspiring freely. Yet they seemed happy. Most of the men looked plain and decent; they wore sodality pins and carried missals. Some of the women had sweet angelic faces. If they were sixty, Lucas calculated . . . born 1932, thirteen at the end of the war. He had picked up the habit of calculating Germans' ages from the Israelis.

It was a cheerful climb, with a smell of sage and jasmine on the wind and desiccated wildflowers underfoot and voices in Hebrew, Yiddish, German. The great walls reduced everyone, confounding all kingdoms. As he neared the ridge, the bells began again.

Following the file toward the gate, he thought of a prophecy, in a *Midrash* someone had related to him. At the End of Days, multitudes would try to cross the Valley of Hinnom to the holy city. Christians, traversing a bridge of stone, would fall to perdition. Muslims, on a wooden bridge, would follow them. Then the Jews would cross, glorified, on a bridge of gossamer. What about me, Lucas wondered, not for the first time.

The top of the trail was paved and provided for by the Jews of Canada. At its end, the mild children of wicked Edom and the pious men of Israel parted in sweet mutual oblivion, the Germans to their hugely unfortunate yellow abbey, the Jews toward the Western Wall. Lucas went his own way, north on Armenian Patriarchate Road. There he encountered more *haredim* headed for the Wall, putting the confusions of Easter behind them. In front of St. James's Cathedral, teenage Armenian acolytes were dressing their ranks for a Sunday procession.

On this conjunction of sacred seasons, the Jews and the Armenians in the crowded street pretended each other's invisibility without colliding. A half-caste apologizing his way through the crush, Lucas was visited by a notion: that only he could see both sects. That where only the unseen mattered, he was reduced to mere utility, to petty observations and staying out of the way.

Passing under an arch where tilesmiths kept shop, he stopped to examine the posters on the wall beside it. They were all in Armenian and many showed the picture of the new president of the Armenian republic. There were also pictures of armed guerrillas with rifles and bandoliers and black-bordered photographs of young martyrs, slain far away in the Azerbaijani war. It was the season of martyrdom in a banner year for martyrs.

In the main street of the Christian Quarter, a promiscuous babble of pilgrims hurried down the sloping cobbled pavement. One group of Japanese followed a sandaled Japanese friar who held a green pennant aloft. There was a party of Central American Indians of uniform size and shape who stared with blissful incomprehension into the unconvincing smiles of merchants offering knickknacks. There were Sicilian villagers and Boston Irish, Filipinos, more Germans, Breton women in native dress, Spaniards, Brazilians, Québecois.

Palestinian hustlers hissed suggestively, offering guidance. Lucas noticed that the Caravan Bar, his favorite beer joint in the Old City, was shuttered. He had heard something about threats. Cutting through the New Bazaar, he became aware of another closing. Above one of the embroidery shops there had been a loft that once sold not only brass pipes and nargilehs but excellent hashish to smoke in them. Now both shop and loft were derelict. Since the intifada, Lucas had taken to buying his hashish where the thin, handsome German hippies bought theirs, at a kiosk near the Arab bus terminal on Saladin Street. The police never seemed to interfere, Lucas had noticed, probably because the seller was one of their informers.

In the courtyard before the Church of the Holy Sepulchre, he was reunited with the mass of pilgrims. Green-bereted troopers of the Border Police were stationed at every approach to the church and on the adjoining rooftops. Under their guns, the Japanese friar was addressing his flock above the noise of the throng.

The Japanese groups were composed largely of middle-aged women who wore dark jumpers and khaki rain hats of the sort once favored by kibbutzniks. The priest would be telling them, Lucas imagined, the story of Constantine and his mother, Saint Helena — how she had discovered the Holy Sepulchre and the very Rood itself. The Japanese ladies were a motherly lot, and Lucas thought they appeared to like the story. Why not, since it had a pious mother, a dutiful son and a miracle? Then, all at once, he found himself calculating ages again. It had occurred to him that the Franciscan and his party might have come from Nagasaki. Nagasaki had been the most Christian of Japan's cities. All through the war, the Japanese had thought the Americans spared it air raids for that reason.

In the sooty, incensed hollows of the church, he made his way through the rotunda to the undistinguished Catholic chapel in the far corner, moving just ahead of the Japanese. A glum Italian monk stood at the door, snubbing pilgrims who tried to smile at him.

Inside the chapel, some Americans with guitars were plinking unhappily away, accompanying their own sad sing-along of a few socially responsible, with-it numbers from the sacred liturgy of whatever cow college town they called home. Like many visitors, they had been unnerved by the inimitable creepiness of the Holy Sepulchre, a grimly gaudy, theopathical Turkish bathhouse where their childhood saints glared like demented spooks from every moldering wall. Lucas, once born, once baptized, put his hand in the holy water and crossed himself.

"Dark is life, is death," he thought. It was all that came to mind. The text was from Mahler's *Song of the Earth* but he supposed it might be considered a sort of prayer.

"My heart is still and awaits its hour."

He still owned an old record, now nearly unplayable, of his mother singing it in German. In any case, he offered it up to whatever was out there, for whatever purpose. Then he made his way through the press of Japanese and across the gloomy spaces of the Anastasis and up the worn stairs to the Chapel of St. James to hear the Armenian liturgy. Theirs was his favorite.

After a while the Armenians arrived in procession, pausing near the entrance of the church so that their patriarch could kiss the Stone of Unction. Then, preceded by youths carrying candles and monks in pointed hoods, the Armenians of the city trooped up to the chapel and the service began. Lucas, as was his custom, stood off to one side.

For a time, he secretly watched the lustrous-eyed worshipers absorbed in their devotions. The night was always dark in their prayers and everybody far from home. Then — because it was Easter for someone, because the Armenian liturgy was sublime, because it couldn't hurt — he lowered his head in the Jesus Prayer. It was another thing he had picked up around, the mantra of the Oriental Christians, a little like repeating *Nam myoho renge kyo* but with a measure of Berdyayevian soul.

"Lord Jesus Christ, Son of God, have mercy upon me, a sinner."

Properly prayed, repeated, the gaze fixed upon the heart, the breathing controlled — it was supposed to be good for you.

At the very moment of uttering this vain hesychastic repetition, while reflecting on the fond, silly regard for religion he had come to Jerusalem to cure himself of, he was startled from his mooning by a dreadful bellow from the rotunda. Then a rasping scream, echoing dismally through the blasted caverns, freezing the pilgrims in mid-bliss. Even the Armenians missed a beat, and a few of the children moved to the edge of the loft to see what the matter was. Lucas followed, looking down over the railing.

"*Anti-Christus!*"

Below, in the candle-lit spaces of the Anastasis, a *majnoon,* a madman, was running wild. Potbellied, bespectacled, arms spread wide, hands dangling, the *majnoon* appeared to be a Western visitor. Around the Chapel of the Tomb he ran, in fluttery, short-legged, birdlike steps. Worshipers fled him. Under the Emperor's Arch and along the wall of the Greek Catholicon, the man ran screaming, setting the hanging sacristy lamps to swing and clatter on their chains. He seemed to be flapping in an attempt at flight, as though he might take wing and sail up to the vault like a church owl. His face was red and round. His eyes bulged sickly blue. A few young Greek Orthodox acolytes in black cassocks were chasing him.

With formidable agility, the madman succeeded in doubling back on his pursuers toward the Chapel of the Tomb. A candle stand full of burning tapers overturned and people fought their way back from the flames. Around and around the tomb he ran, leading the Greeks in a comic rondelay. Then he peeled off and headed for the Chapel of St. Mary. The gathered Catholics gasped and screamed. The friar at the chapel door moved to close it.

Then the *majnoon* began to shout at length in German. Something about blasphemy, Lucas thought. Something about heathen and thieves. Then he began to swear mechanically. "*Fick . . . Gott in Himmel . . . Scheiss . . . Jesusmaria.*" Echoes ricocheted crazily through the interconnected vaults that made up the church. When the Greeks caught him, he switched to English.

"A den of thieves," the deranged German shrieked. "Fornica-tion," he shouted at a prim young Catholic woman in a white man-tilla. "Strangulation. Blood."

Some of the Greek Orthodox posse stomped out the flaming tapers while the rest hauled their prisoner toward the door and the shafts of spring sunlight. A party of Israeli policemen were waiting there to receive him, looking as though they had seen it all before. Around Lucas, the Armenians prayed harder.

The pilgrims pouring out into the forecourt after the service were abuzz with the untoward incident. The soldiers and border policemen lining the route back toward the Jaffa Gate looked more wary and purposeful than usual. Braced for something more serious, they were hoping to herd the mass of tourists out of the Old City. At the same time, they were under orders to let the Christian pilgrims wander at will, as a demonstration of normalcy and order.

He soon drifted with the crowd into the vaulted souks between the Damascus Gate and the Haram al-Sharif. Lucas had come to move confidently through the Old City, although he sometimes questioned his own confidence. He believed his appearance to be more or less foreign, which, in the Muslim Quarter, was a point in his favor. At a kiosk in the Khan al-Sultan souk, he bought an English-language copy of the PLO newspaper *Al-Jihar*. Displayed in hand, it might be a precaution against attack as well as a way of keeping up with the situation.

The Damascus Gate, with its Ottoman towers and passages and barbarous Crusader revetments, was his favorite place in the city. He took a simple tourist's pleasure in the crowds and the blaring taped Arab music, in the rush provided by the open sacks of spices that were piled in wheelbarrows beside the vendors' stalls. To the Palestinians it was the Bab al-Amud, the Gate of the Column, but Lucas rejoiced in the common English name, the suggestion of a route toward mystery, interior light, sudden transformation. He sat for a while over a Sprite, taking in the sensations of the gate, and then set out quixotically in search of something stronger.

Both his regular spot in Christian Quarter Road and the rooftop garden in the souk had inexplicably closed. The one place he found open was a disreputable tourist trap on the edge of the Christian Quarter that catered to *Wandervogel* and other riffraff from the cheap hostels of East Jerusalem. Like many of the bars on the Palestinian side, it displayed pictures of Christian saints lest the Hamas enforcers mistake the management for bad Muslims.

Three young Scandinavian women with shorn hair were drinking mineral water near the street end of the place. He was surprised to find, tending bar in the back, a middle-aged Palestinian named Charles Habib, who had been his host at the Caravan. He ordered a cold Heineken, and Charles served it to him in a frosted glass.

"I've just come from church," he told his host. "There was a *majnoon*."

Charles was a Greek Catholic from Nazareth. He had come to Jerusalem by way of South Bend, Indiana.

"Lots of *majnoon*," he told Lucas. "Plenty."

"I suppose," Lucas said, "God tells them to come."

Charles stared at him without sympathy.

"I mean," Lucas added, "they form that impression."

"The Protestants are worst," Charles said. "They should stay in America and watch television." He paused and regarded Lucas. "You're Protestant?"

"No," Lucas said. He felt uneasy under Charles's scrutiny. "Catholic."

"Every religion has *majnoon*," Charles observed.

Surprisingly, this was a somewhat new concept in town, where screaming infants had burned before Moloch and the gutters on many occasions had run with blood. But each year, it seemed, the equinoctial moon inspired stranger and stranger doings, usually vaguely Pentecostal in spirit, the spontaneous outpourings of many lands. Once, to be a Protestant had meant to be a decent Yankee schoolmarm or kindly clerical milord. No longer. There had commenced a regular Easter Parade, replete with odd headgear. Anglophone crazies bearing monster sandwich boards screeched emptyeyed into megaphones. Entire platoons of costumed Latin Cristos, dripping blood both real and simulated, appeared on the Via Dolorosa, while their wives and girlfriends sang in tongues or went into convulsions.

Locally decorum, in religion as well as devotion, was prized. One Easter an outraged citizen tossed a bottle at some salsa-dancing fugitives from Cecil B. DeMille; the street stirred and the army ended by firing a few tear-gas canisters. At this, insulted heaven opened and there ensued the melancholy penitential drama "Tear Gas in the Rain," familiar to any all-weather student of the twentieth century's hopes and dreams. The Via Dolorosa became a sad place indeed. Its narrow alleys and their inhabitants were soundly poisoned, and many a mournful wet towel went round that night in the city's hospices and hotels.

"Every religion has," Lucas replied agreeably. His surprise at seeing Charles in such a seedy, possibly druggy joint piqued his curiosity. From time to time, Lucas had thought of recruiting him as a source. In his more daring moods, he imagined writing up a story the other guys had thus far left unexamined.

There were rumors, as the intifada ran its course, that some of the *shebab* — the young Palestinian activists who collected taxes for the Front in East Jerusalem — had entered into certain financial arrangements with some hoodlums on the Israeli side. It was a story related to the tales one heard about official corruption in the Occupied Territories. Something of the sort had surfaced in Belfast the previous year, involving connivance between some IRA protection squads and the Protestant underground across town.

Documenting any projected piece on such a subject sounded like dangerous work, but it was the kind of story that appealed to Lucas. He liked the ones that exposed depravity and duplicity on both sides of supposedly uncompromising sacred struggles. He found such stories reassuring, an affirmation of the universal human spirit. Lucas desperately preferred almost anything to blood and soil, ancient loyalty, timeless creeds.

Since rashly quitting his comfortable and rather prestigious newspaper job the year before, he had been finding life difficult. It was constantly necessary to explain oneself. His calling cards impressed new acquaintances as somehow incomplete. Sometimes he felt like a dilettante. And as a freelance he had become less thrifty, less disciplined and more ambitious. Without the constraints of the newspaper format, the stories he wrote went on and on — naturally enough, since things tended to, and things knew nothing of formats or of newspapers, and it was only a beautiful pretense that the daily paper's readers could be informed. A noble pretense, honestly and diligently pretended. Still, there were alternatives, as far as a story went. Fortunately, though the whole world attended the place, there continued to be more people in Jerusalem who liked to talk than liked to listen.

"It's hard to get a drink in town these days," he told Charles.

Charles made an unpleasant face and opened a beer for himself. Then he glanced toward the street and quickly touched glasses with Lucas.

"They say there are more drugs in town," Lucas rashly offered. Charles owed Lucas a few minor favors, mainly having to do with the expediting of American visas for his relatives, and they had an

understanding that, within the limits of a strict discretion, Lucas
might use Charles as a source.

"Correct," said Charles.

"I thought there might be some surprises there. I thought I might
write about it."

Charles gave him a long, dark look and glanced from side to side.
"You're wrong."

"I'm wrong?"

"You're wrong. Because you know and I know what everyone
knows, so it's not a surprise."

"What's not?"

"One," Charles said, "no surprise. Two, you can't write about
it."

"Well . . ." Lucas began.

"You can't. Who you think you are? Who you got behind you?"

It was a question much to the point, Lucas considered.

"Tell me," Charles asked, "do you know Woody Allen?"

"Not personally."

"Woody is a good guy," Charles declared. "On account of that he
suffers."

"Is that right?"

"Woody came to Palestine," Charles said, savoring his ice-cold
Heineken. "He is himself a Jew. But he saw the occupation and
spoke out. He spoke out against the beatings and shootings. So what
happened? The American papers slandered him. They took the
wife's side."

Lucas affected to ponder the case of Woody Allen.

Charles shrugged with the self-evidentness of it all. "So," he told
Lucas, "forget it. Write about Woody."

"Come on," Lucas said. "Woody Allen never came here." The
cold beer made his eyebrows ache.

"He did," Charles insisted. "Many saw him."

They let the subject drop.

"Write about *majnoon*," Charles suggested.

"Maybe I will. Can I bring them here?"

"Bring them. Spend money."

"Maybe I'll just go away somewhere for a while," Lucas said,
surprising himself with his own confiding impulse.

"I won't be here when you get back," Charles said quietly. "Soon
I'm the last Nazareth Habib around. Then, goodbye."

"*Au revoir,*" Lucas said, and went out and wandered on down the Via Dolorosa, past St. Anne's Church by the Bethesda Pool. It was one place he would not go that day; for several reasons, he dared not. Taxis and *sheruts* waited at the Lions' Gate; he passed them. Across Jericho Road, more pilgrims were descending the Mount of Olives. All at once, Lucas found himself out of energy. The force that had impelled him out into the Easter morning was spent.

One of the drivers accosted him, and he bargained over the price of a taxi ride to the Intercontinental Hotel up the slope. He had the notion of looking down at the city. When they arrived the hotel seemed closed; its glass surfaces were soapy and dark. He got out anyway and crossed the street and looked across to Jerusalem. From where he stood, he could see down into the Temple Mount and over all the rooftops of the walled town. Bells began to sound again, from every direction, their tolling scattered on the incessant wind.

The bright onion-domed cluster of St. Mary Magdalen was below him as he went down the steep cobbled road. Turning the corner, he walked along the church's wall and at the next bend found himself surrounded. Worshipers streamed out through the garden gates outside the church. Two small Russian nuns swathed in black were bowing them home. A Russian priest in vestments stood smoking a cigarette beside the church doors, chatting with two Arab men in stiff Sunday suits.

About half the worshipers were Palestinian, but there was a strong Russian contingent among them. The Russians were mostly women. Many were done up in the distinctly Central European overdressed look that Israeli women of a certain age sometimes affected for special occasions, with more hat than one was used to seeing and fashion boots and a little fur in spite of the weather. Lucas was sure most of them had Israeli passports. And though they chatted happily on the way down to Jericho Road, there was about them a kind of guilty wariness. One or two of the Russians seemed to sense Lucas's gaze on them as they walked, and turned to see that he was not one of them.

They would be surprised, Lucas thought, to know how much he and they had in common. Seeds of light scattered in darkness. Whose? Which?

A young woman not much older than a teenager was walking beside him. Their eyes met and Lucas smiled. She had a haunted look and long, dark eyelashes. Then she spoke to him in Russian, and Lucas could only shake his head and keep smiling. Uneasily, she slowed and let him go on. When everyone levitates, Lucas thought, we'll still be here, looking up Mount Olivet, wondering which way to run.

Lucas had recently had a heated conversation with a fellow journalist on a drive through the Gaza Strip, a Frenchman who was a passionate believer in the Palestinian cause. In the conversation Lucas had tried, as usual, to carry water on both shoulders. The Frenchman had told him off, dismissed him as nothing more than an American. And Israel itself was no better, the Frenchman said, than an American colony, more American than America.

At the time they were deep in the Strip, driving between the unspeakable hovels of the Bureij camp that stretched endlessly toward the desert and those of the Nuseirat camp that were spread out toward the sea. All day they had been seeing angry and despairing faces. They were alone.

"If this place exploded now," Lucas had challenged the Frenchman, "which way would you run? If the balloon went up?"

The Frenchman had replied haughtily that he chose not to think in such a way. This had made Lucas angry. As if there were any other way to think.

"I suggest you try running toward Mecca," Lucas had told him. "Me, I'm gonna run for Fink's."

Fink's was a bar on King George Street in Jerusalem where they knew how to make a martini.

Above the Garden of Gethsemane, he left the Russians and turned off toward the vast Jewish cemeteries above Kidron. Among the white tombs stood black-clad figures, some alone, some in knots of two or three. They were religious Jews reciting psalms at the graves of their dead. Lucas found himself following a limestone ridge between the Hellenistic tombs at the top of the ridge and Jericho Road below. Soon he was a dozen rows above one group of three men. Two were elderly, with broad-brimmed fedoras and huge overcoats. The third was younger; he wore dark slacks and a navy-blue windbreaker. A black and gold kippa was pinned in his hair. Slung around his shoulder on a strap was an automatic rifle.

As he watched, the young man with the rifle slowly turned his head as though he had sensed Lucas's presence behind him. When he saw Lucas there, he turned around to face him. His brow furrowed. The two older men beside him were deep in prayer, their heads bobbing together. Lucas walked on past the young man's stare. He was at loose ends, he thought, distracted.

He strolled back through the Lions' Gate the way he had come. Finding himself in the midst of Easter again, he turned left to follow Tariq al-Wad, where things were quieter. Approaching an open juice shop, he had a moment's craving for something cool and sweet. The old proprietor and his nervous, pockmarked son watched Lucas's approach with frowning concern.

"*Tamarhindi?*" Lucas asked. He stepped up to the counter and saw that in one corner of the shop, concealed from the street, a *majnoon* sat with an odd smile. The *majnoon* wore a Western-style suit and a buttoned-up white shirt. He bore a slight resemblance to Jerry Lewis and his delusions gave him the look of buoyant dementia peculiar to Jerry Lewis fools.

The younger merchant served Lucas a small paper cup of tamarind juice as the *majnoon* watched cheerfully. Lucas took it and sat in an unpainted straight-backed chair where he could see the vaulted street.

In the next instant, a plump young mullah walked past, a teacher at one of the madrasahs of the Bab al-Nazir, probably a Hamas neighborhood warden. He had a quietly exalted look. When he saw Lucas there, his face changed. Hot eyes, the brow of Jehu, then blankness, nullity. From his chair, Lucas returned the imperception.

He had been lured into Jerusalem poker, the game of mutually hostile invisibility he had seen earlier that morning in the Armenian Quarter. At this game he was hardly a contender; with his lack of faith and vague identity he could easily be made to disappear. As his friend Charles had pointed out, he had no one behind him. He sipped his swallow of sweet nectar and thought it over.

If he heeded Charles's warning, Lucas considered, and left the corruption and contraband story alone, he had a different piece in reserve: a human rights number in Gaza. It was a place he liked very little to go. Unlike Judea, it had neither relics nor scenery, and the only antiquities were squalid piles in which, for all the world knew or cared, Samson might still be turning a wheel — blind, in irons, supervised by bored, unhappy young men chain-smoking in their green berets and slung machine guns. Gaza's only resource was bad history on a metaphysical scale; it sat on a joint aslant the beam in the Almighty Eye, attracting retribution in advance, forsaken on credit. Long ago Jeremiah had recommended howling as the most suitable public activity there, and the locals had never been allowed to unlearn it.

Gaza was the data that threatened the human reference point, the degree at which informed engagement began its metabolic breakdown. For the journalistic traveler, the big attraction had always been unrequited man, the thing itself. Seven hundred thousand strong, unrequited man could still support a feature.

A woman Lucas knew in the International Children's Foundation had given him a tip about some Israeli hoodlums who specialized in the beating of teenagers and children whom they suspected of rock throwing near the settlements. The beatings were egregious and outside the rules as generally understood by both sides. Two Foundation workers and a UN Relief and Works Agency employee, trying to protect the kids, had also been attacked.

In the hours before dawn the hoodlums would turn up at the alleged miscreants' homes and beat them senseless, usually leaving a few broken bones. At least one of the band was Arabic-speaking, and their leader had assumed the nom de guerre Abu Baraka, the Father of Mercy. He was said to be a North American and a serving soldier in the Israel Defense Forces.

Nuala Rice, the story's source at the Children's Foundation, was an odd number herself. She was Irish, a hard-case aid worker, a veteran of Beirut, Somalia and the Sudan, who seemed to divide her time between good works and various intrigues, erotic and otherwise. Lucas was somewhat smitten with Nuala but their relationship had always proceeded on the understanding that he was not her type.

Nor, he was discovering, was he necessarily the type for freelancing. It was so hard to get it right, working without the assignment, the rubric, the refuge of a word count. No one behind you. And you represented no one, nothing but your own claim to rectitude in a world of mirages, obsidian mirrors and the mist of battle.

He was still pondering it when the mullah wandered back along the cobbled street. The *majnoon* went out from the shop and smiled his Jerry Lewis smile on the young mullah and kissed him. A biblical kiss, Lucas thought. The mullah beamed and glanced at Lucas to see if the foreigner had seen, in turn, the tenderness, the compassion. Life was so self-conscious in Jerusalem, so lived at close quarters, by competing moralizers. Every little blessing demanded immediate record.

As soon as he stood up, the proprietors of the juice shop commenced to haul their corrugated shutters down. Lucas wandered along the old street in the direction of the Haram. The Bab al-Nazir, the Watchman's Gate, was a treasure trove of Islamic history. He had once been conducted through it by a colleague who knew the Mamluk lintels from the Ottoman, and Umayyad from Ayyubid springing.

The one structure he remembered from the previous tour was an ancient building with five windows and a wide arch of rosy stone, as dizzying and inviting a doorway as Lucas had seen in the city. It was close by the Haram gate itself and according to his colleague had been a guesthouse for Sufis visiting Jerusalem. Passing, he saw that the doorway was open and, on impulse, he went in. Inside he found a hallway with an ornate vaulted ceiling supported by columns that looked older than the Crusades. Lucas took off his shoes and carried them in his hand.

The hallway led to a dusty open courtyard in which potted trees grew. It was overlooked by arched windows covered in filigreed screens. Beyond the courtyard was another, even larger one, surrounded by flat, single-story rooftops with trellises and flower boxes planted with marigolds.

When Lucas turned to retrace his steps, he found a child in his path. The child was about five years old, wearing a gorgeous, velvety flowered dress that looked as though it had once clad the ornament of some faraway cold-weather Christian nursery. She was deeply dark-skinned, as black as a West African, her woolly hair arranged in twin pigtails.

"Hello," said Lucas to the little girl.

The child stood motionless and regarded him sternly. Her eyes were huge and profound. Two small wrinkles of disapproval appeared above one eyebrow. When he stepped toward her she fled, padding barefoot across the court, increasing her speed with each stride. Then Lucas saw that lean figures had appeared at the far end of the court. Men in white turbans, tall, black and lean, were staring at him. Some stood in the courtyard he had passed through earlier, and there were others watching from the low roofs where the marigolds grew. From somewhere inside, he heard a trilling female voice.

It occurred to Lucas that he might have gone where he was unwelcome. He was glad he had taken off his shoes. Ahead of him, the courtyard ended in another doorway that he thought might lead to the street. When he followed it, though, it led nowhere, ending at an ocher wall in which the outline of a sealed doorway still showed faintly.

He turned and walked as briskly as he could in stocking feet, back into the courtyard he had just left. The tall men in turbans stood exactly where they had been, motionless. Lucas nodded cheerfully as he went by. The men were utterly without expression, simply alert, offering neither menace nor comfort. He went by them into the first courtyard, not troubling to look over his shoulder, and went back into the hall of columns. The street door through which he had come was now closed, and the hallway was in cool semi-darkness. The street outside seemed strangely quiet. Then the call to prayer sounded from the Haram a short distance away, and its amplified verses echoed among the columns.

Lucas found himself fascinated by the stone vaulting overhead. It was a beautifully fluted half dome, with lacy lines suggesting the metaphysical. He could well imagine it as the work of dervishes; it seemed impossibly old. And how typical of the city, he thought, that it should be tucked away so obscurely, on an unvisited street behind a moldering door.

Absorbed in the fluting overhead, he was surprised by the slamming of a door. Unshod footsteps sounded from an upper story of the inner court. Out of instinct he moved into the shadow of a column.

A young Arab woman appeared in the hallway. She was drawing a wrap about herself, disappearing into a whirl of cloth. As he watched, she went to the street door and opened it, bringing the daylight down on herself.

Her face and hair were still uncovered, and Lucas saw to his surprise that she was wearing a close-cut afro. Her eyes were striking, enhanced with kohl. Leaning against the doorway, she put her sandals on. Flower patterns were traced on her ankles and the brown skin of her feet, and under her djellaba she appeared to be wearing khaki slacks. Lucas pressed himself farther into the column's shadow. He had the feeling that his several weeks of Arabic classes at the Aelia Capitolina YMCA would not support the weight of explanation that might be required for his eccentric concealment.

Struggling with one sandal, the young woman began to sing.

"Something cool," she sang, to Lucas's astonishment. "I'd like to order something cool."

She flatted her fifth very nicely, and Lucas, who happened to know the next verse, was tempted to sing along. Indeed, he could hardly resist. But he watched silently as she put on the second sandal, pulled up the hood of her robe and hurried outside, leaving Lucas in the timeless gloom.

When he got to the street, she had vanished. He wiped his brow. Who knew to what arcane aspect of the city she might attach? The place was full of secrets.

2

THE GYNECOLOGIST'S OFFICE was on Graetz Street, a pleasant street in the German Colony that was lined with carob trees and Norfolk pines. His name was Kleinholz. As a young man he had practiced on the Grand Concourse in the Bronx and been close to the Communist Party. Sonia represented old times for him.

"I remember your father so vividly," he told her as he wrote out the prescription she desired. "Such a handsome devil."

"He was always attractive," Sonia agreed. "Mom had to keep an eye on him." She had the feeling Kleinholz might not have called her father a handsome devil so readily had he, her father, been white. But she had given up keeping score, and in the present situation Dr. Kleinholz could do no wrong. She accepted the prescription with a silent show of gratitude, repressing her fierce impulse to read it and see how many of the pain pills he had written her. They were for the discomfort associated with her period, but Sonia occasionally used them to promote inner harmony and self-fulfillment, and also gave them to her friend Berger.

"Ever go back to the neighborhood?" Dr. Kleinholz asked her. She had only lived in the Bronx for the first year of her life. Thereafter the Barneses had been more or less lamsters, moving from city to city and job to job until the FBI or some local crusaders discovered them and commenced to queer things. They had looked for labor towns: Youngstown, Detroit, Duluth, Oakland, Tacoma. In the course of their travels during the sixties, they had watched the working class disappear while the New Left rose and fell.

"Once," she told him. "It's mainly Hispanic now. What's left of it."

"It was lovely," Dr. Kleinholz said, laughing sadly. "I hope you remember."

She didn't altogether. She did remember being told it was then one of the few neighborhoods outside Greenwich Village where an interracial couple such as her parents might be comfortable. The landlord was a progressive, a friend of the Party. The old Mexican super had been wounded in Spain.

"Yeah, it was nice," she said.

Everyone said that. Almost all the old southpaws were filled with nostalgia. If everything was so nice, she sometimes thought, what were we all revolting against?

Kleinholz nodded and rose slowly from his desk to shake hands with her. Israel was full of throwbacks, and the doc was clearly one of them. With the spectacles on the end of his nose, the white coat and stethoscope, he looked like the family doctor in a thirties movie.

"I have to ask," Kleinholz said. "What are the designs on your feet?"

She laughed. "They're made with henna. When I worked in Baidoa, we sort of picked it up from the Somali women. Just for fun."

"Good," said Dr. Kleinholz. "I was afraid they were tattoos."

"No," she said. "Just henna."

There was a pharmacy on Emek Refaim and she filled the prescription there. He had written her twenty pills. She also bought some colostomy bags, cotton swabs and cans of liquid diet to go visiting with.

Her apartment was a few blocks beyond, in Rehavia. Once there, she showered and put on the clothes she wore to the Palestinian side of town: shirt and slacks under a Nubian robe and a headscarf. It was a cloak of invisibility across the line. On the Israeli side, Arab workmen sometimes stared at her, wondering what an Arab girl could be doing out and about, alone among the Jews.

She took a bus to the Jaffa Gate. There were still a great many Easter pilgrims about. Sonia left them behind, passing through the quiet courtyards of the Armenian Convent and into the Tariq al-Zat. In the Khan al-Sultan souk, she bought some sweet rolls, candy and fruit.

Sonia was headed for Tariq Bab al-Nazir, an ancient narrow street leading to the Nazir Gate, an entrance to the Muslim holy places through which believers and nonbelievers both could pass. Her friend Berger lived in a tiny garden apartment overlooking the courts of the Ribat al-Mansuri, a tarnished palazzo built by an Ayyubid sultan seven hundred years before for Sufi pilgrims. The palazzo had been by turns a prison, a ruin and a tenement block.

In the years before 1967, a Sufi sheikh, an American of Jewish origin called Abdullah Walter, had lived in the same apartment. As a notable convert, Walter had enjoyed the patronage of al-Husseini, the grand mufti himself.

The ownership had changed after the Six-Day War. Walter had gone to California and died there, leaving behind Berger al-Tariq, his friend and disciple. The municipality had torn down half the building and sealed the windows overlooking the Haram. The site's present owner was an Armenian Uniate tile maker who kept a shop on the Via Dolorosa.

Little black children in white watched her heft her basket through the ancient portico and into the courtyard. Once the Haram's Sudanese guards had been quartered in a building across the street, and black people continued to live in the neighborhood. Sonia had a fantasy going in which she imagined that blacks had always lived there, going all the way back, back even to the pharaoh's Cushite soldiers.

That day she had ballpoint pens for the kiddies.

"Hey, homes," she said when two boys ran up to her. "Hey, wass hap'nin'?"

There were four kiddies and each got a pen before she went upstairs.

The interior of the apartment was dark and perfumed with incense sticks. Berger al-Tariq was on a divan, propped up on cushions. Beside him, face down, was a Simenon, *Maigret en Vacances*.

She put her bags in the corner, beside his sink and hot plate.

"Easter bunny's here," she said. "A few things you might need. Can you eat?"

"Not for a day or two," Berger said. "And then I don't know." He made an unsuccessful effort to rise. "May one ask," he asked primly, "has the Easter bunny brought some colostomy bags?"

"You bet."

She watched him light one of the locally made cigarettes he liked. The backs of his long slender hands were freckled and wonderfully lined with outstanding veins.

"What a paltry conclusion to things," he said gaily. "Fucking disgrace."

"You have to go where you can be comfortable."

"I always wanted to die here," he said. "Now I don't think so."

"Have you money to travel?"

Not answering, he waved away smoke. She took the cigarette from his hands and took a drag.

"I can get some," she said. "I have a gig up in Tel Aviv. A standing thing."

She took out the pills, poured a few for her own reserve and handed the packet to him.

"Hey, are you suffering? Are you?"

He laughed and took the pills from her. "I'm suffering. A thing for which I lack talent."

She took a couple of the pills and swallowed them with a swig from his bottle of mineral water.

"What next for you, my dear?" he asked. They had not seen each other for several days.

She inflated her cheeks slightly and puffed. "Don't know, Berger."

"What would you like most?"

"Most of all I'd like to go to Cuba again. I've always missed it."

"Would they take you back?"

"Maybe. Probably."

"But it won't last."

"Actually," she said, "I've thought of working in the Strip. But it's so religious there now. Bothers me a little."

"I failed you," Berger said.

"Don't feel sorry for me. Don't feel sorry for yourself. Those are the rules from which everything flows, right?"

"There's always some kind of blindness."

"I understand," she said.

She had met Berger the year before the intifada, when the Old City had been a magic carpet. Cairo had been a cab ride away. Everyone had been pals, or so it had seemed on the surface. It had been East of Suez, an open sesame of funky treasures where the best was like the worst. She had never understood the Kipling line until coming to Jerusalem.

That had been one of her years of conspicuous underemployment. She had been checking coats in New York, at an Upper East

Side restaurant, singing whenever a gig came her way. It had been the shank of the eighties. She had fallen in among Sufis and they had somehow passed her along to Berger. Together they had pursued the Uncreated Light.

"Yes," Berger told her. "I know you do."

Everything had to end, and it had all ended badly for Berger. The *shebab* regarded him as a sodomite; he had once been a wooer of Arab boys. Gush Emunim had an eye for the madrasah; the militant Zionists were leaning on the Armenian, who was thinking of selling out to them and settling with his relations in Fresno. The Gush had discovered Berger, an Austrian, in solitary residence.

Then he had gotten sick. He had not been able to find the right doctor on the Palestinian side. The idea of an Israeli doctor gave him a feeling he described as "self-consciousness." It was the sort of self-consciousness any compatriot of Eichmann's might feel. Eventually he had gone to the French Hospital in Cairo. Sonia had tried getting some medical names from the American consulates on both sides of town but he had not been reassured.

"I'll go over to Tel Aviv in a couple of days," she told Berger. "Something may turn up. Will you be all right?"

"Yes, I think so."

She gave him a wide-eyed look. "Poor baby," she said slyly. "You'll have to be, huh?"

They laughed together.

"You know," he said, "I'm going out by the same door I came in. It's going to cost me everything I've ever learned in life to get it over with."

"Use it up," she said. "You're lucky to have it."

Her greatest pleasure in Berger was that she could say whatever occurred to her. He looked at her and shook his head.

"How does it go?" he asked. "I have talked the talk. And now I must walk the walk."

"That's the song, Berger."

He lowered a green curtain to divide his sleeping alcove from the rest of the apartment and set about changing his colostomy bag.

"Are you still in hope?" he asked. Their little group had developed its private diction.

She had opened a latticed Moorish door to the small sunny court-yard outside and moved her chair to sit beside it. An olive tree grew from the dry soil in the middle of the court. Two thirsty-looking potted orange trees sat on the loose cobblestones. The sky had a rich blue afternoon light.

Sonia sighed over the light, the green trees, the sumptuous weather. She was content, for the moment.

"Yes," she said. "In hope."

3

IN THE COMMUNITY center more than a hundred young Orthodox men were playing Ping-Pong, *payess* and shirttails flying, eyes ablaze with humor, satisfaction or rage. They were all good, and some were very good indeed. Their games were strenuous and violent. Most were speaking English, and from time to time one or another would cry out, "Christ!" or "Yess!" in the style of adolescent American triumph.

The waiting room of Pinchas Obermann's office could be approached only through the center's table tennis parlor. It was a peculiarity of the complex, located in a new high-rise building in the expanding northern suburbs of Jerusalem.

Two men sat in the waiting room. One was about thirty, in stonewashed jeans and a black shirt with a beige windbreaker. Although it was after ten at night, he wore Ray-Bans under Dr. Obermann's unsteady fluorescent light. A clarinet case rested by his chair.

The second man was older, round-shouldered, melancholy and overweight. He had on khaki trousers, a white shirt with a plaid tie and a tweed jacket.

The younger man was watching the older, unashamedly, never taking his eyes away. The older man, pretending to read a copy of *Jerusalem Report*, fidgeted under the other's scrutiny.

After the two of them had waited for some time, a summoning voice sounded from Dr. Obermann's inner office.

"Melker!"

The voice was peremptory, without any suggestion of healing or solicitude, and projected through the closed door. Dr. Obermann did without a receptionist and a great deal else. The young man gave the elder a last glance and sauntered inside, taking his instrument with him.

Dr. Obermann was red-bearded, crew-cut and thick-bodied. He wore a turtleneck and slacks and army-issue glasses.

"Mr. Melker," he said. He stood to shake the young man's hand. "Or should I call you Raziel? Or should I call you Zachariah? What should I call you?"

"You make me sound like a multiple personality," young Melker said. "Call me Razz."

"Razz," the doctor repeated tonelessly. "I see you have your clarinet."

"Like me to play it?"

"That great pleasure I force myself to postpone," Dr. Obermann said, "until a more appropriate moment. How's the monkey? On or off your back?"

"I'm as clean as the eyelids of morning," said Razz. "I'm happy."

Obermann looked at him noncommittally.

"Take off your sunglasses," he said, "and tell me about your spiritual life."

"You have a nerve, Obie," Razz Melker said, taking a seat and removing his glasses. "Checking my eyes?" He said it good-naturedly. "If I was popping, you think I'd own these shades? Or these clothes? Want to see my veins?" He shook his head in a tolerant gesture. "By the way, with all those little *buchers* out there whapping the balls around, it's a little difficult to talk the spiritual life."

"Think those kids don't have any?"

"Hey," Raziel hastened to say, "they put us all to shame. No question about it."

"I'm pleased that you're clean," Dr. Obermann said. "It's important. Happy is good too."

"Maybe do the odd spliff. That's it." He smiled his pink-edged bad-boy smile and spread his long, jeans-clad legs out in front of him. He wore lizard boots from Africa.

Obermann watched him in silence.

"Want to hear about *my* spiritual life? I still have one. Is that all right?"

"Depends," said Dr. Obermann.

Razz looked contentedly about the office as they listened to the rat-a-tat of Ping-Pong balls. Eyes exposed, he had a blinky, myopic look. The place was decorated with posters from the Palazzo Grassi, the British Museum and the Metropolitan. The show themes were either primitive or ancient art.

"Your patient out there," Razz said. "The elderly dude. Want me to tell you something about him?"

"Mind your business," said Obermann.

"He turned goy on us, right? He's a Christian convert. Or was."

Obermann held Razz's gaze for a moment, then took his own glasses off and rubbed his eyes.

"You know him," the doctor insisted. "You've heard about him somewhere."

"I assure you, man, I never set eyes on him before."

"Be so kind," Dr. Obermann said, "as to not address me as 'man.'"

"Sorry," Razz said. "I thought you wanted to know about my spiritual life. I think I'm playing well too."

"A lot of drugs change hands in those clubs in Tel Aviv," Obermann said.

"You're not shitting, sir. However, as I told you, I don't indulge."

"Very well," Obermann said.

"I'm not about to do that naltrexone treatment again," Razz Melker declared. "Christ, everything Burroughs said about sleep cures is true. They genuinely suck."

"Your father would like you to go home to Michigan."

"I know."

"He's worried about you," Dr. Obermann said. With his glasses resting on his forehead he wrote Melker a prescription for a mild tranquilizer that was part of the follow-up to the naltrexone. Then he dashed off the quick note for the IDF that would assure Melker's continued exemption from military service. "Also, he doesn't think you're making much of a contribution to the Jewish state."

"Maybe he's mistaken. Anyway, his contributions cover both of us."

Dr. Obermann looked at him coldly.

"Tell him I love him," Melker said.

"How's Sonia?" the doctor asked. "Off drugs also?"

"Come on, Doc, she's no junkie. She's a Sufi, a real one. Now and then she dabbles."

"She shouldn't dabble," the doctor said.

"You like her, don't you?"

"I like her very much," said Obermann.

"I know you do. I told her so." He paused to observe the doctor. "You should hear her sing."

"Yes," Dr. Obermann said, "no doubt I should. Are you lovers?"

Razz laughed and shook his head. "No. Want me to fix you up?"

"Impossible."

"How's the book going?" Melker persisted. "The religious mania book."

Obermann wriggled into a disclamatory shrug.

"Am I in it?" Melker asked. "How about the *alter kocker* outside? Is he in it? He ought to be."

"Call me if you have any thought disorders," Obermann said.

Melker laughed and leaned forward confidentially.

"But Doc," he said. "Thought itself is disorder. It disturbs the primal rhythm of the universe. With static. Psychic entropy. The sages —"

"Out!" Dr. Obermann commanded. Melker stood up and took his papers. When he reached the door, the doctor asked him, "How did you know? About that man?"

Melker turned, unsmiling. "He's a musician too. Isn't he? I bet he's a good one. Looks like a bass player. No. Cello?"

"You saw something," Obermann said. "He must have calluses on his fingers. Or something."

"But he doesn't," Melker said. "It's true, isn't it? A musical Christian convert?"

"Why," Obermann asked him, "should he be in my book?"

"I see the roots of his soul," Melker said.

"Nonsense."

"If you say so."

Obermann stared at him. "And what, precisely, do you see?"

"I've explained," Melker said, "what I see and how. I think you understand."

The doctor drew himself up in a Herr-Professorly stance. "What I may understand," he declared, "and what I am able to believe are —"

Melker interrupted him. "Tell me his name."

"I can't," Dr. Obermann said. "I can't do that."

"Too bad," Raziel said. "What's the diagnosis? Schizo? Manic depression, probably. Keep an eye on him."

"I will. But why?"

"Why? He comes from the King, that's why. He rides the Chariot. You know, if you didn't avoid me," Razz Melker said, "if you weren't afraid of me, I might tell you a little about these things."

"I'm not afraid of you," the doctor said. "Your father doesn't pay me to be your pal."

Raziel stopped in the lobby outside to watch the table tennis players, standing by the door that led to the plaza outside the highrise. *Homo ludens,* he was thinking. God's image in every eye. Their youthful energy and passion for play was nourishing, animating the dead of night. Animating the dead also.

His presence made quite a few of the players uneasy; he seemed so mocking and godless. They would have been surprised to learn that once he had been one of them, black-suited, sidelocked, wearing *tzitzit* under his shirt, the fringes a constant reminder of the six hundred and thirteen *mitzvot.*

When he got tired of watching, Melker went out into the desert wind and walked across the empty tiled plaza to the Egged bus stop. All the shops in the little suburban mall were closed except for a *shwarma* stand beside the recreation room. He took out his clarinet and began to play the first notes of *Rhapsody in Blue,* languorously, then explosively — flawlessly, it seemed to him. For a long time there was no one to hear. The lights of the *shwarma* stand went out. He stood and played: Raziel, a phantom busker in some stone city of the labyrinth. But before the bus arrived, Dr. Obermann's older patient joined him at the kiosk.

"Bravo," said the older man shyly. "Wonderful."

"Really?" Razz asked, putting away his instrument and reed. "Thanks." He could sense the man's unfocused strength of soul.

"Yes, you're very good." The man seemed to be making an effort to smile. "You must play professionally."

"How about you?" Melker asked.

"I?" The man coughed with embarrassment. "Oh, no."

"In the States," Melker said, "a shrink would have a back door, right? So we lunatics wouldn't encounter each other at the bus stop."

The man in tweed, the musical Christian convert, appeared to give this observation considerable reflection. He seemed to be still pondering it when the bus drew up.

"I thought you must be a performer," Melker said to the older man as they rode together. "Doctor Obie keeps his weird hours for entertainment people. I thought you might be a musician like me."

"No, no," grumbled the man. "No, hardly."

"What are you?"

The older man stared at him, pretending surprise at his effrontery. "I'm Adam De Kuff," he said. "And you?"

"I'm Raziel Melker. They call me Razz." He looked into De Kuff's eyes from behind his shades. "You're from New Orleans."

De Kuff looked a bit troubled. But he smiled. "How did you know?"

Melker smiled back. "There's a hospital down in N.O. called De Kuff. A Jewish hospital. And a concert hall, right? De Kuff is a grand old name in the Crescent City. A tip-top name."

"In any case," the man said stiffly, "it will have to do. It's the only name I own."

"What is it, Dutch?"

"It was once Dutch, I'm told. With a K-U-I-F. Before that Spanish, de Cuervo or de Corvo. Then it became Dutch in the West Indies. Or off-Dutch. Then plain De Kuff in Louisiana."

"When I meet a fellow madman," Razz said by way of explanation, "it makes me a little crazier."

Adam De Kuff shifted away slightly. But eventually, on the long ride, they fell into conversation again. The bus was almost empty. Its route lay between the Jerusalem airport and the heart of the city, following Ramallah Road, zigzagging to drop and pick up single passengers at new developments like the one where Obermann had his office, stopping at Neveh Yaacov and Pisgat Ze'ev, then skirting French Hill and Ammunition Hill through the Bukharan Quarter and Mea Shearim to Independence Park. The streets it served were nearly deserted at that late hour, bathed in chemical light. Its driver was a surly, sandy-haired Russian.

"Obermann is really a lot younger than he looks," Razz was explaining to De Kuff. "He has an old man's manner because he has an old soul." He had unconsciously adopted a little of De Kuff's cultivated southern accent.

De Kuff smiled sadly. "Don't we all?"

"Has he helped you?" Razz asked. "Pardon my asking, but I think we may have a few things in common."

"He's very gruff. A typical Israeli, I suppose. But I like him."

They rode all the way to the end of the line together, and as it turned out, their conversation lasted through the night. In De Kuff's overstuffed hotel suite they talked about tantric Buddhism and the Book of the Dead, kundalini yoga and the writings of Meister Eckhart. When the Muslim call to prayer broke over the city they were watching the sky over Mount Zion, for first light. They sat in upholstered chairs beside the east-facing window. De Kuff's cello, in its case, leaned against a closet door.

Once, during the small hours, Razz had reached out and taken Adam's hand. Adam had drawn away hastily.

"What do you think, Adam?" Razz had asked. "Think I'm making a pass at you? Relax. I'll read your palm."

De Kuff sat tensely and let the divination proceed.

"Did you go to church yesterday?" Raziel asked when he had seen the man's hand. De Kuff raised his free hand to his forehead. It was as though he had forgotten, at first, to be surprised at Melker's question.

"I went to *a* church. Not *to church*. No longer."

"They do put on a show," Melker said. Still studying De Kuff's hand, he added, "You must be so lonely."

The older man had turned bright red and begun to perspire. "Is that there too? Well, I've learned solitude," he said. "Though neither solitude nor fellowship suits me." The muezzin's second call came from across the valley. De Kuff closed his sad elephant's eyes. "I envy them their prayers. Yes, the Arabs. Are you shocked? I envy anyone who can pray."

"I know why you can't pray," Melker said. "I can imagine what happens when you do."

"But how?"

"Have you told Obermann?"

"Yes. I've tried."

"Obie's good, you know? But I don't think he's ready for you."

"But surely," De Kuff said, smiling, "I'm just another unhappy individual." He seemed suddenly in the grip of an elegant gaiety. Then, seeing Raziel's face, his smile faded.

"How'd you like being a Christian?" Raziel asked.

"I don't know," De Kuff said. He looked stricken with shame. "I felt I had to do it."

"I also," Razz said. "I was a Jew for Jesus." He turned in his chair and took hold of his knee and stretched it. "Hey, I'm still for Jesus. You gotta love the guy."

De Kuff stared at him in confusion.

"I believe I know the roots of your soul," Raziel told him. "Do you believe me?" The older man looked into his eyes. Now I have you, Raziel thought. "Think because I met you at the shrink's I might be crazy?" Raziel asked.

"It does occur to me."

"You went and had yourself baptized," Raziel informed him. "You were a Catholic. Your mother is part Gentile."

"I'm afraid I'm very tired," Adam De Kuff said. "I'll say good night."

"Would you like to sleep?" Raziel asked him.

De Kuff looked at him in trepidation. Raziel got up and stood behind his chair. He put his hands on the heavy man's neck and twisted. For a moment Adam seemed to lose consciousness. Then he stiffened in the chair and tried to stand.

Raziel held him down gently but firmly at the shoulders.

"Learned it from a kundalini *yogin*. Never fails. Kundalini *yogins* don't sleep much, but when they do, they're very good at it. Have a bath and you'll sleep until dinner."

"I do have trouble with sleep," De Kuff said, getting awkwardly to his feet.

"Of course." Raziel patted his new friend's round shoulders. "Someone woke you. Who knows when?"

4

MISTER STANLEY'S was behind the Hotel Best, on the second floor of a concrete building with tinny metal facings and opaque glass windows that presented an art deco curve to the street. It was very late when she finally arrived, a little after three on a weekday morning. The cab driver who brought her from the bus station told her he was from Bukhara. He spoke good English and wanted to know about Los Angeles. L.A. was not a place well known to Sonia. He shook off her questions about Bukhara and the Jewish drummers native to it.

The street on which Mister Stanley's stood was two blocks long. It was the second street from the beach, lined with the back doors and service entrances of oceanfront hotels and postcard shops and snack bars, all shuttered and dark.

A mist of small rain dampened the empty, littered street, and getting out of the cab, Sonia shivered in its unfamiliar salt chill. She had become a Jerusalemite, accustomed to the dry hills. For the trip to Tel Aviv she was wearing her bohemian Smithie getup: a denim skirt, sandals, a black top with her turquoise necklace, an expensive black leather jacket. Crossing the street, she heard laughter from the shadows, low laughter of indeterminate gender.

It was not a meeting she looked forward to. But Stanley settled nothing over the telephone and made it a point of honor to be incommunicado during daylight hours.

The metal grille at the street door was down and she had to rattle it for some time before anyone came to answer. Then an unshaven young man who looked as though he had been asleep appeared and stood looking at her blankly through the grille. Addressing him in her fractured Hebrew, she understood that he was a Palestinian.

After a moment, he lifted the grille without a word and stepped aside to let her pass.

A rap tape went on suddenly. Climbing the stairs, she saw the spastic flashes of a strobe light playing on the well of darkness at the top. There she found an open doorway to the black and blue dance floor. In the middle of it was Mister Stanley himself, etherealized by the flashing light, performing some kind of Siberian cake walk to Lock N Lode's projectile recitation and grinning at her.

"Yo, Sonia! Com-rade! Dar-ling."

Two more young Arabs were sitting on the floor against the wall, watching Stanley perform. They looked agreeably awestruck, like a couple of shoeshine boys in a Fred Astaire movie digging Mister Fred. Sonia raised a hand to shield her eyes from the glare of the strobe. "Someday," she told Stanley, "I'm gonna have a seizure up here."

He came over to kiss her, shaking his head in comic confusion at the coarse poetry on his sound system.

"Listen! What means, Sonia? Whatsitsay?"

There were do-it-yourself prison tattoos on his wrists and the backs of his hands. Links, nets and webs gauged in the mottled, freckling skin. She had to wonder what the officials of ingathering had made of him at Lod. Must have worn his mittens on the flight from Moscow, she thought. He had been rejected for military service because of the tattoos.

"Sonia? Now? Just then. What he's saying?"

" 'Be chillin', muvvafucka, take off my rhyme,' " Sonia reported. "Something along those lines."

Stanley repeated it with a good accent. "What means?"

"A death threat." She had to raise her voice to be heard. "To anyone who steals his rhyme." She shrugged impatiently.

"Awriiight," said Mister Stanley. "Chillin' muvvafucka!" He spread his arms out, winglike and loose-wristed, to dance a few steps more. "Whatsmatter? You don't like it?"

"Sure," she said. "I like it fine. Could you chill that light," she added, "because I think it's giving me epilepsy, know what I'm saying?"

He kissed her indulgently and gave a command in Arabic. When the sound and light were stopped, a tall, dark, strikingly attractive young woman appeared on the dark dance floor, caught by a standing spot overhead. Stanley conducted everyone to a table. One of the two young Arabs brought them a tray with a bottle of Perrier, a bottle of Stolichnaya, and dishes of cucumber slices, olives, Arab bread and what appeared to be caviar.

The woman's name was Maria Clara. When Sonia tried her in Spanish, she replied in a rather genteel accent that she came from Colombia, from Antioqhia province, not far from Medellín. Her features were patrician and tragic. Sonia assumed that she played a role in Stanley's dealings with the Colombian cocaine trade.

"You should hear Sonia perform," Stanley said in English to Maria Clara. "Breathtaking. Soon we make a record."

Stanley's offer was an agreeable fantasy based on his periodic attempts to muscle in on some local record distributorship. Back on the Arbat he had bootlegged American R & B records, and now, as the proprietor of Mister Stanley's, he felt himself an impresario. Stanley and his ambitions had become a troubling constant in Sonia's life. She had not sung in public for twelve years before meeting him. One night the previous spring, she spent an evening in Tel Aviv with an old pal from Friends school and they had gone to Mister Stanley's to try the jazz. The jazz had been sort of east of the Vistula, but Sonia and her friend, a junior officer at the Ankara embassy, were both visibly African American and for this reason had been given the big hello. Stanley had regarded them as an authenticating presence, or at least as atmosphere.

She had been drunk and merry that night. She had been prevailed upon to sing a few Gershwin songs. "Our Love Is Here to Stay." "How Long Has This Been Going On?" It had been a rush. And after that, Stanley had always wanted her there. Stanley had also always wanted her as a mistress — less in his bed, she suspected, than on his arm. As an authenticating presence, or at least as atmosphere.

She had a generous glass of Stoli and a slice of Arab bread and caviar. It improved her mood.

"Really good, Stanley. Appreciate it."

In reply, Stanley presented a vision of himself as stricken Pierrot. He clasped his tattooed hands across his chest and turned the corners of his mouth down. "Sonia," he said plaintively, "I miss you. Why you don't come around more?"

His eyes were bright blue and the skin under them was dark, so that he seemed to be always watching in shadow.

"I want to come back," she said. "I was hoping you could give me a gig."

"But of course," he said happily, and took her hand. "Start any-time. Start tonight. This young woman is a wonderful singer," Stanley told his guest. "Great voice. Makes you shiver."

Maria Clara nodded in somber approval.

"So I'm free next week," Sonia said, wanting to give herself a few days to work up to it. "When do you want me?"

"The night you can start, you should start. Next weekend?"

"All right," she said. "I'd like that. Same deal as before?"

The deal she had had before entailed Stanley paying her five thousand dollars American for seven nights, two performances a night. When he had first proposed the sum, she had thought he was joking. But he had not been; he commanded large sums and he genuinely liked her singing. The amount made it worthwhile to cope with him, at least for a few weeks.

"Same deal," Stanley said.

In addition to large sums of money, he dispensed drugs with vast prodigality, and coping with him meant not accepting any. Sonia's reading was that he would expect nothing beyond minstrelsy for the agreed-upon salary. For free dope, there might be certain expecta-tions, carnal and otherwise. He knew she had worked for the Inter-national Children's Foundation in the Strip, that she had UN docu-ments and access to the UN's vehicles.

"You have a place to stay in Tel Aviv? We can fix it for you."

"I have a place lined up," she told him. It was not exactly true. She knew a pension near the beach that was owned by two old Berlin Spartacists, acquaintances of her parents.

"Maybe you'll be going to Gaza soon?" Stanley asked. "In one of their little white cars?"

She knew he moved drugs there. He claimed to have contacts in the army and in the civil administration, as well as among the local *shebab*. The blue and white UN vans that shuttled between the Hill of Evil Counsel and the Occupied Territories exercised a practical fascination for him.

"I don't think so, Stanley. I think I've worn out my welcome there."

"Well," he said, "if you do, we might work something out. I got friends there." It was as explicit as he had ever gotten. He reached out and took her hand. "Wait, Sonia. One moment. I have some-thing for you."

"It's all right, Stan," she said. "I have to go."

In fact there was nothing but the empty street outside, no buses or *sheruts* for Jerusalem until five or so. He disappeared into a back room, leaving her dithering in Maria Clara's company.

"You're beautiful," said the cool, sad Colombian. She had the gravity of a tango artist. "You mustn't go so soon."

"Well," said Sonia, "thank you."

"You remind me of Cuba. You look like a Cuban. And when you speak, you sound Cuban."

"I'm flattered," Sonia said. "But I'm too clumsy to be Cuban."

Sonia was more or less used to Stanley, but Maria Clara gave her sudden stark chills.

"You know what?" Stanley asked. "We got call from your old boyfriend. The clarinet."

"Ray Melker? How's he doing?" She was about to ask whether he was off drugs, but that might be an awkward question in present company.

"He's in Safed. He gives tours. Now he wants to work. Come down and blow for us."

"Better grab him, Stan. He's a baby Sidney Bechet. He'll be famous someday." She was wondering what it would be like to see Raziel again. Temptations.

Stanley agreed. "You want work, I tell him, you got it."

She left without calling a taxi and walked around the hotel to Hayarkon Street and followed the patterned pavement south along the beach. The turbulent light of day was gathering on the ocean horizon, a mass of twisted clouds and pale gray light. The cold colors of sea and sky confused her sense of place.

A mile or so down the seafront, she encountered a troop of elderly men in bathing suits hurrying toward the ocean. They called to her, thrusting out their hoary hairy chests, puffing themselves up in macho array. One man waved a bottle of Israeli vodka. She stopped and watched them jog together toward the water's edge for their morning constitutional, outlined against the sunrise.

Sonia had a weakness for the old-timers. She had once spent an evening in a bar on Trumpeldor Street where they went in for old Zionist war songs, the "Internationale," Piaf and Polish waltzes; it had reminded her of her parents' world. One bounded by hope. She had begun to think of hope as belonging to the past.

There was a free taxi parked along Herbert Samuel Street, so she took it to the bus station. She caught the first morning bus, filled with civil servants on their way to work. As it climbed into the red and brown Judean Hills, she felt a sense of relief like homecoming.

Who knew, she had to wonder, which was the real world? The plastic town on the make, a city ironically like any other, or the city on the hill where she had settled. In any case, she knew where she belonged.

5

ONE EVENING Lucas had a meeting with a man who called himself Basil Thomas, who claimed to be a former officer of the KGB. He worked in Israel as a kind of journalist's runner, occasionally doing pieces himself under a variety of names, in several languages, but generally providing leads and guidance to other freelancers. Lucas owed his acquaintance with Thomas to a Polish journalist named Janusz Zimmer, who knew everyone and had been everywhere and worked thousands of sources worldwide. The appointment with Basil Thomas took place at Fink's. They shared a table in the tiny space, and Thomas, wearing an outsized leather overcoat despite the mild weather, drank Scotch as quickly as the Hungarian waiter could bring it to them.

The waiter was one of the things Lucas liked best about Fink's. He seemed to have stepped whole out of a wartime Warner Bros. movie and closely resembled at least three of Warners' Mitteleuropean bit players of the period. In the course of being served by him, Lucas had rejoiced in being addressed in a dazzling variety of honorifics: Mister, Monsieur, Mein Herr, Gospodin and Effendi.

What Lucas liked least about Fink's was the extremely close quarters its size compelled. He had found, however, that the place tended to expand or contract according to one's mood and in proportion to the amount of liquor consumed.

Basil Thomas, whistle wetted, was explaining his unparalleled access to the most secret archives of Soviet Intelligence.

"When I say anything you want, I mean anything you want. Hiss. The Rosenbergs. Did they or didn't they, know what I mean?" A salesman, he seemed to hint at some delicious unspeakable aspect of the case.

Yet Basil was a disappointment to Lucas. In setting up the interview, he had imagined a man possessed of some totalitarian chic.

"You have files on Alger Hiss and the Rosenbergs?"

"Not only that. I got files on what's *desinformatsiya,* what's not. I got the Masaryk story. The Slansky story. The story on Noel Field. I got Raoul Wallenberg. I got Whittaker Chambers. I got the basis of your next book."

"So was Hiss really a spy?" Lucas asked.

"Excuse me," said Basil gaily. "This is all scheduled information." Lucas imagined he had picked up the quaint postcolonial term in the course of his travels. "This is the stuff of legend. The story of the century."

Glancing down at his guest's ruddy, hugely knuckled hands, Lucas found it possible to imagine him busting heads in some flaking Balkan capital. An earthy, smiley torturer. On the other hand, he might be nothing more than an amiable trickster.

"Janusz says you know where the bodies are buried," Lucas told Thomas. "That's his phrase."

"Janusz," Basil Thomas repeated wearily, "Janusz, Janusz. Between us," he told Lucas confidentially, "sometimes I think Janusz is a charlatan. I have doubts about Janusz."

"The century's over," Lucas said after a moment. He had gotten drunk through no fault of his own, trying to pace the man, and he was being intentionally unkind. "People may not care about all that."

"How can you say such a thing?" Thomas seemed genuinely shocked. "This is history." He glanced over his shoulder in a gesture of discretion, although everybody in the place — the aged bartender, the Hungarian waiter and the two middle-aged American women at the next table — was clearly listening to every word. "History," he repeated reverentially. "What do you mean they may not care?"

"Oh, you know," Lucas said. "Readers are fickle. With time they lose interest."

"Lose interest?" The possible former agent stared at him as though trying to decide if he was worth persuading. "You're serious?"

"Everyone overrates the significance of his own era," Lucas said for the sake of argument. "Things change."

"Listen, mister," Basil Thomas said. "Knowledge is power."

"Is it?"

"You never heard this? If I own the past, I own the ground you walk on. I control what your children learn in school."

Lucas, childless, was nevertheless impressed. He could not tell whether such thoughtfulness spoke for Basil Thomas's authenticity or against it.

"I guess that's right."

"You guess correctly. That's what I'm offering."

"I think," Lucas said, "it's not for me."

"You don't mind losing the past?"

"I'm losing the present," Lucas confided. "That's what bothers me."

"The present?" Basil Thomas sneered at him. "The present is confusion." He turned in his chair and sighed. "Well, I can go elsewhere." And his covert attention was already surveying the room, spying out an elsewhere.

"Anyway," Lucas said, "I'm not sure I can afford it."

Basil Thomas had plainly expected to be well paid.

"What about the real story behind Avram Lind's dismissal from the cabinet?" he suggested, brightening. "How and why Yossi Zhidov replaces him? What he'll do to get back in? I got a special line on this."

Lucas shrugged. He was not a particularly close observer of domestic Israeli politics.

"I fear for your place in history," Basil Thomas said. "You have the opportunities to make a name, but no. All right," the big man said when Lucas failed to show further interest. "I got something else. Ever heard of Pinchas Obermann?"

Lucas had, but could not remember in what connection.

"The doctor. The doctor who treated the foreigner who tried to burn the mosques. He's a specialist on the Jerusalem Syndrome."

"Which is?"

"Which is coming here and God gives you a mission. To Christians like your good self, only crazy ones."

This time Lucas said, "I don't regard myself as Christian."

"Anyway," Basil Thomas said, "Obermann thinks he has more big stories. He wants to write a book and he wants a collaborator. Only his English is so-so and he'd like an American. For the market there."

Dr. Obermann had an office in the northern suburbs, Thomas explained, but he passed many of his evenings at the Bixx Bar in town and was ready to entertain potential collaborators there.

"Is he connected with Shabak?" Lucas asked. "Shabak" was everybody's pet name for the SB — Shin Bet, the internal security agency.

Thomas shrugged and smiled. "That I can find out for you," he said, although it figured to be something he already knew.

"Well," Lucas said, "the millennium is coming. The city's full of *majnoon*. I'll go look for him at the Bixx."

"Remember where you got it," Thomas said, and in an instant he was fading into the late-century shadows outside.

In the wake of Basil Thomas, Fink's settled down to its customary quiet. The bartender, a melancholy ancient whose beetling brows and Anglophilic dress made him resemble S. J. Perelman, looked straight ahead and wiped glasses. The waiter stood by with a napkin over his arm and an elfin smirk. Lucas finished his drink, paid for Basil's drinks and went outside. There was a spring smell of jasmine along King George Street and Hasidic buskers on the corner of Ben Yehuda.

He would have expected to meet a man like Obermann in some quiet institutional study. The Bixx was a haunt of publicans and sinners near the site of the old Mandelbaum Gate, beyond the Russian Compound. The mysteries of Mea Shearim approached it from one direction, the tense, silent Palestinian city from the other. The walk there sobered him somewhat.

Inside it was reggae night, all smoke, sweat and beer. On the small bandstand, a Rasta quintet was running through the works of Jimmy Cliff. The place was full; there were Viking quasi-maidens, Ethiopians with Malcolm X hats, Romanian pickpockets and American Juniors Abroad in kibbutznik hats. Each boogied according to his covenant. A message board was adorned with calling cards of Moonie missionaries, Player Wanted notices from musical groups, and messages that passing Australians left for each other. Over the bar was a large electric Heineken sign.

The manager, slightly known to Lucas, was a well-spoken American hipster known as One-Name Michael.

"I'm looking for Dr. Pinchas Obermann," Lucas told Michael over the din. "Know him?"

"Sure," Michael said. "Here to get deprogrammed? You don't look like his type."

"Is that what he does?"

"Look," Michael said. He pointed to a table near the end of the bar where a red-bearded man was deep in conversation with a young, sweet-faced blond woman. Janusz Zimmer, the ultra-experienced Pole, was with them.

Lucas made his way to their table and introduced himself to Obermann.

"Mr. Lucas?" Dr. Obermann extended a chubby hand. He was about Lucas's age, bearish and boyish, with humorous eyebrows and watery blue eyes. Physically, he had a morphology one saw among Hasidim; it was easy to picture him in *tzitzit* and suits of solemn black, and faintly surprising to see him without a kippa. But he wore an army shirt and sweater with leather patches at the sleeves and cheap glasses. He introduced the woman with him as Linda Ericksen. It turned out that Dr. Obermann knew Lucas's friend Tsililla Sturm, through the Peace Now organization, which made everything friendlier. "Linda," Obermann told Lucas, "disapproves of Gush Shalom. She's embraced the revisionists. Become a Jabotinskyite."

"That's a fantasy of Pinchas's," Linda said. "I'm not even Jewish. But I've been researching the settler movements on the West Bank and in Gaza, so it amuses him to tease me." Moreover, she told them, she had recently been working as a volunteer for the Israeli Human Rights Coalition.

"Thomas send you over?" Janusz Zimmer asked Lucas. "Clever fellow," he said, without waiting for an answer. "He'll expect to be cut in. He got Pinchas and Linda together also. Connections are his living." Zimmer always sounded a bit drunk, although, keeping track, Lucas observed that he actually consumed fairly little. His way of being drunk was very watchful. Though Lucas did not mention it, connections were Zimmer's living as well.

"Thomas offered me a choice," Lucas told him. "Cabinet intrigue, 'Inside the KGB' or Dr. Obermann and religious mania. I think religious mania is more me." Lucas asked Linda, "Have you had an interesting time with the settlers? They're usually suspicious of the press."

"And of Americans," Linda said. "Maybe because so many of them are former Americans themselves. But I think I've won their trust."

"Do they know you work for the Human Rights Coalition?" Lucas asked.

"The settlers like Linda because she's a midwestern Protestant minister's wife," Dr. Obermann said. "They hope to find a friend in her. And perhaps they have."

Linda struck Obermann affectionately on the forearm. Either they were lovers, Lucas thought, or Mrs. Ericksen was endeavoring to give that impression.

"Pinchas enjoys demonizing the settlers. So many Israelis do. But I think they're perfectly decent people."

Obermann cast a glance heavenward. Linda continued, addressing Lucas. Zimmer watched her.

"Many of the settlers believe what I believe. While they're here, the rights of the Arabs should be protected."

"Notice," Dr. Obermann said, "she says 'while they're here.' As though they could be made to vanish." He got up and went to the bar to buy a round of beers.

The reggae band had struck up the Jimmy Cliff number about the Babylonian captors of the children of Israel requiring songs and mirth. The Rasta version closely followed Psalm 137.

When Obermann brought the beers to the table, Lucas expressed his interest in the doctor's work. He was ready to consider a collaboration. He did not add that he was nearly broke and grossly underemployed. The project seemed interesting, relatively safe and personally congenial. The question — the potential problem — was Obermann himself.

For Lucas's benefit, the doctor summarized a hypothetical story representative of the annals of the Jerusalem Syndrome.

"A young man of scant prospects receives a supernatural communication." Obermann's accent had a Germanic tinge. "He must go to Jerusalem at the Almighty's command. Once here, his mission is disclosed. Often he is the Second Coming of Jesus Christ."

"Are they always foreigners?"

"The foreigners come to the notice of the police. They end up on the street."

"How did you get interested in this subject?"

"I treated Ludlum," Obermann said. "I was doing military service and they assigned me to work with the Border Police. Ever hear of him?"

Everyone had. Willie Ludlum had once been a shepherd in New Zealand. Watching his flock by night under the Southern Cross, he had received tidings that led him to torch the Al-Aksa Mosque in the Old City, filling the streets from Fez to Zamboanga with outraged believers.

"He was sad," Linda Ericksen told them mournfully.

"Willie was quietly insane," said Dr. Obermann. "He was that rare thing, a schizophrenic with manners."

"Didn't he think he was the key to human history?" Lucas asked. "I thought they all thought that."

"Willie was in love," Obermann explained, "on top of his religious delusions. He had fallen in love with a girl on the kibbutz where he was staying, and that's probably what made him violent. But he didn't believe he was Jesus or the Messiah. He thought if he burned down the Al-Aksa, the Temple could be rebuilt. This is a common theme, of course."

"How many such people are there?"

"Ah," said Dr. Obermann, "this depends. All Christians are supposed to believe in the Second Coming and the New Jerusalem. The advent of the Messiah is a fundamental in religious Zionism. So, in a way, all Christians and religious Zionists have a touch of the Jerusalem Syndrome. From a grimly rationalist point of view. Of course this doesn't make them delusional."

"Unless they take it personally," Lucas suggested.

"When they think it involves them directly, there's often a problem," said Dr. Obermann. "Especially when they're here."

"On the other hand," said Lucas, "if they're here — it tends to involve them directly."

"Are you Jewish, Mr. Lucas?" Linda asked brightly. She herself appeared extremely Gentile, a chirpy suburban soubrette.

"Yes," said Obermann with a chuckle. "I was going to ask."

To his horror, Lucas began to stammer. He had not been asked the question for at least a month. Lately his trove of dusty answers and snappy non sequiturs had not been serving him well.

"On a scale of one to ten?" Linda proposed playfully.

"Five?" suggested Lucas.

"How about on a scale of yes and no?" asked Janusz Zimmer.

"My family is of mixed background," Lucas told them with underconfident primness. He thought it might make him sound a little like Wittgenstein. In fact, what mixed had not quite been a family. More of a fuck.

"Ah," said Obermann. "Well, this is what you have to remember in Jerusalem." He raised his left hand and began to enumerate its chubby fingers with his right thumb and forefinger. "First, real things are actually happening, so you have reality. Second, people's perceptions are profoundly conditioned, so you have psychology. Third, you have the intersection of these things. Fourth, fifth, who knows? Possibly other dimensions. Mysteries."

"What about you?" Lucas asked Linda. "What brings you out here?"

"I was a poor preacher's wife when I came here," she replied.

"An actual missionary," Obermann said drily.

"Yes, a kind of missionary. But I tended toward comparative religion. I worked on a dissertation at the Hebrew University."

"On what?" Lucas asked.

"Oh, on Pauline Christianity and its corruption of Jesus' original teachings. In fact, it touches on the Syndrome as a latter-day parallel. It's called 'Raised in Power.' "

"Oh," said Lucas. Some old text came nearly to mind, hung suspended in the half-light of his recollection. He gave it a shot: " 'It is sown in corruption,' " he began, " 'it is raised in incorruption.' " That sounded right. " 'It is sown in weakness, it is . . . raised in power.' "

"So," said Dr. Obermann, "your background is religious?"

"Well," Lucas said airily, "I was a religion major in college, at Columbia." When this seemed not to satisfy them, he went on. "Catholic. My father was a nonpracticing Jew. My mother was a sentimental Catholic. Not really a religious person but . . ." He shrugged. "Anyway, I was raised Catholic."

"And now?" Obermann asked.

"And now," Lucas said, "nothing. Do you come here often?" he asked the doctor.

"Everyone comes here," Linda said.

"Everyone comes here," Dr. Obermann repeated. "Even the eunuchs and abstainers."

"So," Lucas asked, "should I start coming more often?"

"You know," Linda said, "you should talk to my ex-husband while he's in country." She was immediately interrupted by a young Ethiopian with an earring who invited her to dance by raising her at the elbow. Out on the floor, swaying to "The Harder They Come," the pair of them looked like a martial young Othello and his bland but distinctly adulterous Desdemona.

"Her husband was a Christian fundamentalist," Obermann explained. "They both were. Now he works for something called the House of the Galilean. Christian Zionists, good relations with the rightists, something of a moneymaker."

"And she?"

"Officially," Zimmer said, "she's at the university. And separated from the husband now."

"An enthusiast," said Dr. Obermann. "Conversion prone. If she took up Catholicism, crystals, lesbian gardening — one wouldn't be surprised."

"Is she your patient?"

"She was never really my patient. Linda isn't suffering from any kind of disturbance. She's a seeker. When her marriage broke up, we became close."

"Obermann is just cynical," Janusz Zimmer informed Lucas. "He's converted Linda to the cause of himself."

At this point, a hawk-faced man with a shaven skull leaned down and shouted into Lucas's face.

"Yoor the foodie! I remember yoo! When do we do our next interview?"

The hawk-faced man was named Ian Fotheringill. He was an aging Glaswegian skinhead, a former Foreign Legionnaire and African mercenary who had taken up haute cuisine and was employed at one of the big chain hotels. Lucas had once interviewed him for his newspaper. He believed that Fotheringill had formed the impression that he was an internationally renowned food writer who would clear his way to celebrity and the London bistro of his dreams.

"Oh," said Lucas, "soon."

Fotheringill had been drinking heavily. He had red, pointy ears and a tiny nose ring. Seemingly displeased at Lucas's relative indifference, he turned to Dr. Obermann.

"I can make a kosher *sauce l'ancienne*," he informed the psychiatrist. "I'm the only chef in the land of Israel who can make one."

"Aha," said Dr. Obermann.

"They call him," Janusz Zimmer said with a lightning wink, "Ian the Hittite."

Fotheringill began to tell a story in which an American guest at a resort hotel had accused him of using lard in his strudel.

"Lard in the strudel!" he protested to heaven. "Where the fook can I find bloody lard in Caesarea?"

Linda returned from dancing with the Ethiopian. Fotheringill stared at her as though she were a charlotte russe and presently took her back onto the floor.

"You *should* talk to her ex-husband," Obermann said to Lucas. "The House of the Galilean is a very interesting place. Pilgrims go. Victims of the Syndrome. They go for the lentil soup."

"I love lentil soup," Lucas said.

Obermann gave him an appraising look.

"So you're interested in this?" Obermann asked him. "At book length?"

It seemed to Lucas that he could talk his way into an advance without too much difficulty. "I'll think about it," he said.

"My notes are at your disposal," Obermann said. "Or they will be, when we come to an understanding. Ever written a book before?"

"As a matter of fact I have," Lucas said. "It was about the American invasion of Grenada."

"A very different subject."

"Not entirely," Janusz Zimmer said. "There was a metaphysical dimension in Grenada. Some of the people involved thought they had connections on high."

"Reagan, you mean?" Lucas asked.

"I wasn't thinking of Reagan. But I guess it would apply to him and to Nancy."

"Were you in Grenada during the invasion?" asked Lucas.

"Just before," Zimmer said. "And soon after."

"Janusz is a bird of ill omen," Dr. Obermann said. "Where he appears, newsworthiness follows."

"There were cults, as I remember," Zimmer said. "On the island."

"Yes, there were," Lucas said.

"Here also there are cults," said Dr. Obermann. "Not merely a few lost souls, but organized and powerful groups."

"All the better," Lucas said. "For the story, I mean."

Zimmer leaned closer and spoke above the noise of the band.

"Care should be taken," he said.

Lucas was considering the Pole's caution when his attention was diverted by a young woman on the dance floor who was dancing with the Ethiopian. She had the café au lait skin of the Spanish Main and black hair cut in a close afro, partly covered with a Java cloth scarf. Her dress was maroon and she wore a Coptic cross around her neck. She had long legs and Birkenstock sandals and her feet and ankles were decorated with purple geometric designs. Lucas recalled hearing somewhere that Bedouin women wore such designs but he had never seen them. He thought at once of the preternaturally hip young Arab woman in the madrasah the month before. He was certain it must be she.

"Who is she?" he asked Obermann. "Do you know her?"

"Sonia Barnes," the doctor said. After a quick, irritable glance he did look at her. "She used to go out with one of my patients."

"I've seen her around town," Lucas said.

"She's a dervish," Janusz Zimmer told Lucas. "She belongs in your story."

"True," Obermann said.

The girl called Sonia, and Linda Ericksen, the only two women on the dance floor, encountered each other and touched hands in greeting. Linda's greeting was without warmth. Sonia's smile seemed a bit sad and sardonic.

"She whirls very nicely," said Lucas. "Is she really a dervish?"

"Would I make it up?" Zimmer asked. "She's a practicing Sufi."

"Mrs. Ericksen seems to know her."

"Everyone knows everyone," Janusz Zimmer said. "Sonia sings in a place called Mister Stanley's in Tel Aviv. Go and see her. She can tell you about the Abdullah Walter cult. And Heinz Berger."

Lucas wrote it down.

"Dance with her," Obermann suggested.

"I can't. She's too good."

"Wait until you hear her sing," Zimmer said. "Like an angel."

Suddenly Fotheringill noticed Lucas again. His impatient mug interposed itself over Lucas's field of vision.

"What about the poem!" the north Briton demanded. Lucas stared at him in incomprehension.

"The poem about *rillons!*" Fotheringill insisted. "The poem about *rillettes!*" Dimly, Lucas recalled an attempt he had drunkenly made to impress Fotheringill with his credentials as a foodie by quoting a comic poem by Richard Wilbur about *rillons* and *rillettes de Tours*. Lucas had once been a man with a poem for all occasions.

"Oh," said Lucas. "Let's see."

Fotheringill's persistence was unsettling. It was easy to picture him on some blasted moor, slicing off the limbs of fallen cavaliers for their armor while crows overhead sang a ghastly lament.

" 'Rillettes, Rillons,' " Lucas attempted. "No: 'Rillons, Rillettes, they taste the same . . . and yet . . .' "

Memory failed him.

"And yet?" Fotheringill demanded. "And yet what?"

"I guess I've forgotten."

"Drat! I don't like the 'and yet' part. Because they're completely different things, understand!"

Movement by tiny movement, Lucas succeeded in extricating himself from the table while Fotheringill began an embittered discourse on the subject of pastry. He had the necessary numbers in his notebook. Sonia was dancing again as he made his way out the door.

He got a taxi on Ben Yehuda Street and rode it home. Fumbling into his apartment, he turned on the answering machine. It was filled with messages in Hebrew and French for his flatmate and sometime lover, Tsililla Sturm, but the last was for him, and it was Nuala.

"Hello, Christopher," Nuala's brisk Dublin voice declaimed. "I've some news for you about Abu, and I think we may have found the cure for him. So call me in the morning like a good lad."

"Goddam it, Nuala," Lucas told the machine. "What do I have to do? Who do I have to be?"

He suspected that she found him tame and overcivilized, too pale and Catholic. Her taste ran to militants, dark, hot-eyed enragés, cabrones.

Muttering unhappily, he turned the machine off and went to bed.

6

NUALA MET HIM on a ridge in Talpiot, in a café near S. Y. Agnon's house. Across a valley lay the Hill of Evil Counsel, where the United Nations had its offices. On the southern slope, the brown land descended toward Bethlehem. Lucas arrived first and so could watch his friend trudge up the hill. She kept her head down, hands in the pockets of her cardigan, eyes on the pavement. She was wearing a black top and faded crimson Afghan pants. When she removed the sweater at the top of the climb, she looked for a moment like a fashion model in search of a shoot.

As she drew nearer, he saw that one of her eyes was blackened and the skin around it darkly bruised. She sat down at his table with a wan smile.

"Hello, Christopher."

"Hello, Nuala. What happened to your eye?"

"Abu socked me. How about *that*."

"I'd call it a coup. Did you get a gander at him?"

"He was wearing a kaffiyeh over his face like the *shebab*. They all were."

"Sure he wasn't Palestinian? Because there's always a possibility this is some kind of internecine — "

"Balls," she said, interrupting him. "I've talked to every faction in the Strip. I went over it with Majoub." Majoub was a human rights lawyer in Gaza City, a Palestinian activist. "He's in the IDF."

"How do you know he's not just a settler?"

"You're being tiresome," she said. "Because he turns up far from the settlements late at night. He has the use of desert vehicles, maybe even boats. Anyway, I can tell by the reaction of the IDF people. They think he's one of their own."

"How'd you get him to hit you?"

"Oh, my," she said, "thanks very much for the sympathy. He hit me because we caught him. There were stones thrown in Deir el-Balah that day and we expected him there that night. So we lay in wait behind the school. A bright moon there was that night. Sure enough, around eleven a jeep pulls up — a jeep with the serial numbers painted out — and five guys get out. One's a Palestinian teenager in civilian clothes. The other four are in IDF uniforms. They send the Palestinian into the camp and presently he comes back with two young kids. So at that, two of the soldiers crouch and unsling to cover the place and the other two grab the kids. One of the guys has a great billy club. So we broke cover and the Rose took a flashbulb picture."

"The Rose" was a Canadian UN staffer who worked with Nuala at the International Children's Foundation.

"Then it's all shouts and grunts and he hit me. Called me a fucking bitch, too. In English. Or American, anyway. They took the Rose's camera. So I told him, 'I'm on your case, chum.' So he hit me again. The other guys had to pull him off me. Then they gunned it out of town and the Palestinian grass is left on the road running after them."

"And you've reported all this?"

"That I have," she said. "To the army, to Civil Affairs and to Majoub. Today I went up the hill to UNRWA and to see the Israeli Human Rights Coalition as well."

"What did they say?"

"I talked to Ernest at the Human Rights Coalition, and they'll do what they can. Maybe get some questions asked in the Knesset. They'll draft a press release and I've written one for the Children's Foundation. UNRWA can't do much. It takes America, you know."

"Is that where I come in?"

"You could get a piece in a magazine. I know you could. The Sunday *Times Magazine*. You've had things there."

"There are other representatives of the American press here," Lucas said. "They have more clout and more resources."

"But not the soul," said Nuala.

What an odd thing to say, Lucas thought. Can it be she likes me after all? He had never been able to get to first base with her.

"Also," Nuala added, "they have tight deadlines and more pressing stories. Whereas your time seems to be your own."

Hearing that was less satisfactory.

"I don't know," he said. "I've just about resolved to do a piece on the Jerusalem Syndrome. You know, religious mania and so forth."

"Ah," sighed Nuala, "gimme a break, will ya."

"It's quite an interesting story," Lucas said. "Sort of timeless."

"Well, people aren't timeless," Nuala said.

"Sure people are."

"I'm not. And neither are you."

They got up and walked along the muddy ridge. It had been the Green Line once; a rusted half-track marked the place where the Arab Legion's armored column had been stopped in 1948. A cool wind whipped the high ground and Nuala put her sweater back on. Agnon had lived on these heights, Lucas recalled, and his best novel had been called *The Winds of Talpiot*.

"Well now," said Nuala, "how's your love life, then?"

"Poor," said Lucas. "How's yours?"

"Poor fella," she said. "Mine is all confusion."

"Tell me about it."

"Nah. You'd mock and jeer."

"Not me."

Lucas, who fancied her keenly, was painfully aware that he had never been able to generate the degree of menace she seemed to require. In Lebanon, she was supposed to have been the mistress of a Druse militia chief. In Eritrea, she had been able to provide food for the starving through the largesse of her good friend, an insurgent colonel. She was associated in popular lore with Golani Regiment commandos, contrabandists and *fedayeen*. Lucas, who lived a fastidious and anxiously examined life, was not for her.

"Ah," she said, "I know you wouldn't, Christopher. You're a good and gentle person. You make me feel like telling you my woes."

"I wish you wouldn't call me a good and gentle person," Lucas said. "It makes me feel epicene." He put his foot on the rusted fender of an Arab Legion armored personnel carrier and leaned on his knee. "Pussylike."

Her relationship with the State of Israel and its defense forces was singular, he thought. It seemed to give a special resonance to the term "love-hate." But she was good at languages and knew her way around the region like few others.

Nuala laughed her nice Irish laughter. "I'm sorry, Christopher. I know you're a hell of a fella. The girls all adore you, truly."

"Thanks, pal."

"Here," she said, still laughing, "take some of this." She held out a plastic bag full of what appeared to be miniature cedar tips, a dark reddish green. When he failed to take it, she took a pinch from the bag and put it to his lips. "Go ahead, take it. It'll make you even more studly than you already are."

He took the bag and examined it.

"It's khat," she said. "The perfect morning chaw. One gobful and you'll never be without it."

Lucas put the stuff in his pocket.

"I'll tell you what," he said. "I'll talk to Ernest and find out what the Human Rights Coalition knows about Abu Baraka. Maybe I can do something about it. But I think it's going to go the other way. I mean, I think the Jerusalem Syndrome is more for me."

"I suppose," she said. "You're religious."

"I am not religious," he said angrily. "It's a good story."

"Oh, rubbish," Nuala told him. "Of course you're religious. You're the biggest Catholic I ever saw. Anyway, the Jerusalem Syndrome is old stuff."

They started walking again, turning their backs to the winds of Talpiot.

"You're wrong, Nuala," Lucas said. "You may find it boring but it's not old stuff. Religion here is something that's happening now, today."

It was true, he thought, although he had said it often before. Other cities had antiquities, but the monuments of Jerusalem did not belong to the past. They were of the moment and even the future.

"What a curse it is," she said. "Religion."

He wondered how it could be that if she so despised religion she could have made herself so at home in this part of the world. Because it was religion and religious identity that gave the place its passions, upon which she battened.

"I guess so," Lucas said. "Why don't you take your atrocity story to Janusz Zimmer. He's good at that stuff."

"I have," she said. "He claims to be interested." She shrugged.

In this city, as in many others, the practice of journalism was made more difficult by the interlacing sexual affairs that consumed the international press. Nuala and Janusz, who was nearly twice her age, had entertained a brief, crazed liaison that seemed to have ended badly and about which neither would speak. Her present interest was in a Palestinian *résistant* in the Strip, where she worked.

He walked her to the bus stop at the bottom of the hill and waited for the bus with her and kissed her goodbye. Then he began to walk toward town. In about an hour, footsore and depressed, he found the offices of the Israeli Human Rights Coalition in Amnon Square. His friend Ernest Gross was behind the desk. Gross was a South African from Durban whose tanned, athletic appearance and open face made him resemble a surfer. At the same time, he was one of those men prey to sudden, barely suppressed rages, and it was strange because his business was, after all, benign assistance and fairness and mediation. Or maybe not so strange.

"Hi, Ernest," Lucas said. "Get any good death threats today?"

The Human Rights Coalition sometimes received death threats and had accumulated a copious outpouring over the previous month. Its officers had recently taken part in a major Peace Now demonstration.

"Not today," Ernest Gross said. "Yesterday I got one from a psychiatrist."

"You got a death threat from a psychiatrist? You're putting me on."

Ernest sorted through the papers on his desk, looking for it in vain.

"Well, the damn thing's vanished. But it said, like, 'I'm a psychiatrist and I can see your pathetic self-hatred and I'm going to kill you.'"

"Jesus," said Lucas. "Did he send you a bill?"

"In no other country, right?" Gross said. "So what can I do for you?"

Lucas explained what Nuala had told him about Abu Baraka and asked him what the Human Rights Coalition had on him.

"Nuala has a lot of chutzpah," Ernest said in his antipodean cockney. "She'd better be careful."

"Is she right about this? Is the guy IDF, do you think? Are they doing what she says they're doing?"

"Ah," Ernest said, "here it is." He had found the threatening note on his desk. He picked it up and stuck it to his bulletin board with a thumbtack, beside the Amnesty International bulletins and the Peace Now handbills. "Is Nuala right? Well, Nuala's strange. I don't always know what side Nuala's on, and I don't know if she does. But she's a valuable man, as it were. And I think she's right on this one."

"She wants me to do a story on him."

"Jolly good," Ernest said. "Do it."

"I hate it down there," Lucas said.

"Everyone does, mate. The Palestinians. The soldiers. Everyone but the settlers, who claim to love it. And Nuala, of course."

"Actually, the beaches look nice."

"Great beaches," Ernest said. "The settlers have a hotel called the Florida Beach Club. Scandinavian lovelies come to frolic, I hear. Gambol like lambs, with seven hundred thousand of the most wretched people on earth a mere stone's throw away. So to speak. The beach is protected by razor wire and machine guns."

"Anybody else working the Gaza story?" Lucas asked. "I told Nuala to take it to Janusz Zimmer."

"She and Janusz broke up, I understand," Ernest said. "But maybe he'll take it on."

"That was a strange romance."

"All her romances are strange," Ernest said. "Anyway, it would be good if we didn't have to rely on foreigners to do this one. *Ha'olam Hazeh* is trying to get a line on it." *Ha'olam Hazeh* was a left-wing magazine in Tel Aviv. "It's nice when one of our papers takes that sort of thing on. So it's not like we need the rest of the world to tell us about it."

"I think so too," Lucas said.

"Nuala and her UN friends," said Ernest, "they've all been to Gaza. They've been to Deir Yassein and to everywhere else Jews did the kicking. You wonder if they've ever been to Yad Vashem."

"Never asked her," Lucas said. There was an American feminist calendar on the wall beside Ernest's desk, with pictures of great international heroines and red-letter dates in female history. Lucas leaned over to inspect the fetching photograph of Amelia Earhart. "I've never been there myself, actually."

"No?" Ernest asked. "Anyway, we talk to the IDF, and very often they talk back to us. I think I have an idea of how it goes in the territories."

"How?"

"There are unwritten laws. The Shin Bet operate there. They mount punitive strikes and conduct interrogations. They've told us unofficially that they feel entitled to use moderate force in those interrogations. That's the term they use, 'moderate force.' Obviously, this can mean different things to different people. It can mean one thing to a kid from Haifa and another to a kid from Iraq."

"Right."

"They also feel entitled to kill people they believe have killed Jews. Or who've killed one of their informers. It's a respect thing, see. They have Arabic-speaking agents who have to pass a field test, pretending to be Palestinians, hanging around a market somewhere, chatting it up. If they think one camp or village is ready to explode, they'll sometimes use provocation, set it off themselves and come down hard. For a while last year they were killing six rioters a day, and it was hard to believe this was coincidence. Every day it was six."

"I see."

"Shin Bet itself is divided into compartments. Sometimes the left hand isn't acquainted with the right."

"Sounds a little like Kabbala," Lucas said.

"Doesn't it? And there are other organizations besides Shabak and Mossad. Sometimes they're in favor, sometimes out."

"Dangerous work," Lucas said.

"That's what I tell Nuala," Ernest said. "And her friends."

"Well," said Lucas, "I hope they'll be careful. She came back from her last encounter with a black eye."

"I'm sure one of our soldiers roughed her up," Ernest said. "Still, I can't help noticing how often Nuala reports injured. She's always getting hit."

"Are you implying she likes it?"

"Of course she likes it," Ernest said. He and Lucas smiled without looking at each other. "Anyway," Ernest told him as he left, "you be careful too."

He munched on some khat on his walk back to the German Colony. The stuff gave him something of a jolt but failed to lift his spirits. He presumed Nuala used it for sex, and the notion made him feel horny and deprived.

Once home, he settled down to watch CNN. Christiane Amanpour was broadcasting from Somalia. Her cool, classless English voice seemed to impart an order and comprehensibility to the events she reported which they inherently lacked.

The drug had made it impossible to sleep, so he chewed more to ward off black despair, which lurked in the afternoon quiet, in the dove's cooing, the voice of the turtle. Eventually it made him sick. His wheels spun. In a few days Tsililla would be back from London. It was not going well between them, and the break would come soon. His weariness with things was frightening; it smacked of obliteration, a wall of anger and fatigue that felt as though it might sweep him into nothingness. Worst of all was loneliness.

There were times when Lucas was capable of rejoicing in himself as a singularity — a man without a story, secure from tribal delusion, able to see the many levels. But at other times he felt that he might give anything to be able to explain himself. To call himself Jew or Greek, Gentile or otherwise, the citizen of no mean city. But he had no recourse except to call himself an American and hence the slave of possibility. He was not always up for the necessary degree of self-invention, unprepared, occasionally, to assemble himself.

And sometimes the entire field of folk seemed alien and hostile, driven by rages he could not comprehend, drunk on hopes he could not imagine. So he could make his way only through questioning, forever inquiring of wild-eyed obsessives the nature of their dreams, their assessment of themselves and their enemies, listening agreeably while they poured scorn on his ignorance and explained the all too obvious. When he wrote, it was for some reader like himself, a bastard, party to no covenants, promised nothing except the certainty of silence overhead, darkness around. Sometimes he had to face the simple fact that he had nothing and no one and try to remember when that had seemed a source of strength and perverse pride. Sometimes it came back for him.

7

ADAM DE KUFF and the young man who called himself
Raziel set out together from Jerusalem to travel the land.
They did everything and went everywhere together. Sometimes De Kuff would lapse into silences that lasted for days. During
these silences Raziel would talk gently to him, seeing to it that he
carried out the small necessary tasks of travel. De Kuff began to
believe that the younger man knew his every thought. Raziel encouraged him to believe it.

They traveled by bus, they hitched rides or simply walked. They
visited holy and mighty places, eating little and heedlessly, paying no
attention to what was or was not kosher, not observing Shabbat.
They made their way from the Cave of Machpelah to Carmel, from
the Kotel to Jezreel. They saw the sites sacred to early Christian
martyrs and saw the Tomb of the Kings. They went to Mount Ger-
izim for the Samaritan Passover and to the Baha'i shrine of the Bab
in Haifa.

If there were long hours when De Kuff remained silent, there were
others during which he became indefatigably verbal, talking himself
into a state of high excitement that could last all day and all night.
Raziel was able to keep pace with him, fueling his volubility, matching him association for association, until De Kuff subsided in ex-
haustion and despair. When De Kuff's energy was gone, Raziel remained cool and keen-eyed, ready for more, ready for anything. De
Kuff found it frightening. Sometimes, in tears, he ordered Raziel
away. But Raziel never left him.

They talked about music and about history. They told each other
the story of their lives. Raziel had been raised in a wealthy midwestern suburb. His father was a corporate lawyer turned diplomat and

politician. Raziel had gone to the Berklee College of Music in Boston, then left it for life in Marin County. He became the master of several instruments, composed, played with a rock group that had made a record, then gone in for experimental jazz in San Francisco. He had also been a yeshiva student, a Zen monk at Tassajara, a member of a Hebrew-Christian commune. He confessed his problems with drugs.

De Kuff had attended St. Paul's School and then Yale. As an undergraduate, he had changed his area of concentration from history to music, then gone on to take his degree in it. He played with the New Orleans Symphony and with several chamber music societies. He had inherited a large fortune from several generations of De Kuffs in New Orleans; he had a house in the Garden District where he lived alone after his mother died. There was a New York apartment and an elegant summer place near Pass Christian, Mississippi.

Both of them had concluded that at the base of music lay principles of metaphysics that were hidden by the distractions of everyday life. Before long music fell away as one of their topics of discourse and they returned to the subjects they had collided with on the night of their first meeting, prayer and the promise of deliverance, the end of exile and the root of souls.

They talked about Zen and Theravada and the Holy Ghost, the bodhisattvas, the *sefirot* and the Trinity, Pico della Mirandola, Teresa of Ávila, Philo, Abulafia, Adam Kadmon, the *Zohar,* the sentience of diamonds, the Shekhinah, the meaning of *tikkun,* Kali and Matronit under the dread designation of the moon.

They had both tried using Christianity as a bridge between mountains. Raziel offered an image of them both falling, and Jeshu with them, head over heels, his cross reversed and spinning, anti-aerodynamic. Christianity had failed them as Christ had failed, who made his grave among the wicked. Yet, they agreed, his roots extended from the beginning of Creation and the tree would have to grow again. They agreed that each person carried within himself a multiplicity of souls.

Once they went to St. Catherine's Monastery in the Sinai and followed the Steps of Repentance to the summit of Jebel Musa at sunrise. De Kuff prayed at the *mihrab* there, making the Ishmaelite shrine his own. Before them in the direction of Mecca spread the Gulf of Eilat, and to the west the Gulf of Suez, two turquoise dazzles against the blood-red mountains. De Kuff charged up the last steps, coughing and gasping for breath while the darkness turned milky around him, trying to outrun impending dawn.

And because it had seemed a suitable time then, light filling the universe to its far corners, the sun raised up like an offering, Raziel had undertaken to explain to Adam De Kuff the significance of his own name. How the Hebrew letter *kuf* signified paradox — the *zayin* descending, the *reish* hovering above — the soul it represented must experience emptiness and darkness, in the midst of the withdrawing light it struggled always to reach. It stood for holiness descending and contained the secret of Eve. Its value in Gematria was nineteen. How the *kuf* whose value was nineteen followed the *tzadi,* which was eighteen and the secret of Adam. The pairing was completed as *tzaddik,* and this holy term had fallen on De Kuff himself. To the *tzaddik*, the righteous one, fell the task of redeeming the sparks lost with the fall into exile. Any man so signified was compelled to walk through darkness and death and seek out the Uncreated Light. The *kuf* was the sign of Life in Death, the paradox of redemption.

It was just as well to tell him all this then, Raziel said, while they were both bathed in the new light of day, while De Kuff's spirits were high. And if it was really the mountain where Moses had set forth the Law, so much the better.

Together with his name of Adam, Raziel explained, he suggested what was written: "He has set an end to darkness." The secret of the *kuf* was concentrated light. His very name was a channel of perception.

"This is too much for me," De Kuff replied.

Raziel laughed. He told Adam that the letter *kuf* also carried the connotation of monkey, a paradox of another sort. But perhaps, thought Raziel, who was skilled at interpretation, the walker into the place of dead shells, the gatherer of light had to be a kind of clown.

De Kuff's first reaction was anger.

"Why should I trust you?" he asked Raziel. "You say yourself that you used drugs. You take me to the top of a mountain. Beautiful, of course, but rather conventional as the site of inspiration."

He might regret the illusions that had led him to Christian baptism, he told Raziel, that had brought him to stand in the Church of St. Vincent Ferrer, on Lexington Avenue, for the pouring on of water and the laying on of hands. In a room named for a Spanish inquisitor — he, De Kuff, the son of Sephardim! But as a Christian he had become enough of a Jansenist solitary to reject holy places in general as impediments to faith. Like miracles, they suggested people's credulity and trickery.

"You're the monkey," he told Raziel. "You're the one who torments me with notions."

Raziel laughed again. "No, man. You. You're the monkey."

Though it might be too much for him, Adam De Kuff began from that day to believe everything that Raziel told him about himself. Besides terrors, there were raptures. Raziel assured him that his dark world would presently be full of light, an interior morning, brightening by degrees.

De Kuff confessed that he had always wondered about the disorderliness of his own mind, the promiscuity of his thoughts. The doctors to whom he had turned had called his condition bipolar disorder, treated him with psychotropics and even lithium. But he himself had come to speculate more and more on the souls whose essences adhered to his soul — in Jewish mystical terms, his *gilgulim*. Raziel told him to prepare to face extreme circumstances. Things seemed to point to his being an instrument of redemption.

Once, walking in the cool of the evening in the oasis of Subeita, De Kuff was seized by an antic mood.

"What's my problem?" he had shouted, playing the peddler, some imaginary Tevye-esque immigrant forbear, he whose ancestors were the pale *hidalgos, hombres muy formal.*

And Raziel, seeming to joke along at first, had replied, "Your problem is your face is too bright. Your problem is you're too smart to be the one you are. The number of your name could bring down cherubim. You're the Son of David brought back, that's your problem."

That was how Raziel put it to him, finally.

For weeks and weeks they kept moving, as though to illustrate the text that the Son of Man had nowhere to lay his head. De Kuff went without sleep, without rest. He had stopped taking his medication.

Eventually, Raziel moved them in with an old friend, Gigi Prinzer, an artist in Safed. Her house was in the artists' quarter. From it, De Kuff and Raziel would set out each day to wander among the tombs of the sages.

They were hard by the synagogue dedicated to Ari, the Lion, Isaac Luria, on the spot where Elijah had revealed to him the inner meaning of Torah. Not far away was Meron, where Simeon bar Yochai, to whom tradition ascribed the *Zohar,* was buried.

Overcome by the sanctity of the hills, De Kuff would fall prey to fits of weeping. The pious, passing near, glanced at him with approval.

"You'll make me lose my mind," De Kuff told Raziel. "I can't bear the weight of this place."

"If it couldn't be done," Raziel explained, "it wouldn't be asked of you."

"Asked!" De Kuff exploded. "I don't recall being asked. Who asked?"

"I think it's like this," Raziel had said. "Accept it or die. Accept it or go under. And then we wait again. As with Christ. As with Sabbatai."

"But as you know," De Kuff protested, "I can't pray."

"You can't pray. You don't have to. It's all written."

"You're sure?"

Raziel assured him that was why he had been a Catholic for a while. "Moshiach waits at the gates of Rome. Despised. Among lepers. Want to hear the rest?"

"Oh, my," De Kuff said. He took out a handkerchief and wiped his face.

In Safed De Kuff could only sit and cry, as though his borrowed soul aspired to the mountains he could see to the north, as though he wanted to flee the holiness of the sages buried around him, the tyranny of his fate and of the Ancient Holy One. He was always pursued. Now something had seized him again, something unyielding. Jonah.

Gigi Prinzer made her living as a painter of middlebrow religious art, conceived for the bolder among devout spirits, done in desert colors — a little Safed, a little Santa Fe. Gigi had liked Santa Fe and often wished herself there. Now, because she was in love with Raziel, she let them stay.

De Kuff's funds were sufficient to support them, but Raziel could not bear to forgo opportunities to spread knowledge of his recognition, to initiate raps he could dominate. In a tweed sport jacket and an English bookie's cap he accosted tourists at the bus station or the tourist office. His dress and manner promised the alternative tour of Safed, and that was what he provided. Where the competition offered *bubba meisses,* stories of no account, Raziel's strong point was comparative religion. He was soon suspected of being a Mormon or a Jew for Jesus. Interrogators and provocateurs discovered, however, that he could talk Midrash, Mishnah and Gamara with the best of them.

"Who are you?" the *haredim* would demand with customary Israeli tact. "What are you doing here?"

"I am a child of the universe," Raziel would reply. "I have a right to be here."

"You're Jewish?" they would inquire.

"Eskimo," Raziel told them.

On the tours, if he thought the group receptive, he revealed some original notions. The extraordinary Hindu counterparts to Kabbala. How Abulafia's *Light of the Intellect*, with its suggestions for breathing techniques as an aid to meditation, greatly resembled hatha yoga. How the Kabbalistic doctrine of *ayin,* the unknowable element in which the Infinite exists, had its Hindu cognate in the concept Nishkala Shiva, the remote absolute. That there were many more such parallels in Hinduism, and others to be found in Sufic Islam and in the Christian mysticism of Eckhart and Böhme.

Some visitors had left Raziel's Safed tours edified and inspired. But there had been complaints. Sometimes in his enthusiasm Raziel misjudged his auditors. Conservative customers, expecting heartwarming, twinkly wisdom from the ancient sages — or at least something more traditional — had left offended. The Hasidim, a formidable presence in Safed, had been made aware of Raziel's teachings and were displeased.

He and De Kuff also gave occasional concerts in which he accompanied De Kuff on the piano. De Kuff played the lute and chitarone as well as the cello and knew Sephardic melodies with a depth beyond silence. Some clerics went so far as to appeal to the police, who declined to intervene. Raziel was sometimes assaulted, but he could take a punch and he knew a little karate.

Occasionally he would return from one of his tours with one or more guests, who would be given lunch or tea — the price of which they would be politely expected to add to the cost of their tour. Usually the guests were young foreigners, as often Gentile as Jewish. Some stayed for a few days before drifting on. But there were others who stayed weeks.

A young German who had been to Tibet and taught yoga in London joined Raziel in kundalini meditations. Together they in-

structed De Kuff in kundalini yoga. Raziel believed that these meditations were a means of *kavana,* or meditations on the supernal,
which might lead toward *dvekut,* a unity with the Divine Ground.

Kundalini meditations were demanding and further upset De
Kuff's equilibrium. Often in the depths of stillness, pictures formed
in De Kuff's mind that frightened him. At other times they were
inspiring. Raziel made sure that De Kuff always told him what he
had seen.

In some of De Kuff's reports, Raziel recognized elements of *sata-
patha brahmana,* visions of Kali, and Shiva beyond attributes. Raziel assured him it was a good sign, because all these things had their
equivalents in the *Zohar.*

Once De Kuff reported he had seen in meditation a snake devour-
ing its own tail, and Raziel informed him that this was the ouroboros, which in the *Zohar* signified *bereshit,* the opening word of
Genesis. Sabbatai Zevi, the self-proclaimed Messiah of Smyrna, had
adopted it as his special symbol.

Thereafter he addressed De Kuff as Rev, which he sometimes
made sound slightly ironical, and assured him there was no doubt
about his election.

"Funny," Gigi said, referring to the man from Tibet, "we found
this out through a German."

"No, no," Raziel said. "Appropriate. Because it's all written."

"A German?" Gigi asked. "But why?"

"Don't ask me to explain the balance of *tikkun.* Accept him."

Gigi looked to De Kuff for guidance, although he had never provided her with much.

"So be it," he said.

More people came and went. Some Dutch girls who smoked hashish
came briefly, interested only in a place to crash. An American Jewish
girl fleeing her violent Palestinian boyfriend and ashamed to go home
appeared. Gigi would agree to rent to them if they made themselves
scarce and stayed away from the gallery. A Finnish woman who
turned out to be a reporter arrived, took her notes and left.

Once while De Kuff sat weeping, Raziel came up behind him.

"Feeling sorry for yourself? I should add you to the tour."

"Sometimes," De Kuff said, "you seem to hate me. You seem to
make fun of me. It makes me wonder."

Raziel hunkered beside him.

"Forgive me, Rev. I'm impatient. We're both crazy. Isn't it weird the way things work?"

"I want to go back to Jerusalem," De Kuff declared.

"Wait for the light," Raziel said.

That evening De Kuff stayed up late, reading.

The room was decorated with Gigi's paintings and drawings, art from her Perugian period, which had preceded her time in Santa Fe. Pastoral scenes of Umbria in voluptuous brown and yellow forms, warm and handsome, somewhat like Gigi herself.

De Kuff, reading, also had an Italian setting. He was examining his own papers and journals, the ones dating from a period when he himself had traveled in Italy. Spread before him in manuscript on the bed was an essay he had written on Hermetic elements in the paintings of Botticelli. His eye fell on what he had written about the painter's *Annunciation* in the Uffizi:

"The angel's wings appear virtually atremble, one of the great illustrations of spiritual immanence in Western painting. A winged moment of time is captured here, a 'temporal' moment shading into a 'cosmic' one, time shading into eternity. The numinous transforming matter."

Reading the lines made him shiver with longing for the person he had been. An innocent enthusiast, responsible only for himself. Two years before he had been received into the Catholic Church and he had believed himself at peace. Little enough he had known about the numinous then.

"An art lover," he said aloud. He put the paper aside and closed his eyes.

Later, before dawn, he woke up joyful, his room full of light. He went up to the roof and saw the stars. There were meteors on the ridge lines. A sliver of dawn was breaking. At breakfast he declared, "We're going to the city."

"Yes?" asked Raziel.

"This is how it has to be. For a space of time that only I will know, we'll stay in the city. Then we go to Mount Hermon so that it will be fulfilled that we walk from Dan to Gilead. Then back to the city. In the space of the events everything will be revealed. Do you require a demonstration from the texts?"

"No," Raziel said. "I require only your word. You're my world, Rev. I'm not joking. *Nunc dimittis.*"

"What was it like?" Raziel asked his master later, in Gigi's garden. A fresh mountain wind blew, smelling of the pines.

"Light," De Kuff said. "I felt a blessed assurance." After a moment he said, "I think we may see manifestations."

"But what did you see?"

"Someday," said De Kuff, "I'll tell you."

"You can't keep it from me," Raziel said. "I recognized you. I have to know what you saw."

"Get us to the city," De Kuff told him. "Maybe one day you'll know."

"You have to tell me something," Raziel said. "A part. I also have to believe. I've given you my life, Rev. I also have to believe and go on."

"Five things are true," De Kuff said. "Five true things define the universe. The first is that everything is Torah. Everything that was and everything that will be. The outer circumstances change, they're of no importance, but everything essential is written in letters of fire. The second is that the time to come is at hand. And for that reason we'll go first to Jerusalem. The world we've waited for is being born."

Raziel was impressed. He went inside to tell Gigi they would be on the move.

"It's time," he said. "We're a burden on you. And we're getting static."

"I can't go," she said. "All my property is here. I have customers come in from overseas. They don't know about . . ." She waved her hand to indicate De Kuff's theurgical confusions.

"We'll stay in close touch," Raziel said. "Trust us. You'll always have a part in this."

She shrugged and looked away from him.

"Meanwhile," he said, "I guess I'll go down to T.V. and play a couple of gigs. I'll go see Stanley tomorrow. He's usually looking for musicians."

"When you go to Stanley's," Gigi said, "I always worry for you."

"I worry too," Raziel said. "But the light of the eye is stronger than drugs."

"Remember," De Kuff told them, "we have only each other."

"That's the good news, right?" Raziel said, getting up. "Also the bad," he added.

"What about the tours?" Gigi asked. "What if someone calls?"

"Tell them the tours are at an end," said De Kuff. He got up and went back into his room and shut the door. Gigi sighed; she and Raziel looked at each other.

"What will happen?" she asked him.

"We'll live it out," Raziel said. "Check this out, Gigi." He stood and picked up a pocket-sized New Testament that dated from his Jews-for-Jesus phase. " 'Therefore take no thought, saying, What shall we eat? Or, What shall we drink? Or, Wherewithal shall we be clothed? For after all these things do the Gentiles seek.' "

Gigi winced and nibbled her thumbnail. "Funny you should come all this way," she said. "Funny you should come *here* to be a Christian."

"I'm not a Christian, Gigi. I've seen the dark — I've really seen it. I believe in light."

"I was never religious," she said. "I've lost my sanity. Not to mention my business."

The young man laughed. "You became an artist. It wasn't an accident. You don't need a business. To stay here and do *getch* for tourists? And what will sanity get you?"

"The power always fails," she said. "He said it himself. It has always failed."

"It," Raziel said. "What *it?* It's us. We're it." He laughed and frightened her. "It's a game."

"A game," Gigi said. "It's terrible."

When Raziel went upstairs to read, Gigi knocked on De Kuff's door and went inside. He was sitting on the bed.

"He frightens me," Gigi said. "Always laughing. His Christian Bibles."

"People like him don't reassure us," De Kuff said. "They're frightening sometimes."

"I wish I had never met him. Don't you?"

"Too late," said De Kuff.

8

L UCAS'S FLATMATE and occasional lover, Tsililla Sturm, returned early from London. She had been interviewing an
American director who was shooting a film at Shepperton.
Emerging from the taxi in the rosy stillness of a spring morning,
Tsililla looked pale and in pain. Lucas watched her arrival from his
balcony window and went to the door to let her in. He had been
reading Obermann's notes on the Reverend Theodore Earl Ericksen.

"I couldn't telephone," she told him. "Are you alone? I can go to
a hotel."

"Nonsense," Lucas said impatiently. He was somewhat embittered over the flickering out of their affair. "Of course I'm alone. Did
you think I would move someone into your flat?"

"I thought you might have an overnight guest. Why not?"

For a year or so, until the previous winter, Lucas and Tsililla had
been a couple. It had been an intensely reflective, not to say a tor-
tuously examined, relationship. Tsililla had been raised on a Tol-
stoyan-Freudian-Socialist kibbutz in the Galilee, equipped from in-
fancy with such a plenitude of answers to life's questions as to leave
her awash in useless certainties.

Lucas himself tended toward introspection. They had exhausted
each other. As part of their present arrangement, they had set each
other free — a freedom that Lucas found particularly oppressive.
No sooner had things gone wrong with Tsililla than he began experiencing impotence, which declined to set him free. For the first time
in his life, he began to worry about aging and whether his powers
would ever come back to him.

On Tsililla's study wall was a picture of a well-known New York
novelist with his arm around two fetching young soldier girls. One

was the blushing twenty-year-old Tsililla, the second her then closest friend, comrade in arms and fellow kibbutznik, Gigi Prinzer. The touring writer had encountered them at their posting in the Negev and been smitten, whereupon the three of them had managed to parlay a jolly photo opportunity into a ghastly triangle. After an extravaganza of mutual psychic and sexual predation, each against all, the three principals had psychically imploded.

The novelist had gone home, profoundly blocked and in deep midlife crisis, to his wife and the jeers of his cruel psychiatrist. In Gigi and Tsililla's company, he had gathered undreamed-of insights and material but was unable to write a line. Tsililla herself had published a dark novel, which was well received and indifferently translated into French.

The novel had established her career as a full-time writer, although she eventually took up film criticism rather than fiction. Gigi, transformed into Tsililla's bitterest enemy, had gone to the Art Students' League of New York and to the École des Beaux Arts and then become a peace activist and commercially successful painter with a whitewashed studio in Safed. Only Tsililla, Lucas often thought, would preserve such a grisly souvenir as that photograph.

"Shall I get my things out of the bedroom?" Lucas offered. The gesture earned him only a dismissive look, but it was one on which he doted. Her long pale face with its high cheekbones and prominent, full-lipped mouth never failed to stir him.

He was sorely tempted to question her about the trip. He suspected she had contrived to fall in love again. Tsililla had a perpetual affair going with the great *beau monde* of mind and spirit and surrendered herself to it readily. In his jaundiced moments, he saw her as a silly little snob and groupie, and he was inclined to be unsympathetic this morning. But weary from the flight and whatever misadventures, she looked especially desirable. Then, to his perplexity, she came over to the chair on which he sprawled and kissed him on the cheek. He touched her hand in spite of himself.

"Go to bed, my love," he said. "And later things will all be different."

Leaving the bedroom door open, she tossed her traveling clothes in the customary heap at the foot of the bed and climbed under the covers. It was not unusual for her to go to bed at dawn.

"What will you do today?" she asked him from beneath the counterpane.

"I have to go down to Ein Gedi, to this conference. Talk to some Christian sky pilot. Religion and so forth."

"You should do the mud," she said. "Put some on your bald spot."

Anywhere else? he thought. He glared at her, but she was huddled under the covers with her back to him.

"It works," she said after a moment.

"Thanks for the tip, Tsililla," said Lucas.

"Go to Masada."

"Should I? Why?"

"You should. I went when I was in school. You've never been."

The ruined mountaintop fortress at Masada was the place where first-century Jewish Zealots, in rebellion against Roman rule, were reported to have committed suicide rather than surrender to Roman troops. It was a major tourist attraction.

"Masada's a lot of baloney," Lucas told her. "Only Boy Scouts believe it."

Piqued or asleep, she did not answer. But then it occurred to him that he might just go, and even spend a night in the valley. Enthusiasm was, after all, his subject.

In the bathroom, he used the accordion-hinged mirror beside Tsililla's sink to locate his bald spot. Without question it was expanding, brightening in the spring sunshine.

He straightened up and had a look at himself in the larger glass above the sink. He supposed Israel was aging him. Recently colleagues had expressed surprise upon hearing that he had been too young to work Vietnam. But the absurdity in Grenada had been his war, for what it was worth. The Gulf War had literally bypassed him. Overhead.

Lucas was a big man, broad-shouldered, thin-lipped, long-jawed. Once one of his girlfriends had laughed at him, laughed at his face, with the explanation that he so often appeared to be at the point of saying something funny. It was hard for him to believe now that his spare mouth and fixed mug suggested incipient humor. Moreover, his hairline was receding, his forehead claiming more of his face, exposing the strategies in his eyes.

He was not a vain man, but his own appearance discouraged him. Lucas had not engaged his own appearance for some time.

Before setting out, he had a last glance at Obermann's Ericksen file. The meeting was not scheduled until late in the day, so there would be plenty of time to prepare.

The file led off with a résumé of the reverend, apparently prepared by the estranged Mrs. Ericksen. Ericksen had started out as a Primitive Baptist in eastern Colorado, gone to Bible school in California and served a few working-class congregations in the industrial suburbs of L.A. Then he had gone to Guatemala as a missionary for three years and married Linda there. Immediately thereafter they had both turned up in Israel. They had worked with a number of Christian institutions here, as evangelical missionaries to Christian Arabs in Ramallah, at a camp for visiting Christian youth groups loosely organized on the kibbutz model, and as tour guides for church trips. Then, finally, at about the time his marriage with Linda began to fail, he had taken over the House of the Galilean and its good lentil soup.

Calling Ericksen, Lucas had proposed that he join him on one of the H of G's excursions to the shores of the Dead Sea, and Ericksen had agreed. Included with his résumé were many inspirational brochures that emphasized Qumran and the Essenes, with references to the Teacher of Righteousness. The line, barely hinted at in the promotional stuff, seemed to Lucas vaguely unorthodox, if not quite in the *majnoon* category. It suggested a variety of New Age Gnosticism more than old-time holy rolling.

Late in the morning, leaving Tsililla asleep, he packed up his notes and went out. He took along some topical reading for the trip down: Josephus's *Jewish War* and a modern history of the same period by a British historian.

His old Renault was parked at the side of the building's driveway downstairs. As a hopeful precaution, he had equipped the car with two large printed signs that said PRESS in English, Russian, Hebrew and Arabic, purchased from a Palestinian street vendor near the Damascus Gate. Why there should be a Russian rendering Lucas had no idea, but he thought it might not hurt to confuse the issue. He was always trying to project the maximum degree of complexity against a landscape whose inhabitants had neither the time nor the inclination for much. The way to Ein Gedi would take him through the most secure part of the Occupied Territories, but there was always a chance of trouble.

The car's yellow Israeli license plate might well draw stones at the Jericho turnoff; the press sign, designed to placate the rock-throwing *shebab,* sometimes enraged the militant settlers. Cars bearing such a sign were occasionally forced to stop by armed men who interrogated and insulted members of the foreign press, whom they tended to see as Arab lovers. The most militant settlers, Lucas had found, always seemed to be Americans, and they reserved their most furious scorn for American reporters.

But the greatest danger of all, Lucas understood, was not *fedayeen* on *jihad* or enraged Jabotinskyites; it would come from ordinary Israeli motorists, who had, as a group, the aggressiveness, fatalism and approximate life expectancy of west Texas bikers. Their random fury could be neither appeased nor sensibly anticipated.

The city had spread far to the east. Neat, ugly blocks of flats extended into the Judean Hills, and it was nearly half an hour before he reached the open desert. Then all at once there were stony ravines where the ravens might have nourished Hagar. Black Bedouin tents clung to shingled hillsides; demonic goats nibbled along the shoulder of the road. The ridge lines were commanded, every few miles, by army strong points with sandbags and razor wire. Rounding one turn, he came in sight of the green oasis of Jericho below and the pale salty blue of the Dead Sea to the south of it. On the far horizon, across the wide water in the Kingdom of Jordan, loomed the limestone mass of Mount Nebo. It was where Moses was supposed to have set eyes on the Promised Land at last, and died. In some ways, Lucas thought, squinting into the haze, an ideal outcome.

Killing time, he decided to risk a long detour through Jericho, following the main highway into town and pulling off at the compound where the Egged buses stopped and Palestinian vendors sold fruit, soda and gewgaws under the eye of a Border Police post. The breeze was rank and sweet with verdure, and the humidity drew sweat and stirred vague appetites. He bought two large bottles of mineral water and drank one greedily. Even the quality of thirst seemed different in the lowlands. A man in Bedouin robes, dark as an Ashanti, sold him a small bunch of bananas. People of African origin, descendants of slaves it was said, lived in a few nearby villages.

The town was quiet. He had a cup of coffee in the café at Hisham's palace and then drove south, following the straight highway under the cliffs over the Jordan valley. The hotel and spa where the Reverend Mr. Ericksen and his colleagues were conferring had sunfaded flags of the tourist nations on a crescent of flagpoles at the entrance to its driveway. The driveway itself was a desolate sandy track between stands of brush and thorn trees, leading to two beige buildings beside a dun marsh that edged toward the greasy white-caps of the Dead Sea.

A surly young man at the front desk provided him information with studied indifference. The spiritual conferees were off on a junket to the Qumran caves and would not return until late afternoon. Lucas left a message for Ericksen. Until then, he would have a choice of several diversions. He might go out to the caves himself and endeavor to commune with ectoplasmic Essenes. He might hop one of the hotel's tourist buses for the midday excursion to Masada, down the road. Or he might book himself into the whole Dead Sea spritz-and-shvitz, endure the mud bath and the sulfurated showers, perform the belly-up wallow along the salty shore. After a little dawdling, thinking of Tsililla, he opted for Masada.

He read Josephus on the way — the story of Eleazar and the Zealots holding off the Romans to the last, the Roman breach, the self-slaughter of the surviving Jews. For some reason, today the bus to the fortress was filled with Italians, along with a few British and Americans. The guide spoke only English to his charges and on the way told the group about the Allenby Bridge and the Dead Sea kibbutzim and the wildlife park near Ein Gedi. As Lucas had suspected they might, themes of identity emerged early in the expedition. The guide, providing a historical survey in preparation for the fortress, explained the perspective of Herod the Great.

"Herod was a Jew," the guide explained. He was a lean, crusty man in his mid-fifties who wore a plaid gillie's hat. "But in his heart he was a Gentile."

Cringing inwardly, Lucas found himself remembering an ancient black-and-white film he had seen on television as a child. In it, the Indian villain had been adopted by the good Indians, allies of the Americans, but had soon reverted in affection to the bad Indians, who in this movie were Hurons.

"He was born a Huron," the justly suspicious white hero — John Wayne, if he remembered correctly — said of the turncoat Injun. "And unless I miss my guess, he's still a Huron."

A half-breed scout of dubious loyalty, Lucas frowned up at the great red escarpment that towered above the parking lot. While the tour guide led the bus passengers toward the cable car, he took the map the tour company provided and set out to find the trail called the Snake, which led to the top. He had brought a soft khaki sun hat that he took along, together with the books in his day pack and a few bananas and the remaining bottle of water he had purchased in Jericho.

He stopped frequently on the way up; he was out of condition and the sun was high. His skin seemed to wither under the burnished sky. Halfway to the top, he found the shade of an overhang and leaned against the rock to wipe the sweat from his eyes and get his breath. Israeli teenagers in backpacks hurried past him, half jogging up the slope. The wilderness of Moab across the valley shimmered in the near distance.

Walking out on the mesa at last, he felt a stirring of loneliness and spite. Another fateful mountain, he thought, another celebration of blood and bonding. Following the tourist path, he found himself taking comfort in the ruins of Herod's palace, the secular cheer of the fluted columns, the mosaic tiles in the tepidarium. If there had been a place for him at Masada, Lucas thought, it would have to have been with those who would just as soon take the waters as fight over religion. And if he had had to pick a side, he supposed he might have ended up on either, or with both in turn, like Josephus. He might well have found a home with the Tenth Legion — bastards, scum of the empire, including no doubt a few such confused *mischlings,* mercenaries and anti-patriots like himself. He belonged to the late-imperial, rootless, cosmopolitan side of things.

The group with which he had ridden down from Ein Gedi had finished their circuit of the precincts and taken the cable car down. Lucas followed his guidebook from the Herodian synagogue through the Zealot compound to the Byzantine chapel. He walked the walls from lookout point to lookout point, and indeed it was not hard to hear the demotic curses and the cries of butchered families and to picture bloodied *spathas* raised against the blue sky.

He found a shaded bench near the eastern wall and sat down to browse the British historian. The learned don turned out to be a skeptic regarding Masada and its grim intransigence. His line on inspiring tales of the legendary Levant was like Ira Gershwin's: it was not necessarily so.

The historian believed that Josephus, a dramaturge like most classical chroniclers, had invented Eleazar's valedictory to his troops in imitation of Greco-Roman models. In the actual outcome, some Zealots had killed themselves and their families, some had died fighting, others had hauled ass and been cut down or enslaved, or had succeeded in hiding.

Nor had the Zealots been selfless patriots. They had lapsed into banditry and murder, terrorizing the country, killing more Jews than heathen. Lucas had heard something of the sort before, but reading the professor under the spell of the place afforded him renewed relief. People were people, for what it was worth. The fundamental things remained. And the official Masada story belonged to military pageants and state propaganda and the kind of heroic iconography expressed in Hollywood costume pictures with Kirk Douglas clenching his teeth. Or had that been a different movie? He would have to try it all on Tsililla.

Are things better, he wondered, because we know the old stories that sustained us are lies? Does it make us freer? Descending in the cable car, caged in sleek-smelling technology, he watched the parking lot rise from the valley floor. Beyond the lines of tour buses were the buildings of the potash plant that had replaced buggery down in Sodom.

The bus that had brought him from Ein Gedi had left, so he went to wait for the next one. In ten minutes, a local bus came along that was filled with soldiers toting their automatic weapons. Lucas got in and sat across from the driver.

The soldiers proved to be on their way for a bath at the end of their day's duty, and the bus pulled into the spa's driveway. On one side of it was a lot marked by a sign that said NO COACHES in three languages, and it was for this area that the driver promptly headed. Immediately an attendant, a small man in a straw hat and round sunglasses, ran forward to block the bus's path. To the cheers of the soldiers, the driver drove around him. As the bus was parking, the attendant ran after it and planted himself before the windshield, arms outstretched in an accusatory shrug of well-nigh-cosmic pathos. It was the gesture of one who, having seen all folly, challenged the world to destroy the last vestige of his belief in reason. The driver simply sneered and steered around him. Then he turned toward Lucas and gestured at the outraged attendant.

"*Sotsialist,*" he said scornfully.

9

To pass the rest of the afternoon, Lucas took the waters. There were showers and an indoor saltwater pool and a little jitney that carried bathers to the shore. He was surprised to see signs in German everywhere — over some of the doors and blocks of lockers it was the only language of information. Could there be so many German tourists, he wondered, and could so much effort be expended for their convenience? It was unsettling to see the signs among the disrobing rooms and bathhouses and banks of showers.

At the shore, Lucas covered himself in vile-smelling mud, careful to rub some of the stuff into his bald spot. Then he edged over the slime into the oily water and bobbed in it for a while. A dip in the Dead Sea, Lucas found, resembled in its chilly, sticky wetness many of life's other mildly unpleasant trophy experiences.

Rinsing and drying, he found his way to the cafeteria, which was pleasant and had glass walls that commanded a view in all directions. The sun had already passed below the edge of the escarpment to the east, and a lengthening shadow stretched across the fading blue water. He got two beers from the cooler and took a table on the Dead Sea side.

As the afternoon wore on, the cafeteria began to fill with customers. Halfway through his first beer, Lucas became aware that the people at the tables nearest him were speaking German. But they were not Germans, he realized at once — not really. They were elderly German-speaking Israelis, "yekkes," come for the minerals and hydrotherapy. They sat decorously over their coffee and cake, eyeing the other clientele with icy, condescending smiles, interrupting one another, declaiming self-confidently in a language normally half whispered in this land. Almost all looked over seventy, but they were alert, vigorous and sinewy. The men favored short-sleeved white shirts, the women bohemian net shawls about their shoulders. A number of them were staring at him, trying, he supposed, to gauge his story. Sometimes in Israel, Lucas had found, when people had puzzled long enough over your story, they simply came forward to demand it. No one accosted him this afternoon.

Hearing their voices reminded him of walks he had taken as a boy in New York from the Upper West Side to the Cloisters. In Fort Tryon Park there had been a stand that sold good grilled frankfurters and hot mustard to go with them. He had always thought of it as the best hot dog stand in New York, and it was patronized in all weathers by German-Jewish refugees from Washington Heights. Lucas remembered it particularly in winter, when the customers would sit outside, facing the pale sunlight over the Jersey Palisades — the men in their rakishly turned fedoras and fur-collared overcoats, the women in boxy felt hats and tweeds. And if they did not actually sport pince-nez, Lucas still remembered them so.

At nearly six o'clock, he bought himself a third beer and took a table facing east, on the other side of the room, where the view was of the darkening cliffs. In this section were foreigners, Gentiles, and it seemed to Lucas that even with his eyes closed, without discerning the prevailing language of discourse, he would know it. Something guileless and unguarded in the laughter, an absence of irony in the air.

About the time he learned that there were such things as Jews and Gentiles — a fact he had drawn from his mother in the face of extreme reluctance, since it was a matter of some inconvenience to her — Lucas had played a few highly private games involving who was who. For a period during his childhood — following a painful experience at the Catholic school he attended — the question had become an obsession. Of course he had gotten over it.

The incident at school had been devastating in its way. One day, in the fourth grade, Lucas had been playing stoopball outside the school in Yorkville when the subject of neighborhoods came up. Neighborhoods, in the circles where Lucas got his early education, were defined by Catholic parishes. When the game ended, Lucas, who had banged three home runs that afternoon, found himself accosted by the chief of the losing team, a boy named Kevin English. English was an ill-spoken lad and Lucas had once teased him for saying "youse."

"So where do you live?" English had asked young Lucas. "What parish?"

"St. Joseph's," Lucas had replied. "Morningside Heights."

"That's Harlem," English had said.

"No it's not," Lucas had answered. "It's near Columbia University."

"Then it's all fuckin' Jews, then," English said.

"My father's Jewish," Lucas had replied.

English's reaction astonished him.

"Jewish? A fucking Jew?"

Lucas never accepted the Freudian doctrine of repression. It seemed to him, for better or worse, that he remembered everything. Still, he could not seem to recall the spirit — humorous? defiant? confiding? — that had impelled him to make that declaration. He did recall that having made it then and there, he realized at once that he had placed himself in some new cold country of the heart from which he would never return.

The following week, everyone was playing stoopball and Lucas had gotten off a squarely placed hit, smack on the angle, not only high but wide — out of the park, had there been a park. But there were only improvised bases to run — the pointed railing they called "the spears," the manhole at second and, at third, a pair of metal elevator doors level with the schoolyard. So Lucas scored, and so did all three runners on base. As they were exchanging sober handshakes, the custom of the day, English, who had come storming in to cover first, confronted the exhilarated Lucas.

"You Jew fuck! You sheeny kike bastard."

He had known all week it would come back to roost. Only one of English's sycophants joined in. But their attack had been so furious, so venomously *joyous,* so infernal, that Lucas would remember it always. Then there had been a fight between him and English, and he, Lucas, had gotten the worst. This came as a surprise to him, since he had been in the right.

The fight had been broken up by Brother Nicholas, prefect of the grammar school, a dour French Canadian, who had come running out into the street. Brother Nicholas assumed the fight was over stoopball and decreed that the issue be settled by a "smoker" at the end of the week. A smoker was a supervised boxing match through which boys who were weekly boarders at the school settled their violent differences.

He had had a bad feeling about the business all during the day of the smoker. Something had been lost to him somehow, traded for something else unknown.

The smoker was held in a corner of the gym, surrounded by a rectangle of tape. The antagonists were stripped to the waist and wore boxing gloves. Lucas had summoned all the resources of his imagination to invest the event with the pageantry of sports and movies, tournaments and duels and gunfights. But he was without friends. All of his friends were the day students, and the boarders — English's friends — were a hard lot, drawn from the caseload of social service agencies. Lucas was there because his mother was on tour that season. He'd sensed the match would end badly, and it had. He had learned a few new obscenities, which was useful. There was the ambiguous advantage of having justice on his side. But in the end the beating English gave him, whacking him repeatedly on the ear and actually deafening him for a week, made him feel ashamed and deserving of it.

Later the same evening, Brother Nicholas had spoken a few kind words in the school infirmary while putting Mercurochrome on his wounds and icing down his swollen face. The brother had put a stop to the Jew-bastard stuff from the crowd and slapped a few heads.

"So," Brother Nicholas had asked him with Gallic delicacy, "is someone Jewish at home?"

"My dad," Lucas had replied. "Except he's not really at home."

Brother Nicholas had grown thoughtful.

"We must all," he declared, touching the cotton swab to Lucas's eyebrow, "offer up our humiliations." Brother Nicholas believed in offering humiliations to the Holy Ghost, who was apparently gratified or appeased by them.

He was on his own until the following weekend, when his mother came home from her tour, exhausted, throatsore, besieged by migraines. He tried for days not to tell her. But they were confidantes and pals, temperamentally alike, communicators, raconteurs. So he did.

"Why did I say a word?" she demanded of herself. "Why did I have to tell you at your age?" She had told him while waxing philosophical over her third highball during one of their visits to the King Cole Bar at the St. Regis, a goodbye treat for him.

Lucas's mother had then cried so bitterly and lavished such embraces on him that he had rebelled and, out of mischief, pitched her one of the new obscenities he had learned during the bout.

"That English, he's a cocksucker, Mom."

It had shocked her right out of her lamentations. For a more or less kept woman, Lucas's mother was a considerable prude.

A little later on, she set about explaining to him the extreme limitations to which anti-Semites were subject.

"I mean," she said, "the people who dislike Jews" — "dislike" was the most intense word her well-bred instincts made available — "are the most dimwitted, uneducated, unartistic people. No decent person, no person of breeding, certainly no cultivated person, feels that way. Only the most measly, paltry hoi polloi, the lowest, roughest, coarsest of the low, feel such things."

And, who, Mom, Lucas had thought at once, do you think I'm locked up in that joint with? Unuttered, it had remained one of his great unreleased zingers. However, this notion had occurred to her.

"I've got to get you out of that dreadful place," she said.

Snob though she was, she remained a faithful Irish girl, and there was no putting her off Holy Mother Church when it came to education. His father was prevailed upon to underwrite Lucas's transfer to a Jesuit school, whose teachers were all astronomers and poets and veterans of the Belgian Resistance and whose students were cosmopolitans, discreet and even, sometimes, partly Jewish.

But for some years thereafter, as his points of reference and relative sophistication increased, in certain public places — darkened movie theaters of the Upper West Side, for example — he had sat attuned to the unseen audience, trying to gauge from the flimsiest evidence — reaction to newsreels, to pious scenes from New Testament epics, to elements he himself barely understood — whether the people around him were Jewish or not. For practical purposes it was all the same to him; neither comfort nor reassurance would be forthcoming either way.

Sometimes he would turn in the stippled darkness to observe his mother and her reactions to the screen. Her reflexes, sense of humor, vocabulary of gesture and expression were, in retrospect of course, distinctly Gentile. Lucas had never attended the movies with his father. None of this interfered with his Christian ardor, which flourished as he entered adolescence.

Looking up from his beer, he saw a handsome young man approaching him. The man was obviously American, beautifully turned out, dressed for safari in expensive earth tones. He was tall and flawlessly athletic of build, his bronze skin slightly sun-reddened. He wore wire-rimmed round tinted glasses that showed off his fine cheekbones. The German Jews observed his passage with a saturnine alertness. Only at the very last moment did Lucas realize that he must be Reverend Ericksen.

A second man followed a few steps behind Ericksen. This man, though young, had a foxy, unwholesomely rosy face, as if he were suffering from a mixture of sunburn and psoriasis. He wore a dirty white sun hat with a green eyeshade and khaki shorts with ankle-length black socks and dusty black street shoes. He looked as unpresentable as Ericksen looked cool and polished.

Lucas stood.

"Mr. Ericksen?"

Ericksen extended the kind of soft handshake that had become current among well-traveled Americans, replacing the Honest Abe bonecrusher grip of the past. He took a seat across the table. The man with him was named Dr. Gordon Lestrade. Lestrade was British and extended his hand as though the custom of handshakes were pathetically laughable. Lucas explained the mission: an article on the Jerusalem Syndrome. Ericksen looked thoughtfully concerned. Dr. Lestrade smirked.

"Hundreds of thousands of Christians come to the land of Israel every year from all over, Mr. Lucas," Ericksen said. "They come and are inspired for the rest of their lives. A tiny handful are disturbed in some way."

Lucas had the feeling he was receiving a packaged response. He decided to parry with the counter-package. "But religious obsession is fascinating. And it tells something about the nature of faith."

"Religious people are being marginalized by the media," Ericksen declared. "Watch television, go to the movies — the religious person is always a bad guy. Sometimes just a prig but usually a criminal — a lunatic and murderer."

"I'm not pursuing the obvious," Lucas said. He omitted the part about being a religion major. It seemed only to annoy people.

"All right," said Ericksen. "How can I help you?"

"I thought we could start with the House of the Galilean. How you came to be there. What the purpose of the place is."

"Its original purpose was as a hospice for evangelicals," Ericksen said. "They used to be very much outsiders here."

"And now?"

"Now we still put up the odd pilgrim. But we're more involved with research. Biblical archeology. Dr. Lestrade's field."

"Do you work out here?" Lucas asked Lestrade.

Lestrade turned to Ericksen for the answer. His own features were still constricted in an odd, unpleasant smile, which Lucas began to think might be involuntary or otherwise pathological.

"Not very much any longer," Ericksen said. "We bring pilgrims to Masada and Qumran and to the Mount of Temptation."

"I thought you took a special interest in the Essenes?"

"At the moment our work is in Jerusalem," Ericksen said. "Around the Temple Mount. You ought to come see our place in the city. It's in New Katamon."

"Yes," Lucas said. "I know."

"If you like," Ericksen suggested, "you could come out with us tomorrow. We're taking our folks to Jebel Quruntul."

Lucas drew a blank on Jebel Quruntul.

The peculiar Dr. Lestrade came to his assistance. "The Mount of Temptation," he explained. "You probably don't know the story."

"As a matter of fact, I do," Lucas said.

He was at the point of declining the offer when instinctively he thought better of it. He was attracted by the notion of a night in the desert and curious about Ericksen's take for the pilgrims on the Mount of Temptation.

"We're leaving at half past five," Ericksen said. "Can you manage it? Plenty of room in the bus."

"I'll be ready," he told Ericksen. "I have my own car."

It was a slow night around the spa. The cafeteria closed at seven, the buses for the city departed, and there were few overnight guests apart from the members of Ericksen's tour. A wing of the hotel was reserved for them and, wandering in the gardens outside, Lucas could overhear their pleasant chatter. But after nine o'clock a silence and darkness descended on the desert that seemed to suspend life itself.

Walking down toward the invisible sulfurous water, Lucas suddenly heard the flutter of a chopper's engine and saw the sweeping light of a patrol helicopter illuminate the roiling surface a mile or so out. Then it peeled off toward Cape Costigan and the darkness settled down again. He turned around and walked back to the hotel. Beside one of the plastic pillars in front of the rows of doors, he happened on Dr. Lestrade, swathed in towels literally from head to foot.

"Going with us, are you, Lucas?"

Thus swaddled, and with his cryptic smile, Lestrade looked like the statue of a Canaanite deity, a resemblance his black-rimmed spectacles mysteriously enhanced.

"Yes, I guess so."

"Do you actually know what the Mount of Temptation was?"

"Sure," Lucas said. "I've been to the art museums."

"American Jewish, are you?"

"That's right," said Lucas.

"And do you feel a special affinity? That you've come home?"

"Dr. Lestrade," Lucas asked, "are you having me on?"

"No," Lestrade said. "I always ask. Good night." And he was gone like the spectral figure he resembled.

10

B Y THE TIME Lucas was up, early the next morning, the pilgrims of the House of the Galilean were milling about their bus. Most of them were ultra-American. White loafers, lime-green slacks and plaid Bermudas abounded. Pious foreigners in Israel were forever absurdly behind the times, in pursuit of their own national stereotypes. Wandering among them, making a breakfast of the overripe fruit he had bought the day before, he also heard Canadian and antipodean voices, recruits from wherever the House of the Galilean's world-wandering circus played.

Dr. Lestrade approached him. "Look," he said, "can I ride with you?"

Lucas agreed. He assumed the doctor was thirsting for the odd drop of ink. It would be a long time coming, Lucas thought.

They followed the bus off the hotel grounds and onto the Jerusalem and Jericho road.

"Your pilgrims seem to be having a good time," Lucas said.

"Oh, yes. They're Types."

Of course, Lucas thought, though his patriotism smarted, they were that.

"Are they always the same?"

"They all seem the same to me," Lestrade said. "Perhaps not to you."

"They say clichés exist only in art, doctor. Not in life."

"Well, if only we knew each other's inmost souls, haw?"

Which effectively silenced Lucas for the next several miles.

"You a clergyman, doctor?" he asked eventually.

"God, no. Archeologist."

"Specializing in Bible sites?"

"Recently."

"And what's your connection to the House of the Galilean?"

"Scientific consultant."

"Like," Lucas ventured, "searching for Noah's Ark? That sort of thing?"

"Noah's Ark," the doctor repeated. "That's good. No, actually, I'm not a communicant of the H of G. I'm the real thing, in my humble fashion. An actual archeologist. I give a little talk on Qumran and the Essenes."

Before Lucas could apologize, Lestrade went on.

"This is, as they say, the Holy Land." He pronounced the term with a mocking delicacy. "There are actual biblical sites here. I mean *something* happened, eh? Something we're still sussing out."

"Any new findings?"

"Oh, you'd be amazed. Who did you say you worked for?"

"I used to be a contributing editor for *Harper's Magazine.* Now I'm working on a book."

"Oh dear," said Dr. Lestrade, "so am I."

"But mine is on religious sects. I'm not an archeologist. And I might do the odd article."

"Well, working for the House, one tends to specialize. We've been working on the Mount of Olives and the Qumran caves. Also the Temple Mount, of course."

"I thought that was off limits."

"Not entirely. Not to us."

"What's new on the Mount?"

"The House is very interested in the Second Temple and the Holy of Holies. The dimensions and so forth. It's all recorded somewhere."

"The Talmud, you mean."

"Not only the Talmud."

"Where else?"

"Sorry," Dr. Lestrade said. "That's all I'd better say. The House has a public relations officer. Best talk to him."

On the Jericho road, Lestrade got to reminiscing about his adventures educating the Types.

"One of them — well, we're in this Byzantine church near Bodrum, in Turkey. On the wall is a huge mosaic of Christ Pantocrator, J.C., the King of Kings. Staring eyes, upraised arm, come in majesty to judge the quick and the dead. Jesus Christ Almighty, right? So one lady inquires, 'Doctor,' " — and here Lestrade flattened his voice to that of a toneless Yank — " 'how old is this here church?' 'Oh,' says me, 'dates to the seventh century.' 'Really?' she says. 'A.D. or B.C.?' Hee-haw."

"She had Jesus in her heart," Lucas suggested.

"She could have been a fucking Buddhist," said Lestrade, "for all she knew."

It developed that Dr. Lestrade had studied for many years to be a Benedictine monk. Finishing his studies at Cambridge, he had pulled out at the last minute. "Not really for me," he explained.

Following the bus that bore Reverend Ericksen and the Types, they took the Jerusalem highway for a few kilometers and then made the turnoff for Jebel Quruntul. At the junction was a moldering building that had once housed a café. Two toddlers sat in the ruined garden beside it, surrounded by aloe, errant vines and litter. As Lucas eased onto the Jebel Quruntul road, one of the tiny urchins picked up a shard and flung it ineffectually toward the car.

They lost the tour bus for a while, but after a few wrong turns Lucas found it parked in front of the monastery halfway to the summit.

"Thanks," said Lestrade, heading for the bus, which stood with its motor running for the driver's comfort. "This is as far as I'll go. I've heard the lesson and I've seen the view."

Lucas walked through the monastery's dark chapel, with its battery of Oriental saints along the walls. Behind it, at the far end of a walled garden, was a doorway, beside which a disreputable-looking Orthodox monk stood with his palm extended in an unseemly fashion.

Lucas paid his six shekels and started up the limestone path that led to the peak. As he struggled up the steps, the words of the Jesus Prayer kept coming into his mind, matching his labored breathing with the insistence of an insomniac melody. His gut was sore from the bad fruit.

Reverend Ericksen and his tour group were on a rise near the eastern edge of the peak. Ericksen himself stood on a rock above them, his arm extended in a circular gesture. And the view, in all directions, was spectacular and surprising. Across the valley lay the silver strand of Jordan, the land of Moab, to the north Galilee, to the south the Dead Sea. Westward, it was possible to see the outskirts of Jerusalem in the distance, the buildings atop the Mount of Olives.

Ericksen was reciting Saint Luke from memory in a voice like country water. He was giving them Jesus in the desert:

When forty days of fasting were ended, Jesus met Satan, who was out on one of his celebrated walks. For some reason, Satan prevailed on Jesus to accompany him.

"And the devil, taking him unto a high mountain, showed unto him all the kingdoms of the world in a moment of time. And the devil said, All this power will I give thee, and the glory of them, for that is delivered to me and to whomsoever I will give it."

Lucas felt a shiver. The light was blinding and his belly ached. Ericksen took a breath and went on reciting. Dazzled, Lucas broke away from the group and followed a decrepit sign that pointed down the westward face of the slope. Scrambling down, he followed a goat track to an ancient building that appeared to house the toilets.

It was an odd set of privies that the Mount of Temptation provided. There was a water tank outside, but the building itself, partly ruined, much resembled the main building of the monastery down the slope. Inside, Lucas thought he could make out figures on the walls that seemed older than the Arabic and English graffiti scrawled across them. The pain in his guts seemed to be affecting his imagination. Shapes on the wall appeared to sway.

Some kind of desolate, sinister insight flashed across his mind and was gone. Across the room from where he squatted he saw a winged figure in sienna — scales, he thought, scaled wings and claws. It reminded him of nothing so much as the Duccio *Temptation* he knew from the Frick Collection, a painting situated where it was hard to miss, a painting he associated more with lost love and hangovers and rainy New York afternoons than with anything religious. In it, Christ floated under a gold metaphysical sky, dismissing the scaled demon who offered him the world.

The only light in the privy came through the open door. Washing up afterward, he was stricken again by recall: it was the stinking lavatory of the charity school he had gone to and been scalded as a Jew. His memory was of washing up after his fight with English, washing away the blood from his nose and mouth, the salt taste of it. In that moment he recalled also his pale child's face in the dirty communal mirror. It was a bad and unfamiliar recollection. It upset him. He walked out into the painful daylight, breathing in the sweet desert herbs, laurel, tamarisk.

He turned to look at the building he had been inside and touched the wall. There was no way to tell its age. Colonial frontier kiosks from the 1920s could look biblical after a few decades of weathering if they were made of the old stone. But something about the place filled him with loathing — a devil-haunted cloister jakes out of Luther's or his own nightmares, where defiling solitude, childish self-indulgence and shameless concupiscence lay in wait. But worse, the stench of his own childhood, the image of himself as victim.

He ambled back up the *jebel* and waited to catch Ericksen alone. He kept thinking of the temptations of Christ, the curious text and its mysteries. Jesus challenged to turn stones to bread. Offered Satan's powers. Offered the risk of annihilation at the Temple's pinnacle, provoked to summon angels.

"Satan must have been curious about Jesus," he suggested to the pastor. "Being an angel himself. And Jesus being a man. Getting hungry and falling off things."

Ericksen laughed tolerantly. "The whole world was in Satan's power," he told Lucas. "It was about to be redeemed."

"So," Lucas said, "think Satan was fishing for a deal?"

"Yes. Maybe."

"If the world is redeemed," Lucas asked, "why is it the way it is? The Redemption is as mysterious as the Fall. I mean," he said, surprising himself with his own fervor, as though somehow this small-town smoothie would tell him the meaning of it all, "where is He?"

"Satan knew that they would meet again," Ericksen said. "And they will. Satan," he confided to Lucas, "has many names, and his power has never been greater than it is today. That's why the great contest is near."

"Is it?"

"The Messiah of the Jewish people is coming back. He's going to lead the struggle against evil. Then Satan will be known by his true name, Azazel. His forces will fight those of the Lord. When the struggle is over, everyone living will be converted."

"I hate to ask this question," Lucas said, "but who wins?"

"The Lord wins. Azazel will be bound under earth as he was before."

"Was before?"

"Azazel was imprisoned in the earth," Reverend Ericksen declared. "But he escaped to America and he was waiting for mankind there. We Americans spread his power throughout the world. Now we owe Israel help in its struggle against him."

"I thought everyone was going to turn Christian," Lucas said. "Isn't that how it's supposed to go?"

"After the victory," Ericksen said, "Israel will accept Jesus Christ as the Davidic Messiah. But first there will be war and strife."

"So you bring people here . . ." Lucas began to speculate.

The reverend completed the message for him: "To show them the scene of a great temptation. The first temptation was when Azazel tried to murder Moses. The second was when he approached Jesus Christ. The third will be soon, when he assembles his forces and the Messiah returns to combat."

"So we Americans," Lucas said, "we have a lot to answer for."

"We'll pay it back here, helping the land of Israel," Ericksen said. "Well, if there's anything more I can do for you personally, let me know. Otherwise, as I say, we have a PR man."

Lucas passed Dr. Lestrade on the way back to his car. He asked Lucas how he had enjoyed the view and the encouragements.

"Wouldn't have missed it," Lucas told him. "Definitely glad I came."

Dr. Lestrade seemed puzzled but said nothing more.

Driving back to Jerusalem, Lucas stopped at an army shelter to pick up two armed soldiers looking for a ride toward town. One was a fair youth who seemed no older than a teenager, the second was a hard-faced, graying sergeant.

It turned out that the fair soldier had worked in his uncle's T-shirt shop in Islamorada, Florida.

"You could print anything on a T-shirt there. 'Shit.' 'Fuck.' Anything. Then they had to pay. For dirty words, more."

But what the soldier truly wanted to do was build a boat and sail across the Mediterranean and the Atlantic, back to the Florida Keys.

"But not back to the T-shirt business?" Lucas asked.

"Nah. It was rotten. Boring. Embarrassing. But the sea is what I like."

Lucas let him out pretty far from the sea, at a command post across from a settlement called Kfar Silber. The old sergeant was silent and somber. Lucas's impulse was to ask where he came from. But Israel was like the Old West, in that such a question was considered bad form and could open a world of grief, horror, compromise.

At one point, the sergeant took out a pack of Israeli cigarettes and offered one to Lucas. When Lucas declined, he put one in his own mouth.

"Don't mind?"

"Not in the least," Lucas said.

"American?"

"Yes."

"Jewish?"

Lucas hesitated. The sergeant paused in the act of lighting his cigarette.

"No," said Lucas. Not today, thanks.

"Correspondent?" the sergeant asked. Lucas remembered the press sign he was displaying. "Where you coming from?"

"Ein Gedi," Lucas said. "For the waters."

"Like it?"

"I do," Lucas said. "I think it's good for me."

"Sure it's good for you," said the sergeant.

They drove all the way back to Jerusalem together.

11

STANDING under the lights at Mister Stanley's again, Sonia experienced a moment of utter confusion. Who are we? What place is this?

The place was full of Russians. Her backup was bass and piano, the former late of the Kiev Institute. The piano player, who could play every instrument known to man, was Razz Melker, a former junkie, yeshiva student and Jew for Jesus who was now a Jew for someone similar up in Safed. In any case, he was an old flame from her junkier days and a marvelous accompanist who could read your mind and sound your soul. Everyone on stage was clean and sober for the occasion. The house was noisy and boozy.

When the lights were as she liked them, she told the piano player, "*Alef*, Razz, please." So Razz, a mysterian who believed that *alef* invoked the primal waters and the first ray of light, sounded the key in which it all began. And, wondering if her chops were there, wondering if the aging instrument would kindly engage, she threw her shoulders back and brought it up, an old Fran Landesman song called "Spring Can Really Hang You Up the Most."

It came out fine, quieted them, and the end of the first verse drew a little ooh-aah thing that was nice too. She could feel them settling back to enjoy themselves. Now, she thought, if they would just behave. And the applause was solid and, she hoped, not altogether ignorant. Because they had hipsters in Russia too, and a lot of them had come to Israel. And there were other sorts of people in the crowd, including some of her friends.

"So while the theme is spring, comrades," she told them — and you always got a laugh with "comrades" — "the next one is called 'Spring Will Be a Little Late This Year.'"

The title drew applause. Sometimes she sang arcane songs, on the theory that if her shows failed as performance, they might hold up as musicology. But tonight it seemed she was more or less on the money and the room knew what it liked. She gave them "Spring" in homage to the career of Leslie Uggams. It went well.

Sonia's first gig had been in the Village, at a little place called Dogberry's, working for a share of the bar money. After checking coats all evening for the uptown Frenchmen she would hasten out of the Sheridan Square subway stop and down Grove Street and wriggle into the black thing that hung in her tiny dressing room. There had been an upstairs lounge where she performed and a gay piano bar downstairs, so every time a lounge customer got up to pee and opened the hall door, Ethel Merman imitations would resound from the space below.

Her Sufi master in New York had been musical and sent her back to singing. It had been years since her training, and she had had to bring it all back as well as she was able. As a child, she had listened to all the singers. The white ones intimidated her less, so she took some of them as models, starting with Marian Harris and Ruth Etting. Then June Christy, Anita O'Day and notably Julie London, with whom she had fallen in love from afar, and above all Annie Ross of Hendricks, Lambert and Ross, doing Basie and "Twisted." The great soul singers were her true idols but she felt them beyond her. Sometimes, though, she tried to sound like Chaka Khan. And every once in a while, if she had a buzz on, if she thought nobody heard, no one much saw, she might have a shot at Miss Sarah Vaughan, which she dared do only in cold, precise imitation, as ceremony and celebration. In time she actually came to think of herself as something of a white singer, lacking the intensity for jazz but funny enough, salty enough, for cabaret.

She closed the first set with "How Long Has This Been Going On?" after the manner of Miss Sarah and drew a rather rousing ovation.

"Thank you, comrades. Thanks for the prolonged stormy applause."

Then there was a multicultural outpouring of appreciation: some people threw shekels or American bills or flowers. The odd sport even occasionally tossed a low-grade diamond in a cotton handkerchief. She only picked up a couple of roses and kissed her hand to them.

She was on her way to her friends' table when a man intercepted her. He had dark eyes and a tanned, open face and he seemed to contain some peculiar excitement.

"That's the greatest Sarah Vaughan I've ever seen," he told her. "Since I saw Sarah Vaughan."

She gave him a sweet professional smile and said, "Thank you so much."

"My name is Chris Lucas," Lucas said. "I got your name from Janusz Zimmer. You were recommended to me as a student of Sufism, and I wondered if we could chat for a bit." When she failed to answer he added, "You know, it's interesting. Working here. And studying faith."

Sonia was in no hurry to talk to friends of Janusz's. "Sorry," she said sweetly, "I'm joining friends."

"I just meant for a minute or two."

She gave him a little routine that read: Funny, I can't hear you, and you seem not to be able to hear me — and walked delicately around him. She was going to sit with her NGOnik friends.

One of the reasons Stanley favored Sonia's performances at his club was that they tended to attract Sonia's colleagues from the nongovernmental organizations engaged in good works in the area. These were a coven of conspicuously foreign girls from the nicer countries of the world; Sonia had worked with most of them in Somalia and the Sudan. These girls might be Danish or Swedish or Finnish, Canadian or Irish — fair, boreal creatures whose grannies and great-aunts had been missionaries to the hot world and who labored on in the same vineyard, chastened and rigorously nonjudgmental, demystified but no less intense.

This evening, two of the NGOniks were at Sonia's table: a middle-aged Danish woman named Inge Rikker and a toothy, towheaded young rodeo queen named Helen Henderson. Young Henderson was a former serving Rose of Saskatoon, so they all called her the Rose. They both worked for the United Nations in the Gaza Strip. Sonia had been expecting a third, her Irish chum Nuala Rice, who was with an outfit known as the International Children's Foundation.

Inge and the Rose applauded rowdily. Sonia bent and hugged them.

"Hi, guys. Where's Nuala?"

"Back with Stanley," Helen said.

Sonia sat down and poured herself a long glass of mineral water from the bottle on the table.

"Having any adventures?" she asked Inge and Helen. They were both working out of the Khan Yunis camp in the Gaza Strip.

"We're still chasing Abu Baraka," Inge said.

"Abu and his band of merry pranksters," said Helen. "We almost nailed him the other night."

"Who's that?" Sonia asked.

Helen looked at her with a faint frown of disapproval. "You haven't heard of Abu Baraka? I guess you've been meditating, huh?"

"Give me a break," Sonia said. "I haven't been down there in months."

So they told her the story of Abu Baraka, the avenger of Gaza.

"The Father of Mercy, he calls himself. And there's nothing about him in the *Jerusalem Post*." Inge showed them the bleak smile in which her twenty years of recent African history remained unresolved. "Or in the American papers."

Sonia began to feel they were ganging up on her. "Did you complain to the army?" she asked.

"The army says they don't know who he is," said Inge. "Officially."

"And unofficially?"

"Unofficially," said the Rose, "they don't give a shit. They say, 'Give us evidence.'"

"Has he killed anyone?"

"We don't know. If he has, it's gone unreported. He's a crippler. He cripples."

"The attacks are made to appear intracommunal," Inge said. "But our Palestinian lawyer says they make no sense that way. In any case, we have no proof."

"So what if you had? What can you do?"

"Confront the bastard," declared the Rose. "That's my strategy."

Inge and Sonia exchanged looks. The Rose was twenty-five years old. She had worked in the Caribbean, and she liked to drive the back roads of the Occupied Territories in a Jeep Laredo whose bumper sticker read STUDY ARSE ME, an injunction in which neither the Palestinian *shebab* nor the IDF troopers needed encouragement. She understood it to be a Jamaican phrase of defiance. The sentiment had been underlined on her arrival by the extremely tight, faded denim shorts she had planned to wear on the job, until advised of their ungodliness. Muslims in Jamaica, she had explained, never seemed to mind.

Presently a scented French-sounding young man with a gold chain at his neck arrived to conduct the Rose to the floor, where the two of them began dancing to Abba. Inge watched her go with motherly forbearance.

"Fearless," she said.

"You gotta love her," said Sonia, who had her doubts.

"The father's a general, so they say. A war hero."

"No fooling?" Sonia said.

"But not your father," Inge said, and Sonia realized she had been drinking.

"My daddy was not a general," she told her friend. "Not even a colonel."

"What then?"

"A poet," she told Inge. "Really cool but sort of unsung."

Inge kept smiling. "About Abu Baraka," she said. "The Rose would be unwise to confront him. He hit Nuala good and hard last week. At night, his face blacked up. Him or one of his boys."

"I suppose," Sonia said, "some night he's going to kill someone."

"We're working with the Israeli Human Rights Coalition," said Inge.

"One thing you can depend on," Sonia told her. "When the killing comes, the wrong people always get it. It's the first principle of race riots. The wrong people, either side. Well," she said, looking at her watch, "I'm almost on again. I want to say hi to Nuala."

Inge reached out and took hold of her arm.

"But if we found this man," she said, "these men — we could build a case. You and I and the Israeli civil rights groups. I'm Danish, you're Jewish. People might pay attention to us."

"I don't know, Inge."

"As someone said," Inge declared, "to work down there you have to have a center. If you don't, you can't."

"I think that was me," Sonia said. "I said that."

"It sounds like you," Inge said.

Sonia disengaged herself and went into the backstage area to one side of the room. In a small, brightly lit room she found Nuala and Stanley. Stanley was sitting astride a folding chair with his holy fool's smile. Nuala, looking flushed and manic, was sitting on the makeup table with her back to the long mirror. She opened her arms for Sonia.

"Hurrah," she said. "You wonderful girl. I was watching."

They embraced; Sonia thought she seemed preoccupied. Nuala was tall and lithe, with black hair and pale freckled skin. Her eyes were very blue and the sort called piercing. In her early thirties, she had a few wrinkles beside them from a life under equatorial skies. That night she displayed the remnants of a shiner, still slightly swollen and empurpled above her delicate dead-white cheek.

"Hurrah, hurrah," said Stanley, beaming at Sonia.

"What are you two up to?" She winced at the sight of Nuala's eye.

"I thought it was a rifle butt. But I guess it was his fist."

"Maria Clara sends her love," Stanley told Sonia. "She'll be back from South America tomorrow."

Sonia, who wanted nothing to do with Maria Clara, ignored him. "Come and gossip with me after this set," she said to Nuala. "I want to hear about everything."

"Have you missed us, Sonia?" Nuala asked. "We've missed you. But I can't come out, you see. There's a chap in the audience I don't want to run into."

"Who?"

"Oh, the man who just spoke to you. An American reporter. Nice, but I don't want him to see me here."

"Well," Sonia said. "Of course I've missed you." After a moment she asked, "What's he after, the reporter?"

"He doesn't know what he's after. Bit of a lost soul, really. He wants to write about religion. We'd like him to write about what's happening in the Strip."

"He looked interesting." Sonia laughed. "But I stiffed him."

"Well, he's sweet," Nuala said with a laugh and a shrug. "I bet you'd like him. And I think he speaks your language."

Back out under the lights, Sonia thought, What about my center? Nobody home there. Jerusalem was high and dry, no place to tread water; you needed either a job to do or some fancy illusions.

She opened the second set with a Lieber and Stoller song: "Is That All There Is?" It was a favorite of Razz's. Then she did "As Tears Go By" and then her favorite Gershwin songs, finishing with "But Not for Me," in the manner of Miss Vaughan, really getting into it, letting herself go. Her Manhattan adept had suggested that she turn her singing into an exercise, make music her certainty and let it find its *tariq,* ascending like the metaphorical serpent, transforming herself into a horn and the stuff rising straight up, flourishing in the chamber of resonance, emerging through the mask. Useful pictures. It seemed to go well because the room applauded briskly.

Nuala was still hiding in the back room. Inge and the Rose were on the floor, being danced about by a couple of Moroccans.

"Inge says you'll come back," said Nuala.

"Back where?"

"The Strip, where else?"

"Inge may be mistaken."

"Never," said Nuala Rice. "Inge's always right."

"I wouldn't be any use," Sonia said.

"You of all people? Nonsense. Anyway, we need you."

"Nobody's irreplaceable. Especially not me."

"Forget your troubles. Get back with us."

That was the formula, Sonia thought. Some people liked to make their trouble everybody's. Others had to submerge theirs in the great sump of human misery.

"You know," she said, "I probably will go back eventually."

12

S HE HAD A solid last set, sweet and low. Toward the end, to please the Russians, she did two *Porgy* songs, the Gershwin and a Jimmy McHugh. Just before the closing number, Razz the pianist gave her a wink and a nod, inviting later conversation. She wondered if it meant she had been mistaken about his being clean. Or if he was trying to rekindle old fires. They closed with "My Man," which that particular room would conceive as the essence of soul.

After the last number, the jukebox came on and people got up to dance. There was a shortage of women, so she hid out backstage with Razz Melker.

"You all right, Razz?" she asked him. "Got your health back?"

"I'm clean, Sonia." His smile grew even wider and his amber eyes shone. "Life's a miracle."

"Better stay away from Stanley," she said.

When she started away, Razz called after her.

"Sonia?" he said hesitantly. "Something I wanted to ask. A favor."

"Sure," she said.

"We're leaving Safed. We'd like to come to the city."

"You don't mean here?"

"I mean the *city*. J-town."

"Well," she said, "good."

"There's a man, Sonia. You have to meet him. I swear you must."

"Uh-huh," she said cautiously. "Now, would this be a Christian man, a Jewish man or . . ."

"More."

"Wow," she said lightly. "The man we've been waiting for, right?"

"Maybe," Razz said. "I'm a gambler."

"What can I do for you?"

"We have a few people. He has a lot of books. I wondered if you could help us move."

"You mean hustle you up a ride? Offer myself?"

"Hey," Razz said, "nothing sordid. You're my sister."

She laughed. "I'd love a trip to Safed," she told him. "I'd be glad to drive you if I had a car. I sold it illegally. I still don't know if they'll let me out of the country without it. Where will you stay in the city?"

He shrugged happily, and she left him there.

Out in the room a few sports put the moves on her, but since they were all talking at once and getting in each other's way, she managed to pass amiably by. On the way to the table where her NGOnik friends sat, the man who had accosted her earlier appeared once more.

"You can really help me out," he said with a rueful smile. "And I wish you'd talk to me. I like your style so much."

He had been drinking. If he had managed to get drunk on booze at Stanley's prices, she thought, he must be a man of means. But he did not seem to be a casual jazz fan. He had the look of someone who could not order his pleasures.

"Oh, thanks," she said. "Sorry about just now. I was in a rush, see. How's Janusz?"

"Waiting for the next war, I guess."

"Yeah," she said, "Jan is a war lover. I met him in Somalia. He was in Vietnam too, reporting from the Vietnamese side. He flew with the Cuban fighter bombers in Eritrea, writing about it. One day he showed up in Baidoa."

"Interesting guy," Lucas said. "What's he doing here?"

"He lives here. He's Jewish."

"Found his roots?"

"I never thought of Jan as having roots," Sonia said. "What you say you were writing about?"

"Religious enthusiasm. I was told you were a Sufi."

"So you're another guy after religious nuts?" she asked him. "That's *old,* man."

"I'm not a put-down artist," Lucas said, "and I don't go for the obvious. In fact, I used to be religious myself."

"That right?"

"Right," Lucas said. "Can I buy you a drink?"

"I don't like to drink," Sonia said. "Maybe these ladies would like a drink, though. Ladies?" Suddenly Lucas found himself surrounded by Nordic women who looked as though they could handle their liquor. They hastened to accept. It would be an expensive night.

Lucas leaned close to Sonia, to speak above the noise of the jukebox. It was playing Count Basie's "Lafayette."

"You puzzle me," Lucas said. "I mean, what are you doing here?"

"Why shouldn't I be here? I'm Jewish too."

"Are you?"

"What do you mean, am I? You think I'm a little southern fried to be Jewish? Is that what you think?"

"No. I just think it's odd you would come to Israel to study an Islamic practice. Don't you live in Jerusalem?"

"That's right."

"Going back tonight?"

"I get the two-thirty bus."

"Don't do that," Lucas said. "Let me drive you."

She hesitated, then said, "That'd be good. Thank you."

"The bus station is depressing," Lucas said, "at this hour."

Outside, the after-midnight crowd had settled in at the sidewalk tables of the Orion Café, across the street from Mister Stanley's. The Orion's late-night crowd might be described as louche. As Lucas and Sonia went by, the sidewalk trade paused in its vivacious, sibilant conversations to check the two of them out. The customers out front favored pastel sheath dresses, and many had large hairy wrists.

"It's easy to get an extended visa," Sonia said. "And Berger al-Tariq is here."

"And he's a Sufi master?"

"He's the last. You should meet him."

"I'd like to."

She studied him for a moment. "In fact, I could introduce you to some very interesting people here. If you'd do me a favor."

"What would that be?"

"Give me another ride tomorrow. Ride me up to Safed and help me bring some friends down. With their books and stuff."

"Well," Lucas said, "I could do that. OK," he told her. "Deal."

"It's like our piano player wants to move to Jerusalem. He belongs to a religious group in Safed. People who might interest you."

"Good," said Lucas.

On the ride up to Jerusalem, they hit a jackal crossing the road. Its
dying yelps pursued them.

"I hate doing that," Lucas said. "I'll dream about it."

"I'm hip," Sonia said. "Me too."

They rode for a while and Lucas said, "I really meant it when I
said I enjoyed your singing. I hope you don't think I was just butter-
ing you up."

"I gotta believe you," she said. "Don't I?"

"I don't want my name in the paper," she told him a little later on.

"Can't I say you're a really good jazz singer?"

"Nope."

"Well," he said, "I don't work for the papers."

She told him more about the East Side Sufi underground — New
York's, not Jerusalem's — and about Dogberry's and gigs in New
York.

"Do you believe in God?" he asked her.

"Jesus," she said, "what a question."

"Well, I'm sorry," said Lucas. "We were talking religious enthusiasm."

"This is what I think, Chris. Instead of nothing out here, there's
something. It has a nature."

"That's it?"

"That's it. And more than enough."

"Oh," said Lucas, "I like that." It was a familiar enough sentiment, he thought, but she said it nicely. He felt a faint thrill of
sympathy.

"Were your parents religious?" he asked her.

"My parents were members of the American Communist Party.
They were atheists."

Looking at her, Lucas felt he had suddenly penetrated part of her
story. She was biracial, the child of old lefties. The story was on her
face to see.

"But that's belief too," he said.

"Sure. Communists believe that things have a nature. And that
an individual can be part of the process. They believe in a better
world."

"One where they give the orders," Lucas said.

She gave him an even stare, its rigor subverted by the suggestion of humor at the edges. How intelligent and pretty she is, Lucas thought. He allowed himself to believe she liked him.

"What about you, Chris? What's your story?"

"Well, my father was a Columbia professor. Originally from Austria. My mother was a singer. Which is why I like singing, I guess."

"Your father the Jewish one?"

"That's right. How about you?"

"Mom."

"Well," Lucas said, "you're OK then. But the ancients, in their wisdom, included me out."

"What do you care?" she asked. "Are *you* religious?"

"I was raised a Catholic."

"Then you're still one, right?"

Lucas shrugged.

"I'll tell you what," said Sonia. She began to write an address down on a half sheet of UNRWA stationery. "You pick me up here tomorrow and we'll drive up to Safed and we'll meet someone who might interest you. We'll be helping him move down to Jerusalem. On the way, you can ask anything you want."

"OK," Lucas said.

"I hope you don't mind a little light lifting. Ever been to Safed?"

"Never."

"You'll like it. Just wait."

There was already activity in the souks of the eastern city when she made her way to Berger's. Near the Damascus Gate, men with wheelbarrows were offloading sheep carcasses from a refrigerator truck. They stared after Sonia as she went by. She wore the billowing djellaba over her performance clothes. Normally, she would have made arrangements to stay in Tel Aviv with friends of her mother's, but Berger was lonely and dying and needed her.

She climbed the stone steps to Berger's apartment and fished for her keys. Berger was awake when she went inside. The place smelled of his sickness. He watched her around the curtain that enclosed his bed.

"You're seeing the boy from America." His painkiller had loosened his tongue.

"Raziel? Yes, I saw Razz today. We're playing the same gig. He lives in Safed now."

"Safed," Berger repeated dreamily.

Buzz, buzz, she thought. He was really dying. Flies hummed and bounced against the tiles of the inlaid table beside his bed.

"Lean on me," she told him. "I won't let you die alone."

"I think I want to go home," Berger said. "I want to hear German spoken. German without tears."

"We'll get you home, Berger. Don't you worry now."

He relaxed as the pain diminished. When he smiled, she could see the skull inside.

"I think of the lakes. Things like that. What I want to see again. Hail and farewell."

"Yes, my dear," she said. It occurred to her that she had seen a great many creatures die. It must be all right, she thought. It came for everyone. In Baidoa she had watched the babies fade like little stars.

"When I go," Berger said with sudden stoned animation, "someone will come."

"Who will it be?" she asked. "The Mahdi?"

"Don't joke about such things," Berger said.

"But what else is there?" she asked.

Then he himself grinned, like a joker. But the grin drained away.

"When I'm gone," Berger said, "you also should go to Safed."

"I thought you didn't want me seeing Raziel. Anyway, I don't like it in Safed."

"You should be among Jews."

She laughed. "Should I? Well, I probably always will be. One way or another."

Later, when it was light, she moved her chair to the open Moorish door and watched the shadows shorten across the court below. The slim fronds of the olive tree shuddered on a faint breeze. An hour or more passed. When the court was completely in shadow, she got up and brewed some coffee. Berger had only Israeli Nescafé.

His supply of painkillers, stashed in a cedar box on the dresser in the sleeping alcove, was ample. Sonia suspected that he would soon require something stronger. She filled a glass with powdered orange drink and poured in some cold water from a pitcher in the pocket refrigerator. Then she sat on the bed beside him with the drink and another tablet. Sleeping, Berger fidgeted and ground his teeth. When he woke up, he looked at her dully and tried to speak through the rictus of his rigid lower jaw. She got him to open his mouth to take the pill and held the glass to his lips. He drank and began to pant as though he were short of breath.

"Go back to sleep. Go on."

Just before he turned over, he whispered something to her. "Kundry," she thought he had said. She would have to ask him about that, to see if that was what he had said and if he remembered saying it.

"Is that me, Berger? Am I Kundry?"

That would make them Kundry and Amfortas. What a surprise, she thought. How German was the skull beneath the Sufi skin. Thinking of herself as Kundry made her recall Lincoln Center, Good Friday. Her date had been an alcoholic ex-Maoist Swedish publisher. James Levine had conducted. The Swede had alternately slept and wept. He had apparently forgotten the Chairman's thoughts and become a complete moldy fig, a relapsed, sniffling Wagnerian.

She adjusted the covers over Berger's shoulders and bent her head low to touch the quilt with her forehead. He had a smell like the smell that came off a pariah dog she had once seen being stoned by children in Jericho.

"Am I Kundry, Berger. *Moi?*"

She laughed to herself. Kundry. She locked the doors and took off her djellaba and the dress she performed in and her performance jewelry. Then she looked out over the Old City and breathed the name of the faraway Holy One, whose name was being proclaimed over the city, and closed her shutters and lay down to sleep.

13

LUCAS PICKED her up at the Damascus Gate in the bustle of afternoon. While he waited, the *sherut* drivers kept demanding that he move his car.

"Did you get any breakfast?" he asked her.

"I had coffee. Hot and sweet. That'll keep me buzzing. How are you?"

"I'm OK. Hung over."

"Too bad," she said. "I'm not surprised. God knows what Stanley serves out of those bottles."

He told her once again that he had enjoyed her singing. She brushed the compliment aside.

"So what's it like," he asked her when they were on the coastal road north, "following the Sufi way in Jerusalem?"

"There aren't many true Sufis in Jerusalem," she said. "Some Bektashi live in the Strip." She told him about Abdullah Walter and Berger al-Tariq.

They turned onto an inland road to skirt the three-layered congestion of Haifa, and along it the hills were planted in young forest. From time to time they passed the remnant of an Arab village. There were new towns with ten-story high-rises and central squares surrounded by modern vaulted buildings. In some of the squares, the decorative trees were hung with lights.

"Why live in Jerusalem, then?" he asked.

" 'Cause it's holy," she said. He thought she might well have been joking. "And I'm allowed to live there. But if Berger had been in Zurich or somewhere, I'd have gone there too."

"Too expensive. What got you into Sufism?"

"Fear," she said. "Rage. That sort of thing."

"Fear and rage," Lucas said, "are all I know."

After a while she said, "You're half in, half out, aren't you?"

"Of what?"

She did not reply.

"Is that how you feel?" he asked.

"I feel double in," she said. "Proud and simple. Carry it all."

It pleased him, and he laughed. "Everyone should be like you."

"Really?" she asked him coolly. "Like me? Holy cow!"

"Well," he said, "you know what I mean."

Soon they began to climb. The fences of kibbutzim divided the landscape. Vistas expanded. Within an hour they were in high green hills where stands of cedar grew. There were peaks in the distance and the sky seemed higher and bluer than along the coast. A fishtail of cirrus clouds stretched out overhead.

"Beautiful," said Lucas. "I've never been up here."

"Yes," she said. "The Galilee is beautiful."

He asked her about her European friends, and she explained that they were women she knew from working for the United Nations in the Sudan, Somalia and the Gaza Strip.

"I graduated from a Quaker school," she said. "So after college I went to work for the American Friends Service Committee. Then I lived in Cuba for ten years."

"What was that like?"

"I was out in the country. It was a good life. It was plain and friendly and useful."

She said it with such gravity that for a moment Lucas longed for such a life.

"Why did you leave?"

She shrugged, declining to get into it. Having decided that he wanted her to like him, he was reluctant to press her. But there was a story, after all.

"The politics get you down?"

"I'm not an anti-Communist, you know. Never will be. My parents were good people."

"But you left Cuba and . . . the rest."

"Eventually I left. I went back to New York."

And took up religion, Lucas thought, although he said nothing. At that point, he allowed himself to believe that he understood her. She was a person who required the proximity of faith. His understanding, his sense that she was like him in that way, made him feel fond of her. And he had really loved her singing.

"Is that where you studied music?"

"I always sang. I took a few courses with Ann Warren in Philadelphia and then at Juilliard. I studied but it was mostly singing for fun."

Safed stood on two hilltops that commanded the terraced fields of a valley and a view of the mountains of Lebanon. It had narrow streets and cobblestones that sat reverently under the deep blue vault of heaven.

"Lovely light," Lucas said.

"Yes, it's special light. Soaks up your fear and rage."

It was more or less what he had been thinking. He followed the main street as it wound around the principal hill, on which stood the ruins of a Crusader fortress. From the other side of the hill the prospect was even more spectacular. It was possible to see the blue glitter of the Sea of Galilee in the distance, and the peaks beyond it.

"This will do," she said. "Park here."

They were at the top of a narrow street leading down into the artists' quarter. It had been the Arab town.

"Want to come along?" she asked.

"Sure."

The cobblestones were clean and the walls freshly whitewashed. It was a pretty street, Lucas thought, that might be improved by a little squalor. On both sides of the passage were galleries displaying inspirational or religious art: brass menorahs, oil paintings of old men in prayer shawls, dancing Hasidim celebrating life in compositions suggestive of Bruegel. The street was so narrow that the galleries had automated lights to display the paintings.

At the next turn of the alley, a woman stood anxiously waiting, hands clasped at her chest. She was tall and fair, and Lucas thought he recognized her at some remove of time or place.

"For Mr. De Kuff?" she asked them in English, somewhat fearfully.

Sonia assured her that it was for De Kuff they had come. All at once Lucas realized that she was the woman in the picture with Tsililla and the American writer, the second soldier girl.

She led them inside, through a room hung with dark, rich landscapes that seemed to be without religious significance. But in the corner of each, in ocher paint, was a Hebrew letter or series of letters. They were beautifully done. One had *gimel,* the upper fingers of its *vav* like the strings of some instrument, the *yod* at its foot perfectly formed. Another had *zayin,* a third *hei.*

Behind a partition at the end of the gallery, a flight of circular stone stairs led to a windowless room containing a long table and cardboard boxes packed with books.

Two men stood waiting beside the cartons. One was a dark, sleek young man in sunglasses and a leather jacket, whom Lucas recognized as one of Sonia's backup musicians from the night before. The second man was about sixty, slack and round-shouldered in what had once been an elegant gray flannel suit.

"Sonia," the younger man said, "you're like so great. I'll never forget you for this."

"Hey, it's all right," she said. "I sort of carjacked this guy. Razz," she told him, "this is Christopher Lucas. He writes about religion. Christopher, Razz."

"I liked your playing," Lucas said.

"Good," the young man said, "thanks." He stepped aside with a smile to present the other man. "Christopher, Sonia — this is Adam De Kuff, our teacher."

Not knowing what custom permitted, Lucas made a small bow and put one hand to his heart in the Muslim manner. It was hardly appropriate in Safed, but he had taken up the habit. He felt it argued for his good intentions.

"Thank you, both," Adam said to Lucas and Sonia. "It's very kind, very good of you."

He had a pleasant voice, cultivated, southern American. Lucas, watching Sonia, saw no trace of the reserve, the hauteur with which she had fended him off the night before.

"As you see, we have many books," the aging man said. "We should like to take as many as possible."

So Lucas went back up the street and got his car and parked it outside Gigi's gallery on the cobblestone pedestrian walk. It was the sort of thing people did in Israel all the time. But violating even the most grossly secular law in Safed left him with a faintly cosmic sense of delinquency.

They spent the next half hour carrying down boxes of books, filling the trunk of Lucas's Renault. The last articles to go were three cloth suitcases.

"Fine," Lucas said. "Who's coming?"

"Just Mr. De Kuff and myself," said Razz.

Driving, illegally, back up the cobbled alley, they passed Hasidic women in babushkas on their afternoon stroll. At the corner of Jerusalem Street, one of a group of bearded men in black seemed to recognize them and nudged the others. They turned to stare, unashamed and hostile.

"They seem not to like us," Lucas observed.

"That's the posse," Raziel said. "The morality police. They ought to be happy we're leaving."

But the men Raziel had called a posse did not look happy at all. One or two of them stepped into the street to look after the passing Renault.

"Why are they on our case?" Sonia asked. "We're *chillonim*, right?" *Chillonim* was what the Orthodox called irreligious Jews. "They have nothing to do with us."

"Of course not," De Kuff said. "And they have nothing against you. It's us they're after. Raziel and me."

"Why?" Sonia asked.

"A lot of reasons," Razz said. "There are guys here I knew in Brooklyn. I spent some time there. They remember me as a dropout. Also, they didn't like the content of our Safed tours."

"Why not?" Lucas asked.

"We went to the same places their tours did."

"What's wrong with that?" Lucas asked.

Razz showed a humorless smile.

"We threw in a little comparative religion."

"Like what?"

"Like that form is not so different from nothingness," De Kuff said, interrupting.

"Hindu parallels," Raziel explained.

"They didn't care for Hindu parallels?" Sonia asked with a laugh.

"We had complaints," Raziel said. "Someone put the local enforcers on us."

"The Hasidim say everything is Torah," said De Kuff. "We agree."

The religiously minded reporter in Lucas inclined him toward asking Adam how everything was Torah. But before he could compose the question politely, they made a turn onto the main road that led down the slope of Mount Canaan, and the terraced hills spread out before him as far as the distant lake.

"God," he said, "what a view."

"In Safed," Raziel told them, "they say you can see from Dan to Gilead."

"Yes," said his fat, melancholy friend. "From one end of the world to the other."

Beside Lucas in the front seat, Sonia smiled and glanced at him. He felt his heart rise. He was happy to share something with her, even the nonsense of a stranger. At that moment, in that place, it seemed like agreeable nonsense and even possibly more. It was pleasantly evocative, and he thought he would remind himself to ask her sometime what she thought it meant.

"Is it a blessing?" he asked De Kuff. "To see so much?"

De Kuff answered him in some language of Scripture.

"Should I translate?" Razz asked cheerfully. "Or skip it?"

"Sure," Lucas said. "Translate."

"It's Aramaic. A commentary on Genesis." The reverent expository words had an odd sound in his slack hipster tones. Razz was junkielike, thought Lucas, who had known a few. "When it was said, 'Let there be light,' the light was the light of the eye. And the first Adam could see the entire universe."

"But it doesn't really answer my question."

"So think about it," Raziel said, "when you find the time."

He glanced at Sonia and saw that Razz's insolence amused her. It made him feel at once jealous and foolish, a disagreeable sensation, appropriate to adolescence.

"Think about it or not," De Kuff said. Then he seemed to drift into sleep.

"I never get these religious parables," Lucas said. "All the great profound numbers go right over my head. Buddhist koans. Tales of the Hasidim. It's all fortune cookies to me."

"I don't believe you," Sonia said. "Then why come here? Why write about religion?"

"Checking up," Lucas said. "Early warning."

"Of what?" asked Razz.

"The End of Days?" Lucas proposed, on a hunch.

"We're told to look for signs," Raziel said. "See any?"

"I thought you might see a few things I might not see."

"It seems likely," Raziel said.

"What does?" Sonia asked him. "The End?"

"Christopher missing something we might catch," Raziel said. "It's our business, after all. It's all we do."

"Good," Lucas said. "Mine is listening. Trying to get it all down."

"I'll bet you majored in religion," Razz said.

"Very good," Lucas said.

"Which one?" De Kuff asked him.

"It's all right," Raziel Melker explained. "He's joking."

"I knew that," Lucas replied.

Driving back, they went by way of Tiberias, descending from the hills to the plain beside Kinneret. At the confluence of the lake and the Jordan, they passed rows of banana trees on the kibbutz where Lucas's friend Tsililla had grown up. Then they were in the desert, past Bet Shean, on the Jericho road.

"Actually," Lucas told them, "I'm a former Catholic."

"Interesting," said Melker. "You seem Jewish."

Attempting to imagine the ways in which he might seem Jewish to Razz only made Lucas angrier. He had been in a perfectly agreeable frame of mind such a short time before.

"Not altogether," he declared.

Sonia was watching him out of the corner of her eye. "Just passing through, huh?"

"Right," said Lucas. "Working press."

14

O N A C O O L rainy morning a few weeks later, Sonia sat in the small stone showroom of Berger's landlord, Mardikian, the Armenian Uniate tile painter. His shop was off the Via Dolorosa but he lived and worked in a house near the Damascus Gate with a tiny garden and a grape arbor on the roof. Decorative square tiles were hung in rows on the whitewashed brick walls, displaying saints and prophets or the creatures of Eden. The Armenian and his brother painted them in a workshop at the rear, in colors that suggested Persian manuscripts.

He was a man in his seventies, massively boned, with a bald brown vault of a skull secured above his face by monumental brows. From certain angles, he appeared altogether brutal, although his voice was very gentle. They sipped Turkish coffee. From time to time, Sonia had been able to bring him regards from his old Jewish customers in the western city.

Sonia had come to inform Mardikian of Berger's death and to receive his condolences. When the formalities were over she expressed her desire to continue the arrangement. She reasoned that De Kuff's ability to pay well over the customary price might influence Mardikian's attitude.

Her friends, she told the tile maker, were scholars and Sufis like Abdullah Walter. She thought he remembered that Walter had been of Jewish origin but a convert well regarded in the Muslim Quarter.

"Every stranger is closely watched," Mardikian told her with a discouraging sigh. "They claim every stone."

"Who does?"

"All sides. Our property is hardly our own, mademoiselle."

It pleased Mardikian to address Sonia in this courtly manner. He permitted himself a small smile.

"I know that in the United States people are what they choose to be," he said. "It's not that way here, mademoiselle. Here in the Old World we have no choice. That which we are, we are."

"I know what you mean," Sonia said. "Would you rent the place to me? I'm known."

"Your Jewish friends should find accommodation in the Jewish city." Like most people in Jerusalem, Mr. Mardikian believed in a place for everyone, and everyone in his place.

"They want to be in Old Jerusalem, and the Jewish Quarter isn't for them. Some of the religious authorities might be unfriendly."

"But why?" he asked.

"They have their own interpretation of Torah. Of Scripture."

"Is it seen as disrespect?"

"It can be misunderstood," she said.

Mardikian's instincts were plain. Everyone dreaded misunderstandings.

"But these are mature, quiet people," she persisted. "They respect all faiths. They follow the tradition of Abdullah Walter." Her problem was to convince him that she had not been brought into some plan by the militant Jews to acquire another site in the city.

"Monsieur Walter was admired by the Muslims," Mardikian remarked. "But only the older people remember him. And times have changed."

"I would guarantee their conduct," she said. "You know me. The *shebab* know me."

He looked at her thoughtfully until she began to wonder where in fact she stood in the Old City, what people actually made of her.

In the end, he agreed to rent her the place and to let De Kuff and Raziel stay there for the time being. The price asked was much higher than Berger's rent, but Sonia decided to agree to it without demur. Her understanding was that De Kuff was wealthy and could pay.

"I'm sorry to hear of Monsieur Berger's death," Mardikian said again. He always pronounced Berger's name in the French fashion, making it suggest the Follies.

"How complicated it all is," Sonia said when the bargaining was over. They smiled unhappily at each other and he offered her more coffee. Sonia declined.

"I think," Mardikian said, "that each generation is harder than the last."

"We used to think it would be the other way around."

"I also had hope, mademoiselle," Mardikian said, "when, like you, I was young."

It was sweet of him to call her young, Sonia thought. She had trouble imagining him as the victim of blasted illusions.

When he had put the coffee tray away and was at the point of leaving, Sonia found herself in the grip of a sudden impulse.

"What do you think will happen to the city?" she asked.

The old man raised his chin and closed his eyes.

"How is it for you?" she asked. She meant for the Armenians. It was the kind of question her mother would have asked, embarrassingly direct and right-minded. Her mother would have asked after the Armenian *people,* as she would have referred to the Jewish *people* or the Negro *people* or the Soviet *people.*

Having uttered the questions, Sonia at once regretted them. In Jerusalem such questions always had a disingenuousness that no amount of sincerity could redeem. They sounded like hypocrisy or spying.

"I'm well," Mardikian said. He paused for a moment. "We Armenians?. We settle old differences and new ones arise. That's life, *n'est-ce pas?* But it's all right, thank God."

"Good," Sonia said. *Baruch Hashem* and amen, she thought.

It occurred to her that she had missed the Armenian commemoration this year, the procession on April 24 that remembered the Turkish slaughter. She usually made it a point to attend, or rather to follow after, lighting an imaginary candle.

Passing the gate of the Ribat al-Mansuri on her way to Berger's, she heard classical music, baroque or renaissance strings. An African boy in the courtyard heard it too and stood motionless, his face slightly distorted as if he were detecting a peculiar smell. Going upstairs to the apartment, she found Razz and Adam playing a duet on the little terrace that could be opened to the weather. The music did sound baroque, with Oriental ornamentation, De Kuff fingering his cello like an oud. Beside them on the terrace floor was Berger's old violin and antique North African tambourine. Raziel was playing a recorder, gazing down into the courtyard where the black children kicked a soccer ball against one wall. Clouds were gathering in the patch of visible sky. A breeze fluttered the notepad beside him.

Raziel put the recorder down.

"I never knew these people were here," he said.

"Hundreds of years," Sonia told him.

Instead of picking up the instrument again, he began to sing. He sang very well, in a high tenor that he could ease into exotica as required, countertenor, mock contralto, pseudo-Oriental scat. Then he began a song in what sounded like Spanish, but which Sonia recognized as Ladino, accompanying himself on the tambourine. It was as sweet as nougat.

"*Yo no digo esta canción,*" it went, "*sino a quien conmigo va.*"

"If you want to hear my song," she translated it, "you have to come with me." It made her shiver.

"Do you understand it?" Raziel asked her.

"Yeah, sort of. I didn't know you spoke Ladino."

"Only songs."

"They're beautiful."

He moved the cushions on which he reclined and made room for her on the terrace.

"They're Sufi songs. They're the same."

"The spirit," she said, "seems the same."

"Sonia," Raziel told her, "faith is like a sponge. You wring the liquid out, the structure remains eternal. Everything is Torah. This man" — he put her hand in De Kuff's — "is a sheikh, as was al-Tariq. Al-Ghazali was called both a Christian and a Jew. Berger al-Tariq is with us now. He passes your spirit to this man's. The Sufi, the Kabbalist, the saddhu, Francis of Assisi — it's all one. They all worshiped Ein-Sof. The Spanish Kabbalists derived the Trinity from Kabbala. Al-Ghazali knew Kabbala. And you were born Jewish, so the message should come to you from your people."

"I can believe that," she said. "I want to."

"You do believe. You always have. All the things you have believed in the past are true," he declared to her. "What you believed about human suffering, about justice, about the end of exile — they were all true and they remain true. Do you hear me, Sonia?"

"I hear you," she said.

"The things you believed in the past — never stop believing them. You're about to see them come to pass. Do you ask yourself, How can this sick old man here make such things happen?"

"Of course," she said.

"Of course you do. The reason is that his coming has changed everything. The world as we know it is going to disappear into history. You will not — I promise you — you will not recognize it. The reason you believed in the world to come, Sonia, was that you really knew it would come."

"I always felt that," she said.

"Well, you were right. You knew. Now you're going to see it all take place. Sign by sign. His presence here is enough. And you and I and others will make it happen."

She turned to De Kuff.

"Is it true?" she asked him.

De Kuff leaned over and kissed her gently. "Believe only what you know," he said.

Lucas and Janusz Zimmer were drinking at the cellar bar of the American Colony Hotel. Zimmer was one of the few Jewish residents of Jerusalem who frequented the American Colony and the cafés of East Jerusalem. His air of foreignness, his self-confidence, or a combination of the two, always seemed to protect him.

"So you're doing the Jerusalem Syndrome story," Janusz observed. "Excellent choice."

"You sound like a waiter."

"Think I haven't been a waiter? I have been, I assure you."

"And you?" Lucas asked. "What about these IDFs and their lynchings over in the Strip. Gonna cover that?"

"Well," Zimmer said, "if you won't, why not me?"

Lucas experienced a pang of guilt at not working the brutality story. "I should, I suppose."

"Why?"

"Why? Because the Syndrome story is the safer one. And when you start doing the safer one, you're going lame. Time to go home and write travel stories for in-flight magazines."

"American machismo," Zimmer said. "And don't assume a religious story is safer. You could be unpleasantly surprised."

"Well, Ernest Gross at the Human Rights Coalition says an Israeli publication should do the story. For the honor of the country."

"Ah, yes," said Zimmer. "Ernest is a *tzaddik*."

Lucas thought he was being contemptuous, but could not be sure.

"You worked Vietnam, didn't you, Zimmer?"

"I worked Vietnam. And don't forget I was on the other side. I was under your selective ordnance and your gunships and B-52 bombers."

"Why were the Vietnamese so good?" Lucas asked. "Why did they fight so hard? Do you think they were believers?"

"No," Zimmer said. "They just failed to see the funny side. They lacked that American sense of humor. Seriously," he told Lucas, "they were just conscripts. But they never thought of themselves as separate from their army. And they didn't have comfortable American lives to lose. Good soldiers."

"Been back?"

"Twice. If you brought the Communist dead back to Saigon today — or even Hanoi — they'd die a second death. The present regime down there is more corrupt than the last."

"How do you know? Did you see Saigon then?"

"Sometimes I got to Saigon. Remember, we had Poles for a while on the International Control Commission. They could get me the right documents. So I saw the fleshpots. Also the tunnels out at Cu Chi. Amazing. I suppose that was before your time?"

"Just," Lucas said.

"Funny," Janusz Zimmer said, "how we saw the world from different sides. I could never get to the West without a struggle. But wherever what they called 'socialism' prevailed, I was welcome."

"Miss it?"

"I traveled all over Africa for the Polish News Service," Zimmer said. "There wasn't an aspect of African socialism I didn't witness."

"That's not an answer."

"Oh, come on," Zimmer said irritably. "It was ghastly beyond description. Supremos, cannibal potentates, thugs in sunglasses pretending they were KGB. Naturally I wrote about it with enthusiasm and approval. Your side didn't have such great humanitarians either. Your side had Mobutu."

"I wonder what Sonia Barnes would have thought of it," Lucas said.

"In the worst places she would have been killed immediately. Well, not immediately. Raped and tortured first. But she had the sense to be in Cuba. And Cuba was different."

"Was it?"

"Certainly. The most hardened anti-Communists had a soft spot for Cuba. Even me."

"But, Janusz," Lucas said. "You weren't an anti-Communist. Were you?"

"Not at first. I was a Party member."

"And then?"

Zimmer made no answer.

"I used to be a Catholic," Lucas said. "I believed. I believed everything."

Zimmer watched him.

"It's good, no?"

"I don't know," Lucas said. "Do you think it's good? Believing?"

"Depends on what you believe, wouldn't you say?"

"You're so annoying, Zimmer," Lucas said. "I'm trying to talk philosophy. You're giving me common sense."

"Well," said Zimmer, "I'm from Poland, where faiths come equipped with tanks and gallows, gas and truncheons. I'm particular about faiths."

"Fair enough."

"I'll tell you what," Zimmer said, getting up to leave. "You keep me posted on the Syndrome, I'll keep you posted on the Strip."

15

SYLVIA CHIN was a very young, cool and attractive official of the U.S. consulate in West Jerusalem. There were two American consulates in town, and according to journalistic lore they were bitterly divided in terms of Middle East policy. The one on Saladin Street, in what had once been the Kingdom of Jordan, dealt daily with Palestinians and was considered pro-Israeli. The one downtown, which lived with the Israelis, allegedly inclined toward the Palestinians.

Sylvia was California Chinese, her Valley Girl inflections starched at Stanford, a vice consul whose collateral duties had involved the retrieval of quite a few deluded American nationals from variously unsound spiritual enterprises. She was knowledgeable about the religious enthusiasts in town and about cults in general. She was also cagey, with a lawyerly reluctance to opine. At the same time she was genuinely fond of Lucas, whom she recognized as a true admirer.

"Mostly we have individuals," she told Lucas. "Sometimes the families call us. Sometimes they pull a stunt and the police call us. We've had a few disappear."

"What about the groups?"

"Well, the groups I can't formally comment on. It takes all kinds."

"I'm after the more colorful. Or interesting. Or original."

"OK," said Sylvia. "Know about the House of the Galilean?"

"I know a preacher there. Never been to their place."

"Check it out. They're fun."

"Any further comments? Not for attribution. We'd call you 'a Western diplomat.'"

Sylvia shook her head.

" 'An informed observer.' "

She thought about it. "If you stumble on any insights," she suggested, "you might share them with us, OK?"

Her suggestion smacked of the old pitcheroo, Lucas thought. He felt a pang of nostalgia for the Cold War. Who didn't?

"Any time, pal." The notion of lunch with Sylvia was always agreeable.

"They're Christian ultra-Zionists," Vice Consul Chin told him. "Close to the Israeli right wing. Funny, because some of their leadership was once really anti-Semitic. Now they're here and they seem to like it."

"Their thing is 'Repent, the end is nigh,' right?"

"Right," she said. "End-of-the-world type thing. Big moneymaker back home."

"Are they considered legitimate?"

"Well, like, what's legitimate?" she asked with an expression of bright false naiveté. "What about freedom of conscience?" Her expression faded. "You won't quote me by name?"

"Hey," Lucas said, "stand on me."

"The question about religious entities here is whether they have political clout. In country or U.S. or third country, whatever. Christian, Jewish, Muslim or anything else."

"And the House of the Galilean?"

"House of the Galilean is liked by certain quarters here. And liked by the certain quarters back home that like those certain quarters. And has some drag with evangelicals."

"In that business," Lucas said, "it's considered more blessed to give than to receive."

"Right," Sylvia said. "And they're contributors. They don't ask the fat cats for money — they provide it. For political campaigns and whatnot. Investments. Their money comes from cable television pitches and direct mail."

"Interesting," said Lucas. He also asked her if she had heard of a young man named Ralph or Raziel or Razz Melker.

Sylvia knew him at once. "Ralph Melker is a major headache. The Ralph Melker file is a tale of woe."

"Yes?"

"First a congresswoman gets this angry letter about Raziel's group staking out old synagogues in Safed. Complains that they were Jews for Jesus or something. People do that, you know — they see something here and write their congressperson in the States."

"Why not?" asked Lucas. "It's their money."

"The congresswoman sent it to the embassy, and they forwarded it to us. Just buck-passing, no comments on it."

"Naturally."

"As it turns out, Ralph really is a former Jew for Jesus. He's also got a DEA file. I mean, a musician and heavy into drugs. Then it turns out Ralph's old man *also* is a congressman *and* a former ambassador. Active in politics in Michigan, a Democrat. The family sends Ralph over here to straighten him out — they imagine he's reading Torah and working in the vineyards, singing folksongs around the fire. So this is tucked away. Background for us. In case anyone has to cope on some level."

"How about an older man named Adam De Kuff?"

That one called for a short excursion up the diplomatic corridors. Sylvia came back with a shrug.

"*Bubkes* on De Kuff." She had picked up some Yiddishisms in L.A. and it amused her to employ them in country. "But there are people here who go in for what they call 'cult awareness.' They may have heard of him. You might also check with Superintendent Smith at police headquarters. He deals with the prophets and messiahs."

Accommodating as Sylvia was, she declined to let Lucas use the consulate's telephone, even for a local call.

"A no-no," she told him. "And remember, all the free phones are tapped."

In June, Lucas finally moved out of Tsililla's. He had seen little of her since her return from London. For a while she had repaired to a horse farm near Tiberias, ostensibly to ride and work on a film script. They kept arranging to meet and talk things over. When a Canadian journalist Lucas knew was transferred out of town, Lucas arranged to house-sit. The apartment was downtown, near Zion Square, on the eighth floor of a sleek, sinister-looking building that catered to jewelry salesmen. It was supposed to be very secure.

While he had tended to hole up for long periods in the place he'd shared with Tsililla, Lucas now welcomed every opportunity to get out of the downtown place. One day he volunteered to carry some of De Kuff's things to the Old City apartment. Sonia had given him the key.

Sonia's place in Rehavia, in the upper story of a peeling, leafy Ottoman building, was not far from Tsililla's, and not dissimilar to it, at least on the outside. Inside, it was decorated with *santería* figures and Cuban movie posters and mementos of colleagues in various crisis zones. Her souvenir photographs featured groups of toothy young white people in lightweight khakis, posing among thin dark-skinned folk in landscapes that were parched and brown or overbright with fleshy green plants.

Her living room was awash with De Kuff's possessions, books mostly, and bound monographs. Since Berger's death she had been busy transplanting and transposing tomes, his and De Kuff's. The old Austrian had died after several hours in a coma at the university hospital. Most of his last days at home had been spent with Raziel and De Kuff; it was as though the three of them had gone into some psychic space together.

Many of Berger's books, diaries and journals remained in his Old City apartment. His writings were in German, which De Kuff could read and Sonia could not. Sonia had inherited his only possessions of worldly value: a few old Persian manuscripts, his small collection of Islamic art — Kufic rubbings and calligraphy — and his furniture. There had also turned out to be several thousand U.S. dollars in an external account in Amman.

Finally, Sonia had contacted the offices of the Waqf, the Muslim religious authority, to have Berger buried in a Muslim cemetery. The Waqf had not asked for the return of his apartment, which was presumably its property, but it was not yet aware of Adam De Kuff and his followers.

Lucas carried half a dozen or so cardboard boxes down to his car and drove through the east end of the Lions' Gate, which was as close to the apartment as he could bring the car. While parking, he told himself that his yellow Israeli plate would get his car torched one day.

As he carried the first load of books up the ancient stairs, he saw Raziel perched on the terrace watching his labor. He returned without a greeting for the next box.

When he had carried all the boxes up, he saw Raziel smiling up at him from the terrace divan.

"I should have helped you," Raziel said. "I'm sorry. We've been meditating all night."

"No problem," Lucas said. There was a peculiar ornament around Raziel's neck that he had not seen before. "What are you wearing?"

"Oh," Raziel said. He slipped it off and handed it to Lucas. "It's an ouroboros. The serpent swallowing its tail. An Ethiopian silversmith near the Machaneh market did it for us."

"In all the versions of the stories I've heard," Lucas said, "the snake is the bad guy. Except for the Gnostic versions."

He could see the yeshiva boy Raziel roused to disputation.

"The ouroboros is repeatedly cited in the *Zohar*, the *Book of Splendor*. There, it refers to *bereshit*, 'in the beginning.' Actually, '*at the beginning*' is more like it."

Lucas produced his notebook. "May I write this down?"

"Be my guest," Raziel said. "Write this: it means 'in my beginning is my ending.'"

Lucas wrote it. This is strong, he thought as he wrote. Something made him feel that Raziel was not to be despised. It frightened him slightly.

"Are you familiar with kundalini yoga?" Raziel asked.

"I've heard of it."

"The forces we work with are similar. Maybe the same. They aren't forces that allow for half measures or for dabbling."

"But Kundalini is a snake goddess," Lucas said. "That doesn't seem exactly kosher."

"Kundalini is a metaphor, Christopher. The underlying forces are the same. The sages called the outer garment of the world a snake's skin."

Lucas wrote *kundalini* in his notebook.

"I have to ask," Raziel declared. "Is your father Carl Lucas of Columbia?"

"He died three years ago."

"Sorry."

"Sonia tell you that?"

"Not at all," Raziel said.

"You saw an intellectual resemblance?"

Raziel smiled. "Is there one?"

"Yes," Lucas said. "But I'm an epigone. The bastard son, a midget."

"No you're not," Raziel said.

"What about you?" Lucas asked. "Your old man the congressman?"

"Yes he is. A friend of the President. Chairman of the House Committee on Education. So I know what it is to be the son of . . . that kind of father."

"I see."

"And your mother sang," Raziel said.

"Funny," Lucas said. "I'm asking the questions. But you know more about me than I know about you. Yes," he told Raziel, "my mother was a well-known singer, Gail Hynes. She made a good living while she worked. My dad was proud of her. Unfortunately he was married elsewhere."

"I've heard her."

"You're putting me on," Lucas said.

"She sang *lieder*, right? She made some famous records of Mahler and Brahms for Decca."

"Yes, that's right," Lucas said.

"*Das Lied von der Erde*," said Razz. "*Kindertotenlieder.* She was wonderful. As good as Ferrier. You must be proud of her."

"Yes," said Lucas, astonished. "Thank you very much. I am."

"I suppose her career suffered because of her involvement with the professor. Having to be there and so forth."

Lucas could only nod. "She died young," he managed to say in a moment. "Like Ferrier."

"Did she meet your father's friends?"

"Well," Lucas said, "you know, they were stuffy. Bourgeois. German." Lucas laughed in spite of himself. "Once," he told Raziel, "he took her on a trip to Los Angeles on the Superchief to meet all his pals. The Frankfurt school. Theodor Adorno and Herbert Marcuse and Thomas Mann. At least he took her along when he went to see them."

"How did it go?" Raziel asked.

"She thought Theodor Adorno was the guy who played Charlie Chan in the movies," Lucas said. "She asked him, Does it hurt when they do you up Chinese?"

"Wonder what he made of that."

"I would venture to say he was clueless," said Lucas. "Then I understand she kept trying to get the conversation back to Oriental makeup. How she'd done *Butterfly* with the Lyric in Chicago. She drank a little," he explained. "In fact, she drank a lot. In binges.

Made her weight unstable, got her into speed to slim, screwed her voice."

"What did she say about Marcuse?" Raziel asked.

"You mean, what did she think of permissive repression?" Lucas asked. "She thought Marcuse was Otto Kruger."

Raziel looked at him blankly.

"Otto Kruger was one of the actors in the film version of *Murder My Sweet.*"

"You seem to like music," Raziel said to Lucas. "Your mother sang. Why did you never learn to play? Were you afraid of it?"

"I appreciate your having listened so sensitively to my mother's work," Lucas said. "Please don't ask me if I'm afraid of things. By the way, where's Sonia?"

"Sorry," Raziel said. "I think she may be sleeping. She was up meditating with us too." He nodded toward two louvered half-doors.

"Do you think I could see her?"

"Sonia?" Raziel called.

She answered faintly. Lucas went and knocked on the louvered door.

"Come," she said.

"It's me," said Lucas.

"Yes," she said, "I heard you."

She came out wrapped in her djellaba.

"Why are you here?" he asked her softly. "Why did you take them in?"

"Because," she told him, "Berger said I should." Her eyes shone. "Berger knew Kabbala extremely well. He thought of it as Sufic. At the end he called De Kuff el-Arif. That was what he called Abdullah Walter."

"You know what I think?" Lucas said. "I think you're a believer."

She laughed, beautifully he thought. It was pleasing to see her so happy, her sad eyes sparkling.

"I am a believer," she said, "of believers. Because the brotherhood of truth is one in all ages. The sisterhood too."

"Berger say that?"

"Yes, he said it. Raziel and De Kuff say it too. Don't you believe it?"

"Where I come from," Lucas said, "we say, 'Lord, I believe. Help thou mine unbelief.' "

The double doors opened and Raziel came in. Afraid to leave me alone with her, he thought. He felt angry and annoyed.

"So, can I be in your project?" Sonia asked. "Your story?"

"You bet."

"What if I'm boring?"

"I'll risk it," Lucas said. "I'm not easily bored."

"As part of your project, Christopher," Raziel said, "I hope you're studying." Both the familiarity and the admonishing tone annoyed him further.

"Well, I've dropped my Arabic courses at the YMCA. Now I'm at the Hebrew University. Not that it does me much good."

"No?"

"I'm not good at languages."

He was taking classical Hebrew at the university and also a course entitled, with echoes of Broadway, "Tradition." "Tradition" had been recommended to him by Obermann. It was taught by an old Lithuanian Holocaust survivor named Adler and aimed primarily at the young, kids from the United States and Canada taking part in Ulpans and study sessions abroad. There were also a number of Gentiles, some retired clergymen from California, two midwesterners, and a few globetrotting professional students.

The curriculum was partly a review of Jewish beliefs, from the Hasmoneans through Hillel and Philo, Maimonides and Nachmanides, and on to Buber and Heschel. It was informative on the influence of second-century Neoplatonism and on contemporary applications in a rational vein. But Adler's passion, though he attempted to conceal it, was Lurianic Kabbala. In the modernist critical tradition, he ascribed the *Zohar* to Moses de León.

To Lucas's surprise, Adler had approached him for conversation. Perhaps because of personal chemistry, perhaps because Adler had heard of Lucas's father and was proud to be the teacher of such a scholar's son, they had gotten on well, and he had suggested to Lucas a number of books not included in the syllabus. One was a Paulist Press translation of sections of the *Zohar*, and the other, by a Hasidic rabbi, was on Gematria and the otherwise sacred significance of the Hebrew letters. It was, Adler had suggested, a good way to remember and internalize the ancient characters.

Raziel smiled. "Adler. A *mitnag*."

"Not at all," Lucas said.

"But a good man," Raziel added.

In the silence that followed, they heard the house sparrows twittering in the old walls.

"All these Old City houses are full of sparrows," Raziel said, casting his spell. "I like them. Sparrows."

"Why?"

"Because," he said to Lucas, "we're all sparrows here."

Lucas decided it was time to take more notes. He pulled out his notebook and wrote *sparrows.* The word by itself looked unilluminating, so he put the notebook away.

"Where's Mr. De Kuff?" he asked finally. "Will I be able to talk to him?"

"He'll spend the day in *kavana,*" Razz said. "Preparing for *dvekut.*" He looked at Lucas with faint amusement. "Want to say it, brother? Hey, say it, don't be shy. You have a right, it's your language. *Kavana.*" He pronounced the word carefully, glottalizing the opening consonant. "*Dvekut.*"

Lucas realized he must have moved his lips in mute imitation. He was annoyed. But he made himself repeat it aloud, guided by Raziel. "*Kavana. Dvekut.*" He could almost see the characters that formed the words.

"Very good, man," Raziel said. "A person might take you for Jewish."

Sonia laughed, delighted.

By way of rejoinder, Lucas said to Raziel, "I understand you had a problem with drugs for a while."

Raziel fell silent for a moment.

"I told him," Sonia admitted. "I told him about myself too."

"I was a common junkie," Raziel said.

"And a Jew for Jesus?"

"What about you?" Raziel asked. "Who were you for? Who are you for now? What if I ask you why you drink?"

Always smiling, Lucas wrote in his notebook, ignoring the insolent counter-questions as best he could. *Patronizing arrogant but probably sincerely nuts.*

"Don't go to Obermann," Raziel said urgently. "Come to us. She knows your *tikkun.*" Lucas saw that he meant Sonia. Lucas wanted to explain that he was not a patient of Obermann's but a collaborator. But he was so amazed at the notion of Sonia's knowing his *tikkun* that he said nothing. Raziel had fixed him with a blazing lover's look, a seducer's.

"She does?" Lucas looked at Sonia. "Really?"

From his courses at the university he knew that *tikkun* referred to a primal accident at the beginning of time. According to the doctrines of the mystic Isaac Luria, the Almighty had absented himself in the first and greatest of mysteries, bequeathing to his exiled, orphaned creation emanations of himself. The force of these emanations was beyond the capacity of existence to contain them. Since the beginning, the goal of the universe had been to restore the divine balance, to restore the *tikkun,* a cosmic harmony and justice, and the task had somehow fallen to mankind to set right. And each person, some Kabbalists believed, labored under his own *tikkun,* a microcosm, a succession of souls, through a process of reincarnation called *partsufim.*

"I do," Sonia said. "I think."

Nonsense, Lucas thought. But it made him feel close to her.

"If you know my *tikkun,*" he asked, "what should I do to square it?"

"What should you do to be saved?" Raziel asked, smiling. It was the question the rich young man had asked Jesus, in Luke. Though he had never been wealthy, Lucas had often identified himself with the same rich young man.

"Open your heart," Sonia said. He could not help staring at her. Was she saying this particularly to him? Or was it some New Age formulation? He was falling in love with her.

Absurdly, he wrote it down. The call to prayer sounded. *The brotherhood of truth is one in all ages.* It was in the Koran. He was intensely aware of Raziel's watching them.

"You're quoting from the New Testament," Lucas told him. "Do I assume you're still kind of Christian?"

"Christianity isn't the faith of the Redemption. Maybe it was once. The Talmud says, 'On the eve of Passover they hanged Yeshu.' That's all it says. Yet in Kabbala, we have a thousand clues about him. And he was only one of many."

"I daresay," Lucas observed, "that that's an unconventional reading."

"You were devout," Raziel said, "as a boy. Wasn't he, Sonia? See, I'm guessing," he told Lucas. "But she knows."

"Yes," she said, "I think he was. He was always close to us."

"You were always close to us. Every soul that inhabits you partakes of us. You're a little like the Rev. The mixture of shells and light makes you confused and unhappy. One side employing the force of the other, merging. You're one of those people who hears the sun come up."

How flattering, Lucas thought. And in spite of oneself, what fun! To be special. To be part of a process that was beautiful and mysterious. To be chosen. In his secret heart he found it congenial, and the child in him somehow wanted to believe it, there in Jerusalem among the timeless stones. So beguiling. And it was surprising what authority the young Raziel could bring to bear.

"Tell me this," Lucas asked. "What is Mr. De Kuff to you? Or," he asked Sonia, "to you?"

"Ever read Marx?" Raziel asked. "*The Eighteenth Brumaire of Louis Napoleon?*"

In fact, Lucas had read it. He had thought no one would ever ask. "As it happens," he said, "I've read it. Didn't he say history always repeats itself twice? First as tragedy wasn't it? Then as farce?"

"Life is tragic and absurd," Raziel told him. "The same figures eternally recur. This is a secret of Torah. Maimonides himself says the Messiah comes again and again until faith is strong enough."

"And you're saying that Mr. De Kuff in there . . . ?" he pointed to the other room.

"Who was Yeshu?" Raziel asked. "Who was Sabbatai?"

"They were false messiahs," Lucas said. He felt, against reason, that he was blaspheming.

"They were not false. Man was false. The world was false. So the *tikkun* was not restored. So it was not 'on earth as it is in heaven.' "

"And we always fail our messiahs?"

"Depravity is the mystery of creation," Raziel said, smiling. "We change, we fail, but the Torah remains, never changes under its garment. The chance to restore *tikkun* comes again and again."

"Well," Lucas said, "I guess you could say that Marx was interested in restoring *tikkun*, right?"

"You could," Raziel agreed. "You could also say Einstein was. Or that you are. And we, Sonia and I."

"All in pursuit of *tikkun*?"

"Or maybe," Raziel said, "*tikkun* is in pursuit of us."

Marx, Einstein, Lucas wrote in his notebook. *Us after tikkun, tikkun after us. Him, me, Sonia B. Always fail our messiahs.*

"Don't you know it's true, Chris?" Sonia asked him.

"He sees," Raziel said to her. "And don't be offended," he told

Lucas. "We're all mutants here. De Kuff became a Catholic, communion every morning. I was with Jews for Jesus. Sonia is a Sufi, she was a Communist."

"And," Lucas asked, not bothering to write, "is the actual Torah known to us?"

"Only the garment," Sonia said.

"Only the garment," said Raziel after her.

"And me?" Lucas asked. (What about me?) "Am I part of this?"

"Yes," Sonia told him. "You always have been. Since we all stood at Sinai."

Serious mindbending, Lucas wrote in his notebook. He still wanted to please Sonia.

"Don't be impatient, Chris," she said. "Remember where you are. That it's Jerusalem. What happens here is unlike what happens elsewhere. Sometimes it changes the world."

"Well," he announced, "I better be going. I enjoyed your playing. I enjoyed our talk." And he walked, a little unsteadily, out to the street.

"He's one of us," Raziel told her. "He has a place in what's to come."

She watched Lucas go out of the courtyard.

"Rest awhile," Raziel told her. Obedient, she went to her old room.

He knocked on the door of De Kuff's room and went inside. The old man seemed to be sleeping, but after a moment Raziel realized that he was awake and suffering. Watching him, Raziel considered the depths of the old man's loneliness and desperate desire for prayer. Whenever he detected De Kuff's thoughts, he would speak them and, inevitably, achieve surprise. If it was manipulative, he thought, it could not possibly be in a better cause.

"If only," De Kuff said, wiping tears from his eyes, "there was something I could do." Recently he had subsided into a weepiness over which he had little control. No one could say he was not a man of sorrows.

"You struggle," Raziel told him. "You suffer. The rest is for us." He made a fist and opened it, the gesture he used to denote the universe entirely.

"But I can't," De Kuff said desperately. "So often I can't believe the things you tell me."

"You have to believe," Raziel said. "If you stop believing, we're lost."

The notion that he might be losing De Kuff, losing the Redemption and his place in it, terrified him. Long ago, only a boy, he had prayed for the preservation of his own life with a detachment that made his parents suspect him of being suicidal. They had sent him to a child psychologist, and the psychologist had told him to record his dreams.

Once when Raziel and the psychologist were talking, the subject of the dream journal had come up.

"I don't keep it because you tell me to," young Ralph Melker had exploded in rage.

"Why then?" asked the psychologist.

"To examine them," Melker had declared triumphantly. "To see who I am."

In studying what he had no business studying, and with no more than the most elemental knowledge of Gematria, he had read that the sixteenth-century Kabbalist Hayyim Vital had done the same, hoping to discover in dreams the roots of his soul. Which naturally had floored the shrink: the family, that of a politician, hadn't seemed that religious.

"Will I ever be able to pray?" De Kuff asked Raziel.

"You're too close. Your life is worship."

"I think I would like to go to the Wall, to the Kotel, again."

"One day you will," Raziel said. "And they'll follow you." It was hard to keep the old man's spirits up when he had such desperate trouble with his own. "You'll walk through the gates of gold and I'll be with you."

But Raziel could not picture what it would really be like. The phrases of prophecy were clichéd and formulaic. General rejoicing. Music never before heard. The square would become hip and the rough places plain.

At his core Raziel believed. He had labored so hard to work it out. He had endured so much terrible silence, listening for the slightest sound from inside. Once he had been told by a wise Hasid: wait in the worst of times, wait for the whole text, the whole *alef-beit*, wait for the end. The last letter, *tav*, was love. Love was understanding. He had taken over De Kuff's life and given up his own. Now they would have to wait for the *tav*.

16

THAT NIGHT in his new apartment, Lucas stared at his scant notes. He felt shaken, frightened and alone, pursued by unreasonable yearnings. He could imagine they were a part of his nature, inherited and nourished over a vast span of time.

But if he felt personally beset, the *story*, the project, was fine. There would be plenty to write about. If there was a danger, it was in the very size of the thing.

He felt he had a clear line on Ralph Melker. A little too sensitive as a boy, a little too intelligent, religious. He had to sympathize, Lucas did.

A boy of promise, a believer, and he discovers music. But with the music, drugs. And from these he has to make his own return — to be, in a sense, his own messiah.

Lucas knew a few things about junkies from his time at Columbia. He had done some recreational popping; some of his friends had been strung out. Kicking was murder, just getting through the day.

For such terrible days Raziel, like many, had required Grace. And then he'd found her, standing there atop the Twelve Steps, lovely as the poets dared describe her. Grace was by Botticelli, descended from Cora and Persephone, but essentially Christianized. Grace was amazing, ineffable, unmerited, feminine, worshiped smooth by Gentiles until she embodied the quality of mercy that Shakespeare thought had to be explained to uncomprehending Shylock, a slave of the Law. No matter if one beheld her as the Divine Presence, the Shekhinah. The Shekhinah could never be one's very own — unlike Grace, who could be yours alone, like Mom. And dependence was so Christian, so weak and sweet.

Thus grace abounding descended upon young Raziel, got him his music back, picked him up, then estranged him from the tents of Israel. But Raziel always wanted more. To be apostate and messiah and Mingus too. And if any boy from Pontiac Park could do it all, that boy was Ralph Arthur Melker. A terrific musician.

It was strange, Lucas thought, that messiahs would keep showing up among the Jews — of all people — whom ruin, expulsions and sheer annihilations had made so notoriously cautious and critical. (And what about me?) Yet after six thousand years of articulate speculation and competitive humor, in Israel a miracle was still worth more than an aphorism.

And how insightfully sly of Raziel to detect the election of someone else, to choose a lost humble soul, a diffident wounded seeker like De Kuff, and be his John the Baptist.

Only the garment, he could hear Sonia saying. Yes, the *story*, the project, was going fine. But he had come to understand, listening to Raziel's hot and cool junkie ramblings, that there were problems for him here. Because of who he was. Because it was Jerusalem, where the Judean wind praised the Almighty, every sultry breeze infested with prayer, every crossroads laboring under its own curse. Where the stones were not mere stones but resided in the heart and were wept upon or given in place of bread. Lucas had confidently and wrongly thought himself beyond all that. In fact, it was part of him, his inward man. Raziel was right: it was why he had come. He himself suffered from the Jerusalem Syndrome. There was another Willie Ludlum inside him, another consecrated buffoon. Raziel had called it: he was a sparrow like the rest of them.

Raziel, Lucas realized suddenly, called them all. Sincerely nuts — maybe, but he was a prodigy. There was something second born about him.

Lucas had a drink and looked up "sparrow" in the concordance to his King James Bible. It was the best he could do, since his reference books had been scattered in exile, and unlike his elderly classmates at the Hebrew University, he scarcely knew *tannaim* from *amoraim*, Mishnah from Gemara. On his way home he had noticed for the first time that the city was full of the obnoxious birds.

The Bible spoke specifically of only three sparrows. Two were in the Old Testament, both in Psalms. The first was in Psalm 84, and, lucky creature, it had found a home in the love of the Lord. But the other, in Psalm 102, was forlorn and dreadfully alone. Its heart was smitten and withered like grass. It watched in dread from a rooftop while the owls of the wilderness, the pelicans of the desert, circled overhead, equally unhappy.

Sparrow three was the one in Matthew and Luke, the two-for-a-farthing creature that took the well-known Fall — the one not to worry about, since God had it covered. The one we all hoped stood for us.

Fragments of poetry returned to him, "Cape Ann," by the Jew-despising Eliot.

> O quick quick quick, quick hear the song-sparrow,
> Swamp-sparrow, fox-sparrow, vesper-sparrow
> At dawn and dusk . . .

Just the thought of vesper sparrows, the shadow of their name, made him hear chanting from the woods on summer evenings. A sweet summoning, the call to prayer.

Later the same night he went out to Fink's, to get drunk again at close quarters. It was a quiet night, the bartender looked particularly downcast, the waiter sighed often and sang softly in Hungarian.

"Now where does anyone get off," Lucas asked himself, aloud but discreetly, "calling me a fucking sparrow?" People often talked to themselves in Fink's.

The bartender appeared to shrug, more tweedy and Perelmanesque than ever. The waiter muttered and snapped napkins. The Druse anchorman of the evening news was huddled with some colleagues at a corner table.

" 'There's a special providence in the fall of a sparrow,' " Lucas recited. Of course that was Shakespeare, not the Bible. " 'Not a whit!' " he declared. " 'We defy augury.' "

"Jolly well done," said the sad bartender.

17

ONE SUMMER MORNING, Lucas followed Dr. Obermann on rounds at the mental hospital at Shaul Petak, which catered to religious maniacs. It was just outside the western city, a practical-looking building in the Israeli socialist-realist style, an architectural mode that might be expected to banish religious, philosophical, poetical or any other sort of speculation.

They met some famous figures from Scripture. Noah was present, glancing uneasily at the smoggy sky. Samson, unbound but closely supervised in a room of his own, sneered at Lucas's philistine lack of conditioning. There were several John the Baptists, their animal skin bikinis exchanged for hospital gowns. There were returned Jesus Christs, all disappointed at their long-awaited receptions, and some Hebrew messiahs, one of whom had been George Patton in another existence.

"The morning is usually their best time," Obermann explained to Lucas. "Not for them, actually, but for the student of the malady. Of course medication renders them subdued. Samson, for example, is already on a high dosage of Haldol and he's still ready to pull the temple of Dagon down."

"Do you think he saw that movie?" Lucas asked. "With Victor Mature?"

Dr. Obermann treated the question as beneath his notice.

"The thing about crazy people," he told Lucas, "is that they're just like anyone else. Some are naturally interesting, witty, imaginative. Some are pedestrian and tedious — they drone on. I assure you, there is no one on earth more boring than an elaborately deluded paranoid schizophrenic who is also literal-minded, undereducated and stupid."

"Obviously," Lucas said, "you're not sentimental about your patients."

"I?" Obermann asked. "Sentimental? I should say not. I've seen far too many."

"I understand," said Lucas.

"But I can tell you this," said the doctor. "We can't blame crazy people for the troubles of the world. It's the nominally sane individuals who cause most of human misery."

With the doctor's wisdom in mind, Lucas betook himself to the House of the Galilean. The House was in New Katamon, where it had been the villa of a wealthy Arab merchant. It had a carved gateway with verses from the Koran and a massive wooden door that opened onto a garden with fruit trees. The original key to the door was undoubtedly displayed on a parlor wall in Abu Dhabi or Detroit, to be brandished on appropriate occasions. Or, if the family had been unlucky or improvident, it hung in some hovel outside Gaza or Beirut.

A row of joined stone cottages ran along the garden wall. Their doors were ajar, and as he made his way across the garden to the organization's offices, he stopped to peer inside one. Surely they were the servants' quarters of the Palestinian merchant's family, and yet all traces of Arab occupation had been removed. What had replaced the Middle Eastern style of furnishings provided an ambiance that was neither Israeli nor American but rather British colonial. The House of G had been in possession of the villa for less than twenty years, yet the occupants had seemingly — and surely without specific intent — assembled every loose piece of the British Raj remaining in the Levant since the days of Ismail Pasha.

The tiny room Lucas saw looked as if it had been inhabited by the proprietor of an imperial summer hill station, homesick for his cottage on Windermere. There was wood paneling and willow-patterned china, comfy overstuffed sofas and oak tables with Irish lace doilies and a day bed with a Welsh bedspread. The prints on the burgundy walls depicted Highland cattle and heroic lighthouse keepers' wives. Facing each other across the dim, single-windowed space were some of Peters's views of Jerusalem and Holman Hunt's *The Scapegoat*.

Waiting at the entrance to the main house, Lucas expected an Arab servant to answer his ring; instead, a young, apparently American girl appeared. She was tall, blond and virginally deferential, her prettiness marred only by a mildly eczemic rosiness of complexion. They shook hands and she introduced herself as Jennifer.

Jennifer led him into a thick-walled office lined with beautiful Turkish carpets and appointed with Scandinavian furniture. The room, which must have been the effendi's countinghouse, was short on daylight and so lit by sleek ceiling lights. At one end of the room was a scale model of some ancient edifice, like the Egyptian temples under glass at the Metropolitan Museum in New York.

A man in an ugly brown lightweight suit, wearing a tie the color of faded broccoli pizza, was seated at one end of a long mahogany desk. At the other end, like a consort sharing a throne, was a horse-faced woman in a yellow pantsuit, with short dark hair and prominent teeth.

The man rose. "Hi there, fella."

Lucas thought they must be acquainted, but after a moment he realized that they were not. The woman rose seconds after her partner.

"Welcome to the House of the Galilean," she intoned, somewhat in the manner of a flight attendant. He had a strong feeling she must once have been one.

"I'm Dr. Otis Corey Butler," the man declared. He was barbered and tanned, with a tough, sensible Scotch-Irish face like a North Carolina farmer's. Handsome. It was a shame about his tie. "This is my wife, Darletta, who I'm proud to say is also Dr. Butler."

Lucas introduced himself to the Drs. Butler.

"Dr. Ericksen suggested that I call on you," he said. "I'm researching religious movements in the city."

"Dr. Ericksen isn't with us any longer," Darletta replied. "Whom did you say you represented?"

"I'm working on a story for the *New York Times Magazine*." And in fact he had had a vague conversation with someone there a few months previously. "I also hope to do a book one day."

"I want you to have a press kit," Dr. Otis Corey Butler said. "You'll find our story and especially the relevant biblical quotations. Some of this material is hot off the press, and you'll find fresh information about our projects that's never seen print before. I'm sure you'll find it a help. In fact," he added, "there's little left out."

He was the kind of hustler, Lucas realized, who was used to

having the hacks take his press kits and run with them, or even lift them whole. No doubt, Lucas thought, he imagined himself a literary man.

"Do sit down, Chris," said Darletta, when he had stood thumbing through the pamphlets for a while.

Lucas's eye fell on one project that involved the preservation of Aramaic as a spoken language. It appeared there were some villagers somewhere in the wastes of Iraq who still spoke it.

"This is interesting," Lucas said. "Spoken Aramaic."

"We've been subsidizing teachers to preserve it among the children," Darletta explained to him. "We were able to continue our efforts all through the Gulf War."

"Aramaic," Dr. Otis Corey Butler told Lucas, "was the language spoken by Jesus Christ himself."

"Yes," added Dr. Darletta, "the very words spoken by Our Lord were in that tongue."

"Are you of Jewish heritage?" Dr. Otis Corey Butler asked Lucas. "Or otherwise?"

"Jewish," Lucas said, "and also otherwise. Is the fund to preserve Aramaic well subscribed?"

The couple looked at him blankly.

"I mean," Lucas explained, "does it bring in a great many contributions?"

"The project," Dr. Otis Corey Butler said, "supports itself." He had withdrawn a degree of affability from his voice.

"And you solicit in church magazines?" Lucas asked. "And through the mail?"

At the mention of the mail, the Drs. Butler looked distinctly alarmed.

"Yes," said Darletta. "We do."

"Deductible, is it?"

"Certainly it's deductible," Dr. Otis Corey Butler said. "It's a religious charity. We've got to feed and clothe these Iraqi kids too. They live in great poverty."

Lucas continued thumbing through the press kit. There was a great deal about the Mountain of God and the very stairs that Jesus himself climbed. An American astronaut had climbed them and declared himself more excited than when he had walked on the moon.

Dr. Otis Corey Butler cleared his throat.

"What did you mean," Dr. Darletta asked, "Jewish and otherwise?"

Scanning the pamphlets, Lucas found one that referred to the remains of the Second Temple and, by extension, to the First, that of Solomon. There was a great deal about Qumran and something about language studies, but the central project of the H of G seemed to be a rebuilding of the Temple of Jerusalem on the Temple Mount. It had to do with the coming of the Messiah. Yet it would be possible to read the handout, Lucas thought, even do a sweet story using its inspirational diction, and not quite realize the notion at the core.

"I mean my background is mixed," Lucas said. "Do I understand," he asked them, "that your organization proposes to rebuild Herod's Temple in the Haram?"

"The Temple was the Lord's," Darletta said in a tone that might be insisting that he buckle his seatbelt before takeoff. "Not King Herod's."

Where have I been? Lucas asked himself. The House of the Galilean had been sitting here with its color handouts and palatial villa, spades at the ready, years before he had come to town and he had paid it no attention. It was the very story for a man of his background, a wandering *mischling* and religion major.

"I knew there was a Jewish project to rebuild the Temple," Lucas told the Butlers. "I've been to their place in the Old City. I didn't realize they had a Christian counterpart."

In the Jewish Quarter, an American rabbi named Gold ran a sleek showroom where, for a fee, one could have a window, a wing or a menorah of the coming Temple named for one's Uncle Jack or Aunt Minnie. That a Christian equivalent existed, that this was the purpose of the House of the Galilean, was news to him. He would have to press Sylvia Chin a little harder, he thought. None of the clips on Willie Ludlum mentioned the House of the Galilean's development plans. Lucas decided to raise the awkward association and get it over with.

"That New Zealand fellow," he said, "Ludlum. The one who torched the Haram. He'd been staying with you all, had he not?"

Dr. Otis Corey Butler looked philosophical, Darletta somewhat pissed off.

"Ludlum was a disturbed individual," Dr. O. C. Butler said. "His delusions were his own."

"Do you think the government would let us stay here," Darletta asked, "if anyone thought we were responsible for attacks on holy places?"

The answer presented itself to Lucas with startling and unwonted clarity: It would depend on which government. And on which holy places.

"Ludlum was mad as a hatter," Dr. Otis Corey Butler said. "But when he came to us, we couldn't turn him out on the street."

"Not that you'd have known it at first," Darletta said resentfully. "He was quiet. Wrote in his journal. Called everyone sir and madam."

"When he seemed alienated, we communicated with the N.Z. embassy," said Otis Butler. "But he didn't have a family back home. He hadn't broken the law. Finally a kibbutz took him in, one catering to Christians."

"Look," Lucas said, "let me be sort of a devil's advocate. Destroying the mosques would make it possible for the Temple to be rebuilt. Doesn't it look as though Ludlum took what he heard here and carried it one step too far? Or," Lucas suggested, "a little prematurely. Of course, there are also a number of Jewish extremists who've called for the destruction of the mosques."

"Mr. Lucas, Mr. Lucas," Otis Butler declared, "as I'm sure you know, every great Judeo-Christian doctrine has been perverted by negative forces. Satan tempted Christ himself."

"I suppose," said Lucas.

"We and Rabbi Gold are aware of each other. We both oppose extremists. We join in renewal projects. We reject confrontation. In our brochure you'll see a statement by Rabbi Gold making plain that Christians will be able to contribute to the rebuilding of the Temple and that they will be able to offer sacrifices there. The Court of the Gentiles will be restored. Only the Jewish priesthood may enter the sanctuary. We accept this absolutely. Only the wicked and idolators will be forbidden to approach God's house."

"What about the mosques?" Lucas asked. "What happens to them? And what about the Jews? Aren't they supposed to be converted at the end?"

"Apples and oranges," Darletta Butler told him.

"You're mixing apples and oranges, Mr. Lucas," said Otis Butler. "Our Christian policy toward the renewal of Israel at the End of Days is determined by Scripture. It's in Romans 3:9 and Romans

9:3. In Galatians 10:4, 5, 6 and 7. In Daniel and Ezekiel and Jeremiah . . ."

Lucas looked from Otis to Darletta.

"And in Hebrews 8:12, 13, 14 and 21," she said, with the smile she might once have employed to demonstrate an inflatable life vest. "Also in Jude, Thessalonians and Timothy."

"We enter the last days," Dr. Otis Corey Butler said softly. "We enter in faith. We don't know what the end will be like. Now, some people worry that their relatives and friends will be on a freeway when the Rapture comes. They picture trucks flying through the air. We've been in the Holy Land long enough not to be literalist. Only the Lord knows what plans He's made to provide for his Muslim children and their houses of worship. Only He knows how He will resolve His everlasting covenant with Israel. All the righteous will share. Our weapons are spiritual. Our means are patience, brotherhood and prayer. We aspire to light the way for the Light of the World."

"I see," Lucas said. He was impressed and even a bit jealous. The Butlers made him feel credulous and naive, as though if he were only a little more intelligent and energetic, he might find a place in their schemes. They had the humor and detachment to make a good living from things he somehow could not keep from taking seriously.

"Doesn't it say somewhere a third of mankind will be killed?" he asked.

"It predicts terrible tribulations," Dr. Otis Corey Butler said contentedly. "And soon."

His wife smiled. Lucas wondered what she could be thinking.

From the House of the Galilean he went over to the Human Rights Coalition office to see Ernest Gross. Linda Ericksen was at the copying machine, looking pale and shaky.

"Everything all right?"

"Oh," she said, "we had a bunch of self-righteous creeps showing us horror movies."

Ernest had just had an information-exchanging session with a delegation from the International Council of Churches on the subject of Abu Baraka and the killings in Gaza, as recorded by the UN, the NGOs and Ernest's own organization. The session had left him out of sorts too.

"They come here to hone their Christian self-esteem," Ernest told Lucas, taking him to the inner office. "Jews are bastards, that's all they want to know. They look at me like: why haven't I turned to Jesus?"

"Think *they* go to Yad Vashem?"

"Who cares?" Ernest said. "I don't want them there."

"You know," Lucas observed, "there's such a thing as burnout. Especially in your business. Maybe you should take a break."

"Thanks."

Lucas reflected on the fact that he himself had not made the short trip to the Holocaust memorial of Yad Vashem. There were many reasons that he had not gone yet, but they could not be compacted into an explanation.

Several days earlier, Ernest had acquired a video of some uniformed Israelis in Jabalia shooting a Palestinian up the rectum and had duly run it for the Christian philanthropists.

"Want to see it?" he asked Lucas.

"I suppose I should."

The video's effect was odd. One moment everyone — the policemen and the man about to be shot — seemed engaged in good-natured, if somewhat physical, hijinks. Rolling on the ground, actually laughing, or appearing to. The man's expression might have been a grimace or a desperate attempt at conventionalization. Everyone was fully clothed.

Then a sudden convulsion, and the Palestinian turned deathly pale, his teeth set in a rictus. The shot appeared to kill him instantly, a mercy for which Lucas was grateful. He had watched with dread but the thing was over in seconds, before the event it recorded could be properly absorbed.

"Dumb of them to get taped," Lucas said when it was over. "Who took it?"

"I can't tell you that. But they brought it to us."

"And you know that's Abu's merry band?"

"That's what they called themselves for the Palestinians. They're looking for a reputation." He put the recorder on rewind. "It's being bootlegged around town. The Spanish or the Italians may run it on their news. The police won't comment. Unofficially they say it must be an accident, that they were threatening the bloke and it went wrong. *Our* police sources say it's Abu all right."

"Too bad you don't have the shooter's face on the tape," Lucas said. "Of course, it could have been an accident."

"Oh, the guy they shot probably did it to somebody else," Ernest said. "An informer. On the other hand, maybe he simply bears some unfortunate resemblance to some other fucking Arab. I mean, where does it stop?"

Some time before, under the last government, after a particularly bloody day for the population of the Gaza Strip, Lucas had found occasion to quote the late Golda Meir to Ernest. Mrs. Meir had said that she could forgive the Arabs anything except making the Israelis cruel and brutal, as the Arabs themselves presumably were. It had once been a much-cited quotation.

"That statement," Ernest had informed him, "marks the lowest point in the moral history of Zionism."

Until then, Lucas had always thought of Meir's reflection as thoughtful and sympathetic. It was not every day he learned something. Later, an Israeli journalist had referred to the Meir statement as "moral kitsch" and it was rarely heard thereafter. If there were still *tzaddiks,* men raised to judgment, Lucas thought, Ernest seemed to be one, as Zimmer had said.

"That killing was done in broad daylight, and the men were in uniform. They're getting bolder. They're trying to touch something off." He looked over at Lucas. "Going to write it?"

"I had something else in mind. Religion."

Ernest looked at him as if he had lost his mind. "You're such a man of leisure. Other reporters work for a living."

"I have a real story to go with. A nonviolent story. I'll leave the Strip to Nuala."

"She should watch it," Ernest said. "She's reckless."

"Really," Linda Ericksen said. She agreed without turning from the copier.

18

ADAM DE KUFF woke to the radiance of the newly risen moon. Going to the window, he saw its light silvering the battlements of the Haram. The lambent Dome of the Rock reflected a shimmering vault of sky. The scattered light bore fragrance — jasmine, roses.

"He wraps himself in light as in a garment," recited De Kuff.

In the interstices of different orders of dreams, De Kuff had seen the lions guarding the Name. Instead of fear, he had experienced exaltation. And now, this night, the splendor of the sky.

His room had been Berger's. On a littered dresser stood an oil lamp. A tarnished mirror with a cracking wooden frame was propped against the wall beside it, and De Kuff's first impulse, when he had lit the lamp, was to inspect his own face in the glass. Inspired though he was, he hardly dared. He realized from the beating of his heart how it must appear, how it would shine.

He lit the lamp all the same, avoiding his direct reflection. Around the mirror were artifacts and externals of his quotidian life. There were the appropriately flesh-colored lithium carbonate tablets from an elegantly antique drugstore on Madison Avenue, years old and perhaps literally poisonous now. His journal, in a child's dappled black and white copybook, bought in the same shop as the prescription, from the same smiling clerk. And what he ironically called his sacramentals: kippa, *tallit, tefillin.*

He had inherited Berger's prayer beads. Beside them lay a band of saffron-colored cotton cloth from a temple in Sri Lanka, and incense sticks and, wrapped in a silk cloth, a crucifixion icon in imitation of the one by Dionysius the Monk at the Ferapont Monastery in Russia. He removed the cloth from the crucifix, avoiding the sight of the suffering Logos depicted there as he avoided his own eyes in the glass. Taking his *tefillin,* he bound them in the manner of the ancient *minim,* the accursed Gnostics and Nazarenes. In a dream he had seen how it was done, the wearing condemned in the Mishnah as *minnut,* a secret sign of Yeshu as high priest and Messiah.

In the mirror, at the edge of vision, he could see his bustling rhythms reflected, so much impatient writhing. After prayer, he allowed himself to face the mask of flesh there. The glow was mainly of blood, but it was his eyes and not the lamp that lit the room.

And outside, the night!

No prayer or meditation could contain him. He sat wide-eyed, knuckles against his lips. The worst thing about the exhilaration, he had long ago decided, was its loneliness. Once his notebooks had given him an illusion like companionship. No more, after so much suffering.

He dressed haphazardly, his heart swelling. Ecstasy. For a moment he stood outside Raziel's door, wondering if the young man was asleep. They had not exchanged a word for days. But De Kuff's desire was toward the streets.

He jogged over the cobblestones, pulling on his expensive tweed jacket on the run. His face was upturned. Intersecting lines of glowing sky met among the close crowding rooftops. Innumerable stars. He ran across a small courtyard. Luminescence spread overhead. Sheer space was divine, an emanation. Isaac Newton had believed it.

From the shadows at the end of the courtyard, a ragged, angry voice called after him in Arabic. The single voice raised others. Street dogs yapped. Here and there the alleys of the city trapped a smell of hashish.

At a turn in the Tariq al-Wad, he saw the lights of the Border Police post and heard military Hebrew crackling from the post's radio. Under an arcade, two men were sliding open the corrugated shutters of their stall. A young man with Down's syndrome, wearing a white religious cap and standing in the light of a bare bulb, screamed at him and gestured with a broom.

The sky was still blue-black and star-scattered when he approached the Lions' Gate. The morning's first taxis waited there and a half-dozen International Harvester buses, their huge noxious engines running. Palestinian companies operated the buses between

West Bank towns and the city they called Al-Kuds, The Holy. De Kuff hung back in the shadows, a few hundred feet from the well of noise and light at the gate.

For the first time since coming to Jerusalem, he had a sense of the Spirit of God close by. The Temple's Holy of Holies had been inside the Haram. He felt himself drawing strength from its otherness and fearfulness. He felt newly elected, called from the depths of that starry night toward Mount Moriah.

From the arching shadows, he watched faint lights burning in the Franciscan Monastery of the Flagellation down the street. The lights made him imagine chanted plainsong. After a few moments he was sure he actually heard it, the *"Regina Coeli"* of Franciscan Matins: *"Ave Maria virgine sanctissima."*

With its imagined cadence in his ears, he walked to the gate that enclosed the plaza of the Bethesda Pool and the Church of St. Anne. The sky above the Mount of Olives began to glow.

In the quickening light De Kuff saw a row of reclining bodies against the wall of the seminary across the cloister. They were young people, and most appeared to be foreigners. Some of them looked ragged and impoverished; others appeared to be prosperous tourists. They must be an overflow, he thought, from the night services at the Holy Sepulchre and the nearby hostels. Some were asleep, some stared at the sky, a few watched him.

He walked across the stone square in front of the locked church to the edge of the dry ruins that had been the Bethesda Pool. As light gathered over the Mount of Olives, De Kuff felt that he could hear the sunrise, its rhythms and subtleties, the mingling of elements it contained. He thought he might be experiencing the *sefirot,* the divine emanations. Sweat poured from his body. In spite of his confusion he felt grateful.

He sat down on a stone step overlooking the Pool and took the tweed jacket off and folded it beside him, with the lining out. Light drifted all around, riffled like water, musically ringing.

The Pool had once served the Second Temple; then it had been called the Pool of Israel. Each year, it was believed, an angel descended in season to trouble the water with its wing. The water was good and healing. Beside it, Jesus cured a paralytic.

In a temple of five colonnades, Serapis had been worshiped there, the great syncretic god of the East. Serapis was at once the subsumation of Apis and Osiris and Aesculapius, a son of Apollo. He stood crowned with a wheat measure, attended by Anubis the jackal-headed, wielding the staff with twined snakes.

De Kuff settled himself cross-legged on the ancient stone. Bathed in the rosy light, he raised his hands above his head and let them rest, palms up, on either side. His arms were short and flabby but his hands extremely delicate, lithe and sensitive. A musician's hands, a physician's.

As the dawn prayers reached him from the Haram, De Kuff closed his eyes to see the shining *sefirot*. He and Raziel had been looking for them in the sounds of Muslim prayer since coming to the Old City. This time the *sefirot* were there for him, the myriads of the *Zohar,* the Uncreated Light.

He had no idea how long he stayed in *kavana.* When he looked about him, over a dozen youths had gathered around the place he sat and were either lost in their own meditations or just watching, as though waiting to hear what he would say. He stood up and smiled at them and picked up his jacket. A solemn young blond woman helped settle it around his shoulders.

He was dizzy from sitting in meditation and unsteady on his legs, but his heart ached with joy. He felt consumed with love for the motley youths who crowded around him. Had he spoken to them? They were looking at him with concern, stepping back to let him pass.

Heading toward the street, he saw that the Church of St. Anne had opened, its altar candles lit for the early Mass. St. Anne's was a church of great austerity. Its lack of decoration and massive hewn stones gave it an almost modern aspect. After Jerusalem fell to Saladin it had been used as a mosque, and an inscription from the Koran remained over the lintel. De Kuff went inside the church and stood under its great vault, breathing in the faint traces of incense, the candle smoke and old stone.

And suddenly, in that church-mosque-temple by the Pool of Israel, he thought he knew what it meant to say that all was Torah. And what it meant to know that the world to come was at hand. The mystery of Torah was far stranger than anyone believed. It was the eternal reason that there was something rather than nothing. It underlay everything, in forms more various than anyone had dared conceive. The knowledge nearly knocked him to the floor.

As he stood swaying in the center aisle, the young blond woman came up to him again.

"Please," she said, "you will come later? You will come later and hear us sing?"

"If you like," he said. She gave him a timid smile. She had watery blue eyes, like Van Eyck's Saint Ursula.

Her smile vanished as if she were afraid of offending him. He patted her hand and went outside into the plaza. A few of the youths followed after him.

He had become a Catholic once, received into the Church at St. Vincent Ferrer on Lexington Avenue, a church that strained to evoke what St. Anne's conveyed in every stone. He could still remember the winter afternoon of his baptism and reception — the hysterical confusion, kneeling in a shrine named for a Spanish Dominican inquisitor. It had been unwise, premature, a useless apostatizing. He had been without guidance then. He had thought in those days that it was not possible to have it all — a false economy. In those days he had believed in austerities, mortifications, humiliations. Often, he still found life harder without them.

Now he could stand anywhere on his own terms and represent in his own soul the obviated differences between Jew and Greek, male and female, bond and free. The world to come was within him, represented in his person, available to all. If they imagined that they had taken hold of the *sefirot,* bound some in their churches to worship, what matter?

He began to recite from the *Zohar.* The young foreigners, at Bethesda for sunrise, began to gather round. The time had come, De Kuff thought, to reveal a part of the truth.

19

A T F I N K ' S one evening Basil Thomas, the go-between and former KGB officer, treated Lucas to a prolonged complaint about life in Jerusalem.

"One is a secular type of guy," Basil Thomas lamented, "one feels an outcast. One might as well go somewhere and be a Jew, if you see what I mean."

"It doesn't bother me much."

"How," Basil Thomas inquired haughtily, "would it bother *you?*"

Basil Thomas also imparted the information that Dr. Obermann had broken up with the former wife of Reverend Ericksen, the unsuccessful American missionary. Linda Ericksen, according to Basil Thomas, had taken up with Janusz Zimmer.

"What do you make of Zimmer?" Lucas asked after they had talked awhile. "Has he made *aliyah,* or is he just hanging out?" Of course, Lucas thought, one could have asked that about hundreds living here.

"This is an interesting fellow," Basil Thomas admitted. He spoke softly, without his usual bluster. "Very knowledgeable. A gifted journalist." Lucas thought his discretion represented some kind of political caution but asked no further. Then Basil Thomas said, "Ayin."

"What's Ayin?"

"Nothing," said Basil Thomas. "Ask Janusz."

Lucas's next meeting with Obermann took place at the Atara, a café on Ben Yehuda Street. The doctor seemed downcast. During their conversation the subject of the estranged Ericksens did come up.

"If we want a disgruntled Galilean," Obermann said glumly, "you should interview Ericksen. I hear he's leaving the country."

"How about his missus?"

"Linda's with Jan Zimmer."

"Oh," Lucas said. "Sorry to hear that. I mean . . . I suppose she's a restless soul."

Obermann raised a hand in dismissal. "With Zimmer," he said, "she'll lead a more adventurous life. In any case, if either of us is going to interview Ericksen, it's got to be you."

"Think he'll see me?"

"Try," Obermann said. "He's moved in with the archeologist, Lestrade, down at the Austrian hospice. I have the number."

Lucas took the number and bought some telephone tokens from the Atara's cashier. No one answered at the hospice.

"Go anyway," Obermann suggested. "I would. Maybe you can surprise him."

Lucas walked it, by way of the Damascus Gate. The Austrian hospice was in the Muslim Quarter of the Old City. Passing through the foyer of the hospice, he noticed an enormous plaster crucifix on the wood-paneled wall. He had to wonder if, back in the late thirties, there had not been a portrait of the Führer adjoining it, at a mutually respectful distance.

Ericksen was sitting among potted thatch palms on the rooftop terrace of the adjoining building. He was not the man he had been on the Mount of Temptation. His tan had paled, and a loss of weight had scaled his features to a death's-head pattern. A newly prominent Adam's apple gave him the look of an unsound American rustic.

"Dr. Ericksen . . ." Lucas began, slightly out of breath from the stairs.

"I'm not a doctor," Ericksen said. "I'm not anything."

"Sorry," said Lucas. "I tried to telephone but there wasn't an answer. I wanted to talk with you before you left." Ericksen never glanced at him. "Do you remember me? We talked at Jebel Qurun-tul."

Finally Ericksen turned, slowly, shielding his eyes.

"Yes, I remember."

"Well, I heard you were leaving. I had hoped we could talk."

"All right," Ericksen said.

"Got an offer back home?"

"I don't have any offers. I'm leaving church work."

Lucas stopped himself at the point of asking Ericksen whether he wanted to talk about that decision. It was always the wrong question.

"Why?" he asked instead. "Is the decision a result of working at the House of the Galilean?"

Ericksen looked, at that moment, like a man who had been slapped.

"You're a reporter," he told Lucas.

"Well, I'm writing about religious developments here. I thought you might be able to help me."

"Who," Ericksen asked exhaustedly, "do you represent?"

"I'm writing a book," Lucas told him. "About religion in the Holy Land." It was not a phrase he commonly used.

"Are you a Jew?"

"I'm a lapsed Catholic," Lucas said, "of partly Jewish background. I have no ax to grind." That, he thought, was a good one.

"What do you want to know about the House?"

"Well, on leaving, do you believe you've done something worthwhile?"

"Even if they were honest," Ericksen said, "nothing they do would be worthwhile."

"Can I quote you?"

"Sure," Ericksen said. "Why not?"

"What is it they actually do?"

"They make a lot of money. A lot of Christians give them money. Jews too, now."

"Did you get any?"

"Yes," Ericksen said.

"What's the money for?"

"Various things. Lately Gordon Lestrade is reconfiguring the Second Temple. Who did you say you represented?"

"The world," Lucas said. "Reconfiguring the Temple?"

"I think you do represent the world," Ericksen said, and laughed. Lucas attempted to laugh along.

"They're trying to reconstruct the Herodian Temple. There's a Jewish effort and a Christian one."

"Why a Christian one?"

Ericksen gave him a look that seemed to express surprise at how little Lucas knew about it.

"American fundamentalists are very interested in Israel and the Temple. The rebuilding of the Temple will be a sign."

"Of what?"

"Oh," Ericksen said with a grim smile, "of things to come."

Lucas tried to remember what he knew about eschatology and millenarian doctrine. He had forgotten a great deal.

"A lot of Christians genuinely believe these things. But the people at the House — Otis and Darletta — they're just promoters. I don't know about the Jews. Perhaps they believe."

"In what?"

"I don't know. The coming of the Messiah, I guess. If they build it, he will come."

"Like in the movie?"

"I suppose," Ericksen said. "I didn't know they still made those religious movies."

"And Lestrade?"

"I don't know what Lestrade believes. He used to be a Catholic like you."

"And he's doing the reconfiguring?"

"He takes tourists out on digs. But his main work now is on the Temple Mount. Lestrade claims he can rebuild the Temple on the basis of his research."

"Reconfiguring it?"

"Look," Ericksen said, "rebuilding the Temple is what the House of the Galilean is all about. That's what they claim to be doing."

"I thought you were missionaries."

"If we were looking for converts," Ericksen said with a smile, "the rabbis would drive us out. They don't care for us anyway. And the Muslims would kill us."

"So you never made any converts?"

"We converted a few Christians to our kind of Christianity. And we made a lot of money."

"You sound very disillusioned," Lucas told him. "Have you just had it with the House of the Galilean? Or have you lost faith?"

Ericksen looked at him without expression.

"When Linda and I came here," he said, "we both believed it very much. We came to witness."

"But . . . something went wrong."

"There's a power here," Ericksen said. "A terrible power."

"But," Lucas asked humbly, "it's good, is it not? We're all . . . supposed to believe in it."

"We're supposed to believe in the power of evil. Most people here do. Most people everywhere. It makes them stronger."

"The power of evil? Do you mean the power of God?"

"Whatever you call it. It makes you stronger until you think about it. It took Linda," he told Lucas. "It took her body as a thing to fuck. Next it's going to kill me."

"Excuse me," Lucas said. "Let me take a little jump. Are you talking about God? The Jewish God?"

"I was wrong when we spoke on the mountain," Ericksen explained. "The Jewish God is Azazel. Always was. I never knew it. Azazel, God, Jehovah, the evil thing — it belongs to them."

The reverend, Lucas thought, resembled his former wife. Their eyes were very similar, with transparent irises through which his passion visibly burned, while hers lay invisible as Azazel.

"I like the people who wear the serpents," Ericksen said. "The black girl and her friends at Bethesda. Do you know them?"

"Yes," Lucas said. "I like them too."

"Do you know why they wear serpents?"

"I guess I don't know. I'd like to hear you tell me."

"Because," Ericksen said, "when the first Adam was destroyed, the serpent came to free us from Azazel. But Azazel set all women against him. Christ was the serpent come again. The serpent, the snake, is our only hope." He dipped his hand under the V of his collar. At the end of a thin chain hung a tiny ouroboros, essentially the same one Raziel and Sonia wore. "See, I have one. Would you like one also?"

Lucas, who was untalented, began to try and draw it in his notebook. Then it occurred to him that he might have many future opportunities to do so.

"I don't know," he said. "I guess I'll have to think about it."

20

THE DAY AFTER De Kuff's Pauline expedition to the Bethesda Pool, Janusz Zimmer arranged to meet Sonia at her apartment in Rehavia. She had been spending most of her time over in the Muslim Quarter, at Berger's. She and Zimmer were old acquaintances. If she had not taken up with Raziel, if she had not become a Sufi of Berger's, they might have been more than that.

Sonia had no idea what was on Janusz Zimmer's mind. For a while they talked about the places in Africa they had both been. Nairobi. Mogadishu. Khartoum.

"We're both old Reds, aren't we?" Zimmer asked her. He was drinking a bottle of Israeli brandy he had brought, and he seemed to be getting sentimental. It was midafternoon. The light outside grew richer, the shadows under the eucalyptus grew longer.

"I suppose we are," she said. "But not the only ones in town."

"Among the few in Jerusalem," Zimmer corrected her. "Most of our old comrades live in Tel Aviv."

"Tell you the truth," said Sonia, "I always thought you were just faking it. I never believed you were actually a Marxist-Leninist."

"To tell you the truth, Marx and Lenin opened my eyes when I was a youth. Remember, we were still fighting a civil war with reactionaries in Poland when I was a young man. The Americans were parachuting weapons to them. There were pogroms. So, for a period, I called myself a Marxist Leninist."

"And you became disillusioned."

"To make a long story short," Zimmer said, "I became disillusioned. But of course *you* had the good fortune to be in Cuba. Where everything is wonderful."

"Please don't put down Cuba," Sonia said. "It hurts me."

"But the bottom line is, it's a police state, yes?"

Sonia shrugged, declining to argue it.

"So you embrace Sufism and whatnot," Zimmer said.

"Well, not much whatnot," Sonia told him. "A lot of Sufism."

"And now you're with these Jewish-Christian, Christian-Jewish Jews, so called. Isn't that right?"

"Are these friendly questions, Jan? Are you asking as a reporter? Or am I supposed to exercise self-criticism?"

"We'll pretend we're back in the Party," Zimmer said.

"Jan, I was never in the Party. My parents were."

"We'll pretend we're back in the Party," Zimmer repeated, as though he knew better than to give weight to such demurrers. "Exercise self-criticism. Why do you have to chase these phantasmagoria?"

"My beliefs are my own business," Sonia said. "These days."

"Is it because it's Jerusalem?" Zimmer asked. "Because what happens here is unlike what happens elsewhere? And sometimes it changes the world?"

She was startled and a little hurt. "Chris Lucas told you I said that."

"Yes," said Zimmer, "Lucas and I keep in touch. But what you say is right, Sonia. What happens here *will* change the world. This time it will."

"What do you mean, Jan?"

"The Party — the Party lost its soul when it lost us. I mean the Jews, because you're as much a Jew as I am. It was our hope, our passion for *tikkun olam,* our courage, our devotion that made the Communist Party everything it was. At least everything good. The Stalinists, the murderers, were all mainly Gentiles. There were Jews among them, yes. But essentially they were all anti-Semites, regardless."

"Jan," Sonia said. "Are you pitching me? Are you hitting on me? Are you asking me to help you bring back the Party or telling me I should be a better Jew or asking me for a date or what?"

"I'm telling you this, Sonia. There are organizations in this country whose work it is to see that this becomes a better place."

"Everybody has different ideas about that."

"We might possibly be of like mind. You might be able to help us. Where there was a Red Orchestra we now have a Jewish Orchestra, a network organized as well as anything that was organized in

Europe against the Germans, or here against the British. I want you to join it, or at least to help. I owe it to you to ask."

Sonia looked at him in wonder. "So you haven't given up on the perfect world?"

"I have not," Zimmer said. "I will not. But it won't come from Moscow. Maybe we can do the job here."

"What do you propose to do?"

"If you will commit, you'll learn more. Surely you know how it goes. On the basis of need to know."

"I guess I'm a Jew," Sonia said. "My mother was. She used to say that you didn't have to be Jewish to be a Jew. That a lot of people who weren't Jewish were, as far as she was concerned. So I guess I'm like her. My country's here, sure, but my country's in the heart too. I don't believe in a perfect world, but I believe in a better one."

"My poor baby," Zimmer said. "You've become a liberal."

"Hey, Jan," she said, "I'm a person of color, you know. And sticking up for the Palestinians in this country, who are a despised minority here — that just may be my way of being a good Jew. So if a Jewish underground means what I think it means, no thanks."

"Let me give you one last piece of friendly advice," Zimmer said. "Stay out of the Gaza Strip."

"Jesus," Sonia said. "You're off the deep end, aren't you? I worked there, Jan. I may very well work there again."

"So be it."

"I'll tell you what," said Sonia. "We'll forget this happened — this conversation. I won't mention it. So we can stay pals."

"That would be considerate," Janusz Zimmer said. "And I certainly hope we can stay pals. I'm not sure."

"You know," Sonia said, "they say the truth is one."

"Is that a fact?" Zimmer asked her. "Yours or mine?"

21

OR WEEKS, on the days that he was well enough, when the spirit upheld his frail body, De Kuff went to the Pool of Bethesda. For years, Bethesda had been a gathering place for a great variety of strange pilgrims and seekers. Anyone passing it in the dawn hours would see scores of foreigners assembled, singly or in groups, most of them appearing to be in the grip of some torment or illumination, watching, mumbling prayers. Some faced toward the medieval church during its early Mass, kneeling as the consecration took place inside. Some of them read their Bibles, either silently or to a small group of companions. A great many simply sat or took the lotus position, palms upturned, listening to the proclamation from the Haram of the oneness, the mercy and compassion of Allah.

The people who oversaw the area or lived or worked in it had become used to the morning and evening assembly. Since the first dawn De Kuff arrived on the scene, proclaiming the truths of the universe, the attention of this group of religious wanderers had come to focus on him. Also, their numbers increased. The larger crowds and the appearance of this new, radiant, ungainly figure attracted attention from several quarters in that city of impossibly delicate balances.

The sheikhs of the nearby Haram, the priests of the adjoining churches, Greek and Latin, all became uncomfortably aware of the transformation taking place around Bethesda. Members of small, militant Jewish congregations asserting the sacred nature of the whole city sometimes wandered, armed, down to the Via Dolorosa for a look at De Kuff. The police took note but did not intervene, as long as De Kuff and his hearers remained off the street itself. If his preaching were to be prevented, it would be up to the various institutions that owned sections of the courtyard to complain collectively. And collective legal action was difficult for the divided sects.

De Kuff became a more and more familiar sight at the Pool, and certain of the eccentric pilgrims became regulars and waited for him every morning.

As the summer went on, De Kuff's crowds grew larger and larger. One morning, he decided to inform his listeners of the third principle of the universe. He had already preached two. Sonia and Lucas were in the crowd. Raziel had stayed back at Berger's apartment, playing his clarinet to the courtyard.

"Why is there something rather than nothing?" De Kuff asked the crowd. It fell silent at his words.

"That which is at the core of the universe utters words," he proclaimed. "The wind takes the words and scatters them. They take a million million forms like snowflakes. But the essential words remain, regardless of their infinity of superficial meanings in a blind world."

"I like that New Orleans accent," Lucas whispered to Sonia. "Sidney Lanier must have sounded like that, you think?"

But Sonia was transfixed.

"If I say everything is Torah," De Kuff declared, "I say that life has myriad forms but only one essence. Its essence is inscribed in imperishable fire. Now the letters, the words, they whirl like leaves. But under the multiple disguise" — he smiled triumphantly — "one essence, one truth."

It seemed to Lucas that the crowd grew closer to him at the words "one truth." As if it were a cold morning, as if they were cold and he and his words warmed them. Especially the words "one truth."

De Kuff had a second principle of which to remind them.

"The varieties and mysteries of the world will now be solved. That which began as imperishable words will become again imperishable words. The End of Days, the world to come, is at hand. In the world to come, the snake sheds its skin, the wool divides from the linen, all things. No more shadows on the wall of a cave. 'For now we see through a glass, darkly,' " he said mischievously, " 'but then . . .' "

He waited for a reply, and someone in the crowd said, " 'Face to face.' "

"Face to face!" De Kuff shouted in delight. "When everything is Torah. And the Messiah comes. Or Jesus returns. Or the Mahdi.

And all know," he said. "And all partake. And there are no shadows."

"This is far out," Lucas said.

"No," Sonia said, "it's simple."

"Maybe it's simple if you've believed in the dialectic," Lucas said. She was lost to him again.

There were other things, De Kuff said, other things everyone must know. The time was ripe, the fullness of days was come. The pangs of the world being born were being felt.

The crowd grew excited.

"Jesus," said Lucas, under his breath.

And there was more. De Kuff preached Hagar in the desert. When Hagar beheld in the desert the insight at the core of the universe, she could not believe she would not die.

"Can I see the Lord of Seeing, can I see El Roi, and live?" De Kuff had Hagar ask.

Then he talked about the Death of the Kiss. Because the new world was being born, because certain things could not be seen, understood, witnessed, without a kind of death, each person had to embrace the Death of the Kiss. In the Death of the Kiss, each died to the world. A kind of death in life must be practiced. It was a death, but it was life more abundant. It was being more alive to something else.

"In the beginning," De Kuff said, "is the end. In the end is the beginning is the end. In the beginning . . ."

Lucas saw Sonia fingering the ouroboros at her throat.

"He's exhausted," she said. "He'll never come down."

And indeed, De Kuff, his face glowing with mad enthusiasm and drawn with fatigue, went lurching across the courtyard. Some of the more enthusiastic of his regular following made as though to follow him. An old woman in black. A few weeping Russians. Some young European hippie types. Lucas thought he spotted the German *majnoon* from the previous Easter. Suddenly De Kuff stopped in his tracks.

"The prophets died the Death of the Kiss," he declared. "And I will. And I will die to the world and all who follow me. And where I was, the old world will disappear and things will become the word of God incarnate. And this is what we mean when we say the world will become Torah."

The Gentile crowd praised the Lord. But at the gate that led out of the Pool enclosure to the *tariq,* an elderly, well-dressed Palestinian man, his features flushed with rage, was struggling with some men his own age who sought to restrain him. There were catcalls in Hebrew from the upper story of a nearby building. Someone threw a stone. De Kuff came up to Sonia.

"Do you remember the song, Sonia?" he asked her.

"*Yo no digo esta canción, sino a quien conmigo va,*" she said. She looked at Lucas, dry-eyed but obviously in a bit of a state. "It means," she told him, "if you want to hear my song, you have to come with me."

De Kuff had wandered off again; he had gone, pursued by his followers, out into the Via Dolorosa. There was a scuffling match between the disciples and a few people in the road. A police jeep started slowly up the cobbled street from the Lions' Gate. Lucas and Sonia fought to stay behind De Kuff. As they struggled to follow, he went through the door of the French Catholic hospice next door to Bethesda.

"He's going to get himself in big trouble," Lucas said. "And you along with him."

"We should get him out of there," Sonia said.

The crowd around them was mainly Palestinian now, as the Muslim Quarter began its working day. Boys were pushing wheelbarrows full of eggplants and melons over the cobblestones. Passersby, seeing all the agitated foreigners, stopped to ask what was going on. Lucas and Sonia went into the hostel and found De Kuff in argument with a French Sister of Notre Dame.

The interior of the hostel was redolent of France. Lucas breathed in the aroma of floral soap, sachet and varnish. There were fresh cut flowers at the reception desk. The first guests had come down for breakfast and were speaking French, adding the smoke of their first Gauloises to the mix, along with the smell of coffee and croissants.

A sleepy-eyed Palestinian youth behind the desk had put aside his copy of *Al-Jihar* and was staring in disbelief at De Kuff as the old man, all courtesy and deference, spoke to the nun in French.

She had gray hair and wore a seersucker dress with a black apron and dark cap. She looked over De Kuff's shoulder to assess Lucas as he came in. Her face clouded with suspicion.

De Kuff was clearly and confidently informing her that he might, upon occasion, require a room.

"Why are you here?" she demanded sternly in English. "What do you want with us?"

Lucas thought he understood what was happening. The French nun had recognized them, or at least De Kuff, for Jews. The Palestinian clerk, a non-European, was unsure.

"From time to time a bed for the night, Sister," De Kuff said. "No more than that."

"But why?"

"To be near the Pool," he told her. "And the church. In case of need. If the time comes."

"I wish I could believe you were only an enthusiast," the nun said. "I'm afraid you have come to dispossess us."

"You're mistaken," said De Kuff.

When the Palestinian clerk came around from behind the desk, she placed a restraining hand on his chest and addressed De Kuff.

"We have been here for three hundred years and even before that. Our rights have been confirmed by every authority. Your government is committed."

"You're mistaken," De Kuff said kindly. "I understand your mistake. You take me for an Israeli militant. But I was once a Catholic like yourself. I can show you a certificate of baptism."

He reached inside his jacket and fumbled for the thing and eventually found it among the mysteries of his pockets. He withdrew a decorative little folder in an envelope with a gold cord, with the signature of the friar who had baptized him.

The nun took it and put her glasses on to read it and struggled with the corded envelope.

"I must stay here," De Kuff said. He was becoming agitated. "You have to understand. I need to be close to Bethesda. I require its blessing."

He hurried from the room and into the refectory where the French pilgrims were having breakfast.

"If you could have seen the things I have seen this one morning," he announced, "you would glorify the Holy Ancient One for the rest of your lives. What you have come here for — I have seen."

The pilgrims at their café au lait and croissants stared at him.

"Who are you?" the nun asked Lucas. "Who is he?"

"I'm a journalist," Lucas said.

The nun cast her eyes heavenward and touched her brow.

"A journalist? But why are you all here?" she asked again.

"Only because he's our friend," Sonia said, "and he's not well." The nun stared then at Sonia and the coiled serpent at her throat. "In fact, he's a good man who believes in all religions."

The Sister of Notre Dame laughed bitterly. "Do you say so? In all?"

She turned away from Lucas and pursued De Kuff into the breakfast room. "What is it you want, monsieur?" she asked in measured tones, as though the language of clarity might put everything in order. "Why must you be near the Pool? Or St. Anne's?"

"To meditate," De Kuff shouted. "To pray. To hear my friends sing. And I can pay."

The nun puffed out her cheeks and exhaled, in the French manner. "I don't know what to think of you, monsieur. Perhaps you are ill." She turned to Lucas. "If he's ill, you must take him home."

De Kuff seated himself at the refectory table and rested his head in his hands. Sonia went in and sat beside him.

"Come on, Rev. Let's go."

"I told them," he said, "about *mors osculi*. I proclaimed the Death of the Kiss and I thought they would be afraid. But everyone was strong and it was all joy."

"I know," she said. "I was there."

"Presently," De Kuff said, "I'll lie down."

The nun sat down across the table from them.

"I think you *are* ill, monsieur. Where are you staying?" she asked Lucas in English. "A hotel?" The ouroboros, which De Kuff also wore, plainly made her unhappy.

"If I can rest a moment," De Kuff said. "Suddenly I'm very tired."

"You must understand," the nun said more gently, "the situation is very dangerous. An intifada is in progress. There are incidents every day. It may become dangerous. Do you understand?"

"We understand," Lucas said.

The nun was still working on the gold cord that sealed De Kuff's baptismal certificate.

"You must have seen others the same way," Lucas suggested to her.

"Yes," the nun said. She checked out his collar to see if he had one of the same necklaces. "Many," she said — relieved, Lucas thought, that he did not wear one. "But never such eyes."

"He's a good man," Sonia said. "He loves the holy places."

"So it seems," the nun said.

"We have to get him out of the Muslim Quarter," Lucas said. "People are thinking territory, period. Someone will hurt him."

"All right," Sonia said, "take him to my place in Rehavia for today. We'll find him a place somewhere."

Standing over De Kuff, the Sister of Notre Dame unfolded the certificate of baptism De Kuff had given her.

"St. Vincent Ferrer, New York, New York," the nun read aloud. "*Ah,*" she said, as though things had been instantly made clearer, "*vous êtes américain!*"

22

ONE MORNING, at her apartment in Rehavia, among her souvenirs of famine, pestilence and war, Sonia played Meliselda's song for Lucas on her guitar, singing along in Spanish and Ladino.

He had risen early from a sleepless night and gone over to her place. It was one of those Jerusalem desert days that could be a thing of dewy beauty at dawn and leave you suffering through a *hamsin* all afternoon.

"*Meliselda ahí encuentro,*" Sonia sang. "*La hija del Rey, luminosa.*"

And it always ended: "If you want to hear my song, you have to come with me."

Sitting there, he realized how unlikely it was that, within the limits of his life as he foresaw it, there would ever be a woman to whom he would be more attracted, whose company and person he would desire more. He allowed himself to entertain the notion that her credulity, as he saw it, was a factor that could be overcome. As far as believing impossible things went, she could do it for both of them.

"I've got the whole group in a hospice out at Ein Kerem," she told Lucas. "Keeps them from wandering into the Old City, getting in trouble."

"Doesn't he still show up at the Pool?"

"Sundays at dawn," she said. "He hires a Palestinian car service to take him there and back. Not just a *sherut*, a full-dress limousine. He pays for the hospice too."

"Probably safer," Lucas observed, "if people think he's rich."

"Well, he is. It's handy. And I think he's converting his driver."

While the mood was still light, Lucas asked, "To what? I mean, what is it you characters believe?"

"All right," she said. "What do we believe? We believe that every-thing is Torah. That means —"

"I know what he means by it, Sonia. I heard him. Platonism, it's called."

"We believe that a time of change is here. That a new world is coming."

"That's what your parents believed."

"That's what my parents believed in. And look at me."

"They required a revolution."

"We do too."

"A sort of figurative revolution."

"No, man," she said. "The same revolution. Except it won't re-quire weapons."

"Why not?"

"Because we believe that in our end is our beginning. That we have to stop being in the world the way it is. And if we want to change it, it will change."

"Right," Lucas said. "The Death of the Kiss. I wish that didn't sound so much to me like poisoned Kool-Aid. What else?"

"I think I know the rest," she said. "But I can't say it. Not until he does."

"Of course not."

"I'm sorry, Chris. Sorry if I sound like I'm blowing bubbles. That's me."

"Yes," Lucas said.

"Look at it this way," she said. "We're in Jerusalem. What hap-pens here affects the inner life of the whole world. Isn't that true? Weren't you brought up to believe that? Even if you were brought up Christian, you must have believed that what happened here defined human existence. Doesn't it feel true sometimes? The specialness of our people's story? The teachings that come forth from our experi-ence? I mean, think about it."

"I will," Lucas said. "Now let me ask *you* something. Do you really think there's a thing in the sky that cares whether the pass-ing asshole down below is Jewish or not? It loves one set of little tiny figures down on Earth more than an identical set of little tiny figures? It imposes hundreds of really special, utterly meaningless responsibilities on them? Some . . . some eternal, immortal oversized paperweight with a beard and wings who loves his little buddies the Jews?" He made binoculars of his hands and inspected the Spanish carpet. "Hooray. There they go. I mean, come on. This celestial leftover doorstop from the gates of Nineveh, except he's not under the sand, he's up in the sky? Forget it."

"History is history," Sonia said. "This people — ours, Chris — played an irreplaceable role in the moral history of humanity."

"Sonia, the universe does not care whether you're Jewish or not. Paranoids, Nazis care. Professional Jews and anti-Semites, people who need someone to hate. It's an imaginary condition, Sonia — it's in the heads of people who require it. Bigots. Chauvinists. God's own franchise, the cosmic home team? Give me a break."

"I'm sorry," Sonia said. "I don't think you really see it that way. Because then what are you doing here? What are you after?"

"Writing a book," Lucas said.

"I don't know how different we are," she said, "you and me. You try to act like you're content not believing anything, and I don't think I buy it. Me, I've spent my life learning to believe. To believe so it matters. You think I'm deluded. I think somebody has to be pretty deluded to be as without faith as you say you are."

"If I wasn't deluded," Lucas asked, "what would I have faith in?"

"History, maybe? Your own inner consciousness?"

"I don't think I have an inner consciousness," he said. "Just an outer one."

"Really? No inner resources? What do you do when shit gets impossible?"

"I drink. I go nuts."

"I understand," she said. "I used to do drugs."

"Me too."

"Chris," she said, "listen to me a minute. For all of civilization, Jews have been coming forward to speak for change."

"Oh, Sonia," he said, laughing, "don't you think I know the spiel?"

She put up a hand, palm outward, to override his protest. "Sorry. You get the spiel." She went toward him, then shrugged and folded her arms and half turned away, as if to make what she would say not be the spiel. But of course it was. "Because life is shitty, Chris, for most people. So you have Moses, you have Habakkuk, you have Isaiah, Jesus, Sabbatai, Marx, Freud. All these people were saying, Understand and act on it and things will change. What they were saying was true, man. Their lives failed, but *they* didn't fail.

"A hundred years before they burned Giordano Bruno in Venice, they burned a Jew named Solomon Molkho in Mantua. He was a Gnostic, a Sufi, a magus. He said when the change came the Dragon would be destroyed without weapons and everything would be changed. So we believe it's going to happen. Happening."

" 'So have I heard,' " Lucas said, " 'and do in part believe it.' Except I don't think I do anymore."

"Are you serious? Or do I just get some Shakespeare for my spiel?"

"I don't know," Lucas said. "Is it to Raziel you owe all this?"

"Raziel only speaks for the Rev. It all happens inside him."

"*Inside* him?"

"On the level of emanations. Through the souls inside him. He's the one who does the fighting. With Pharaoh. With the Dragon. Hell," she said, "I wish he'd shut up and not go out and do his numbers. But he's suffering so much he can't stand it."

"He'll get burned like Molkho."

"He might. And this stuff doesn't come from Raziel. The Sufis always knew it. And the Jews, in a certain way, always knew it, because that's what Torah is. It's a formula for making things one. For bringing us back where we belong. A lot is concealed in it."

"How is it that suddenly Raziel and the Rev are party to the big picture?"

"The way we all know the important things we know," Sonia said. "The old Jews used to say a wise person had a *maggid,* a spiritual counselor from another world. But a *maggid* is just something from your subconscious, from collective memory. Telling you something you already know.

"So poor old De Kuff's learned to recognize the souls inside him. And Raziel recognized *him.* Adam, the poor lamb, he fought it as hard as he could. It's a terrible fate to stand between the worlds. It's like madness."

"Don't you think," Lucas asked, "it *is* madness? No more than that?"

"No, I don't," she said. "Because I've seen this before. I've studied it half my life. Berger, before he died, recognized him. I recognize him too."

"All right, all right," Lucas said with a shrug. "So what's up? What's going to happen?"

Sonia laughed. "I don't know, man. Any more than you. Change. And me, I think it's gonna be beautiful."

Lucas walked across the room to inspect her collection of Third World photographs. Happy, hopeful faces among the wretched of the earth. On one table she had propped some photographer's proof sheets against a lamp. There were scores of images, hundreds, each one a child, dark, emaciated.

"Who do you have to be to get your picture in the house of a *maggid?*"

"Well," she said, "if you're one of those kids, you have to be dead. Because they all are. During the famine in Baidoa."

Lucas picked up one of the proof sheets and looked at the long, huge-eyed faces. The lines of a poem came to him, and he said them for her:

> "Go smiling souls, your new built cages break,
> In Heaven you'll learn to sing ere here to speak,
> Nor let the milky fonts that bathe your thirst
> > Be your delay;
> The place that calls you hence, is at the worst
> > Milk all the way."

"Milk all the way," she repeated. "How about that?"

"It's an old poem. By an old dead white guy. Richard Crashaw. 'To the Infant Martyrs.' About yet another Middle Eastern misunderstanding."

"I wish I'd known it in Somalia."

"No you don't, Sonia. Then you'd be like me. And instead of doing things and believing in things, you'd just know poems about them. Well," he said, "I have to go. I have a meet later with the doc."

"Wait, Chris. Sit down. Go ahead," she insisted when he only stood and looked at her. She spoke to him with the mock sternness of an old-fashioned southern schoolmarm and sat across the room from him, arms around her knees.

"Why do you hate yourself so much? What do you feel so bad over?"

"I don't know," he told her. "Maybe I'm dragged because it's a shitty world. As you just pointed out. Want to tell me my *tikkun?*"

"It's gonna be changed," she said. "We'll be free. Because where the spirit of the Lord is, there is liberty."

"I like it," he said.

"Do you?"

"Yes," Lucas said. "Of course. I was always religious. I was always feeling sorry for myself, and not even just for myself. So I really like it. I'm weak. I'm sentimental. Gotta have a Santa Claus. Yeah, I could be one psalm-singing fool." He stood up and turned away from her. "Yes, sure, I like it. I really do. And I like you. I like you very much."

"Yes, I know you do," she said, "because I know your *tikkun*. I like you too. Will you come back?"

"Yes, I will," Lucas said. "And I'll taunt and abuse you until I've made sure you've lost your faith."

"Because misery loves company?"

"Because you're too hip and beautiful and smart to believe this garbage. It's dangerous. And because misery loves company, and if I can't have all these pretty dreams and illusions, I'm going to take them from you."

"But, Chris," she said, laughing, "they're my joy. They make me happy."

"Well, I don't want you happy. You're too good a singer. I want you like me."

23

IN THE AFTERNOON he went over to the Atara to see Dr. Pinchas Obermann. There the tables along Ben Yehuda Street were all full, and people had pulled out chairs from the inside parlor to sit in the faint breeze. Obermann was at his usual cramped inside table. Lucas gave him a report on Reverend Ericksen and the returning serpent.

"Gnostic," Obermann said. "Yahweh is the demiurge who controls the world. The serpent is wisdom. Jesus came to free the world from Yahweh. Basically Greek anti-Semitism."

"He's not just bitter," Lucas said. "He's lost his mind."

"Working too close to the light," said Obermann.

"That," Lucas agreed, "and having his old lady fucked seven ways from sundown."

Dr. Obermann was not offended. He looked thoughtful. He, after all, was the cuckold now.

"Apparently," he said, "there really is such a thing as the missionary position."

"I guess it's how they teach you to fuck in Bible college."

"Do you mean," Obermann asked, "that American evangelicals are instructed in unrewarding sex techniques?"

"Just kidding," Lucas said. "But who knows?"

"Well," said Dr. Obermann, "Linda's learned her way around it. By the way," he told Lucas, "I read your book on Grenada." Lucas saw that he was holding in his hand the book that he, Lucas, had thought was long out of print. "Don't be surprised. I looked you up on Nexus. And I use a book service."

Like the Ministry of Defense? Lucas wondered. Or Mossad? He had spent three months turning out a book of reportage on the United States' invasion of Grenada, Operation Urgent Fury, which event he had covered for the *Baltimore Sun*. The book had done him little good and attracted scant notice, but he had worked on it honestly and well.

As a writer, Lucas suffered from a combination of indolence and perfectionism, so it had taken altogether too long to write. By publication time, its revelations of ineptitude and petty corruption among some of the military's special-operations elites had been mainly obviated.

Lucas was a good listener, a man of his word to whom talkers liked to talk. Unfortunately, within a few months of Urgent Fury the derelictions to which his sources had led him had been either successfully covered up or piously disclosed. For public consumption there had been a few autos-da-fé: designated fall guys had quaveringly owned up to obscure oversights couched in deep military diction. A few manly sobs had been swallowed before sympathetic congressional committees. There had been some undesirable transfers and early retirements. A number of Lucas's sources had been hunted down and covertly punished.

Moreover, his publishers had felt the book dwelt a shade too heavily on the role of Afro-Caribbean religion in the island's contemporary history. But Lucas had done his best. His life had been largely promise, subverted by false starts, underconfidence and incompleteness. The book was the only thing he had ever really finished. He was quite proud of it.

"It was just a paperback," he told Dr. Obermann. "Trading on the headlines. Sort of a quickie."

"It was a smart book," Obermann said. "A wise one. I don't know much about the Caribbean or the American army, but I believed what I read in it."

Hearing this greatly pleased Lucas.

"So I'm encouraged," Obermann said. "I picked a good one. And are you . . . still enthusiastic about our story?"

"The people who really interest me are Raziel and De Kuff."

"And Sonia," Obermann added. "You like the girl." He poured a little *schlag* in his coffee.

"Yes," Lucas said, "I do." The summer's parade of young tourists and students wandered past the Atara. The adepts of the café ignored them, except to gaze on the more outstanding of the young women. "I'm inclined to focus on De Kuff and his group to the exclusion of some of the others. They're more interesting."

"We might do that," Obermann said.

"But," Lucas said, "you naturally prefer a story that goes somewhere. Something like this . . . people drift in and drift out. It trails off into nothing."

"Where are they?" Obermann asked. "These followers of Raziel and De Kuff."

"In a hospice at Ein Kerem. De Kuff's paying. He's quite wealthy apparently."

"Are they still wearing the ouroboros amulets?"

"Yes, they are. Sonia too. Do you think it relates to what Ericksen's on about?"

"Yes," Obermann said between bites of coffee cake. "In a way. They're heretics, very radical heretics by the standards of normative Judaism. But of course the ouroboros appears in the *Zohar*."

"I'm unclear about their theology. It's obviously messianic. I gather they revere Sabbatai Zevi and Jacob Frank and Jesus."

"Yes, it follows. They probably see all those figures as a single recurring soul. Reincarnated now in De Kuff."

"How did that serpent business get in the picture?" Lucas asked. "It's haunting."

"When the Almighty is rendered ineffable," Obermann said, "and lost to us, some emanating force remains latent. But it can only be quickened by a congruous force — this is basic chemistry."

"In which I —"

"In which you did so badly at school. Never mind. To the Hindus, the serpent Kundalini represents Shakti, the consort of Shiva. Through Shakti, the immanent Shiva becomes the life force. Some people worshiped the serpent in Adam's Garden."

"Not Jews."

"Certain Jews," Obermann said. "Heretics. *Minim*. The Gnostic Elisha ben Abouya. But remember this: in Kabbala also the serpent stands for the force that quickens the First Power of God. It brings time around to its conclusion in eternity. A holy serpent signifies the God of Faith. An eternal, eternally renewing serpent that changes the immanent into Primal Will. Like it?"

"It's neat," said Lucas.

"In Gematria, the term 'holy serpent' has the same numerical value as 'moshiach.' De Kuff's wearing it — Raziel got him wearing it, maybe not just for himself but for every *moshiach* past and present. An eternal salvific force. Not just one Jesus. Not one soul. Many."

"I must have studied this stuff," Lucas said.

"I don't think so. Maybe you should meditate. Or maybe not. Anyway, that's what you're dealing with here."

"It doesn't sound like it's going to go away."

"Not until Jews go away. Or God goes even further away and ignores their schemes and antics to bring him back. So," Obermann said, "even if it trails into nothing, it'll be something."

"It sounds like a disaster waiting to happen."

"The universe moves from disaster to disaster. An insight the Marxists owed to Wagner, who owed it to physics."

"So tell me," Lucas said, "where does all this stuff come from?"

"What is above? What is below? What was aforetimes? What is to come?" He fixed Lucas with a sidewise interrogative stare. "He who asks those questions — better for him not to have been born. So said the great sages."

"How do we see it?"

"Man is formed in a likeness," Obermann said. "He perceives what he resembles. The shapes he sees are determined by his nature." Obermann stared at Lucas. "You're not having second thoughts? You're still committed to the book?"

"Yes," Lucas said, "I'm still committed."

Lucas paid, as he had become accustomed to doing, and they walked toward Jaffa Road.

"Did you know," Lucas asked, "that De Kuff preaches every Sunday in the Muslim Quarter?"

"In front of St. Anne's? At the Bethesda Pool?"

"I guess so. We found him right next door."

Obermann seemed complacent. "It's a hangout. The temple of Aesculapius. More snakes. Also the Pool of Israel."

He put a hand on Lucas's shoulder, lurching off in the direction of Jaffa Road and his bus home to Kfar Heschel, a new suburb over the Green Line. "Listen, we'll do something good together. Something worthy. By the way, I sent you some books you probably can't get at Steimatzsky's or the university. Oblige me and take care."

Lucas felt excited going home. It would be something worthy, that would be the thing. Obermann's books were waiting for him at the disagreeable concierge's office.

"Christ!" the concierge said, as though he had had to carry anything anywhere, which was most unlikely. "What you got here?"

"Diamonds," Lucas told him.

All through the afternoon and into evening he sat on the narrow terrace off his kitchen and chewed some of Nuala's khat and read the material Obermann had given him. In it, Jerusalem sounded like a crazed congress of wonders. There were Gentiles like Willie Ludlum, a religious incendiary whose passionately inane musings on the universe filled a police file longer than the Gospels of Mark and Matthew combined. There were the Guardians of the Beauteous Gate, who planned on rebuilding the Temple by selling off memorial wings to prosperous Americans, and the Bearers of the Mark of Cain, a cult of German hippies bent on atonement, who sounded like the Nazis' revenge on themselves. There were the keepers of the House of the Galilean, with whom Lucas was already acquainted, and the Lost-Found Black Oriental Children of Zion, most of whom came from Bakersfield.

Some took the Great Pyramid as their inspiration, others the True Sepulchre or the Lance. All seemed to rejoice in colorful nomenclature. There were Pyramid cultists from Oregon called the Silent Seekers of the Oak and Vine, and a covey of Panamanians identified as the Most Chaste Athletes of the Holy Grail.

There were also numerous solos, male and female, who had mistaken themselves for Francis of Assisi or Teresa of Ávila or Peter the Hermit. But among the Jews, who were on the whole conventional, there was no one like De Kuff or Raziel.

The material was solid. Early the next morning, he called an old girlfriend at a publishing house in New York and talked up the book.

During their conversation, he surprised himself by singing the project like a garden full of nightingales, raving as confidently as Elijah on Mount Carmel before the four hundred and fifty prophets of Baal, as though he wanted nothing more than to write the stuff.

"It sounds quite, quite wonderful," said his old girlfriend, who herself sounded more like the Boston Athenaeum each year. "I bet I can sell it."

"Well," Lucas said, "let's keep in touch."

It might all be as simple as that, he thought. For his literary skills, such as they were, and his Americanizing sensibility he could have Obermann's trove of demented God-strivings, along with whatever he might turn up on his own.

24

THE FOLLOWING DAY, sleepless before first light, he started taking notes on Obermann's material. Then he had some coffee and a roll, and took his after-breakfast walk in the neighborhood around the railroad tracks, among the little gardens of oleander and tamarisk.

Back home, he made a cup of Turkish coffee and looked at the paper. On the bottom of page four was a story he had overlooked.

AMERICAN CHRISTIAN CLERGYMAN DIES IN FREAK FALL FROM OLD CITY TOWER

The early Byzantine aqueduct tower between the Spafford Hospital and the Bab al-Zahra, or Herod's Gate, in the Old City wall was the scene of an unusual accident early Thursday. A man identified as the Reverend Theodore Earl Ericksen, a minister of the Independent Evangelical Church in North America, apparently fell to his death from the parapet of the tower in spite of a chest-high barrier on the Old City side of the wall. Mr. Ericksen's body was discovered many feet from the base of the wall, at the edge of the Bethesda Pool complex near Herod's Gate, a site frequently visited by Christian and "New Age" visitors to the Old City. Residents of the area reported seeing a man on the parapet at various times during the night. Guards of a nearby madrasah, alerted to the possibility of a rooftop prowler, had searched the roofs and adjoining tower several times, without result.

Mr. Ericksen, 36, who came from Superior, Wisconsin, USA, had lived in Jerusalem for three years and was affiliated with the House of the Galilean in New Katamon, a Christian study group. He leaves a wife, Mrs. Linda Ericksen, also of Superior, who is employed with the same organization.

Police are investigating the death, and a coroner's inquest is scheduled for two weeks time. Meanwhile the Ministry of Tourism has declared the area around the aqueduct tower structurally safe for visitors and plans no new construction in the wake of the tragedy. Mr. Chaim Barak of the Ministry said today that while tourists were encouraged to visit the walls, it is safest to do so during the day and in groups.

Instead of going out again, he called Obermann.

"Yes, I saw it," the doctor said. "He felt betrayed."

"I think that's the word," Lucas said. "Too close to the light, you said."

"Poetic of me. Well, I'm distressed. He could have had another life."

"You think he was mugged or something?"

"He didn't fall accidentally," Obermann said. "He would have had to jump or be pushed."

Uneasily at first, Lucas went back to the books he had bought at Steimatzky's or taken from the English stacks of the Hebrew University library to accompany his course there.

He had Adolphe Franck, Gershom Scholem on the cosmology of Isaac Luria, Daniel Matt's translation of the *Zohar* and a dozen or so other books. Some were pious, some secular, some antiques, others contemporary. Most were Jewish, some Christian, including a few on Spanish Christian Kabbala and on the work of Pico della Mirandola. He had been riffling through them for weeks and actually read a few.

Lucas, a collector of obscure lore, discovered several things he had not known before. Having studied with Adler, he was able to comprehend the formulas by which Sabbatai Zevi and Jacob Frank had derived their own divinity through the holy serpent; both men included the ouroboros in their signatures.

He also learned that by adding the Hebrew letter *shin* to the Tetragrammaton, one could transform the name of God into the name of Jesus. That the Sephardic Kabbalist Abraham Abulafia had suspected himself of being the Messiah, and he visited the Pope to inform His Holiness of this development and walked out of the Vatican alive. That a number of the monks of San Jerónimo in Castile had been arrested by the Inquisition for conducting a seder during Passover of the jubilee year 1500. And that nearly all the great Spanish mystics were of Jewish origin, including Saint Teresa, Saint John of the Cross and Fray Luis de León.

Increasingly, the Kabbalist formulations delighted him, even as revised in the ravings of Raziel and De Kuff. At one point in the afternoon, he got up to have a drink, but instead of drinking he returned to Scholem, *On the Kabbalah and Its Symbolism.* How true it was, he thought. As true an explanation for things, psychologically speaking, as he had ever entertained. More sublimely persuasive than the Thomistically encumbered Catholicism that had managed to constrict his nature from the age of seven. Though of course it was never a question of what was or was not *true* — ludicrous word.

Then it occurred to him that the notion of some great divine withdrawal, of sacred emanations remaining, all these things were not more true than his mother Christianity but were in their way the same — an essence underlying any form truth might assume.

He went to his copy of Pascal's *Pensées* to look up something he half remembered.

"The universe is such that it bears witness everywhere to a lost God," Pascal had written, "in man and outside him and to a fallen nature."

Jansenism. The chain led him from Port Royale to Descartes. The proof of God by ontology. Its formula held that if you could well and truly imagine the Old Boy, he must, by Jove, be there. The proof by ontology, in turn, made him feel like having a drink again — brought out the never-to-be-ordained Irish Jesuit in him, or possibly reminded him of sneaking a bottle into church dances. So he filled a glass with Glenlivet and sat watching the stones of the city subtly change their hue in the withdrawing light.

Descartes by the hot stove, went the story. Here I am — Descartes by the Hot Stove — so there's got to be a God. I'm dreaming it up, so it's got to be there. Freud's method. I think, therefore I am. There's a process, so I've got to be part of it. No question, he thought, ontology went better with a drink, which was probably why so many of the clergy had a problem.

But there *was* a process, was there not? There were things rather than nothing. And if the process did not end with one, as plainly it did not, where did it end? Was all this rage for ultimates utterly damned, all this longing without hope of rest, the thirst unrequited? The notion of thirst called for another drink.

Then it came to him that the idea of a great absconded Creator must reflect, had to reflect, some actual state of things. That the emanations of crown and holy wisdom and mother understanding, of greatness, power and love, of dread judgment, beauty, mercy and endurance, of majesty, the kingdom of God and its foundation were perfectly and obviously present, simply were. And were even in him, in his base darkness. Drink in hand, he thought: What fun to entertain such beliefs, how lovely and satisfying.

Moreover, he asked himself how much of a stretch it would be to imagine all this as his by right of birth. As a Jew, which, he decided, he might well choose to be. But even if he chose not, how nice to have it all. To inherit on both sides of the street, the Shekhinah along with Mother Church and Irish oatmeal, the blessing *and* the porridge.

Walking home from church on Sunday once, he and his mother had encountered his father's wife. The two of them had been coming from St. Joseph's on La Salle Street, amid the projects of Harlem, where his mother took him in spite of the fact that her snobbery might otherwise have inclined her to go to St. Paul's Chapel, Columbia. And there on the sidewalk, Mother in her white straw hat and performance-standard gloves, and he in his suit and bow tie, like a wee pale replica of the little black kids going to storefront churches, had been accosted by Mrs. Lucas, the esteemed professor's crazy wife. She had been darkly handsome, in manner Teutonic, resembling the actress Lilli Palmer, as even his mother admitted.

The encounter had been bitter and included words unsuitable for Sunday. He would always remember the phrase *that unfortunate child*. Something something my husband something something *that unfortunate child*. Him. Inconveniently, they all lived in the same neighborhood. Slice of life. Upper West Side.

Loneliness settled on him as the light of day receded, and after a while he went out. Every night he felt the same crepuscular restlessness. There were no sunset rituals for him, only a desperate necessity to hurry darkness. He had become impotent sexually, intellectually. Eve be sudden, dawn be soon. But there he was, the professor-doctor-father's son. And it was Jerusalem, the place of the thing itself, the home of Uncreated Light. Walking a little dazedly through the twilight city, he had reached the Ottoman fountain in the Hinnom Valley before he realized that he was headed for the Western Wall.

In the lighted plaza before the Kotel, Sabbath crowds had gathered. Lucas, who had not thought to bring a hat, took a paper kippa from the gray-bearded army chaplain who stood by the guard post at the top of the stone stairs leading down to the plaza.

Pale Hasidic men were dancing in a ring in the area between the south end of the Wall and the Dung Gate. At the base of the Wall, the worshipers stood four deep. All around the lights were warm and welcoming, Shabbat arriving, so the song went, like a bride. Lucas wandered among the rejoicers in his paper yarmulke, feeling he must be invisible to them. In his heart he belonged to what the Kabbalists called the other side, the dark shell of things.

At the center of the plaza, he faced the Wall across the reverently covered heads of the crowd. It was easy to see it as shimmering, its sacred geometry ascending toward the darkness that separated the upper from the lower worlds. Lucas let his eye follow it toward the void. According to the faithful, the Shekhinah, the Divine Presence, hovered there.

"We are incapable of not desiring truth and happiness," Pascal had written, "and are incapable of possessing them." And if it was easy to imagine the soul's longing, the exile shared and mitigated by the spirit of God, it was equally easy to imagine terror before Otherness, the bright wings of the Lord of hosts.

"Woe to the wicked," proclaimed the *Zohar* he had read the same day, "their desire and attachment is far removed from Him. Not only do they separate themselves from Him; they cleave to the other side."

For a long time he stood watching the others pray, and he felt dizzy, reduced. He moved to the mouth of one of the cavernous rooms at the north edge of the plaza. The space was filled with praying old men; their voices echoed off the ancient surfaces.

He went outside again. A dark young man with thick glasses, wearing a straw cowboy hat, approached him.

"Excuse me. You're Jewish?"

Lucas looked at him and shook his head. The young man, one of the worldwide army of Lubavitchers, hurried on to someone else.

25

I N THE PRAYER AREA near Wilson's Arch, at the corner of the Western Wall, Janusz Zimmer and Raziel Melker stood side by side, holding their prayer books, *davening* as they spoke. Raziel wore a cloth cap and a black coat; the fringes of *tzitzit* showed beneath it. Zimmer wore a kippa and a coat like Melker's.

"I think we've established an identity," Melker told Zimmer. "I'm watched, I know it. I think my father employs a security firm. We fit into the space Berger occupied."

"It's good that De Kuff is preaching. If you're going to be a cult, you have to start attracting converts. The streets are full of seekers. And foreign nationals are ideal because their governments will want to bail them out after the event."

"What about the Baptists, or whoever they are? Are they happy?"

"They aren't Baptists. They aren't even Pentecostals. They're hustlers. If they make money, they're happy. What about Sonia? Is she going to the Strip anytime soon?"

"As a matter of fact, she's going next week."

"Good," Zimmer said. "We'll try and see that she goes on a regular basis. With Nuala Rice whenever possible."

"Why?"

"Because," Zimmer said, "I have it on good authority that Nuala is bringing in explosives. If Sonia goes, it's going to look like you and your friends. Since you're being so kind as to take the fall when . . . it happens."

"You surprise me," Raziel said. "I wouldn't have thought you would be mixed up in something like this."

"Good," Zimmer said. "We surprise each other."

26

LUCAS HAD TURNED away from the Wall and was headed for the Zion Gate when he ran into Gordon Lestrade, the House of the Galilean's archeologist, just past the military checkpoint at the edge of the plaza. With his slack, colorless hair combed to one side and his flannel slacks and blazer, he looked like a figure from the world between the wars. "Excuse me," he said to Lucas in a cockney whine. "You're Jewish?" He grinned at his own mimicry of the Hasidic proselytizers.

"I'll do," Lucas told him, "until Jewish comes along." Discovering he was still wearing his paper kippa, he reached up and took it off and crumpled it.

"What are you doing here? Tracing the faith of your fathers again?"

"How about you?" Lucas asked him.

"I often come on Friday night. It's inspiring, up to a point."

"At what point does it stop being inspiring?"

"Come," said Lestrade, pulling at Lucas's sleeve, "let me show you something."

He took Lucas to a corner of the plaza that was under excavation. They climbed over a wooden barrier and onto exposed earth. Lestrade put his face close to the bricks of the wall. On one of them an inscription had been covered with a sheet of plastic.

"What is it?" Lucas asked. "Hebrew?"

"Aramaic, actually," Lestrade said. He was a bit wobbly with booze. "It's Isaiah. It says, 'You shall see and your heart shall rejoice and your flesh shall flourish like the grass.' "

"Is it very old?"

"Early Byzantine. They're saying it's from the time of the emperor

Julian, who favored the Jews and encouraged them to build another Temple. Which apparently was begun and then destroyed at
Julian's death, and this may have been part of it. Whoops, here
comes Shlomo."

"Shlomo" was a military policeman, who brusquely waved them
away from the excavations. All Israeli soldiers and policemen, it
turned out, were called Shlomo by Lestrade.

"What are you up to? Come have a drink."

Lestrade's apartment was in one of the Christian hospices of the
Old City. His invitation was issued in a faintly contentious spirit, as
though he were morally certain Lucas would be reluctant to go there
after dark.

Lucas had a look at him in the floodlights around the Kotel plaza.
At first glance, Lestrade gave a portly, forthright, somewhat ho-ish
appearance, but his eyes had a drunken slyness.

"Sure," said Lucas. "Love to."

At night the streets of the Palestinian Old City, on the anniversary
of the intifada, *were* more dangerous for foreigners — which was
not really dangerous enough for Lucas to give Dr. Lestrade the
satisfaction of declining his invitation. Passing through the plaza
checkpoint, Lestrade showed the Israeli soldiers tending it his usual
sarcastic grin. Lucas wasn't sure whether or not the grin was vol-
untary; either way, it annoyed the Israelis and gave their passage
through the checkpoint the slightest edge of potential violence.

It was the first time Lucas had experienced Israeli soldiers as
anything like adversaries, and it was not pleasant. The soldiers'
English was fluent. When Lestrade addressed them in Arabic, they
turned thuggy and insolent.

"Why did you assume they spoke Arabic?" Lucas asked when
they had cleared the barrier.

"Because they do," Lestrade said cheerfully. "The big one is from
Iraq."

"You're sure?"

"Oh, I can tell," Lestrade said.

They followed El-Wad toward the Muslim Quarter through
hushed, darkened streets, along which the shops were shuttered.
There had been anti-Israeli demonstrations all day.

Lestrade's small apartment off the Via Dolorosa had belonged to
the caretaker of the Austrian hospice. It consisted of two rooms and
a small roof garden planted in grapevines, with a potted almond

tree. The larger of the two rooms had a domed ceiling. Lestrade had decorated the place with Russian icons, framed verses from the Koran and Circassian daggers. There were a great many books, in several languages.

They sat in the sandalwood-scented living room. Lestrade threw open the shutters and poured grappa for the two of them.

"How's tricks, Lukash?" Lucas was rather surprised that Lestrade had remembered his name. He found it impossible not to take the alveolar Magyar pronunciation as a patronizing insult. In any case, his father, a native Viennese, had never employed it. "How's the book coming?"

"All right, I guess." The comfortable surroundings and the drink rendered him confiding. "How's the reconfiguring of the Temple?"

"Oh, dear," Lestrade said. "Someone's been talking. Singing. Blabbing."

"I don't think your work is such a secret in town. A lot of people follow the doings at the House of the Galilean."

"Yes," Lestrade said. "Like your friend Obermann. The great Jungian. Preposterous fraud."

"We're doing the book together, actually. We're thinking of putting you in it."

"Is that a threat, Lukash?"

"I thought you'd be pleased."

"I'm not concerned with the American-Jewish press. And I have no problem about working with Brother Otis. I'm an archeologist. If a university doesn't support my work, I have to find someone who will."

"Why is it," Lucas asked, "that a university won't support your work?"

"They do," said Lestrade. "They have. However, I don't suffer fools gladly and I tend to separate myself from invincible ignorance. As a result, I take my backing where I find it. Within reason, of course."

"Within reason?"

"That's what I said," Lestrade told him.

"Do you really know the dimensions of the Holy of Holies and its location?"

"The dimensions are in the Talmud. An informed archeologist can translate them to modern terms."

"Has it been done?" Lucas asked.

"Yes. By me."

"And the location?"

"Can now be calculated. Through research of mine which I'm not prepared to share or discuss."

The Englishman went to his sixties-vintage record player, put on a side of Orff's *Carmina Burana* and turned the volume up. Then he refilled their glasses.

"The ordinary observer," Lucas said, "would wonder why you're doing your work under the sponsorship of an American fundamentalist group."

"Would he?"

"Sure. Instead of a university or the Ministry of Antiquities. Or even the Vatican."

He was nearly shouting, not out of aggressiveness but from the necessity to make himself heard above the music. Lestrade would be playing Orff for company, Lucas surmised, because the composer's work was legally forbidden in Israel. Glancing at Lestrade's record collection, Lucas saw that it seemed to lean heavily on similarly problematic music: it featured highlights from *Der Rosenkavalier* and quite a lot of Wagner.

"The people at the House of G," Lestrade said, "are quite ready to let me work unobstructed. Being American fundamentalists, they have good relations with the Likud government and they're able to smooth away certain objections. I myself have some connections with the Waqf. I'm provided with whatever I need."

"The pay is probably competitive too. By the way, I read in the paper where you lost your roommate."

"My roommate?" asked Lestrade, puzzled.

"Don't tell me you've forgotten him. The Reverend Mr. Ericksen."

"Oh," said Lestrade, "Ericksen. Of course I haven't forgotten him. I simply never thought of him as a roommate. He moved in here when that little tart threw him out."

"Is that why he killed himself?"

"He was very frightened, Lukash. He was frightened of the invisible world. Principalities and powers. He was frightened of God. He thought he was damned. That he knew too much."

"Did he know about the configuration of the Holy of Holies?"

"Oh, shit," Lestrade said in frustration. "I don't mean it in any melodramatic way. I mean he thought Yahweh was his enemy. That

God despised him as an Edomite and took his wife to give to an Israelite and was about to slay him. And of course he'd always been rather fond of Yahweh. And presumably of his wife."

"But *did* he know a lot about the Temple's structure?"

"He'd been shown around. He knew more than many of them. They were going to use him as a fundraiser in America, so he had to give lectures with slides and so on."

"I see," Lucas said. "And meanwhile you get whatever you need."

"Whatever I need," Lestrade repeated slowly, over the expressionist chanting.

It seemed to Lucas that Lestrade was an unstable character, hence a journalistically desirable figure. It might also be inferred that a man who loudly professed not to suffer fools was a man who talked too much. Lucas's own strategic role, then, should be that of a fool. Insufferable enough to unbind a few inner demons, but not so insufferable as to be thrown, drinkless, into the street.

"What puzzles me," Lucas said, "is why American fundamentalists would be so interested in the Second Temple."

"Never heard of millenarianism, Lukash? Have you come so far to have the commonplaces of Yankee Bible thumping explained to you by the likes of me?"

"Guess so," said Lucas.

"Revelation," Lestrade said. "The Apocalypse. Last book of the New Testament. Heard of that?"

"Certainly," said Lucas.

"Shouldn't be in the canon. Not a grain of faith, hope or charity in the fucking thing. One long, meandering lunatic image after another but, on the whole, typical of Jewish prophetic literature at the time of J.C. And typical of early Jewish Christianity.

"Now, amid the flaming swords and sparkling whirligigs and falling stars, we have a core of prophecy so nonsensical and non sequitous as to defy interpretation by the maddest of mad monks. Actually, the monks left it alone, because Saint Augustine didn't care for it and the medieval Church didn't want the rabble reading it and going all funny."

On the record player, the swan about to be roasted for the feast lamented its fate in academic Latin.

"With the Reformation, however, every dork and yoik at every muddy crossroads read the fucker and swooned with insights meant for him alone. Nowhere so much, Lukash, as in your adopted country."

"The United States is not my adopted country, Lestrade. I was born there."

"Good for you. Anyway, in our story a time of tribulation ensues. We're talking grave tribulation — famine, pestilence, nuclear war. The forces of good battle the forces of evil. Upon which a thousand-year regnum ensues. Baddies defeated, goodies exalted. Christ comes back, the much-vaunted Second Coming."

"Does ring a bell," said Lucas.

"Only question is, does Christ come back before or after the tribulations? If you believe *before,* you're a pre-millenarian. You believe in the Rapture. Familiar with the Rapture?"

"We see it on bumper stickers. People are advised to be ready when it comes."

"Ah," said Lestrade, "sound advice. But hard to follow given the avalanche of strangeness that's going to descend."

Lucas knew something more about the Rapture than he was presently prepared to allow. He had first heard it talked up on late-night radio stations while driving through the desert. Then it began to turn up on Christian television, and there were cassettes, in several of which he had invested. They were both breathlessly sensational and boring. Then, since his conversation with Otis and Darletta, he had researched it further.

As Lucas understood it, the Rapture, when it came, would be distinctly cinematic. The returned Christ would gather up his own. The upgathering would be of a literal nature. One of these mornings, in order to be spared the final trials, the born-again would wake up singing, as it were, spread their wings and commence to fly. They would be rapted, like cosmic chipmunks in the talons of their savior, drawn irresistibly heavenward into the Everlasting Arm. Godly motorists would be wafted from the controls of their cars.

Since born-again Christians tended to be concentrated in states with high speed limits, things would get ugly. One moment Mr. Worldly Wiseman would be spouting cynical, superficial observations from the passenger seat. Then his motor-pool buddy, Christian, one of the elect, would vanish from behind the wheel and there would be nothing in the driver's seat except a pair of white loafers and plaid golf slacks and a polyester sport shirt, none of them necessary in the world to come.

Mr. W. W. would stare terrified and confused at the wildly spinning unhanded wheel beside him, like Stewart Granger beholding Pier Angeli transformed into a pillar of salt in *Sodom and Gomorrah*. Soon the car and Mr. Wiseman (or was it Weissman?) would hurl driverless into a wall of consuming flame. And that would be only the beginning.

"War," Lestrade was saying. "Armageddon up there in Megiddo. The Emperor of the North, blah blah. Well, someone's got to fight the good fight. And for the pre-mils it's going to be the Jews, operating out of the Temple. The rebuilding of the Temple is a sign of the Rapture's imminence, and it'll be GHQ for the Final Conflict. When the war is over, the surviving victorious Jews will accept Christ. The thousand-year reign of the saints will commence."

"How do the religious Jews see all this?"

"Some of them believe that if they rebuild the Temple, the Messiah may be prevailed upon to appear. The more militant would like to get all those mosques off Mount Moriah and start pouring cement."

"And relations are pretty good between what you call the premils and the messianic Jews?"

"Very warm and fuzzy on the face of it. For one thing, the premils are making a fortune marketing this shit in the States."

"Your employers?"

"There are a number of Jewish religious entrepreneurs as well. But primarily the Jewish extremists are building up a political constituency in the States. Until metaphysics takes over, they can work together. Raising money. Building support."

"Quite a story," said Lucas. "What if I write it?"

"Why don't you? Of course it's been written, but it never seems to take hold. Everybody knows about Jewish extremists and American Bible thumpers. No one takes them seriously."

Lestrade put on the first cut of *Götterdämmerung*.

"Really, Lukash, write it. It's an American story. They're all Americans. The pre-mils, most of the Jewish Temple builders. Anglo-Saxons, the Israeli press likes to call them." His face was flushed with booze or anger or amusement.

"Someone once said," Lucas said, finishing his grappa, "that there are no antiquities here. No past. Everything is present or future." Lestrade refilled his glass. "So I suppose it's just another chapter in the ongoing story of the city."

"Part of the story now. Since you people got here."

Does he mean Americans? Lucas wondered. Or Jews? Does he mean me? He decided to ask.

"We people, Gordon? Which people?"

"Like the grappa?" Lestrade asked.

"Smashing. Do you mean Americans or Jews? Jews were always here."

"Oh, you know," Lestrade said. "It's a continuum. The one is virtually the other, if you see what I mean."

"Not exactly."

Lestrade studied him through an Italianate haze of the drink. "Oh, shit. You're going to get fucking politically correct in the American manner." A surprising measure of anger seemed to have descended on him. "You're going to turn into a special-pleading nit."

"Who," Lucas asked, "me?"

"Yes you, cock. Moralizing is your only form of discourse. That's why there are so many hypocrites among your people. Present company excepted."

"*My* people?" Lucas asked. "I wish you'd stop thrusting identities on me. I mean, it's a drag. I'm only one fella."

"Yes, of course," Lestrade said contemptuously. "Sorry. By the way," he asked, "who are those people living in Berger's old *zawiya*? The old Jew and his followers? The pretty chichi girl you like? People over here used to think she was old Berger's wife."

"No," Lucas said. "Nobody's. They're sort of Jewish Sufis." He let Lestrade refill his glass. "What does 'chichi' mean?"

"They wouldn't be ultra-Zionists involved in a takeover, would they? Kachniks trying to set up a yeshiva in the Muslim Quarter?"

Lucas began to wonder if Lestrade was asking out of his own curiosity or for the information of his contacts on the Muslim side.

"They're innocents. I think their beliefs come from Sheikh Berger al-Tariq. They're mainly Americans."

Lestrade put a hand on his breast. "Heartbreak Hotel," he declared. "American innocence again."

"Think of them as New Age types."

"Charming," Lestrade said. "I like them already."

In *Götterdämmerung,* the Siegfried motif sounded. Lucas had always been moved by it. The promise of human transcendence, of great things to come.

"Like them or not, they have a right to be here."

"Surely," Lestrade said. "And a whole army to protect them. Two whole armies." He poured more grappa. "Just, why can't they do *their thing* in California?"

"They're Jews," Lucas said. "This is Judea."

"That's the settlers' line. And screw the natives, right?"

Lucas's job, as he well knew, was to inquire into Lestrade's researches around the Temple Mount. But the man himself was a distraction.

"They aren't settlers," he said. "By the way," he asked the archeologist, "what did you mean by 'a continuum'?"

Lestrade seemed to have forgotten.

"You said 'a continuum,' " Lucas repeated. "You said . . . the one is like the other. Americans and Jews."

"Ah, yes. The rationalist continuum. A long story. A sort of theory of mine."

"Tell me," Lucas said. "I can ponder it on my way home."

"Peoples given to fiddle," Lestrade said. "Tinkering. Mental monkey-fingeredness. Never mind."

Lucas went over and turned off the record player.

"Go on, man. I'm writing a book."

"There exists," Lestrade said, "a certain dreadful energy. A certain instinct for cheerful intrusion that no doubt is seen as helpful. Helping other people out from under the weight of their illusions. Even if these illusions are thousands of years old and have produced much that is beautiful. Even if they represent the creative force of a race." He winced slightly at his last sip of grappa. "I suppose this is on the record?"

"I suppose so," Lucas said.

"Well," said Lestrade, "I'd best be careful. Employ my well-known tact."

"Definitely."

"A certain despising of other people's excellence. A desire to subvert their culture and their leaders. A noisy, assertive triumphalism that might uncharitably be called vulgar. I realize of course that as an American you don't believe in vulgarity. And at a certain point this becomes profoundly . . . profoundly hostile."

"Just to keep things straight," Lucas said, "to whom are we referring at this certain point?"

"The Americans and the Jews. Two peoples who may or may not

exist, exactly. We sort of have to take their word for it. Talking tradition, tradition, tradition. But actually rather shallow-rooted. Moralizers, a light to the Gentiles, a city on a hill. Two peoples very congenial to each other.

"But what they can't stand is other people's social order. Bonds and faith and blood — they hate it. They want to liberate everyone. They want to rationalize. They want to help out — bless their little cotton socks. Idealistic, optimistic folks.

"So it's no accident this brave little colony is out here, this far-flung outpost you set up together. Of course I'm not talking about you personally."

"Oh," Lucas said, "I don't know about that. Here I am."

"So a perception grows in the world at large," Lestrade went on, "of enmity. A hostility to your continuum that you perhaps fail to understand. For example, there's a song — I heard it sung in Nicaragua once — about the Yanqui, enemy of humanity. Terribly unfair, but there it is. And for quite real reasons."

"So what do they sing about Jews in Nicaragua?" Lucas asked.

"You're being ironic, Lukash. Good for you. Well, I'll fucking tell you what! They sing about La Compañía," Lestrade said. "And they don't mean the Jesuits. United Fruit. Sam the banana man. Mr. Eli Black." He bit his lip. "What I mean is that this energetic collaboration is perceived as hostile on a fundamental level to many people. To a broad spectrum of the human race who do not have the enlightened privilege of being American or Jewish."

"This may be a naive question," Lucas said, "but isn't this sort of what Hitler believed?"

"I'm glad you asked me that," said Lestrade. "Have you read *Mein Kampf*?"

"No."

"No. Have you read Alfred Rosenberg's *Myth of the Twentieth Century*?"

Lucas shook his head.

"Well I have, you see. And I don't happen to subscribe to the theories expressed in those works. Nor do I happen to advocate murder, nor am I myself a murderer. So a little healthy resistance to the American philo-Semitic juggernaut doesn't make one a Nazi. Nor a practitioner of genocide. Nor a so-called anti-American. The self-pity of the mighty — it's so pathetic."

Lucas considered his answer.

"You shouldn't call people chichi," he said after a moment. "Regardless of what you think of them. Certainly not to their friends."

"Sorry. Old colonial expression. No offense."

"Right," Lucas said. He looked at his watch and found that it was almost one. A long length of dark street lay between him and the Jaffa Gate. "I better go."

"Have another. I'll go to the gate with you, if you like."

"No thanks," Lucas said. He would be damned, he thought, if he would let himself be chaperoned. But he took the drink, to equip himself for the solitary walk. The grappa was excellent, as smooth as any liqueur, a world of taste away from the raw stuff of his own experience. Lestrade was, after all, a connoisseur of things.

"You know," Lestrade told him as they stood on the steps in the spice-scented air, "your Jewish Sufi friends are up to something with Otis and Darletta at the House of G. I've seen at least one of them there."

"Really?" Lucas said. "I wonder what?" He was not sure what to believe. He decided to ask Sonia about it.

"Just a tip," Lestrade said. "Goodwill gesture."

"Thanks," Lucas said. "Next time you'll have to tell me more about the Temple."

Lestrade tapped his swollen forehead. "Sure thing," he said in a flat American tone. "Can't I walk you to the gate?"

"No thank you," Lucas said.

When they had said good night, Lucas made his way uphill along the dark cobbled street. A single naked light strung from a wire burned above sharpened potsherds at the top of a stone wall. Beyond its barren gleam, a medieval darkness prevailed, through which he had to follow the contours of the buildings. Arches along the route formed black passageways that stank of piss and ambush. In one, he heard half-suppressed, unsound laughter and caught a whiff of hashish. The sky above was as lightless as the streets.

Lucas walked trembling with rage, his teeth clenched, his jaw locked. Although for much of his life he had studied and written about war and disorder, he was not comfortable with conflict at personal range. Anger did not suit him.

It was with some relief that he reached the galleries of Al-Wad, among which a few dim lamps burned at intervals. Looking north, he could see lights behind the quarter's shuttered windows all the way to the Damascus Gate.

Entering a narrow street leading to the Khan al-Zait, he found himself passing the juice shop he had stopped at weeks before, the shop where the young retarded sweeper was employed. Its metal grate was closed to the empty street, the far end of which was darkness. As Lucas approached, two men appeared from the shadows. His blood quickened. Caution weighted his steps. Something about the place and the men's bearing promised badly.

Nevertheless he plodded on, giving the pair his best casual glance, practiced in a few tight spots, one that exuded confidence and avoided eye contact. Of course in the darkness eyes went unseen. He registered the fact that they were Palestinians, that one of the men wore a suit and the other was in shirtsleeves. The two of them passed and he breathed easier for a moment, home free. Suddenly there were steps behind him. His relief had been premature.

"Oh, sir," said a false, insinuating voice, its menace smooth with sarcasm.

Lucas chose not to turn around.

"Welcome, sir," said the man behind him.

He stopped then and turned. It was the man in shirtsleeves. Lucas felt they had met before, but the shadows were too deep for him to be certain. The second man was hanging back, at the edge of an arcade.

"Hello," said Lucas.

"Hello, sir," said the Palestinian. "You are welcome."

He could picture, rather than see, the man's insolent smile. A hand was extended. He took it, and the man's thumb and forefinger lightly encircled his wrist.

"For what are you looking, sir? So late."

"Nothing. I'm on my way home."

"You are living here? From where do you come?"

"I live here," Lucas said.

"Please, where is called here?"

"Al-Kuds," Lucas said. The Holy. So as not to call it Jerusalem.

"And from where have you come?"

"I'm an American journalist. On my way home from a friend's house. From the house of Dr. Lestrade."

"Welcome, sir," said the man, who had not let go of his hand.

"Thanks," said Lucas, and he turned to go.

"Welcome, sir. Are you drinking?"

He was being told he smelled of Lestrade's grappa.

"Thanks," Lucas said again. "Good night."

"Welcome," said the man. "Welcome to Al-Kuds. All places to drink are closed."

"So I see," said Lucas. When he started up the street the man kept pace with him.

"Welcome to Al-Kuds," said the man.

"Thanks again."

"Why come here to drink alcohol?" the man inquired. His tone of mixed unction and contempt had not varied.

"I joined a friend," Lucas said, although he thought it might be a mistake to try and explain.

"What friend?"

This time he made no answer. The man kept walking with him. Lucas listened hard, trying to tell whether the second man was trailing them. He might be serving as a lookout.

"Welcome, sir. But the places to drink are gone."

When they did it, Lucas thought, they did it with a knife. In the last case, he remembered, a male Dutch tourist had been dispatched with an ordinary kitchen knife. The man had either been mistaken for an Israeli or was the nearest available infidel. Perhaps, Lucas thought, he'd had liquor on his breath.

"Welcome, sir," said the citizen, laughing. The street grew darker as they went. Various questions occurred to Lucas, in no particular rational order. Was the mocking conversation good or bad, a prelude to murder or the alternative? If there was a knife, would it penetrate his lung? Ought he to respond or simply walk on?

"I think you are courageous person," said the man in the dark street. "Here is very nice. In the day it is very nice. But at night, very dangerous."

"What do you want me to do?" Lucas asked. "Hold your hand?"

It was rash of him to mock the citizen; he had forgotten about being drunk. But he was still angry and mortified at his own fear. The man, at least at first, was too pleased with himself to realize he had been rudely addressed.

"You are welcome, sir. I will walk with you."

"Suit yourself," Lucas said.

"What?" the man asked, less unctuously. "Shall I hold your hand? As friend?"

"Excellent," said Lucas. "We shall go about together. Heard of Shakespeare? Like him? A great American writer."

"Oh, sir," said the citizen after a moment's reflection. "You are laughing. You are joking."

Up the narrow street, about fifty yards away, Lucas saw hard white lights on stanchions and the outline of a jeep blocking the way. It was one of the mobile police posts that the Israelis had set up in the Old City during the intifada. A few border troopers usually occupied a market stall commanding a field of fire, sandbagged it and set up communications.

Lucas made for the lights. He tried hard not to appear to hurry. The man beside him had hold of his wrist, and as they got closer to the police post, he tightened his grip and began to pull back.

"We will go," he said. "We will drink. Find girls."

"How about letting go of me?" Lucas asked.

"Where you are going?" the man asked angrily. "Welcome. We are friends."

He stopped and Lucas pulled his hand away. Plainly the citizen wished not to approach the police post. He was only a passing wit, a wise guy showing off before a pal, flaunting his aggressiveness, patriotism, insolence to foreigners. His English.

"What fun it's been," Lucas told him. "Thanks for the walk. Thanks for the welcome, too."

There were two Israelis at the post, regular soldiers rather than the Border Police, and quite young. Both were curious about Lucas and his late-night stroll. One was polite and friendly, one not so. The friendly one was fair, with a French accent. The unfriendly one asked Lucas for his passport and for a hotel key before motioning him up David Street. Lucas had to explain that he was a resident of the city.

Halfway up the sloping thoroughfare, he paused to get his breath. Looking down toward the police post, he saw one of the soldiers watching through binoculars, talking into a field telephone. The policemen at the Jaffa Gate watched him pass with professional hauteur.

The taxi he hailed outside the gate had come up from East Jerusalem; its driver was an Arab who kept a red-checked kaffiyeh on his dashboard.

"Where you are going?" asked the driver. "What country is your home? Where you are coming from?"

"From church," Lucas told him.

In the apartment, most of his books and private possessions were still in boxes. The furniture came with the place: an algae-colored carpet, a few canvas chairs and some butt-scarred blond-wood tables. It was deeply depressing.

He sat on his unmade bed and turned on his message machine. Obermann was on it, and Ernest from the Human Rights Coalition, and, to his surprise, Sonia, proposing a drive to the Gaza Strip. He was too tired and dispirited to wonder what it might mean. Or to wonder about Lestrade's claim about one of Sonia's religious friends turning up at the House of the Galilean.

During the remainder of the night he dreamed of crowded streets whose symbols were Hebrew characters. The letters were nowhere displayed, but to find one's way it was necessary to know the vowel points. Then there were people all around, and though it was broad daylight in the dream, he could not tell what anyone looked like.

After a few hours, he heard the muezzin in Silwan, and the church bells.

27

THAT EVENING in Tel Aviv, a party of gay American sailors showed up in Mister Stanley's and provided Sonia a marvelous audience. They stayed reasonably sober and listened to her numbers in a hush of admiration and applauded generously. At the same time, she had the feeling they knew what they liked.

There were a dozen or so, their drinks paid for by two prosperous South African Israelis who designed beachfront apartments for investors and aspired to some California of the mind. The sailors were variously suburban sophisticates and tough veterans of the inner city, sibilant and acne-scarred. Sonia's favorite was a bespectacled, light-skinned Afro-American named Portis, a Sixth Fleet disc jockey who slipped her good requests and knew every verse of the show tunes without feeling compelled to sing along.

Stanley was delighted. As it turned out, he was entertaining Maria Clara on one of her flying visits from Colombia. The two of them shared a table at the back and applauded wildly. Maria Clara smirked and sparkled unremittingly. Halfway through Sonia's second number, Nuala Rice of the International Children's Foundation came in and sat alone at the bar. Sonia joined her between sets. The South Africans sent free Cape province champagne.

"Come in on your own, Nuala?"

"I'm on an airport run to Lod. Thought I'd stop by. By the way," she asked, "are you still going to come to the Strip with me next week?"

"Yes, I'd like to. Are you still looking for the rogue soldiers?"

"Oh, yes," said Nuala.

"I want to get down to Zawaydah. Berger used to say there were Sufis there. The Nawar."

"The Nawar are gypsies. Tinkers. They'll be Sufis if you want them to be."

"Well, I thought I'd have a look anyway. And I wanted to keep in touch. And," she added, "I wanted to bring along a reporter friend I know."

Nuala laughed. "Christopher, you mean? I know Christopher well. Thought he'd become a religion writer."

"Yes, he has. But I'd like to take him along."

During the next set, Nuala disappeared. Sonia did an impression of Sarah Vaughan singing "Over the Rainbow" and followed it with "Something for the Boys." Then she ran through the Gershwin songbook and finished up with the Fields and McHugh version of "I Loves You, Porgy." The place had crowded up and she had been mainly on the money.

For encores she did "Bill" and "Can't Help Lovin' That Man." "The Man That Got Away," though requested by Portis, was beyond her. For nearly half an hour after the final number, she stood around the dance floor while the sailors took each other's pictures with their arms around her.

The performance and the adoring sailors gave her a lift. She had slept very little or not at all for the past week. Each night she went over her conversations with Raziel. There was no way to pin him down, no way, literally, to make him stop his verbal entrechats.

Each night too she thought about old De Kuff at the Pool, holding forth in his sweet Louisiana voice about the revelation of Torah to the world. She was not as convinced as she made herself sound for Lucas. The more closely she tried to examine the things that preyed on her mind, the more elusive they became. The *maggid* was hard to summon.

On her way to Stanley's office to get paid, she encountered Raziel himself. He was dressed for town, in his shades, seated at a front table with one of Stanley's regular musicians, a bass player from Winnipeg.

"You come in to score?" the bass player was asking him.

"I'm clean and sober," he told the man. "Right, Sonia?"

"That's my man," she said.

"Scary," said the bass player.

In the back, Stanley paid her off. Nuala and Maria Clara were with him.

"I call myself Sky," Stanley announced to everyone.

Sonia watched the flexing of his black jailhouse tattoos as he counted out her wages in crisp, fresh American bills. He had declared a bonus, slipping her a few hundred over the agreed-upon sum. She was not in the mood to object. "What you think? Sky! Sky is the limit. Sky all around. Blue Sky smiling at me."

"Really cool," Sonia said, gathering up the money. "Who suggested it?"

"Is a character in *Guys and Dolls*. A cool guy. Gambler. I like the character. Guy like me."

"We went to see *Guys and Dolls* in New York," Maria Clara said gushingly. "It was so typical. We thought of you."

"Luck be a lady-y!" Stanley sang. "Also, we went to Rainbow Roof." He gave a little whistle. "That's the kind of place when I'm a kid I'm dreaming about."

"America is so problematical," Maria Clara said. "They are without formality, so one doesn't know what to expect. The men without charm, but I think the women are sweet. But they are so strong and the men are weak."

"Did they really know about the Rainbow Room in the Soviet Union, Stanley? During your childhood?"

"What?" protested Stanley. "Everyone knows Rainbow Roof! Everyone always knows it. Anyway — Sky! Me. And the place — Sky's! Sky's Joint."

"Rainbow Room East," said Sonia. She knew Stanley's sense of humor, regarding his own dignity, had limits. She had once seen him beat a porter senseless with a broom handle for liberties of deportment.

"I like the black Americans the best," Maria Clara said. "We thought of you, Sonia. The way they move. And the others, the Yanquis, are so clumsy. Such a country. They themselves don't understand it, isn't it so? Like big children."

"I like there," Stanley said. "They have great shit. And not so tough as in the movies."

"Yeah," Sonia said. "Can't live with 'em, can't live without 'em, know what I'm saying?"

"Fucking right!" said Stanley Sky. He was delighted. "That's right absolutely."

Maria Clara tottered over on her heels. She was wearing skin-tight spangled pants from a Paris designer. She took Sonia by the chin. "You are so deep by your eyes. I know you are deep. But not what you are thinking. Stanley, eh?"

"She's my Sonia," Stanley Sky said. "My Sonitchka."

When Sonia started to leave, Stanley stopped her. Raziel waited in the doorway.

"Sonitchka! You're going to Gaza, yes?"

"Thought I would."

"Maybe you get UN car, yes? Because I got something I want to take there. But I can't go 'cause I'm Jewish guy. They fuckin' kill me, right? I don't know no one. But you could take down. In UN car."

"I can't get a UN car, Stanley," Sonia said. She was about to say she would not care to carry packages for Stanley but thought better of it. "I'm going down with Nuala. She's got a Children's Foundation car."

Stanley made a face. "Nuala . . ."

Maria Clara made one too. "Nuala, I don't like her."

"Nuala is always fighting with the soldiers," Stanley said. "Always pissing them off. I don't like to have her bring things."

"I'd like to help you," Sonia said. "I don't think I can."

Maria Clara looked wide-eyed at her effrontery. Stanley kept his smile. "So don't worry," he said. "It's all right."

After the show, Nuala was waiting for her. The streets near the oceanfront still had a few restless strollers and loiterers in search of comfort. They sat down at one of the Orion Café's curbside tables.

"So, are you seeing Christopher?" Nuala asked.

"Not really. How about you?"

Nuala shook her head.

"You're in Stanley's a lot. Becoming a jazz fan?"

"It makes a change from the Strip," Nuala said.

"I miss you," Sonia said when the coffee came. "I miss Somalia. I guess that's a terrible thing to say."

"Not to me," Nuala said. "We were useful. What about the revolution?" she asked after a moment. "Miss that too?"

"I thought it was over."

"Never," Nuala said. She looked up and down the deserted street as though someone might overhear. "Never," she whispered. "Not for me."

Sonia frowned into her lukewarm espresso. "This is going to sound sort of corny," she said. "But I think something very important is happening in Jerusalem."

"And what would that be? The Second Coming or something?"

"Jerusalem doesn't mean to me what it means to you," Sonia told her friend. "I believe in the specialness of it. And I think I may have found what I came for."

"Oh, Sonia," Nuala sighed. "Well," she said, "to each her own, I guess. That's the way you are."

"Weren't you ever a believer, Nuala?"

"Me? Of course. I was going to be a nun like every little twit in County Clare."

"You don't believe anymore?"

"I had a selfish, sickly belief. A little girl's. Now I'm a grownup, I hope. I believe in liberation. That if it's possible for me, it's possible for everyone. And I won't have mine until everyone does."

"I understand," Sonia said.

Nuala walked her to the late-night *sherut* stand and put her on the road to the *yekke* guesthouse in Herzliya where she would be spending the night.

"By the way," Nuala asked, "how are your contacts on the Hill of Evil Counsel? Do you think you could wangle us a white UN car?"

"Jesus," Sonia said, "Stanley just asked me that. What's up?"

"I don't know about Stanley," Nuala said. "I'm on the IDF's list. Certain days they hold me up for hours. With a white car, sometimes if they're busy they'll wave you through."

"I'm out of contacts up there," Sonia said. "You've got your NGO credentials."

"Right," Nuala said. "No problem there. But the thing is, we may need your help. For old times' sake."

"Nuala, I can't get a car."

"But maybe you can ride through with me. Bring someone else along. I mean, the more of us the better."

"I don't know, Nuala. You're not running guns, are you?"

"You'd always know," Nuala said, "what we were doing and what we had."

"You don't have something going with Stanley, do you? Some dope thing?"

"Stanley's not my type," Nuala said. "Though I like his tattoos."

"All right," Sonia said. "I'll help you however I can if it doesn't involve hurting anyone. Call me."

Nuala smiled and leaned forward and kissed her.

28

I N O N E O F the visitors' cottages serving the House of the Galilean, Janusz Zimmer and Linda Ericksen sat side by side on the Welsh plaid bedspread Linda had carefully replaced after she and Zimmer had made love on the day bed. It was the same cottage Lucas had looked into the previous month, the one featuring Holman Hunt's *Scapegoat* on its wall.

Now the wall cottages were reserved for visiting evangelists and their chief financial supporters, layers on of hands, charismatics come to recharge their charismas, translators of Aramaic, and other friends of and collaborators with the House. Both Zimmer and Linda qualified.

"It would have been better for us, my love," Zimmer said, "if we had lived in a less urgent period of history."

"There's supposed to be a Chinese curse," Linda said. " 'May you live in interesting times.' "

"Well, I have inherited it," Zimmer said. "I was born before the Holocaust, born against reason. And now this remains for me. My only blessing is that I have you to help me."

"I'm hardly a blessing to anyone," humble Linda said. "I certainly wasn't a blessing to poor Ted. He needed me here in this place and I abandoned him. I know I contributed to what happened."

Zimmer made a few soothing noises. He could not bring himself to contradict her.

"But he didn't belong here," she said. "And I know I did."

"Yes," Zimmer said.

"I've hardly studied. I haven't been brought into the faith."

"Well, if we used the term 'baptism,' " Zimmer said, "yours would be a baptism of fire."

Linda stood up, went to the center of the room and folded her arms. "All right," she said, Ruth among the alien corn, "what do I have to do?"

"This much, my love," Zimmer said. "Nuala Rice goes regularly to the Gaza Strip to pick up drugs. In return she brings weapons."

"You know about this?" Linda said in horror. "Why don't you inform the authorities?"

"You mean Shabak? We have some contacts in Shabak. I'm afraid I have to tell you that the authorities are well aware of this traffic. It's their way of arming the one PLO faction they think they can control and that can keep order down there."

Linda was shocked beyond measure.

"But the drugs will be used by Jewish people."

"A few scum. Most of it will be sold in Haifa and Nazareth. At least that's what they say. In any case," Zimmer told her, "your job is essentially this: you will use your Human Rights Coalition status to get into the Strip. As often as you can, get Sonia Barnes to go with you, and try to see that she's on record as accompanying Nuala Rice.

"We want the association between those two made clear. For example, you might tell her there's information on the beatings of the rock throwers in Jabalia and you aren't able to go. Ask her to get the information for the Human Rights Coalition. As a favor to you.

"If possible, she should spend the night there. Shouldn't be difficult, because Nuala's Arab boyfriend lives in Jabalia. If they get in trouble with the IDF, with someone who isn't in on the scheme, we'll send you over to get them out."

"When will this be?"

"We're not sure. But soon."

"The purpose," Linda suggested, "would be to stop this traffic?"

"The purpose is to destroy the enemy shrines on the Temple Mount. To wipe them away and build the Temple of the Almighty."

"My God," Linda said. "There'll be riots. There'll be war."

"In religious terms, put it this way: sometimes the Almighty wants us to live in peace," Zimmer said. "Sometimes he requires of us war."

"How?" Linda asked. "How will it be done?"

"That you'll know when the time comes." He laughed. "I've already told you more than you should know."

"Anything," Linda said, trembling. "Anything you want of me."

"Yes, I know, my dear," Zimmer said, smoothing her hair. "I

expect very much of you, and I have no doubts where you're concerned. But for the rest of the way, we'll do it like we did it in the old days. You'll know the details as required. In the meantime, you can continue your studies."

"I will. I'll do whatever you want me to," Linda said. "If it's for this land. If it's for you."

"I assure you," Janusz Zimmer said, "there will be a place for you in what is to come."

"A place with you," she told him.

Zimmer laughed. "Well, insofar as these things are up to me, yes."

Linda, whose sense of humor was not highly developed, glared at him briefly. But she softened. "It's funny that in that time with Pinchas Obermann, a scoffer, a cosmopolitan, I should find faith. I couldn't have done it without you, Jan."

"Maybe," Zimmer said, lighting a cigarette, "maybe it was meant to be."

PART TWO

29

ON THE MORNING of his trip to Gaza, Lucas decided he should see Yad Vashem. Before setting out, he went to a bakery off Ben Yehuda Street and had coffee and a circular apple concoction whose recipe the management had brought, half remembered, from Mitteleuropa. It was sunny and there were cheerful crowds in the street. He left his car in its garage and went to the memorial by taxi.

Afterward, Lucas would recall it all in great detail. On that particular morning, certain things stood out immediately. One was the photograph, the largest in the historical section, of the grand mufti of Jerusalem reviewing the befezzed and tasseled Muslim storm troopers of the Bosnian SS. It made a connection with the day's headlines.

His worst moments were occasioned by the children of the camps. Some of them had tried to make little picture books in bright colors about fairies and princesses, as though they were safe at home and not imprisoned for slaughter by fiends. Above all, he felt simple shock and perplexity, and he was reassured that everyone there seemed as perplexed as he. Strangers avoided eye contact. Earlier, he had asked Sonia to go with him, and she had explained to him the necessity of going there alone. It had not taken him long to understand that she was right. On the pavement outside, he wept.

At the monument, beside the unhewed stones and the eternal flame, he recited prayers from a book an unkempt man had sold him for six shekels. "O Master of the Universe, creator of these souls, preserve them forever in the memory of thy people."

There were, inevitably, questions for Lucas. Where might he have been? What might he have done? How might he have behaved and ended up? Was he a *mischling* of the first or of the second class, and which was which? He could never keep it straight. What had become of his father's family? Carl Lucas had never told him, never referred to it.

It might be, he thought, that the world divided there, into the race of those somehow responsible and those somehow not. It was a division personally difficult for him. But around it spun a fallen universe of shame. Everyone would always look into its darkness as deeply as they could or dared. Everyone wanted an answer, a guide for the perplexed. Everyone wanted death and suffering to mean something.

Nuala was at the wheel. Sonia sat in the back with the book she had brought on her lap: *Their Eyes Were Watching God* by Zora Neale Hurston. She had managed to procure them a UN minivan after all.

"So I went," Lucas said.

"You went to Yad Vashem?" Sonia asked. "You gonna do Yad Vashem and Gaza on the same day? Trying to make yourself tired of living?"

"I was free. Killing time."

"So you went," Sonia said. "No surprises, right?"

"Oh," Lucas said, "I wouldn't say that."

Nuala, driving, said nothing.

"I hear there's a good fish restaurant in Gaza," said Lucas.

"Good fish," Sonia said. "No beer."

"So what's our agenda?" Lucas asked.

"The Foundation is working with some local self-help groups in Al-Amal," Nuala told him. "They've established their own school and a clinic and we're helping them out. Bringing them down some toothbrushes. Toothbrushes are hard to get in the Strip. Soap. Everything's overpriced. Israeli made. A little like America and Cuba. Anyway, I thought you might want to have a look. Spend the night."

"What about this squad of head-breakers you told me about? Are they still active?"

"Abu and his gang were in Rafah last week. Of course they could turn up anytime. Too bad you decided against that story."

"You can't do them all."

"Well, we've got lots down here," Nuala said.

Their time on the road drove Lucas to reflect yet again that Nuala Rice would never make him easy company. There was the problem of the keen, unsentimental attraction he felt for her, not untinged with a kind of resentment and rueful perversity. Beyond that, she had the female adventurer's snobbery, with not a grain of mercy for the timid or contemplative or conflicted. She was the walking embodiment of performance anxiety — moral, sexual and professional.

For reasons unclear, Nuala had them stop south of Ashkelon. They parked in front of a brown, featureless warehouse and Nuala held a quick colloquy with a short, powerfully built man who looked like an Oriental Jew. She handed him something in a manila envelope.

"Who is that guy?" Lucas asked Sonia as they waited in the van. "He looks like a *shtarker*."

Sonia shrugged.

"Who was that?" he asked Nuala when she was back behind the wheel.

"Oh," she said, "he's a vegetable wholesaler. He buys from a Palestinian cooperative. We carry messages, help with the barter."

"Is he a music lover?" Lucas asked. "Because I think I've seen him up at Stanley's."

"Not likely," Nuala said.

Lucas glanced back at Sonia and saw her troubled eyes returning his look.

"Sometimes," Nuala told them, "our cars are all that gets through. The curfews can last weeks. We carry a little of everything."

Sonia, holding Lucas's gaze, raised her eyebrows. The cargo behind her, in unmarked wooden boxes covered with tarpaulins, was now difficult to imagine as consisting of toothbrushes and aspirin.

"Of course," Lucas said.

The border between the State of Israel and the occupied Gaza Strip had always reminded him of the line between Tijuana and greater San Diego. There, too, ragged men the color of earth waited with the mystical patience of the very poor on the pleasure of crisply uniformed, well-nourished officials. Some months before, Lucas had come down for the dawn shape-up at the checkpoint, and he had not forgotten the drawn faces in the half-light, the terrible smiles of the weak, straining to make themselves agreeable to the strong. Unlike Tijuana, none of the niceties of mutual sovereignty concealed the raw dynamics of Gaza. There were automatic rifles, razor wire and hedgehog barricades, the wielders of power, the supplicants and the schemers against it.

Like most Israeli soldiers, the border guards at the Gaza checkpoint disliked UN vehicles and the people who rode in them. They took their time inspecting Nuala's and Lucas's passports.

"Johnnie Walker Irish," the soldier who looked at Nuala's passport took occasion to remark. "You like Johnnie Walker?"

In that ongoing war, a special venom was reserved for attractive women associated with the other side. Pretty Jewish girls drove some Palestinians crazy, even to the point of murder. An Arab construction worker had killed a beautiful teenage woman soldier with a sharpened trowel half a block from Lucas's old apartment. And Israeli soldiers often spat the rage of Jehu on those they considered the Arab-loving, Arab-fucking *shiksas* of the United Nations and the NGOs.

"They seem to think Johnnie Walker is an Irish whiskey," Nuala said when they had been passed through the border. "They were on about Johnnie Walker Irish in Lebanon. They had a faceoff with the peacekeeping force there."

"A few shells got exchanged, as I remember."

"An Irishman was killed when they fired on UN positions," Nuala said, "and the IDF said he was drunk. They called the UN Johnnie Walker Irish."

"How much time did you spend in Lebanon?" Lucas asked. "I've never heard you talk much about it."

"A few months," she said. "Every day was different, if you know what I mean."

"I suppose you enjoyed it."

"I was in the mountains when your battleships were shelling the Druse villages. The USS *New Jersey.* I didn't enjoy that much."

Beyond the wire, they crossed into a no man's land of low dry grass and plastic rubbish. Past it on their right were the neat white boxes of an Israeli settlement called Eretz, its approaches overseen by sandbagged emplacements and heralded by the Star of David flag. It was the main road to Gaza City.

"Do you think you got a line on what was going on there?" Lucas asked.

"Cold War, wasn't it?" Nuala said brightly. "America defending the Free World against Communism. Israel helping out as usual. The mountains were full of Druse and Muslim Bolsheviks, plotting to nationalize the stock exchange or something. So you sent those battleships."

"Now I remember," Lucas said. "And the Marines."

"Bloody murder," Nuala said.

She was definitely not, he felt sure, referring to the massacre of the U.S. Marine peacekeeping force near Beirut airport. The mountain villages of Lebanon had been shelled by the U.S. Navy, as far as Lucas could remember, because their inhabitants had been perceived as allies of the Syrians, who were allies of the Soviet Union, an evil empire then bent on world domination. The battleship *New Jersey* had done much of the shelling. Later, some Lebanese Shiites had captured a young American sailor on a highjacked airplane and, learning that he was from New Jersey, burned him for hours with cigarettes before killing him. Perhaps they had confused the state with the battleship, as they confounded their enthusiasm for torture with virility. When the boy was finally dead, they had photographed each other in manly postures, flexing their biceps, flashing amphetamine smiles, then left the film behind. It was the sort of disarming behavior that endeared such types to Mossad and the CIA, whose assassins nevertheless managed to murder a few of the wrong Arabs in revenge for the revenges.

"Find out anything else?" Lucas asked.

Nuala was testy. "More about naive American meddling? That was enough."

The villages had been shelled on behalf of a Lebanese faction that at the time had been perceived as "pro-Western." Since then, the term had become totally meaningless; it had doubtless been fairly meaningless at the time. Lucas had once vaguely understood who the "pro-Western" faction were and how they had figured as "pro-Western." Now he could not quite remember, and it wasn't likely many other Americans could either, least of all the former President who had presumably ordered the shelling.

"What the hell do you mean, 'anything else'?" she persisted.

"Oh, you know," Lucas said. "Like was Kahlil Gibran really a good poet?"

"Please," Sonia said.

"Kahlil Gibran?" Nuala demanded. Though she suspected him of baiting her, she could hardly resist the subject: her empathy with the Third World and its poets. "Well of course he was. A very great poet indeed. And a great man as well."

"Really? I always thought his stuff was drivel."

Rounding on him, Nuala nearly ran their van off the shoulderless road. "How can you be so bloody contemptuous? How dare you?"

"C'mon, kids," Sonia said. "Let's not fight."

"*The Prophet* always sounded like drivel to me," Lucas said. "Maybe I'm mistaken."

"Oh, Christ," Nuala crooned gently. She was not responding to Lucas. They had all seen the tower of black smoke rising from what seemed to be the center of Gaza City.

"Should we go around?" Lucas asked.

"Yes, we better," Nuala said. "Maybe we can skirt around Beit Hanoun."

"Don't you think we should see what's up?" Sonia asked. "That's sort of what we're here for."

"I have a delivery for Al-Amal," Nuala said. "I've got to get it through."

"I think we should go through town," Sonia said. "If they close the roads, we're better off at UNRWA's headquarters."

Nuala sighed and wiped perspiration from under the line of her dark hair.

"All right," she said, a little despairingly. "Mind driving, Chris?"

For no reason that he could see, Lucas walked around the car and took the wheel. He did not care for driving in the Strip, but it seemed only right that he should make himself useful.

When he pulled out, they followed the main road. On their right, across a set of derelict railroad tracks, appalling hovels of mud brick, cement and corrugated iron stretched as far as one was inclined to look, in a welter of cooking fires and strung laundry. Knots of grim children stared at the van.

"Where are we?" Lucas asked.

"Jabalia camp," Nuala said.

"There's gonna be an IDF checkpoint at Jabalia town," Sonia said. "Slow down."

The checkpoint appeared around a curve and consisted of piled sandbags, razor wire and two jeeps with mounted machine guns. Lucas's sudden braking and its attendant squeal sent the soldiers there into combat mode. When the van had stopped, he saw an armored personnel carrier and another jeep in the dunes some distance off the road, ready with covering fire for the checkpoint. The men in the vehicles were sighting down the guns, a trigger's weight from welding Lucas and his passengers to the upholstery. Behind the wheel, he took a deep breath and closed his eyes.

For a moment no one advanced from the checkpoint. Then a blond young soldier, hatless but in a flak jacket, moved out, his weapon held chest high. His comrades were covering him, watchful. The young soldier took a quick angry look at the UN logo and the van's passengers.

"You got a fucking problem? Going so fast?" He had a slight Slavic accent.

Another soldier advanced from the barrier — an officer, Lucas thought, but it was hard to tell with the Israelis. While the first soldier backed away, rifle cocked, the officer put out a stiff hand for their papers.

"Where to?" he asked when he had inspected the documents.

"Al-Amal," Nuala said.

The officer looked at her curiously and checked a list secured to his guard belt. It was as though he had been told to expect her. Then he took note of the others.

"Lukash?" He looked at Lucas's press credentials. "Sonia Barness?"

"Barnes," she said. They had a brief exchange in Hebrew and he waved them forward to the barrier. The APC rumbled forward to let them pass.

"Drive slower," Sonia said to Lucas. "Just a suggestion."

"Good thought," he said. "What did he say to you?"

"He said have a nice day. More or less."

"What do you think he meant by that?" Nuala asked.

"Hard to say," Sonia said. When Lucas turned around she winked at him. How cool she was, he thought. "I think he was wishing us luck."

Jabalia town was a collection of shapeless stone buildings with a marketplace by the side of the road. At its principal intersection a knot of Muslim women turned toward their van and began to cheer. Lucas was astonished.

"We appear to be the good guys," he said.

"Good guys," Nuala said scornfully.

"It's the car," Sonia told him.

And indeed, as they drove deeper into Gaza City they passed more people — cloth-swathed women carrying babies, market workers, schoolchildren — who briefly turned from the column of black smoke that increasingly blotted out the desert sky to wave and applaud.

"The car?" he asked.

"It's a UN van, remember."

"Of course," he said.

Driving through crowds that cheered them, Lucas became exhilarated. Their innocent, earnest van displayed twin pictures of the great world itself, portrayed from its nonconfrontational polar perspective, wreathed in boughs of peace. And people were actually waving. Take up the good guy's burden, he thought. Something new.

"Slow down," Nuala said, "because we're getting into it." She spoke quite deliberately. "If the army asks you where you're going, tell them Al-Azhar Road."

There were a great many people in the street as they inched the van forward. No one was cheering any longer. Now Lucas could catch the stench of the burning rubber, and with it another smell, a sweet skunky musk not immediately unpleasant but charged with something dangerous and unreasonable. Tear gas. It reminded him of Easter in the rain.

"Keep going," Nuala said. "Maybe we can make Al-Azhar."

"Everyone all right?" Lucas asked.

"We're fine," the women said together.

Around the next corner, a shabby concrete mosque thrust its angular minaret from among the rickety shapeless buildings around it. An amplified voice, transcendent with anger, sounded from the tower, echoing in the empty spaces below. Now they could hear shouts and shattering glass and the rattle of stones against pitted walls. From nearby came the explosive thud of launched grenades. Smoke, blended with the bitter gas, drifted before the windshield and Lucas rolled the windows up.

At an intersection, a crowd of women in blue robes were carrying on, wailing, raising fists to heaven. Some wrapped their headdresses over their mouths, less from piety, it seemed, than because of the fumes. When they saw the UN van, they all ran toward it.

Lucas slowed to a roll. Outside, the women pounded on the roof of the van, on the hood, the windows.

"Stop," Sonia said. When he stopped, she and Nuala got out and were engulfed by shrieking women. A few of them went around to the driver's side to shout at Lucas. Out of politeness, although the gas and the smoke were getting bad, he lowered the window. A woman reached in and scratched his face with her nails. Their sheer frenzy set his head spinning and dimmed his vision. He was stunned, vertiginous, stained with their tears.

"Go," Sonia said as she and Nuala climbed back in the van. "They've shot a kid, I think."

The heart of the thing itself was a block away. Out of the smoke came a chanting, howling gang of teenagers, boys in ragged hand-me-downs — Purdue sweatshirts, ripped sweaters and khakis. There were three or four dozen. The youngest among them might have been twelve, the oldest around seventeen, and they were straining to support the slender, supine body of a youth like themselves. The young man they carried was fuzzy-lipped and deathly pale, his eyes were milky and unfocused, his teeth bared and set. He was bleeding from the ear.

"Shouldn't we get him to a doctor?" Sonia asked in a low voice.

"He's dead, Sonia," Nuala said.

Up the street, an enraged voice over the minaret loudspeaker carried on, beside itself, summoning all hell. Competing with its grim measures now was a second amplified voice, a cold, bored police voice in Arabic, reading what Lucas assumed was the riot act.

Driving on, they lost sight of the fallen boy. The crowd of youths had retreated ahead of them and disappeared in the turns of the road. Smoke and gas were growing thicker, the stones fell closer about Lucas. CS fumes were truly like skunk: if you'd never been dosed there was a brief psychological immunity, but once the stuff took hold you were immobilized. Rifle fire sounded behind them.

"We're in between the army and the crowd," Sonia said calmly. "How shitty!"

Suddenly IDF soldiers were all around; an officer stepped out in the road ahead and put out the flat of his hand to halt them. When Lucas slowed, the soldiers flowed around the van from behind, advancing along the reeking, peeling walls, moving cautiously, covering each other's moves, checking the rooftops and their backs. Two soldiers moved directly in front of the van and raised their weapons to fire gas canisters at the withdrawing mass of young men. Taking aim, they posed like archers in an ancient frieze, squinting up at the declining sun. The propelled gas grenades exploded from their launchers with a disastrous thud, like sprung rivets. A few came back, spinning against the blue sky, sputtering and smoking, in the hail of rocks from the shadows at the far end of the street. More soldiers moved in, firing from one knee, discharging what Lucas assumed were rubber bullets — there was no sure way to tell — in the direction of the crowd.

"We should get out in the square," Nuala said.

"Right," Sonia said. She took some wads of Kleenex from her bag, wet them with bottled water from the seat beside her and passed them around.

At the next intersection, an officer crouching against the closed shutters of a café waved at them to halt.

"Keep going," Nuala said. Lucas speeded up and crossed the intersecting street with angry shouts behind. He also heard more firing close by.

A rain of fair-sized stones met them halfway down the next block. When he pulled over to the side, the stones stopped coming but the smoke was thicker than ever.

"Maybe we should turn around," Lucas said.

Neither Sonia nor Nuala said anything.

"I'm from out of town," he said, turning in the driver's seat. "That's why I'm asking."

"We have to go on," Nuala told him.

"Right," he said, and put the car in gear.

At the far end of the street, visible through the smoke, was a sight Lucas had some difficulty making sense of. A skirmish line of troops had secured the entrance of an alley, firing gas grenades and whatever ammunition their rifles contained. Behind them, a larger body of soldiers in riot gear were milling about in the time-honored military tradition of hurry up and wait. In front of the Israeli firing line, a small white jeep was parked. Hanging limply from its radio antenna was the blue and white flag of the United Nations. Beside the jeep stood a tall sweating man in a plain, uncamouflaged khaki uniform and blue beret. His shoulder displayed a flag patch with a white cross on a red field. A Dane. He stood, arms folded, legs wide apart, frowning at the ground, lips pursed in an attitude of intransigence.

The soldiers, in their helmets and flak jackets, contrived to fire around him. Two Israeli officers were shouting at him at once. One seemed reasonable, the other less so.

"Want to walk home in the desert?" the more reasonable officer asked him. "Fine. Because we'll bulldoze your goddam jeep."

"A violation!" the other officer shouted, appealing as to heaven.

"Interference with the security forces!" He swore in Arabic, Hebrew being lacking in obscenities for the occasion.

The Dane shifted his stance and shrugged.

"How can you do this?" the unreasonable officer demanded. "How? How?"

"We're resisting a criminal attack," the reasonable officer explained. "We're resisting criminals, you're creating an international incident. It's not your business, Captain."

From time to time one of the soldiers in the mass of troops at the rear would also shout at the Dane, but most watched without expression. A few appeared amused. After he had been shouted at for a while the Danish captain condescended to reply quietly. Lucas and the women in the van could not hear what he said. Stones still flew from time to time, coming from somewhere up the alley under siege. The Dane and the officers who were shouting at him ignored them in soldierly fashion. The air reeked of burning rubber.

"Let me go out and talk to them," Sonia said. "I think I know the UN guy."

When she got out, Lucas got out with her.

"Look," Sonia said, "someone's got to stay with the van. Otherwise the soldiers will just shove it off the road."

"I'll stay," Nuala said.

Lucas and Sonia made their way through the smoky street to the alley where the officers stood. The two Israeli officers were not happy to see them. The less reasonable one raised his arms in exasperation.

"What now?" the reasonable one asked.

"Hullo," said the Dane to Sonia and Lucas. "Are you my reinforcements?" He appeared to be joking.

"We were on our way to Al-Amal camp," Sonia said, "but we're stopping at headquarters in town. What's up?"

"I have explained that I must stay," the Dane said. "But these gentlemen are opposed."

"None of you have business here," the reasonable officer said. The unreasonable one nodded fierce agreement.

"What happened?" Lucas asked.

"This," the Dane said, "is under dispute."

"Do you want us to stay?" Sonia asked.

The captain looked at the van in which Nuala sat and then at Lucas and Sonia.

"No," he said. "I want you off the street. Headquarters knows I'm here."

"Will you let us pass?" Sonia asked the two Israelis.

"No!" shouted the unreasonable officer.

"Certainly," said the reasonable one. With a courtly gesture he offered them the street ahead, smoky and laced with stones. "Pass."

They got back in the van and drove by the alley unharmed. Some of the Israeli troopers muttered after them.

"What's going on?" Lucas asked as they drove out of the smoke.

"They're murdering Palestinians," Nuala declared.

"What's going on," said Sonia, "is that they've got a bunch of the *shebab* cornered up that alley and they want to go in and whale on them. So they'd like Captain Angstrom out of there. But Angstrom, God bless him, is being an asshole."

A kilometer away, the smoke had dissipated and the streets of Gaza City were deserted. Other columns of smoke, more than half a dozen, rose from various points of the landscape.

The army had concentrated its forces around the university, near UN headquarters, so they had a few more checkpoints to negotiate. They found headquarters on an emergency footing. In the dusty courtyard stood an old Laredo with yellow Israeli plates and a bumper sticker that said STUDY ARSE ME.

"The Rose is here," Sonia said.

Inside, Helen Henderson, the Rose of Saskatoon, was in conversation with a Canadian called Owens, who was chief of the Social Services Department of the field office of the United Nations Relief and Works Agency for Palestine.

Sonia introduced Lucas and asked them what had happened in Daraj, in the southeast of Gaza City, where the riot was. A radio transmitter carried muffled voices over static, speaking in English.

"Someone raised a Palestinian flag," the Rose told them. "The army came. The *shebab* threw rocks. That's as much as we know. Captain Angstrom's up there."

"We saw him," Sonia said. "I think there was a fatality. We saw a boy who appeared to be dead."

"More than one," Owens said. "We have reports of three."

"We have to go to Al-Amal," Nuala told Owens. "Can we get through?"

"I wouldn't use the inland road. The whole Strip's hot and it'll be dark soon. There'll be a curfew and a lot of paranoia. The army might let you through over on the coast. Or they might not."

"They're supposed to let us through," Nuala said. "They're obliged to."

"Yes," Owens said, "well, good luck. Do you have a radio?"

They had no radio. Owens told them to keep their heads down.

The army did in fact let them pass by the Beach camp checkpoint, and their drive from Gaza to Khan Yunis featured sunset on the sea. A half mile off Deir el-Balah, the searchlight of a helicopter played on shrimp boats, gliding theatrically across the dark swells from vessel to vessel. The sea was smooth and they could hear it gently breaking on the nearby beach. There was another camp close to the shore; darkness somewhat dissolved its squalor and menace, encouraging illusions of tranquility. The evening call to prayer echoing from its loudspeakers sounded tragic and fateful, resigned, remote.

The name of the Compassionate and Merciful One still hung over the mud-brick hovels when they encountered the first of the settlers' resort hotels. Beyond the sandbags and razor wire, its poolside glow was green and lush, and there were strings of colored lights along the beach.

"Who would go there?" Lucas wanted to know. "It's so close to the camp."

But there were customers. Long-legged blond women in bikinis and gauzy wraps strolled in the verdant shadows. A man with fair hair to his shoulders carried a young woman to the edge of the pool and dropped her in.

"They're mostly Europeans there," Sonia said, "because that hotel's not religious. Israelis go to the others. They're a good buy."

"But you can see the camps."

"And smell them," Nuala said. "It doesn't bother everyone."

Turning from the young Aryans at play across the wire to the dark mass of the camp, Lucas had to consider what he had seen that morning. Images of Gaza and Yad Vashem would be forever confounded in his mind, although he understood perfectly well that it was a cheap equivalence, already a cliché of the place, trotted out for the record by every aspiring athlete of the sensibility who passed by. But the chain of circumstance connecting the two shaped the underlying reality. Blind champions would forever turn the wheels in endless cycles of outrage and redress, an infinite round of guilt and grief. Instead of justice, a circular darkness.

It occurred to him that Sonia had been right about going to those two places the same day. He had been trying to balance some imaginary scale, and no doubt anyone who saw Yad Vashem might imagine the necessities of Gaza. On the other hand, the two were utterly unconnected, because history was moronically pure, consisting entirely of singularities. Things had no moral. If you had to have a side, it was better to see only one — choose according to your needs and simply ignore or deny the other. Comparisons, attempts at ethical calibration, induced vital fatigue.

"But it must be so strange," he said, "to go to the beach over there. With your back to all this."

"Some people probably like the drama," Sonia said.

"Drama indeed," said Nuala sternly. Lucas and Sonia exchanged a secret glance.

"I'm sure some of them moralize," Sonia said. "Come here and frolic in the surf, then go home and bitch about the cruel Israelis."

"Sounds about right," said Lucas.

"We'd have tourists in Cuba," she told him, "leftists, don't you know. *Gente de la izquierda, socialistas.* You could find them on the Malecón, looking for girls or boys to fuck them for dollars. Then they go home and say, How about me, I spent my vacation in Cuba. *Para solidaridad.*"

"Some of the tourists fall in love with the settlers," Nuala said. "They come back again and again."

"Listen," Sonia said to Lucas, "want to go swimming tomorrow? So you can tell the tale? Maybe we can fix it up."

"It seems frivolous," Lucas said.

"You'll earn it. We'll all go. Right, Nuala?"

"Maybe," Nuala said. "If there's no curfew in Gaza."

"It's not exactly what I came for. Is it permitted?"

"You mean by the Koran?" Sonia asked. "By the Torah? Take your pleasures where you find them, Chris. If someone offers you a swim, swim."

"It's a date," Lucas said.

There was an army checkpoint at the edge of the protected coastal road, and they approached it with great discretion.

The noncom in charge, when he had finished inspecting their

passports, addressed them in American English. He was earnest-looking and bespectacled, like a young doctor or a college instructor.

"You shouldn't be on the road at all. I hope you know you're spending the night here."

On the outskirts of Khan Yunis, the army owned the light. Lucas eased the van through narrow alleys, trying not to outrun his own parking lights, steering by the occasional glimpse of a kerosene lamp behind a partition. Helicopters scurried about in the darkness overhead, showering brilliance on the landscape below. The high beams prowled in zigzag patterns over the camp, illuminating columns of smoke, sometimes lighting the flight of a solitary runner. Radios crackled, bullhorns sounded. A parachute flare drifted earthward out in the desert, beyond the southern boundary of the camp. There were shots.

"Turns out to be a big night," Sonia said grimly.

They parked behind a run-down stucco wall that enclosed the ruins of a garden that had been part of a British army hospital during the Second World War. A drooping UN flag hung over its gate, lit by a row of half a dozen bare bulbs, a couple of which were dark and broken. Signs in Arabic and English were pasted around the entrance.

It took them some time to gain entrance; they had to pound on the heavy wooden door and depress a lever that only intermittently rang a little bell. Then the door opened and a young Palestinian in a white doctor's coat peered out at them.

"Rashid," Nuala said.

At the sound of her voice and the sight of her the young doctor broke into a radiant smile. She stepped forward and stood before him. Neither of them moved for a moment. Then Rashid took a quick glance over his shoulder, as if he were concerned who might see them, and put his hand over his heart. Lucas saw his look change from a formal polite gesture into something fateful and passionate and meant for Nuala alone. He wore a stethoscope around his neck, and the breast pocket of his white smock was filled with ballpoint pens, some of which leaked and had empurpled his white coat. His hands were stained with ink.

"You have come," he said to her.

"Yes," Nuala said. "And brought everything. And friends along with me. Oh," she said when she saw the condition of his coat, "you'll ruin your jacket. Your pen's leaking."

There was something boyish and fond about the way he laughed at her admonition. In his happiness, he welcomed Sonia and Lucas warmly into the dimly lit foyer, trying not to touch them with his ink-stained hands. In one wing of the old building babies were crying. Lucas noticed that two other Palestinian men were standing at a desk on the far side of the room as though reluctant to approach.

"So," Sonia asked Rashid, "are you with the Children's Foundation?"

Rashid, though no less delighted, seemed confused by her question. He turned to Nuala.

"He's a new assistant administrator," she told Sonia. "Sent over from Hebron the other week."

"I have just finished a residency," Rashid told them, "in America. In Louisville, Kentucky."

"That's great, Rashid," Sonia said. "Congratulations. I didn't know you shared space with UNRWA," she said to Nuala.

"Oh, we don't," Nuala said. Her speech was hurried, her eyes averted. "We're just over in Al-Amal."

As they stood awkwardly in the foyer, they heard the engine of the van start up outside.

"Is that our car?" Lucas asked.

Rashid smiled at him in silence. He turned to Nuala.

"Yes, they're moving it out of the road. It'll be safer over at our place. Tomorrow," she said, "I'll show you around our shop."

"Sure," said Sonia. "We should all turn in."

Then Nuala and Rashid, walking stiffly side by side, went back out into the contentious night. From the darkness, young Palestinian women began to unload the UN van.

"They're taking the stuff," Lucas said. "Is it all right?"

"Let them," Sonia said. "It's meant for them."

Sonia said nothing as they walked toward the desk, where a second Palestinian physician waited, an elderly man with a blue blazer on under his white coat. Sonia knew him; he was Dr. Naguib of UNRWA. She introduced Lucas as her friend, a journalist. He and the man exchanged a soft, silent handshake.

"I hope you'll have room for us," Sonia said to Dr. Naguib.

"We have only the office beds for you. Perhaps we can put one in the hallway."

The office beds turned out to be two camp cots with Swedish sleeping bags on them, which were stowed under a desk in the office of the Education Department. Lucas and Sonia sent Dr. Naguib away when he tried to help them wrestle them out.

"The bath is just outside," Naguib said, pointing down the hallway. "But the water there is not good. And you must be careful tonight because of the patrols."

"We have water," Sonia said. "Thank you, Dr. Naguib."

"We don't have to shlep one into the hall," Sonia said. "The doc won't care."

"I should have brought a bottle of Scotch," Lucas said when Naguib was gone.

"Not appropriate," Sonia said.

"Just as well," Lucas said. "It keeps me awake." He lay down on the cot and cradled his head on his hands. Sonia sat down on one of the office chairs.

"Once upon a time," Sonia said, "I would have brought some Percodan."

"Is that what you like?"

"Used to be. I don't use them anymore."

"Why'd you stop?"

"The Rev told me to quit."

"De Kuff? And that's good enough?"

"Good enough for me," Sonia said.

He was at the point of pursuing the question of De Kuff's role in her life when something closer to hand occurred to him. "Tell me," he said, "what's going on with Nuala?"

"I guess she's got something going with young Dr. Rashid."

"Oh."

"Uh-huh," Sonia said, and laughed quietly. "He's cute, too. Clean-cut kid. Good for Nuala."

"She might have told us," he said. "What are we supposed to be, the beards or something?"

"Good question," she said. She stood up and turned out the light in the office. "Who knows?"

Sometime later, he made his way down the hall in the direction Dr. Naguib had pointed and let himself out into the night to find the toilet. He slid a shoe in the doorjamb to keep the outside door from locking on him. He was edging toward the little shed when the noise of a motorbike exploded in the silence. As it passed the naked lights over the main entrance, he saw that there were two riders on the bike: a man up front and a woman riding pillion. Nuala.

Within seconds, with a roar and torrent of wind a helicopter was prowling overhead. The tin roofs of the alley rattled in unison, the street refuse flew in an eye-stinging whirl, dogs howled. A great column of light descended and he saw the running lights of the chopper only a couple of dozen feet above him. Breathless, he huddled in the moist darkness of the washroom, waiting for the big machine to move off.

Back inside the dark Education Department office, he stood outside the cubicle where Sonia lay. Surely, he thought, she must be awake.

"I just saw Nuala taking off with Rashid," he told her.

"She's probably going to Al-Amal to spend the night with him. And tell his people she brought them what they need."

"I hope they make it."

"They will," she said without opening her eyes.

He went and lay down on his cot in silence. After a moment, he got up.

"I think now," he told Sonia, who lay with her eyes closed, "I think I'd like to hold your hand."

"I'd like you to hold it," she said. Her eyes remained closed.

He went over to her and took her hand and kissed it.

"Now I have to tell you," she said, "that we are deep in Islamic territory. And we must do nothing to give scandal." She shifted so that she rested her face against his arm. "So if you have any unseemly impulses, you better forget them."

"And I suppose there are nasty little kids on the lookout for non-Islamic behavior," Lucas said.

"Damn right," she said. "Especially among infidel women. And they sneak up to windows."

"What will we do, then? Will you sing for me?"

"No fucking way, Jim. After hours."

"Then I'll tell you a story," Lucas said. "Would you like that?"

"Uh-huh."

"So one time," Lucas said, "before the Second World War, this tourist goes into Notre-Dame in Paris. Someone's playing Bach's Fantasy and Fugue in G. An angelic rendering. So the tourist goes up into the choir loft to see who's at the keyboard, and who do you think he sees?"

"Fats Waller?"

"Hell," Lucas said. "You knew."

"Damn right," she said.

"So Fats says, 'Just trying their God box, man.' "

Sonia had begun to cry.

"Poor Thomas Waller," she said. "He loved Bach. He loved the organ. After his radio show was over, he played it on his radio station for hours. For free. Uncredited." Tears rolled down her cheeks and she opened her eyes to wipe them.

Lucas patted her shoulder. It had been a strange day. He had gone to Yad Vashem. He had come through the smoke of Gaza. Now he was listening to a woman in God's most ancient wilderness, weeping for Fats Waller.

"I think it's great," he said after a moment, "that you're crying for him."

"I always cry for him," she said. "He was sort of like my daddy. They knew each other when Daddy was young. I cry for them both."

Lucas kissed her gently and went back to his cot and fell asleep at once.

30

LONG BEFORE, during the years of the British mandate, part of the cellar of the main building of what was now the House of the Galilean had been taken over by one of the Arab merchant's sons as a radio room. The boy had been a ham operator with vast resources, and he had equipped the cellar lavishly, turning it into a cross between an American commercial broadcasting studio and the radio shack of an ocean liner. He had performed live together with his brothers and sisters, singing Arab songs and continental ballads of the day, staging and reading his own radio plays.

The young man's relaying equipment was long gone; his rig had been closed down by the British during one of the emergencies and his expensive gear confiscated in 1939. But the trappings of an old-time studio were still there — baffled walls, curving tweedy sofas, spare modernistic tables and cylindrical lamps.

There was a long horseshoe-shaped table like a newspaper copy desk, and Janusz Zimmer and some of his associates had just held a meeting there.

The representative of the principal organization in attendance was an American rabbi from California who had lost one son to drugs but redeemed the other to militant religious Zionism. His group had committed itself to armed violence against the Palestinians and, if need be, against the Israeli state.

Its sages, consulting the tractates as the youth division trained with modern weapons, had come to the conclusion that only the strict and literal application of the most militant adjurations in the Torah could bring about the return of the Messiah. The return centered, they believed, on the expulsion of idolaters and aliens —

according to the letter of Numbers 33:55 — and the reestablishment of the Temple and its priesthood.

The rabbi's organization regarded itself as the only serious participant in Janusz Zimmer's plans, and was so seen by Zimmer. It had a few small but avid cells in the army and the bureaucracy and especially among the pioneers in the harsher settlements of Gaza and the West Bank, where the Arabs were many and the amenities few. The other outfits, whose representatives had been in attendance at the radio shack, both Zimmer and the American rabbi regarded as potentially useful idiots.

One of these groups, founded by another American, in this case a renegade Hasid, had its roots among the Essenes and the Books of Jubilees and Enoch. It made an effort to proselytize among Ethiopian Jews, for whom those texts held great importance. Its aim was to restore the balance of time as conveyed to Moses by the angel Uriel, so that the feasts might be celebrated as the Almighty desired. The introduction of the solar calendar had caused the destruction of ten thousand false stars that whirled in torment in some subcelestial sky. This group, too, required the rebuilding of the Temple, where they believed the solar calendar would prevail and the feasts be properly observed.

Another sect in attendance, represented at the meeting by its founder, was the creation of Mike Glass, a junior-college professor of Jewish background who had grown up in an anti-Semitic New England town and lived a secular life. After teaching poly sci and coaching football, he had turned to Jewish studies following the breakup of his marriage.

He had come to the Apocalypse through his readings of Scripture, the agrarian pessimism of Wendell Berry and the predestinarian poetry of Larry Woiwode. The history of Israel, he felt, provided evidence of divine election and the human depravity from which only God's choice could rescue humankind.

Raziel Melker had also attended, representing, in a way, the disciples of Adam De Kuff. Neither De Kuff nor Sonia, nor anyone else close to them, knew about Raziel's association with Zimmer and his attendance at the meeting.

The officials of the House of the Galilean knew the purpose of the meeting and the intentions of the participants but did not choose to be represented at their deliberations.

When the other delegates had left, Zimmer and Linda Ericksen,

Raziel and the rabbi from California remained seated at the horse-shoe. It was plain that the presence of Raziel and Linda troubled the California rabbi, whose name was Yacov Miller. In a few minutes, Zimmer asked them to leave.

"You should adjust to Linda," Zimmer told the rabbi bluntly. "She wants only to be of service. But she is, finally, an American woman. She will resent being ordered out of rooms."

"The 'American woman' is not an ideal of ours," Rabbi Miller said. "You obviously trust her completely."

"I don't give my trust easily," Zimmer said. "If I did, I wouldn't be alive and present at this moment. She has a rare sense of dedication. Great rectitude."

"I hope you don't mind my pointing out," Miller said, "she's a multiple adulteress. Supposedly a religious person, she shamelessly took up with that man Obermann. And now," said the rabbi, with the interrogative tone of a religious disputant, "she comes to us?"

"You're supposed to be a religious person as well," Zimmer said. "Don't you understand the soul when it searches? Don't you understand the female temperament?"

Miller only looked impatient.

"Have you never heard," Zimmer asked, "that the power of Din seeks souls from the Other Side?"

Miller bridled, flushing. "I have no interest in Kabbala. It's medieval superstition. And I distrust, shall we say, the lingo."

"Well, you're not dealing with the president of your congregation and his wife in the suburbs," Zimmer said. "If you want to break some eggs, you better get used to meeting colorful characters."

"Like that Melker, I suppose."

"You don't like Melker?" Janusz Zimmer asked. "A pity. I like him far better than I like you. But we put up with each other."

"I wonder about him," said the rabbi, blushing in full measure now. "I distrust him."

Zimmer fixed Miller with his falcon stare. "You want the redemption by violence. You're ready for war, for death and maiming. Have you ever seen it?"

Miller declined to answer.

"Have you?"

"I've never personally witnessed combat," Miller said. "Many of our group have."

"I didn't ask you about your group." Zimmer leaned his hard mask into Miller's angry face. "I have seen it. All over the world. People burned alive at roadblocks. Starvation. The water torture, caged rats eating people's brains, young boys and girls bleeding to death, dying of thirst. It makes you thirsty to bleed in the desert. Never knew that? Ever had to elicit intelligence from fanatics?"

"I believe God will preserve his people," Miller said.

"A war where only one side will suffer and die — is that what you expect?"

"I don't know what to expect," Miller said. "I have faith."

"Miracles."

"Yes," shouted Miller, "miracles! How else?"

"The miracle of dynamite," Zimmer said. "That boy has access to explosives. He will procure them. If the attempt fails, his group will assume responsibility."

"Why?" Miller asked. "It sounds crazy."

"In the event of failure," Zimmer said, "the investigations, the accusations, the name-calling will never end. With success, the country will unite. If necessary against the world."

"But why? Why would he do it, this hippie? I won't ask how."

"You won't, Rabbi? Suspect drugs are involved? You could be right."

"I have only to look at him to suspect that," Miller said. "Young Mr. Hip with the dark glasses. But what about the assuming of responsibility? Why would he do that?"

"Because he's what you look down on. A mystic. I think he believes if the act is performed no one will be hurt on any side. As you say, a miracle."

Miller sneered. "How can he believe such a thing?"

"You despise him, Rabbi? You who believe in bloodshed where God sees that only the right blood is shed? In a one-sided war? *Gott mitt uns!* I suggest you not despise him. He may be deluded and drugged out, but he has more humanity than you."

Miller brooded for a minute.

"Sure thing," he said at last. "OK, you got it. I won't despise him. To tell you the truth, the element that most puzzles me is this: What moves you, Zimmer? What are your hopes?"

"I wouldn't expect you to understand."

"Condescend," said Miller. "Try me."

Zimmer stood up abruptly and went to the wall consoles where most of the radio equipment was. "I wonder if they listen in," he said.

"The goyim upstairs?"

"I don't suppose they're interested as long as the money comes in."

"I agree," said Miller. "But you haven't answered my question." He kept his seat at the end of the horseshoe and watched Zimmer pace up and down.

"My father believed in the brotherhood of man," Zimmer said suddenly. "He gave his life to the Communist Party of Poland. Then two years before the war Stalin abolished the Party and shot its leaders, my father included. Then came the Nazis. Everything had to be rebuilt."

"And I suppose you were right there. With your Polish brothers who love you so well."

"We rebuilt over and over," Zimmer said. "When one structure we rebuilt was destroyed, we rebuilt again. Over and over our plans foundered on human nature. Not just Polish nature or Jewish nature. On the mediocrity of human nature that betrays its better self, its best ideals, that is unworthy of itself everywhere . . ."

"Over and over," said Miller, "the people betray the covenant. Even us, to whom so much is given. Without the coming of the Promised One we'll always fail." He seemed unable to stop blushing, and it was hard to tell which prevailed in him, anger or embarrassment. "I'm sorry about your father," he told Zimmer. "But it's an old story. And I'm sorry for you."

"Are you?" Zimmer asked. "How kind. Now tell me, Rabbi. Here you are in the Promised Land. Is it what you hoped for?"

"It will be," Miller said. "That's what we're doing here today."

"Shocking, the mediocrity of everything — is it not? The country of a people with such gifts? Without their genius European civilization — and not only European civilization — would have been impossible. And yet here you have a corrupt bureaucracy, ugly cities, vulgarity. Cheap tabloids, bad art. Everything made by the hand of man looks second rate. Not quite the light to the nations we had in mind. Or hadn't you noticed?"

Miller trembled with fury. "Excuse me, I'm not a European aesthete like yourself. It's too bad while the world is occupying itself in murdering us we can't find the leisure to provide an artistic and cultural renaissance for its edification. So that when we're destroyed the goyim might grow contrite — 'Poor Jews, they were so talented. Too bad they had to be driven from the earth.' " Then he stood up, to address Zimmer from, so to speak, his own level.

"The mediocrity that concerns me is a moral mediocrity. A refusal to accept our covenant, to create a Jewish nation that will truly light the world. Then maybe we can have the pretty pictures you require."

"Has it not occurred to you, Rabbi," Zimmer asked, "that the one thing might have to do with the other?"

"All that has occurred to me," Miller said, "is that what should be a Jewish land is not one. Yet."

"You're an intelligent man," Zimmer said. He flipped one of the wall switches on, then switched it off. A small red light came on and went out. "You question my motives? I'll answer you. I have a choice and I cannot escape it. That is, I cannot escape it and live. I've seen a lot of dying, my friend. I know the difference between life and death, and for me it's one or the other. I don't propose to stop living until I'm dead."

"All," Miller said, "very personal."

"Yes," Zimmer agreed, "very personal. Now I have the choice of meditating all my life on what I've seen and learned. Perhaps I can transcend it through insight, eh?"

Miller only watched him.

"Or I can be part of the process of becoming. The relationship between this land and the Almighty I leave to you, Rabbi. But I don't propose to watch this country, the country of my allegiance, remain a pawn of hypocrites in the west or the refuge of mediocrity. We engage in the process of becoming or we die. We have an adventure before us and a historical destiny, if we can seize it. In that process of becoming I can and I will lead."

"In that process," Miller said with a slight smile, "you may be sure you'll be judged. Who knows? You may be chosen."

"Not I only, Rabbi. Fools who expect God to do their fighting and dying for them will be disappointed. The force at work here is history. History will judge us as men and as a nation. If we prevail, maybe you'll have your Zion."

"You're an odd kind of Jew," Miller said. "I suppose Vladimir Jabotinsky was like you."

"I'm no Jabotinsky, Rabbi Miller. But I'm sure if Jabotinsky had his way, the clergy would have stayed out of the way and awaited the

Messiah. Recruiting the religious element wasn't necessarily the benefit some people think. In my humble opinion."

"Mr. Zimmer," Miller said, gathering up the notes on which he had done no more than idly doodle, "who ever said your opinion was humble?"

31

THE AL-AZIZ lying-in center in Khan Yunis had been a place of shadows the night before, but in the morning it seemed charged with insistent life. Babies squalled from the maternity clinic in the other wing of the building. On a quick excursion to the washhouse, Lucas observed that the alleys beyond the compound were peaceful enough. Smoke from breakfast fires drifted toward the smoggy sky, although there were few people in sight.

When he and Sonia had stowed their cots, Dr. Naguib took them on a tour of the clinic. Amid homespun nursery decorations, dozens of shy, ample Palestinian women rested with their infants, everyone swathed in a vast profusion of sheets, curtains and robes. A few of the women smiled at the visitors, most stared evenly or looked away. Babies were everywhere.

Lucas bowed and beamed, trying in vain to experience the good cheer he was dutifully projecting. The women's plump pale faces, uniformly encircled by scarves, had a charmless interchangeability. The raw, unlovely newborns wailed. Strolling the ward with a politician's smile, he felt pity and vague despair. It must be only awkwardness, he told himself, a foreigner's embarrassment.

Adjoining the lying-in center was a children's ward. The children were mainly toddlers, one or two with sleepy mothers attending them in plain folding chairs beside their beds. Communal toys hung suspended from the ceiling: stuffed animals or leering rubber dolls in bright ugly colors.

"We have bad water," Dr. Naguib told them when they went back into the foyer. "This is our major trouble in Gaza. Politics aside," he added.

Outside in the compound, Lucas saw no sign of their van. Dr.

Naguib, who had a grid of small scars on his face, continued to walk with them.

"Years ago we lost many. Dehydration, enteric fever. There was malaria here. Diphtheria. Trachoma was very common."

"And now?" Lucas asked.

"And now it is better," the doctor said. "Now the U.S. will pay its dues at the United Nations again and so people say things will improve." He laughed pleasantly.

"Can that be true?"

"Of course not. But the U.S. should pay for everything, I think." He gestured toward the sea. "Yes, for everything. Why not?" He was a Christian and a native of Gaza. He had studied in Iowa. "That is my opinion," he told them good-naturedly. "To my mind, the Americans should pay. Now they have the world as they want it."

Lucas thanked him and congratulated him on the clinic.

"The maternity clinic belongs to us," he said, "to the United Nations. But the pediatric side is the Children's Foundation's. All Nuala's doing."

"They're lucky to have her," Sonia said.

"She is a blessing," said Dr. Naguib as he went off.

They were standing in the shade of a date palm that was the only green thing left of the British army's hospital garden. Sonia kicked at the ground and hunkered down at its base. Lucas got down beside her.

"Remind you of Somalia?"

"Somalia was much worse. Of course there, too, we had bad water. But it was very, very bad water. All the children died."

"Not all of them, surely."

"Oh, yes. All of them. Practically every goddam kid. Next thing to it. Slight exaggeration. They hardly had time to be born before they died." She looked at him sidewise. "Like in your poem. They learned to sing before they learned to talk."

"And that's where you learned to paint your feet."

She laughed. "Yeah. Because you had to do something far out, understand what I'm saying? Paint your feet like the women there. Had to do something like that."

Para solidaridad, he thought, though he had the sense not to say it.

"Sometimes weird, inappropriate food would arrive. Useless shit the kids couldn't eat. Caviar! So we'd open it and gorge and party.

Put on the tapes and dance." She shook her head. "We were trying to keep from losing it."

"I understand," Lucas said.

"So you really went out to Yad Vashem yesterday."

"Seems like a long time ago."

"Well, I told you," she said.

"Yes, you did. You said don't go there and come here."

"I said not on the same day."

"Maybe it's not such a bad idea," Lucas said. "We'll put it on the moral tour."

"Will there be moral tours?"

"For the press. And the press will recycle them for everybody's breakfast. Put the folks on buses, show them both sides. That way," he explained, "everybody will understand everything."

"Believe it'll help?"

"I think I have to believe it. It's my job."

"Then why joke about it?"

"Because what else is there?" Lucas asked. They stood up. "What about Nuala, Sonia? What's she up to?"

"I guess she's in love."

"We already know that," he said. "What else?"

Sonia only turned away.

"Well," said Lucas, "let's go find her."

In a tent adjoining Nuala's pediatric clinic, they found a young mullah at work in a white-curtained compartment. He was being assisted by two other men of religion, both considerably older than he. A middle-aged Muslim woman, her eyes closed, reclined on a hospital bed while the mullah's assistant held up a plastic bottle of intravenous solution. The mullah was reading the Koran aloud. More Muslim women sat on benches around the tent, waiting their turn.

"What's happening?" Lucas wanted to know. "Can we go in?"

"Better not," said Sonia.

"What's he doing?"

"He's an exorcist," she said. "He's casting out devils."

"With an IV?"

"I think that's how you do it," Sonia said.

They found Nuala and Rashid drinking tea in front of a little tin-roofed mud-brick hutch at the edge of the compound. They sat at a huge splintering wooden table that looked as though it had stood in someone's parlor for a hundred years. Nuala hastened to bring them cups and Rashid explained exorcism. He was wearing a newly laundered white coat.

"In the plasma bottle a hole is made. Through the hole are read verses of the Koran. Then the djinn will depart by way of the big toe."

"Always?" Lucas asked.

"Yes," replied Rashid. "If the djinn is a Muslim."

Lucas laughed politely and realized at once that no one else was smiling.

"It is true," Rashid said. His tone was calm and pleasant and he did not seem offended.

"And are the afflicted always women?" Sonia asked.

"Often," Rashid said. "That is usual."

"And why do you think that is?" Sonia inquired.

Nuala laughed protectively. Lucas noticed her touch Rashid's wrist for an instant and then take her hand away.

"That is their way," he said smoothly. Lucas thought there might be irony there for those who fancied it. Or not, if not.

"The way of women," Sonia asked, "or of djinn?"

"Maybe of both," Rashid said. "But this is true in the West, is it not? The possessed have usually been women, isn't it so?"

"What if the djinn isn't a Muslim?" Lucas asked.

"Then it must be converted."

"I seem to remember hearing in Somalia," Sonia said, "about possessed women being beaten to death."

"Not here," Nuala said. "We don't allow that."

"In Somalia the djinns are beaten," Rashid said. "The women suffer by accident. But we don't beat djinns here because Ms. Rice will not allow it." He pronounced the trendy honorific *miz* humorously, self-consciously.

"Would you like to look around our setup?" Nuala asked.

"Yes," Lucas said. "Certainly."

"Why don't you go with Rashid?" Sonia said to Lucas. "I'll stay here and gossip with Nuala."

Rashid took Lucas back to the exorcists' tent and they stood and watched the process for a while. The mullahs and the waiting women ignored them.

"Usually reporters want pictures," Rashid said. "But you haven't a camera."

"I don't use one much."

"Good," said Rashid. "Because you would have to pay the exorcists. And the pictures have been misused in the West." They left the tent and walked out of the compound toward the camp outside. "Words are better, I think."

"For some things," said Lucas. "Tell me, what other religions are the djinn?"

"They may be pagans. They may be Christians or Jews. The Israelis send us many Jewish djinn. To bedevil us."

"What are *they* like?" Lucas asked.

"They are as in the novels of Mr. I. B. Singer," Rashid said as they turned into the street. "They are as represented there."

Back at the grand open-air table, Nuala poured Sonia more tea.

"It's all quite sanitary," Nuala said. "I hope Rashid makes that clear to him. We get them fresh IVs and antiseptic. It's the popular religion, you see. And the religion of the people — you have to go along with it."

"Is that what Rashid says?"

Nuala laughed. "Yes. And it's what Connolly said in 1916. And it's what's happening now, in Latin America."

"So Rashid is a secularist?"

"Rashid's like me," Nuala said. "He's a Communist."

Sonia began to laugh and wiped her eyes. "Jeez," she said, "you're breaking my heart."

"Does that sound so quaint, then?"

"It sounds a little quaint, yes. I mean, it makes my heart beat faster. But you know it's not on, don't you?"

Nuala looked glum.

"I mean, Jesus Christ, Nuala. You think they're gonna pray five times to the dialectic? You see the vanguard of the working class anywhere?" She looked up and down in a stylized manner. "You see the working class anywhere?"

"And you're religious yourself," Nuala said bitterly.

"I always have been," Sonia said.

"You'll never make much of a Muslim."

"I guess I'm not exactly a Muslim," Sonia said. "I guess I'm sort of a Jew." She thought she heard Nuala give a little gasp. "What's the matter with that?" she asked. "Don't you like Jews?"

"I haven't been granted the opportunity to know many socially," Nuala said, "in my field of endeavor."

"Well, you ought to start with someone other than Stanley," Sonia said. "Don't you think?"

Nuala said nothing.

"What are you doing, Nuala?"

"You mustn't ask me too much," Nuala said.

"What did you bring down in the van?"

"I'll have to explain it another time."

"Just because it's a United Nations van," Sonia told her, "doesn't mean it won't be searched. And whoever gets it for you will land in the shit. Like me."

"If there was time," Nuala said fiercely, "I'd have explained. And I will."

"Nuala, there are informers everywhere."

"Right," said Nuala. "So I have to trust you. Can I?"

"What was in the van?"

"Ah," said Nuala, "what do you think?"

"Guns."

"Yes, weapons. Weapons of defense for those who are defenseless."

"Why did you involve us in this?" Sonia asked. "Why did you involve Chris? And why me? I don't support killing no matter who does it."

"Keep your bloody voice down," Nuala said. Then she asked Sonia softly, "Is it wrong? Is that what you're telling me? We have to protect our children. We have to protect ourselves from fanatics, Muslim and Jewish both."

"I don't know," Sonia said.

"Well, bloody decide," Nuala told her. "Decide now and that's an end to it."

Sonia began to pace back and forth on the sand, numbering her fingers. She was half aware that it was exactly what her mother had done, pondering the purge of the Browderites and the Hungarian Revolt and Khrushchev's secret speech.

"It was wrong to deceive me. It was wrong to involve Chris."

"An unstable character," Nuala said.

"Maybe," Sonia conceded, still pacing. Then she stopped and slapped the back of one hand against her palm. "To get guns for Rashid's militia isn't necessarily wrong. But it could be a mistake."

"We're all that's left of the Communist movement here," Nuala declared. "If we're unarmed, if we're neutralized, the working class has no voice. With weapons we can police our camps and keep order. Without them we're helpless and the camps will be run by fanatics or the corrupt. This is the bloody Middle East, as your Israeli friends are always saying."

"I'm not taking part in armed struggle. I'm not saying it's wrong. Once I might have. But now I won't."

"Trying to be neutral, are you?"

"I may give it a shot," said Sonia. "Some kind of peace isn't impossible." She stood watching Nuala brush the dark disordered hair from her eyes. The Rebel Girl, she thought. Maybe I envy her. "Tell me this," she said. "If guns come in — what goes out?"

"Money," Nuala said. "Or dope. The Bedouin sometimes bring it in. Or it lands by boat."

"And ends up on the streets of Jaffa."

"Oh, don't give me that," Nuala said. "The Shin Bet connive with the dealers all the time. Here and in Lebanon. And we don't have the Soviet Union anymore."

"Right," said Sonia. "So what are me and my nice white UN van hauling today? Will there be a couple of kilos of kif under my ass while the boys point those Uzis at me?"

"Only Stanley's money," Nuala said. "I'll carry it."

"I won't do it again, Nuala."

"You won't say anything?"

"Think I'm a snitch?" She went over and put her arm around Nuala's shoulder. Well, she thought, that's the end of that. "Better be careful, baby."

"Just a little sedition and regicide," Nuala said, joking uneasily. "Christ, I was raised to it."

They walked back toward the camp.

"Know what the slaves used to say in Cuba?" Sonia asked her former friend as they went. "*Que tienen hacer, que hacer no morir.*"

"Meaning?"

"Meaning, What you gotta do is not die."

"Sound advice," Nuala said.

When Lucas returned from his tour with Rashid, he and Sonia and Nuala started back. On the way they saw fires burning in Nusei-rat and Eshaikh Ijleen. At the UN military beach club they stopped for a beer; both Sonia and Nuala were known there. The Danish officer they had seen in Gaza City the previous day was drinking beer alone at a table, watching the surf. He was boozy, sunburned and blond, and his rosy foreignness glowed like virtue itself. Lucas tried to buy him a beer, but he was too drunk to communicate.

Afterward they went to the fish restaurant to have dinner with the Palestinian lawyer named Majoub. Ernest Gross of Israeli Human Rights was with him, along with Linda Ericksen, who was still volunteering her time with the IHRC.

"Christ," Lucas asked Gross, "how the hell did you two get down here?"

"Usual way. We took a taxi from the checkpoint. Bloke knows me. Always use him."

"He is welcome," Majoub said. "Everyone knows him."

But in fact, Majoub was being polite. Ernest, pretty obviously an Israeli to the Palestinian eye, took a considered risk in coming to Gaza, especially late in the day. The lawyer Majoub was at some pains to engineer his comings and goings and his safety depended to some degree on Majoub's own influence in the community. Nor were Ernest's enemies all Palestinians, although any attacker would very likely be one. There were those who would savor the irony of such an attack.

"I want them to get used to seeing Linda," Ernest said, "so we're introducing her around."

"First time in the Strip?" Sonia asked pretty Linda.

"Well, I've been to some of the settlements," Linda told them. "Interviewing. But this is my first time in Gaza City."

"A somewhat different perspective," Lucas said.

"Yes," said Linda. "Of course, they could keep their own streets in better condition."

No one said anything for a while. Lucas sneaked a look at Majoub, who kept on eating and appeared not to have heard.

"Linda," Sonia said. "There's a water problem here. Also a military occupation problem. There aren't many sewers. People are living on forty cents a day."

"I'll bet white people say that in Harlem," Nuala said. "Eh, Sonia."

"They say something along the same lines," Sonia agreed. "Soweto too, I understand."

"We were in court today," Ernest said, "Majoub and I. Anyway, before the civil administrator."

"And as usual," said Majoub, "we lost. We always lose. I personally have never won a case."

"What was the case?" Nuala asked. She and Sonia had been quiet on the drive.

"We asked for a hearing on the confiscation of an ID," Ernest said. "A soldier took the man's card from him for whatever reason. No reason, says the man himself. He doesn't know the soldier's name or his unit. So he can't get to his job in Ashkelon."

"You came all the way down from Jerusalem for a hearing about an ID card?" Lucas asked.

"We had a lot to talk about," said Majoub. "Our report to Amnesty is due."

"Is overdue," Ernest said. "See any evidence of Abu Baraka?"

"Not particularly," said Lucas. "But I believe in him."

"We must all," Ernest said, "believe in Abu Baraka."

"Right," Sonia said, watching the port lights come on, an Israeli navy searchlight sweeping the old harbor. "Especially on an evening like this."

The shrimp was excellent. Everyone said it was a shame about the impossibility of beer or wine.

"One day," Majoub said, "we'll drive over to Alexandria. There one can still have wine."

"For the time being," said Sonia.

"Last ID case I had," Ernest said, "the poor bugger claimed a soldier ate it. Laughed out of court, right? But we asked around and what do you think?"

"Some smartass kid ate it?"

"You got it. Scarfed the thing, lamination and all. So the bloke loses his job."

"Funny," Nuala said without humor.

"Well, it is kind of funny," Lucas said, "in a dreadful sort of way."

"Funny," said Nuala, "unless it's you."

Lucas raised his glass in salute. "Someday," he proclaimed somberly, "somewhere, somehow — everything will be funny for everyone."

32

ONE DAY, with De Kuff and the others safely sequestered in Ein Kerem, Sonia was cleaning Berger's old apartment in the Muslim Quarter when two young men who claimed to represent the Waqf, the Islamic religious authority, arrived. Sonia offered them coffee, which they sternly declined. Both wore djellabas and white religious caps. One was short and dark-complexioned, the other sallow with a thin fringe of beard that served to frame his face. The pale one had large, expressive eyes and a prominent nose. Taken together, his features had a fey, slightly grotesque fascination. Sonia was immediately reminded of photographs she had seen of the young Frank Sinatra. She thought the man might have learned his antique English in India or Pakistan.

"Here was a madrasah," he explained to Sonia. "Here also lived al-Husseini, the beloved. And Sheikh Berger al-Tariq, of blessed memory, who was your friend. We thought you were as we are, a believer."

"We made allowances," said his companion, the dark one.

"We're here to learn," Sonia said. "To pray and to study. This is why I came. This is why I invited my friends."

"Which," asked the Sinatra-like man's companion, "is your husband?"

Before she could improvise a respectable answer, the man spoke again. "If you are here to study and to learn, you, the friend of the beloved Berger al-Tariq, then surely you must know that the study of studies, the end of learning, is Islam."

Everyone kept silent. The second man uttered a quick blessing.

"I have no husband," Sonia said. "I live without my family. I also loved Berger al-Tariq, whom I bless, but he was not my husband. I revere Islam and so do my friends."

The two men watched her for a moment.

"What is it," the dark man asked, "that the old man tells the Christians? Why do they crowd around him?"

"They even come here," the pale one said.

"He has had a vision," Sonia said. "He speaks to everyone. Not only to Christians."

"To Jews?"

"Yes."

"To believers?"

"He reveres all faiths. He adds nothing of his own. He encourages Muslim belief."

"But he is a Jew," said the man with the face like young Sinatra. "We are told this. And you," he said to Sonia. "You as well."

"Abdullah Walter was born a Jew. A great sheikh. The friend of al-Husseini. This was his house. I am his follower. My friends believe as I do."

"As the house of al-Husseini, it should be the property of the Waqf," said the dark man. "But it is owned by a Christian, an Armenian who follows the Pope of the Franks. And inhabited by Jews."

"To me it's Berger's house," Sonia told them. "Everything here honors him."

"The old man speaks before the Christian church that was the mosque of Salah ad-Din. We see him there."

"We think there is irreligion," said Frank Sinatra. "Irreligion in the house of al-Husseini. We also think the house will be taken by the Jews."

His voice was measured, but Sonia saw his faint tremble of rage and knew that the cause was lost. The Waqf was nominally a force for moderation, answerable to the Jordanians. But plainly there would soon be trouble.

When it grew dark, she turned on the electric light and began sorting through the things that she felt an absolute need not to abandon in the move. Much would have to be left behind, although she had done her best to disperse Berger's property among his relatives and taken what she could herself.

After nine, when it was completely dark, the telephone rang. She had been going through Berger's uncompleted writing projects, half listening to the singing and dancing from a bar mitzvah celebration that reverberated distantly across the massive network of stone steps and walls that divided her chamber in the old mufti's palace from the Kotel plaza.

"Hello?"

It was Chris Lucas, wanting to see her.

"Do you mind coming here, Chris? If you think it's not safe, I'll meet you somewhere else."

"Forty minutes," Lucas said. "I'll walk it."

He hung up before she could caution him not to come from the Kotel side. In fact, that was how he came, on the theory that if Lestrade could use the old Cardo road, so could he.

The African boys were gathered around a lamp in the courtyard as he went up the stairs. One of them had a Game Boy in his hand.

"Were you followed?" she asked him.

"No more than usual," he said. He had never thought of himself as being followed in the city.

"This may be our last evening here, Chris."

She told him about the visit from the Waqf and that she thought it would no longer be possible to stay.

"I should have brought some champagne," Lucas said. "To cultivate beautiful memories."

"I'll have memories, all right." Then, from the way she looked at him, he thought she had grown angry with him. "I had a fantasy. I thought of us living here."

"You mean you and your growing band of pilgrims? Dangerous work, Sonia. And a little overcrowded."

"I meant you and me, Chris. The two of us. When things come to pass."

"Oh," he said, "you mean in the Age of Miracles. The New Order of Ages. Like it says on the money."

"Don't laugh at my fantasies," she said. "Not if you want to be in them."

He reached out and drew her to him and kissed her. "I'm not in a position to laugh," he said. He ran his hands over her and held her close, unwilling to let her go. He felt hopeless and desperate, as though there were no way to keep her. "I would if I could."

"Holy shit," she said. "Must be love."

"That's how I see it," Lucas said.

She stood facing him and rested her hands on the front of his shoulders, his collarbone, and patted a rhythm. "Chris," she said, "the Rev doesn't even want me to see you."

"The hell with him, then."

"At least that's what Raziel said. He says the Rev feels that if you won't wait with us, you don't deserve our company."

"If I won't sing alleluia, I don't get a pomegranate. And naturally you let these people control your life."

"It's how religious communities sometimes work. If I were part of a Sufi community in New York, it would be the same."

"Hey," Lucas said, "if you'll actually come with me, I'll join up. I'll play the tambourine, dress as Santa Claus, eat with my hat on, you name it. But I have conditions too."

"Such as?"

"Such as you've got to sing for me sometimes. And I get to keep working on the book. When it's done we go back to New York."

"I don't want you to pretend to believe, Chris. I want you to open yourself. Then we can be together. Really."

"Ah, Sonia," Lucas said. He laughed and ran a hand through his thinning hair. "What are we going to do? Because I really do love you. Maybe," he said, "we better take it by the day."

She slid away when he tried to embrace her.

"I think we both have empty places in our lives, Chris. Don't you agree with that?"

"I thought we could help each other with that."

"I do too. I do. But there's more to things than you and me."

"I'm not used to believing too many things before breakfast, Sonia. That's the difference between you and me."

"But you were religious. You told me."

"I was a child. I also believed in the tooth fairy."

"I wish I could hold you down and whup you," Sonia said. "And when I let you up, you'd see."

Lucas sat down on Berger's stained, carpeted bed and poured himself a glass of the late master's plum brandy.

"Let's hear it from you, then, Sister Sonia. How does it look to you? What's happening? What must I do to be saved?"

"It's simple," Sonia said. "Well, OK, it's not simple. But we've just had the twentieth century, right? We tried everything. Philosophy. Making life into art. Everything got further and further from how it was supposed to be."

"You mean there was a plan the whole time? Everything was supposed to be a lot better? Someone obviously fucked up on a major scale."

"Yes. We did. Sure there was a plan. Why else is there something rather than nothing?"

"Because it happened that way."

"Some things are better than others," Sonia said. "Some things make you feel good, some don't. Don't tell me you've got a problem with that."

"Not me."

"What makes you feel good is being closer to the way things were first created. They were created as God's word. He stepped aside and made a place for them and for us. The secret of that is in Torah, in the words themselves, not just in what they mean."

"A lot of people believe that," Lucas said. "It doesn't have to come between us."

"Over the years a man comes to speak the words of Torah and change our lives to the way they were meant to be. Moses came. Jesus. Sabbatai Zevi. Others too. Now it's De Kuff."

"Oh, come on," Lucas said. "De Kuff is just a manic depressive. He's manipulated by Raziel."

"No, baby. Raziel only found him. The ones like De Kuff are always men of great suffering. Always despised. Always struggling."

"So what now?"

"Now, the Rev has to struggle like Jesus on the cross. The prophets say that his struggle takes the form of a war, but it's a war without weapons. When it's over, it's like we'll be home. The whole world will be home. My parents knew that. They just didn't know how it was done."

"I'm not telling you you can't believe that, Sonia. I just want to be with you."

"But first they need me here, baby. To bear witness."

Eventually, he coaxed her to him.

"We'll take it by the day," he said. "If you need me, I'll be here."

"You still think I'm crazy," she said.

"I don't know what's crazy and what's not. I'll tell you what," he said. "I'll listen to the Rev if you go talk to Obermann. Try looking at things his way."

"Obermann?" She laughed at him. "Obermann is just a cheap

seducer. The biggest cocksman in town. What am I going to learn from him, other than the obvious?"

"Well, he's a Jungian," Lucas suggested meekly. "Anyway, this is the city of seduction. Everyone's pitching."

"And meanwhile the two of you write your book?"

"It won't spoil the process, will it?"

"I don't know."

"Anyway, the book might turn out very differently from the way I expected," Lucas said. "I might end up seeing things your way."

"You're bribing me with hope."

"I'm bribing myself. I'm trying to keep my own hopes up."

And that was it, he thought. It was all a series of rooms one never found one's way out of. You had to be content with that, or die, or go completely crazy.

They had just gotten into bed when the door opened to a key and a dark young woman dressed like an American entered the apartment. Someone they could not see followed behind her.

"What a pleasant place," she said. "How very nice."

When she came upon them in the bedroom she betrayed no embarrassment whatsoever. She had a bright, unfriendly smile.

"How about this?" she said to someone in the next room. "The grand mufti's very own digs. La-di-dah."

"Just a little portion of them," Lucas said. "Would you mind telling me who you are and what you're doing here?"

The person with the woman was a young man who wore chinos and a kippa and carried an automatic rifle.

"We're prospective tenants," he explained. "We're interested in the apartment." He had the same smile as the woman. "We have a use for the premises and we wanted to get a jump on the competition. Just look around before you give it back to your Arab friends. Or your Christian-Hebrew, Hebrew-Christian friends. Or whatever they are."

"Next time," Lucas said, "make an appointment."

"Next time," the young man said, "you won't be here, smart guy."

They really did look a lot alike, Lucas thought. They might have been brother and sister.

The woman wandered around, writing in a notebook as if she were taking inventory.

"Great place," she said again, leaning into the bedroom again with her unpleasant smile. "Thank you so much for letting us see it."

"Yeah," said the young man as they went out, "thanks a million, kids. Have fun."

From the sounds on the stairs outside, there were other people with them. It had been a reconnaissance in force.

"Obviously," Sonia said, "we're sitting on some prime real estate."

"I have the feeling," Lucas said, "that it's just been priced out of our range."

"I guess we don't want to be here," Sonia said, turning on her stomach, "when the Waqf and those people start fighting it out over the place. Poor Mardikian. I wonder if he'll get his price."

"He'll probably be leaving town," Lucas said. He reached up and turned off the old-fashioned beaded lamp. "Anyhow, 'sufficient unto the day is the evil thereof.'"

But it was not as simple as that. Somehow, in spite of the force of his passion, he could not make love to Sonia. It was what he had wanted more than anything, and now he found it beyond him. To be sure, there were a thousand exculpatory reasons. The confusions between them, the peculiar midnight raid. A man could be forgiven. But for some reason, Sonia took it badly. She wept and punched him and hid herself beneath the pillow. He got out of bed and started getting dressed to leave.

"No, no, please," she said. "Please don't do that. I don't know what's got into me."

"I'm sorry. This happens to me sometimes."

"It's because of things . . ."

"I guess it is. Those two characters. The whole mess."

"No, no," she said. "It's exactly like everything else. What the Rev said about us is true. It's impossible."

An icy liquor of despair froze Lucas's heart. He felt at once panic-stricken and childishly disappointed. His childhood disappointments had been painful.

"Ah, baby," he said, "it's just the fuckupedness of things. It doesn't mean anything."

"Yes it does," she said. "It's standing in the way of the Rev's struggle."

"Oh, Christ," Lucas said.

But she would not answer. Finally she said, "It can't happen yet. Maybe it can never happen. I don't know. I shouldn't see you."

"I want to see you," Lucas said. "Any way you want it."

"I don't know," she said. "I just don't."

Lucas went and got the bottle of plum brandy and put it beside him on the floor and drank until the first call to prayer sounded.

33

LUCAS WENT HOME through the early morning markets, by way of Jaffa Gate. In the middle of the morning he called Sonia.

"I don't think we should see each other," she told him. "I think it will turn out the same way every time."

Lucas held the phone against his chest to reject her message. Eight stories below him, an occasional vehicle sped headlong through the half-deserted streets. He felt like crying out in shame and pain. She was out of her mind, in the clutches of lunatics, and he was not man enough to save her.

"I need to know how you are," he said. "And where you are."

"For your book, you mean?"

"Yes," he said bitterly. "For my book."

"Well," she said, "I'll try to keep in touch."

"You should be seeing Obermann," Lucas said.

"No thanks. But maybe you should."

When he did see Obermann, with a selective report of what was happening, Obermann told him she was being manipulated.

"By Melker," the doctor opined. "He's a sly one. He wants her for his acolyte. Don't give up."

"I've got to take a break from them," Lucas said. "I've never felt so wretched in my life."

Obermann gave him a prescription for Prozac. "Keep working," the doctor advised him. It was sound, if self-serving, advice.

So Lucas kept working on the book, read Scholem's history of Sabbatai, read in the *Zohar* and about Jacob Frank's orgiastic rituals. Every few days he left a message on Sonia's answering machine. Then, during the last week of summer, he got a call from an American magazine asking him to report on a conference in Cyprus. The theme of the conference was "Religious Minorities in the Middle East."

He desperately needed a break from Jerusalem and its syndromes, in spite of the fact that the De Kuff story continued to unfold most interestingly. The old man was becoming a well-known figure in the city, and his statements were more and more provocative. The number of his followers was growing.

The police prevented him from holding forth in the Old City now, and he had been banned from the space in front of St. Anne's. He held some meetings in New City parks, billing them as concerts. At each gathering De Kuff and Raziel played Sephardic music.

Walking through Yemin Moshe the night before his departure for Cyprus, Lucas had an English-language flyer for that evening's session pressed into his hand by a young man he had never seen before. The advertisement was accompanied by something like program notes, which Lucas guessed had been written by Raziel Melker.

"If all art aspires to the condition of music," the flyer said, "so all true music aspires to *tikkun* and reverently reflects the process of *tsimtsum* and of *shevirah*."

The English text rendered the Hebrew words in the original, but Lucas had learned enough to recognize them. *Tsimtsum:* the expansion and contraction of the divine entity, like an anemone in the cosmic tidal pool, or the pool itself. *Shevirah:* the process underlying creation, the breaking of the vessels designed to contain the divine essence, the result of man's failure. And *tikkun:* the righting of things, the end of exile for God and man.

The strange announcement filled him with sadness and longing. It was definitely, he thought, time to leave town for a while.

Instead of flying from Lod to Larnaca, he took the bus to Haifa and then a slow, stinking ferry to Limassol. Amid unwashed backpacking Teutons, he read the conference's handout. It was written in a Gallicized translator's English.

"The opportunity is foreseen," it said, "for interventions and discourses illuminating the actual situations confronting the minorities of the region."

Droll, thought Lucas, and filed the thing away for use in his piece. The night was moonlit, and waves lapped against the rusting bow. The Teutons smoked hash and drank arak, sang, got sick, hallucinated, smoked more.

"Groovy shit," they shouted through their tears.

So it went until morning, when they were off Limassol. Aphrodite's maiden landfall was an ugly line of pastel hotels under a whited-out sky. The goddess was still big there; her scallop shell and cestus — not to mention her naked Olympian behind — were featured in many hotel and restaurant motifs. Goons in shades watched the ferry landing, but it was nice to have a break from strict monotheism.

Along the marine parade he saw beet-red, short-haired English youths — airmen from the base outside town. They reminded him of the seconded British junior officers who had commanded Caribbean troops during the Grenada invasion — off the record, of course, and on the sly. The British had not even bothered to deny the reports in his Grenada book, probably because they had never heard of them. By late afternoon, a minibus had conducted him to the hotel near Larnaca where the press was being put up and he was on his tiny, brittle balcony, sniffing iodine and sewage, regarding the wine-dark sea.

The conference had been bruited about for years, its proposed venue forever shifting to accommodate the high-beam scrutiny of eager assassins and nervous secret policemen. Originally planned for Cairo, it had been rescheduled for Malta, then Antalya in Turkey, then Izmir, then finally — to the fury of the Turks — to Greek Cyprus. Its sessions took place in a drab retreat above the Stavrovouni Monastery, overlooking the Larnaca–Limassol road. Still, the pine- and olive-covered slopes were pretty, and it was possible to see the blue ocean far below.

Minorities in the Middle East — the whole notion, Lucas considered, was so fraught with ironies as to render the topic laughable in a ghastly way. The ironies were unsubtle: poison gas, vultures puking on rooftops, car bombs.

Nevertheless, some right-minded hustler had put the unlikely thing together. Everyone loved a junket, and there were airline and hotel kickbacks to be had, and Cyprus afforded a few licks — girls, booze, a break for the God-fearing, though they would have preferred Geneva.

So an assemblage of various savants was scheduled to convene the next day at the Stavrovouni Palace, apparently the only building on the island not dedicated to Aphrodite and convenient to a fragment of the True Cross.

They were predominantly elderly, Frenchified or Anglophilic intellectuals, but some were men of courage. A few actually represented minorities. There would also be mistresses, Lucas assumed, informers, spies and double agents, dealers in pursuit of bland cover and professional government apologists. Some of these latter would have packed suitcases full of hard currency, their life's acquisitions, to be opened only in Switzerland, behind double-locked doors in their suites at the Beau Rivage. There, beside the *lac,* they hoped to shake the sands of the desert from their pointy Italian shoes forever — if only they could make it out of Cyprus alive.

The Stavrovouni had closed its lobby bars in deference to religious sensibilities, but its terrace café served beer and wine. After the first session, Lucas became a regular.

The first meeting was the customary tower of babble — the droning of professors, recitations of Arab poetry, attacks against imperialism and its agents, who were responsible for transforming the peaceable kingdoms of the East into places of distress. Each local tradition was declared to be more tolerant than the next. Perfidious Albion was anathematized, also the Pentagon, along with the Elders of Zion. The translators, more used to corporate negotiations, lost their way in the meaningless courtesies and compliments and tropes.

That evening in the café, above the bright, sour sea, Lucas found himself dining with a scented old professor, representative of some antinomian sect from the Caucasus. Gnostic? Sabean? Hashishian? In any case, the old man drank wine. They shared a bottle of retsina.

"The minority situation in the United States is well known," the old professor declared. "But we in the Middle East, unlike you, have never had slaves."

"Really?"

"Servitude in our part of the world was never opprobrious. Rather, it was benign."

Lucas had been drinking for a while.

"Someone," he said, "once told me that at Darfur there was a house where African children were castrated for service as eunuchs."

The old boy shrugged patiently.

"I mean, not just a lean-to, you understand," Lucas continued, "but a huge fucking warehouse where they processed kids. And for every kid that survived the operation, fifty died. But the place still made money."

"A practice adopted from the Byzantines," said the scholar.

"Maybe, maybe not. Or else adopted like crazy," Lucas said. "Like it was the greatest thing since sliced bread. If you'll pardon the expression. And they worked half of Africa. Coptic monks specialized in the operation. And dervishes. Regional minorities. Probably had to get by somehow, what do you think?"

And he went on about it.

"Who do you think you are?" asked the dignified old man at last.

"Ah," said Lucas, "you got me there, fella."

At the next sessions and in the corridors he was whispered about as a representative of the CIA. He thought it reflected badly on the agency.

On his third night there, with the translator-deconstructed prattle ringing in his ears, he fastened on a piece of wisdom: foolish, drunken, insolent behavior did not play in the Fertile Crescent, and he was out of control. There was even a phone in the room to get him in further trouble. Moreover, he already had what he needed for the piece.

At the airlines office he found the flights to Lod and Haifa booked and decided to endure the ferry once more. In Limassol, he was killing time, strolling the streets of the waterfront, when, rounding a corner near the Lusignan Castle, he encountered Nuala Rice. When he stopped she simply walked around him. Not a glance, instant incognito.

Walking on, he wished he had been cooler and not stopped at all. Even better would have been not to have met her. Turning at the next intersection, past chips shops and signs for Wall's ice cream, he saw that the street ended at the landing where the hydrofoil to Beirut was tied up.

Might Nuala have been coming from Beirut? It was on her map of adventure. An Irish girl, alone, with the right connections would have no reason to stay away. If she had business there.

Then, on the Haifa ferry, he saw Rashid, her friend from Gaza. Nuala was nowhere in sight. He and Rashid avidly avoided each other, but Lucas was puzzled. Shin Bet or Mossad, or both, surely had agents in Limassol, and in Beirut for that matter. Surely the ferry was watched. It was such a small world and there were too many secrets.

Late that night, he got himself into a pocket hotel in the lower city of Haifa and looked over his conference notes until they disgusted him. Then he had recourse to the Bible, idly checking notions. Somewhere in the night, not far from his open window, Deadheads dwelled. He heard "Box of Rain," "Friend of the Devil," "Sugar Magnolia." The album, *American Beauty,* was twenty-two years old now. He had been living on East Fourth Street with a woman who went to graduate school at NYU.

Psalm 102, the one with a sparrow in it, was mournful stuff and even carried a warning preface: "A prayer of the afflicted, when he is overwhelmed, and poureth out his complaint before the Lord."

"I am like a pelican of the wilderness: I am like an owl of the desert. . . . I watch, and am as a sparrow alone upon the housetop."

Lucas felt suitably afflicted and ready to pour out his complaint, had there been anyone around to drink it with. The hypocrisy and shallowness of his Cyprus encounters throbbed against his nerves like an impending toothache.

During the night, two things occurred to him that could be looked into from Haifa, which might or might not cap the minority story. One was the headquarters of the Baha'i, on the slopes of Mount Carmel, and the other was Father Jonas Herzog, a man of French-Jewish origin who had applied for and been denied Israeli citizenship under the Law of Return. He lived and worked in a Benedictine monastery up above town.

Just after sunrise, Lucas took the funicular railroad to the uppermost level and strolled toward the Persian domes of the Baha'i sanctuary. There was dew on the olive trees and riotous bougainvillea. Doves lowed on the whitewashed walls, and below the sea sparkled.

The world in the morning, he thought. So encouraging. Despair was foolishness. But he was foolish.

There was a touch of self-conscious Orientalism about the Baha'i holy place and the tomb of the Bab. "Orientalism" had been a word much invoked at the Cyprus conference. Obviously this place was meant to suggest the great Shia shrines of Persia. Why not, since just beyond normative Shiism lurked the Aryan speculation, the paradoxical symbols, the universalist urge that had sometimes burst forth in heresy.

The oneness of God and the brotherhood of man — such liberation in that reduction! You had to wonder what it had felt like to be the Bab, to see it all converge. A thousand years before him, the Karaite Jew Abu Issa al-Isfahani, another Persian, had argued for the resolution of monotheism, Moses, Jesus, Muhammad. And with them, of course, al-Isfahani himself. With a little imagination it could all be made to connect with De Kuff.

He took off his shoes and went into the martyr's tomb, accompanied by an attendant. The silence, the dimness, the streaming light — a touch of Isfahan, a touch of Forest Lawn.

The attendant was an American black in a blue polyester suit who had what looked like a razor scar on his face. Maybe he had done hard time, Lucas thought, got religion in the slammer. He spoke pleasantly and well, with a southern intonation, reciting the story of the Bab, the history of the faith. Lucas paid more attention to his voice than to his words.

"Peace, brother," the man said when Lucas made his contribution and was leaving.

A fierce dude. Peace was worth nothing to those who had never known war. On this man's lips it sounded green and golden. Nothing was free.

"And to you, peace," Lucas said.

Maybe the Baha'is had some dark, crazy side, he thought, walking down the hill. Intrigues over power and money, cultish connivings. But on such a pleasant morning it was nice to imagine there was nothing like that. He walked the winding residential streets of the upper city to the lower reaches of town and sat at a café to watch the water. In the afternoon, he telephoned the Benedictines to ask if he might have an interview with Father Jonas Herzog. The monk on the phone informed him that Father Jonas no longer gave interviews.

"It wouldn't necessarily be an interview," Lucas said. "I'd just ask him to comment on a recent conference. And," he added, "I have a few personal questions."

The monk, sounding dubious, replied that Friday was a busy day for Father Jonas, who had administrative duties and had in addition to hear confessions. Lucas thanked him and resolved to try confession.

The monastery church stood among poplars, half a mile's distance from the Baha'i shrine but out of sight of it. It was not particularly old: a Neo-Romanesque structure looking a little like St.-Germain-des-Prés and representing another concession to the French by the Ottomans. A busy road ran past it, on which traffic slackened only slightly with the advent of Shabbat. Haifa was a mixed and generally secular city.

A Palestinian in a patched cassock, standing just inside the doorway, politely asked Lucas his business.

"Just thought I'd pop in," he said.

That seemed to do it. He had not been able to bring himself to ask the hours of confession, but once inside, he saw he was on time. Lines of Palestinian teenagers in family groups stood against both walls of the church, waiting for their turns in the confessional, boys to the right, girls to the left. Priests were identified by plastic strips on their confessional doors, which stated their names and the languages they commanded: Father Bakenhuis, who received penitents in Dutch, French, German and Arabic; Father Leclerc, who advised in French and Arabic; Father Waqba, who understood French, English, Arabic and Coptic.

Jonas Herzog's booth was halfway to the altar on the right hand side, but none of the kids were waiting for him. There was no strip on his door and the booth was empty. A queue of assorted foreigners stood nearby along the wall. Lucas turned to the sextant.

"What language does Father Jonas speak?" Lucas asked.

"All languages," the sexton replied.

Like the devil himself, Lucas thought, and took a seat in an adjoining pew. Ancient the place might not be, but it had the smell of cool old stone, incense and mortifications.

Then the man entered who must be Herzog. Lucas had read that he was sixty, though he looked even older. Out of the splendor of the Holy Land's light he came, and into the gloom of apostasy, genuflecting before the sacrament, bowing to the cross. He appeared cramped and stooped in his black and white Benedictine habit.

Herzog carried his own strip and hung it on the confessional door. It displayed his name in Hebrew characters, along with the Arabic and roman. Yonah Herzog–Jonas Herzog, OSB.

One waited long for Herzog. When the last penitent had gone and Lucas got to his feet, he was preempted by the sudden arrival of a young European woman. She was simply dressed, a pretty blonde in a white sundress and a cotton sweater that covered her shoulders. She wore a white scarf over her fair hair. German? She appeared somewhat distraught.

She looked married, Lucas decided, a young matron, a vice consul's unfaithful wife or an unfaithful vice consul. There were so many ways to be unfaithful in this place, so many unforgivable couplings and covenants to betray. Sleeping with a married colleague, or a dashing Palestinian guerrilla like Rashid, or her Shin Bet control. She would naturally go to Herzog, who knew the price of betrayal and its fascinations.

Her confession went on for a long time. Lucas could hear it only as a murmur in what sounded like French. Then the young woman came out and walked to the altar to say her penance in the ancient way.

Lucas rose, his stomach in a knot as though he were a child again, and went into the darkness and knelt alone with the crucifix. Then Father Herzog's sliding window opened. He could see the man's keen profile and the glint of steel-rimmed glasses in the semi-darkness. Suddenly he had no idea where to begin. Although he had no intention of confessing, he tried to remember the formula for confession in French.

"It is twenty-five years since my last confession," he heard himself say.

"Twenty-five years?" asked Father Herzog, with only the faintest surprise. "And you want to confess now?"

Lucas had to try and puzzle out the French and then the nature of the question.

"Are you guilty of a crime?" the priest asked.

Un crime. It made him think of Balzac.

"No, Father. No great crime. As they go."

"Preparing to receive the sacraments?"

To which the only right answer was yes. But instead Lucas said, in English, "No. But I wanted to talk with you."

"I, in my person, am not at your service," the priest said in English. "I'm here as a priest."

"I have questions of a religious nature."

"I have only the sacraments to offer you," the priest said. "And only if you are a baptized person."

"I am," Lucas said, "and also . . . like yourself . . . of mixed background."

Herzog sighed.

"If you could give a few minutes," Lucas said, "I think it would help me. I could wait. We could make an appointment."

"Are you a journalist?"

"I happen to be a journalist," Lucas said. "Yes."

"And your topic is religion?"

"War, mainly."

"Since the court's decision, I no longer give interviews."

"Then I won't ask you for one," Lucas said. "Only for advice. In private. Off the record."

"Do you want to hurt me?" Herzog asked, almost humorously.

"No."

"I see. Well, I have to ask. If you can wait, I can see you after confessions."

"Yes," Lucas said, "I'll wait."

So he left the booth, like a good child, and sat in the same pew he had occupied before. The process was infantile, but there was no way around it.

The young blond woman was still at the rail saying her penance, and he envied her the prayers. When she went out, crossing herself, he wanted to follow her. He wanted her faith and her secrets, her life. He felt altogether alone.

No one else went to Father Herzog for confession. Lucas fell asleep in the pew and awoke in an empty church with the priest in the aisle looking down at him. The light in the doorway had faded.

"Sorry," Lucas said.

"*Bien.*"

"Should we go somewhere?"

The priest sat down beside him.

"Here will do. If it's all right."

He seemed very French, courtly, ironic.

"Sure," said Lucas, and moved away slightly.

"You mentioned a mixed background. Is this a problem for you?"

"I was Catholic," Lucas said. "I believed. I should understand faith but I can't remember it."

Herzog gave the faintest shrug. "One day it may occur to you."

"I feel tempted by it," Lucas said. "But I can't quite recall how it goes."

It was not at all what he had intended to say. He had cornered himself with his own interviewing strategy. Sometimes, an editor had told him once, you have to tell them the story of your life. But this was beyond that, out of control again.

"Then you have to pray."

"I find prayer absurd," Lucas said. "Don't you?"

"It's childish to pray like a child," Herzog said, "if you're not one."

"Tell me about being Jewish," Lucas demanded. "Does it have a spiritual dimension?"

" 'There is neither Jew nor Greek,' " Father Herzog quoted for him, " 'there is neither bond nor free, there is neither male nor female; for ye are all one in Christ Jesus.' "

"I know that," Lucas said. "But Jewishness must mean something. It's always been the conduit between humanity and God."

"What Paul is telling us," Herzog said, "is that we are alone with God. Which does not mean we have no responsibility to man. Our moral landscape is human. But finally we are all individual men and women, waiting for grace.

"We cannot make our condition less lonely. You ask me why God revealed himself through the Jews? I suppose we could find social and historical reasons. But the fact is, we don't know why."

"Do you feel as though you were a Jew?" Lucas asked.

"Yes," said the priest. "And you?"

Lucas thought about it at length. "I don't think so."

"Good," said Herzog, "because you aren't one. You're an American, are you not?"

Lucas felt dismissed. Being an American, he felt like telling Herzog, does not necessarily make my condition more trivial. "But I feel," he said, "that part of me has lived before."

After a moment, Herzog said, "Not everything we feel is revelation."

Embarrassed, Lucas prepared to risk humiliation. Working press, he thought. He had a card; he could go anywhere, say anything. Their voices echoed off the stone.

"In the Kabbalist rabbis," he told the priest, "I find the greatest interpretations of life and truth I've ever heard. And I find it brings me back to religious feelings I haven't had since . . ."

"Since childhood?"

"Well, yes. And I wonder if these aren't things I've always known. I mean always."

"First time in Israel? You can choose to be Jewish. It can be arranged. Not by me, unfortunately."

"I understand the one in terms of the other," Lucas said.

"I suggest you not tell a rabbi you're so moved by books you cannot possibly understand in a language you don't read. He'll throw you out of his study."

"Is it true," Lucas asked, "that we have to lose one life to gain another?"

"Unfortunately," said the priest.

"But you claim to go on being Jewish."

"Because I am. That is my condition. My problem, my means of grace."

"What about me?"

"What about you? You're one American in a world of poverty and pain. What more do you want?"

"To believe. Sometimes."

"Look," Herzog said, "all I can tell you honestly is what any priest — the most bigoted, the least enlightened — could tell you. Trust in God. Try to pray. Try to believe and perhaps you will believe. If you seek God, some say, you've found him."

So they sat in silence for a little while and Herzog cleared his throat and was about to go.

"As a journalist," Lucas said, "as something we call background, not for attribution — what did you tell the court?"

The priest put his hands on the bench in front of them. "That in Israel I had the right to Jewish nationality. No more."

"That was . . . intrepid. Because you must have known you would disgust them."

"Yes, of course," the old priest said. "A *melamed*. And the Jew turned monk is an old enemy. The bad son, the evil child, the avenger who denounced the Jews and set off public disputations and the burning of the Talmud. Of the Kabbala, for which you have a fondness."

"Wasn't it what you expected?" Or wanted, Lucas thought.

"I failed to make my case."

"When I read about your case," Lucas said, "I thought about Simone Weil. What she would have done."

"Ah, yes," said Herzog.

But, Lucas thought, he knew what Simone Weil would have done. She would have gone to Gaza and lived there, outraging everyone.

"She refused baptism," Lucas said, "so in a way she remained Jewish. Is there a place for her in the world to come?"

"Yes, as a saint," Herzog said. "There was no place for her here."

"Too bad," Lucas said, "we don't have bodhisattvas in our religion. Whatever it is."

Herzog walked with him to the door.

"I'm sorry I can't help you, sir. But as you see, I can't. I can't give you a faith with bodhisattvas and the Kabbala and Our Lord. No doubt in America there is one."

They stood beside the crucifix over the holy-water font beside the door.

"And the Kabbala," Herzog said, "is indeed beautiful. In the end, the Christians took to it themselves. Reuchlin and Pico and the Spaniards, even under the Inquisition. One day, if you have the discipline, you may understand it and it may help you."

"Why did you come here?" Lucas asked the priest. "Why did you go to court?"

"Because it's holy. And to pray for my parents in their own land. Although they were not religious."

"They'd turn over in their graves," Lucas said.

"They have no graves."

"Sorry," said Lucas. "Is it true you were hidden in a Catholic school?"

"In Vence," said Herzog. "My parents left me under a crucifix. And I asked them, my parents, 'What happened to him?' I meant the man on the cross, the Christ figure. I was then ten years of age and had no idea what a crucifix was. We lived in Paris. After the liberation I was not yet fourteen. The prefect told me who I was. That I was a Jew. That my parents, my family, had been delivered to the Germans and murdered by them. And I felt — what can I say — a recognition."

"But you couldn't leave the Church?"

"Oh," Herzog said with a little shrug, "I didn't care much about the Church. The Church was men, people. Some good, some not." He looked at the floor.

"Then why?"

"Because I was waiting," said Herzog. "Waiting where I had been left. At the foot of the cross. Out of spite or devotion, I don't know." He laughed and put a hand on Lucas's shoulder. "Pascal says we understand nothing until we understand the principle from which it proceeds. Don't you agree? So I understand very little."

"We're supposed to believe that Christ has gone on to reign in glory," Lucas said.

"No," said Herzog. "Jesus Christ suffers from now until the end.

On the cross. He goes on suffering. Until the death of the last human being."

"And that," Lucas said, "brings you here?"

"Yes," said Herzog. "To attend. To keep on waiting."

From the steps of the church, the evening smelled of car exhaust and jasmine.

"I realize that in this kind of world," Lucas said, "I have no business being so unhappy. I realize also that on a religious level I'll always be a child. It's absurd and I regret it."

For the first time Herzog smiled.

"Don't regret it, sir. Perhaps you know Malraux's *Anti-mémoires*? His priest tells us that people are much more unhappy than one might think." He offered Lucas his hand. "And that there is no such thing as a grownup."

34

A S HAD BEEN the case at Safed, various God-struck and
otherwise intoxicated drifters came and went at their bungalow in Ein Kerem. One who stayed was a Dutch former
nun named Maria van Witte, who in the religious life had been
called Sister John Nepomuk. Often about were two long-armed,
slack-jawed brothers from Slovakia whose names were Horst and
Charlie Walsing. Lucas had thought they were Germans, but they
turned out to be Jewish — German-Jewish Hungarians. One was a
musician, apparently of some reputation; the other seemed mentally
retarded or autistic. In spite of the difference in their cerebral com-
petence they appeared virtually indistinguishable, although no one
in De Kuff's circle had any particular reason to distinguish between
them. Oddly, Ian Fotheringill, the author of kosher *sauce l'ancienne,*
also appeared from time to time. Occasionally Helen Henderson,
the Rose of Saskatoon, came with Sonia. Her background had been
Pentecostal, but it was entirely devotion to Sonia that brought her.

Veterans of alien abduction, reincarnated priests of Isis, putative
pals of the Dalai Lama, all put in an appearance, lounging under the
garden tamarisks in Ein Kerem.

Among the more memorable visitors were a father and son named
Marshall. The father seemed anywhere between sixty and eighty, the
son about the same age. Although Jewish, the elder Marshall knew
long passages of the New Testament by heart. When the Marshalls were around, private detectives stopped by the place, inquiring after them. Marshall the younger had taken over all family
financial transactions, and indeed all numerical calculations of any
kind, since his father, a Kabbalist, was obsessed with numbers. Lucas, who was there almost every other day, heard from Obermann

that Marshall Senior was some kind of criminal, wanted in America, who had either gone insane or was pretending to have done so.

De Kuff paid attention to no one except Raziel and Sonia, and Raziel let anyone who showed up at Ein Kerem stay at De Kuff's expense.

One evening, all of these figures and many more gathered in a nearby garden, owned by the Sisters of Notre-Dame-de-Liesse, for what was advertised as a concert.

The afternoon before the concert, Sonia went over from Rehavia and found Raziel meditating behind his dark glasses in the bungalow garden. Not wanting to disturb him, she took a seat in the shade of the wall, under an olive tree.

"Big night," Raziel said after a moment.

"Is it?"

"You're going to sing for us."

"Wait a minute, Jim," Sonia said. "Who says?"

"The Rev says you have to sing."

"Uh-huh. Do I get scale?"

"Take no thought for the morrow," Raziel said, his eyes still closed.

"Standards in order? Rogers and Hart?"

"The Rev wants Ladino songs. He wants 'Meliselda.' "

"Razz," she said, "don't be saying 'the Rev wants.' It's what *you* want. I know that. And I don't speak Ladino."

"So fake it," he said. "Make it olde Spanishee."

"You're bad," she said. "I don't know about you."

"It's a big night," Raziel said, sitting up. "Really it is. Because it's not just a concert. It's the night he preaches the mystery. The fourth one."

"I thought he'd do that in Bethesda."

"It's too dangerous. It'll be dangerous enough here."

"What is the fourth mystery?"

"Come on, Sonia. You know."

"If the first is 'Everything is Torah,' and the second is 'The time to come is at hand,' and the third is 'the Death of the Kiss,' what's the fourth?"

"You know it as well as I do. And he hasn't told me either. Anyway, it's something you already believe."

"All right," she said. "Let's see the songs you want."

*

That night Lucas went to Ein Kerem with Obermann. He had finished his Cyprus conference piece, writing on khat. He was tired and depressed.

"He's been mixing his message with music lately," Obermann said of De Kuff. They parked on a side street near the concert site. The small Arab village of Ein Kerem had been enveloped by Jerusalem and transformed into a kind of far-flung, dry-land Sausalito. By dusk, the smog sometimes drifted off and the evenings were again herb-scented. "His crowds have grown very numerous. He's an attraction."

"I used to see him at Bethesda," Lucas said. "What does he do now?"

"He casts his spells. His Neoplatonic version of Torah. Kabbalistic mysticism. He has a good voice. And the music can be wonderful."

"Aren't there complaints?"

"Complaints. Hecklers. One day he'll probably go too far. You know, they never seem to pass the hat. I wonder where he gets his financing."

"It's his own money," Lucas said. "Apparently he owns a chunk of Louisiana."

As usual, there was no charge for the concert. In the garden at Notre-Dame-de-Liesse, a makeshift stage and an acoustic shell had been set up among the cedars. Rows of wooden planks lined the opposing slope, on which spectators might seat themselves in reasonable comfort if they brought cushions and were careful of splinters. There were no enclosing walls, so as many people as cared to might gather within sound of the stage.

As the area began to fill up, Lucas wandered in the crowd, sensing the same faint but infuriating aura of bliss that tended to infuse De Kuff–centered events. The people who had turned out were mainly young. Many of them were foreign Gentiles, but there were plenty of youthful Israelis and American Jews. Gathered in one section were some Black Hebrews, from their colony at Dimona, in the Negev.

There was a smell of patchouli oil, a fragrance he had hardly breathed since his own youth. Scattered among the spectators were some older couples, who gave the appearance of being single and on their first date, and even some who looked as though they had come for the music. Under a stand of carob trees beside the stage were a few rowdies in kippot who, Lucas thought, might have come to heckle.

When it was dark, with night birds trilling and stars overhead, Horst and Charlie Walsing, Raziel, De Kuff and Sonia came out on the stage with their instruments. De Kuff was playing bass and oud, Raziel clarinet. Horst Walsing had a violin; his handicapped brother, Charlie, a tambourine.

From the adjoining grove, the religious rowdies began to shout insults in English.

"Go home!"

"Excuse me," a youth with a cockney accent kept shouting. "Excuse me! Excuse me! Any of you lot Jewish? Excuse me!"

They began to play Sephardic music, to which Raziel kept imparting a faint klezmeric flavor. Eventually the hecklers quieted down — all but the cockney boy.

"Excuse me!" he kept shouting.

During the performance, Lucas did his best to resist the music, but afterward he could not get it out of his head. The pieces were settings for words he could not understand. Lucas found the first songs laced with irony, with jokes and comic congruities. Later, some were ineffably sad, as if they were in search of a complementary refrain, like the song of the chanting sparrow. The chanting sparrow's song required an answering call, or else hung over the woods and meadows, incomplete. There were still nightingales in the Jerusalem Forest nearby, and they filled a few of the silences.

Overall, the melodies were mournful and sweet, as sweet and passionate as Bruch's and faintly reminiscent of them, but often ragged, naked, shocking — those were the words that occurred to him. Sometimes symmetrical, but more often unpredictable. Charlie Walsing's beat was arbitrary, though it seemed somehow to work for the music. There was, Lucas thought, an element of madness, a din. It was the sort of music that might subvert a particular cast of mind, uncover its uncertainties, awaken its serpents. His own mind might serve as an example.

Lucas was trying to consider the music as something to write about. But that was hard to do, because it was she, it was Sonia, that it stood for. Whatever its sources were, Raziel had adapted it for performance, presenting the order of the pieces to form the narrative he required, and above all arranging it for Sonia's voice. Lucas could not make it be about anything but her. Thus, for him, it was about believing, about surrender, about angels and fallen stars and wandering spirits. About wild hopes and the mold of dreams. Its melodies replaced her, became her presence and occupied her space until she seemed an instrument played on the edge of control. They forced her to shift the focus of her voice from throat to chest and back within the same passages, trilling, ululating. Watching, he could see how the long songs taxed her physically and how they were working on her emotions. He knew that because of the way they worked on his own.

The same lyric seemed to turn up in every song, whether it was about Meliselda, some metaphorical king, broken vessels or the demands of unyielding love. The two lines of verse he could more or less understand:

> If you want to hear my song,
> You have to come with me.

He could not resist imagining her singing it for him. He would never be free of her, he thought. At the same time, she was on the other side of darkness, beyond him, beyond his capacity for believing, beyond anyone like himself, so unequipped for magic. Unready now even for tomorrow, let alone the world to come.

If he walked toward her, he thought, there would be nothing where she stood on which to place his feet. She was the leap he could not make. If the End of Days was at hand, she was the fate he would encounter there, the fall he would be condemned to take from the bridge over Hinnom. Although he could not cross, neither could he go down altogether, only turn in thwarted love, suspended. Half believing, half being. Would she know he was out there in the darkness? Or had she passed, by that music, to some stone heaven of the Jews, the sapphire hall of a presiding angel, where love unmade itself and everything was called by different names? She had left all his messages, from Cyprus, from Haifa, unanswered.

> Yo no digo esta canción,
> Sino a quien conmigo va.

Lucas sat transfixed. Even Obermann, next to him on the bench, gave himself over to the music, his round unmusical figure swaying to it.

When he looked around, he could see the power the stuff had over its listeners. Many in the crowd were wearing the ouroboros medallion. Obermann had noticed that as well.

"Some silversmith is getting rich," he said. "Can these people know what it means?"

Lucas was not the man to ask.

"It's in the *Zohar*," Obermann said. "Among the Hellenized syncretists, the snake stood for Serapis. One might go on."

He was prevented from going on by the concertgoers nearest them, who shushed him. The heckling had continued too, blotted out for Lucas by his meditations on Sonia, but persistent.

Then De Kuff and Raziel went downstage together. De Kuff's arms were raised to the crowd. Behind him, Sonia had taken the tambourine from Charlie Walsing and beat it in De Kuff's path.

"The circus!" a heckler shouted. "The clowns!"

De Kuff was chanting verses of poetry, perhaps from the *Zohar*. Whatever it was, it suited his voice beautifully. But hearing him was difficult because the hecklers in the grove, held a bit in check by the music, rallied now against him.

"The words change," De Kuff shouted, his face red and shining with perspiration, "but the song is eternal. The words are a cipher concealing the truth beneath them. A covering for the holy light where it threatens the darkness of this world."

The hecklers began to sing "Onward, Christian Soldiers," to which many knew the words. "Excuse me!" shouted the insistent Londoner.

The crowd gasped, laughed, shushed one another.

"A mystery!" De Kuff shouted.

At the side of the stage, Raziel spoke to Sonia.

"This is where he does it, Sonia. This is number four."

Raziel and Sonia grinned at each other. She rang four beats on the tambourine and rattled it into shards of silver.

"Excuse me!" shouted the youth among the carob trees.

"All mysteries are the same mystery!" De Kuff informed them. "Whether we worship the Holy Ancient One, whether we worship the *sefirot,* we are the same. There is one truth! There is one belief! There is one holiness! And at the birth of things to come, we all, through birth, through *partsufim,* we all stood at Sinai. There is not Israel! There is only Israel! The mystery is one! You are one faith! You are all believers in one heart! Not to believe together is to cease to be!"

At that, even the hecklers stopped teasing and paused to work out the doctrine. When they began to shout again, their rage was multifold.

"This is what comes from under the serpent's skin!" De Kuff said. Sonia struck her tambourine.

"It was written that I would shock you. I show you Uncreated Light among the wilderness of empty shells. Linen among the wool."

Onstage, Raziel whispered something to the old man. De Kuff turned to Sonia and took her by the hand and presented her to the crowd.

"This is Rachel," he said. "This is Leah."

The wind rose, a sudden force in the surrounding pines. Sonia looked up at the stars.

"Goddam you!" shouted the religious boy from London who had been shouting "Excuse me."

Raziel came forward.

"Thank you for coming. You're here to be one with us. Look into your hearts!"

There were screams and cheers. People cried in anger and for joy. The garden grew disorderly.

De Kuff, Raziel and Charlie Walsing began to play again. Sonia crooned to her tambourine. People who appeared to be sympathizers formed a line around the stage.

Lucas fought his way through the shifting crowd toward Sonia. He was thinking that he had always been good at cutting out of his life the people he thought threatened him with destruction or madness. His own hold on things, he believed, was so tenuous that it was necessary to be ruthless. Now watching her on the stage, transformed into the dervish she had aspired to be, he thought he could never let her go.

And the space toward which he labored made a strange sight. The crazed Walsing with his tambourine. His brother, who looked that night as if he had gotten lost on the way to Lincoln Center. De Kuff with his burning crimson face and Raziel in his shades and black hipster drape. Sonia, as Rachel and Leah, her eyes shining. He could imagine the letters of the Torah as fire in the night sky. It was what the music was about. Some kind of inspired nightmare fallen from another world.

"You believe," Raziel said to Sonia on the stage. "I hear your faith."

"Yes," Sonia said.

"The power at work here is like music," he told her. "It transcends ordinary reality the way music does. Whatever happens, Sonia, keep singing. And you'll sing us through the Redemption. You'll sing us into the world to come."

"Songs," she said. "It's all I know."

Lucas came up to her.

"Why won't you take my calls?" he demanded. "Will you just never speak to me?"

"She will now," Raziel said.

Lucas ignored him.

"I've got to talk to you," he said to Sonia. "Anywhere you say. Anytime."

"Yes, all right," she said. "I'm sorry I didn't get back to you. I'm so confused."

"It's all right," Lucas said. "I'll call you tomorrow, out here. Will you see me?"

She put a hand on his elbow and took it away quickly. "Sure I will."

"That's all I ask."

Some policemen were overseeing the clearing of the garden. Looking for Obermann, Lucas encountered Sylvia Chin from the American consulate. She was in black, wearing a jade amulet whose patterns suggested sacred geometry, and she looked very sleek and fey. There was a tall graying man, apparently European, with her.

"Hey, how was Cyprus?" she asked.

"Crummy."

"The conference."

"Edifying like you wouldn't believe."

"How about tonight?" Sylvia asked. "Pretty edifying too, huh? Smell the patchouli? See all the kids on Ex?"

"I didn't notice anyone stoned. You mean the kids who were heckling?"

"Of course not, silly. The kids who were heckling say their prayers every morning. The kids up front. Like in the mosh pit. Crying and carrying on."

"I didn't notice."

"I saw the Mr. Marshalls with De Kuff. Both of them."

"Who are they?"

"Well, one Mr. Marshall is a crook from New York we're trying to extradite. A hustler in *shmattes*. The other Mr. Marshall is his son. They've become De Kuffites."

"I guess they're going to plead insanity," Lucas said. "And they're looking for an alibi."

"Could be," she said. "The old guy lost all his money at the track. So they made him factor his payments. People ended up paying him *and* the factor. So everybody went to the D.A. Like millions." Then she was gone.

"What do you think?" Obermann asked Lucas as they left. "Feel a blessing?"

"He's going all the way, isn't he?"

"He seems to be going all the way. Gnosticism. Syncretism."

"What's next?"

"I think," Obermann said, "I think I know what's next."

"What?"

"Let's wait," the doctor said, "and see if I'm right."

"There's nowhere for this to go," Lucas said. "It has to crash, doesn't it? And it's dangerous. Here in Israel, of all places."

"Here," Obermann said, "these are not abstract or academic matters. So it's dangerous. And also dangerous to the self. These people are only people. They can be swept away."

"But if the end was coming," Lucas said, "someone would have to approach the fire."

"You sound like one of them," Obermann said. "Maybe you should let yourself go. I see you and Sonia are speaking again."

"I don't have any choice," Lucas said. "Not at the moment. I can't leave her to this. I mean, where she is now."

"Send her to me," Obermann said.

"I don't think so."

"Tell her," the doctor said, "in all the stories lies a warning not to draw near. Kundalini destroys. Actaeon is torn to pieces. Uzzah is killed by the ark. Remember it yourself."

"I don't need a warning," Lucas said.

"Maybe not. But try not to lose your mind. We have a book to write."

"I'll try."

"We have a stake," Obermann said. "And I don't trust the devious Raziel. I don't want to see some wretches like Otis and Darletta put them on the road and steal the old man's money."

35

U NDERSTAND," Sonia told him the next day, "you have to make a choice. And I don't think you're capable of choosing me."

"You're just parroting what these people tell you to say."

"I was your lady if you wanted me. It didn't happen because it couldn't. Not with you despising what I believe."

"I don't despise what you believe," Lucas said. "I'm really attracted to it in a way. And I certainly don't despise you."

"Well, I think you do. Raziel says it's what came between us. It always will."

"Do you have to tell that asshole everything that happens in your life?"

"He's my guide."

"Your *guide!* For God's sake! He's a junkie manipulator. He can't have sex because he's on drugs. And he doesn't want you having any."

"He's quit drugs, Chris. And — I'm sorry to say this — I didn't see you setting any fires the other night. And I think Raziel is right about the reason. It's because you refuse to open yourself."

"Thanks for being sorry to say it," Lucas said.

That night, she consented to go with him to a concert at Mishkenot, the outdoor arena overlooking the illuminated walls of the Old City.

A quartet of Russian immigrants finished their set with Shostakovich's String Quartet in D Major, the one he had written after seeing Dresden and dedicated publicly to the victims of war and fascism and, in addition, privately, to the victims of the regime he pretended to celebrate. The Russians were four women of stern aspect; the first violinist had a tragic homeliness and a style that was almost sacerdotal in its decorous passion. Lucas thought both she and her playing inexpressibly beautiful. Yad Vashem, the Gulag, Gaza, exile, cruelty, compassion. Sometimes her eyes were closed as she played, at other times open in witness to some great sadness. To hear her, Lucas thought secretly, was to be close to the Shekhinah.

"You can't hear that," Sonia said, "and not believe that God moves through his people. And through his people he touches history."

"Yes you can," Lucas said. "Of course, it's nicer to believe."

"Oh, Chris," she said. "What does it take for you?"

"Art is not supernatural. It's not religion. It's not even real life. It's just beautiful."

He drove her back to Ein Kerem. When she got out of the car, she stood beside it for a moment.

"I could make you happy, if you let me," she said.

"I believe you, Sonia. Being with you makes me happy."

It was not quite what he had meant to say, and it was not quite the truth. She was the object of his desire and his loneliness.

"Our souls have the same root. Over the years we keep doing this. But until you believe and understand, you'll be miserable. The way you are now."

"Maybe you're right," Lucas said.

He drove back to the garage he had rented off Jaffa Road. His apartment seemed especially ugly and cold; he sorely missed Tsililla's place in the German Colony with its adjoining arbors and gardens. He stood at the window and watched the empty streets of downtown Jerusalem through the rain that had begun to fall.

The next day was pleasant enough for the Atara to put tables outside. But Obermann kept to his usual table, inside, next to the espresso machines.

"I'm going to write something about Herzog," Lucas told his collaborator.

"He's not really a victim of the Syndrome," Obermann said. "But he's an interesting case."

"An interesting man," Lucas said.

"You identify with him?"

"I don't claim the status of a Holocaust survivor," Lucas said. "I don't know if 'identify' is the right word. There's something about him waiting by the cross for his parents. Waiting where they left him."

"Yes, I see."

"Something short," Lucas said. "Because he came here searching. Out of a loyalty that's rejected."

"Despised and rejected," said Obermann. "Good idea. Do it." He looked at Lucas critically over his Turkish coffee. "You don't look well. Are you all right?"

"Yes, I think so," Lucas said. After a moment he said, "I went to a concert with Sonia last night."

"Good," said Obermann. "At least they're not cutting her off from the outside world. As yet."

"I won't let them."

"My dear fellow," Obermann said, "they'll give her the wood and the nails and she'll build her own prison. Too bad you're personally involved. But believe me, I understand your situation."

"Because of Linda?" Lucas shook his head. "Funny, I have trouble thinking of you as a pining lover."

"You think because I'm a doctor I'm without emotion?"

"Sorry," Lucas said. "Also, if you'll excuse my saying so, I don't care for Linda Ericksen very much. I find it hard to imagine getting emotional about her."

"She's a popsy," Obermann said. "A little American popsy. But one can grow fond of a popsy." He stirred the sugar cubes in his coal-black coffee. "And I wonder what she talks about with Zimmer. I wonder a great deal about Zimmer. By the way," he asked Lucas, "has Sonia said anything to you about the Ebionites? Or the Clementine Recognitions? Do you know about them?"

"I've heard of them somewhere. A long time ago. In school, I guess. Sonia hasn't mentioned them."

"No? Hasn't she told you that you and she were Ebionites in another life?"

"She did say our souls had the same root. And she claims to know my *tikkun*."

"The Ebionites are an obsession of Raziel's. Soon, if I'm not mistaken, you'll hear about them from Sonia."

"That's a depressing thought."

"The Ebionites," Obermann said, "were Hebrew Christians — I mean ancient ones, from the days of the Jewish church, the church of James. The Recognitions were part of their scriptures. Raziel believes De Kuff and Sonia carry the souls of Ebionites. He seems to believe it about you too. He believes the Messiah will come from that root. That's why he's fixated on De Kuff. At least that's my opinion."

"Do you really think she's so under Raziel's influence?"

"I'm afraid so. At the moment. But I think she likes you. After all, she's telling you you share a soul with her."

"Any time," Lucas said.

In the afternoon, he drove out to the Hebrew University library to see what he could find about Ebionites and Clementine literature. Every word they had, as far as he could determine from the catalog, was in German. There was a single monograph in English, a summary that presented Christ as a Jewish Gnostic *aeon* who had appeared to Adam as a snake, and then to Moses. Jesus' soul was destined for subsequent appearances until finally, at the End of Days, he would return, inhabiting a different personality, as the Messiah.

Tracking the concept of Jewish Christians, Lucas discovered that Walter Benjamin had written on Pico della Mirandola's mystical derivation of the Trinity from *bereshit,* the opening word of Genesis. It gave him a strange sensation to see the reference: Benjamin had been a mentor of his father's, someone he associated with the old man's circle.

When evening came, he wandered again into the Old City. There was a crowd of foreigners around the doors of the Anglican hostel and the Christian Information Service. Urchins emerged from the shadows to pester them with false information and misdirections. The blind beggar called Mansour moved among them, seizing foreigners by the lapels, demanding *baksheesh.* Mansour was a legend in the city. He had been blinded with an awl, it was said, by a crazed American girl he had accosted. Many Palestinians believed that the girl had been a setup, her act a brutal lesson meant to undermine Palestinian male confidence, and that she had been repatriated unpunished by the Israeli government. In the souk, Lucas found his Palestinian acquaintance Charles Habib behind the counter of his café.

"No beer," he told Lucas at once.

"No beer?"

"No beer. Respect for the martyrs."

"I see," Lucas said. "But you stayed. So let me have a Turkish coffee."

"Arab coffee," Charles reminded him. "How's your writing? You do Woody Allen or the *majnoon?*"

"*Majnoon.*"

"Good," said Charles. "Did I tell you I got my niece coming over from Watertown, Massachusetts? She can teach me the American modes. My job will be to keep her out of trouble."

"Why's she coming over?"

"My sister wants her to see the situation. I told them, forget it. Better she knows nothing about it."

In a back mirror Lucas caught a fleeting glance of a young blond woman. He could have sworn it was the same woman he had seen in Haifa, at Jonas Herzog's Benedictine monastery. He turned and saw her from behind, her exposed fair hair unmistakable among the evening crowds. She seemed headed up the little loop in the Via Dolorosa that led to the square in front of the Holy Sepulchre. A moment later he thought he saw Sonia too, thought he recognized her shawl and the indent of her cheek.

"I have to go," he told Charles abruptly.

He stood up and went out after the illusions he had glimpsed. They were nowhere to be seen among the swarm outside the church. Searching that crowd, he suspected that both the young woman penitent from Haifa and Sonia had been creatures of his imagination. He found himself going into the church with all the tourists.

A young man in a black suit and matching tie immediately approached him.

"Will you be with us for the vigil?" He sounded like a midwesterner, or possibly Canadian.

He looked over the young man's shoulder for Sonia or the other woman. They had vanished in the shadows and intersecting planes of the church. Incense wafted, candles flickered. The place never ceased its effort to beguile the tenth-century mind.

"Maybe," Lucas said.

"You'll have to be here from nine on."

"Right," said Lucas, and went past him. In the unlikely event that Sonia had chosen to pass a vigil in the Holy Sepulchre, he had the feeling that she would make her way to the roof, where the Ethiopians had their chapel. But when he climbed the stairs that led to the rooftop monasteries, he found the door at the top bolted shut.

He had not been in the Holy Sepulchre since Easter, the day of the *majnoon*. The dimness was filled with foreign pilgrims, and he supposed the image of the blonde from Haifa had been a projection of their presence in the city. Or a portent, he thought. The angel of loneliness, calling him to a vanished home. Some strange reversal. And he had seen Sonia there simply for wanting to see her.

The pilgrims wandered, bewildered, drowning in the gloom, awash in the wake of the awesome events they struggled to believe in. Lucas lost track of time. When he went toward the door, the young man who had addressed him coming in barred his way out.

"I'm afraid it's locked."

"What?"

"It's locked. For our vigil."

Lucas looked at him blankly.

"It stays locked until four," the man told him. A sickly grin broke out across his thin, ungenerous features. "We don't have the key, you know."

To his horror, Lucas realized he had arrived on one of the nights designated for nocturnal vigil, during which groups undertook to remain in the church through the hours of the night. It was true that no one in the church had the key. Each night it was taken away by one of two designated Muslim families of the city, who kept it until dawn. Neither fire nor flood would let them out. He was immured.

"Jesus Christ," Lucas said. "Shit!"

The young man stepped back in horror and loathing. A wave of invisible indignation reverberated through the half-darkness.

"You can try to find a sexton, I suppose," the young man said with an air of Christian submission.

Lucas went off in search of authority. There were only bewildered tourists and dank chambers where candles guttered. It was like trying to find his way back from the hereafter.

Eventually Lucas happened on a group of kneeling Palestinians in work clothes, surrounded by a welter of mechanical equipment. There was a huge, dirty gray tube that looked like the creation of Hollywood sci-fi, a giant maggot from space. Near it lay some blowers and metal joints. But the Arabs were so rapt in prayer that Lucas was reluctant to disturb them. He sat down on a corner step near the crypt of Saint Helena and confronted his awful situation. Near the Chapel of the Franks, the pilgrims were gathering for prayer. They began to chant in cut-rate plainsong, their nasal, New Agey monotone informed by a dreadful gusto that sounded as though they might still be going strong at dawn.

Lucas remembered the *majnoon*. If he went well and truly berserk, it occurred to him, if he leapt and shouted and screeched, they might be terrorized into releasing him. On the other hand, he thought, glancing around, he was probably under the jurisdiction of the ecclesiastical authority of the Six Christianities rather than that of the State of Israel, at least until dawn. Misbehavior might subject him to ghastly admonitions or severe antique confinements. Chains. The rack.

Jesus Christ. Shit.

The Christians chanted lustily. Then, all at once, a sound like no other he had ever heard exploded in the place. It was like a sour note from a transcendental off-key calliope, as if all the reprobate jackhammers of hell were gearing up to vaporize the universe.

The wailing echoes were magnified beyond imagination by the cavernous hollows of the church, transformed into a cacophonous lament for history, or perhaps a very loud twelve-tone Mass, an apology of some sort for the crimes and follies of religion.

Lucas got to his feet. He was aware of the Christians calling out in protest, but he could not hear their voices for the great sacred noise.

The Palestinian workmen who had been praying before the Catholicon were gone with their equipment. Approaching the Chapel of the Franks, he saw the heart of the matter under dispute. The Orthodox patriarch of the church had chosen this night to launder his stone property — let vigils and mouthings of schismatics be damned. The proprietors of the vigil, priestly-looking foreigners in lay clothes, were remonstrating with the work crew. From the beatific smiles of the Arabs, who kept the steam coming, it was apparent the remonstrances were in vain.

The young man who had been at the door saw Lucas and shouted at him.

"Can you believe it? They're steam cleaning it! Tonight of all nights!"

It was very hard for the two men to hear each other, so they had to strain.

"Maybe," Lucas suggested at the top of his voice, "maybe they're getting ready to sell it!"

Then he went off to find a place to curl up and hide.

36

THAT EVENING, Janusz Zimmer and Yakov Miller, the leader of the militant settlers' organization, sat under the olive trees in the garden of the House of the Galilean. Dov Kepler, the heretical Hasid, and Mike Glass, the junior-college professor and football coach, were with them. The religious Jews had removed their kippot to blend in with the Christian atmosphere of the House.

Sitting apart, about twenty feet away, in stiff chairs like those the men sat in, Linda Ericksen and a young man named Hal Morris sat side by side. Hal was clean-cut, North American–looking and so shy that, in pretty Linda's presence, he could do little but stare at his shoes.

"The rest of our equipment should come in this week," Zimmer told his council of war. He addressed himself principally to Rabbi Miller. "Everything we need for the removal. Lestrade will give Otis the structural layout and Otis will give it to me. Then we have a number of specialists to plant the material in the right places."

"What are they using?" the man from the West Bank asked. "Just out of curiosity?"

"Gelignite. Made in Iran."

"Will it go off?"

"Want to go and see?"

"I'm concerned with the loss of life," the eccentric Hasid said. "Our soldiers are stationed around the Haram. The Kotel plaza might be damaged."

"It will be minimized. There's nothing we can do about the soldiers. The Kotel will be all right."

"Jews were killed in the bombing of the King David too," Yakov Miller said.

Mike Glass frowned and rubbed his forehead.

"Very true," Janusz Zimmer agreed. "Now, if you don't mind," he said to Miller, "I'd like to talk to the young man you brought me."

Miller called to Hal Morris in Hebrew. The young man, whose command of the language was not expert, looked up startled and pointed questioningly to himself. Laughing, Linda urged him to stand and follow orders.

"You too, Linda," Janusz Zimmer said. "Both of you join us."

"We have some necessities arriving from the Gaza Strip," he said. He looked around at his fellow conspirators, resting his eyes longest on Miller. "This is where you come into our closest confidence," he told young Morris and Linda. "Linda knows this, you perhaps do not. We propose to destroy the enemy shrines on the Temple Mount."

"And rebuild the Temple," young Morris said, his voice breaking. "I've been told."

Miller looked at him with a pride that was like love. "Has a day been set?" he asked Zimmer.

"I was going to ask also," said Dov Kepler, the Hasid. "Some days, I'm sure you know, are more propitious."

"The Ninth of Av would be appropriate," Mike Glass said. The Ninth of Av was traditionally a day of lamentation among Jews. Both the First and Second Temples had been destroyed on that day.

"Tisha b'Av indeed would be," said Miller. "But it's a day lately when security is extra-tight. Although religious people would be observing the fast. That's a plus."

"A *rosh hodesh* at least," said Kepler.

Zimmer only watched them.

"Tisha b'Av is soon," Miller said. "Would we be ready?"

"A wonderful day that would be," Kepler said happily.

"No significant days," said Janusz Zimmer. "There's always the chance of some extra precaution. And a greater tendency to talk."

"Think of it," said Miller. "A holiday in the heart. Perhaps a new one for Jews everywhere. And then for people everywhere. Perhaps Tisha b'Av would be ended forever with the rise of the Temple again."

"It's so exciting," Linda said. "So wonderful to be a part of."

"*Baruch Hashem,*" young Morris said.

"Your black Sufi friend has got to be in the Strip again," Janusz Zimmer told Linda. "She's got to be seen there. On the day we move the explosives, you'll go out there on behalf of the Human Rights Coalition. Get Ernest Gross to let you go if you can. If he won't, just go. And you, Mr. Morris, ever been to the Gaza Strip?"

"No," he said, flushing. "Is it worse than Hebron? I've seen that. I've seen Arab hate before."

"Do you know what the Israeli Human Rights Coalition is?" Zimmer asked him.

"It's a leftist, atheist organization," the young man said, "of pro-Arab Jews."

"Think you can give a good impersonation of an IHRC field-worker? Because we'll want to pass you off as one. That's how we get your friend to Nuseirat," he told Linda. "Tell her you need company. You're going to help Hal interview some witnesses to the sad beatings of the poor, oppressed Arab youths. With tapes, of course."

"And will there be interviews?" she asked.

"Kfar Gottlieb will round up some cooperative Arabs." Zimmer turned to young Hal Morris. "This is something you have to remember. You don't call them Arabs in the IHRC. You call them Palestinians. Like the anti-Semitic and left-wing press. That's the politically correct term."

Morris laughed. "Well, I'll work on it."

Janusz Zimmer kept looking at him.

"Are sure you want to be part of this? How old are you?"

"Twenty."

"In school?"

"Finished with undergraduate school. In the fall I start medical school at Hopkins. I feel doctors are needed. But I'll be here as much of the time as I can."

"You're convinced this is the right work for you?"

"Medicine?"

"Not medicine," Zimmer said. "This. What we're doing."

"He's convinced," Yacov Miller said. "What do you want from him?"

"It's like getting to be here in the earliest days for me," Hal Morris said. "Like the war for independence. Nothing makes me happier."

"All right," Zimmer said. "As long as you're sure. From now on, your name is Lenny Ackermann. Understand?"

"Lenny Ackermann," said Hal. "Right."

"Don't be too sure you'd have liked the old days, Lenny. The ambiance was very left wing."

When the meeting was over, Zimmer and Linda were leaving the grounds of the House of the Galilean when they happened to encounter Dr. Otis Corey Butler.

"*Shalom, chaverim,*" Dr. Butler enthused.

"Good evening, Dr. Butler," said Janusz Zimmer.

"I just thought I'd mention," Dr. Butler said. "I don't know whether it's important or not. You know the journalist, the American fella? I don't know whether he's Jewish or not."

"Neither does he," Zimmer said.

"Well, someone put him on to us out here. It turns out he's writing a book on the Jerusalem Syndrome, as he calls it, with Pinchas Obermann."

Linda, somewhat alarmed, looked at Zimmer. Zimmer appeared unconcerned.

"Good," he said. "He's picked an eventful period. For the 'Jerusalem Syndrome.' "

"I just thought you'd like to know."

"We knew," Zimmer said. "Didn't we, Linda?"

"Yes," she said uncertainly. "I suppose we did."

"If he should come again," Zimmer said pleasantly, "do let us know."

The next day Pinchas Obermann was sitting in the Atara when he looked up from his coffee and saw Linda Ericksen standing over him. Although Obermann was at his usual table, she seemed surprised to see him and behaved as if their meeting had taken her by surprise.

"Linda, my dear," Pinchas said, "please sit down."

He signaled for the waiter, who at first did not come. Eventually, when his curiosity about the young foreign woman at Obermann's table overcame his predisposition to be alone with his thoughts, the waiter condescended to approach and inquire into their desires. Linda ordered café au lait.

"I understand," Linda said, "that you and Christopher Lucas are writing a piece on what you call the Jerusalem Syndrome."

"A book," Obermann said. "Unfortunately, we can't claim to have coined the term."

"I have to ask you," Linda said, "if my husband and I appear in this book."

"No one appears by name."

"But many people would be easily recognizable."

"People familiar with the field, or the theme, might recognize individuals."

"This seems to me a violation of privacy," Linda said. "Possibly hurtful to careers."

"No," Pinchas Obermann said.

"What do you mean, no? Of course it is."

"What you're saying is, people who know the people will see what they know in print. People who don't know the people will see case histories."

"Oh, come," she said. "It's a small world out here. And in the field."

"I fail to see," Obermann said, "how a book like the one I've described differs from all the other books on all the other human subjects in the world."

"I know you so well," she said. "Too well to fall for your rhetorical techniques."

"What rhetorical techniques?"

"Come on, Pinchas."

"Neither your husband nor any of your boyfriends is going to come out looking bad. Nor you. So don't worry."

"Funny, I don't find that assurance very comforting."

"I was the one you left Ericksen for," Pinchas said. "You think I'm going to demean myself?"

"Honestly, you're so weird," she said, "it wouldn't surprise me."

"Linda," Obermann said, "don't worry. You'll enjoy the book. It'll be a souvenir of your youth. Of your quest."

"You are the most cynical individual I've ever encountered."

"You should know me well enough to know I'm not cynical. Maybe you think I wasn't fond of you."

Linda stirred her coffee. "I'm still fond of you, Pinchas. Of course, my life is with Janusz now. But we're not enemies, are we?"

"Enemies? I don't know. I don't write defamatory books. You shan't find yourself mocked or attacked."

"But you're not still fond of me?"

Obermann looked at her. She fixed him with an expectant smile, as though they should both be resigned to her universal appeal.

"No. Not fond."

She smiled stiffly. "Not fond? What then?"

"Not fond," said Obermann.

"Look, Pinchas," Linda said. "I'm not going to give you any trouble. But Janusz is a hothead. He's not young but he's plenty tough. You should be careful."

"You wonder what I know — is that it?"

"I wouldn't want to see you and your friend get in trouble."

"If I didn't know you were so fond of me, Lindaleh, I would be tempted to call this little chance visit a threat."

Linda laughed unpleasantly. "A threat? A threat! Now really."

"What shouldn't we say? What should we conceal?" Obermann asked. "That the characters in the House of the Galilean are con men? That they're in with Moledetniks and worse? Anyway, what's that to Janusz? Or to you?"

"Maybe we think you're turning your back on what the country stands for. And this book that you and that other man are writing is part of that."

"Maybe I think what the country stands for is my right to sit and drink a cup of coffee without religious fanatics breathing down my neck. Like people do in other countries like this one, where religion is practiced and personal freedoms are guaranteed."

"Freedoms," she said, with scorn.

"One thing Israel should guarantee me — I shouldn't have to argue theology with Swedes. Especially ones from Wisconsin. Before noon. By the way," he asked her, "did you know that Vladimir Jabotinsky translated Poe into Hebrew? 'The Pit and the Pendulum'? Have you learned the Hebrew word for 'nevermore'?"

"If you stop being a smartass, Pinchas, we might have a story for you and your friend that will knock this country's enemies on their ear. A purely secular story, I assure you. Involving the UN, the NGOs, arms and dope smuggling. About how these organizations engage in terrorism and blame it on Israel."

"If it's a secular story," Obermann said, "we can't use it. Anyway, what's the point of this stick and carrot? What are you afraid of? Why are you threatening me?"

"This is not," Linda said through clenched teeth, "a threat."

"What then? A greeting? A hello?"

"Goodbye, Pinchas," Linda said.

37

WHEN LUCAS AWAKENED, a little girl was standing in the candlelight of the chapel in which he had gone to sleep. She was honey-haired. Her skin was fair and flushed as though with cold. She had bright blue eyes and a slender, pointed nose that was flushed at the tip. The effect was elfin and not unattractive.

"Did you light all those candles?" Lucas asked her sleepily.

"Yes," she whispered. "Is it good?"

"Very nice," Lucas told her, sitting upright. "Wow," he said, "you lit a lot of them." There were upward of fifty candles burning in the small chapel. Smoke swirled around the uneven ocher ceiling. The roar of the steam-cleaning apparatus which had resounded in his sleep seemed to have stopped.

"There was once a fire," said the girl. "Many died. Standing together."

She wore an odd kind of uniform. It had a high-necked blouse with three buttons on the collar and bouffant sleeves narrowing to tight white cuffs. Over this was a smock that stretched to her ankles with a white apron over it. A wide-brimmed straw hat with a blue band rested on her shoulder blades, attached by a cord around her neck. Stuck in the band was a tiny bouquet of lupines and cornflowers.

"The fire that comes from on high," she said. She had long, thin upper teeth. Pearly white. Her name, she confided to him, was Diphtheria Steiner. She was Rudolph Steiner's daughter.

"Yes," Lucas said. "The Holy Fire of the Greeks. It started a panic. Many, many years ago. In olden days." "Olden days" was the term Lucas's mother had used to refer to the past.

"Many died standing together," the girl repeated. "And many were burned alive. Piled by the gates."

"Who told you about it?" Lucas asked. He could see dim figures around him in the adjoining chapels. He heard distant chanting. When he looked at his watch, he saw that it had stopped at ten. It was a thirty-dollar Timex. He wondered if the women he had impulsively followed into the church were also confined by the vigil, or engaged in it.

"God's will," the child said. "God's fire." There was a heraldic device sewn on the breast of her smock on which he read the words *Schmidt* and *Heilige Land*. "Yet it was not from God the fire came."

She seemed to be posing him some sort of riddle, and Lucas felt that he ought to find a moral for her. He was not good at talking to children.

"We always have to be careful," he explained, "with fire. Even in church. Lighting candles."

"The prophets of Baal could not call down fire," she said. "Not one escaped."

"Prophets of Baal?" Lucas asked. "Never mind the prophets of Baal. Just be a good girl and behave yourself."

"And go to heaven when I die."

"Right," said Lucas. "You'll die and then you'll be in heaven." He stood up and stretched. "What are you doing here? Are you with a group?"

"It was a false miracle," the girl said. "Is that right?"

"They're all false miracles," Lucas said. "Well, I don't really mean that. I mean, we don't know what makes things happen."

"God punished the Greeks for the false miracle."

Lucas was annoyed. "Who told you that? It's not very Christian. I mean, you're supposed to be Christians together. We, I mean. Nobody punished anybody."

"Is it not right to punish?"

Lucas began to look about him for another place to wait out the vigil. The kid was tiresome and he felt exhausted, almost as though he could not put one foot in front of another. The fatigue made him sit down near the carved mausoleum beside which he had been resting. The carving on it showed a bound figure. Christ, bound to be scourged, perhaps.

It reminded him of a carving he had seen years before on a parish church in England, traveling with his then fiancée. A bound devil. A very ordinary little devil, almost a stick figure, confined in bonds, licked by little flames. It was a strange thing to put on a sarcophagus, he thought, unless the person entombed had gone to hell.

The child, who was tall, stood a head higher than Lucas when he leaned back against the tomb.

"Well," he said, and closed his eyes wearily. "Is it not right to punish?" He tried hard to make sense of it. "I guess you have to punish people to make them behave. That's human nature. But," he added, "you can't punish people before they do something wrong. Only after. I mean, you can't punish people in advance."

"Not one of the priests of Baal escaped," the girl from Schmidt's declared.

"It's just a story," Lucas said. "People used not to be able to think straight." The child only looked at him with her politely pleasant half-smile. Being presentable for the grownups. "Unlike now," Lucas said. "Now we have it all figured out."

"God wanted to kill Moses," Diphtheria declared. "He wanted to kill him at the inn."

"Ah," Lucas said. "No he didn't."

"But the wife of Moses cut the baby on the little place. And with the blood touched Moses there."

"Come on," said Lucas sleepily, "they don't teach you that in school. What are you doing here, anyway?"

"Blood and fire," said the child. "Ice and oranges for diphtheria. God makes his enemies die."

"God makes everyone die. That's what makes him God."

"In the mind is the source of all," the Schmidt's girl said. "Papa tells us."

"He does?"

"What we think is what shall be," she explained. "In the mind is the future."

"What an awful notion," Lucas said. "I suppose you had diphtheria long ago."

But she was gone. It took him a moment to admit the possibility that she had not really been there. Or perhaps she had been a djinn. She had seemed a malign figure; it was agreeable to believe she did not exist.

His wanderings led him around the wretched little ark and cross some Victorian Englishman had built over what was supposed to be the tomb of Christ. The chanted beads grew louder as he went.

Through the arched entrance of the Franciscan choir, he saw half a dozen friars kneeling in front of a group of pilgrims. One of the friars led the prayers in French, with an accent that might have been Spanish or Italian. Lucas went next door to the Magdalen chapel and listened. The chant took him back to boarding school, the fight with the boy named English, the Jew business, his own fervent tearful prayers. He had believed absolutely.

There were icons of the Magdalen on the walls and paintings in the Western manner, all kitsch, trash. Mary M., Lucas thought, half hypnotized by the chanting in the room beside him; Mary Moe, Jane Doe, the girl from Migdal in Galilee turned hooker in the big city. The original whore with the heart of gold. Used to be a nice Jewish girl, and next thing she's fucking the buckos of the Tenth Legion Fratensis, fucking the pilgrims who'd made their sacrifice at the Temple and were ready to party, the odd priest and Levite on the sly.

Maybe she was smart and funny. Certainly always on the lookout for the right guy to take her out of the life. Like a lot of whores, she tended toward religion. So along comes Jesus Christ, Mr. Right with a Vengeance, Mr. All Right Now! Fixes on her his hot, crazy eyes and she's all, Anything, I'll do anything. I'll wash your feet with my hair. You don't even have to fuck me.

You had to wonder what she'd make of her picture on the wall times seven. Amusing to show her around the place. What do you think, kid? Like it? Everybody remembers you and your old gang. We talk about you all the time.

And all the time, the rosaries resounded nearby.

"*Contemplez-vous, mes frères et mes soeurs, les mystères glorieux. Le premier mystère: la Résurrection de Notre Seigneur.*"

They were to meditate, *s'il vous plaît*, on the resurrection. The rosary, school, the Magdalen. It got him thinking about his mother. She would surely have been delighted by a resurrection.

She had died on the young side, still in her fifties, of what was, to her, an unmentionable cancer. She had winced to talk about it, not because it was fatal — she had never believed in death — but because it was breast cancer, and her combination of superstition, prudery and vanity had kept her from doctors and eventually killed her. She was the type for the disease: unmarried, with only one child, and not that much of a sexual history. A nonsmoker, because she had been a professional singer from her teens, but a bit of a lush, favoring rare brandies and champagne, though except for the breasts she kept her figure to the end.

She had studied in Europe, she liked European men, blossomed under their compliments. Her musical sense of measure rendered her at ease in the presence of formality; she liked a formal occasion and liked the undoing of it that made it fun in the first place. She was a wonderful dancer.

Herr Professor Doctor Lucas, of Mainz and the Humboldt University in Berlin and Columbia, was the man for her. Of course he was married. It was wrong, but she refused to worry and she had wanted a child so much. So *voilà* sits that homunculus himself, still intact, if a bit conflicted, in the Magdalen chapel in the middle of the world. He was neither a musician like his mother nor a scholar like his father. He believed, though, that he had inherited a number of their separate qualities. Self-doubt, impatience, bad judgment, a sumptuary nature, a drinking problem, a bald spot.

I should say a prayer for her, he thought. She had been a great one for prayer, drunk or sober.

A free spirit, a fun-lover full of dire predictions and grim proverbs she used as expletives in times of stress. "A moment's mirth to wail a week." She had liked that one. And, more folksily, "Sing before breakfast, weep before dinner."

But she also said, seeming very pleased with herself, "Smart men often like to cook." The professor doctor was no mean hand in the kitchen. His wife never cooked. Sometimes he took Lucas's mother to Voisin. Sometimes he came and cooked for them.

And never songs so sweet as the songs with which she sung him to sleep, everything from Gaelic ditties to *lieder* to *Don Carlos*. The two of them, Lucas and his mother, Gail Hynes, a not unknown mezzo-soprano, lying in the dark, she singing and he swooning, yes swooning, on her breast. And his only rival the professor doctor, whose tread might sound on the stair, come to lure her away with the honey of Lucas's own generation. And later, in the fourth grade, the bad school and the Jew business.

He could remember the last of her, encoffined. Very happy she looked, rosy as life under the cross Father Herzog served, on all that satin, amid all those flowers in the gold dress the professor doctor liked. As though she had died without a mark on her, her skin as milky white as the princess Isolde's, her fine high cheekbones emphasized and just a hint of the boozy swelling under her chin.

Only to be conveyed to St. Raymond's Cemetery and buried in that hateful, mean, black ground stinking of consumption and Irish spite, surrounded by the dwellings of cops and grafting school janitors, beside her parents, Grace and Charlie, and her alcoholic little brother, James John. How could anyone imagine the professor doctor in such a place, among those dead? But he went, while the family eyed him. Her rich Jewish lover, a bloody tycoon, a mogul, a banker, a merchant prince. Cocked their gray eyes on him — her eyes, the eyes Lucas had brought to see Jerusalem — and smiled the sympathetic smile of a conquered race, and went home and moaned of their humiliation.

That night, his father, who was merely a spendthrift Columbia professor, took Lucas to his club.

"We have both suffered a terrible loss. I loved her very much. I don't know if you can know, at your age, how it was. She was more to me than I thought possible."

How much did you think possible? Lucas had wanted to ask. But he had only met his father's gaze with affirming gravity.

"I hope that you feel affection for me. You are my son. I have always loved you."

Then Lucas, drunk on the club's martinis, had answered with the words he thought the moment demanded.

"I love you too, Carl."

It sounded like the movies, only worse. So embarrassing and inappropriate. Had the waiter heard? Yet it was strange. His father so solicitous and behaving just as he had behaved with Lucas's mother. But Lucas loved his father, who was obtuse but, all in all, sort of lovable.

"I'm all right," Lucas had said. "I mean, I'm an adult." Thinking: Want to play Claudius to my Hamlet, Carl?

At their next meeting they talked about Shakespeare, which Carl adored but which Lucas believed his father imperfectly understood. Lucas had a secret theory that Carl sometimes missed the point of things, owing to his latter-day English. Carl believed he spoke better English than anyone in America.

"Do you think Claudius might have been Hamlet's father all the time?"

"I like it," said Carl, "and the ghost from hell, yes? But Shakespeare would have told us. Anyway, don't ask me, dear boy — it's a young man's play."

Funny, Lucas now thought in the Holy Sepulchre. Hamlet's father's ghost from hell? It was like the serpent preaching liberation in the Garden.

Lucas's father, late in life, was only gradually giving up the notion of a homosexual conspiracy — whose original founder was Senator Joseph McCarthy — to rule the world. Lee Harvey Oswald had been involved.

"I always assume you're not homosexual," his father had said. "Is it so?"

Lucas had laughed at him. "Jesus Christ, if I was gay, don't you think you'd know it? Hey, what is it, Carl? My show-tune records? My walk?"

Then later, the girl Lucas was sleeping with, a Barnard student who waited tables at Mikal's, had told him, "You know, your father made like a serious pass at me?"

"That prick! Report him."

"What? Are you kidding?"

"I'm kidding," Lucas had said. "He's a great old dude. Only don't sleep with him."

At the memorial for Gail Hynes, they had put up a photograph of her lifted from a Town Hall poster twenty years old. In it she appeared not only beautiful but radiant, eyes high, as though she were beholding the spheres and about to sing their music. Seeing the picture on its tripod at the front of the hall, Lucas knew at once the quality of the moment it captured. In a second, she would dissolve in giggles. She always looked at her most spiritual at the point of breaking up. Onstage giggles had been a problem with her. And at the same service, they played her rendering of *The Song of the Earth*. *Abschied*. The dying fall, her sad reluctant surrender of life. Echoing, as over some still, melancholy alpine lake. *Abschied. Abschied.* Rapture. Only the dying Kathleen Ferrier had done it better. Carl had rashly insisted on having it played. Whereupon, needless to say, everyone present had totally lost his or her shit. Orgiastic weeping had ensued. A few pure fans had mixed with the mourners; people were fond of her.

Resurrection, he thought among the flickering tapers of Christ's Tomb, how it would surprise and delight her. How well she would carry it off, with a formal bearing and a delighted smile, in the gold dress, completely concealing her distress at discovering herself in Queens. It would please her so much to be alive again.

Then, above the cadences of the rosary, he heard the echoing report of a sliding bolt and the crash of wood against stone. The main door had been opened and the vigil was over. He walked toward the gray morning light. Spilling across the stone floor, it caught columns of whirling dust and smoke. Instead of going out, he stopped by the Stone of Unction and looked toward the chapels of Calvary.

The believers liked to think that Christ had been crucified there and that Calvary was the tomb of Adam.

"Since by man came death, by man came also the resurrection of the dead. . . . And so it is written, The first man Adam was made a living soul; the last Adam was made a quickening spirit." It sounded a bit like De Kuff.

He went into the street, where the air was fresh and dewy, the chill mountain air of Jerusalem as yet unsullied by exhaust fumes. From the Haram just up the street, the call to prayer resounded, and he thought, I will never get out of this crazy place.

Would he trade his sanity for faith? Only in Jerusalem. Elsewhere, faith wouldn't get you on the metro, the vaporetto, the IRT. But in Jerusalem, not so. You could walk everywhere, there was plenty of time — eternity, in fact. If he stayed, he thought, he knew what might be coming. He was aware of a certain slide, a slackening of the critical faculties. He had taken to meditating on phenomenology, pursuing phantom temptresses, conversing with German elves. He was drinking too much. Hearing Sonia doing "If you want to hear my song, you have to come with me."

The company in which Lucas walked to the Pool included junkies and lunatics of every age and nation. Half of them had spent the night in the Holy Sepulchre and would spend dawn at Bethesda, meditating on the mysteries of the rosary, the attributes of Allah, the *sefirot*. Such self-confidence they all had! Such single-mindedness. Lucas was in awe of them as he stood by the doors of St. Anne's to watch them pass. The light in their eyes was not their own.

Then all at once his breath seemed to have been drawn out of his body, sucked up and out, as napalm was said to dissolve its victims' oxygen. He staggered off the cobblestones and leaned against a doorway near the Monastery of the Flagellation. Terror seized him. It was as if he had not found, would never find, his way out of that ghastly church.

How? How could anyone believe that there was a covenant and a redemption to come, that this parched crescent of fundamental desire and loss, this most uneasy bargain of a place, could be called The Holy? Its monster of a God had effortlessly, fondly formed the fleet carnivorous lizard, the eyelids of morning, the submersible, red-eyed rage of Behemoth. His symbol was the crocodile. He was the crocodile.

The place he had wandered into, apostate wayward Christian, wandering Jew. It was lousy with prayers, in the mosques, in the reconstructed Temple to come, in the flickering crackhouse light of the church — all of them, behind their talk of mercy, nursing bloody vindicating covenants. Dominion of the blood and the sepulchre. The first shall be last, the crooked straight, universal revenge.

Land of the dear Lord who favored tornadoes for transport, and you just had to believe in Him, the old charmer, on all those sunless, chirpy mornings with a solid insect horizon. He did it all for the improving terror of the least of his devoted servants, of course. Then he lacked the class even to keep from boasting about it to them in the depths of their despair.

But in the invisible roaring giant of this land we must believe, the dread Ancient One. Blessed be He for being as close as the fucked universe came to love or mercy. This Alice in Wonderland character on the throne of being, a cosmic psychopath in a spinning layered chariot, all we have to love, worship, cherish in the world beyond ourselves, our maws, our own orifices.

And the land itself had to be believed in, famous for its election among the nations, its stone bread and harsh rectitude and the mute stone witnesses that stood in its deserts attesting thereof. But redemption? Worshipful? Holy?

Not me, Lucas thought. *Non serviam.*

After a while, he felt a little better. He had parked his Renault on Saladin Street, up on the sidewalk, Israeli style. Only a few feet from the car, he saw that his rear window had been smashed and the paint around it was blackened and blistered. Someone had hit it during the night, maybe because of the yellow plates, maybe because someone had seen him park and wanted a relationship.

"Aw, fuck," Lucas said. He looked around but there was no one in sight. "Diphtheria, you little rat." Diphtheria Steiner, Diphtheria von Heilige Land, a wee Nazi djinn.

"Diphtheria, you baby demon moppet, you evil little bitch," he said to the air. "You trashed my car!"

38

"Did you know the Black Panthers?" Linda asked when they had cleared the Beit Hanoun checkpoint.

"I was still a kid in the days of the Panthers," Sonia said.

"But didn't you admire them?"

Sonia was nervous and unhappy at finding herself in the Gaza Strip with Linda Ericksen, hostage to her own promise to provide safe transportation.

"The Panthers weren't one thing, Linda. It wasn't like you were talking about the CP or the CIA. They were street guys. One man was sometimes very different from another. Different chapters went different ways. A lot of times they'd been infiltrated. There was manipulation and doublecross. But, yeah," she said, breaking into a smile, "I admired them then. They were beautiful. Some of them were very bad."

"You mean *baaad*," said Linda with merry complicity.

"Well, I mean that," Sonia said, "but I also mean bad. If you ever heard the tape of them torturing Alex Rackley in New Haven, I don't think you'd like it."

"But you can't tolerate informers, can you? You have to be that way to combat infiltration, right?"

The day before, Linda had announced that a few members of Abu Baraka's special squad were ready to speak for the record and she had been delegated to arrange a meet. Sonia had called Ernest Gross, who was away at a conference, and also Lucas, who was not at his apartment; she had succeeded in reaching only machines. But the prospect of a statement from Abu Baraka's men seemed worth the risk, and she could hardly let an innocent like Linda set off to record

it. Now, driving by the smoldering garbage of Jabalia, she was having regrets.

"I can't make those decisions. That's why I'm not a revolutionary."

"I thought you were close to the Communists."

"Really? Who told you that?"

"I can't remember," Linda said, shifting in her seat. "I don't
know. I inferred it."

"Yeah," said Sonia. "I was born that way."

Slowing to let a knot of children cross the road, Sonia considered
her history as a red-diaper baby and suddenly remembered one of
her mother's stories. She found herself smiling into the children's
hard, curious stares as it came to her. The night of the Rosenbergs'
execution, her mother had taken Sonia's older sister, Fran, to Union
Square in her carriage. They had arrived just as the cops had turned
off the protest rally's sound system. Then there had been a rush, the
cops shoving the crowd back toward the Fifteenth Street pillars, and
Helen, her mother, had picked Fran up and run with her like a
football toward Fourteenth Street, and the carriage had been pushed
along by the milling crowd, Odessa-steps style, Fran liked to say.
And that was the last they saw of the baby carriage — a fifty-dollar
carriage from Macy's, and some Bowery bum had undoubtedly appropriated it to collect his deposit bottles. Later, she could remember
coming home from first grade to hear her parents arguing over
Khrushchev's secret speech of several years earlier.

When the last kid was across the road, she started up the Land
Rover again. For some reason, the UN insignia seemed not to be
working its magic. Everyone who passed, even the children, seemed
tense and hostile.

"And you were in Cuba," Linda said.

"Yup."

"Didn't they send you to Africa? Didn't they try to use your . . .
background?"

"How do you mean?"

"Oh, I don't know. Look, I don't mean to be cross-examining
you. I think everything you did is wonderful."

"Like what did I do?"

Linda laughed again. "It seems to me that you've spent your life
working for people. And you're still doing it."

"People," Sonia repeated. "*The people.* But I'm not still doing it,

Linda. Just trying to get my own head straight." She scanned the distance for any concentration of smoke that might indicate a disturbance. The car was equipped with a radio this time, and she raised UN headquarters in Gaza City for the traffic and riot report. The UN duty officer was a Canadian whose voice she failed to recognize.

"I'm headed for Nuseirat," Sonia told him. "I have Miss Ericksen of the Israeli Human Rights Coalition, a U.S. national. How's my road?"

"Might have a few problems. Nothing up your way as yet. You'll have one checkpoint on the inland road. Check in if you go past Deir el-Balah. Who are you, by the by?"

"I'm Sonia Barnes, U.S. national. I'm a Communist."

Both the Canadian duty officer and Linda got a kick out of that. The Canadian seemed to think it less funny than Linda did. "Eh?" he inquired.

"I hope you know what you're doing," Sonia said to Linda. "I owe folks for the use of this vehicle. I'd hate to see them get in trouble."

"It's all arranged," Linda said.

"I have to tell you, I wish Ernest hadn't been out of town."

"It's a unique opportunity," Linda said. "Our informant said he had pictures and everything else. I brought a video camera."

"You know," Sonia said, "I haven't been very active on this side of things lately. I've been helping friends."

"Yes, that wonderful-looking Mr. De Kuff. He seems so spiritual. That must be inspiring."

Sonia had a quick glance at her passenger. Linda was smiling so enthusiastically, she seemed not to see the cinderblock hovels and the soiled canvas flaps or smell the foul smoke and the pit toilets.

"You must have come this way before if you went out to the settlements," Sonia said.

"No," said Linda. "We went by way of the beach."

"Really? Did you go swimming?"

"Yes, it was great," said Linda.

"Where was that?"

"Oh, I don't know," Linda said. "One of the settlements. Somewhere on the shore."

"Didn't it smell?"

"What, the water? The beach?" She thrust out her long jaw and pursed her lips. "No, it was terrific."

"Didn't you get the feeling that the guy who calls himself Abu Baraka might come from one of those settlements?"

Linda looked startled. "Absolutely not," she said. "In fact, they have a good understanding with the local people."

"Is that what one of the settlers told you?"

"Well, yes. But I didn't see any reason to doubt it."

"I think you'll find," Sonia explained, "that when the settlers say they have a good understanding with the local people, they mean that they've got the local people terrorized. 'A good understanding' means the Palestinians understand who's boss."

"Well," Linda said, "the locals do steal sometimes."

"I hadn't thought of that," Sonia said. "I bet you're right. Sure enough."

For reasons that Sonia could not quite remember, Argentina camp had a rough reputation. It was set about with IDF checkpoints and surrounded by razor wire searchlights and machine-gun emplacements. From what Sonia could see, it seemed composed of the same gray sheds and littered, pitted roads as the rest of the camps. There was a front gate with IDF soldiers manning a sentry box, and the road into the camp devolved into a spiral of sandbags. A few civilians in sharp khaki tropicals watched as the soldiers gestured to the UN vehicle to stop.

The soldier checking identification looked at both Sonia's and Linda's. When he saw Linda's he called out, "Human Rights Coalition!" One of the civilians walked over and looked at Linda's card, then at her passport, and then at her.

"Supposed to be an Israeli organization," he said.

She shrugged prettily.

"You got to have an appointment to come out here," the man said. "We're not equipped for surprise visits."

"I thought we had one."

"We have no problem with IHRC. When there's an appointment, it's kept. Today there isn't one."

"What do you suggest we do?" Linda asked.

"I suggest you go back and make an appointment. Then come."

With a smile to match his sarcasm, Sonia put the car in reverse while the soldiers on duty looked idly on. A short way down the road, a young man in a white shirt came up to the wire and waved at them. He seemed to be indicating a turnoff.

"Oh, good," Linda said brightly. "He'll let us in."

"Linda," Sonia said, "that guy was Shabak. Or something equally heavy. He wasn't fucking around. You don't play games with them."

But the young man in the white shirt was indeed indicating a turnoff that led to an entrance from which sandbags had been removed. He was opening a gate. Sonia stopped the car.

"Christ," she said, "I don't like this. Something's weird. You know," she said to Linda, "let's just go back across the line."

But Linda was filled with passionate intensity. "No, no. Look, this kid is letting us in."

"I see that," Sonia said. "But I don't like it. I'm not a big fan of the IDF, but I like them to know what I'm up to. I don't believe in sneaking in."

"It's arranged," Linda insisted. "We arranged it."

Linda, biting her lip, was not convincing as an arranger.

"You arranged it? You arranged it without telling the IDF spokespeople?"

"Yes," Linda said, seeming to seize on the notion. "That was the whole idea."

A soldier in a watchtower was observing them through binoculars. He shouted something in Hebrew through a megaphone. From a nearby mosque sounded the call to prayer. The young man in the white shirt waved to the soldier in the watchtower and pulled the log-and-wire gate aside. Sonia drove the UN car just inside the arc of the gate and the young man closed it. She was trying to remember what she had heard about Argentina camp.

"He's an American like us," the young man told Linda. He seemed to be indicating the soldier in the tower. "He's giving us a break. Come on, quick."

They left the car and the man led them through the camp. Sonia liked this less and less. For the most part, the alleys seemed a bit more squalid than those of other camps in the Strip, although here and there some enterprising soul had transformed his hovel into something like a bungalow. The buildings were not the standard-issue 1948 UN model, and a few of them had television aerials. So there was electricity in the camp, probably a generator. The place seemed to be at once dirtier and better provided for than the others Sonia had seen. Unlike at the beach, Linda began to notice the smell. She crinkled her nose.

The man, who seemed to want to avoid eye contact, took them to a little square where a few local youths, surly and druggy, looked at them with indifferent hatred. Narcotized hatred always had a special quality, Sonia thought. Impersonal, almost abstract, even philosophical. It appeared superficially less threatening to those whose job it was to contain it and was often preferred by them. The downside was its way of seeming to extend from the dull eyes of the haters into dimensions beyond the context at hand, through the seven spheres, from the corner of Perdido to the bottom of the sea. Infinitely implacable, because there was no reasoning with dead souls. That was what hell was about.

The camp had a school with the plaque of the Israeli Ministry of Education. It appeared closed, but most state schools had been closed since the intifada began. There was also a small health center. Sonia and Linda followed the young man inside.

The center also seemed unattended, although the equipment in it was clean and bright and the receiving station orderly. There was a metal chair and table with a kidney-shaped aluminum bucket. Beside the chair was a bed covered with a laundered green sheet. On the wall over the bed was a framed drawing of a stylized Bedouin encampment that looked as though it might have been taken from an American children's Bible.

Against one wall, cardboard boxes were stacked to the ceiling. Each carton bore a stenciled label of its contents in a Scandinavian language. Touching the stack, Sonia realized the boxes were all empty.

"Who runs the medical operation?" she asked.

"Well, we used to," Linda said. "I mean, the House of the Galilean. Now it's part of the camp."

The young man, who was tall and reddish-haired and on the nervous side, introduced himself to Sonia as Lenny. He did seem North American.

"Who did you say you were with?" Sonia asked him.

"Human Rights," Lenny said. "Middle East Watch."

He kept not looking at her. This, Sonia had come to realize, usually meant something, though it was often difficult to decide what. Shyness, morbid hypersensitivity and homicidal racism could all assume the same aspect. But she did not for a moment believe that he had anything to do with human rights or that he worked for Middle East Watch.

It turned out that he was supposed to be from California. He said something about Long Beach. All in all, he sounded like a man who had a job to do and people to deal with and just enough goodwill to manage it, with none to spare. Sonia was too anxious to listen. The whole thing was distressing. Lenny did seem fond of Linda, though, and she of him.

"Lenny works with us in Tel Aviv," Linda explained.

"That's great," Sonia said. She went to the door and looked out on the little square. The decrepit young Palestinians looked back sidewise. It was an especially scroungy and demoralized place, the generator notwithstanding.

"Did you say you brought a video camera?" she asked Linda.

"Yes. It's in the car. I'll get it."

"Our cars get hit too," Sonia said, "and that parking lot's unprotected."

"Let me," Lenny hastened to say. "I'll go."

"I'll get it," Sonia said. "I have to get something of my own."

She hurried out and down the alley that led to the gate before they could stop her. In one of the hovels, someone was watching CNN. She heard the voice of Bernard Shaw.

A few kids were already circling the car when Sonia got to it. Linda's video camera was in plain view on the front seat. Sonia climbed in and tried raising UNRWA headquarters at Zaitun, in central Gaza City. She got the Rose of Saskatoon.

"Rose! Sonia B."

"Hey, Sonia!"

"Meet you on three-eleven mike hotel."

Switching to the peacekeeping force's military frequency was against regulations. Moreover, it was monitored by the IDF. There was a chance, however, that switching over to it might purchase a little time and salutary confusion.

"This is UNRWA on three-eleven mike hotel," the Rose's voice said.

Over the line, one of the PKF officers started bitching at them for being on a restricted frequency.

"Rose," Sonia said, "we're over at Argentina camp. Can you get over here?"

"Negative," the Rose said. "I'm alone right now." There was a pause. "Maybe I can. Wait."

Sonia took a deep breath and asked the big hard question. "Was anyone supposed to be taking statements about Abu Baraka today? The beating of juveniles by the security forces? Some kind of meeting in the Argentina camp set up by IHRC?"

"I don't know anything about it. Better ask Ernest."

"Ernest is out of the country, Rose."

"You're not actually in Argentina camp?"

"Well," Sonia said, "on the edge like."

"It's nasty over there," the Rose said. "Smelly. Stinky. And they don't let anyone in."

"I'm hip," said Sonia. "I'm supposed to be waiting for Abu. Or something."

"Something's screwy, Sonia. Stay out of Argentina camp."

"Well, I'm with this Linda Ericksen person."

"Swede?"

"No, she's American. She's supposed to be arranging an interview with Abu."

"Fuck that noise. Where are you?"

"Well, I'm like ocean side of the main gate. At a side gate. I think it's just outside Nuseirat."

"Oh," said the Rose, "bloody Nuseirat."

"Something wrong?"

"Hang on," the Rose said. "I'll be over as soon as I can."

39

WHEN SONIA ARRIVED at the dispensary with Linda's camcorder, three crestfallen Palestinians were standing in a row in the examining room. A broad-shouldered smiling man with a fierce mustache and cheap sunglasses was with them.

"These were beaten," the man with the fierce mustache said humorously. "I am called Saladin. I beat them."

The beaten Palestinians looked ratty and frightened, without dignity. They seemed to be toeing an invisible mark on the floor. One wore a brown army-style sweater, extensively darned and full of holes. The darning was old and unraveling; it looked as if someone had once cared enough to repair his sweaters and then just given up. He alternately picked at it as though for vermin and grabbed its sleeves to wrap it more warmly about himself. The second junkie seemed to be on the nod and appeared at the point of passing out on his feet. The third had a slack smile. Although it was warm, they wore long-sleeved garments. The man with the sweater had a nasty abscess on the back of his hand.

Christ, thought Sonia, they're junkies too.

"What a coup!" said Linda. She was filming it all.

"Great," said Lenny.

"When are they coming to town?" Sonia asked. "Because I know Chris Lucas is going to want to talk to them. This is really his story in a way. And there'll probably be television, right? Because the government's been denying this."

"Oh, we'll never get them to town," Linda said.

"Never," Lenny added.

"Yes," said Linda, "this will have to be it."

"This?" Sonia said. "This is all the Coalition needs? That's impossible."

"I am Saladin," the grim old mustache repeated. "I beat them."

"This man was in the Border Police," Lenny explained. "He's a Circassian from Mount Carmel."

"I thought you were only coming out to make some formal arrangements for interviews," Sonia said, trying to stay calm. "Are you telling me that was it?"

"Well," said Linda, "this will give us something for a joint statement. The Human Rights Coalition and UNRWA and even Amnesty International."

"No, it won't," Sonia said. "It isn't anything."

"Chris can interview them later if he wants," Linda said. "I doubt we can bring them back today."

It was likely, Sonia thought, that both of them knew perfectly well that Lucas had dropped the Gaza Strip story. Probably, she thought, she should have taken him into her confidence before. But there had been personal considerations, and she had not wanted to be a snitch.

"Well, Helen Henderson is coming over," Sonia said. "As a witness. We have to wait for her." She looked through the front door and saw the pale, dirty faces of children framed in it, watching them, unafraid. "I thought you were just a volunteer, Linda. I thought you just did, like, typing for the Coalition."

"Well," Linda said happily, "this is my big chance." A little too happily, Sonia thought. With a little too much force and venom. Something was taking its course, like the song said. Call me Clueless Barnes, she thought.

"Since when did the UNRWA people get involved?" Lenny asked Linda.

"They're not involved," Linda said. "She must have called them."

"Did you call them?" Lenny asked Sonia.

"Well, yes. I thought we needed witnesses."

"You're a witness," Lenny said. "Linda and I are witnesses."

Saladin, the Circassian from Mount Carmel, saluted and marched the three junkie plaintiffs outside into the square. The children lined up to watch them pass. It was a semi-military procession, a parade.

"We should get out to the car," Sonia said.

"Yes," said Linda. "As it happens, we're expecting someone too."

Lenny went along behind them, carrying a cardboard box with a wooden handle. They got to the car in time to catch two children in the act of trying the doors. The children peeled off in no particular hurry.

The soldier in the watchtower was gesturing at them, pointing to his watch. Lenny gave him the thumbs-up sign and started hauling the gate open again. Linda helped him. Then Lenny climbed in the back seat with his box. They drove the UN car out onto the road and parked it.

A moment later a heavy UN truck appeared, driven by a tall, dark-skinned soldier with frizzy hair piled under his blue beret.

"Are you my folks?" he asked. "You have something for me?"

It developed that they had, and it was Lenny's box. Leaving his motor running, the soldier climbed down from the cab. He had a big smile for Sonia. Perhaps for that reason she helped him take the box out of the back seat. It was very heavy.

"Where you from, dear?" the soldier asked. "You ain't from here, are you? You ain't an Ethiopian girl?"

"American," Sonia said, handing over the carton.

"No fooling? How about that?"

"How about you?" she asked him.

"I'm Fijian. Long way from home."

At the edge of the road, Linda was fiddling with the camera. For all Sonia knew, she was filming them.

"What do you think of that woman taking your picture there?" Sonia asked the Fijian.

"Reckon it's all right. She's done it before. Hey, I knew you was from Canada or the U.S. Where you live?"

"I live in J-town," she said.

"Come down to Tel Aviv tomorrow. Come to party. We've got Fijian blokes. Canadians. All kinds."

His name, it turned out, was John Lautoka, a Micronesian rather than an Indo-Fijian, and he was quite handsome.

The guard in the adjoining tower now addressed them through his bullhorn. He seemed to be growing impatient.

"I think he's telling us to fuck off," Sonia said.

"Right," said Lenny, "let's do it."

From the edges of Nuseirat they could hear the amplified voices of muezzins.

"I don't want to be boring," she said, "but what was in the box?"

"Oh," Linda said airily, "stuff for Ernest. Tapes, videos. Paper."

Beyond Argentina camp's wire, a Laredo with the white letters

UN taped to its sides whizzed past them and made a U-turn to the gate. It was the Rose and Nuala. The Rose climbed out; she still had the STUDY ARSE ME bumper sticker on her jeep but her attire was more modest. Nuala got out the other side.

Nuala and the Rose looked at Linda briefly. They had all seen each other around.

"I'm Lenny," said Lenny.

"What'd you want to come to Argentina camp for, Linda?" The Rose phrased her question in the sort of friendly, cheerful and helpful Canadian manner that brought an accusatory pall over the entire exchange.

"Well. I work for the Israeli Human Rights Coalition," Linda said. "And there are men in that camp who claim to have been beaten. So we made a tape."

"Not in there you didn't." Nuala strolled over to her. "Ernest would never send you in there. Aren't you one of those American Christers?" She turned to Lenny. "Who're you, friend? What do you have to do with Argentina camp?"

It seemed odd, Sonia thought, that Nuala would not know Lenny if he was one of their contacts.

"Who told you to pick up here?" Nuala asked the Fijian driver, John Lautoka, who had been picking his teeth and comparing the Rose's and Nuala's structural dynamics.

"I was told what I was told," the man said.

Three separate covert conversations ensued. While Nuala questioned Lautoka, Sonia took the Rose aside. Lenny and Linda were left looking left and right in the middle of the dirt road, holding their own counsel.

From the watchtower, the soldier who was supposed to be American whistled between his teeth and pointed at his wrist to indicate a contracting supply of time. Lenny waved him off impatiently. The soldier shouted something.

"Do you know what this place is, Sonia?" the Rose asked. "This Argentina camp place? It's where they keep their snitches. No one in there is going to talk to a reporter or a rights worker."

"She filmed these guys," Sonia said. "I thought we were making some kind of preliminary contact. She told me Ernest sent her. And Len had a friend on guard duty."

"Shit too," said the Rose. "That's not likely. I wasn't going to tell you this," she said. "Nuala's running dope into T.V. They get guns in exchange."

"I know," Sonia said. "And I suppose Shabak does too."

"They've been doing it for years," the Rose told her. "Shabak will play one faction off against another, and whoever's considered useful at the moment gets guns and money. But to keep the Americans from finding out, they work through dope dealers like Stanley. The IDF has orders not to interfere."

"I suppose they each think they're getting the best of the deal."

"Everybody knows. Except us. UNRWA. And even we know, if you see what I mean. The Americans probably know too. Shabak was using Hamas the same way. To screw the Muslim Brotherhood. Until it blew up on them."

"Where does Linda come in?" Sonia asked.

"It doesn't make sense. It's all worked out between the Communist faction of the PLO and the Shabak control. Nuala and Rashid handle it from this end. The Israeli Human Rights Coalition would never be involved in something like this."

"Maybe they're dropping the Communists?"

"I don't know, Sonia. It's scary."

Sonia saw black smoke rising over the hovels of Bureij town. Burning rubber.

They heard amplified voices from the mosques, although it was not the hour of prayer. The voices sounded enraged, almost hysterical, aged voices distorted and shrill. From the shabby precincts of Argentina camp, a pathetic wail of fear — the fear of grown young men who had lost their fighting spirit, their strutting vanity, their feigned self-confidence, their self-respect and finally even their adulthood — ascended like a foul prayer over the filth and stink of their quarters. The Israeli soldiers on guard shouted them down in mocking consolation. Everyone turned to watch the smoke.

Nuala was questioning John Lautoka.

"You were supposed to pick up in town," she said. "Who told you to pick up here? Was it Walid?" Walid was the name one of their controls used, though he was an Israeli and not a Palestinian.

"No. An IDF soldier I never saw before. But he used the right codes."

From his watchtower, the sentry whistled again and pointed to the horizon.

"I've got to go," Lenny told Linda. "Will you be all right with them?"

"I'll be all right," Linda said. "But where will you go, Lenny?"

"Kfar Gottlieb. I'll get a ride from the camp in the next army jeep," Lenny said. "I've had enough of these people."

"You should come with us," Linda said. "You'll be seen and you won't be able to work out here again."

Lenny smiled. "There won't be anyone out here except us, remember?"

"Ride with the soldier in the PKF truck," Linda suggested. "He can drop you at the checkpoint outside Nuseirat, and there's always someone going to Kfar Gottlieb from there."

"No," Lenny said, "I don't mind being seen by the Arabs, but I shouldn't be riding with *that* element. It's all right for you. I'll wait here for an IDF vehicle."

"For heaven's sake," Linda said, "don't dawdle. Look at all the smoke."

The fumes were ascending now from every direction, black and unacceptable as Cain's sacrifice.

Nuala opened the gate for John Lautoka and his truck and called for everyone to leave.

"Bloody hell," she said, sniffing the stench of rubber. "Here we go again!"

40

ON HIS WAY home from the burnt ruin of his car, Lucas
went to a police station to report its trashing by fire. The
Israeli policemen had not exactly hooted and jeered at him,
but their manner had not been overly sympathetic either. It had been
a hell of a way to start the day, a most uninspiring climax to a
night's vigil.

There was a cut-rate car rental office near the police station, so he
stopped there and filled out the paperwork for the rental of a Ford
Taurus. Rental cars were not always readily available, and since he
was likely to need one soon, it was just as well to get the process
under way.

Arriving in his apartment, weary and disgusted, he turned on the
phone machine and heard Sonia's voice on it. She was going to the
Strip. Linda Ericksen had arranged for her to videotape the confessions of Abu Baraka. She had tried to get Ernest to go there with
them, but he was out of the country. She was meeting Abu at a place
called Argentina camp, near Nuseirat.

He sat on the bed for a minute or two, pondering Sonia's message.
Then he tried calling the offices of the Israeli Human Rights Coalition. Ernest was away, as it turned out, but the North American–
sounding young woman he spoke with was familiar with Abu
Baraka's pastimes. She felt able to assure him that nothing as news-
worthy as a statement from Abu Baraka himself was in the offing.
Had it been, Linda Ericksen, a foreign volunteer who had more or
less withdrawn her minor services from the organization, would not
have been detailed to deal with it. He thought about it for a moment
more, then decided to pick up his rental car.

Two hours later, he was leaving it at a parking lot on the Israeli

side of the Green Line. He crossed into the Strip on his press credentials and hired a *sherut* to take him to Argentina camp. The driver, a
young man who spoke a little English, was torn between his insistence that he knew of no such destination as Argentina camp and his
determination not to lose Lucas as a fare. Since there was no such
place, the driver made it clear to Lucas, it would be expensive to go
there.

On the way, he entertained Lucas with fragments of Shakespeare:
"To be or not to be . . . Tomorrow and tomorrow and tomorrow . . .
Ripeness is all . . ."

The horizon before them grew progressively more hazy. Then the
haze became smoke, and at first it seemed to be part of the eternally burning trash fires that wafted out of the camps' dumps. Eventually, both Lucas and his driver recognized it as rubber smoke, the
kind of smoke that signaled flaming barricades. The driver slowed
down.

Out of the smoke came a sweating, blackened man; he was hurrying along looking straight ahead, swinging his arms in a military
fashion. He looked out of place, to say the least.

The driver turned to Lucas. Lucas, who had been preparing for an
argument with him over proceeding further, was surprised to see
him smiling unpleasantly.

"A Jew," he said. For a fraction of a second, Lucas thought the
man was talking about *him*. Then he realized that the Jew in question was the unlikely pedestrian they had passed. They drove for
another few minutes, and to his great relief Lucas saw two white
vehicles parked behind a barbed-wire gate off the road. Sonia,
Nuala, Linda Ericksen and the Rose were gathered beside them.

"I got your message," he told Sonia.

"Thanks, Chris," she said. "You probably shouldn't have come."

"Forget it," he said. He paid the driver and got out. His driver lost
no time in hauling ass the way they had come. The departing taxi
added its exhaust fumes to the gathering smoke.

"We're turning back," Nuala told him from the lead car. "We're
going the way your driver went. I want to get home to Deir el-
Balah."

"I think it's popping that way too," Lucas said. "Maybe we can
get there by the coast road. By the way," he asked Nuala, "who was
the guy walking along the road? I think he might be in trouble."

Linda Ericksen had been sitting on the passenger side of Sonia's

Land Rover with the door open. She got to her feet. "Oh," she said, "Lenny!"

"Who's Lenny?"

"We don't think we know," Sonia said.

"You've got to help him," Linda said.

"If he's not known," Nuala said from the lead car, "he's in trouble."

They decided to leave the Rose's Laredo to the security of Argentina camp and make for Deir el-Balah in Sonia's UN vehicle. Nuala, for her part, was worried about Rashid.

They packed themselves into the Land Rover. Nuala drove, with the Rose and Linda beside her. Sonia and Lucas sat in back.

Nuala was scanning the burning landscape, counting off the towns that seemed to be in flames. Bureij. Maghazi. There was smoke everywhere. They began to hear small-arms fire.

Linda stammeringly told her story about documenting Abu Baraka's crimes for Sonia's benefit.

"They've got to be more careful with their snitches than that," Nuala said to Linda. "I'm sorry, I don't buy it."

"Why would you?" Linda asked her furiously. "You're with the *fedayeen*. You're one of them. You too," she told the Rose. "Lenny's a genuinely concerned individual. He's with the Human Rights Coalition."

"Is he?" Sonia asked Lucas.

"I don't know," Lucas said. "I don't think so."

By the time they had gone as far as Bureij, they had not seen a single Israeli vehicle or soldier. The IDF might have concentrated some forces at the approaches to Argentina camp, but they had clearly pulled out of the concrete slums of Bureij, closing down the highway northward, strengthening their checkpoint and waiting for reinforcements before going in. For the moment, the *shebab* had free rein of the noisome lanes and had even come out on the road.

Some of the youths were running along it, jogging parallel with the Land Rover. Their faces were veiled in their kaffiyehs; each kaffiyeh's color expressed the wearer's political affiliation, Lucas had been told. The Arafat people wore a black check. The Communists, under Nuala's Rashid, naturally favored red. Hamas wore Islamic green. Green was the prevailing color now, here in Bureij.

It was the first time Lucas had ever seen the *shebab* rampant. Some of the boys spun in ecstasy. Some threw their heads back and screamed at the smoky sky.

"*Allahu akbar!*"

They had not quite the friendliness toward UN vehicles Lucas was used to. Some of the men who had unveiled their faces had terrible smiles. Many wept. How shall it be with kingdoms and with kings, Lucas thought. He forgot the rest. He did not roll up the window, in spite of the smoke. He did not avert his gaze from them.

"*Allahu akbar!*"

The wretched of the earth, the avengers of oppression, the beloved of God, blessed be He. Up ahead he could see the IDF checkpoint beyond smoke and wire, and the soldiers retiring toward it from the town, covering their withdrawal squad by squad. Rocks flew, and gas grenades, and he heard the small whiz of bullets, rubber and the other kind.

"*Allahu akbar!*"

And maybe for these army kids, the undertrained reserve soldiers of the IDF, temporarily outnumbered, it was as it had been for the toughs in the Antonia Fortress of the Old City, in the first flush of the Jewish Revolt, when the Zealots came for them in the name of Sabaoth. The same God inspiring the same strokes. Mercy was His middle name — except on certain occasions, during special enthusiasms.

"Christ," Lucas said, "is this it? I mean, is this the one?" He meant the one he had planned to observe on television in Fink's while his French colleague ran to Mecca. No one in the car answered him.

Along the side of the road, a howling ancient was hurried along by veiled youths. He shook his fists and it appeared that the young men might be having trouble keeping pace with him.

From the mosques, from the alleys, from the road: "*Allahu akbar!*"

Linda was crying.

And suddenly they were in a relatively quiet stretch. Piles of tires burned unattended. The army had pulled back to fixed positions while the Palestinian crowds were closer to the town center. A souk, its stacks of produce displayed in place, stood deserted. Nuala braked and they stopped briefly at the mouth of what seemed to be a deserted alley.

Turning into the alley, they were surprised to see men and boys racing among the market stalls. The young men were not shouting slogans, and they appeared very grim. Something about the charge of the scene fascinated Lucas. In the next instant they watched a stall overturn and heard a wordless cry. Then a voice shouted:

"*Itbah al-Yahud!*"

A kind of silence fell. Then it was repeated.

"*Itbah al-Yahud!*"

The phrase was being chanted over and over, roared by men, ululated by unseen women.

Lucas knew immediately what it meant, although he had never heard it said or screamed or sung before. Why had he known? He saw that Sonia knew too. Down in the alley a grinning middle-aged man was jumping up and down in place.

"*Itbah al-Yahud!*"

Kill the Jew!

"They have someone," Sonia said.

Lucas knew that she was right. And that this particular *Yahud* was not an abstraction, not the *Yahud* squatting in the estaminet, blistered in Brussels, patched and peeled in Antwerp. Not the Rootless Cosmopolitan or the International Financier. He was one man alone, run down by a mob, carrying the whole fucking thing by himself. A Jew bastard such as young Lucas had once been.

"*Allahu akbar! Itbah al-Yahud!*"

"It's Len!" Linda shrieked. "It's Lenny!" She might have caught a glimpse of him.

Nuala pulled over to the narrow shoulder. Everyone got out and stood in a milling circle beside the car. Locals, hurrying to the spectacle, paused to regard them with surprise.

"Why would he walk alone in the Strip?" Sonia asked. "Is he out of his mind?"

"He was afraid of getting in trouble!" Linda shrieked.

Lucas and Sonia looked at each other.

"Getting in trouble?" Lucas asked.

"What are these two doing here anyhow?" Nuala asked, apparently meaning Linda and Lenny. "Christ, maybe we can get him loose. Take the car and follow me."

Nuala got out and Lucas drove, with Sonia beside him. The Rose and Linda were in the back.

"Give it the horn," Nuala called to Lucas. "And don't run me over." Lucas began to pummel the car horn. Nuala walked ahead of him with one hand on the fender. After a minute the Rose opened the back door and got out on the road to slog beside Nuala. Slowly, absurdly, they advanced up the alley where an ecstatic crowd was beating an unseen Jew. Finally, Lucas decided he could drive no further.

"We might as well get out too," he said to Sonia. Linda crouched ashen-faced in the back. "Come with us," Lucas told her. But she stayed where she was.

Now he was reluctant to leave the car. The crowd was out of control, and though he took the keys, he knew that it might be gone or ablaze when they got back, and Linda with it.

"Stay together," Nuala told her troops. "We'll try to get him."

And maybe they would, Lucas thought. Nuala was good with crowds; she was a Communist, after all. He was looking about him in unfocused hope of some formless mercy, sanity, forgiveness, understanding. But there was nothing around them except the mass of hovels of cement and hammered tin and dirty plastic, stinking for miles from the desert to the sea.

"*Itbah al-Yahud!*" cried the mob.

Linda locked the car behind them.

"Lenny?" Lucas shouted. He was trying to remember who Lenny was. But it hardly mattered now. He was the Other here, the prey, the pursued. A man like himself, like himself in every important way.

A group of youths approached to intercept their passage. Lucas thought of the Dane he had seen weeks before, standing up for the lives of the cornered Arab kids. He tried to ease forward but the crowd pressed against him. He could still hear the sounds of struggle and pursuit in the next arcade.

Sonia began to speak in Arabic. The youths confronting them shook their heads grimly and avoided her eyes.

"Please let us pass!" Lucas said. "We have a job to do here."

They stared blankly, leaving Lucas to contemplate his own declaration. He supposed it was pretty meaningless, even had the crowd been able to understand it. As though they were there to pave the street.

Meanwhile, Nuala and the Rose were shouldering their way into the melee, shouting, shoving, ignoring copped feels, slapping impersonally at the hands that clutched their thighs and the hem of their shorts, as though swatting insects. It was Eros and Thanatos in the worst way, the men displaying their virility by grinding their teeth in the women's faces, presenting masks of sweaty, smiling rage, one hand clenched in a fist or brandishing a rock, the other clawing at the women's private places. Lucas and Sonia formed a secondary line, fighting forward. Lucas turned and got a last look at Linda, hysterical in the back seat of the car. Nuala had succeeded in reaching the end of the next alley, and it was clear that she could see what was happening there. She was frowning, tight-lipped. She began to shout and tried to move forward.

"*Itbah al-Yahud!*" the crowd screamed. Just at the moment when it looked as if Nuala would round the last stall and wade through to the action, she went reeling backward, one hand to her eye. Lucas found himself on the weak end of a shoving match with three young men who had put green-checked kaffiyehs over their faces. Someone grabbed him from behind and held him. He saw Nuala coming back through the crowd. This time it parted for her.

Then Lucas saw the things they had taken up: trowels and mallets and scythes, some dripping blood. Everyone was screaming, calling on God. On God, Lucas thought. He was terrified of falling, of being crushed by the angry swarm that was whirling around him. He wanted to pray. "O Lord," he heard himself say. The utterance filled him with loathing, that he was calling on God, on that Great Fucking Thing, the Lord of Sacrifices, the setter of riddles. Out of the eater comes forth meat. The poser of parables and shibboleths. The foreskin collector, connoisseur of humiliations, slayer by proxy of his thousands, his tens of thousands. Not peace but a sword. The Lunatic Spirit of the Near East, the crucified and crucifier, the enemy of all His own creation. Their God-Damned God.

An old man emerged from the crowd. He wore the white cap of the *haji* and leaned on a carved stick. He had a Bedouin face, long and grave. At his approach, the youths released Lucas. Was he the Almighty Beard-Winged Celestial Paperweight's earthly representative?

The old man spoke softly, nodded courteously. And when Nuala remonstrated with him, he raised his chin in the least ambivalent gesture of the place. No hope.

"He says we're in danger," Nuala told them. "He says the Jew is a dead man. If we stay we'll bring the troops, and the troops will kill everyone because of him."

"The Jew is a spy," one of the youths shouted in English. The old man nodded agreement.

"Sorry," Nuala said to her friends. "That's it."

She had a large welt over her eye and a bloody nose and they did not argue with her. To Lucas's profound gratitude, the car and Linda were where they had left them.

"Was it Lenny?" Sonia turned to ask when they were climbing in.

Nuala took a cautious look at Linda and nodded. The Rose was crying, big tears coursing down her milk-fed, tanned cheeks. There was blood on her shirt.

"Was he alive?"

Nuala only gave her a grim look.

As they drove, Linda slumped over into the space between the seats and cried and retched.

"Do it out the window, love," Nuala said. "Better not stop, you know."

Finally Linda said, "We could have saved him. If we'd had a gun."

For a moment, Lucas was afraid Nuala would say something unkind about Americans.

"Who was he?" he asked her.

"Christ," Nuala said, nursing her injured forehead. "They half broke my bloody leg as well, the fucking wogs. Lenny? I don't know who he was. Who was he, darling?" she asked Linda. "You have friends over here? Work for Shabak? For the CIA?"

Linda just kept sobbing.

"You're bleeding," Sonia told Nuala.

"Well," Nuala said, "I'm a bleeder. Thin skin."

"Like a white fighter," Sonia said.

The rough humor of the revolution, Lucas supposed. Meanwhile, he could still half hear it.

"*Itbah al-Yahud!*"

After a few miles they saw an army checkpoint ahead, heavily reinforced. Half-tracks and regular deuce-and-a-half trucks were pulling up and soldiers were fanning out from the road.

"We've got to tell them about Lenny," Linda said.

"Stop!" said Nuala. "Pull over."

Lucas did as he was told. Nuala and the Rose, who seemed to have recovered, stepped out of the car.

"Sonia," Nuala said. "Tell her."

"Make her understand," the Rose said.

Sonia turned in her seat and spoke to Linda.

"Linda, Lenny has been killed by now. People who work in the Strip can't afford to be seen as informers for the IDF. They can't provide intelligence for the soldiers. Even to be thought of that way."

"You can't!" Linda screamed. "You can't just let those animals kill a Jew!"

"This is tough," Sonia said, looking up at Lucas.

"I see," he said.

"We tried to save Lenny," Sonia said. "We failed. He's dead now. If the soldiers were guys we maybe knew or trusted we might . . . I don't know. But these guys" — she nodded toward the checkpoint, where the Border Police and Golani Regiment paras were assembling — "these guys the Golanis are very tough soldiers. Special soldiers. If we told them what happened, they might blame us. They might even, accidentally on purpose, what with the riot, kill one of us." She glanced up at Lucas, in case he failed to understand who that would probably be. "It happens."

"But that's not the point," Lucas said.

"It's not the point," Nuala said, kneeling outside the car. "If we tell them, they will go to that village and they will kill ten for the death of one Jew. They will torture kids to get names out of them, and the names won't always be the right ones. They will kill, and some of the people they kill will be innocent. That's what they do. They think it's justice."

"But we don't think it's justice," Sonia said quietly. "Because we believe in . . ." She looked at the dun sand and shook her head.

"Human rights?" Lucas suggested helpfully.

"That's it," said Sonia. "Human rights."

"Righto," said Nuala. "That's why we're here, see. So we're going through that checkpoint, God willing, and we're not saying a bloody word."

"You are shits," Linda told them. "I'm reporting you."

"No," the Rose said earnestly. "You don't understand."

"Linda," Nuala said. She beckoned Linda toward a point in the distance that would cause her to put her head outside the car window. "Have a look at that."

When Linda stuck her head out to look, at what she presumably hoped was aid, solace, resolution, Nuala hit her with a solid, considered uppercut. Linda's eyes teared, then glazed over.

"Settle back," Nuala said to her gently. "Settle back, darlin'."

She climbed in beside Linda, and Lucas started the car.

"Make it quick," Nuala said. "She's not unconscious."

"Could of fooled me," Lucas said.

At the checkpoint, a paratrooper captain elbowed the young reserves who were inspecting their identification out of the way.

"What were you doing back there? Where are you coming from?"

"We had a hardship case at Argentina camp," Sonia said. "Bureij is going up. We have two injured people here and our radio's out."

"So where do you think you're going?"

"Back to base," Sonia said, "if we can make it to Gaza."

The officer shook his head in disgust. There was another Golani officer present. Lucas watched him observe that Sonia was American and black, and this moved him to sympathy.

"If they won't let you through Gaza," the other officer said, "you might want to take the coast road to the line. Especially if your people are hurt." He looked into the back seat. "Is it bad?"

The captain barked an order at him and he moved off. Ignored, they drove away. They were almost a mile along when Linda, her jaw swollen, began to scream. She screamed and screamed.

"Hold her," the Rose said.

"Jesus!" cried Nuala, because Linda had succeeded in working her way from Nuala's rough embrace and jumped out of the car. They had been doing about 20 miles per hour on a bad stretch. By the time they were out of the car, Linda had scrambled to her feet.

"Linda, please, baby," Sonia said.

But she flashed them the fierce eyes of a child and brushed her bruised knees and ran, making for the Israeli post as though the devil himself were after her — which, Lucas thought, was just about the way she saw it — while the four infidels milled about ineffectually.

"She's not safe on the road," Sonia said.

"Well, hell," said Nuala, "we can't hold her prisoner. But we're in deep shit now."

"Know any Sufi prayers?" Lucas asked Sonia.

"This is one," she said. But that was all she said, so he concluded that their situation represented some variety of Sufi prayer. Obviously, it was a demanding religion.

They were driving among fires. Young men veiled in green-checked kaffiyehs appeared beside the road again. Suddenly an IDF jeep loomed behind them, right out among the racing demonstrators. It nearly forced them off the road. In it, next to the driver, was the kindly Golani officer who showed concern for their injured. The officer leaped out.

"You sons of bitches," he shouted. "You Nazi swine! You oversaw the killing of a Jew!"

"Now . . . ," said Lucas.

"You shut the fuck up!" said the officer, trembling with rage. "You threw that girl out of the car. You left . . ."

Then someone called to him and he could not go on. Some of the crowd of Palestinians had noticed the army vehicle. Soon, Lucas thought, they would notice that it was isolated and unprotected. The officer and his driver, in spite of their anger, became aware of this.

Just before he ran to attend to whatever business demanded his attention, the officer gave them a last look of such hatred and fury that Lucas's heart shriveled in his breast. Someone would die for this, it was plain. Possibly him.

"We'll have your names," the officer shouted as the jeep bore him away. "We don't forget." The rest of what he said was lost. Had he used the word *momzer?* Maybe. Maybe Lucas had imagined it. More army vehicles sped by, the soldiers in them looking with glum hostility at their UN car.

They drove disordered roads through more towns where tires were burning and the mosques echoing with *jihad.*

"God, he looked fierce," the Rose said. She meant the officer who had stopped them.

"Yes, he did," Lucas said. "I mean . . ." He had been about to say "put yourself in his place." Then he figured, fuck it. He was tired of imagining his way into everyone's situation.

"I hate them all sometimes," the Rose declared. "Both sides."

"I know what you mean," Lucas said.

41

A T JUST ABOUT the time oily black night commenced its
descent on them, they ran clean out of road. Sonia had
raised Gaza City headquarters on the radio, and the Dutch
officer there suggested they make for the UN distribution center in
Eshaikh Ijleen, on the coast. But after they had gone a few kilometers they discovered that the track ahead was blocked with a barrier
of burnt automobiles four cars wide and there was no shoulder
beside it. The hulks were piled wire to wire.

They got out and edged their way along the wire until they were
past the pile of charred metal. Then they began to trudge toward
Eshaikh Ijleen. The last of the day's heat, fed by fires, laid twilight
mirages in their path. Lucas kept thinking he could see the ocean.
They came to a kind of town.

"Used to be an Orthodox church around here," Nuala said. "We
had dealings with them. The priest was a Greek who sympathized
with us."

Lucas could not tell whether she meant Palestinians or Communists.

"What happened to the church?"

"Hamas burned them out," she said.

The abandoned town had been a Christian camp. The church
building and the priest's house beside it had been vandalized,
the murals of mournful Byzantine saints defaced with graffiti, the
domestic fixtures and fittings stripped. An ancient photograph of a
woman carrying a parasol and wearing the fashions of the early
twentieth century lay on the red-dusted floor. Nuala picked it up.

As they walked on toward the coast, they saw dozens of fires
burning against the mottled sunset. Again Nuala recited the names
of towns. Nuseirat. Deir el-Balah.

From inside the Netzarim wire, illumination rounds traced automatic fire. Someone had got hold of a flare gun and was amusing himself firing off parachute flares. Each explosion produced cheers. Children scampered under the canopies of pretty light.

"Looks like a bloody fun fair," Nuala said.

As darkness gathered, they stopped to rest beside the road. By now they could no longer tell what lights signified or distinguish army positions from towns in the grip of riot.

"We're on our own," Nuala said. "We'll have to get through the night. The PKF will probably close all the compounds." She had taken the map from Rose's Laredo and tried reading it with her pen flashlight. "There's another small camp down the road," she said. "Rashid has a couple of cousins there. Somebody might remember me."

Leaning over to have a look at the map, Lucas saw that they were not far away from the coastal camp where he had gone on his first journey to the Strip. It was one of the poorest and most benighted parts of the place.

At the entrance to the small camp was a pile of tires buttressed by gasoline cans, an instantly inflammable barricade. About a hundred feet beyond it, a group of youths were gathered about burning trash cans. In the light of the flames, he could see figures laid side by side under blue sheeting. The figures appeared to be corpses.

All four of them walked toward the tire barricade. Lucas took the map from Nuala. He ought to keep it as a souvenir, he thought, in case they got through the night alive. It marked a place where seven hundred thousand people passed each night in prayer by the light of trash fires, demanding their own revenge and protection from everyone else's. A major energy resource, Gaza, forty kilometers long by six wide, had more than enough fear and rage to sustain human nature for the next millennium. Beaches, too.

As he walked toward the villagers, Lucas noticed that all the men around the fire began to shout at them and point at Lucas.

"What's wrong with them?" he asked the others.

"Damned if I know," Nuala said. "Better wait here."

So Lucas waited on the far side of the tire barricade while Sonia, Nuala and the Rose tried to parlay with the citizens of the camp. The citizens were screaming. They drew back the sheeting to reveal the numbers of their dead. Every few minutes, one of them pointed at Lucas. They appeared not to want to hear what Sonia and Nuala had to say to them. Eventually, the three women came back around the barricade. On the way in, a few of the Palestinian men had shifted tires and barrels to help them through. On the way out, no one helped them.

"So?" asked Lucas.

"So," Sonia said, "let's get out of here."

There were distant sirens. And now, again, the voices of muezzins.

"They have something against me?" Lucas asked.

He turned to catch a glimpse of someone from the camp stealing up behind them. In the firelight, he could see the boy had a bad eye — from viciousness or madness or plain strabismus. Apprehended, the youth skipped away, giggling. A cry went up from the men around the fire.

"They don't like you," Nuala said. "Start moving. Don't run."

"Oh, shit," the Rose said.

They kept walking jauntily along, heads held high.

"Should I sing something?" Sonia asked.

"No," said Nuala. "They'll think you're an Israeli. They always sing."

It seemed to Lucas that not even Israelis on a neo-Hegelian walkabout would sing in the present circumstances. Now a helicopter raced overhead, the roar exploding out of darkness, its fiery spotlight spinning theatrically over the ground.

"The people back there," Nuala explained to Lucas, "they think you have the evil eye. And that you're a spy. And a Jew. And that we're protecting you."

"Oh," said Lucas. "Why do they think that?"

"I don't know," Nuala said. "They seem crazy. The mullah seems crazy."

That seemed to be all she could tell him. Glancing from the road, he saw a couple of dozen people running along beside the wire. They seemed a jolly crowd, and he was the object of their attention. They were laughing and screaming, pointing, celebrating him.

"Why me?" Lucas asked, dry-mouthed.

"Oh, there are rumors," Sonia said. "They've had a few people killed, probably by snipers from the settlement across the way. There are actually provocateurs in the camps."

"The mullah says you're not a man," Nuala told him calmly. "He says you're something else."

"What?"

"I don't know. Not a man. A spirit, like a djinn."

"But still Jewish, right?"

"Right," said Sonia. "No cure for that." She sighed. "Maybe it's a camp for *majnoon.* Anyway, we won't stop there."

"Good," Lucas said.

When the helicopter went by again, Lucas said, "Do you think there's a chance the army would help us out?" He supposed he was beginning to see the point of the Israeli army.

"Us?" Nuala said. "*You,* you mean. Don't count on it. If you're press, they think you came here to make them look bad. And one of their own just got killed. They may hold you responsible."

Maybe we were responsible, Lucas thought. If we had notified the soldiers, Lenny might have been rescued. But foreign volunteers in the Strip did not run to the soldiers with information.

"Look at it this way, Chris," Sonia said. "They're not here to help you."

"You know how he's looking at it," Nuala said. "He's an American. His money buys their guns. His spies work with theirs. He thinks they owe him."

"That's not what he means," Sonia said.

"No," Lucas said. "I suppose I mean that they're people more like me, in the end. They may not be the Knights of the Round Table, but they won't kill me for being a Jew. Or a djinn."

Across a dark field more fires burned.

"You can't trust them," Sonia said. "The fact is, you can't trust anyone. Some Israelis would help you. Some wouldn't."

"I wasn't proposing pissing off to the army and leaving you three here," Lucas said testily. "I just wondered if it was worth trying to get help from them."

"The fact is," Nuala said, "we're in different situations. For each of us it's different."

They stopped again to watch the distant fires.

"Why do you think Linda got us out here?" Lucas asked. "What was on her mind?"

"We're going to find out," Sonia said. "Really soon."

"Maybe PKF will send out a patrol," Sonia suggested. "That would be nice."

"Amen," said Lucas. Someone, he thought, amid all this religion, ought to say a prayer for all the poor bastards in the world who were awaiting the ministrations of little white UN vehicles along the fucked, rutted roads of the world, and the unfortunates in control of them.

Down the road, the sound of chanting came from the direction of the village of the *majnoon*. Its tune did not particularly lift the spirit.

Turning around, Lucas saw what could only be a crowd of Palestinians advancing through the darkness. They were carrying all manner of lights — flashlights, kerosene lamps, open flames on torches. They seemed to be shouting at once. In that desert night, Lucas thought, one might actually imagine them as God's army, or Gideon's, the elect of the Lord, His host. It was undoubtedly the way they saw themselves — on the march in search of God's enemy and theirs. Him.

"They think we're getting away," Lucas said. Everyone walked faster.

They jogged through the darkness, following the faint luminescence of the road. Lucas began to think about necklacing and the uses the hostile imagination might contrive for shears and pruning hooks, all the punishments prescribed for creatures who, like himself, pretended to be human beings but were not. He found Sonia's hand and they jogged together toward the top of a small hill. For a while the smoke cleared. There were a million stars overhead, like evil angels.

At the very crest of the hill they must have been outlined against the sky, because a hearty liberationist cheer broke from the pursuing crowd. It was easier running downhill. The Rose had the penlight and was trying to read her map on the run.

"If we can get a mile and a half down the road," she said breathlessly, "there's a camp called Beit Ajani. It's supposed to be under PLO control."

"Whatever that means," Sonia said.

"Well, we don't know what it means," said Nuala. "But we'd better get down there and run for it."

So they sprinted for the gates of Beit Ajani, with the entire population of what appeared to be a camp for the insane at a quarter-mile's distance behind, waving their torches and gasoline cans in merry pursuit. They were close enough now for Lucas to hear what they were chanting.

"*Itbah al-Yahud!*"

He thought he heard a chain saw.

Inside Beit Ajani camp there was no one in sight. The place had an open gate that led off the road, so the four of them tried to push it closed behind them. Although it was made of only wood and wire they could not, all heaving together, get it to budge. Something invisible in the darkness held it immovably open.

They started running along the rows of shacks. Beit Ajani was a camp of the poorest kind; the core of each house here, too, was one of the cement structures the United Nations had built in 1948, when the place was under Egyptian rule.

"Where the hell is everyone?" Lucas asked. Not so much as a single light showed anywhere in the camp. Meanwhile, the crowd from *majnoon*ville had halted at the open gate, still waving its lighted wands and dreadful weapons, chanting its slogan.

"There are people here," Nuala said. "Lying low."

"Cooking oil," Sonia whispered. "You can smell it."

They were crouched against the line of shacks. Nuala stood upright.

"*Salaam,*" she said loudly. "*Masar il kher. Kayfa bialik?*"

"Who's she talking to?" Lucas asked.

Then he saw that she was talking to an old woman, who was peering at them from behind a quilted cotton curtain. The old woman said something in reply. She was trying to see Lucas in the darkness. The noise of the mob was growing closer. It sounded as though they had come in through the gate.

"*Itbah al-Yahud!*"

The old woman stepped aside and let the women — Nuala, Sonia and the Rose — stoop to enter her hut. When Lucas tried to follow them, she barred his way with her arm.

"It's a *daya*'s chamber," Nuala said. "A midwife's surgery. He can't come in here."

Lucas paused and looked back toward the camp gate. He no longer saw the crowd that had been behind them, only saw the lights they carried and heard their war cries. They had turned down a different alley.

"Well, he can't stay out there," Sonia said. "Listen to them!"

Lucas looked into the dim *daya*'s room. The plastered walls were painted with homely grape-leaf patterns and blue five-fingered palm prints such as those found in North Africa. The *daya* herself looked African. The only light in the place came from her cooking stove. She stood firmly in the doorway, her hands on his chest, pushing him away.

"*La,*" she trilled at him. "*La, la.*" No entry.

But she seemed ready to take the foreign women in without question, in spite of the trouble outside, the state of siege, the mob in the street. Something about the way the woman acted made Lucas think Nuala, Sonia and the Rose would be safe with her.

"I think you'll be OK here," he said to Nuala.

"What about you?" Sonia asked.

Nuala spoke to the old woman in Arabic. She shook her head in refusal.

"I don't know," Lucas said. "I'll show them my press pass or something."

With a peculiar gentleness, the old woman closed the door on him.

"*Itbah al-Yahud!*" sang the crowd in the distance.

Walk or run? Lucas wondered. He might pretend he was out for a stroll. At a T junction at the end of the alley, he went in the direction he sensed was away from the mob. An old man, collecting water at a communal tap, encountered him in the darkness and shrieked.

"*Masar il kher,*" Lucas said politely.

Suddenly he was very thirsty. He recalled the verse from the Ottoman fountain in the Valley of Hinnom — "All that is created comes of water" — one of the dozen verses of the Koran he knew, one of his tiny store of artifacts of this quarter of the world, where he had chosen to represent himself as such an expert. They were in the desert and he had not taken a drink all day and they had left a thermos in the Land Rover. He doubled back and drank from the tap while the old man whimpered at him.

When the mob sounded close again he began to run; he thought his breathing must sound terribly loud. If they burn you, he wondered, was it better to scream? To start screaming right away, just commence yelling bloody murder even before it hurt? Maybe you could use up energy that way and have a little less left to be converted into pain. Maybe such an unseemly display would shame them. No, they would only be amused by his cowardice.

What about trying to tough it out? Courage was so admirable, so transcendent. He had always admired it in others. Might he have a shot at aplomb? Fuck your necklace, fuck your burning gasoline. Let me show you how a half-Jew dies. With class. A little alienation maybe, but class. Like Cary Grant in *Gunga Din* at the temple of Thuggees.

"*Itbah al-Yahud!*"

At the end of the next alley, he came up against barbed wire. On the far side, beyond a couple of acres of what looked like spinach, burned the lights of a settlement. The camp's wire beside him did not look impossible to negotiate, but he was not inclined to venture onto the settlers' hard-won plantation at the height of an insurrection. They were likely to be aggressive defenders of their turf.

Eventually, though, there was no more to Beit Ajani camp. The last alley came to a dead end, and the rutted streets seemed to turn back to where the armed *majnoon* prowled. So he had no choice but to make a bloody-forearmed crawl under the lowest rung of barbed wire, out of Beit Ajani and into the spinach. The grim discipline of the lights arrayed across from him suggested mine fields. Might people mine their spinach? In Gaza, maybe.

Anyway, he kept running. Avoiding the camp, avoiding the road, avoiding the settlement. When another helicopter swooped overhead, he ducked and buried his head in the vegetation. Insects burrowed in the glare across his closed eyes.

Every once in a while he would pause for breath. If only, he thought, he had brought more water. Several times he thought the mob had given up; he would bend his ear to the landscape and listen hopefully for some kind of silence, a benign silence under the small-arms fire, under the muezzins' exhortations, under the helicopter's roar. A private silence in which no one pursued him. But the chant kept resounding; no matter how far he ran, they seemed always out there behind him, determined to expose him. He began to stop believing in himself as a human being. Who, he thought, would care to be one?

When the copter that had passed him in the spinach field discovered the *majnoon* mob that was chasing him, he ran, laughing to himself. Let the flying ones destroy the ones on foot! Let the ones on foot drag down the others!

Maybe, he thought, he had been imagining the chant for hours; the phrase had been echoing in his head so long. But no, there it was when he stopped again.

"*Itbah al-Yahud!*"

He was so thirsty. How did it go? "Nor let the milky fonts that bathe your thirst be your delay." Milk all the way. The American Dream. Lestrade would be amused.

Shadowed against the lights of the settlement and the rising moon, he saw a minaret at the far end of the field. There were faint lights at the base of it, and beyond more lights — aluminum lamps at regular intervals, which he thought might just mark the coast road. If he could just get through the night without falling into the hands of the mob, he thought, some passing UN vehicle might give him a ride.

Then the field in which Lucas stood burst spectacularly into light. The helicopter was overhead again — he could hear its radio crackling coordinates and instructions. Then someone began to shout over a loudspeaker. The shouting was in English, Lucas realized, and directed at him. He stood still and raised both his arms as high as they could be made to stretch, shoulder joints to fingertips.

"Press!" he yelled up at the chopper. Blowing sand got in his eyes. Twigs and small rocks swirled around him in the wash of the rotors. "*Periodista! Journaliste!*"

As he stood, arms outstretched in the whirlwind, a great shout went up from the crowd of Palestinians on the Beit Ajani road. They had lost him in the darkness of the field, he thought. Now they had located him again in the helicopter's searchlight.

For a few seconds the copter spun above him like a fury. He could see the mob's agitation, but the pounding engine drowned out any noise they made.

"Mr. Reporter?" the man said over the loudspeaker. "You're the reporter?"

It sounded like rescue.

"Yes, sir!" he shouted to his heaven-borne new pal. "I'm Lucas." He wanted to explain that they were chasing him, shouting "*Itbah al-Yahud.*" He wanted to explain everything. The helicopter was descending now, and the furious whirl of stinging shards and dirt stirred up by the rotors increased.

"Don't move, Mr. Reporter. Just wait right there!"

"OK," Lucas said, choking. In spite of being half suffocated, he was anxious to be agreeable. Although he could no longer hear the crowd for the engine noise, they appeared ever more agitated.

"Wait right there!" the loudspeaker said. The man sounded a little too earnest and helpful. "We'll pick you up first thing in the morning. Got it? Don't go anywhere, understand?"

"Yes!" Lucas shouted at the top of his voice. Then it was dark again, and he could hear the mob on the road. The helicopter was disappearing over the settlement. Within seconds it was a mile away, and Lucas understood that he had been the subject of some rough, soldierly humor. And the crowd was at the wire now, climbing it, piling under, trying to hack through. Lucas hesitated for a moment, then began running through the spinach. Someone started firing from the line of lights at the settlement's wire. Cries of pain and outrage came from the Arabs.

He ran until his breath was spent, falling, rolling, clambering upright. The spinach field ended at a high brick wall, which enclosed several domed buildings together with the minaret he had seen. Leaning against the brick, Lucas rested, eyes closed, trying to determine whether he was really hearing the chant of the same crowd. When he had taken a few breaths, he crawled along the wall's edge to look back across the field he had skirted. Sure enough, the crowd was still assembled, waving their lanterns and flashlights, banging on what sounded like trash can lids. Now they seemed to be facing the settlement, directing their slogans to it. Every once in a while, a shot would ring out from the lighted perimeter on the far side of the field. Then screams and lamentations would go up from the mob, a waving and flaunting of lights and torches.

Now, at least, he had put to rest the question of what to expect from the army. But with luck, he thought, he might stay where he was, leaving the settlers and the demented villagers to entertain each other. The coast highway was tantalizingly close, but there was not much likelihood of his finding friends there. He had an odd feeling that he had been in the same place before, during one of his earlier expeditions to the Strip. He had done an interview, it seemed to him; it had been the day of the angry Frenchman.

He traced his way along the wall with his hands, trying to step carefully over the talus and litter at its base. In the scattered light, it appeared that the minaret looming above him was surmounted with the metal remnants of a cross, bent and hanging half detached along the stucco wall. A Christian enclave, but not the same one they had stopped by earlier. And this one did not look deserted; he had seen faint lights around it.

The previous year, Lucas recalled, on his outing with the French militant, they had examined the ruins of a Christian ghetto much like the one he had come to. It had been just outside a town called Zawaydah. He leaned back against the wall to rest, trying to remember the details of the place, wishing he had brought the water. There were still shouts and stompings on the road beside the spinach field;

the mob seemed still to be out in force. Plainly, he was the event of the year. Listening hard, he realized that there were people right on the other side of the wall from where he rested.

He stood up and climbed on some fallen bricks and tried to hear the people beyond the wall. They were speaking softly, almost secretly, as if they, too, were in hiding. The language they spoke sounded like neither Arabic nor Hebrew, although he could not be sure.

Who were they and what did it mean? In the Gaza Strip, it was possible to happen upon almost anything. Most of it, at least in the opinion of those whose business it was, went better unwitnessed. Across the spinach field, the army helicopter had returned and was circling over the lights of the settlement's wire.

Lucas climbed on the brick pile and chinned himself to the top of the wall. What he saw on the other side was the remnant of a church garden that had been converted into an automotive junkyard from the days of Laurel and Hardy. There were barrels of spare parts and engines piled against each other and a dozen cars and buses in various stages of disassembly. An International Harvester truck stood in the center of the space, with its front end hoisted on a block and tackle between two sickly palm trees. At one end of the garden was a covered shed lit by kerosene lamps in which there were rows of workbenches covered with tools.

The yard was full of people who seemed to be camping out. Families lay together in sleeping bags. Men slept in upholstered armchairs with exposed springs, their feet propped on cartons. Women were nursing infants. There was an air of watchful dejection about the place.

As silently as possible, Lucas lowered himself again and tried to decide what use the place might be to him. On his last expedition, he recalled, an old man had been trying to sell him an interview. The old man claimed to be a mukhtar of the Nawar people, the local tribe of gypsies. A self-proclaimed gypsy. Lucas had taken him for a hustler.

Now, with the mob of crazies still prowling the road and a helicopter full of practical jokers overhead, it occurred to Lucas that he might want to find himself a gypsy and purchase an interview after all.

42

WHILE THE MOB ran up and down on the road outside, calling on him to reveal himself, surrender and be disemboweled, Lucas drank strong tea and arak with the mukhtar of the Nawar people, who practiced Bektashi Sufism. Among their useful enterprises was fortunetelling. Lucas readily consented to hear his fortune.

"You must pay," the mukhtar declared. Lucas was briefly alarmed, thinking that retribution was the sum of what life held in store for him. He had always expected to be made accountable. But the mukhtar was only pointing out that his psychic services were a negotiable item, subject to a fee.

"Certainly," Lucas agreed.

"How much will you pay?" asked the mukhtar. His name was Khalif.

Lucas, rather indiscreetly, looked in his wallet. He had a little over two hundred dollars in U.S. currency and shekels.

"Fifty dollars," he proposed.

"You will pay one hundred dollars," the mukhtar announced with the authority of one who saw the future.

"OK," Lucas said.

He put out his hand and the mukhtar felt along his life and fate lines. Then he put his hands on Lucas's temples.

"You will live long," the old man said.

"Good," said Lucas, though the noises close at hand did not seem to diminish.

"You will have unhappiness yet five years. You will wander the world among those who do not love you. But Allah, praised be He, will protect you as he protected others like you. At five years you will embrace Islam. You will be Darwish of the Bektashi."

"I suppose it's possible."

"Yes. You will have a wife. She is Darwish. She will instruct you. A wise woman of great faith."

"What will she look like?"

"Beautiful. Like a woman of the Howitat. Her skin is dark. She lengthens her eyes with kohl."

A bare electric bulb swung in the breeze above them. The mukhtar's kaffiyeh was spotless and his mustache barbered and lacquered like a Hungarian hussar's.

Lucas expressed amazement at the mukhtar's preternatural insights. He admitted that he was acquainted with such a woman.

"Believe," the mukhtar said. "Honor what is holy. Then your unhappiness will stop."

For an additional fee, the mukhtar offered to provide his special, informative feature-length discourse on the Nawar, Darwish of the Bektashi. It was a service he had often provided the visiting press, and it would cost another hundred dollars. Lucas did not take notes, distracted as he was by the nearby disturbances. He assured the mukhtar that his memory was excellent.

"Nawar," Khalif informed him, "is not a good name. It is a dirty name. Truly we are not Nawar. We are al-Firuli."

According to the mukhtar, the al-Firuli and their cousins, the Zhillo, had come from Albania with the khedives in the nineteenth century. They had fared well in Egypt and Gaza until the overthrow of King Farouk, who, as a descendant of the khedives, had been their patron and protector. The al-Firuli had been in Gaza since before the refugee camps, the mukhtar said. The Palestinian refugees sometimes oppressed them, as they themselves were oppressed by the Israelis. In the past the al-Firuli had made their way as musicians and dancers. Their men and women danced together and told fortunes. Since the Islamic revival, fortunetelling and mixed singing and dancing had gone into decline. And since the intifada had begun, a state of war had existed. Neither weddings nor Bihram was celebrated with music, out of respect for the martyrs. There were only funerals, and the al-Firuli did not do funerals.

The mukhtar made the Nawar view of things sound attractive and open-minded. They celebrated life, using wine and arak when they could be had. They honored Muhammad, Moses and Issa, all prophets of God.

In Tel Aviv, Khalif explained, people could be found who spoke a language the al-Firuli understood. These people in Tel Aviv spoke Romany. The Nawar language was called Dumir. Many of the younger Nawar no longer spoke it.

Lucas asked Khalif if he had been to Tel Aviv. Khalif answered ambiguously about his own travels. But many of the al-Firuli had been across the line, he admitted. They went to Tel Aviv and to Jerusalem. In Jerusalem, they went to churches and mosques and other public places to tell people about themselves. Lucas assumed he meant that they went there to beg.

It developed that Khalif had heard of Yad Vashem. The al-Firuli went there as well. Lucas ventured to ask him if he knew the significance of the place.

"The Jews were killed," Khalif said. "Many died until they came here."

He said he had heard that it was a magnificent place, built of precious metals, as great as any mosque.

"But it's not a place of worship, exactly," Lucas said. "It's a monument. To Jewish martyrs. In remembrance." The shrine there was of unhewed stone, he told the mukhtar. Not of precious metals.

Khalif said he thought he had grasped the message there. "The greater the grief," he said, "the greater the revenge will be. When one man grieves, he wants to see the grief of his enemies. He thinks, Why should I weep and not another man?"

Khalif noticed Lucas's distress at receiving this information.

"You are sad? You are a Jew?"

"I am sad," Lucas said. It had been a sad day and night for him, he explained. Of Yad Vashem, Jews, Romany, al-Firuli, he said nothing. It was a hopelessly long story. What am I, he thought, a missionary? Things had quieted down on the road.

Paying again, Lucas observed that the frenetic West had much to learn from the ancient wisdom of humble peoples. The mukhtar complimented Lucas on his humility and readiness to learn. The mukhtar had wide experience of Western peoples. Lucas, he believed, was an exception, different from the others.

Just before dawn, Lucas heard the morning call to prayer sounding throughout the great valley of ashes. This time there was no raging muezzin's song, no calling down of wrath upon abominations, no *Itbah al-Yahud*. Only the beauty of the summons to devotion, the admonition and promise to the faithful that prayer was better than sleep. Of course, it was only a recording. But as it sounded, the first rays of the sun appeared over the desert, and the road was quiet and at peace.

Khalif came by the place he had been dozing. "The day will be better," he said.

"Good," said Lucas.

A young Nawar drove him up the road in the dawn light, the same road the crazed villagers had scoured for him the night before. A military helicopter passed overhead and hovered for a minute. Presently they would be ordered off the road.

After a while, Lucas recognized the outskirts of Eshaikh Ijleen, where the UN distribution center was said to be. The Nawar let him out there and he began to walk down the road. The sky was still full of smoke. Somewhere not too far away, Lucas thought he detected an iodine smell that might have been the ocean, seaweed, the shore.

An hour after sunrise it was extremely hot. Lucas, who had not brought a hat, felt the sun bear down on his bald spot. Mirages shimmered along the road. A cloud by day would be handy, Lucas thought. A pillar of fire by night.

He did not think it made sense to try to get back to Beit Ajani, where the women had taken refuge in the old *daya*'s house. Better to try and duck into the shadow of the UN or some NGO presence and make contact from there. They ought not, by his reckoning, to be in any immediate danger.

As he walked down the road, four stick figures emerged from a mirage in the road before him. When they drew closer, he saw that they were four young Palestinians. Their clothes were dirty and blackened, as though they had been too close to a fire. One had a kaffiyeh with a black band and was carrying a gasoline can. The sight of the gasoline can annoyed Lucas.

The young men approached him, staring impolitely. He could tell little about them. They might have been Palestinians from town, or Bedouin, or even Nawar of the al-Firuli.

"You are Jew," one said to him as they passed.

"You are spy," said another.

"You are shit," said the young man with the kaffiyeh who carried the gas can.

"Shit," said the fourth, who presumably spoke the least English.

Why argue? Lucas thought. Everyone went his way and Lucas, at least, did not look back. It was no worse than similar encounters he had had in the Caribbean.

The next vision to take shape in the glare was a self-propelled gun, stopped by the side of the road, with a blue and white Star of David flag on it. It was dusty and forlorn-looking but turned out to be a patrolling IDF vehicle. A hatch opened and a young man in a tanker's helmet stuck his head out. He then took the helmet off, reached into his sweatshirt pocket for sunglasses and squinted down at Lucas.

After a puzzled moment, he said, "Identification."

Lucas showed him his passport and press pass.

"You got a little trouble?" the soldier asked drily.

"Well, I ran into a barricade last night. Had to leave my vehicle."

"It's probably burned now," the soldier said. "Lucky you weren't in it."

Lucas smiled in appreciation of the joke. "You're right there."

"You think I'm joking?" the soldier asked irritably. "A civilian was murdered last night. Attacks all over the Strip. In the West Bank also. Even in our own cities. In Lod. In Nazareth. In Holon. A young girl was killed, the *skezzin*."

"In the Strip?" Lucas asked.

"In Tel Aviv itself," the soldier replied.

"Well," Lucas said, "as you can see, I'm lost and I'm a foreigner. I'd like to call my office back in Jerusalem. Do you think you could give me a lift to a UN post?"

The soldier looked troubled. A second young soldier appeared in the hatch, fanning himself with his beret. The open hatch was killing the gun's air conditioning.

"I'd like to help you out," the first soldier said. "But something happens and you're with us, we're in Lebanon." He scanned the horizon. "Look," he said, pointing across the spinach field to the nearest settlement. "That's Kfar Gottlieb. They have a phone. They'll help you out."

The second soldier said something offhand in Hebrew, which amused his comrade but which Lucas could not understand.

"We *think* they have a phone," the first soldier translated. "We don't always know what's allowed with them."

They spread an army blanket, cool with the tank's interior currents, on the blazing metal of their vehicle and Lucas rode on top of it to Kfar Gottlieb. At the settlement's gate, the soldier commanding the self-propelled explained Lucas's situation. The armed sentries there opened the gate so Lucas could enter. Except for their kippot, the sentries wore khaki uniforms that were identical to the soldiers'. They were grim and silent.

Lucas shook hands with the two soldiers who had given him the lift and passed through the gate.

"I didn't think I'd make it," he told the sentries. There were three of them. Two were in their mid-twenties, the third was in his mid-fifties. They made no reply whatever to Lucas's attempt at conversation. Soon a jeep arrived from the settlement's headquarters, summoned by walkie-talkie. The jeep was driven by a handsome dark-haired woman with a khaki bandanna. The older sentry motioned for Lucas to get into the jeep and sat down beside him. They drove in silence through the fields of spinach. Beyond the spinach were fields of tomatoes, and beyond them rows of grapefruit trees and then bananas.

"So this is Kfar Gottlieb," Lucas said, again trying conversation with the couple in the jeep.

The older sentry looked at him blankly. "That's right," he said. His voice seemed without accent or expression.

They drove for nearly half an hour before they reached the neat rows of stucco houses among which the settlement's headquarters stood. Getting out, the sentry ordered Lucas from the jeep with the same peremptory gesture he had used before. Although the man kept his machine gun strapped to his shoulder, Lucas felt himself somehow a prisoner. The woman in the khaki bandanna drove off without looking behind her.

"I'd like to get in touch with the people I was traveling with," Lucas said pleasantly as they walked into the air-conditioned trailer that seemed to be the settlement's main office. "Some folks from the International Children's Foundation."

The man with the machine gun stopped in his tracks and stared at him with the same blank look, informed now with a lurking rage.

"Children?"

"Yes, I —"

"You a reporter? We have children here. You want to do a story about our children?"

"I've been working in the camps."

"Oh, the camps," the man said. "I understand. Sure. Those children."

"It was a hell of a day," Lucas said, still hoping to be pals. "Dangerous for everybody."

"That's right," the man said. "In fact, one of our brothers was killed. One of our children."

"I'm sorry," Lucas said.

"He wasn't a child," the man explained. "He was a beautiful young man. I hope you don't think I'm a faggot."

Lucas thought it best not to answer. He was obviously in trouble again.

"Of course if you're gay," the man said, "I don't want to insult you. I want you to think well of us. That's very important to us, what the world thinks."

"You've certainly . . ." Lucas looked around at the verdant fields, in search of an observation. Sprinklers on movable sections of irrigation pipe made ranks of misty rainbows stretching into the haze on the horizon. "You've certainly grown a lot of spinach." He was frightened and very tired.

The man laughed appreciatively, a hearty, false laughter. "A lot of spinach. That's good. Yeah," he said, "we've made the desert bloom." He waited a beat. "The young man who died, who was murdered by that scum — he was new here. At the same time, he was one of our children. Maybe that's hard for you to understand?"

"Of course I understand," Lucas said. He might, he thought, have rashly allowed some irritation to creep into his voice. "Why shouldn't I?"

"You should," the man said. "And you will."

"How," he asked the man with the gun, ignoring the prediction, "did it happen?"

"Mister," said the man, "we're gonna start asking you about that."

43

LYING ON the tiles of the cool bright room, Lucas had occasion to reflect that until a few moments before, no one connected with the business had really troubled to hurt him. The several straight-armed shots he had just taken from the jolly-faced red-headed man in front of him were the most solid he had ever stopped — this was far worse than the time he had been mugged drunk in Morningside Park. He had no intention of striking back, but the man had a little homily for him anyway.

"You do not ever strike a Jew," the red-headed man said. "For you to raise your fist, to attempt to injure a Jewish person, is to direct an injury against the Almighty Himself."

"I never heard that," Lucas said, starting to his feet.

The red-haired man had a colleague in the room with him.

"Now you heard it," said the colleague. He was a much shorter man and lacked his associate's good-humored appearance. He was short and squat and hard-eyed, with dark hair and a slight potbelly. He seemed aware of his own effect.

Lucas hauled himself onto the stool that had been provided for him. It was a three-legged stool, one on which a fighter might rest between rounds or a class dunce might be exhibited. At Kfar Gottlieb, Lucas could imagine it being used for both purposes. Looking into the hard light, he saw that the red-headed man who had been hitting him was wearing bright red boxing gloves. The man's colleague noticed Lucas's surprise.

"He's an athlete," explained the colleague, who seemed to be in charge. "So he needs to protect his hands."

"I thought maybe he played the violin," Lucas said. This proved entirely the wrong answer. Whappo, and he was on the floor again, numb-nosed, tasting cartilage, looking down at his own blood.

"I do," the red-haired man said. "I'm shopping for a fiddle. Want to be one?"

Helping himself back onto the stool, Lucas thought about respiration, wondering when his own might be restored. It reminded him of the time he had run out of air during a night dive at Sharm al-Sheikh. He'd hit the surface not a moment too soon and seen the black sky and the huge desert stars. Then he had pulled the regulator from his face and settled back in the BC's rubbery embrace, savoring the sweet air. Yet for some mysterious metabolic reason, the air was unavailable. He had floated on the black surface rasping, breathing what might have been the air of Uranus, for all the nourishment it had given his poor lungs.

The room they were in had been pitch black and moldy on their arrival. Its single fluorescent overhead light showed it to be lined with ceramic tiles. It was a hideaway of some kind, a bunker. Strive as he would, it seemed twenty seconds before Lucas had his breath back.

"So," asked the dark-haired man, "why were you beaten?"

The answer, he believed, was "because of Lenny," though he did not volunteer it. Discretion came hard to Lucas, who tended to think slowly and aloud, but it was time to try a little harder.

"You saved my life," he told the men in the room. "If you hadn't taken me in, I might have been killed. So I don't really know why you're beating on me. I'm an American journalist, just as it says on the pass."

"Jewish?" the red-headed man asked.

It was hard for Lucas to keep from laughing. Over his few years in country he had been asked the same question every which way from Dan to Gilead, from just about every angle. Just when he had thought there could be no more variations in delivery, readings of the line, inquiring inflections, he would encounter a new one.

The red-haired man's version had not been particularly hostile. Rather, it was faintly welcoming.

"Partly," Lucas said. "My father was not an observant Jew. He practiced Ethical Culture. My mother was a Gentile."

Why am I telling these assholes the story of my life? he had to ask himself. It was one thing to be afraid, but this forfeiting of moral authority was humiliating. Still, he could penetrate his own logic. As long as he could believe in their relative virtue, he might reasonably expect them not to kill him. That expectation was the only possible place to work from. He was aware, however, that the revisionist underground groups during the British mandate had killed far better Jews than he. Real ones.

"How come you're not in the government?" asked the red-haired man. It was a joke between the man and his colleague, and Lucas thought it would be indiscreet to smile. Also, he did not wish to be hit again.

I'd be good enough to get in under the Nuremberg Laws, he thought. If I'm good enough to get gassed, I ought to be good enough for you. But he said nothing. One day, if he stayed alive, he might get to use the line. He had taken about all the punching out he felt he could manage.

The two men in the closed room spoke together in Hebrew, and Lucas passed out briefly. When his head cleared he found himself focused on the boxing gloves. He remembered the boxing matches, the smokers, he had had to fight as a child in the wrong school. He had been compelled to slug it out with every professed anti-Semite in the school, beginning with the boy named Kevin English. There had been a dozen.

How peculiar, he thought, how uncanny to be remembering all that here. To be calling up that childhood jungle world with its greasy stinks and godly Jansenist doom in a place like Kfar Gottlieb. But had they not certain things in common? Religion. The heart of a heartless world. How sentimental of Marx to call it that. And here at Kfar Gottlieb they had religion plus. Nationalism. Automatic weapons. Spinach. Lucas wanted it all to mean something. The idea that it did not made him angry.

"So what do you think you're doing, Lucas," the dark man asked him, "in this land of ours?"

"I'm a journalist," Lucas said. "You've seen my credentials."

"Sure, and you're like the rest of them," the red-haired man said. "You're here to defame the religious community. Maybe we can't stop you from doing that. But when you cause the death of a Jew, you incur a debt of blood. That we can do something about."

"We did everything we could do to save that man's life," Lucas said. "He walked away from us. The mob got him and we couldn't get him back."

"That's not what Linda Ericksen says. She says you went through an army checkpoint and said nothing. That you struck her, kept her from informing the army."

"That's not exactly what happened," Lucas said.

So they brought in Linda, swollen-eyed and post-hysterical.

"They hit me when I tried to tell the soldiers," she said bitterly. "They're responsible for his death."

"Linda," Lucas began, "you know better than that." But he understood there would be no convincing her. He was unsure himself what had happened. No one's sense of justice was likely to be satisfied.

"Look," Lucas told his two interrogators when Linda was outside the room. "I don't know who Lenny was or what he was up to, but I did my best for him and so did everyone else in my party. He walked into that camp by himself."

"What do you mean, you don't know what he was up to?" the dark man asked. "What were you doing with him?"

"My understanding was that he was taking Miss Ericksen and Sonia Barnes to talk to some Palestinians at Argentina camp. Miss Ericksen's a volunteer with the Human Rights Coalition. Sonia Barnes drove her out in a United Nations car."

"Yes?" said the red-haired man.

"When things started getting out of hand — when the riot started — I went out by taxi to look for Sonia. The next thing, we were in the shit."

"Why you?"

"Because I'm Sonia's friend. I'm writing about her."

"Writing what?"

"I'm doing a piece on religious groups in Jerusalem. Sonia has friends who belong to one."

"A cult," the red-haired man said.

Lucas shrugged. "It's a relative term." You should know, he thought.

"That's what you're writing about?" the dark-haired man asked. "Cults in our country? Like Ethical Culture, maybe?"

"I've been writing about religious obsession," he said.

"So who's supposed to be obsessed," asked the short, dark man, "out here? Not us, I hope."

"Present company excepted," Lucas said. He was feeling faint again. "Could I have some water?"

They brought him a cup of heavily chlorinated water. On the wall behind them, he noticed, was a banner displaying a crown over a palm tree, with the letters *bet, daled, gimmel.*

"So why are you so interested in Linda?" asked the red-haired man. "She comes out here and you show up."

"I've been interviewing Linda and her ex-husband for months," Lucas said. "I came out yesterday because Sonia Barnes called me."

"And why is Sonia interested?"

"We're going in circles," Lucas said. "Sonia got the NGO car. Linda asked her for it. Because she was supposed to be investigating the beating of kids by the guy who calls himself Abu Baraka."

Lucas tried to determine, as quickly and silently as possible, what the two young lions across from him wanted. At first he thought he was being beaten because of Lenny's death. But there seemed to be something about him they wanted to know.

"Who else did you see yesterday?" the dark man asked him. "Outside of Arabs."

Lucas thought about it. It was reasonable to conclude they knew whom he had seen.

"Nuala Rice from the International Children's Foundation. Helen Henderson from UNRWA. Lenny. Linda and Sonia."

"You've been on Linda's case," the dark-haired man said. "You interviewed her ex-husband. You met her through Pinchas Obermann."

"It's a small country," Lucas said.

"You think you have a source in the Shabak?" the red-headed man asked. "I can tell you that nothing happens in Shabak or Mossad or anywhere — anywhere — that we don't know about. By the way, how come you quit your newspaper job?"

"Oh, that," said Lucas. "That was personal. And I don't have a source in the Shabak."

"You're being manipulated," the red-headed man said. "We can give you a better story and a chance to help the country. Or we can close you down."

It seemed to Lucas that he could understand their wanting to kill the Abu Baraka story. Because surely Abu Baraka was one of them. Or, more plausibly, several of them — their squad of enforcers. But what was the better story?

"This guy," he chortled, "this guy is a Mossad type. *Shaygetzy*-looking *petzle.* What do you think?"

The other man paid no attention to his friend.

"You claim to be an honest journalist. Well, let's see how honest you are. We can give you the story of a plot against the State of Israel," said the red-headed man. "And a plan to slander the active religious community."

Lucas did not reply.

"What's the matter, Mr. Lucas? Not interested?" He swore in Arabic. "To these bastards of the glorious free press, if the Jews fight back against terror, if they defend themselves against murderers, they're no better than Nazis. The Jews' place is to be a victim. Otherwise the world is out of joint, right, Mr. Lucas?"

"That's not my position," Lucas said.

"Your friends in this cult, Lucas, these foreign women and the men controlling them, are a bunch of drug runners and terrorists."

"I would have to see evidence of that," Lucas said severely. At the same time he had a nasty feeling he was about to see something like it. It sounded distressingly like Nuala, as though she had finally run out of slack.

"That, Mr. Lucas," the dark-haired man said, "is what you're going to see. And when you do, we're going to require justice of you, understand? You claim to be innocent of our comrade's death. Maybe we'll give you the benefit of the doubt. But we expect you to see to it that the truth of this story gets told. You were being programmed for a campaign of lies. Instead, you'll write the truth."

"Because," said the red-haired man, "the truth is wonderful. But you owe us more than the truth. You owe us a life for a life."

"I don't," Lucas said. "I haven't killed anyone."

"Sorry, friend. A man died. You were responsible. That one death could lead to others. The stuff on your hands — it's blood." The red-haired man made a gesture with his head that included the dry flats beyond the wall outside Kfar Gottlieb, beyond the fields of fruit and spinach. "There isn't anyone here who wouldn't die to keep holy what belongs to us."

"So we're giving you a story and the chance to break it," his colleague said. "From now until this is resolved it's important that you work with us. What do you say?"

"I don't know," Lucas said. So they produced Linda again, who told him about the hashish. Nuala and Sonia brought it through every week, she explained. They brought back weapons for Palestinian militias that sometimes collaborated with Shin Bet, like the Black

Falcons or the Communist faction. They also sometimes brought Mister Stanley's Colombian cocaine for the militia's elite. Recently they had provided explosives from Iran for De Kuff's band of syncretists, who had some demented scheme involving the Haram. Linda claimed she had happened on it by accident and Sonia had confessed all to her.

But, Lucas thought, nursing his jaw, if anyone had destructive plans for the Haram, it would be the militants of Kfar Gottlieb, the superpatriotic creators of Abu Baraka — hardly De Kuff and Raziel's group of Kabbalist aesthetes, of that he felt reasonably certain.

Lucas, not in the mood to argue, decided to sort it out later. Meanwhile, Linda cried a lot and Lucas said OK to whatever they told him.

Sometime during the night Ernest from the Human Rights Coalition showed up at the settlement's gate. He had driven from the border with a nervous Palestinian driver to pick up Linda. The *chaverim* allowed Lucas to go along.

"How did you end up *there?*" Ernest asked Lucas.

"Long story," Lucas said. "I thought you were away."

"I was at a conference in Prague. But when I got back yesterday, I was told that Linda was here."

"Told by who?"

"We have some contacts here," Ernest said. "Not everybody who lives in Kfar Gottlieb shares the prevailing ideology. But I had to come myself."

He turned to glance at Linda in the back seat, who was pretending sleep. Ernest had had to come himself because he was one of the few people who could pass in increasingly precarious safety from Gaza City to the settlements.

He and Lucas exchanged a look.

"Did anyone get the women out?" Lucas asked. "Sonia?"

"Nuala and Miss Henderson are back at the Children's Foundation compound. Sonia's at the beach."

"The beach," Lucas repeated dully.

"You'll see," Ernest said. "So, what are they saying in the settlements? You look like you got roughed up. You can get some first aid at the beach."

"We can stop looking for Abu Baraka. Abu Baraka is them. What beach?"

"Figures," said Ernest. Linda fidgeted, as if in her sleep. "What else do they say?"

"They say God is on their side. And they're trying to plant some story on me."

"They're the left hand of God," Ernest mused. "The right one too."

"You know what I think," Lucas said. "God's going to get His fucking hand cut off someday." He was startled by a scream from Linda. He turned and saw she had put her hands over her ears.

"I guess there should be a trial," Lucas went on. He was half asleep himself. "After the Gnostic revolution, when the *tikkun* is restored, we'll put the Old Dear in a cage in Pisa and test His sanity. I personally don't think He'll score very well."

"Ask Him where he's been," Ernest suggested.

"A cage in Pisa," Lucas insisted. "Ask Him where he's been and what the fuck He thinks He's doing with his bombs and booms and thunder, and us running shitless around ground zero while He rings our hats. Ask for a poetry sample. He made Leviathan, but can He scan? I mean, I'm sorry, but desert sunsets and similar shit are not poetry."

"But He is poetry, Chris," Ernest said. "And the bombs are ours, not His. Anyway, He's got to be better than Ezra Pound."

"Two bearded old bums," Lucas declared, "and they both belong in cages."

"What about the settlers in Kfar Gottlieb?" Ernest asked. "Do they think God wants peace or war?"

"As far as I can make it out," Lucas said, "sometimes He wants both. Usually at different times."

"How can you laugh at that?" Linda demanded angrily, although they hadn't been, really. "It's historically valid."

44

FRESH FROM the wrath of the prophets, Lucas found himself at the foggy edge of the cold Philistine Sea, wandering among Hellenized youths wearing tiny, tight bathing suits. He had just reclaimed his rental car, showered, changed his shirt and put on a pair of baggy khaki shorts from his overnight bag. He was looking for Sonia, who was somewhere on the beach.

The Hellenized youths were mainly off-duty members of the Israeli navy. Their base straddled the Green Line, lying partly in the Gaza Strip and partly in Israel proper. Finally Lucas came upon Sonia, playing in one of their volleyball games. She wore a pale blue bathing suit. When he called her out, another girl was waiting to take her place in the game.

"Sort of consorting with the enemy, aren't you?" Lucas asked her.

"Who? These kids? They're no enemies of mine. I often stop here on the way to the Strip. They've always got a spare pass."

"Just another one of those anomalies of war, I guess."

"Chris, I'm not at war with anyone. What happened to your face? It's all swollen."

"I don't think anything's broken except my bridge. I have to try and bend it back into shape. I've got a loose tooth."

"Did you get hit?"

"I got beat up at Kfar Gottlieb. Ernest tells me I'm not the first reporter who's been beaten up there."

"We should get some disinfectant cream or something."

"It's all right."

He took her by the arm and walked her along the water line, the wash of the slow waves breaking at their ankles.

"I just had it put to me that you're running hash between T.V. and the Strip."

"Who put it to you?"

"Hell," Lucas said, "I was hoping you might deny it. It didn't sound true."

"I do deny it," she said. "Of course I deny it. Do you really imagine I'm some kind of crazy drug queen?"

"Well, no," Lucas said. "But the settlers say it. What are they talking about?"

"About Nuala," she said.

"Shit," said Lucas. "I knew it! And you've been riding with her."

"I didn't know about it until the last time I came over. She's not doing it for profit, you know. It's some setup between Rashid and the Party fraction and Shabak. What do the settlers care? They must know that kind of shit goes on."

"Well, if you were after Abu Baraka," Lucas said, "it would be a way of making trouble for you. Because Abu Baraka is them. It's the settlers at Kfar Gottlieb. And the same goes for Nuala. She can't collaborate with dirty deals and crusade against the settlers at the same time. It just confirms all their suspicions."

"Who told them anyway?" Sonia asked.

"Linda. She's one of them. I mean, she was there when I got jumped on. She says she's seen large quantities of hash move and Nuala's carrying it."

"That rotten little milk-white bitch," Sonia said without force. "How about her? But she hasn't seen anything. I don't believe it. Someone told her."

"Well, there's more to it. They're blaming us for Lenny's death. They also say Nuala was running explosives. And they seem to think you were in on it. That the explosives were going to Raziel and De Kuff. Your guys."

Sonia laughed. "Explosives? They can't believe that."

"I don't know what they believe. But they want to lay a story on me. A news story. About a plan to damage the Haram. A sort of Willie Ludlum thing."

They had come to the rolls of razor wire that marked the end of the beach. The two of them stood looking down at it for a few moments and then about-faced and began to walk back the way they had come. Suddenly Sonia bolted from his side and was running into the waves, losing her footing, gaining it again, throwing herself headlong at chest level into an oncoming wave, disappearing, then appearing on the far side of the break. She swam parallel with the shore for a couple of minutes, then eased onto a wave and rode it to shore, staggering out of the surf where Lucas was walking.

"How many rides have you taken with Nuala?"

"I can't remember."

"How many?"

"Half a dozen over time. That was it."

"Enough to be recognized. And probably photographed. Why didn't you tell me she was running dope?"

"How could I tell you?"

"I don't know. I was riding with her, though. You might have tipped me."

"I thought you were tight with Nuala."

"Not really."

"Well, if they've got me," she said, "they've got you. Especially after yesterday."

They walked on. "You should have confided in me," he said.

"What do they want you to do?"

"Stripping it down, I'd say they want me to write something. A version of something."

"A true version of something?"

"Their version of truth. In their version, I think I'm off the hook. If I write it."

They walked up from the water and Sonia went through security into the women's locker room to change.

When they had driven halfway to Jerusalem, leaving the coast road, Lucas said, "It must have to do with the Abu Baraka business. You and I and Nuala are all involved in it. We're a weak link."

They drove on in silence for a while.

"I had a dream," Lucas said. "At least I think it was a dream. Maybe it was a hallucination. I was talking to Rudolph Steiner's little daughter, Diphtheria."

"There's a lot of bad Ex around," Sonia said. "Really. Down in Tel Aviv. All over. Someone's slipping it in the felafels. Or maybe in hash. What did little Diphtheria have to say?"

"She seemed to think like Linda Ericksen. One thing she said, though — she said, 'What people think, will be.' "

"Gosh," Sonia said. "Remember when we thought that was good? Where did you get the bad Ex?"

"I don't know. I had the dream in the Holy Sepulchre."

"It's a creepy place," Sonia said. "You shouldn't go there."

They fell silent for a few miles.

"I had a funny conversation with Janusz Zimmer a while ago," she said. "Like he was warning me about this. About some kind of underground."

"I'll call him," Lucas said.

"Be careful," she said. "He seems sort of off the deep end. And he's been keeping company with Linda."

"Christ," Lucas said. "Who's who? What do people want?"

It was hard to tell who anyone was and what they wanted because the emergency basis on which the state proceeded created constant improvisations and impersonations. Organs that were not in fact of the state represented themselves as being so. State organs pretended to be non-state, or anti-state, or the organs of other states, including enemy ones. Many people with firsthand knowledge of official security and military procedures had separated themselves from the relevant organizations, or partly separated themselves, or were pretending to have separated themselves, or had turned militantly against the relevant organs while pretending to work for them, or were working for the relevant organs while pretending to have turned militantly against them, or were unsure whither they had turned. Some people worked simply for fun or money. Then there were the pious and the patriots.

"Do you really think they care," Sonia asked, "if anyone knows they're slapping Palestinian kids around? People like the settlers at Kfar Gottlieb don't care that much about world opinion."

"I think somebody wants something on you, Sonia. I think we should see Ernest. I don't like this crap about the Haram. If anybody wanted to blow the place, it would be them. To build the Temple, right?"

"There's a demonstration on the Ninth of Av," she said. "During the summer, the day both Temples were destroyed. There always is. The faithful demonstrate. The Palestinians demonstrate. People get killed, usually Palestinians. You know," she said, "I better have a word with Nuala."

"While you're at it," Lucas said, "check with Raziel."

45

B ACK IN JERUSALEM, Lucas drove Sonia to the bungalow in Ein Kerem. The place was quiet, the garden deserted.

"I'll be back," he told her. "Get some rest."

He drove the rental car to the garage of his downtown apartment building and went upstairs to shower and change clothes and minister to his wounds with aspirin and Band-Aids. It occurred to him that he might find a way out of their political difficulties by invoking nationality.

Despite what many in the region believed, and despite America's patronal relationship with the State of Israel, it was often difficult to bring the superpowerful weight of the Republic to bear on behalf of its private citizens. It helped to be perceived as a person of particular value, but since Israel was chock-a-block with individuals whose names and organizations resounded with political mellifluousness at home, the competition was stiff. Influence talked; snide journalists and colored ex-Fidelistas hoofed it.

Given the situation, Lucas was compelled to fall back on the goodwill of his crony Sylvia Chin. Although she was a small, solitary device in the giant machine of U.S. diplomatic research and information, he had found her disproportionately clever, discreet and resourceful. When he called her at the office, she agreed to meet him at a café on the edge of the Machaneh Yehuda market.

Sylvia arrived in a modest silk dress, her slender throat adorned with an amber necklace. An expertly applied film of ointments concealed a tiny scar left by the nose ring she had worn in Palo Alto and removed on the day of her foreign-service exam. The hucksters of the market sang Ruritanian songs to her.

"Christopher," she told him at once, "I think you're in trouble." She frowned at his swollen face.

"I went to the Strip the other day. I saw some shit."

Sylvia looked coolly around the café.

"Did I tell you about our big drug enforcement operation here? Not just down in Tel Aviv but up here."

"I think you've referred to it."

"Well, I'll tell you, Chris, when the Latin lovers of the DEA get their big flat feet in the door, nothing gets them out. Now they're being romanced by Shabak and Mossad, which is really an irony when you think about it."

"Why's that?"

"Well, the last time Mossad helped out the DEA was in Thailand, when it penetrated a major heroin operation as a special favor to Uncle Sam-san. Mossad took the sucker over and ran it themselves, for spare change. So you'd think DEA would learn something."

"If DEA ever learned something," Lucas said, "the entire international narcotics industry would collapse."

"Right," said Sylvia. "Well, let me tell you something. One of your NGO buddies, the Irish girl, and her main squeeze the doctor, came to us for a visa yesterday. She seemed to think we owed her one. I think it was because her Shabak control told her we'd fix her up. She's bandying your name around quite a lot. You better watch it. You made a couple of significant shit lists."

"Great," Lucas said.

Sylvia leaned forward slightly and lowered her voice. "Something struck me during my conversation with Nuala. Our chat about her visa. Know what it was?"

Lucas considered the question for a moment. "If somebody over there really wanted to help her," he said, "they'd get her —"

Sylvia raised a finger to her lips and very quietly finished his sentence for him. "A false passport. Phony papers. They wouldn't send her *shnorring* for a visa."

"They're cutting her loose," Lucas said.

"In the old days, the Soviets might have fixed her up. Not now." She smiled, largely, it seemed, for the benefit of anyone who might have been observing them. "She expects to see you over in Tel Aviv tonight. I would say maybe don't go."

"What about Sonia Barnes?"

Sylvia dabbed a sprig of mint from her upper lip.

"It doesn't help anything that Nuala Rice and her boyfriend are CP. Or what's left of it. It doesn't help either that Sonia has this Party background and spent all those years in Cuba."

"Maybe you can straighten it out," Lucas said to Sylvia. "If you think they were used."

"Maybe," she said. "But you know, Chris, sometimes things get so twisted they're beyond straightening out. It's like nobody ponders information anymore. There's more information available than there is stuff to know about, if you know what I mean."

"Of course," Lucas said. It seemed to him he knew that as well as anyone.

"Machines are dumb," Sylvia said, "but they never forget. Like elephants. Who put the jalapeños in their trunk. Who was a Communist when. Who lived in Cuba."

"So they're going to throw Sonia to the wolves?"

"Let me tell you this," said Sylvia, "and you can pass it on. Nuala and the Palestinian doctor are fucked. I don't mean to be cold-hearted, but they're really not my job. We go to bat for them, people will think they worked for us."

"Any good news?" Lucas asked.

"Maybe. Sonia might get off through Raziel, because his old man wants him home in one piece and we're supposed to make that happen."

"How?"

"Well, it'll be tough, because the DEA guys made him for a junkie at a hundred feet. But we try to keep tabs. The old man is paying a private security service called Ayin to watch him. Just happens to be the same one the New York bail bondsmen used to skip-trace the Marshalls, *père et fils.*"

"Small worlds," Lucas said. He thought of the tile room where he had been interrogated, and the structure of his newfound universe seemed a series of such rooms, expanding endlessly, aeons presided over by their demiurges.

"Ayin likes to tell us it's well connected," Sylvia went on. "They mean they're close to Shabak and have some political savvy. That's what they sell. Now, I don't know what Raziel's up to or what the Israelis have against him, but I very much doubt they would do anything too bad to him, considering his old man. Sonia's best bet is to stay close to Raziel. Maybe yours too. Be a working American reporter. A not very well-informed reporter."

"I hear you," Lucas said. "But what started this, what first got me and Sonia in trouble, as far as I know, was some settlers beating up on kids in the Strip. A story I didn't even follow up on. Is someone really so bent out of shape over bad publicity," he asked her, "that some settler, some soldier, bashes a kid or even kills one and the world finds out? Is that such a big deal to anyone of importance?"

Sylvia made a little half-shrug, raising her eyebrows, lifting her fingers from the tabletop. "I wouldn't have thought so. But Sonia's close to this dope connection. Also, we're getting a buzz that there's another plot to blow the Temple Mount. If Raziel or Sonia is anywhere near that, I don't know if anybody can help them. Because you know what could happen?"

"That's ridiculous," Lucas said. "They're like Sufis. They believe all religions are one. They're nonviolent."

"Good," Sylvia said. "I hope you're right. But don't come running to the U.S. consulate if the Temple Mount blows, because there won't be one standing."

"So where do I find you?"

"It's not funny. I lost an old roomie — my sorority sister — in the explosion in Riyadh. She went back to Iowa in sections. When I hear the sacred boom, I'm one step ahead of the mob of martyrs. My English will desert me. I know the exact distance to the nearest kosher Chinese restaurant and how long it takes to cover it in heels, and that's where you'll find me. Selling noodles."

"They wouldn't be involved in anything like a bomb plot," Lucas said. "That's not their thing at all. They follow this old guru."

She looked at him in a way that might fairly be called inscrutable and said, "OK, Christopher. If you say so."

He drove at once back out to Ein Kerem. There was no one in the bungalow except Sonia, who was packing a bag.

"Going somewhere?" he asked.

"I called Stanley about doing a few gigs. I need some money of my own."

"Do you still believe the world's about to be set free? Maybe nobody will need money. Maybe the cash nexus will be obviated."

"Don't laugh at me," she told him. "If I've been kidding myself the whole time, well — I've been wrong the whole time. I've been wrong before. But what if I'm right?" She took a deep breath, out of fatigue or stress or to keep from crying, Lucas could not tell. "Every day is different. Some mornings I wake up and I'm as sure about things as I am about my right hand. Others, I think I must be out of my mind. You know how it is, don't you, Chris?"

"I guess I do," he said. "But if you can possibly help it, I don't think you should go over to T.V. In fact, maybe you should leave the country altogether."

"No," she said. "I won't be doing that. I promised Stanley I'd perform tomorrow. Nuala will be there. She's waiting for some documents and she wants to get together. Then the Rev wants to go into meditation up to Galilee. Somewhere in the mountains."

"I suppose we're due for the last mystery. The one that's going to change everything."

She only nodded wearily.

"And you're going too?"

"I've come this far," she said. "I guess I'll go the distance. You should come with us. For the purposes of your book."

"Is that a personal invitation?"

"Yes," she said. "I'd like you to come. I'd like you with me. But no one's here, so I don't know when this will happen."

"I'm going over to Tel Aviv tomorrow to see what I can find out from Ernest. I'll stop by Stanley's."

"All right," she said.

She walked him into the garden.

"Tell me something," Lucas said. "Has anyone in your group — Raziel or even one of your passing-through people — ever said anything to you about destroying the mosques on the Temple Mount? Maybe to rebuild the Temple? Something like that?"

"Never. Where did you get that idea?"

"Sylvia Chin at the U.S. consulate asked me about it. There's a buzz around. Some people might connect it with your group."

"Us? Raziel? Raziel couldn't set off a firecracker. He's never done a violent thing in his life. Look," she said, "we've had a lot of crazies crashing here, but I've never heard of anything like that."

"I thought so," Lucas said. "That's what I told her."

46

THE NEXT DAY, Lucas threw some gear into his Ford Taurus and prepared to drive through the hills to Tel Aviv. Before setting out, he tried calling Dr. Obermann, to ask him if he thought Raziel could be involved in a bombing plot. He planned to say little over the telephone, just arrange a sit-down meeting.

To his disappointment, he was informed by recorded message that the doctor would be away for the week, had in fact gone to Turkey, where he could be reached in direst emergencies only at a number in Bodrum, between 1200 and 1300 and after 1900 each afternoon. The recording went on to give the name and phone number of the psychiatrist who was covering for him.

Lucas, in some anxiety, was determined to try the man himself. So he called Bodrum.

"What are you doing in Turkey?"

"Ah," said Obermann, "filling in for an anthropologist colleague. Conducting a tour of Germans through the ruins of Ephesus." The doctor waxed lyrical. "Ephesus, home of Diana. Not the wholesome huntress of the Attic Greeks but the Oriental abomination —"

"Listen," Lucas said, cutting him short. "I need to ask you a few things about some of our friends." He was trying to compose relevant questions that would not give away too much. In practice, Lucas had found, genuine discretion over the telephone was damnably difficult for one not raised to it. Conversations dissolved into childish, transparent evasion.

"Indeed?"

"Your former friend, the Frau Pastorin — she wouldn't be of the messianic persuasion, would she? Explosively so?"

"If you mean Linda," Obermann said, "she does have an apocalyptic side. Her tendency, though, is more toward implosion."

"I see," said Lucas. "How about Raziel?"

"Raziel," Obermann said, "is capable of anything."

"Shit," said Lucas.

"Spot of bother down there?" Obermann asked.

"You might say that."

"Here, one gets perspective. The Temples of She, the ageless archpaganess sister of Cybele, whose devotees mutilated themselves."

"I feel a little abandoned," Lucas said. "Could it be you know something I don't? Are you making yourself scarce for a reason?"

"Hold fast to your role of observer," Obermann said. "Forget romance."

"Thanks," said Lucas.

"No need to be sarcastic," Obermann told him. "Do as I say and you'll be fine. Think about it and you'll see what I mean. Ever been to Ephesus?"

"Never."

"Saint Paul preached to the Jews here," Obermann said. "He told them it was better to marry than to burn. There's a synagogue — he may have been to it."

"I'm afraid for Raziel," Lucas said. "He may be having an important religious crisis."

"Don't carry packages. Don't forward messages. Don't go alone to lonely places. Limit your responsibilities until you feel better."

Lucas liked the sound of the last part. But before he was out of his apartment and on the road, his downstairs buzzer rang and Linda Ericksen, the Frau Pastorin, was at his door. To his annoyance, she arrived in the apartment with the same American couple who had burst in on him and Sonia at Berger's place in the Old City. The woman had her bright, unfriendly smile and the man had his automatic rifle.

"Chris," Linda said, "I want you to listen to what Gerri and Tom have to tell you. Do you remember them?"

"Sort of. I was in bed."

"Mr. Lucas?" the man asked pleasantly. "How would you like an exclusive?" He turned smiling to the woman who might have been his wife. "Are they still called 'exclusives'?" he asked her.

"I think so," she said. "I'm out of touch."

"You'll get a call to meet a man you know who'll explain a few developments. Afterward a fax will go out. But only you will have certain confirming details."

"Isn't that exciting?" the smiling woman said.

"Yes," Lucas said. "Really." He wondered who "the man you know" would turn out to be.

"If you want to stay out of trouble," the American said, "cooperate and confirm. Don't change any of the wording of any document you're given."

"You know," Lucas said, "I'm working on a book. Not doing spot reporting. Who am I supposed to peddle these details to?"

"Believe me," the man said, "you won't have any trouble moving the release when the time comes. The world will come to you."

Lucas thought he saw the woman flash her companion a cautioning look.

"You know," Lucas ventured, "if I had some insight into the background here, I might be able to help the world out a little more. Isn't there something I ought to know about what this concerns?"

"Frankly," the happy hard case of a lady told him, "no. Because you happen to be severely compromised. I won't bother to point out why."

"In other words," her friend said, "do as you're told and you can keep out of trouble. And stay away from the wrong people."

"You never know who's who," Lucas said.

"Check with us," the man said. "We'll keep you informed."

"Really," the woman said. "Who do you think you are?"

Fortunately, there seemed no imperative for Lucas to frame an answer. Linda gave him a look of triumphant virtue and the three of them left.

47

I T WAS A HOT, hazy day on the coast. The beaches were unusually crowded for a weekday and the traffic was more or less out of control. Lucas sat with Ernest Gross in an imitation English pub near the British embassy. Except for its ferocious air conditioning, the pub's ambiance was fairly convincing, and the beery smells and lukewarm bitter contrasted strangely with the room's temperature, which was that of a meat locker. On most workdays, English-speaking Israeli youths came to flirt with female Sloane Rangers from the embassy, but that afternoon there were mainly tourist couples in flight from the weather.

"Well," Ernest was saying, "someone's going to cop it for Hal Morris."

"Hal Morris? I thought his name was Lenny something."

"No. Hal Morris. 'Lenny' was apparently a nom de guerre."

Lucas decided to tell Ernest about the events in Gaza and about his conversation with Sylvia Chin and with Linda's friends Gerri and Tom. It was necessary to trust someone. At least for Lucas it was.

"The fact is," Lucas said, "he walked into it. Literally. And God knows what he was up to."

"What do you think was supposed to happen?"

"I have no idea. Nuala claims her friends had some arrangement with Shabak. They were playing one Palestinian faction against another. I don't think anyone was supposed to get killed."

"There's got to be retaliation," Ernest explained. "Normally they'll pick a Palestinian from the town where the incident took place. Someone with PLO connections."

"There's no way to tell who in that mob killed Lenny — or Hal."

"They don't worry too much if they get the wrong man," Ernest said. "They reckon whoever they get is probably guilty of something. Or would have been eventually. And if he didn't do anything, he probably wanted to."

"That's a terrible policy," Lucas said.

"It's short-sighted. That's what we're always telling them."

Lucas drank his beer and listened to Elton John compete with the air conditioning.

"I don't want to take the fall for Hal," Lucas said. "And I don't want Sonia to. We weren't responsible."

"You think I can fix it for you?" Ernest asked.

"I think you have a few connections. I was hoping you might plead our case where it counts."

Ernest said nothing.

"Nuala wasn't responsible either," Lucas said. "She did what she could for the kid."

"I can't go to them about Nuala," Ernest said. "If her people had a deal with Shabak, whoever got her into it will have to get her out."

"Something's up, you know," Lucas said.

"Yes," Ernest said. "Something soon. Rival demonstrations maybe. A provocation. Something."

"Do you think it involves Sonia's people?"

"Have you asked her?"

"Yes."

"Of course," Ernest said, "she may not be aware of anything."

"And Pinchas Obermann's leaving town on me."

"He was your guide, was he? Through the mysteries?"

"We're doing a book," Lucas said.

After a few minutes, Ernest looked around at the frigid pub with distaste.

"Come on, mate. Let me take you somewhere more authentic."

They went out and got Lucas's rental car and drove along the beachfront toward Jaffa.

"Stop here," Ernest told him.

The place was called the Café Vercors, on Trumpeldor. Although it was just sunset, its main room was crowded and the tables commanding a glimpse of the Mediterranean were all full. They took a seat in the back.

"My favorite place in Tel Aviv," Ernest said. "Come here all the time."

Looking around, Lucas saw that he and Ernest appeared to be the youngest people in the place by a considerable margin.

"I like this town myself," Ernest said. "It may not be one of the Mediterranean's beauty spots, but it's the real thing. It's actual Israel."

"I don't know it well," Lucas said.

"No, you're an aesthete. Religious fanatics and aesthetes live up in J-town."

"You live there too," Lucas reminded him. "What's your excuse?"

"Closer to the action."

"We better enjoy it while we can," Lucas said. "Before they pave it over around us."

On the floor people were dancing to a polka. They were wonderfully spry. The women tended to wear large jewelry and low-cut blouses and gypsy skirts, a bohemian look. Almost all the men wore plain white shirts. None of them wore kippot, though there were a few Greek fishermen's caps. The dancing was in the Central European manner, with dips and arches, the men bending stiffly at times to one knee. Everyone seemed to enjoy himself immensely. The place reeked of Gitanes, Gauloises.

When the polka was over, a sexy woman in her late sixties stepped out onto the floor and began to sing: "*Non, je ne regrette rien . . .*"

"So," Lucas asked, "who are these people?"

"You've never been here? Sonia never brought you?"

Lucas shook his head.

"Ever hear of the Red Orchestra?"

"I guess so. The Russian resistance's spy network during World War Two?"

"That's right. Well, a lot of what's left of it is here," Ernest said. "People the Gestapo didn't get, that Stalin didn't shoot after the war — they come here most nights. The men who fought in the Byelorussian forests. The ones who put the limpet mines on British patrol boats in '46. They're here."

Lucas laughed. "*Non, je ne regrette rien,*" he repeated after the singer. "But I suppose they have a few. Regrets, I mean."

"This is the way I always pictured Israel before I came," Ernest told him. "This and the kibbutzim. After a day in the orange groves I thought everyone would gather and sing the 'Internationale' or 'Bandiere Rosse' or 'The Song of the Hammer.' I was down there in South A. getting slapped around by Afrikaner goons, going from jail to house arrest. What did I know?"

"Well," Lucas said, "here it was. Waiting for you."

"I thought the whole country would be like the Vercors, with the same sort of people. Sometimes I think there was a time when it was."

"It can't be an easy thing," Lucas said, "to make a country. It's tough enough to make a café. Or to make one be the way you imagined it. Unless you only let certain people in and keep the rest out."

"Right," Ernest said. "And what's the use of a café like that?" He looked around, content. "They say James Angleton came by when he was visiting. Heard about the place and wanted to see it."

Surveying the room, Lucas saw Janusz Zimmer in a windowed corner, watching the sea. On his table was a half bottle of Israeli vodka and a plate with bread and lemon slices beside it. "Look," he told Ernest. "Zimmer. Shall we buy him a drink?"

He had not thought about consulting with Janusz Zimmer. Suddenly it seemed a salutary notion, providing he could manage a little strategic probing and keep a few secrets at the same time. Then he was startled to recall that Zimmer had been keeping company with Linda Ericksen.

"Best leave him in peace," Ernest said. "Jan and I — sometimes we get into it."

"Really? Is he critical of your work?"

"I don't think he's really against us. I always thought of him as a left-winger. Lately we seem to get into arguments about what the country's about."

"I thought that was the national pastime."

"It is," Ernest said, and no more.

"What about Linda Ericksen?" Lucas asked. "She's volunteering for you. She's seeing Zimmer. And she has some very . . . odd friends."

"What sort of odd friends?"

"Well," Lucas considered, "what's the word? Militant? Reactionary? Fascistoid?"

"I knew she was spying on us for someone," Ernest said. "And by the way, she passed the word about Sonia and you and the alleged drug smuggling."

"She was with Lenny in the Strip. She claimed to be there on behalf of your organization."

"If she's doing that," Ernest said, "I'll have to give her the heave-ho. I can't have that false-flag shit. But I hate to, in a way. One conduit less — if you see what I mean."

"Do you think Zimmer might be behind her?"

"Behind her or not, I think he's just fucking her, frankly. But who knows? It's a shifting political landscape. Janusz is ambitious. And very political."

"Tell me," said Lucas, "when you and Janusz argue over what the country's about — who says what?"

Ernest only shrugged. Clearly, he did not care to talk about it, at least not then and there.

"Let me ask you this. If I say 'bombing the Temple Mount,' what do you say?"

"I say it's an ongoing fantasy. Ongoing plot. People scheme to do it. The government — at least all the governments so far — scheme to stop them."

"Janusz wouldn't be into something like that, would he?"

"Janusz," Ernest said, "isn't a bit religious."

"And that takes care of the question?"

"Well, it should," Ernest said.

They both watched Janusz Zimmer drink his vodka across the room and stare out to sea.

"What about you?" Ernest asked Lucas. "Why did you come here?"

"I don't know," Lucas said. "Maybe because I was a religion major."

"Like it?"

"Do I like it?" He had never, ever thought in such terms. "I don't know. It's a workout."

"You may find it difficult to live anywhere else," Ernest said. "Wait and see."

Outside, where the twilight teemed with riddles, the sun had disappeared beneath the Philistine Sea. A woman in the middle of the floor, the same woman of timeless seductiveness who had sung Piaf, was singing a song in Spanish about a Moor with a grenade.

"Out of the eater came forth meat," Lucas found himself reciting silently, "and out of the strong came forth sweetness."

"I know a few people with intelligence connections," Ernest told him. "We try and make ourselves useful to each other. In a good cause. I'll put in a word with them about you and Sonia. In the meantime, in case there are plans afoot of which we know not, you might have a trip out of town. Go diving. Walk in the desert."

"Funny," Lucas said, "I've just had a walk there."

When they left, the chanteuse was singing "Golden Earrings" in Yiddish. Every man in the Vercors shed thirty years.

48

SONIA WAS WALKING along Allenby Street toward the seafront when a shiny black Saab hung a U-turn from the oncoming lane and pulled up beside her. Janusz Zimmer was at the wheel.

"Like a lift?"

"OK," she said. "I'm going to Stanley's."

"Mister Stanley's," Zimmer said with amused scorn. "Get in." When she climbed in beside him, he asked, "Singing tonight?"

"Well, I'm billed," she said, "but I can't do it. Thought I'd break the news to the boss and throw myself on his mercy."

At Ein Kerem she had gotten a call from Raziel. De Kuff's retreat to the mountains of Galilee was to take place at once. The disciples would rendezvous at the hotel in Herzliya where Fotheringill cooked, proceed the next day to a guest kibbutz near the Lake of Kinneret, and go northward from there.

"Why is it," Janusz Zimmer asked her as they drove up Hayarkon beside the sea, "that you never take my advice? I told you to stay out of the Strip."

"And I didn't," she said. "And now I'm in trouble. Any connection?"

"It's all right," Janusz said. "You shouldn't worry. You've been useful anyway."

"Useful to who?"

"Useful to the country. To its higher interests."

"I don't know how you figure that, Jan."

"Why can't you sing tonight? I was hoping I'd get to hear you."

"We're going to Galilee. To look at the mountains."

"It'll be cold in those mountains. De Kuff going up there?"

"For a while."

"I'll give you another piece of advice. Let's see if you've gotten any smarter. Stay up in Galilee. If Mr. De Kuff wants to come back, let him come back himself. Stay and pick wildflowers."

"Listen, Jan. I want you to tell me something. I keep thinking about that sort of weird conversation we had. When you told me to stay out of the Strip. And about an . . . orchestra."

"What about it?"

"You don't know anything about a scheme to blow the Temple Mount, do you? So the religious types can build the Temple?"

"Do you?" Zimmer asked.

"Not a thing," she said. "That's why I'm asking."

They pulled up by the alley that led to the second street from the water, where Mister Stanley's was located.

"Enjoy Galilee," Jan Zimmer told her. "Take a long, well-earned rest."

Then his car pulled away, turned the corner of Hayarkon and disappeared.

49

WHEN LUCAS ARRIVED at Stanley's, a man whose hair fell in cascades of salt-and-pepper curls around his shoulders was playing Monk's "Bolivar Blues" for a half-filled room. Stanley was standing unhappily at the bar, nursing a vodka and tonic, eating pistachio nuts.

"Hey, book writer," he said to Lucas. "What you're doing to my Sonia? She won't sing for me."

"She got religion, Stanley. Didn't she tell you?"

"Got to get her back," he said. "Maria Clara's coming in from Colombia. She has a present for her. And every time Sonia leaves, the customers go crazy. Sonia! Sonia!"

"I can imagine."

"You know something?" he confided to Lucas, "the Americans are buying people. They send a detective around, they want to find Razz Melker, guy used to play clarinet for me. Then they want this old man from New York, Marshall. They got reward."

"Big reward?"

"Big reward for Razz. For the old man . . ." He shrugged. "Peanuts."

"I don't suppose," Lucas said, "anyone wants to buy me?"

Stanley regarded him with quickened interest.

"Just a joke," Lucas said.

"The world is full of things and people the Americans are paying for," Stanley observed. "Someday they'll run out of money."

"And it will all stop," Lucas said. "The end of history."

Nuala Rice was sitting just outside the door of Stanley's office. Lucas took a seat at the same table.

"Christopher!" she exclaimed when she saw him. "I've been try-ing you and trying you. We have to be out of here, the lot of us."

"Where's Sonia?"

"She won't be here tonight. She went to see her friends in Herz-liya. She left a note for you."

On the slip of paper Nuala handed him there was only the name of a kibbutz and two dates, that of the next day and the day follow-ing that. The kibbutz was called Nikolayevich Alef. It was on Yar-mouk Road, the note said, south of Tiberias.

"Thanks," Lucas said, and put it in his pocket. Kibbutz Niko-layevich was where Tsililla and Gigi Prinzer had both grown up.

"What about you?" he asked Nuala. "Is Rashid with you?"

"He's sleeping," she said. "You know," she told him, "we went to the U.S. consulate yesterday. They didn't want to know us."

"Is that surprising?"

"I don't know," she said, a little helplessly for Nuala. "Our con-trol sort of implied the Americans would give us a visa." She low-ered her voice. "We got the word from him to clear out. He said he'd help us."

"Good," said Lucas. "But where is he now?"

"He's getting us the proper documents. They'll get us out."

"What did the American consulate say?"

"They said we'd have to wait for visas. Like everyone else."

"The State Department doesn't like giving visas to PLO people," Lucas explained. "It's politically incorrect."

"Shabak can fix it," she said.

For a revolutionary, he thought, she had a moving confidence in the goodwill and capabilities of the secret police.

"Just out of curiosity," he asked her, "how do you justify working with them?"

"How can they justify working with us? Sometimes there are coincidences of interest."

Coincidences of interest in that corner of the world, he thought, were ropes of sand. But he had to assume she knew that as well as he did.

50

THEY STOPPED at the four-star hotel in Herzliya where Fotheringill worked as a chef. Raziel conducted them across the lobby under the stares of elderly diamond dealers.

First Raziel himself, in his dark slacks, black shirt and wraparound sunglasses, supporting the Rev by the arm. Then Miss van Witte, the former nun, in prim seersucker. The two slope-shouldered Walsing brothers. The Marshalls, father and son, in their increasingly tattered two-thousand-dollar suits. Sonia, in sandals and jeans. Helen Henderson, the Rose of Saskatoon, in khaki shorts, hiking boots and a short-sleeved shirt that matched the shorts, carrying a backpack on a metal frame. She was obviously determined to share Sonia's fortunes, come what might. And Gigi Prinzer had come out to join them, finding accommodation up the coast with friends in Ein Hod.

"A circus," a guest in the lobby muttered.

They were given a shabby but extensive suite in the back, so that De Kuff, as usual, had a small bedroom to himself. Their view was not of the ocean but of a juice-processing plant and the misty fields of grapefruit trees around it.

Shortly after they arrived, the two Marshalls fell to quarreling over a set of black ledgers, such as might keep the records of a basement moving company or a New York bodega. Finally the younger Marshall prevailed by brute force, seizing the books from the older man's grasp.

The Walsings changed into their bathing suits and set out for the swimming pool, where they would be sure to astonish the reclining diamond merchants further. They looked like a pair of hulking, pale

Teutonic ghosts dispatched from Valhalla on a mission of atonement or revenge.

Helen Henderson, who had caught a cold, dealt with it by downing vitamin pills and attempting meditation.

Later, while his son was sleeping, the older Mr. Marshall crept across the carpet of their suite and rescued one of his ledgers. One aspect of the older Mr. Marshall's religious obsessions centered on the number thirty-six, along with its variants and multiples. Sitting with the ledger on his lap, his eyes showing white, he tried to connect the name of De Kuff with the year, and the date of the year with the ninth day of Av, so that the ninth might be seen to occur out of season. His ledger was the abstraction of loving discourse on thirty-six, and his encoded notes the digest of reflections on the mystical properties of the Hebrew thirty-six, *lamed-vav,* and also of three, nine, and eighteen.

On other pages he had copied or summarized incantations, the names of the firmaments, encampments, thrones and presiding angels whose powers might be brought to bear against his enemies and persecutors. One of the spells, which he had had frequent occasion to use against various officials and auditors in the Southern District of New York, was an imprecation against creditors:

"That you will plug," it asked of the deadly angels, "his mouth and make his planning vain, and he will not think of me nor speak of me, and when I pass in front of him he will not see me."

The elder Mr. Marshall — and his son as well — could do complex calculations in their heads. They could also count cards in blackjack and had been banned from several casinos. The younger Mr. Marshall had created several computer programs.

In the tiny kitchen area, the former Sister Maria John Nepomuk van Witte was brewing herbal tea, her copy of Elaine Pagels's *Gnostic Gospels* folded face down on a stool. Below her was a letter from her former companion in the Sisters of the Common Life, who was now a member of the Netherlands parliament and an open lesbian.

"In that forest they wear strange shoes," said the letter — a proverb from her province meant to apply to both of them.

Sonia leaned against the window, singing to herself and looking out over the misted citrus fields. Was the mist ground fog or pesticide? Did it matter, in the condition to which the world had come?

Raziel spent the day with a word for each of the Rev's followers. He read to Helen Henderson from the *Zohar,* taught her to meditate on the letters of the Tetragrammaton. *Yod-hei-vav-hei.* To visualize black fire against white fire and fix the sacred characters in mind, silently breathing in the *yod,* exhaling the *hei,* taking in the *vav,* letting out the final *hei,* creating the deepest of silences, a space in which nothing intervened between the devotee and the ineffable object of devotion. He disputed points of Torah with the younger Marshall, predicting new, unexpected interpretations in the world to come. He talked of the works of Hildegard von Bingen with Maria van Witte.

"Yo, Sonia," he said, finding her sad at the window. "Wassup, home?"

"You tired, Razz?" she said.

"We're almost there, kid."

"I hope so," she said. She looked at him. "I still believe. Am I thinking straight?"

"Sonia," Raziel said, "don't worry. Very shortly the world will be unrecognizable. The world as we know it will pass from history."

She closed her eyes and opened them again.

"Must be the child in me," she said. "I have to believe you."

Then he left her to go in to the old man. De Kuff lay on a sofa bed, in his stocking feet, his overcoat draped over his frame. Under the coat, his arms were crossed at his chest.

"How are you, Adam?" Raziel asked.

"Losing my strength," De Kuff said. "I think I may be dying. I think I might like to die."

"I understand," Raziel said. "Better than you think. But we have a ways to walk. We have one final mystery to impart."

"Do you really believe?" De Kuff asked him. "Don't you think we might have been wrong?"

Raziel smiled. "We've given our lives over to it, Adam. We have nothing else."

"That doesn't mean we were right," De Kuff said. "Only that we ourselves are lost."

"Don't give up, Rev. Wait for the time of the final mystery. Remember, wait for the *tav.*"

"How I wish we could have been spared," the old man said.

Raziel went over and took his hand.

"Do you wish it for me, too? You're kind, Adam. But we weren't spared, and you really are who you are. Wait yet a while."

De Kuff closed his eyes and nodded.

The doorbell rang and the people scattered about the suite froze and looked at one another. Raziel went and opened the door. Ian Fotheringill stood in the hall, in his white chef's tunic and toque. Raziel left the door ajar and stepped out into the hall to join him.

"You have it?" he asked the Scot.

Fotheringill handed him a package wrapped in butcher paper and Raziel put it in his pocket. Then the two of them stepped into the suite.

"We'll only be staying a few hours," Raziel announced. "Anyone want to wait here while we go up the mountain?"

No one did. Each of them wanted to go as far up as they could manage.

Raziel approached Sonia. "He needs somebody. He needs you for a change. Tell him what he has to hear."

"I wish I knew what that was."

"You do, Sonia. You always have."

Sonia got up and went into the room where De Kuff was resting. He was lying on his side, weeping.

"Are you suffering?" she asked, taking his old, cold hand as Raziel had.

"Very much," he said.

"This is the struggle without weapons," she told him.

"I may fail. If I fail, I'll die. But it's all right." He turned onto his back and looked anxiously up at her. "You have to take care of all these children." It really seemed, she thought, that there was not much life left in him.

"Sure," she said. She sat down on the bed beside him.

"Among Sufis," Sonia said, "the struggle without weapons is called *jihad*. It's not the *jihad* of Hamas or what the *shebab* call *jihad*. But it's *jihad* all the same."

She saw his eyes come alight.

"Is there anything we can do for you?"

"We have to go," he said with sudden urgency. "To Galilee, to the mountain. And then to Jerusalem. You see, I'll do everything that is required. If it doesn't happen . . ."

"If it doesn't happen, it doesn't," she said. "One day it will."

In his own room, Raziel locked his door, cooked up the heroin Fotheringill had brought him, tied off and found a vein. He felt a childlike rush of gratitude; creation in that instant became again a

place of comfort, and he had found some quarter of a caring, providing world.

The necessities of his task had brought him back to drugs. Every
day he lived in fear that De Kuff would be lost to him, that he would
have no place in the process that he had made himself believe in. The
process, his perfectionism, had brought him to drugs for relief again,
just as, once, music had.

He had not been able to take the contradictions, the intersections
he had been compelled to negotiate, connecting the pious routines of
orthodoxy to conspiracy with swindlers and men of violence. Un-
aided, he had not had the strength.

Every day he had been casting formulaic prayers into the void of
the unknowable. Every minute of each day had been shadowed in
paradox. He had sought out forbidden Sabbataian texts that reversed the meanings of Torah, to force it from its traditional interpretations. He had traced the memory palaces of the ancient *min*
and meditated on the sidereal tables and astral metaphors of Elisha
ben Abouya, the accursed Gnostic Pharisee. He had consulted tarot
and the *I Ching* in search of Kabbalist parallels. His motto, alibi,
guiding text, had been the words written on a scroll of Qumran, the
words of the Teacher of Righteousness: Depravity is the mystery of
creation. To liberate into the world the ultimate goodness of God
and man, it was necessary to walk deep into the labyrinth.

Sometimes, he thought — pitying the old man, himself and the
ragged circle of believers — it was so hard to believe that there had
ever been or would ever be anything resembling redemption or rec-
onciliation under Jerusalem's heaven. Anything at all but that rich,
indifferent blue, the first and holiest of unresponding skies. But
behind it the sages had discovered the *ayin,* the substance wherein
holiness itself was concealed and that Raziel, for all his confusion,
believed in absolutely, joyfully.

But in the end, he had needed drugs again to realize it and to
believe — to be at once Jew and Christian, Muslim and Zoroas-
trian, Gnostic and Manichean. The creed he had worked out was
antinomian. He himself, in his heart, was not antinomian enough to
be the priest of so contradictory a sacrifice, not depraved enough or
magus enough to bring the process to fruition. And he had constantly to conceal the violent aspect of the plan from De Kuff, from
Sonia, even from himself in the midnight hours.

Like the fighting Zionists, he had believed in the imminence of the final redemption. The signs had come. Even the charlatans of the House of the Galilean subscribed to that, or pretended to. Raziel did not in fact think that it would come to violence. He had believed there would be intercession, although the forms of violence had to be employed. Now he could feel it all dissipating into illusion.

Finally, he supposed what he worshiped was the butterfly, the sweet blood butterfly that spread its motherly wings against the window of his needle. It was all that could raise his sick, impoverished, tied-off heart. The thing had failed, but he had not the courage to tell them. Above all, he could not face De Kuff. He watched his own blood in the glass.

How lovely, how symmetrical, the lovely language, the Torah, the dreams of the Nazarenes. He had been an athlete of perception. Now, perhaps, it was all almost over.

51

EXHAUSTED, driving the rented Ford Taurus, Lucas overtook them at a campsite run by Kibbutz Nikolayevich Alef. It was one of the oldest kibbutzim in the country, dating from Ottoman times. Until 1967 it had been practically astride the Jordanian border and subject to regular attacks. Once it had been on fire with conflicting ideologies, but it had survived all and become a kind of country town. Part of it still subscribed to the old kibbutz collectivism, part of it functioned on the principle of a moshav.

Nikolayevich Alef was surrounded by orchards and fields of sugar cane and streams beside which papyrus grew. Lucas was glad to leave the Dead Sea road for its shade and birdsong. He found De Kuff and his followers in the dining hall, eating by themselves. A nearby table full of teenage girls watched them in desperately suppressed merriment, exchanging hilarious whispers at the pilgrims' appearance. The girls bit their lips and pressed their faces into the Formica tabletops so as not to be caught laughing.

De Kuff and his followers were definitely a scene, but few others in the huge cafeteria-style place paid them any attention. Most of the residents were commuters, to Tiberias and Jerusalem, professionals and civil servants, men dining alone or married couples, both of whom sat with their briefcases at their side.

The kibbutz did not keep a kosher dining hall, and the special of the day was shrimp. Lucas thought it looked institutionally overcooked and was probably frozen. De Kuff and Raziel ate theirs with enthusiasm. Sonia had salad. The Marshalls also ate shrimp, wearing their hats and looking grim. They ate the fried tails along with the rest.

It might be said now that among the group there was neither Jew nor Gentile, male nor female, bond nor free. A circus. But at Kibbutz Nikolayevich Alef their circus was more comical than scandalous. At one end of their table were Sister van Witte, eating slowly, her hands crippled with arthritis; Helen Henderson, the Rose, blowing her nose in a tissue; the awful Walsing brothers; and the unlikely Fotheringill, who had brought some bread and cheese to share. At the other end sat Sonia, Raziel, old De Kuff and sad Gigi Prinzer, sipping her kibbutz orange drink.

Standing in the doorway of the dining hall, Lucas was moved by the sight of them. He tried to remember how long he had known them all. A few months, no more.

Raziel looked up and saw him. He said something to Sonia. She pushed her plate aside and came to him.

"You got my note," she said. "You went to Stanley's."

"Yes. We have to talk."

She looked at him with some concern. "You're all fucked up, you know that? You look sick and you look tired."

"Scared," Lucas said.

"Come in and eat something," she said.

"I don't like cafeteria food," Lucas said. "Not since the Belmont closed."

"Where was that?"

"Twenty-eighth Street, I think. It's been a while."

They went out into the sweet-smelling garden. Azaleas bloomed.

"We're in trouble. I've been to see Ernest and I've been to see Sylvia."

"I was afraid we might be," she said. She seemed, to Lucas, more calm and composed than she had any right to be. "Is it over Gaza? Or the Haram story?"

"I still don't really know."

"What do they say?"

"That Nuala and Rashid are in very bad trouble. And that we're better off because we connect with Raziel. By the way," he asked her, "have you by chance asked our young leader if his revelation involves some . . . some mishap at the Temple Mount?"

She laughed uncertainly.

"Well, no. But it wouldn't, would it? I mean, Raziel is an ex-junkie and all, but he's a gentle guy. And you don't think the Rev is some kind of bomber, do you?"

"No," Lucas said. "But I thought it might be worth asking. Just on an unlikely notion, sort of."

"You want me to ask him?"

"Yes," Lucas said. "Because it seems to me that . . . if history is going to be resolved, the rebuilding of the Temple should figure in it."

"We don't think that way, Chris. That's not our way of seeing things."

"Ask him anyway," Lucas said. He sat down on the mess hall steps. "Is there somewhere I can sleep?"

"I'm in a bungalow with Sister van Witte," she said. "You can sleep with us, I guess."

"OK," Lucas said. When she started back inside, he called her. "Sonia! What did he say to you when I came in?"

"Who, Raziel? When?"

"When I came in, while you were all eating. He said something to you when he saw me."

"Oh," she said. "Well, you know how he is. Always sort of scheming. He said to get you to come with us. Up the mountain."

"Right," said Lucas. "Scheming."

When Lucas had gone to put his gear in the bungalow, Sonia approached Raziel outside the mess hall.

"Razz?"

"Yo," said Brother Raziel.

"Just around like, you haven't heard anything about, well, about some plan for destroying the mosques on the Temple Mount?"

Raziel did not seem surprised. "Did Chris ask you to ask me that?"

"He did, actually. There seems to be some plot like that around."

"There always has been," Raziel said. "Goes back a long way. In Jerusalem people are always tearing something down to build something else in its place. Back to the Babylonians, right? The Ninth of Av. Pull down one temple, put up another. Pull down their guy, put up our guy. Pull down the temple, put up the church. Pull down the church, put up the mosque. Profane the sacred. Sanctify the secular. Goes on and on."

"But we have nothing to do with one, right? These plots have nothing to do with us, do they?"

"Sonia," Raziel said. "We aren't here to destroy anything physical. The change that involves us is spiritual. It's a transformation in kind. A miracle. Regardless of what people may have heard. Or what they think."

"So you're telling me," she said, "that I'm right about that, yes? We have nothing to do with any destruction of the mosques?"

"I give you my word, Sonia. Not one of us will harm a human soul. Not one of us will harm another's property. I swear it. Is that good enough?"

It was getting dark. They heard the teenagers laughing at them from the direction of the communal swimming pool.

"Yes," she said. "Of course it is."

52

AT THE AIRPORT in Cyprus, Nuala and Rashid were picked up by the man they were told would meet them. His name was Dmitri, and because the deal involved Russian friends of Stanley's, they had expected a Russian. But Dmitri was a Greek Cypriot, a small, wrinkled man with a long, comically fluted nose. He was also less cosmopolitan in appearance than they had expected. He was dressed like a village artisan, with a stained old-fashioned English tweed cap.

Dmitri took Rashid's cloth bag; Nuala was wearing her backpack. At first they could get no English out of him, which for a Greek Cypriot was absurd.

When the car weaved its way through town, left the coast road and headed north, then turned off again, she complained.

"Just a mo, Dmitri," she said. "Could we ask you where we're meeting our friends. I thought it would be in Larnaca."

According to her sense of Cypriot geography, they were headed toward the mountains and the border with Turkish territory.

"Road to Troulli, madame," Dmitri said. "But you will not be going all the way there. Your friends are at the monastery."

Nuala looked into the darkness. The headlights caught tiers of cactus plants in flower along the road.

"A road to no-town, they say in Ireland," she told Rashid.

"They are secretive and they know their business. It's best." If he did not sound completely confident, neither did he sound frightened. Nuala decided to keep a weather eye on Dmitri.

They took a left fork from the main road, and before long there was hardly any road at all. Dmitri stopped the car at a cattle grid. Like a chauffeur, he got out and walked around to her side and opened the door. After a moment's hesitation, the two of them stepped out onto the muddy road, invisible beneath their feet.

"It is *ekklesia*. *Temenos*. It is *Ayios Yeorios*."

About a hundred yards up the sloping path, a lamp showed, disappeared, showed again. Nuala turned back and saw Dmitri standing beside his car. The motor still turned; the headlights made two reassuring columns of light. The beams widened bravely in the darkness until their rays scattered among the tiny night-winged creatures that flitted against her cheek. There were cicadas and the smell of cows and manure, a country smell that, except for the piney bitterness of sage and scrub oak, reminded her of home.

"They wait," Dmitri called up to her. "Russki."

"It is OK," Rashid said. "Yes! I see it's OK."

She looked for his face in the darkness and saw his jaw thrust out, his arms raised. When he took her hand, she felt in his touch the show of manhood, the straining of his muscles summoning courage. As they walked on, she suddenly knew that they were going to die in the darkness ahead. For a moment she wanted to run — she could run fast, had learned to run in her dusty boots over the dry ground of the Middle East. Fighting the revolution, living to fight another day. But she did not run.

"Well," she said, "we're together."

"Yes," he said. "See? It is OK."

They closed in on the dark buildings, and the beam of the flashlight probed and withdrew to a red glow where men stood.

"*Salaam aleikum*," a voice said.

And happily, Rashid replied, "*Wa aleikum salaam*." He knit his fingers in hers. "Yes. These are Russians."

He seemed so sure. Yet she thought there was something strange about the old familiar greeting coming from Russians, from men who were associates of Stanley's or Party comrades.

"Madame," the same Russian voice said, "come with us please."

Come with us please but there was no church, no *temenos*. It was just a stable. Half hypnotized, she held on to Rashid's hand and followed the glowing translucent shield around the torch in the man's hand that swayed as he walked ahead of them. Then they were under a stone roof and for a moment she saw the stars through a lancet window and mixed with the other smells was a smell of old stone and faint incense so that it might have been a church once, a long time before.

Then Rashid pulled his hand away and she stood alone, not comprehending. Then the sudden sounds of struggle. Yet she stood alone, untouched. And then he shouted and she thought, It shall be rain tonight. Let it come down.

And when the knee went into the small of her back and the hand over her mouth, she still heard his boyish, boastful curses and threats, his posturing. In part, she knew it was for her benefit. A doctor, a Communist, a leader of his people, her life's love and still, in the Arab way, a favored son, a boy who could not, even in extremis, stop performing.

There were several men and they shone the light on her. Her arms were pulled tightly back, and over her head they forced some kind of canvas harness. When she resisted, they twisted her arms without mercy until both were bent at the elbow, paralyzed behind her.

"Nuala!" Rashid shouted. He had never learned to say her name correctly.

"Yes," she said. "Here, my love." And she threw her head back and shouted, "Rashid!"

While they called each other's names she was lifted, with strange gentleness by the elbows. There were two men, one at each arm. They carried her up a flight of stone steps, and through the lancet window she briefly saw the stars again. Then the men in whose hands she was turned her away from the window and she saw that she was on a ledge. There seemed to be hay on its hard stone floor. But perhaps it had been a church, the choir loft.

"Rashid!" she shouted. He called back to her. For a moment — maybe she had been encouraged by the gentleness with which they had lifted her — she wanted to address the unseen men who had made her prisoner. Then, when the noose was set around her neck, she knew it had been the gentleness of hangmen, an executioner's discretion. They were roping her ankles together.

It was a dirty, terrifying place to die. One of the men said something to her, but she was too frightened to understand. She heard Rashid call her name again, and he too now sounded afraid.

"Rashid!" she called, hardly able to speak. Her throat was dry, the rope tightened around her neck. She struggled against fear as she had struggled against the harness that held her. Here we are, my love, she thought. She could not tell him it was over. More than anything she wanted him with her, his courage not to fail him in that awful place. Because they were both people of the conquered world, and the gallows that had finally come for them had shadowed all the history of their peoples. "Be brave, my love!"

He called on God.

"Power to the people," she said, although she knew the phrase she had chosen to die uttering had become a joke. "You have been naught," she tried to say, tried to think it. "You shall be all."

Such a dirty, fearsome place. Then she was swinging free and breath was all she cared about, all, it seemed, she had ever cared about, the air of that filthy-smelling place, but there was none to be had. So with her breath all the thoughts of her devotion were expunged while the angry men stood watching her in the beam of their light and she wondered if she would ever ever die and then a deeper darkness, in its mercy, came.

PART THREE

53

IS BED HAD a comforter, and he woke to the sun through lace curtains and a chorus of warblers in the eucalyptus grove outside.

The bungalow was empty, the other beds in it made up. He found Sonia sitting on a child's swing in the eucalyptus grove, shielding her eyes to see him against the morning sun.

"Want breakfast?" she asked him.

He shook his head. "Where is everyone?"

"Raziel and the Rev left for the Golan with the Rose. She's young and strong and she helps out, and it might keep her out of harm's way. The rest of the gang is staying here. We rented them a couple of bungalows. I'm waiting for you."

"Waiting for me to do what, Sonia?"

"We're going up the mountain."

"Really? And what do we do when we get there?"

"I sing. You listen. You're a reporter, are you not? You protect me. Then, if everything works out, we go to Jerusalem."

He turned away from her and saw Fotheringill, working under the hood of a sixties-era Volvo, talking to himself.

"You seem hesitant," Sonia said, taking Lucas by the hand. "Got any other ideas?"

"I guess not," he said.

When they were on the road in his rental car, Lucas asked, "What does he think he's going to do in the mountains?"

"He has to meditate before he makes the last . . ."

"Pronouncement?" Lucas suggested. "Revelation?"

"Yes, that's right. And then go back to Jerusalem, because it's written that he pass from out of Dan."

He glanced at her from behind the wheel. There was no irony in what she said; she still believed. Sooner or later it would have to end, he thought. Then, when the lights came on, what would be left of her? As for himself, by now he wanted it not to end. He wanted them both to be subsumed in ongoing mystery.

"Perception is functional," he said. "That's true, isn't it? Things aren't defined by what we see every day, are they? What we see every day could be false consciousness."

"That's the spirit," Sonia said. "Now you're getting it. Anyway, the Rev needs me. He said he did. And I want you to come."

Before long they were passing the shops and hotels of Tiberias. There was a small amusement park along the Lake of Kinneret. Shy Arab families wandered uncertainly among the rides. Lucas noticed that the women wore bandannas and mantillas instead of *chadors*.

"Christians," Sonia said.

"That's the South Lebanon Army on R & R. This is where they come."

When they passed Migdal, where Mary Magdalene had been a country girl before she went wrong in the big city, a single faint bell was sounding near the lake.

Dirt roads ran down through rough fields to the water, bordered by tamarisks and eucalyptus. A few miles ahead, Lucas saw the arches of a lakeside church.

"What is it?" Lucas asked.

"Someone's church. I forget whose."

The church and adjoining monastery were the rosy color of Jerusalem stone but they did not seem very old. They were Neo-Romanesque with red roof tiles and a spotless courtyard and fountain out front. He pulled off the highway and guided the car down a dirt road toward the lake. When they reached the water, he saw that they had followed the wrong road; the church and monastery were across a rutted pasture enclosed by wire.

Bells were sounding, bells of every register, from funereal profundo to a tinkling Eucharistic chime. The sound whirled on the lake wind, singing the bright sky, announcing the slow-moving formations of heavy clouds on the far shore.

A tall monk in white was closing the wooden church door.

"Benedictines. I want to go," he announced. "I want to go to Mass."

"If that's what you want," she said, "I'll go with you."

Lucas began to struggle with the wire fencing that enclosed the field, cutting his wrists and arms.

"Hey," Sonia said. "Watch it."

He fought the wire as though he were engaging serpents, until it was subdued and he could hold up the bottom strand for her to crawl under.

"Take it easy," she said. She wriggled through on her back with barely an inch to spare. "Hey, maybe we should get in the car and backtrack."

"No," Lucas said. "We'll never make it." He was growing more and more excited. "We've got to hump cross-country."

Sonia was brushing herself off. She had cut her knee on the wire. "You really feel the need, Chris?"

"You don't have to go," he told her. "You stay. Drive back around and I'll meet you at the church."

"No," she said, "I'll go with you."

So the two of them scrambled across the field of high tough grass, brambles and clodded red earth that lay between them and the monastery. It was hard going and they both cut themselves further. Lucas was breathing hard.

"Chris," she said anxiously, "what's wrong with you?"

"This is the place of the loaves and fishes," he said. "Where the multitude was fed."

"Oh," she said, "I know that one."

"I've got to make that Mass," Lucas said. "I've absolutely got to."

"You look . . . you look beside yourself," she said, panting to keep up with him.

"Maybe I am."

But when they reached the building, its great wooden door was ponderously secured. Lucas pulled at the great ring handle. Locked. He pulled harder, then pushed. A sign on the door said RUHIG, and under it, GESCHLOSSEN FÜR GOTTESDIENST.

He went to the other door. It had the same sign.

"They have to let me in," Lucas said.

"No they don't, Chris."

"The hell they don't," he shouted. From inside he could hear faint Gregorian chant. The doors, he thought, must be very thick. He began to pound on them with the side of his fists.

"Let me in, you German sons of bitches!"

His eye fell on a date on the cornerstone of the church: *1936*.

"Jesus Christ," he shrieked, "1936! You bastards, let me in! Let me in! Look," he told Sonia, "they're keeping me out. They won't let me in." He pounded until his wrists hurt and his hands were numb.

"You have no right!" he shouted. "You have no right to keep me out! Look," he said to Sonia, "1936!" He pounded some more, until it was impossible to imagine no one heard him. The faint chanting inside continued. He began to kick the door.

"Chris," she said, "please stop."

"The fucking sons of bitches!" His shouts echoed along the tranquil Sea of Galilee.

"Huns!" he cried. "They should be on their knees every minute in this country. They should live on their knees here. Imagine them not letting me in!"

He got to his own knees.

"Because I'm in trouble. I'm in need."

"Yes," she said, helping him to his feet. "I see. I see you are."

They stumbled back over the hard ground toward the car. "You can cry if you like," she said. But he only bit his lip and pressed on, wild-eyed.

They drove to the Franciscan chapel outside Capernaum. A friar was sweeping the steps beside it that led to the ruins, and they nodded to each other. Lucas and Sonia walked along the shore and sat by the remains of the ancient synagogue.

"So what was that about?" she asked when he had calmed down.

"Beats me."

"You say *I* need to believe. What about you?"

"I don't know. I've been drinking too much. I'm out of Prozac. I've got a cold."

"We'll fix you up, poor guy."

"It's all an undigested bit of beef," Lucas said.

"Say what?"

"An undigested bit of beef," he said. "Like Jacob Marley's ghost."

"Jacob Marley?"

"You never heard of Jacob Marley? *A Christmas Carol*?"

"Oh," she said. "Him."

He took an empty water bottle they had brought and filled it from the lake.

"What is it?" she asked.

"Water," he said. " 'Over whose acres walked those blessed feet which fourteen hundred years ago were nailed for our advantage on the bitter cross.' "

"Better not drink it," she said. "Never mind who walked on it."

They drove into the hills north of the lake.

"You have to be ready for this to fail you," Lucas counseled her. "When it comes to nothing, you still have to go on living."

"It won't fail us," she said. "But it might be the other way around. *We* might fail. It's hard to make everything be music. But music will always be there."

"Is that what it's like? Making everything be music?"

"Making everything be music *again*," she said. "The way it was in the beginning."

"You know," Lucas said, "all the grief of the twentieth century has come from trying to turn life into art. Think about it."

"If we try," Sonia said, "we can make things the way they were. The way they were is the way they're supposed to be. That's why we have art. To remind us."

He could not resist the little flutter of mindless hope. In what? In nothing he could remotely conceive. Did it not matter that Raziel was the flake of flakes, De Kuff a dying reed, Sonia so good and smart she turned foolish? That they were at the heart of a Middle Eastern setup devised by deluded masters? It mattered, all right. But he could not resist the little flutter.

That afternoon, they caught up with De Kuff, Raziel, the Rose and their Dodge van at a campsite in the Hula Valley. There were tents to rent, and the Rose helped them put theirs up. She was good with tents, a young outdoorsy woman — which was, Lucas supposed, why Raziel had consented to bring her along.

"I wish he wasn't so unhappy," the Rose said. She meant De Kuff.

"It's chemical," Lucas told her. He watched her ponder this information. "Why did you come?" he asked her.

"To help Sonia. And maybe now to be with him. I think there's a lesson for me. And I want to say I was here."

With darkness had come a slight chill. He had brought a bottle of The Macallan, and he took occasional comfort from it. Their tent was enormous, of canvas, and of an old-fashioned sort that could accommodate camp tables and cots. Sonia furnished it with a rented air mattress and some Bedouin skin rugs and cushions, orphans from Berger's apartment.

He found her lying on one elbow, looking at peace. Dry oak leaves were caught in the curly bush of her hair.

"So here we are again," he said.

"So here we are again. A love supreme."

"So," he asked her, across the glowing Coleman lamp, also rented, that hung between them, "what is this? What are we doing out here?" Peter the Hermit's army, he thought. A long trail of bozos had preceded them.

"You're working," she said. "The working press. You're reporting on religious mania."

"Right," he said. "And this is the real McCoy. Primary process."

"Would you like me to sing 'Michael, Row the Boat Ashore'?"

"So you're actively believing it all? Right now? This minute?"

"Uh-huh. And you — you're amazed. Going around amazed. What's real? What's not? Are you real?"

"I get drunk every night," Lucas said. "I hallucinate Rudolph Steiner's daughter, Diphtheria, who says —"

"What we think, will be," Sonia said helpfully. "Diphtheria's right. She's just a little djinn, just a little demon. But, you know, Theodor Herzl said, 'If you will it, it is no dream.' She's got something there. So repeat after me: The force of human will. Go ahead, repeat it."

"No," Lucas said.

"Where shall wisdom be found?" she asked him. "What is the place of understanding?" She put out her hand.

"You know, do you, Sonia?"

"Yes," she said. "With me."

The tent smelled of apples. The lantern flickered between them.

She had on a djellaba, decorated with stars. Her raiment, he liked to call it. When she took it off, he saw the serpent on the chain around her neck dangling to her breasts. She climbed under one of the skin rugs and held her arms out to him. He sat down next to her.

"Come on, Chris. You're real. I'll help you believe."

"I don't think you will," he said. But he bent beside her until they both lay on the mattress, against the skin — she under it naked, he in his clothes, on top.

"Yes I will," she said. "It's good. It's right."

And, taking off his jacket, glumly unbuttoning his shirt, he had the sensation of playing out an old losing hand. But the Bedouin goatskin blanket, which he had thought would be foul, was soft and sweet-smelling, and the feel of her body beneath it made his mouth go dry. So he continued undressing, in a thrill of despair, and lay naked beside her. Wisdom. The place of understanding. *The depth sayeth, It is not in me; and the sea sayeth, It is not with me.*

She still had on her underpants and the chain. Lying on her side, facing him, she lifted the pendant from around her neck and set it down beside them. Under the skin, she took his hands and led them to the warm smooth silky swellings of her derriere. Each hand found its own way around to her waist and down her belly from the navel. He went down to her and took off the white panties and pressed his mouth against her thighs and groin and pudenda.

Pulling back a moment, he said, "You have to bear with me." He had said the same thing before. It had hurt him so much that it made him sick to hear himself say it again. "I'm slow."

Slow and sometimes so slow you wouldn't know he was there at all.

"A love supreme," she sang. When he had made her wet with his mouth, he bent his knees and rose up against her, on fire, rampant, like the boy with the Shulamite, sick with love. *Return, return, that we may look upon thee.*

And she sang and screamed and afterward Lucas cried the tears of a happiness he could not measure or analyze or otherwise molest with self-examination. It was really as though she commanded the depths where wisdom lay.

"You see what I'm saying?" she said.

When she was sleeping he went out to see the stars against the distant mountains. The lamp burned low. The clouds over the Golan had parted to reveal Andromeda, cradling her galaxy in the flawless sky, and her stars Alpheratz, Mirach, Almach. The Arab names sounded of the *Zohar,* jewels of the curtain under the Throne of Glory.

So why not, he thought. And among the stars, her astral correspondence, the star of my lover, my sister, my spouse, in whose depths is the place of wisdom.

The man who believes in nothing ends by believing in everything. So said Chesterton, his abandoned Catholic mentor. Let it be done as she says, he thought. She was the soul of truth; she deserved it. He felt as if he had been near to death and come alive. Yes, let it be as she says. Let me believe. In the washhouse mirror, he saw, for the first time, the serpent pendant around his neck.

In the morning, they started after the Rose had broken camp for Raziel and De Kuff and hurried them on the road north, along the top of the Hula Valley. They saw wild pigs running near the lake, and a soaring osprey. The mountains of the Golan drew closer. Papyrus grew beside the water. Pelicans made their geometric, card-trick pterodactyl dives.

"The pelican of the desert," Lucas said.

They had reached the edge of the Paz petrol roadmap Lucas had been using to navigate. Its corner sections were worn away and missing.

"Do we have a decent map?" Lucas asked.

"Just this," said Sonia. She handed him the rental car company's map. It was not very detailed.

"This is the kind of map that killed Bishop Pike," Lucas said.

"The one for us," said Sonia.

54

RAZIEL AND DE KUFF stood at the edge of a Druse village. A manure-flecked road led from the stone houses of the village to the black-rock pastures where some goats and thick-wooled sheep grazed. Far below, at nearly a vertical angle down the slope, the Druse had their orchards.

The village headman and his son had come out to speak to them. The vaulting mountain sky furnished a chilly gray dawn.

The elder Druse spoke a little French. His son worked at a concession in the Hula Valley and had some words of Hebrew. Raziel was trying to persuade them not to turn the pilgrim group away. The Golan Druse were caught between their hospitable instincts, their resentment toward Israel and their fear of army and police spies working for Israel, Syria or both.

"Tell them we're scientists," Raziel advised De Kuff, who was speaking French to the older man. "Tell him we've been sent by the Ministry. To study the sources of the Jordan."

"In the Holy City," De Kuff said to the old headman, "we were told that voices spoke from the mountain." He used the Arabic name for Jerusalem, Al-Kuds.

The headman looked at him blankly. "*Privé*," he said after a moment.

"Only to the river," De Kuff said. "Only to cross."

The older Druse looked at the Dodge van. The Rose was asleep in the back seat.

"Friends will move our car across the mountain," De Kuff said. He took out his wallet. "We'll pay."

Father and son looked at the wallet in his hand. The older man said something to his son, and the youth turned and started walking toward the village. Raziel leaned against the van, a hand shading his wraparound sunglasses from the sky's gray glare. De Kuff stood in the attitude of Muslim prayer, facing the slopes of Mount Hermon. After a few minutes the headman's son returned with three other men about his father's age.

"We can offer them as much as we have," De Kuff said breathlessly. "What does it matter?"

"Take it easy, Rev. If you give them too much, they'll get scared and call the Border Police."

"They're honest men," De Kuff said, looking fondly at the villagers.

"Keep them honest," Raziel said. "Just don't wave money around and make them crazy."

But De Kuff gave a fifty-dollar bill to everyone. Raziel had no idea where he'd gotten the cash. The Druse looked at the bills with hope, dread and suspicion. There were many counterfeit American fifties in the Middle East, and even on Mount Hermon people were aware of it.

When the headman had agreed to let them pass through the fields, De Kuff signaled to Raziel to awaken the sleeping Rose. His gesture was kingly; it was one of his enthusiastic days. She climbed out, blinking prettily, and smelled the mountain air.

They were standing beside the van when Fotheringill drove up in the Volvo. He motioned Raziel to his car. He was holding a sheaf of papers in an open manila envelope that had a disc-and-string seal.

"Some of Lestrade's tunnel maps," the Scotsman told him.

"OK," said Raziel. "You got something else for me?"

Fotheringill gave him another package wrapped in butcher paper. In exchange, Raziel gave Fotheringill his keys.

"Right," said Fotheringill. "There's a park headquarters across the valley. The park's been closed since the Gulf War, but I can leave your car there with some of the maps in the glove box. I'll leave the rest in the Volvo for the cops to find." He got into Raziel's van and gave him a humorless grin. "Be careful of mines, eh? They're mainly marked."

"Good," said Raziel.

When Fotheringill took off up the road, Raziel helped De Kuff ease himself over into the Druse pasture. They started walking toward the line of valonia oaks and oleander that marked a stream. On the higher slopes there were dwarf olive trees and two mighty terebinths, one of which was scarred by lightning.

There was snow on the brow of Mount Hermon. The Golan

peaks enclosed the narrow valley in which they walked. Mount Sion and Mount Habetarim loomed to the north, below the shoulders of Hermon, and toward the Syrian lines and Tel Hamina, the mountains called Shezif and Alon.

De Kuff breathed deeply. His face was radiant and his eyes full of tears.

" 'Naphtali is a hind let loose,' " he told Raziel. "This is his kingdom."

"I told you, Rev, the time was near. You have to trust me."

They would go to every tribe now, down from the highlands of Naphtali to Dan to as far as Gilead, and what was written would come to pass.

Raziel was thinking that his next name might be Naphtali. It was all the same, he considered. The closing of the circle, the serpent finding itself, the resolution of the noosphere. Things themselves come to consciousness. Faith was easy in the mountains. It required a congenial landscape. But now, for Raziel, faith required an interior landscape too.

"Here it is," De Kuff said. "This is the source of the river."

They both sat down and drank of it from their right hands. Raziel too, although he was left-handed.

"Yes," Raziel said, laughing. "The waters of Merom."

Around them grew waist-high mint and flowering nettles, a wealth of ferns like the carpet of a rain forest, and wild fig.

"We'll go up," De Kuff said, looking at the snow fields high above them. "We'll go up and meet them."

From the next ridge they could see a Syrian observation post at the base of the next mountain. They came to a track that was marked in Hebrew, Arabic and English as a military road. A short way beyond it was a sign lying flat in the brush that warned against mines. The letters on it were so weathered as to be almost illegible.

Raziel was looking for a place where they could spend the night without hauling their gear down for a campsite, where they could watch through the night with a section of the river to themselves, with only a fire.

It did not take him long to find a spot. It was close to the Syrian lines, but at least they had the passive permission of the Druse. The nearby park was indeed closed. Almost any flat spot where there was dry brush for fire, one within the sound of fast water, would do. Also, he would be able to fix comfortably there.

55

HAVING DRIVEN off the map, Lucas was trying to make his Ford Taurus behave like a vehicle of adventure.

"If I'd known we were going in for alpine touring," he told Sonia, "I would have rented a four-wheel drive."

Nearly all night they drove the frosted wadis, avoiding flooded streams and sandstone precipices. Toward morning, Lucas let Sonia drive, and when he woke up they were on paved highway heading north, under the mass of Mount Hermon.

"Love these military roads," she told him.

"We're probably in Syria," Lucas said.

After an hour and a half, they came to a strange series of kiosks resembling small alpine chalets. In the largest one there was an attended snack bar and a little boarded-up souvenir shop. A few souvenirs had been left out in the weather on the splintering counter: a cheap print of Jesus walking on water, a photograph of the rebbe of a Hasidic sect.

A cold, unceasing wind blew down from the peak, rattling the fragile buildings. Sonia had brought some bread and the makings of falafel from the kibbutz and they ate some.

They were just finishing when the inevitable Fotheringill pulled into the desolate parking area in the Dodge van. Sonia saw him first, over Lucas's shoulder. Her mouth full of dry falafel, she pointed to the car.

Fotheringill was wearing commando fatigues and his hair appeared to have been cut even shorter. He parked the van and sauntered over to them.

"Where's the Rev?" Sonia asked him.

"Down the river a mile or two. Follow the path and you'll see him on the near bank."

Lucas walked over to the shattered wooden railing and looked out on the valley. He saw white smoke rising from a spot a few miles below.

"You surprise me," Lucas said, turning to Fotheringill. "I didn't think of you as a religious man."

"It's just him," said Fotheringill. "How he is. Great bloke."

It seemed a less than inspired endorsement. But who knew?

"Then it's me protecting him," Fotheringill said. "Such a fine wee man as he is, he needs someone to keep him from harm. From the evildoer, eh? Fucking evildoer, eh? So that's me, see. Makes up for the wrong I've done."

"Like your fallen soufflés," Lucas suggested.

"Right. And Angola," said Fotheringill. "By the way, did you ever remember that poem? About *rillettes de tours?*"

"No," Lucas said.

Grasping at reeds and morning glory vines, they descended the muddy path. On the far bank, to their right and below, the slope was covered in vineyards that Lucas thought must belong to one of the Golan kibbutzim. There was a smell of mint along the course of the stream. The stones were slippery with moss and crushed pennygrass. The wind from the mountain never quit.

They followed the stream for a long time, and as they went the grinding of rapids below them became louder. Finally they came to a falls where the stream crashed precipitously about six feet, into a clear pool more than deep enough to swim in. There was a little meadow beside it, and in the meadow, indifferent to the wind and mud, De Kuff was sitting by himself, his head lolling on one shoulder.

Raziel rose from the bush ten feet farther down the stream.

"Like winter camping?" he asked.

"It's not winter," Sonia said.

"Well, nearly. But it'll never be winter again."

They followed him to the next descent of the stream. Beside a second, smaller falls, the Rose was making tea in a blackened pot set over a fire.

"It takes a long time to boil," she said, "at this altitude."

When the water had boiled long enough to be served, she poured some into a variety of receptacles that included army mess tins, broken souvenir mugs and fruit jars. It seemed to be some kind of herbal tea.

They brought their tea upstream and Raziel sat down at a respectful distance from the old man, who was sitting with his head between his knees. The others followed Raziel's example. Lucas could only watch the stream and ask himself what he was doing there. For an answer he looked to Sonia. She eased beside him.

"What should I do, Chris? Want me to sing to you?"

Raziel spoke without raising his head. "Sing," he told Sonia. "Sing for him."

Sonia sang a Converso's song about the soul ascending like music, the music ascending through the seven spheres of the lower *sefirot* to its ineffably distant home:

> "*Traspasa el aire todo*
> *Hasta llegar a la más alta esfera,*
> *Y oye allí otro modo*
> *De no perecedera*
> *Música, que es de la fuente y la primera.*"

Overhead, clouds drifted just out of reach, turning the day damp and cold.

"I should have brought my guitar," she said, and shivered.

"You don't need a guitar," Raziel said, still not raising his head.

She lay down on her side and let her cheek rest on the grass. Reaching out, she took Lucas's hands in hers. She did not sing then, but recited softly, almost in a whisper:

> "*Cuando contemplo el cielo*
> *De innumerables luces adornado,*
> *Y miro hacia el suelo*
> *De noche rodeado,*
> *En sueño y en olvido sepultado . . .*"

"You make me almost understand," Lucas said. "But of course I don't really. It's illusion."

"Sure, baby. I'm a fool and you're another.

> "*El amor y la pena,*
> *Despiertan en mi pecho un ansia ardiente;*
> *Despiden larga vena*
> *Los ojos hechos fuente.*"

"What's it mean?"

"Oh, well," she said. "About how love and grief and yearning make you cry. They do, don't they?"

"Sure. Actually," Lucas said, "I cry a lot. More than I ought to."

"How can anyone cry too much?"

"Did you cry in Somalia?" Lucas asked her. "I'll bet you didn't."

"It isn't a place you cry. But I did later. I mourned them all. And there were so many."

"But you're not a fucking weeper like me, Sonia. Anything can set me off. *Our Town. Madame Butterfly.* A good single malt."

"I thought you were gonna cry when those Germans wouldn't let you in their Mass," she said. "Then you looked ready to kill someone."

"Fear and rage," Lucas said. "That's all I know."

"You're a good lover."

"God bless you. Nobody's ever said that to me."

"Funny," Sonia said. "My father lived all his life in fear and rage. Real fear and real rage."

"Mine are real too," Lucas said. "Less deserved, maybe, but real. I'm real. Sort of."

"I believe you," she said. "You're angry and you're scared. And real."

Lucas took his bottle out.

"I'm sure your father's life was a great deal harder than mine," Lucas said. "I'm sure it would have finished me in no time."

"He cried easily too," she said. "It wasn't different for him. I mean, it wasn't different somehow because he was black."

"I know," Lucas said, "I think."

"I wasn't there for my old man," Sonia said. "I was too dumb and vain and shy with him." She held on to Lucas's hand and rolled over on her back. The clouds had parted. "There's a saying from Kabbala: 'To contemplate truth without sorrow is the greatest gift.' "

Raziel had been listening. "I was going to give that to you," he told them. "Whatever happens, I wanted to make that possible for all of you."

Looking at him, Lucas realized two things. One was that there was not the remotest chance that this hipster fiddler could provide the contemplation of truth or of its shadow to anyone, unless it was in the form of music. The second was that there was something potent, something psychotropic, in his tea.

Old De Kuff struggled to his feet.

"A prison," he shouted. "Yes, a prison!" He knelt and ripped handfuls of mint and clover, asters and mushrooms from the place he had been sitting. "Beautiful!" he told them. "But it's nothing."

He got to his feet. "It's not holy," he shouted at his little band. "No land is holy. All earth is exile. The redemption is in the mind. *Tikkun* is in the spirit." He walked toward them. "What is it?" He took Raziel's face in his hands and looked into his eyes.

"What is it in your eyes?" He then went to Sonia and put his fingers under her chin and stared at her. "Don't look away," he said sternly. "And you," he said to Lucas. Lucas let the old man cup his hands around his ears and met his tired eyes. "Sparks," he said, and laughed. "Sparks. The sparks are beautiful. In each of you. Who can deny it? Who, looking into your lovely eyes, can deny it?"

"Or in yours," Sonia said.

"It comes from the Almighty," De Kuff said. "Power, wisdom. The sparks, in the humblest of you. It shines." His strength spent, he sat back down in the grass.

"What is he talking about?" Lucas asked Sonia.

"I guess he's talking about being Jewish," she said.

"I see."

And seeing the old man in his transport, tossing the grass of Jordan in the air, Lucas for a moment believed. There was a quality. There was a way in which certain people, even against their will, shared in the light at the source of creation.

Beside the river, he no longer knew what he believed or denied. Then he remembered the tea. He tried to recall the Shema. It was very short, short and powerful like the Jesus Prayer. He had never been instructed in it, only heard it around: Hear, O Israel: The Lord is our God, the Lord is One.

De Kuff laughed. Charming, knowing, southern laughter. "Nothing is wasted," he said. "The redemption is unarmed. The battle is with the self. The land is in the heart."

"Is it time?" Raziel asked. "Here are the mountains." He waved his hand toward the summit of Hermon. "The mountains of Naphtali. Are you ready?"

With an energy Lucas would not have believed, De Kuff rose and stood to his full height. The river at his feet seemed to gain in force and velocity, the water to sparkle with rainbows.

"Let them prepare the Temple for sacrifice," he shouted. "To me it is given. Blessed be the Ancient Holy One."

The Rose of Saskatoon, Sonia and Raziel looked up at him with joy. Lucas, in amazement, watched the river change its form.

Raziel rose to stand beside his master.

"He who gives the salvation unto kings and dominion unto princes, whose kingdom is an everlasting kingdom, who delivered his servant David from the destructive sword, who makes a way in the sea and a path in the mighty waters, may he bless, preserve, guard and exalt evermore our Lord and our Messiah, the Anointed of the God of Jacob, the Celestial Stag, the Messiah of Righteousness, the King of Kings. Behold him!"

"He raised me up to be the Lamb of God returned," De Kuff declared, "as it was foretold of Yeshu. And he has appointed me the Mahdi of the Merciful and Compassionate that the truth be made one! So as the Almighty is One, so also are the believers! The kings are resurrected! The vessels are repaired! The *tikkun* is restored!"

"Hallelujah," cried the Rose of Saskatoon.

Lucas was thinking that he would give anything to believe it all.

"We'll go now to the city," Raziel said. His voice trembled. "We have no choice. Let them all understand. This man is the Gate, the Bab. He is Moshiach. He is the Second Coming and the Mahdi of the believers."

"I'm certainly glad I came, then," Lucas said. "But you ought not to let him take on so much. He doesn't look up to it."

"No?" Raziel said. "All the same."

"And you?" Lucas asked. "What does this make you?"

"I was going to ask," Sonia said.

Raziel laughed and pointed a finger at her, as though he had caught her up in some error of calculation.

"Me? We'll go up the river and we'll talk. We three."

Lucas was suddenly reminded of something he had neglected to point out.

"You put something in the tea," he told Raziel, "didn't you?"

"Oh my God," Sonia said. "Look at the river!"

The river, as they stared at it, was reversing itself, forcing its way with the same unnatural speed it had assumed as they came down, upward now toward the high lake at its source. The more they looked at it, the more the thing was undeniably so. It surged backward against itself from the banks outward, until its own main stream turned back with great violence, charging up the falls and toward the mountain.

"He is mighty," De Kuff declared, raising his voice. "He is the Master of the Universe. He is One. He is the three great *sefirot*. He speaks continually in the darkness." Then he seemed to lose his way.

"The meaning of Job," Raziel said, like a prompter.

Somewhere a lone sheep was bleating.

"The meaning of Job," De Kuff shouted, "is that the Master of the Universe abandoned Job to Satan's kingdom. And Satan's kingdom is the world of form, the world of things.

"Because all flesh is grass," De Kuff called out to the mountain, "and all the beauty of the lilies is delusion. The only beauty is invisible. The only true world is the unseen world. This was the world of the first Adam. And the Jordan's turning in its course means the end of illusions."

"Raziel," Sonia asked softly, "did you put something in the tea?"

"Don't spoil it," Raziel said. "He needs the nourishment."

"Raziel?" she asked. "Ralph, what did you put in the tea?"

"Herbs," said Raziel. "The herbs of the mountain. Of the Jordan."

"Stop," old De Kuff shouted. He was holding clods and tufts of grass in either hand. "Wait. Are you afraid for me, my boy?" De Kuff asked Lucas. His voice was at its gentlest. He seemed amused and relaxed, a charming, comfortable old man.

Lucas was thinking that he wanted nothing more than that this old man should be the resolution of life, the healer of his wounds, the resolver of all uncertainties. But it was only the tea.

"What are you doing?" Sonia asked Raziel. "Who do you think you are?"

"Come on," Raziel said. He beckoned them to follow him upstream. He put one hand under the old man's arm. They were both smiling.

In the next meadow up, he turned on Lucas and Sonia.

"Want to know who I think I am, Sone?"

"What's he going to do?" Lucas asked Sonia. "Baptize us? Because in my case — "

"I'll go," the Rose said. She began unbuttoning her shirt. "I'm ready. There's nothing wrong with the tea," she told Sonia. "I made it."

Sonia turned to Melker. "Why did you put shit in the tea, Raziel?" she demanded. "You a damn fool or what?"

"Think of me as Din. The Left Hand. The Spoiler."

"You?" Sonia asked. "You?"

"Oh, come on," Raziel said. "I put a little Ex in the tea to stimulate the force. For those of us unfamiliar with Olam Hademut. Our non-Sufis who have never beheld the Alam al-Mithal. The unhip who don't know from *mundus tertius, mundus marginalis.*"

"You gave it to the Rev. You'll kill him."

"Never happen," said Raziel. "I didn't."

"Like hell," she said. "You gave it to him, for Christ's sake. To Chris."

"Well," Raziel said, "a little boost."

"I don't believe you. And what about me?"

"Abulafia said," Raziel informed her, " 'Womankind is to herself a world.' But there's nothing in yours either."

"I hate to spoil a nice country prayer meeting," Lucas said. "But it's cold and we're stoned and that's usually time to say, like, adieu. So how about canning it? Because on the whole —"

"It was a drug," Sonia said without expression. "How could you do it to me?" she shouted at Raziel. "You got me fucked up, you prick."

"Sonia, sweetheart, there's nothing in your tea but a little mint. Some people have trouble seeing the middle world. By that," Raziel explained to Lucas coolly, "I mean what exists between the material and the spiritual."

"Lately," Lucas said, "I have trouble *not* seeing it."

"It's unforgivable," Sonia told Raziel. "It destroys everything."

"Only," Raziel said, "because everything needs to be destroyed."

It seemed to Lucas that everyone was getting higher and higher, but he could not really tell if Raziel had taken the drug or not. The stream seemed to be running faster and faster. Was there not a theory about Jesus being a psychedelic mushroom? Or was that only a joke? Or was there a theory *and* a joke?

"Sonia," said Raziel, "who are you to talk? Last year, the year before? Weren't you blowing with me? Don't say you couldn't hear it in the sound. The synergy. You were doping. You were bringing opiates into the five worlds. Your Sufi stuff and your pills."

"I stopped. Things let me."

"A love supreme," Raziel sang to Sonia mockingly. The song she had sung for Lucas the previous night. It told him something he had long suspected. "A love supreme."

"What do you want from us, Raziel?" Sonia asked.

Everyone fell silent.

"I mean, if this is just more getting loaded," she said, "where's it supposed to go?"

"We have to go to the city," Raziel said. "That's next. You'll have to trust me."

"Sorry," Sonia said.

"You know," Lucas said as they climbed, "the last time I got high this way I was listening to Miles Davis. *In a Silent Way.* I wish I could hear it now."

Just below them, Helen Henderson fell to her knees.

"Please," she said, "somebody help me! I'm scared."

"Before Redemption," Raziel told them, "tribulation. How did you expect the Redemption to look?" He raised his voice. "Want to see the chariot? You'll see it. Want to see the temple rise? You'll see that too."

"Do you believe him?" Lucas asked, steadying himself against a dwarf almond tree.

"She believes me," Raziel said, fixing his eyes on Sonia. "She knows everything requires the resolution of opposites. She was raised on the dialectic. The Law does not change but its surface changes, its garment changes."

"Do you?" Lucas asked her again. Sonia kept looking at the river. "Do you believe him?"

"Out of these shells we build," Raziel said. "Trust those who know. Out of this confusion, out of this ugliness, a love supreme, Sonia."

"I wanted it," she said to Lucas. "I want it so much. But it's bullshit. It's *trayf.*"

"Forget it," Lucas told her.

"So you see the angel Sandalfon," Raziel said. "We've studied this. The world of shells, Gentile women, idolatry, the man who's been to Rome. The death of the whore. Violence."

"The death of . . . ? What violence?" Lucas asked. "You sound like the guys at Kfar Gottlieb. Are you?"

"Them?" Raziel laughed. "They have no part in what's to come. No more than the fools at the House of the Galilean. The pre-millenarians, the post-millenarians. But they're necessary and they're going to do what's necessary."

"And what now?" Sonia asked.

"Our king goes to the city, and we go following."

"Almost in time for Christmas," Lucas said. Sonia clung to him.

The river running beside them still seemed at the point of manifesting a great holiness. Something Lucas felt himself unworthy to see. Something dreadful that he required. He was having trouble letting go of it all. He so wanted to believe.

"Don't be afraid," Raziel said to them.

"Oh, that river," Sonia said. "Oh, Jesus! I wish it could take us back."

"It's the Jordan," Lucas said. I see the god coming up out of the earth, he thought. As though Raziel had raised up the prophet Samuel. If he had, he would be punished for it. But Lucas could not shake off his own terror. The fear of holiness.

When he looked up the bank, he thought he saw a yeshiva boy in *payess,* shaking a small, pale fist at him, spitting. A Jewish djinn?

"How dare you come to this battlefield!" the boy shouted down to him.

"I hear words in the river," Sonia said.

De Kuff was having trouble climbing now, sliding on the wet earth and sharp rocks of the gully. And Helen Henderson was hanging back, crying, terrified.

"Was it this bad?" De Kuff asked Raziel. "Was it like this when I came before?"

"Yes, my king," Raziel told the Rev. "We have to go up now."

"Once," the old man said with sudden restraint, "I had a breakdown."

"It's your tea," Lucas said. "Go lie down."

De Kuff let Raziel help him along the bank. It was getting stormy and also getting late. It rained briefly. Lucas and Sonia still held each other.

"We wait. Into the night. Maybe until morning," Raziel told them. "Then we go to the city."

"If we could get the car nearer," Lucas said, "we could get the old guy out." In the light from the gray sky he tried to read the little Avis map. Perhaps, he thought, they had put themselves back on it. "This road," he said, pointing with his finger, "it goes down the next valley. If it's a road. If it's not a river or a dry wadi. We might get the car closer."

"I need you," Raziel said to Sonia. "I need you to help me get the Rev up to the car. Regardless of what you may think of me now, I need you."

"Go ahead," Lucas told her. "Go with him. I'll stay with the Rose."

"It's not going to work," Raziel said. "I've known for a while. It's going to be spoiled again."

"If we get over the next ridge," Lucas said, still trying to get the lines on his map to stop quivering, "we might come to the road. And get the car and pick everyone up. It looks closer. Of course, on one of these maps," he said, "it's hard to tell."

"I don't want everyone to leave us," Raziel said.

"All right, all right," Sonia told him. "I'll help you get him back to the city. Chris can get the Rose out."

"I'll meet you at the car," Lucas said to Sonia. "Wait for me."

"No, no, I'll see you back in town," she said. "I want to take care of it."

De Kuff was muttering to himself. Lucas went down to where the Rose was cringing, naked now, beside the river. "Be careful," he said to Sonia. "I need you too."

56

THE ROSE had taken her clothes off, either in preparation for baptism or out of an ecstatic impulse. She was a tall, muscular girl with angel eyes and a strong jaw. Lucas handed her her clothes one by one and she got back into them.

"I don't think I want to go up the way we came," she told Lucas. "I'd rather go that way. Where it's open."

Lucas looked at the Avis map again, unsure whether the area he had marked out on it corresponded in any way to the wilderness they found themselves in.

"All right," he said. "There might be a road out there. It's bound to go up to the park entrance."

They spotted a series of partly dry rocks on which to ford the river and teetered across. The Rose, though under the influence of Raziel's tea, was naturally agile and sure-footed. Once across, they hopped from tussock to tussock over a swampy depression until they gained dry ground. Then it was easy going to the top of a ridge — easier for the Rose than for Lucas.

Below them stood a valley of bones — rocks, really, in mossy granite clusters that looked like dolmens in fairy rings. There was a distant line of struggling trees, olive and tamarisk, below the face of a cliff that marked a spur of the mountains.

"There are altars in the rock," the Rose told Lucas. "And a waterfall."

At first he thought she was hallucinating. But when he looked at the rock faces it seemed that he saw niches there, patches of marble against the darker stone.

"It's supposed to be the birthplace of Pan," he told her. "And the source of the Jordan."

"Oh, no!" said Helen Henderson. "How far out!"

He was delighted to have news that improved her spirits. The Banyas spring was on his map and was reassuring — it indicated that they were still in Israel, rather than in Lebanon or Syria.

"Do you mean," the Rose asked, "that these are the altars of Pan? *The* Pan?"

"Yes," Lucas said. "Idolatry and sudden fear. So close to the river Jordan."

There were, in fact, a great many goats about.

"Long ago," Lucas said by way of stoned conversation, "a late Latin poet tells us, a mighty voice was heard round the world: 'Great Pan is dead!' it said. Or words to that effect."

"Oh, no!" said the Rose. She seemed to be taking the news badly. So Lucas said, "Of course the gods never die. And this isn't necessarily Great Pan. This is Banyas Pan." Banyas, it seemed to him, was near a road. His Avis map concurred.

While Helen contemplated the death of Pan, they set out across the valley toward the line on the map. The part of the way that had looked like desert turned out to be wetland — craterlike marshes filled with rushes, sinkholes caused by the runoff of winter snow from the slopes of Hermon. Other parts were grown with aloe and cactus, so dusty dry it seemed they had never been impinged upon by the smallest rain.

There were sheep grazing in the grassier sections. Their long, starveling antelope faces peered from within abundant folds of dark, dirty wool. The sheep were all horned, and the horns of male and female alike twisted asymmetrically from narrow skulls. Unmatched and unbalanced, their horns made the sheep look even more unkempt and unhusbanded. Vestigial horns, brittle and useless, good only for trapping their possessors in thorn bushes.

Wearily they made their way across the marshes, the sinks and the stony places.

"Where did you meet Raziel?" the Rose asked Lucas.

"I was writing a book. I interviewed him."

"And do you believe the things he says?"

"No. How about you?"

"I liked listening to the Rev," she said. "He seemed wise and kind. I never understood the things he said. But I'm not clever."

"You'll be forgiven everything, Helen," Lucas said. "Just keep trucking."

"I have no regrets," she said.

"Do you know the story of Uzzah and the Ark? Did they teach you that in Sunday school?"

"The soldier who was struck dead for touching the Ark of the Covenant? Not too much."

"Do you think," Lucas asked as they eased through a marsh with earthen pads crowned with brown cottony plants, "that God told Uzzah to try and save the Ark? Do you think he took him aside, appeared to him in a ring of fire and said: 'Uzzah, today on the way to J-town the Ark will start to fall. And you my beloved Uzzah, you my special lamb, have got to keep it from falling. Otherwise terrible shit will happen to the whole world'?"

"Goodness," the Rose said. "I have no idea. I've never thought about it."

After about an hour and a half, they were approaching the tree-line at the border of the Hula Valley, within sound of fast-moving water. Climbing in soft, black-ribboned sand, Lucas happened on a goat that was lying, snakebitten, on its side at the top of a hillock. Its tongue lolled despairingly, its eyes were glazed and spectacularly bloodshot, and it watched with indifference as Lucas approached. Drawing closer, he saw that a large camel spider was feeding at a hair-matted wound in one flank. A swarm of bees crawled over it, wings folded against the rain.

It made Lucas think of the Holman Hunt, *The Scapegoat*. Even the landscape was a bit the same.

There are no metaphors here, he thought. This was whence it all came home, where things themselves resided and the only symbols were the holy letters of a book. He thought all this must constitute a great difficulty. He wanted to talk to Sonia about it.

Over the next rise, they found themselves looking down at another stream, brown and swollen. The path beside it looked frequently used — a clear, mainly dry track of hard-packed earth supported by a rocky shoulder and crisscrossed with boot prints. On Lucas's road-map, the stream was indistinguishable from a nearby road.

After a minute or so they saw headlights and what looked like a decrepit minivan, perhaps a Druse *sherut*, climbing the mountain switchbacks, its engine laboring harder with each shift of gears. The cliffs on the far side were over a mile away. On the map, among the line of contours that roughly corresponded to the cliffs, the word *Banyas* appeared in tiny, quivering antique letters.

The sun, low on the oppressive horizon, broke through the sodden clouds and lit the cliff face ahead of them to a polychrome shimmer.

Lucas and the Rose stared in wonder at the lovely mountain. There were indeed altars in the cliff face, their contours outlined in the brief sunlight.

Suddenly the Rose broke into a run.

"Hey!" called Lucas. "Hey, it's getting late. It's raining."

"Oh, please," the Rose shouted without breaking her formidable stride. "I've never been here. I've got to see it."

"Shit," said Lucas, and took after her, panting, dodging sheer rocks and deadfalls. Occasionally he caught sight of her towheaded figure ahead of him, her bright hair bobbing in the rain. She was going to the god. Lucas watched her vanish in the gloom of the small forest of twisted cypress and tamarisk. Gone. Turned into a tree. But after a minute he heard her again.

"Oh!"

She had found a place to stand, a moss-grown root that afforded a clear view of the Panic altars in the cliff.

"Oh!" she said. "I hear it." She looked terror-stricken.

"You're really scared," Lucas said. "It's probably just the tea." He himself was becoming increasingly uneasy.

" 'Afraid?' " She cried, and laughed. " 'Afraid! Of *Him?*' " And what was in her eyes? he wondered. She appeared thoroughly demented. " 'O, never, never! And yet — and yet — O, Mole, I am afraid!' "

Lucas at once understood. They were in *The Wind in the Willows*. She thought she was Rat encountering Pan, the Piper at the Gates of Dawn. Why not, he thought. What shone in her radiant cornflower eyes was unutterable love. If he tried, Lucas figured, he might hear elfin music.

Helen Henderson clasped her hands beneath her chin and recited: " 'Lest the awe should dwell — And turn your frolic to fret — You shall look on my power at the helping hour — But then you shall forget!' "

She turned to Lucas. " 'Forget, forget.' "

"Whatever," said Lucas.

"We sang that at camp," she explained. "We chanted it at Brownies."

"Fantastic," said Lucas. "And now you're here."

Israel had something for everybody.

As they blundered back up the wooded slope, he was amazed by the rough territory they had run across. It was a miracle neither of them had broken a leg.

An Egged tour bus was coming down the road. When it pulled to a stop beside them and the door opened, Lucas could see that it was only half full.

"Can you take us?" Lucas asked the driver. "Just up to the park entrance?"

"But the park is closed," the driver said, "for the war."

Eventually, overcoming his bureaucratic instinct toward inutility, the driver let them on. The tourists were mostly elderly Gentiles. One of them, an English speaker, found himself sitting next to Helen Henderson.

"Out in the rain, were you?" he asked. "Seeing the castles?"

"We forget," she told him.

When they left the bus at the park entrance, there was no one in sight. A line of cars stood beside the deserted concession stand, including Lucas's Taurus and Raziel's Dodge van. Lucas was surprised to see the yellow Volvo Fotheringill had been driving that morning.

When they opened the Dodge to get Helen Henderson's second backpack, Lucas found a few sheets of paper under the seat on the passenger side. In the car's overhead light, the sheets seemed imprinted with a building plan of some kind. A series of tunnels and chambers with dimensions and notes in several languages, like the working guide to an archeological dig. On each side was a single Hebrew word.

Kaddosh. Holy.

"Know what this is?" he asked the Rose.

"I don't," she said. "That guy Fotheringill brought them."

It had gotten dark. There were lights on the road that led down the slopes to Katzrin.

A vehicle approached, a Border Police jeep. The officer in it lectured them about wandering around unescorted. The park had been secured for the emergency, and only a few authorized tour groups were permitted into the area.

"I don't know how you got in in the first place," the officer said.

"There are sensors and machine guns that fire automatically. There are mine fields. We picked you up on the detectors halfway to the Litani."

One of the policemen shone a red-banded light on their passports and then into their faces. His beam lingered on Helen's eyes, which were wide, the pupils visibly dilated. She put up a hand to shield them.

They drove the rented Taurus straight down from the pitch-black peak of Mount Hermon. Lucas discovered that he was still more or less stoned. He assumed this was true of Helen as well.

"Life is a little like a children's story," he wisely advised the young Rose.

"Oh," she said, "but life is so hard on children."

And about that, he thought, she probably knew more than he did.

"Well," Lucas said, "if it's not *The Wind in the Willows,* maybe it's *Alice in Wonderland.*"

"But why *Alice in Wonderland*?"

"Well, because *Alice in Wonderland* is funny. It's funny but it has no justice. Or meaning, or mercy."

"Right," the Rose said. "But it's got logic. There's a chess game behind it."

She had him there.

57

THEY STOPPED for coffee at Kibbutz Nikolayevich Alef. No one was waiting there for them. Gigi Prinzer had apparently taken the rest of the party down to Ein Kerem. The Rose decided that she would ride back with Lucas.

"Be careful around Jericho," the young woman in charge of the kibbutz's guest facilities warned them. "It's nighttime and you've got the wrong color plates."

Miles behind them, on the Jordan road, Sonia was driving the Dodge van southward. Raziel sat beside her. Old De Kuff slept in back. Sonia had been for putting him to bed at the kibbutz, but De Kuff had insisted on being brought to the city without delay. Now the strength was ebbing from him.

"It's almost out of our hands," Raziel told her.

"What are you telling me? That it was all some fantasy you drew us into?"

"It is not a fantasy."

"Let me ask you something awful," Sonia said. "Are you back on the spike?"

"You got it," he said.

"Oh, Razz," she said. "How long?"

"What I want you to do, baby, is I want you not to cry. You'll remind me of my mother."

"You know what's funny?" she said. "I gave up everything. Reefer. Martinis. Because of him. Because things would change."

"I did too, Sonia. I was just as clean a week ago as when I saw you in Tel Aviv."

"You know what I thought when you loaded that tea, Razz?"

"You thought I was hustling *shmeck?*"

"Like it all came to me. You had the Rev, unlimited funds. Then I find out Nuala's moving for Stanley. Then Linda Ericksen gets religion on us."

"Our own religion too," Raziel said.

"Our own religion, because she fucks religions like Nuala fucks the ghost of Che Guevara. And then I hear about the bomb and I think, Who's in the middle of this action? My man Razz, and he's been kicking the gong the whole time and we've been a pack of marks."

"But you thought wrong, Sonia. I had a miracle in my hand. I quit too. Because things would change."

"So what happened?"

"Great things, awful things were happening. It was true, baby. All true. Never let them take that from you."

"So it wasn't just a hustle?"

"Just a hustle? Maybe the universe is a hustle. What is this thing called love, you know what I'm saying? I'm telling you the doors would be opened. I'm talking about redemption."

"You said he had five mysteries to preach. Is that still so?"

"He's revealed all five. Now he has to accept his identity in the city. But we're running out of time."

"What do you mean?"

"I mean I set certain events in motion. I didn't think we could fail. But now I see we're like all the others. We're trapped in history. Losers lose, kid. Story of my life. I had the power but not the strength. Know the difference?"

"The power," she repeated, trying to understand. As though it would help. "The power but not the strength?"

She picked up one of the diagrams that were lying all over the van — on the seat, plastered to the mat, behind the sunscreen. "This is your friends' diagram of the Temple Mount, right?"

"That's right."

"So there is a bomb. You lied to me."

"Everything is written, Sonia. This is a spiritual struggle. A struggle without weapons. But struggle is conflict, and conflict is dangerous. It was why I used the tea on him. I was afraid he would fail us. I needed him ready to declare himself."

"Now listen, you have to tell me everything. Everything you know about where they put it."

"Sonia, Sonia," he said impatiently. "If we succeed, there are no weapons. Those characters think they're planting a bomb. But there are no bombs in the world to come."

"Right," she said. "Just flowers, I suppose."

"I said no one would get hurt. I meant it. I'm sure."

"How come you went back on the spike?"

"I lost my nerve. Last minute. I thought if we spiritually fail, only historical things would happen. Just more of the shitty history of the world. Instead of everything we dreamed of."

"What's going to happen, Razz? What have you done?"

"I don't know. More grief, more history. The process isn't moral, only the result."

"You never should have stayed here, Razz. Why did you?"

"Because I was the only one who knew the score. Because I found the old man. Why me? Don't ask. But he was revealed to me."

"It must have been your music," she said.

"Maybe that," Raziel said. "And you were with me. I'm a weak vessel," he told her, "but I had the power. And I had you. You believed me. And you loved me a little, didn't you?"

"I loved you," she said. "Everybody loved you once, Raziel. You were our prince."

And she could not keep from crying then because the faith, the hope, the love were draining out of her. And no one was going to save her soul but she was going to have to take care of everyone else again, as always. And it had all been nothing. A little feel good. A little dream and so good night.

"Funny world," she said. "Where things go on repeating themselves. And how are we supposed to know?"

"Funny world," he said.

Then, suddenly, she could not — would not — let it go.

"Razz?"

"Yeah, baby."

"Razz, maybe we can still do it. If you did everything right. The process."

"I told you the process, kid, and you laughed at me."

"I'm not laughing. Maybe we can make it happen. Maybe! If you did everything right."

So Raziel himself laughed. "Sonia, you're wonderful. If you'd been with me all the way, we'd have done it."

"I was with you," she said.

"You're gonna save the world, Sonia." He laughed again. "You tell the girl you've blown it. She tells you maybe not. You're one crazy mixed-up chick, baby. If you'd have been with me, I swear we'd have come across. Clean out of history."

"I got nowhere to go, Razz. I'm still here."

"Sonia," Raziel said, "you're not kidding, are you?"

"I'm afraid not," she told him.

"This is how it is, Sonia. We're caught between worlds. I don't know if I can get us out."

"Tell you what," she said. "You get us out of between worlds. I'll drive."

"Everyone so far has failed," Raziel declared after a few miles. "But someday someone won't. The process . . ."

"Right," she said. "The process."

"I couldn't believe it," he told her. "In the old man's eyes — the way out. The world we've been waiting for."

"Freedom?" she asked.

"Music," Raziel told her. "It was all music."

"All right, then," she said. "Music."

"Drive faster, home," he begged her. "I don't want you to see me fix."

58

A T NIGHT, the village of Ein Kerem was surrounded by the lights of the high-rise apartments of the New City, which had drawn closer and closer around it. The inhabitants of the apartments facing the valley often did not trouble to draw their curtains after dark. Anyone looking up at the lighted windows would have a sense of good lives lived behind them, lives that were civilized and comfortable. It was possible to make out bookshelves and prints and paintings on the walls.

The buildings themselves were not attractive, so they looked best at night, illuminated by the high-bourgeois taste and respectability of their inhabitants. There were still nightingales in the Jerusalem Forest nearby. Their flutings and repeated, intricate riffs could soothe and stir the heart. The forest was a mellow place, charged with benign possibility.

Only a few of the lights in the nearby buildings were on when Lucas arrived at the bungalow with the Rose. The eastern horizon was tinged with a glow the color of Jerusalem stone, and the call to prayer was sounding from a loudspeaker in the village.

He went quietly from room to room but could find no sign of De Kuff, Raziel or Sonia. The other regulars were all still in bed. Only Sister John Nepomuk van Witte was awake, reading a picture book about Sulawesi, where she had lived for many years.

When Lucas telephoned Sonia's Rehavia apartment there was no answer.

"I'm putting you in charge," he told Helen Henderson. "I would suggest everyone lie low until things get sorted out."

The Rose was herself again. She had ridden south in thoughtful silence.

"Which things?"

"Things," Lucas said. After Helen had bathed and gone to bed, he made a few more fruitless calls to Sonia. Then he lay down on the living room floor and slept fitfully until morning. At eight A.M., still unrested, he called Obermann, who was back from Turkey, to ask if he could come over. Obermann demurred; he had rounds at Shaul Petak. They compromised by arranging to meet at the hospital. On the way out, Lucas brought one of the building plans he had found in the van.

"You look terrible," the doctor said when Lucas was in his hospital office.

Lucas explained that he had taken Ecstasy at the source of the Jordan, borne witness to the Messiah's First and Second Comings and visited Pan with Rat and Mole.

"Ecstasy? How did you drive back?"

"In fragments. But I made it." He handed Obermann one of the diagrams. "This suggest anything to you?"

They spread the worn copy on a desktop from which Obermann had removed a pile of file folders. It still appeared, to Lucas's utterly unpracticed eye, to be a kind of blueprint, the outline of a building showing three elevations with the dimensions marked in meters.

With one exception, the verbal indications on the sheet were in English or transliterated Arabic. There was a rectangle indicating the Bab al-Ghawanima, which Obermann identified as an ancient gate through the wall of the Haram. The single Hebrew word on the sheet was one that Lucas had deciphered as *kaddosh* and translated as "holy." There on the rough sheet, in the language God had spoken to Adam, its curt, fiery-tongued characters had a daunting aspect. *Mysterium terribile et fascinans.*

On another grid of the chart was a word in Greek: *Sabazios.*

"It's a chart of the Haram wall," Obermann said. "It probably marks the latest excavations."

"What about the *kaddosh?*"

"A holy site. Maybe someone's idea of where the Holy of Holies was."

"And Sabazios?"

"Sabazios is a Phrygian god. I can't remember his particulars."

"Think this is about planting a bomb?" Lucas asked.

"That," Obermann said, "would be a conceivable hypothesis. I gather from our telephone conversation that you've had some run-ins with our Linda."

"Yes indeed. I think she's involved."

"Frankly, I think you're right. She's conversion prone and over the top. When she goes, she goes."

"I spent a little time wondering what really happened to her old man," Lucas said. "If I were you, I'd wonder too."

Obermann sighed. "I thought Janusz Zimmer would occupy her questing nature. But maybe she's broken with him. Or maybe there's something about Janusz we didn't know. Anyway, she's aware of our book."

"Aware of it? She wants to fucking write it for us." He told Obermann about some of his adventures in the Strip and at Kfar Gottlieb.

Obermann picked up one of the diagrams Lucas had brought him and examined it further.

"Sure," he said. "This could be a blueprint for a bomb. Where did you get it?"

"Up in the Golan. In one of our cars."

"This is the kind of survey they did at the House of the Galilean," Obermann said. "It must have come from Linda."

"I think they're setting up De Kuff and company," Lucas said. "And they're planning to use us to do it. We're supposed to buy the package. And then sell it."

"The second coming of Willie Ludlum."

"Exactly. Well, I'm going up to the House of G. Maybe you'd like to inform the police? On the theory that they don't know about it?"

"I have a few friends," Obermann said. "I'll inquire."

"And keep trying Sonia's, will you? I think she's got Raziel and the old man over in her apartment and they may not be picking up. Lying low. But she'll need to check in before long."

"Right," said Obermann.

Before calling at the House of the Galilean, Lucas made a quick trip to his apartment to change clothes. He called Sonia's place again but reached only the machine. Then he turned on the bathtub tap and called Sylvia Chin.

"I hate to talk business on your private line," he told Sylvia when she answered. "But for your information — and the information of whoever's tapping your phone — someone's about to do a

Willie Ludlum on the Haram. Very soon. Hear anything more about it?"

"I can't say what we've heard, Chris. But I can tell you this. Your friend Nuala's dead. So's her lover, Rashid. They were strung up in a ruined convent in Cyprus. According to the Cypriots, whoever killed them used rope from the days of British rule. Official imperial rope. An execution. What are you going to do?"

"Take a bath," he told her.

When he got to the bathroom, his legs went weak. He stood stunned, holding his hand under the running water, undone by the necessity of judging its temperature, incapable of that much measured consideration.

Nuala had required consuming passions. In Jerusalem she had found one and, sure enough, it had consumed her. He remembered Rashid talking about djinn. And Ericksen haunted by the force he claimed would kill him. What he was experiencing, he thought, might be described as fear of the Lord. This emotion, it was written, was the beginning of wisdom. Of course it had been rash of him to refer to the Almighty as an invisible winged paperweight. He wondered if wisdom might not be, at long last, presenting itself to him.

59

LUCAS'S NEXT VISIT was to the House of the Galilean. It seemed no longer to be associated with the cause or personality of any one specific Galilean; moreover, it was closed. Its plaques and signs were gone. Palestinian workmen were applying a conditioning coat of wash to the walls.

"House of the Galilean?" Lucas asked one of them.

The Arabs only stared at him, curious but afraid. He drove back to his downtown apartment and played the message machine. Whose hearty, authoritative tones should he hear from the device but those of his old friend Basil Thomas, the purveyor of "scheduled information." Thomas had already troubled himself to drop by Fink's once, in vain. He would be there again tonight, he declared. Lucas decided to meet him.

As the roseate Jerusalem evening came on, Lucas made for cocktail hour at Fink's. There indeed was Basil Thomas, looking every bit the genius of the receding century in his leather policeman's coat. When he saw Lucas, his features assumed a well-informed, let's-see-you-walk-away-from-this-one expression.

"This is hot," Thomas said. "Schedule A. Most secret."

Lucas bought them both a beer.

"You're going to see disturbances all over the city."

"Why's that?"

"Oh," said Thomas, "some anniversary. But don't leave them out of your account. And be prepared."

"Something about the Haram?"

"We'll meet tomorrow," Thomas said, "you and I. We'll meet here and I'll have a handout for you that you will value. Few in this city will be more informed than you."

Lucas at once realized that he had to go back across town to check his sources there. Not that his other sources were extensive. There was Lestrade, if that Christian soul was still in town. He had to remind himself, with a mixture of frustration and dread, that Pastor Ericksen was dead, like Nuala and Rashid. Thomas did not seem to be bluffing. He had been chosen as a conduit.

"This wouldn't involve an attack on the Haram, would it?"

"Mister," said Thomas, "I don't even know what I'm going to tell you. If I did, I wouldn't, if you see what I mean. It would be rash and there wouldn't be a percentage in it."

"Then what do you mean about disturbances?"

"A free prognostication," Thomas said. "Exchange for the drink."

"OK," Lucas said. "I'll be here if you will."

The rush of dusk was in progress at the Damascus Gate. The sky was fading; a promiscuous lingering light shone from a variety of sources, illuminating the caves and stalls of the city. He felt closely watched. Beside the moneychangers' stalls, the man selling *Al-Jihar* was in some agitation; he had a headline to chant, an Extra. He seemed ambivalent about selling the paper to Lucas. At first he said he had no English version. Eventually, it turned out, there was one. The edition looked like a throwaway, with day-old news inside. But the front page was covered with sixty-point type, green on white, and it read, "Defense of the Holy Places in the Name of God."

The words caused Lucas further theological anxiety, of the sort that could be construed as virtue. Fear of the Lord. Appropriately, it was time for prayer. Amplified up and down the darkening streets, the muezzins sounded genuinely angry.

On Tariq al-Wad, Charles Habib was closing up his café. It had been months since the Caravan had sold its last Heineken to a disoriented tourist. Charles seemed astonished to see Lucas, but for a moment Lucas thought his old acquaintance might pretend not to know him. Instead, Charles beckoned him inside and closed the shutters. They went to the rear section, which Charles maintained as his city apartment.

Charles owned a number of apartments in Jerusalem and in Nazareth. They were always occupied by groups of his relatives, who seemed to live on some updated, urbanized and intercontinental nomadic model, appearing at intervals from Austin, Edinburgh, Guadalajara. In the room farthest from the street a group of elderly

Palestinian women in flowery housecoats were gathered by a television set. There was a huge unconnected bathtub on the floor in front of them, and as they watched, they were putting blankets in the water to soak. Lucas noticed that the windows were all shuttered and reinforced with stacks of wooden crates.

Among the women helping to saturate the blankets sat a pretty teenage girl in a denim jacket and a Boston Red Sox cap, reversed. When she saw Lucas come in, she separated herself from the older ladies and, over their protests, came to sit with Charles and Lucas. Charles did not discourage her.

"I thought you went back home," Charles said to Lucas. "Do you know what's going on?"

"I was hoping to ask you that," Lucas said.

Absent-mindedly, Charles introduced the teenager. "This is my niece, Bernadette Habib," he said. "My brother Mike's daughter, studying at Beir Zeit. She's from America."

"Watertown, Mass.," said Bernadette. She shook Lucas's hand in Watertown fashion.

"What do you think, Bernadette?" Lucas asked her. "What do they say at Beir Zeit?"

Recently, at Beir Zeit, the secular PLO ticket had defeated the Muslim fundamentalists in the university's student elections. It had been considered a good thing.

"The Islamic kids say the Israelis are going to trash the Haram," Bernadette said. She wore tiny earrings and a cross around her neck like Madonna's, but of course their significance would be very different in Jerusalem than in South Beach. "Did you hear the sermons all day?"

"Mr. Lucas doesn't know Arabic," Charles explained.

"Really," the young woman observed unsympathetically. "Not many Americans do."

"Did the sermons get all this started?" Lucas asked.

"*Haredim* came to the Damascus Gate in the morning. They overturned stalls. They beat people, even Europeans. They said they would destroy the Muslim holy places."

"It sounds like provocation," Lucas said, thinking the militants might want the confusion of a Palestinian riot to cover the action. Increasingly, outside, one seemed to be taking shape.

"What is America going to do?" Charles asked Lucas. "The Haram is going to be taken over. Everyone says so. It will be war."

"I don't know," Lucas said. "They don't know any more at the U.S. consulate than we do."

"No one believes that," Bernadette said.

"No one," Charles added.

"How about you?" Lucas asked Bernadette.

She shrugged. "Maybe the government thinks one thing and the CIA thinks another."

The wonders of a junior year abroad. A sophisticate, Lucas thought. "We still keep the embassy in Tel Aviv," he said. "That means something."

Bernadette gave him a look of polite indulgence. She was regularly a student at Holy Cross in Worcester, doing her year at Beir Zeit, during the periods when it was open. Lucas had discovered that there were hundreds of Arab-American students in the country, a mirror image of the young Jewish students who came.

"At school — at school here — we read, like, Noam Chomsky?" Bernadette told Lucas. "Ever heard of him?"

"Of course," Lucas said.

"Really? Because most Americans haven't. We read his book *On Power and Ideology*. It's all stuff like you never hear."

"Don't they read Chomsky at Holy Cross?"

"In poly sci, I think. About Latin America. I didn't even know he wrote about the Middle East."

"Ever talk to any of the Jewish kids over here?" Lucas asked her. He gestured, as people did, toward the other side of town.

"Sometimes. But it's all different here," she said. "Everybody's scared. A lot of their kids carry guns. They think we're bombers. Like, we're American, they're American — but nobody's American here."

It occurred to Lucas that, if it could be managed, a year spent in the Third World as a non-American might be a salutary addition to every young American's education. It might be coupled, as absurd counterpoint, with a compulsory reading of M. Bourguignon's great work of travel, sociology and armadillo observation, *L'Amérique*.

"You should get to another part of the city," Charles said. To Lucas, Charles always pronounced the phrase "another part of the city" with distaste. By it he meant the Jewish part. "Otherwise, I can put you up on the floor."

"Do you really think there'll be a riot?" Lucas asked.

Charles gestured toward the tub full of blankets.

"Some people think," Bernadette told Lucas, "that they'll come down here and kill us all."

"The old women," Charles said, "they say it'll be like 1948."

"Over there," Lucas said, gesturing toward the western city, "they think you'll come and kill them."

"Sleep with your passport," Charles told his niece. "Everyone sleeps with their passport."

"Sleep?" Bernadette asked. "You've got to be kidding."

Charles walked Lucas to the street and let him out through the metal shutters.

At that point, Lucas reasoned that the most significant man in the city, the one person to see regarding scheduled information, would be the great digger himself, Gordon Lestrade.

Going farther into the Muslim Quarter, he began to hear chanting. He passed groups of young men gathered at the ends of the streets leading to the gates and walls of the Haram. There were a few Palestinian flags in sight, but most of the young men Lucas passed had rallied to large green banners. Across some of them were emblazoned the lettering of the Shahada: There is no god but God, and Muhammad is the messenger of God.

The chanting increased as Lucas walked. Laughing children collided with him, seemingly on purpose. No one appeared to be going home to bed; the streets were crowded but the shops were closed. There were lights everywhere, but none were the sort that provided comforting illumination. The beams of cheap flashlights hovered nervously; there were camp lanterns, detached car headlights, colored spotlights, strings of lights hanging from the mosques.

Nowhere was an Israeli patrol in evidence. Lucas found himself drawing dire and threatening looks. Little missiles struck him as he walked, mostly from behind, but a few from the darkness ahead. There was nothing hurtful or sharp, only an intermittent rain of small, dirty things, invisible insults. It was like Gaza again, except that this was Jerusalem.

Through it all, the amplified calls — desperate, imploring, enraged — kept sounding from the holy places. Lucas began to feel that the moment he had so long imagined was at hand, the time of hard truth when he would have to decide whether to run, and which way. Like Herod, in his heart he hardly knew.

Arriving at the Austrian hospice, where the Via Dolorosa entered the Muslim Quarter, he heard, to his uneasy satisfaction, the shimmer of Richard Strauss drifting down into the disorderly streets from Gordon Lestrade's rooftop apartment next door.

The main entrance of the hospice had been barred, along with the ground- and first-floor shutters. But the wooden door of the alley that led up to Dr. Lestrade's quarters, though locked, did not yet have its shutters in place. Lucas began to pound on it, trying for a rhythm at once emphatic and discreet. The streets were getting out of hand. Bands of martyrs in search of dispatch raced past, shouting at the top of their lungs.

After a moment — out of prearrangement, curiosity or rashness — a Palestinian porter opened the door.

"You are for Dr. Lestrade?"

"That's right," Lucas said.

"You must hurry," said the porter, stepping aside.

Up in the apartment, Lestrade was rushing about, in a mood more evocative of *Till Eulenspiegel* than *Rosenkavalier*, which was in the player.

"My fucking plants!" he cried. "Can I count on the hospice to water my plants?"

"Sure," Lucas said. "They're Austrians."

Lestrade turned, startled. Whoever he had been expecting, it was not Lucas.

"What the hell are you doing here?"

"Well, I'm covering the story."

"Are you bloody mad or what? By the way, get out of my house."

Dr. Lestrade's possessions, of which there were a great many, had been gathered in the living room for transporting. He had suitcases and ancient steamer trunks that looked as though they should read "Port Out, Starboard Home." There were many wooden boxes of books and some cardboard ones.

"I can't believe you're leaving Jerusalem," Lucas said. "I thought it was home."

"It was," Lestrade said. He looked at Lucas in utter frustration. "Listen, old man, would you mind leaving? I'm in a terrible rush. And I'm not in the mood to answer questions."

"Sorry," Lucas said. "But what happened to the House of the Galilean?"

"Closed, gone, kaput. I arrive for work in the morning only to be told by this bloody native that I'm redundant. They've got my files, my work. I wasn't allowed to make copies on the job."

"You don't get to keep copies?"

"Oh, I've got a few copies, all right. And I'm not the only one. But the rights to publish belong to the House of the Galilean. I mean, they were my publishers."

"Why'd you sign the rights away?"

"Christ, man! They have this huge publishing house! A television channel! They were going to make it a bestseller over there. And worldwide! 'Secrets of the Temple' thing. Millions of videos."

"Well, you can sue in America."

"Which means I'll have to go there," Lestrade said bitterly.

"It's not so bad now," Lucas assured him. "Thousands of English people live in New York and they hardly ever see an American."

"Anyhow," Lestrade said, his outrage gathering, "none of your business. I'm off."

"Where to?"

"Look, Lucas," Lestrade said, "do you mind?"

The commotion in the streets seemed to be increasing in volume. Lestrade went to his rooftop garden and looked over the side of the building.

"Shit," he said. His spite and impatience gave the word a special, nasty excrementality. "Hello, goodbye, fuck off and Bob's your uncle. That's what I got from the bastards."

"You did better than Ericksen."

"What are you talking about?" said Lestrade with a sneer. "Bloody Ericksen's dead."

There was a knock on the door leading to Lestrade's quarters and the Palestinian attendant appeared, looking unhappy and frightened. He spoke to Lestrade in Arabic, whereupon the professor stepped aside to let two men pass into his apartment. Lucas saw that one of them was the hawk-faced Ian Fotheringill.

"Hullo," said Fotheringill to Lucas.

"Hello," said Lucas. The little greetings covered their mutual distress at meeting. Lestrade seemed disturbed that the two knew each other. Increasingly, everything seemed to disturb him, which was understandable, given the sounds from the street below.

The man with Fotheringill was broad-chested and mustachioed, a

Middle Easterner of indistinct nationality. Nothing about his features or his dress bespoke his loyalties. Looking at him, Lucas wondered if he had not seen him before, in the Gaza Strip.

"Bloody lot here," Fotheringill said, looking indifferently at Dr. Lestrade's luggage. "Never get all that down."

"Never get it down?" Lestrade retorted in outrage. "Never get it down? Never get my luggage down? I should bloody think you would."

But Fotheringill was staring at Lucas.

"I've got to ask," he said. "It's tormenting me. Ever sort out that poem about *rillons* and *rillettes?*"

"Oh," Lucas said, "right." He scratched his chin. " '*Rillettes, Rillons,*' " he recited, " '*Rillons, Rillettes* . . . The dishes are the same, and yet . . .' "

But it was still gone. He had forgotten it.

60

A FEW HOURS after Pinchas Obermann finished his rounds
at Shaul Petak, he succeeded in reaching Sonia at her apartment in Rehavia. She sounded as if he had wakened her
from sleep.

"Just stay there," he told her. "I'm coming over." He brought
with him the curious diagram Lucas had picked up in the Golan.
When Sonia saw it, she matched it with one of the sheets she had
found in the van.

"It's a diagram of the chambers of the Temple Mount," Obermann told her. "There's probably a bomb in place now."

Raziel was sprawled on her sofa. He tried to rise but could only
pull himself upright against the arm of the sofa.

"Where's Chris?" Sonia asked Obermann.

"He went looking for Dr. Lestrade at the House of the Galilean.
He's trying to find out where the bomb is."

"Linda!" Sonia exclaimed.

"Yes," said Obermann, "we think so."

"Who's Sabazios?" she asked him.

"Sabazios Sabaoth. Yet another syncretic god. Like the one you
and De Kuff and your friends were creating. A golden calf, if you
like."

"Might someone put a bomb on him?"

"Someone might. Where's your perfect master?"

Sonia indicated a bedroom. Obermann went in to see the old
man.

"Are you Moshiach, Mr. De Kuff?" he asked.

"I never thought so," De Kuff said. "Raziel saw my *tikkun*. I
thought what must be, must be."

"Yes or no, please. Moshiach? Not Moshiach?"

"If I am not," De Kuff said, "if I cannot succeed in discharging my responsibilities, I'm going to die."

"Do you think you're ill?"

"The souls in me are suffering. They force their way through my body. They cry and scream. They demand that I take my place among them."

"Who are the souls?"

"Yeshu, who was the Christ. Sabbatai of Smyrna. Elisha ben Abouya. There are others."

"Do you see them?"

"I hear them. Above all, I feel them."

"And when they force their way through your body, does it hurt?"

"Yes," De Kuff said. "Great pain."

He made a note of the last time De Kuff had taken lithium: it had been six months.

"Don't you think Ralph Melker — Raziel — abused your confidence?"

"He's young for the responsibilities thrust on him."

"You're very concerned with responsibilities," Obermann observed.

"There is no more to life," said De Kuff.

Obermann decided to put the old man in the hospital until some more permanent provision could be made for him.

"I'm going to give you something to help you sleep longer. You're still very fatigued. I'll get you some liquid and then I'll give you a sleeping pill."

When he went out to get some juice from the refrigerator, he found Sonia on the phone. Her Danish friend Inge Rikker, the NGO-nik, was calling from Tel Aviv to tell her about the deaths of Nuala and Rashid. Obermann poured out some canned tomato juice while Sonia told him about the executions.

"They must blame them for a death," Obermann declared.

"They might as well blame me," Sonia said.

"They will have enough blame left for you," he told her.

In the bedroom, De Kuff took his pill with the juice and soon passed into sleep.

Dr. Obermann went into the living room and had a look at Raziel.

"His pupils are dilated. He's on heroin."

"He's been back on it for a week or so," Sonia said.

"Maybe longer than that, eh?"

"No," she said. "Only the last week."

"You knew?"

"No. Not until yesterday."

"Excuse me for asking, but," Obermann said, "you attended his every word. He brought you messages from the gardens of the cherubim. You're a New York musician — and you couldn't tell he was on *shmeck?*"

"I wasn't looking for it, Doc," she said.

"No," Obermann said. "You were looking for magic."

"That's about it."

"The new moon you were looking for."

"The new moon," Sonia said. "That was it."

Obermann called Shaul Petak to make arrangements for De Kuff's admission and quickly prepared to leave.

"If there is a bomb and it does go off, better stay inside." When Sonia failed to answer, he looked at her and shook his head. "But of course that's not what you'd do, is it? You'd be out on the streets. I'm talking to the wrong person."

"Is the Rev all right?" she asked.

"De Kuff? I think he's physically all right. I want him in the hospital. If you people are quite finished with him."

"Don't nod out on me," Sonia said to Raziel after Obermann had left. "I thought this was a struggle without weapons."

He had found his works and done up again. He told her that a red heifer without blemish had been born in Galilee — the Temple sacrifice required for the purification ritual.

"I don't know anything about the bomb," he said. "I don't know where it is. I didn't care."

"Why not, Raziel? How could you not care?"

Because, it turned out, he had not believed the bomb would go off, not really. Not literally. A power would prevent it.

At the same time, creation was wrought in smash. Only in chaos could the balance be restored. An explosion that mirrored the accident at the beginning of time.

So he had taken it upon himself to surrender the city to the agency of destruction, to the prevailing of Din, the Left Hand. He had trusted in the transubstantiation of all form, in all things returning to the substance of the first Adam.

There would be no death, only change, a liberation from appearances through the power of love. All categories would be obviated. Human nature and the world that had formed around it would lose all but their divine aspect. Without knowing it, the destroyers of matter would transform matter into light and liberate all things from their fallen imperfection. All the unheard music would be heard, everything holy, everyone redeemed. It would end as it had begun, in praise and rapture.

"Rapture," Sonia said. "That sounds like those fundamentalist missionaries."

"A catastrophe," he answered. "A catastrophe without victims."

A struggle without weapons, a sacrifice without blood, a storm without rain. The vision had endured for centuries. It was promised. It was foretold.

"He will wipe every tear from their eyes," Raziel said. "There shall be an end of death, and to mourning and crying and pain, for the old order will have passed away. Behold, I am making all things new. All things new," he said. "Tell me you never heard that before. Tell me the heart that believed this was not a Jewish heart!"

"I wouldn't know, Razz. Sounds like it."

"I couldn't wait," Raziel said. "I recognized him, then I failed him. I went to the tarot. To conjury. Finally I needed the drugs. I couldn't pull him through. So I left him to fail. But I wasn't wrong about him, Sonia. Only about myself."

"I could forgive you the tarot and the conjury," she said. "Even the drugs. But why the people with the bomb?"

"I thought I had to let them use me. I thought they would provide the negative force. And I would provide the rest. A scheme in free fall."

"Old story," she said.

"The story of the century," Raziel said. "The story of our lives. Life into art. Art into something more."

"Will it happen again?" she asked.

"Until we get it right."

"The violence is the hard part," she said.

"You need it," Raziel declared. "But it's the step that's hardest to finesse."

It turned out that he was essentially ignorant of the details. He knew next to nothing about the gelignite, the assembling. He told her as much as he knew or could remember. Doubt had terrified him back to opiates. Everyone had been using each other. Zimmer. The boy, Lenny. Linda.

"And Nuala," Sonia said. "And me. We never knew what we were doing. We've been seen crossing. How could you have done that to us?"

"I agreed that the blame could be placed on us. As before it was placed on Willie Ludlum."

"You mean Willie Ludlum didn't burn the mosques?"

"Sure he did," Raziel said. "No question about it. But there have been other bombs since then. Not everyone who went away was necessarily involved. Not everyone involved went away. I thought I knew what would happen this time. I let the ones who were planting it think we'd take the fall. It was our last chance."

He lay on his back, his works beside him, and literally beat his breast. The penitent junkie, she thought, watching him. The stuff of a stained-glass window somewhere, in the great ecumenical temple to come, a figure from the twentieth century's martyrology.

She kept looking at the diagram Obermann had brought and the one she had found on the ride down. She was almost certain she knew of the Bab al-Ghawanima; it was an old name for one of the Haram gates near the madrasah that housed Berger's apartment. It had been next to the section of the building that had been torn down to enlarge the Kotel plaza.

The militant friends of Linda Ericksen had been anxious to take it over, and perhaps not only because it was loose real estate. It was just possible that there was an approach to the foundations of the Haram from that area. Possibly through one of the building's layers beneath the street.

She thought Raziel had passed from consciousness. But when she stood up, he called to her.

"Sonia, don't leave me."

She went over and took his hipster sunglasses off and switched off the light beside him.

"Poor Razz," she said. "You should have stayed with music. You could have saved the world a little. Lived rightly. Loved mercy. Saved yourself, too, and maybe me."

"I promised," he said. "I was promised. More."

61

SORRY," Lucas told Fotheringill. The poem simply eluded him.

"No matter. Coming with us, are you?"

"Not me," Lucas said. "I've just been interviewing Professor Lestrade."

Fotheringill looked at the professor reproachfully.

"Have you, then?" he said. "Well, maybe you'd better ride along with us after all."

"Where?"

"Cairo," Fotheringill said. "Great town. Know it? We've got our own *sherut*. Right, Omar?"

The man he had addressed as Omar nodded. He was not much of an actor, and while he might succeed in giving the impression of a man who was about to take someone for a drive, it was hard to believe that it would be a very long one. In spite of whatever destination Fotheringill had promised Lestrade, no one was going to Cairo, of that Lucas was sure. For one thing, the Gaza Strip would not remain open.

"Don't you think they'll close the Strip?" he asked Fotheringill.

"Why should they do that?"

"Haven't you noticed? There's something of a riot in progress."

"Then we go through Negev," said Omar. "Cross at Nitzana. Or Taba."

"Taba," said Fotheringill. "That would be a bonny drive." He turned to Lucas. "Professor Lestrade can continue his studies in Cairo. He has arrangements there."

"Myself," Lucas said, "I wasn't planning a trip to Cairo."

"Weren't ya?" Fotheringill asked. "Well, you can ride with us partway. Out of the trouble, see. Maybe you'll remember the words of that poem."

"Maybe," Lucas said.

He was trying to think of a way out. In the streets around him, a virtual *jihad* was starting up, which meant that someone had already spread the words that were meant to start the war — the holy one, the war at the end of the world.

It also appeared to him that Fotheringill and Omar were about to dispose of Lestrade, who probably knew as much as anyone about the planting of the bomb. They would be armed. And he had walked into it.

"I'd better use the phone," he said cheerfully.

"You'd better fookin' nae," Fotheringill told him. "I mean," he added, more politely and in standard English, "it would be unwise."

"I hope we don't have to go through bloody Taba," Lestrade said. "If there's one place I despise, it's Eilat."

"Don't you have something stored in the hospice?" Lucas asked. "Equipment? Shouldn't we check with the porter?" Fotheringill and Omar watched him stand up.

Lestrade was unhelpful. "I don't think so, Lucas. Everything's right here."

Having got as far as the roof, Lucas called across the narrow space that separated the two buildings. During their exchange, Lucas was fairly sure he had heard Lestrade address the porter as Boutros.

"Boutros!" he shouted at the top of his lungs. The noise in the street had not abated. "Boutros, can you help us, please?"

Over the street cries, he was pleased to detect a surly answer. Fotheringill and Omar looked at each other.

"It can be done here," Fotheringill said very slowly, probably to accommodate Omar's English. "Right here, understand?"

But by the time Omar had translated it all in his head, Boutros, the Austrians' Palestinian porter, was at the door.

"How about helping us get some of this gear downstairs, Boutros? There's so much of it. And I'll get the car."

Boutros, who had plainly been asleep, looked horrified. Then his expression changed from astonishment to rage.

"Look," said Lestrade, again unhelpfully, "that's not his job."

"Sure it is," Lucas said. He assumed a colonialist stance. "Omar,

you and Boutros get the bags. The professor and I will get the car."
He nearly lifted Lestrade off his feet.

"But I don't know where the car is," Lestrade protested. When
Omar and Fotheringill stood up, Lucas shoved Lestrade out on his
rooftop. A broken bottle landed a few feet from them. There were
police klaxons sounding from the streets beyond the walls.

"They aren't going to take you to Cairo, Lestrade," Lucas told
him. "They're going to kill you. Either at Kfar Gottlieb or in the
desert."

Fotheringill stood watching with some amusement while Lucas
conveyed the news.

"What?" Lestrade asked. "Kill me? Kill me? What?"

Omar and Boutros were arguing over something. It might even
have been over who would carry the luggage.

"Kill you," Lucas continued. "And me. The way they killed
Ericksen. Ericksen and I are Americans, Lestrade. You're only a Brit.
Brits die all the time, like ordinary foreigners. Killing an American is
heavy shit. So you can reason that if they've already got Ericksen
and they're going to get me — you've had it."

Of course, Lucas was bluffing. Americans were beginning to get
killed all the time now too, just like all the other ordinary foreigners.

"What?" Professor Lestrade kept demanding. "What?"

Lucas noticed that Fotheringill, who was now standing beside
them, appeared increasingly amused. He was either a glutton for
entertainment or extremely stupid. Perhaps, Lucas thought, he was
crazy. Or perhaps his amusement was derived from the ease and
speed with which, as an ex-SAS man, he could dispatch them all.
There was no time to waste.

Above all, Lucas was concerned with saving himself. But it would
be a good idea, he thought, if he could get Lestrade out with him.
For one thing, Lestrade would know where the bomb had been set
and might be able to help unset it. For another, although Lestrade
was a prick, a fascist and an anti-Semite, it would be the Christian
thing to save him. Or the Jewish thing. The Judeo-Christian thing.

From where he stood on Lestrade's roof, Lucas could not make
out the regular Border Police post over the Damascus Gate. It was
probably manned, he thought, but blacked out. If things had gotten
bad enough, it was possible that the IDF had pulled back temporarily from the Palestinian parts of town, to secure Jewish residential
areas.

But IDF doctrine was not defensive even in the short run. It was likely that regardless of the riot's extent, the Army would shortly be taking up positions inside the walls, in Palestinian areas. There were also scattered Jewish enclaves in the Muslim Quarter, yeshivas and flag-showing oddments like General Sharon's apartment. They would shortly come under siege, and the IDF, being the IDF, would risk a great deal to prevent any loss of Jewish life if Palestinians attacked them.

"How do you propose to get to your car?" Lucas asked Fotheringill. A tissue of fiction remained around the idea of Fotheringill's driving them to safety, and Lucas decided to keep it in play.

"You let me worry about that, laddie."

Omar had gotten rid of Boutros, harried him back to the Austrian hospice. But where, wondered Lucas, could Fotheringill's car be? It was impossible to drive the Old City streets as far as the hospice. They would have to walk through the mob. And even then, driving would not be easy.

The thing was to keep Fotheringill and Omar from killing them right in Lestrade's apartment. They had that option, should they decide it necessary. The riot would cover untoward events.

"Well," Lestrade said, "I suppose there's no hope for my poor plants. So I'm ready, what?"

The Old City walls, thought Lucas. The IDF would surely have secured them. There would be spotters along the length of them, unseen. In the distance, he heard the chant of the IDF's Golani Regiment.

From the direction of the sound, the elite Golani troops were coming through Herod's Gate. They would either be securing a strong point or getting someone out. They might also be the opening wedge of a major attack on the rioters. If anyone was using rubber bullets that night, it would be the reserve units in the rear. The Golani favored bullets of the full-metal-jacketed variety.

"Golani," Omar said to Fotheringill. Fotheringill looked at his watch.

What, Lucas wondered, if the commandos came within earshot and he called for help? It might get them out, free of Fotheringill. It would also alert the rioters of their presence. But the rioters were a lesser evil. Then he thought of what had happened to Hal Morris in Nuseirat.

Suddenly there was a crashing of wood and glass downstairs, and for a moment Lucas thought the crowds might be rushing Christian hospices, the Austrian one included. But the shouts of the men who came charging up the hospice steps and across the landing to Lestrade's were in Hebrew. And the men who rushed into the apartment were in uniform.

Golani, Lucas thought. He would never think badly of them again. At least for publication.

The soldiers filled the apartment and crisply took up positions on the roof. Neither Fotheringill nor Omar seemed disturbed or even surprised by the arrival of the IDF.

"See here," said Dr. Lestrade, "this is Christian property."

He's going to do it, thought Lucas. He's going to formally protest having his ass saved. Lucas could still hear the cadences of troops a few blocks away. There were shots. Then he noticed there was something slightly askew about the conduct of the soldiers in the flat.

For one thing, although at least one of the men wore a Golani patch, they did not have the squared-away look of the paratroopers. They must, he thought, be an outfit that had been called in to support the general offensive, a kind of rescue squad. Some of the men were wearing *tzitzit*. Others looked incurably civilian, even by IDF standards. They seemed defeated by their own equipment, its snaps and buckles, and held their weapons haphazardly. They might be volunteers, Lucas thought, scholars and urban settlers from outside the Jewish Quarter, on a mission to rescue their brothers and colleagues. In which case, Lucas wondered, what were they doing here? He counted ten of them.

"Car secure, then?" Fotheringill asked one of the soldiers.

"Follow us," one of the men answered in North American English.

So they were, Lucas saw, not regulars but reserves and guerrillas.

"Watch these two," Fotheringill said. He meant Lucas and the deeply confused Dr. Lestrade. "They're the passengers."

One of the military men took Lucas by the sleeve.

"And this bastard," Fotheringill said, pointing to Lestrade.

Something occurred to Lucas. "Surely," he asked Lestrade, "you knew about the bomb?"

"Bomb?" asked Lestrade, inflecting the very pinnacle of irritated outrage that was his inheritance. "*Bomb? A bomb?* Certainly not."

It was difficult not to believe him.

62

WITH RAZIEL passed out on her sofa, Sonia had another look at the diagram she had found, tracing the passages marked on it.

"*Kaddosh!*" she said aloud. Then she found herself thinking of the stairway that led down from the madrasah where Berger had lived. It struck her as altogether possible that the passages marked a connection between the cellars under Berger's and under the Haram. The apartments once belonged to the grand mufti, after all.

And Berger had said something, it seemed to her, about connecting passages. Then, of course, the two intrusive young militants, presumably the people with whom Raziel had involved them, had shown a particular interest in that building, an interest that might have had its technical side.

She might, she thought, add her intuition to what the police knew about the bomb plot. But if she simply picked up the telephone and started telling a voice on duty what she suspected, she might succeed in doing no more than getting arrested. And although she really believed in the complicity of Shin Bet with the bombers, it was never clear whom one was talking to. She decided to get to the madrasah and see what could be done there.

On Sonia's television set, the evening news was reporting disturbances in the Old City. It was also announcing curfews in sections of town and ordering the members of certain security units to duty. Sonia knew that if she was going to go, she had better get moving before the police closed off the streets completely.

She changed into the clothes that gave her the run of the eastern city and drove the Dodge van into the center. She parked illegally at a construction site at the Old City end of Jaffa Road and set out for the Jaffa Gate. It might, she knew, be the last she saw of the van; civil disturbances consumed automobiles as Moloch had devoured infants in his day. She slid open the side door, took from the van's utility chest a flashlight, a wrench and a hammer, and carried them beneath her djellaba. Hurrying by the police post at the wall, she passed unhindered and turned right toward the Armenian Quarter.

The gates of the quarter were secured by the time Sonia arrived — the Armenians hunkering down for trouble. From every mosque in the city, loudspeakers gave forth sacred rage. There were rifle shots, cries of grief and anger, the ululations of women.

At the passageway's turning near Zion Gate was an IDF checkpoint. Sonia had a Palestinian identity card she had bought from a moneychanger near the Damascus Gate, but she spoke both Hebrew and Arabic haltingly. The card identified her as a resident of the Old City.

The soldier who searched her bag was a fair-haired Ashkenazi who took her bad Hebrew for granted. She told him she was going home from her hotel maid's job in the western city, and he let her pass. In the squares and spotless plazas of the Jewish Quarter, married couples had gathered, listening to the growing roar of the riot. Here and there, groups sang patriotic songs. It was "Never Again" in tableau vivant — quiet, armed determination. Everyone more or less faced the Western Wall and the Haram beyond it, the enemy's shrine and temple, whence he would come with his heart full of murder.

There were not many children in sight. One of them, a boy of about ten with a crew cut and sidelocks, spat toward Sonia's skirts as she hurried past him.

The next checkpoint she had to pass was in the tunnel that led from the Western Wall plaza to the bazaar of El-Wad. It had been strongly reinforced with busloads of soldiers; a line of armored personnel carriers were pulled up against one wall of the tunnel.

A middle-aged bearded reservist who looked like a rabbi quickly checked her card and directed her into the deserted labyrinth. Its length was full of echoing, threatening noises, and when she emerged from it, she saw flames. For no reason she could imagine, someone concealed in the shadows of the burning building threw a fist-sized chunk of metal at her; it hit a wall, ricocheted and rolled over the cobblestones. Perhaps because she was a lone woman, coming from the Jewish Quarter.

El-Wad in the Muslim Quarter was crowded, lit by flashlights and camp lanterns. She heard unpleasant laughter and the frightened boastfulness of young men. A helicopter appeared overhead, its beam illuminating the pale, contorted faces of the youthful rioters, taking them by surprise. A whirl of curses like winged insects flew up toward where it had passed, as though drawn by the rotors.

The wooden street door of the building where she had lived with Berger was bolted. Some time before, the place had been taken over by Israeli militants, who had connected it by a series of walkways with a street off Jewish Quarter Lane, and as far as she knew the militants still occupied it. A Star of David had flown from one of the interior balconies, visible from the street. Now it was gone.

There seemed a deserted quality to the place, which made her wonder whether anyone at all had found a purpose for it. She tried sounding the ornate Ottoman-style knocker on the carriage gate. When she had knocked for a minute or so, she heard the bolt sliding free.

The door opened and a tall, thin young man of Christlike aspect stood before her. It was not likely that the young man would soon come in glory to judge the quick and the dead; rather, his slack smile and purple mantle suggested contemporary, vulgar notions of the Christian savior. His mantle appeared to have been appropriated from the window of a no-star hotel, its curtain rings still in place. His smile, though genuinely welcoming, gave evidence of lax oral hygiene.

"Praise Jesus," he told Sonia.

"Right," she said, and passed inside. There was no sign of the Sudanese children who lived in the madrasah before. It seemed to have become a refuge for the homeless: all along the courtyard, pallets and bindles were stashed, sometimes attended by their owners, who variously wept, prayed or slept. It seemed an odd use for the militants to find for their Muslim Quarter property.

"What happened to the young Israelis who took the building over?" she asked him.

They had gone, the youth said. Scientists excavating the ancient foundations of the buildings across the street had replaced them. Now these savants too were gone.

"What are you people doing here?"

The young transcendentalist explained that his friends were being paid to watch the tunnel entrances until such time as the scientists might want to use them again.

"Tunnel entrances?" Sonia asked.

The young man led her to the foyer she had passed a hundred times when Berger was in residence. Three narrow rising steps followed the base of one of the building's columns, forming a little alcove the local children had used in games of hide-and-seek. But now there was a rectangle of burlap over the opening. When Sonia brushed it aside she saw that the aboveground steps were only the top of a flight that curved down into the damp darkness beneath the quarter's streets.

Ten steps down was another wooden door, and it was locked fast. Any number of attempts on her part, assisted by the young pseudo-Christus, failed to shake it. Finally, with more assistance from the young man and his friends, she succeeded in forcing it open. An intoxicating smell of ancient stone ascended from the spiral passage.

The street that led to the Bab al-Ghawanima was about fifty yards away. She shone her flashlight on the diagram and saw that any tunnels branching out from the old madrasah might well lead to the foundation of one or another of the Haram's bordering buildings.

The property had belonged to al-Husseini during the British mandate; there was every reason to think he had found a network of passageways useful during the strife of that period. And if the militants who had seized the madrasah had finished their work, it made sense to conceal their access to the Haram in what appeared to be a derelict gathering place for the religiously deluded, behind a series of locked doors.

Following the beam of her light, she set out. After a dozen steps or so, she realized that the squatters of the madrasah intended to follow her down.

"Beat it," she told them. "Fuck off. Not you," she told the Jesus look-alike when, chastened, he started back with the rest. "You come with me."

The steps, their well narrowing, descended for what seemed a hundred feet, deep enough for Sonia to feel the pressure in her ears. A utility lantern was burning at the mouth of a passage that seemed to descend gradually from the foot of the stairs. From somewhere not far away, but distorted by the hollows and vaults, came a sound like the cries of a crowd and what might be gunfire.

Sonia entered the passageway, humming "Makin' Whoopie" as she went. She had not gone thirty feet when the passage divided again. She had a look left and right in the flashlight beams, but it was little help. To follow the line of the Bab al-Ghawanima, it seemed that she ought to bear right.

"What's your name, sir?" she asked the imitation of Christ behind her.

His name turned out to be George.

"Would you stay right here, George? See, you're just in the light of that lantern, so if I find you, I can find my way out of here. Will that be cool?"

George hastened to accept this assignment.

Soon the passage divided again, and again she bore right. Then it triplicated, and after few more paces doubled again. This time the right-hand passage led to what at first looked like a false chamber. But there was, she saw, an aperture low on the wall that seemed to lead back to the enclosure from which she had just come. Probing it with her beam, she saw that it was on an incline that subvented the adjoining chamber. The whole surface had a slight downward tilt, so anyone advancing along the system of corridors moved gradually deeper beneath the street.

Getting prone on the floor, Sonia began to elbow her way into the passage she had found. In a short time she was aware that it contracted around her, growing narrower as she went along. There was something organic about its structure, as though it replicated a kind of living creature.

After a while the narrowing was too much for her claustrophobic instincts; she started backtracking, digging in her knees for leverage, wiggling her behind, shoving backward with the palms of her hands. Back in the chamber from which she had started crawling, she breathed dust that savored of centuries. But when she shined her light on the floor, she saw that there were fresh footprints in it, the tracks of walking shoes or army boots, but also those of plain street shoes.

She found no one at the dimly lighted intersection where she thought she had left her assistant. The passageways were an intentional maze. She hesitated a moment before calling out to him; she did not relish hearing the sound of her own voice in that buried place.

"George?"

His answer, when it came, seemed so distant and atremble with echoes that it chilled her heart. It was an acoustical trick of the place.

"Can you turn up the light?" she called.

She could not make out what he said in reply, but the light burned no brighter. Her flashlight was losing its power, the beam fading and yellowing before her eyes. And in the passageways, the ones through which she thought — but was no longer sure — she had come, she could not find her way at all.

63

TWO GUERRILLAS took hold of Lestrade and thrust him toward the door.

"See here," Lestrade said, "what about my luggage?"

"His luggage," the North American who led the squad repeated tonelessly. "What about my grandfather's luggage, you prick," he said. "Worried about your luggage? It'll be held for you. We're like your German friends. Very honest."

"Bring a toothbrush," one of the other English-speaking men said. "And warm clothes. And we'll give you a postcard. You can write home."

"Look, I'm a reporter," Lucas said. He nearly said, I'm Jewish. He had been very close to saying it, trying to remember the Shema.

The leader looked at Fotheringill.

"Take them both," Fotheringill told the man in charge. "Let's get the hell out of here."

Being shoved down the wooden stairs inside the ancient stone tower, Lucas had a picture of himself as he might be somewhere in Europe, circa 1942, being shoved down an old flight of stairs by soldiers.

I'm not Jewish, he would be saying. They would pay no attention.

Lestrade had an exculpatory formula as well.

"Listen here," he told everyone. His inflection now was humorous, as though he were inviting everyone to join him in merry laughter at the absurdity of it all. "I don't know a thing about any bomb, you know."

The street, which before had been crowded with young fighters shouting out for martyrdom, was deserted. But close by there was more shooting and the noise of sirens, chanting soldiers, chanting rioters. A holy war, Lucas thought. And he had gotten himself in it.

All at once, Dr. Lestrade began to shout in Arabic. Two young men holding lanterns appeared at the mouth of an alley. And suddenly Boutros, who had seemed so put upon and sleepy moments before, came charging out of the hospice at them, wild-eyed, beside himself.

"*Itbah al-Yahud!*" he shouted at the top of his voice.

One of the Israelis fired at him. The burst was high because Fotheringill had knocked the barrel of the rifle upward with his forearm. The spent cartridges rattled on cobblestone. Then Fotheringill swung the butt of his Galil into the porter's jaw. Boutros groaned and sank to the pavement of the Via Dolorosa. Another Israeli began shooting into the alley where the two other Palestinians had appeared. They withdrew, apparently unhit.

The whirl of light that had momentarily filled the street vanished, and the area was now in deep darkness. Lucas saw Fotheringill take an automatic rifle from one of the less coordinated men of the squad.

"I'll fire a burst, then you'll go for the gate." He paused. "I hope you know your bloody way."

"We know," the North American said. "It's not far."

Fotheringill opened up with the Galil, sending ricochets along the narrowly parted walls, breaking glass, shattering flowerpots and trellises, sending stray cats running.

"Move out," he commanded.

Lestrade, disinclined to run, got a rifle butt in the kidneys, which served to jump-start him. Lucas ran out of sheer instinct.

At the first intersection, it was apparent that something had gone wrong. The two streets met in the kind of crazy quilt of light that had accompanied the rioters. An angry crowd had gathered there, and Fotheringill fired over it. Some of the lights disappeared, others withdrew. There were screams and curses in a variety of languages, several of them European and including English. A number of the other Israelis also fired, some high, some not.

Lucas hugged the wall, squatting in the confusion of rifle shots.

"Where are they?" Fotheringill shouted. He meant Lestrade and Lucas. Temporarily, at least, they had slid out of his operational control. Good old fog of battle. Lucas tried to make out Lestrade.

Searching for their prisoners, the squad had halted its progress. It was appallingly ready, however, to make do with covering fire.

"Stop!" a woman screamed. An English voice. "We're press." She was answered by a couple of wild rifle bursts.

There was enough light for Lucas to make out what had happened. A press pool had sneaked in behind the army and attached itself to a group of rioters. In the unearthly brilliance of a television lamp, Lucas recognized a seventyish Palestinian man who worked as a guide for foreigners, specializing in the Haram. His name was Ibrahim. He was learned, multilingual and shamelessly greedy. He had undertaken to conduct the foreign press through the opening hours of the holy war.

"Oh, shit," the Englishwoman shouted. "Kill the lights before they shoot the lot of us."

"Halloo!" Lestrade shouted from somewhere in the blackness that descended. "Are you British? I'm British."

Sacred identities were being proffered like so many junk bonds in the ancient darkness. They did not seem to trade for much.

"Yes," said the brave girl at the intersection. "Come over here. You'll be right with us."

When the last light disappeared, Lucas stood up and bolted for the corner. He ran straight into Lestrade, who was strolling triumphantly in the center of the street while Fotheringill and his Israelis apparently kept trying to kill him in the dark. Bullets rattled and whistled in every direction.

Colliding, Lucas put both arms around the professor and dragged him down. Like Jack Kerouac, Lucas had briefly played football for Columbia, although he was not very talented. Dragging the professor by the collar, he crawled over the invisible foul stones.

"Halloo!" Lestrade kept calling. "I'm British!"

"Shut the fuck up," Lucas advised him.

Hands came out of the dark and pulled them forward, and in an instant they were around the corner. There were more lights at the end of the street. He could see Palestinian flags under the lights, but no sign of the army.

"So," said the female reporter, whom Lucas could not see. "Who's British, then?"

"I am," said Lestrade. "I'm a researcher with a valid visa and we've been brutalized and murdered."

Lucas could sense rather than see the other reporters drawing near. It was what George Bush would have called a feeding flurry.

"Look," he said. "We've got to get out of here. Those men are not the IDF. They're killers."

At this intriguing intelligence, the shadowy press corps moved out toward the street Fotheringill was busily shooting to pieces.

Lucas stood up and grabbed Lestrade.

"It's us they're after," he told the Englishwoman, who had stayed behind. "We have information they don't want known. They're going to kill us."

"I beg your pardon," she said.

"Come on," he said to Lestrade. "If you want to go on living. They know about you and the bomb." He took the man by the arm and began running him toward the Damascus Gate, the direction where the next set of lights burned.

"What?" Lestrade asked. "Bomb? What?" He sounded genuinely confused but he ran along with Lucas.

"Just a minute," called the English reporter behind them. "Just a minute." For a moment it looked as though she would run after them. Lucas then realized that it might be useful to have her around. Possibly fatal to her, but useful.

When they arrived at the next lighted corner, the woman had not followed. There were no reporters at this corner, and the young men in charge of it looked at Lucas with an unpleasant intensity. He began to wonder if he would actually have to utter his obverse credo: I'm not Jewish. Denying two valid identities in one night was hard even for Lucas. Nevertheless, people did such things during holy wars. It was to counter this kind of ignobility that shibboleths had been invented. Somewhere, a wakeful rooster crowed above the disorder.

On the positive side, Lestrade spoke Arabic and began to do so, volubly. Unfortunately for Lucas, there was no imagining what manner of fatally offensive absurdities such a man might blabber.

While he was waiting for the practical effects of Lestrade's narrative, he saw the young woman come up from the street where Fotheringill and his company were shooting it out with themselves in the dark. She was tall, dark-haired and rather pretty.

With her, brandishing his stick, was Ibrahim, the Palestinian guide, whom she had somehow commandeered. Lucas's first thought was that the old man would cost her employers a fortune. Afterward —

if there was an afterward — he would demand at least twice what he had agreed to.

The woman was checking over her shoulder. Something more was up, at the corner, and there were lights again, lights of the army's sort.

"Golani," she said. "They're taking that street."

So Fotheringill and his ersatz troops would have to fade, and he and Lestrade were saved, for the time being. He would really have to do something nice for the Golani. A friendly feature.

"Thank God," Lucas said. *Baruch Hashem.*

The English reporter turned up her nose in a disapproving manner. "Oh, thank God for Golani? You must have seen a side of them I've never. But of course you're American, right?"

No, I'm not, Lucas thought. He tried to think of something to be that was less disagreeable.

"There are Israeli terrorists down there killing people," he said. "They tried to murder us. Golani at least is under discipline."

The young woman looked unconvinced.

"If you don't believe me, ask your countryman."

But Lestrade was busy unfolding a tale that held the young Palestinians at the corner rapt. Lestrade, Lucas realized, was either an idiot of transcendent proportions or an extremely slick, if somewhat eccentric, master operator. Either would serve at times, he had come to realize, and it was possible to be both.

"I'd like very much to talk to him," the young woman said. "Where were you when this all began?"

"I was interviewing Dr. Lestrade," Lucas said. "I'm also a journalist. My name is Chris Lucas."

"Sally Conners," said the young woman. They did not shake hands.

He saw that she was going to ask a question about Lestrade, then saw her decide not to. She seemed reluctant to ask questions of a foreigner — an American admirer of the Golani Regiment, yet — about a fellow countryman. Honorable, Lucas thought, but unprofessional.

In the meantime, the Palestinian guide was visibly torn between his fear of Lucas as a possible rival and his desire to expand his fees. Yet, Lucas thought, it would be very useful to have a Palestinian around, especially one as well known as Maître Ibrahim. Among other things, the old man was selling the security of his company.

For Lucas, it was annoying to have to share the eyewitness aspect of the story, especially with an Englishwoman. On the other hand, his "exclusives" were more trouble than they were worth, and beside the point now. A little collaboration and corroboration were not necessarily a bad thing. The more he thought about it, the more it seemed to him he would never be able to approach the Haram without the Palestinian, and someone would have to pay him off several times over.

When Dr. Lestrade had finished regaling the assembled Palestinians with his recent adventures, he allowed himself to be interviewed by Sally Conners.

"Well, I had to pack in a great hurry," he told her. "Then this man appeared" — he indicated Lucas — "and the man who had arranged to drive me turned out to be . . . well, I don't know."

"Dr. Lestrade is an expert on the construction of the Haram and the holy sites beneath it," Lucas told her. "Since so many people feel the Haram's about to be blown up, he must have been leaving to avoid controversy. That was it, wasn't it, Lestrade?"

"Well, no," said Lestrade. He thought about it for a moment. "Well, yes. I mean no one's blowing up the Haram. Sensationalistic nonsense. Native rumors. It's a survey for the American Bible-thumpers."

"Blowing up?" asked Sally Conners.

Lucas left her to press Lestrade, who was awkwardly composing a narrative in which he was a marginal figure, brought in arsy-varsy. He found the old guide waiting impatiently, in fear that his clientele would evaporate amid disorder. There was more firing and, over the Armenian Quarter, like some celestial portent, a flare climbed in the sky. Someone must have shot off a flare gun because the someone owned one and the time seemed right. The people on Lucas's corner crouched warily.

Lucas spoke confidentially to Ibrahim. "All the reporters are looking for Salman Rushdie. Everyone knows he was brought here. But no one knows where he is."

Ibrahim looked at Lucas without expression; it was impossible to surprise him with any information, however improbable. He immediately appropriated to himself all intelligence of whatever kind, and his primary assessment involved not accuracy but resale value.

"He was seen at the airport," Lucas continued in his rash, over-confiding manner, "accompanied by Israeli and American bodyguards. Don't you think he must have come to witness the destruction of the holy places?"

Without doubt, the guide liked it. His faded-flannel blue eyes shone in the mixed light. His next utterance was oracular.

"He is here," Ibrahim pronounced. "I have seen him."

"I suppose," Lucas suggested, "the Israelis and the Americans will make him mufti or something. He'll approve a new construction of the Dome and the Aksa in Mecca."

"This is right," said the learned old fellow. "But more is involved." He raised his voice. "Salman Rushdie!" He shouted. "Rushdie has come!"

There was a moment of astonished restraint, and the gathered young men began to cry out and rend their garments.

"Salman Rushdie?" asked the young Sally Conners. She had grown annoyed at having constantly to revise her perception of events. "That's rubbish."

Her observation was not well received. Her own guide grew angry at her.

"He is here!" shouted Ibrahim. "He has come!"

64

S ONIA TRIED following her own sandal prints in the dust. The prints turned out to be ephemeral; there were other tracks and wet spots in the stone. She could no longer remember whether the ground she had covered was of masonry or just rocky earth. She made a slow, careful attempt at retracing her way and then a headlong series of instant intuitive decisions. Neither got her free. On the contrary, after her two attempts she felt farther away from mad George and his light than she had been when she started.

"George!"

Was she hearing laughter? Noises underwent strange distortions as they passed through the walls and passages and grottoes of the place. "George?"

In some chambers there was hardly any echo at all. In others, whatever she called out was repeated in unnatural multiples that would sometimes stop for a few seconds and then resume at a distance, diminishing as the sound was carried farther and farther away.

Not one of the cubicles she passed through was large enough for her to stretch her arms out in front of her. She felt a rush of panic in her throat. Her legs went weak; she thought it must be fear. She cried.

Already her mind was unsteady. She kept thinking that the darkness around her would consume her and turn her into the nothingness it was itself, as though she had come to some ancient order of things where chaos was in the process of being separated from time and event. Chaos was cold.

As long as the light lasted, she thought, she would probably be all right. With darkness, she imagined she would begin to come apart. The place had the kind of darkness that could get inside you and hide you from yourself.

Keep moving or stay still? She decided to keep moving, trying to guide herself by the noises she thought must be coming from outside. They were unrecognizable, ugly noises and it was impossible to tell whether their source was even human. But, she thought, they were better than silence in this darkness.

"George!"

The answer she got did not come from the Christlike youth. Something about the shape of the walls and ceilings gave it a quality like a voice at a séance or that of a stage magician. It was a voice she vaguely recognized.

"What are you doin' down here, Sonia?" the voice wanted to know. "Not looking for us, I hope."

"I'm lost," she told the voice. The reverberations made it impossible to recognize any voice.

"Who sent you here, Sonia? Was it Lucas?"

"No," Sonia said. "Where are you?"

"Too bloody clever," the man's voice said. He was speaking to someone else. It was as if she weren't supposed to hear him.

Suddenly she heard a serpentine hiss cast its weird sibilant echo in the same room she occupied.

"Sonia!" Now she heard what sounded like the voice of Fotheringill. He spoke softly, without dentalizing, as though he were communicating in a mode of speech to which he had been trained. "Stay wi' me. Back toward the wall."

It was Fotheringill. She froze in her tracks, uncertain whether to answer.

"I'm lost," she said. The unseen Fotheringill hissed at her, demanding silence. She began to edge toward the nearest wall.

Coming under Fotheringill's mercy, she felt like the prey turned over to a predator for protection. But out of panic, fearful loneliness, unreasoning hope, she could not resist doing it.

"You're not lost," the other voice, the one from above, declared. "You're in the temple of Sabazios."

At the same distance, through the same stone filter, she heard laughter and mutterings of affirmation. There were men with him. It sounded as though there were more than a dozen, but all the clues were unreliable.

"Why are you here?" she whispered to Fotheringill. "Do you know there's a —"

Another quick, viperish rush of breath cut her off.

"Sonia?" asked the voice from overhead. "Is someone with you?"
She did not answer but only kept backing toward the wall.

"Your king has become a Muslim, Sonia," said the voice close by.
"Did you know that?"

"Well," she said to the voice, "it's all the same to him."

Still hidden, Fotheringill hushed her again.

"Is it?" said the other unseen man. "You'll have to explain that."

When she felt the dusty wall behind her she edged along it, trying
to find a door to the next chamber, deathly afraid of encountering
Fotheringill. She was trying to keep track of both of the men's
locations and figure some concept of her own. It was more than she
could handle.

At last she felt a turn in the wall. It seemed to be an opening and
she crouched and rushed through it.

"But you know how he thinks," she called out to the secret
speaker. "That it's all the same."

She decided to repeat her technique of moving along the walls.
With her flashlight off, she had to take each step into utter darkness.
There were only sinister, ambiguous voices, somehow promising
common humanity in that place, so far from everywhere.

"Who are you?" she called out. Another sibilant silencing from
Fotheringill. Wherever he was, he was tracking her, like a cat, in the
blackness.

There had to be a pattern to the maze of chambers, and someone
confined here long enough, she thought, might work it out. She had
no idea whether Fotheringill knew his way around the passageways
or not. She knew, she realized, very little about him. She also had the
feeling he was much closer now than he had been before.

Then, again from above, she made out a buzz of small curses and
comments that seemed to accompany the second voice.

"I'm here to learn," she shouted. Perhaps, she thought, she was
discovering something about herself — that, at any risk, she could
not abandon herself to darkness and silence. This time Fotheringill
did not interrupt her.

"You're nothing but a black drug addict," the voice above her
said. It was just a bit clearer now. European, accented. "The country's full of people like you. In the Negev, with your fucking soul
food. You're not Jews."

There was a subdued mutter of anger overhead. It was as though
some kind of justice was descending on her. In that darkness, full of

unseen men, she was tempted to call on Fotheringill. One of the gang.

"I've got as much right here as you," Sonia called. In this particular place, it seemed a questionable assertion. This time Fotheringill hissed at her again.

Someone was going to hurt her, Sonia reasoned. She had lost all sense of where anyone stood, what the plot had been about. She had expected the police or Shin Bet or Mossad. Someone.

"Aren't the police here?" she shouted. Shouted it at the top of her voice.

"Sonia!" she heard Fotheringill whisper at close quarters. "Don't."

It sounded as if he were offering support. But surely, she thought, he was part of Raziel's disastrous plot. He was not alone; he was doing something illegal and desperate. Most likely, she thought, he was planting the bomb.

From somewhere outside she heard noises she could not interpret. A crowd. Machinery. The sounds were impossible to track; at times they seemed to come from overhead, other times below. Occasionally they seemed to approach, then withdraw, infinitely.

They'll hurt me, she thought.

All at once she heard a rustling and scuffing somewhere in the darkness, the rattle of metal gear, weaponry, faint but audible.

"Sonia," Fotheringill called, "stay where you are. We'll find you." Along with the threat was a fearful reassurance in the way he said it.

To hide or to run? She was afraid to turn on her flashlight; she had no idea how far away Fotheringill and the others were. On the other hand, she could see absolutely nothing, and the only way for her to get into a different chamber was to feel along the wall for it.

The sounds were so confusing now, and she didn't know whether she would be moving toward or away from them. George and his light, if he was not somehow part of the plot, might as well have been miles away.

She decided to try and move away from where she thought the men were. It stood to reason that they knew their way around the warren, and that if she tried to hide, they would find her.

Facing the wall, she slid her way along its damp, uneven surface until her hand encountered vacancy or an angle. Then she would step into whatever opening offered itself. Sometimes it would be only a niche in the chamber, sometimes a low door that led to an adjoining chamber. The scuffle of boots and packs and weaponry sounded farther off now. There was still a distant roar from some-where outside. Her only concern had become escape.

When she had made her way through about four separate cham-bers, she came upon one that struck her as special. For one thing, the tiniest sound created a disproportionately long echo, which made her think the place was uniquely spacious, floor to ceiling. For an-other, it had a peculiar smell, one different from the ancient stone dust she had been inhaling for the past hour or half hour or however long she had been in the tunnel. She had lost all sense of time.

The smell in the chamber was compounded of metal, chemicals and sweat. Her sudden sense of it made her freeze in her tracks and hesitate in her manual soundings of the walls. But she stayed at it until she felt a niche again and reached out before stepping into it. Her hand brushed something smooth. Unlike the walls, it was not coated with dust or sand. It seemed, she thought, to be a figure made of metal, and it represented a form that was somehow familiar to her. She needed both her hands to encompass it.

Reaching behind the figure, she felt a ceramic shape that was detectably a human form. It seemed composed partly of folds that were those of a garment, and there were odd excrescences around it, but whatever it was, it was intended to represent something human. She turned on the flashlight.

She was in a chamber with a ceiling about eleven feet by fifteen. Its walls were decorated with frescoes she could not make out but that appeared immeasurably old. The foremost figure she had felt in the darkness was the metal working of a human hand. The hand's last two fingers were curled against the palm; the first three were raised as in benediction.

The statue behind the hand was a figure like Hermes. In its left hand it held a staff around which two snakes curled. Its face, care-fully worked, had a beatific smile, reminiscent of a bodhisattva's. It wore a cap, like the figure of Liberty in the Delacroix painting of the Revolution of 1830. Its right hand was extended in a ges-ture identical to the lone hand that stood in front of it. On the wall behind it was an inscription in Greek.

"This," the voice from above her declared, the soft, cultured European voice, "is where you belong."

65

ALMAN RUSHDIE!" the old guide Ibrahim was intoning, like a muezzin. "Rushdie has come!"

"But that's utter rubbish," Sally Conners repeated.

"It's arrant nonsense," said Lestrade. His sense of security seemed to have renewed his attempts to bring the funny side to bear. "It's poppycock."

"I think you're Salman Rushdie," Lucas told Lestrade. "I think the CIA has disguised you. Planted a homing device in your socks. I think you're going to die. Look at his hooded eyes," he told Sally Conners, pulling on Lestrade's boozy underlids. "Look at his receding hairline. His shifty eyes. Behold," he shouted to the crowd. "Behold . . ." He had no idea how to say "behold" in Arabic, but it sounded appropriate.

"All right, all right," said the terrified Lestrade.

"If I get killed out here," Lucas told him, "you're getting it first. You think my Jewishness is amusing? How'd you like to sample Christian martyrdom?"

"See here," Sally Conners said. "Leave him alone."

Everyone was asking Ibrahim where Salman Rushdie was. He seemed to have gone into a trance state, like a psychic, to locate the accursed one.

"Maybe we can surprise him," Lucas told the gifted ancient, "at the Bab al-Hadid. His guards may have taken him there."

"No!" announced the guide. "He is atop the Mount of Olives. He comes by helicopter."

"Look," said Sally Conners, "the rest of the press is following the army through the streets. That's what we should be doing. There'll be shootings. Atrocities."

"He is not atop the Mount of Olives," Lucas told the guide. "He is in the Bab al-Hadid. If you want to be paid, you better fucking look for him there."

Ibrahim checked to see if anyone was in earshot. "But the bomb . . . ?"

"We have professors who can unmake bombs."

Ibrahim looked grave.

"Do you want to make money tonight or just get blown to shit?" Lucas asked him. "If you don't help us get there you'll regret it."

"I fear no threats," said Ibrahim. "I am old."

"Good," Lucas said. "Do it for the money. And to save the holy places."

Clearly, the old man did not trust him. Nonetheless, he announced that Salman Rushdie was lurking in the Bab al-Hadid.

The crowd cried out for Rushdie's blood. Outside the walls there was more rather than less commotion, and the intensity of the gunfire inside the Old City seemed to have increased. Had Hamas or the PLO gone over to armed resistance?

"You must pay me," Ibrahim said, taking Sally Conners aside, "much more than agreed to go to Bab al-Hadid."

"But I don't want to go to the Bab al-Hadid," she said. "Or the fucking Mount of Olives either. I want to follow the Golani Regiment from the Palestinian point of view."

Lucas looked around him to make sure that Lestrade had not escaped in the confusion. But the professor's instincts had kept him among fellow Franks.

"Lestrade," Lucas said, "tell her she wants to go to the Bab al-Hadid."

"Well, you see," Lestrade said, "there's a tunnel there. A new excavation."

"Don't you get it?" Lucas asked Sally Conners. "They got a Western fall guy to excavate, then they planted the bomb. It's going to be another number like the mad Australian."

The young woman absorbed this information.

"Won't it blow up?" she asked. "I mean us too?"

"Probably," Lucas said. "But you'll get a look at the tunnel. And we have experts working on it already. For example, the professor here is an expert. And so am I."

"What are you," she asked, "the CIA or something?"

"I'm a religion major," Lucas told her.

"Death to the blasphemer!" the guide was shouting. "Death to Salman Rushdie!"

He could speak without fear of contradiction. So they all hurried off down El-Wad toward the Bab al-Hadid, Lucas and Lestrade and the old guide Ibrahim and the young English reporter — who did not for one minute believe that Salman Rushdie had been brought to Jerusalem to see the holy places explode — all followed by a crowd of nearly a hundred shouting Palestinian men and boys.

One street they attempted to traverse was in a state of war. Hastily made Molotov cocktails sailed down from the rooftops like ravioli malfatto, exploding in air, in the streets or in the hands of their makers. There were cries and flaming trellises in the rooftop gardens and the smell of burning lemons. Golani gunners were laying down fire along the walls while their snipers tried to pick off would-be Davids among the enemy host. A young man fell screaming onto the street, his kaffiyeh and Oakland Raiders sweatshirt on fire.

Lucas and his party tried another street. Lucas pulled Lestrade behind him. The English reporter did the same with Ibrahim, who nonetheless attempted to assume a proprietary attitude.

"The north and west side of the blessed Haram," he shouted, "forms best-preserved medieval Islamic complex in this world."

There was a burst of what sounded for all the world like Thompson submachine-gun fire. Ibrahim pressed his face to the street and covered his head with his hands.

"Christ," said Sally Conners. "A Thompson gun. It sounds like Belfast used to."

"Belfast without the Guinness," Lucas said.

"Oh, *please,*" she sighed with girlish disdain.

The crowd of Palestinian youths behind them advanced, gathering enthusiasm as they came. One waved a Palestinian flag. Again Lucas was reminded of Gaza.

"Look," he said to the guide, "we've got to get to the Bab al-Hadid. There must be a shorter route than through the streets."

Without raising his head, the guide spoke in a croaking voice. "Over the rooftops," he said. "From Bab al-Nazir."

"But the army will take the rooftops," the English reporter said. "It's the first thing they'll do."

"They'll defend the Jewish Quarter first," Lucas said. "Then they'll occupy the Israeli establishments around the Muslim Quarter. They may take up positions around the digs."

"Over the rooftops," Ibrahim insisted.

"Yes, he's right," Lestrade said. "We can go by rooftops as far as the Haram wall. But the army will take all the buildings that command the wall plaza, the whole upper level there."

"How do we get up there?" Sally Conners asked. "Knock on doors?"

"We follow the *shebab*," Lucas said. "Don't you think?" he asked the guide.

Ibrahim looked into the gloom ahead, rose from his haunches and shouted to the youths who lined the sides of the narrow street. There were no lights on anywhere. Only the helicopter beams that shot by overhead lit the alleys and arches of the Old City.

"*Al-jihad!*" the old guide shouted. "*Al-Haram. Itbah al-Yahud!*"

"*Itbah al-Yahud?*" asked the reporter. "What's that?"

"Don't you speak Arabic?" Lucas asked.

"I do somewhat," Sally Conners said. "But I don't recall the phrase."

"We'll talk about it later," Lucas told her. "It's a patriotic song. Sort of like 'The March of the Men of Harlech' or 'The Wearing of the Green.' "

"What?"

"I'm sorry," Lucas said. "I'm a bit demented by the day's work. It means 'Kill the Jews.' "

"Oh, I see," said Sally Conners.

Someone, a woman, her head thickly covered, opened a door for them and everyone passed through — several dozen of the *shebab,* the guide, Lucas and his reporter colleague, along with Dr. Lestrade. They raced past landings that smelled of tahini and perfume, through someone's bedroom and onto the rooftop. Ibrahim, waving his cane, tried to make a show of leading the way, but the *shebab* raced ahead of him. He looked anxiously around for the foreigners who had contracted to pay him.

"It is this way," he shouted. A helicopter's beam shone out of nothingness and clouds of gas blew from a neighboring roof, the stuff intensifying in seconds from a spice to a reek to a blistering of the sinuses. A rain of gas canisters descended one building away, their cylinders rattling and exploding under the monster staccato of the copter engines.

Lucas took a last look at the stars — it was a cool, clear night — and covered his eyes with his forearm. With a stiff wind from the east, the stuff might blow away. On a second adjoining roof, in the direction of the Haram, the *shebab* were blindsided again. The canisters caught them exposed, dosing the crowd thoroughly and cracking a few skulls and elbows with their weight. The young men moaned and cursed; the helicopter swerved and came back for another pass. Lucas and his party on the rooftop sat tight until the chopper found other prey among the stalls in the al-Quattanin souk.

Ibrahim began to scream in classical Arabic about the day of sorting out and the evil angel Eljib and killing the Jews and the djinn.

"Please, sir," said the English reporter, "may we proceed?"

Struck dumb with wonder and gallantry, he leaned on his cane and bowed, one hand on his heart. A bullet, the real thing, whistled by within two feet of their rooftop position.

"My God," said Sally Conners. "No wonder they kill six people a day in the intifada."

"Six," Lucas explained to her, "is a strong number."

66

ONIA HEARD a noise above her and shined her light on a pair of army boots appearing through a passage that seemed to lead straight up into the ceiling. In the next moment, the wearer of the boots lowered himself through the hole and landed, knees bent, with massive grace right beside her. She turned her light on him, but the man had brought his own. He turned it on her.

It was pointless to run, so she stayed where she was. In the light of the man's torch, she saw that at the statue's feet was a paratrooper's rucksack, looking at first like a packed parachute. But the top flap of the pack was partly open, and beneath it she could make out a complex of colored wires and bulky batteries. As a child of the revolution, Sonia knew a bomb when she saw one.

A group of armed men were letting themselves down the passage through which the first man had come. A few of them landed with the same éclat as their leader, but most were non-professionals and failed to land on their feet.

"Well, you found it, didn't you?" the leader said to Sonia while his men organized themselves. It was Janusz Zimmer.

"Uh-huh," she said. "That's right, man. And I've called Shabak and I've notified the Border Police and they are about to come down on your ass."

"Have you really?" Zimmer asked. "You saw that as the right thing to do?"

"That's right," she said. She was looking around the chamber to see if Fotheringill was still with them, if she could make out any sign of him.

Within seconds there sounded through the chambers a tremendous clash of metal and a tumbling of stones like a wave receding over a rocky shore.

"That's them, mister," Sonia said. "You call it."

Except she did not really believe that it was Shin Bet or the Border Police. She found herself thinking, of all things, about "The Fall of the House of Usher," which she had once read Poe had based on something he had read about an Egyptian temple-tomb situated on an island in a swamp.

"The tunnel's collapsing," one of the men in the group said, without much interest.

"No it's not," Zimmer told him. "You — you are fucking collapsing."

Then came a mighty voice, one without the faintest transcendent quality. It was plainly a police bullhorn. It had two messages, one in Hebrew, the other in English.

Sonia was too astonished to speak.

"Shabak," one of Fotheringill's band said. "She did it."

"She did it," Zimmer said calmly.

"Jew fighting Jew," one of the men in the group said. "Jew killing Jew. This is what we feared."

"No one's killing anyone," Zimmer shouted. "Put your weapons down." He shone the beam around the chamber and called off eight or nine names. "Walk toward the tunnel entrance."

The men hesitated.

Fotheringill appeared behind a flashlight as though he had spirited himself through the wall.

"Do it," he called out in a military manner. "You heard the man."

"How about Lestrade?" Zimmer asked him.

The men he had brought down into the chamber milled about in some confusion.

"Lestrade's provided fer," Fotheringill told him. "We didn't drive him out. But the town's bagged. He'll be with Lucas and the press."

"So you thought you'd pop over?"

"Aye. Thought I might be useful like."

"All of you take cover," Zimmer said to the men who had come down with him. "The army is nearly through. Watch out for ricochets. We don't want any misfortunes."

Most of the men in his company did as they were told.

"We're betrayed," said one of the men. It was the junior-college football coach from New England. "You're a traitor," he told Zimmer. "A Christian — Christians, all of you."

"Not really," Zimmer said. "She's a Sufi. And this gentleman," he said, indicating Fotheringill, "works for me."

"The soldiers of Ahab," the football coach said. "The soldiers of Manasseh." He put the light on Sonia. "The soldiers of our Jezebel here."

"You're the soldiers of Saul," Sonia proclaimed. "And I'm the Witch of Endor, how's that? I think she was black like me. And I can call up the prophet Samuel like she did, and the prophet Samuel would call you traitors against God and the Jewish people and the land of Israel. I come from a long line of rabbis."

Fotheringill laughed. "She's barmy," he told his boss, Zimmer. "But I love her."

67

ODGING searchlights, stones and the odd stray bullet, the crowd of *shebab,* followed by Lucas and Sally Conners and Ibrahim the guide, made their way over the dark rooftops of the Muslim Quarter toward the Bab al-Hadid. Some of the roofs sustained fragrant gardens, some were derelict. There were accordion rails for the protection of children and sometimes lines of broken bottles set in cement, to pierce the flesh of evildoers. The streets below were swarming with an increasingly excited crowd.

Approaching the Bab al-Hadid above a narrow street, they encountered a charge of mounted police who turned a crowd headed for the Haram into a Pamplona-like stampede, with young buckos running before the horses or crowding against doorways. At the end of the street, the mounted police turned smartly to avoid being separated from their own lines and rode back up the same alleyway, administering baton whacks to some of the kids they had missed the first time through. At another point, a force of soldiers had a contingent of *shebab* trapped in an alley and were amusing themselves firing gas canisters into it. Now and again an empty canister would come flying back, but the rioters seemed to have picked themselves an unlucky refuge.

At this point, against Lucas's inchoate advice, the young men with whom they were traversing the rooftops were unable to refrain from tossing everything loose and handy down onto the ranks of soldiers below them. This in turn provoked an enraged charge by a flying squad from the far end of the street, who smashed through the doors of the street-level dwellings and made for the roofs. Everyone scattered, including Lucas and Sally, who were now operating in a kind of uncoordinated alliance, Ibrahim in pursuit of his fee, and Dr.

Lestrade, who obviously preferred not to be the solitary representative of Western Christendom among an angry crowd prepared to drink the wine of paradise.

Not all the soldiers found their way immediately to the rooftops, so it was possible for the four of them to maneuver across several roofs and across the souk on the arching roof that covered its stalls. Lucas had a look over the edge of the first building they came to on the east side of the souk and found it full of soldiers and police, apparently being held in reserve.

For better or worse, they had put the hot side of the riot behind them and were back of the Israeli lines. But in every direction from the lighted vital center the army and police were holding, a huge crowd, partly visible through its own mixed media of homespun light and powerfully audible in its chanting, was pressing dangerously against them. The shots, the rattle of stones and the popping of canisters continued.

Discovering himself where he was, Ibrahim expressed his unhappiness. He was good at being unpleasant — as became a man used to raising his prices after a deal was made — but the talent gave him little comfort at this time and in this place.

"They are destroying the Haram," he declared. "You must pay me."

Sally Conners winced at this non sequitur. Crouched beside a potted pomegranate tree, she searched her fanny pack and came up with about a hundred dollars in shekels.

Ibrahim screeched imprecations.

Lucas gave him three American twenties. Like a baby bird, he chirped for more.

"I don't know if I should let you do that," Sally said. "I hired him."

"Good," Lucas said. "I'm firing him, and it's worth every penny." He turned to Lestrade. "Would you like to give him something?"

"I?" asked Lestrade. "What? What? I give him something?"

Ibrahim immediately homed in on Lestrade. They quarreled in high-flown Arabic until Lucas physically removed the professor from the rooftop. Pushing open a door, they found themselves in a room full of crying children. A dozen, Lucas thought, and not one of them over four years old. They huddled together on huge mattresses placed on the floor.

A woman swathed in layers of cloth was hiding, not very successfully, behind a curtain at one end of the room, ostrich fashion, keeping her face averted. Lucas, Sally and Lestrade headed for the street. They were not far from the Bab al-Hadid. The Border Police squads ran past them, paying no attention. From the roof, Ibrahim hissed down at them like an animated, alienated gargoyle.

"Salman Rushdie is not here!" he croaked malevolently, as though to disappoint them. There was a large Palestinian crowd not far away.

"Do you know where you're going?" Sally Conners asked Lucas.

"The professor here knows," Lucas told her.

Suddenly, they knew not how, the Palestinian crowd had broken through and they were now part of it. The mob's purpose seemed to be to penetrate the barriers at the Bab al-Hadid, make an end run around the police lines and hurl itself against the Haram wall.

In a burst of youthful athleticism, Sally Conners took off with the rioters. Lucas, with Lestrade following, raced after her. Sally had a volatile effect on the mob. Some of the young men looked delighted with her, others infuriated, many appeared to register both reactions, by turn or in combination. In any case, the Palestinian charge was contained by soldiers who waded into it, using their rifle butts liberally.

Lestrade, Lucas and Sally were shoved to one side. Lucas cowered, protecting his head with his arms. Lestrade, breathless, panted and crossed himself. Sally Conners stood tall, like Nurse Edith Cavell before the Hun, ready to take her medicine.

An angry officer accompanied by two troopers approached them. Perhaps because of Sally, no blows were struck.

"Who are you? Where do you think you're going?"

Farther down the street, protected by metal barricades and under massive white lights, soldiers were operating Michigan loaders under the guidance of gray-haired men in civilian clothes. They seemed to be digging up the cobbled street close to the Haram wall.

"Press," Lucas said.

"Press? You're engaging in disorder. I saw you. Staging riots to write about?"

Then the officer stalked off, leaving them in custody of the two soldiers, who stared at them in slack-jawed menace. In a moment, the officer returned with a civilian.

"No press here!" the civilian declared. "The area is closed. How did you get here in the first place?"

The officer spoke to him in Hebrew.

"You led that crowd in here. You could be responsible for deaths. You're under arrest."

"Wait," Lucas said. "Is there a bomb under the Temple Mount?"

The Shabak man looked at him closely. "Who told you this?"

"We think there is," Lucas said. "This man," he said, indicating Lestrade, "is an archeologist. He thinks he knows where it's planted."

The representative of Shin Bet looked doubtfully at Lestrade.

"Well," Lestrade said. "I've an idea."

"An idea," the Shin Bet agent repeated.

"A good idea," Lestrade said.

"Basically," Lucas told them helpfully, "he knows where the thing is. He can take you to it."

"Well, yes," Lestrade said. "The chamber of Sabazios. That would be my guess."

The Shabak man went away without a word.

"That is all nonsense, isn't it?" Sally Conners asked. "About Salman Rushdie?"

"I have to tell you," Lucas said, "I don't see him."

"Do you really know where there's a bomb under the Temple Mount?" she asked Lestrade.

"Yes, I think so," the professor said.

"Crikey," said Sally Conners. As discreetly as possible, she hugged herself with joy.

68

THE BOMB that lay at the feet of Sabazios was one that looked vaguely familiar to Sonia. She once had a boyfriend, a dropout from Long Beach State and a Maoist militant, who had quit school to organize the shipyard workers at the San Diego Navy Yard. At the time, it had become the most radical and Maoist-influenced shipyard in the country. But Bob Kellerman, the militant, had given it all up for nitrous oxide and drowned in his own bathtub.

Bob Kellerman had showed her how bombs were made, with gelignite and acid batteries and telephone wire. She had sat together with several other adepts to assist in, or at least to watch, the process, and somehow they had not blown themselves to kingdom come like the comrades in Greenwich Village some years earlier.

It was a similar bomb. Its timer was an alarm clock that did not show the correct time.

"Who made the device?" she asked Fotheringill.

"Never mind," Zimmer said.

"And the statue is Sabazios?"

"Correct."

"So you thought that was a good place to put it," she said. "One of the American *chaverim* make it? Ex-cop or something?"

"Doesn't matter now, does it?" Zimmer looked at the clock timer in the rucksack.

The sound of earth-moving machines grew louder and closer. Shots were fired inside the foundation, the reports echoing endlessly. Something that might have been a tear-gas canister rattled over the stone.

Zimmer took Sonia by the arm and led her in the direction of the noise. Fotheringill was crouched with his Galil, covering the men in the chamber.

"What about the bomb squad?" Sonia asked. "What about the soldiers who come in here?"

"What about the Temple rising again?" Zimmer said. "Don't worry about a thing."

He shouted something in Hebrew down the tunnel. The noises stopped abruptly, all at once. Zimmer shouted again.

In the next few seconds the chamber was full of light and helmeted policemen. The men who had come down with Zimmer backed away from their piled weapons. Then Sonia saw Lestrade and Lucas in the glare of floodlights.

"This is the place," Lestrade said. "Now for God's sake, don't harm that statue."

"Get back!" the soldiers ordered. They shoved Lucas and Lestrade aside and began to shout at Sonia and Zimmer's captured band.

Lucas saw Fotheringill in a shaft of light.

"Jesus," he said. "I remember it."

> "*Rillons, Rillettes,* they taste the same,
>   And would by any other name,
>   And are, if I may risk a joke,
>   Alike as two pigs in a poke."

"What the bloody hell are you talking about?" Sally Conners asked him.

Lucas was entranced:

> "The dishes are the same, and yet
>   While Tours provides the best *Rillettes*
>   The best *Rillons* are made in Blois."

"Fotheringill!" he called. "Did you get that?"

But then he, and Sonia, saw that Zimmer and Fotheringill were gone, vanished from the chamber, and though she probed every corner with her feeble light, there was no sign of them. What she did see, just before turning off the redundant flashlight, was the football coach making a run for the pile of weapons.

One of the soldiers took off to intercept him. Before the soldier could stop him, the coach seized an Uzi, pointed it at Sabazios's feet and, diving forward, fired a burst into the packed rucksack.

There was a dazzling eruption of white flame, and the room filled with chemical smoke. Everyone hit the deck. When the flash came, it mocked the soldiers' lights and blinded everyone.

69

AFTER AN AMOUNT of time he could not judge or measure, Raziel came to consciousness on Sonia's sofa. He got to his feet, staggering among her photographs and Kilim rugs. It was still night. When he went into De Kuff's room, he found it empty.

Raziel's footing was unsteady. Sometimes things seemed in motion on the edge of vision, and he was not always completely certain what room he was in. But eventually he was straight enough to determine that the old man had truly taken off, simply put his covers aside and gone. He would be making for the Old City, Raziel thought. For the Bethesda Pool, the source of prophecy for him. It was the night of the bomb, of the unmaking of all their plans.

Raziel composed himself to the point where he could struggle to a public phone at a bus kiosk near the railroad station. He took a token from his pocket and called a taxi. He did not tell the dispatcher where he wanted to go. Over the shoulder of Mount Zion, he could see fires reflected in the sky and hear distant sirens and the report of weaponry. He stood beside the enclosed kiosk and stared at the lighted sky. Drivers passing on the road slowed their vehicles to look at him in suspicion and dread.

The taxi that arrived was driven by a sullen man in his twenties with a fake silk shirt, open at the neck to show his chest hair and the variety of gold-colored chains around his neck. He did not care for the appearance of his fare, and when Raziel opened the door and climbed in beside him he recoiled as though from an assault.

As they drove downtown, the driver peered fearfully at the agitated Jewish crowds in the streets. It was as if he were lost in his own city. As it happened, it was not his city: he was a Gentile from Romania.

"I would like to go to the Lions' Gate," Raziel told him.

The Romanian volubly refused. When Raziel realized that his driver's mind was not about to be changed, he got out of the taxi and set out on foot for the Old City.

At the Jaffa Gate, things seemed less tense than elsewhere. The security forces were in control there, although it was easy to hear the shots and cries and rattling canisters in other parts of the Old City.

Edging along the army's lines on David Street, he looked for a place where instinct might promise him an easy crossing. He found a few unconfident-looking young soldiers near the Muristan and showed them his American passport and let them search him. The soldiers permitted him to proceed into the deserted quarter of market cafés.

As he hurried toward the Pool, army patrols and jeeps passed him from time to time. The soldiers bellowed at him to step aside, get out of the way, stay off the street. But the soldiers were preoccupied with a fiery struggle close by that he could not see.

He could sense the inhabitants of the Christian Quarter huddled behind their massive doors and dark barred windows. There were people on the rooftops too. Several shouted down at him. Threats, warnings.

Approaching the end of the Via Dolorosa, almost at the Lions' Gate, he saw a noisy milling crowd of Palestinians. A line of policemen and soldiers stood between them and the gate. Raziel found that he had put himself on the inside: the crowd stood between him and the gate and the Jewish troops that held it.

Above the shouting, he heard a voice he knew. It was the voice of Adam De Kuff speaking from the upper quadrant of his interior universe, strong, unafraid, joyful, thoroughly delusional. Raziel shouldered his way through ranks of astonished Palestinians until he saw the man himself.

The gates to the Pool and the courtyard in front of St. Anne's Church had been forced open. De Kuff and the crowd that surrounded him all stood within it. About halfway between the crusader church and the ruined temple of Serapis, De Kuff, standing on a cement bench, addressed the enraged Palestinians.

He wore what looked like an army jacket that fitted him so badly its cuffs stopped a little past his elbows. He had hugely baggy army trousers and untied muddy boots whose laces coiled around his ankles and twisted underfoot as he shuffled passionately from one end of the bench to the other like a dancing bear. There was a kippa on his head and a white scarf tied around his forehead like a turban and he crooned at the top of his voice.

The watching Palestinians stared as though De Kuff represented a spectacle beyond imagining. All of them were men, and there were more than a hundred. Some were laughing. Others occasionally shouted at him in anger. A few seemed frozen in cold rage.

From the army line, a policeman with a bullhorn was saying something, amplified in Arabic. Overhead, a helicopter scattered its whirling lights. Because of the angle of the walls of the adjoining madrasah and the smashed gates of the church courtyard, De Kuff in the small plaza was aslant the line of vision of the soldiers and police assembled nearer the city gate.

Raziel kept trying to force his way closer to the old man. He had the notion of taking him away from there, before the thing failed utterly, before all spells and mercies were suspended, before whatever grace that had touched their pilgrimage was withdrawn and the violence and raw holiness of the place overwhelmed everyone.

The holiness was in fact gathering to strike. A man with the white turban of the *haj,* a turban like the one De Kuff's scarf might be thought to mock, came forward, beside himself.

"Perish the hands of the Father of Flame," cried the *haji,* in a language neither De Kuff nor Raziel could comprehend. "Perish he!"

De Kuff himself understood only that he was in the place he knew and loved best, the scene of his successes, the ancient Serapion and Pool of Israel. All that day he had been trying to reach the souls within himself as they weaved in and out of his consciousness. He had begun to think that everything he had ever believed about soul and mind was wrong. There was no way to exercise control.

But there at the Fountain, his souls were manifest and his heart was full, and in the completeness of his joy he had no choice but to tell about it. It was necessary to tell everyone, anyone, no matter how distressed or distracted they might be by politics or by the illusions of separateness and exile that burdened everyone. He felt elected and protected by God, ready to support the Ark in the holiest of places. He used the metaphors that were employed in this city, although, in a way, it might have been anywhere.

"Call me as you like," he explained to the angry crowd. "I am the twelfth imam. I am the Bab al-Ulema. I am Jesus, Yeshu, Issa. I am the Mahdi. I am Moshiach. I have come to restore the world. I am all of you. I am no one."

There were screams of terrible passion. "Perish he! Death! *Itbah al-Yahud!*"

Some soldiers had seen him, and a flying squad from the police lines set out, using batons and rifle butts as deemed necessary to rescue him. The squad advanced as far as the plaza gate but was stalled by the crush there and retreated. A few onlookers were left lying on the ground. There were cries of outrage and the men in the crowd closest to De Kuff seemed to blame him. People began to throw stones.

"Death to the blasphemer!"

De Kuff opened his arms to them. For a moment those who were advancing on him stopped. Raziel, shouting, shoving, tried to get through.

"You don't have to listen," Raziel said to the crowd. "It's all over. Rev," he shouted to De Kuff, "it's all over! Another time, man. Another soul. Another street."

The men who were taking hold of De Kuff, pulling him down as he tottered on his bench, also laid hands on Raziel.

"Another day!" Raziel told them. "Another mountain!"

The soldiers near the gate attempted a second charge. Savage as it was, lay about them as they did, they could not break through and penetrate the crowd to extract De Kuff and Raziel.

Then a few reserve soldiers fired live rounds. Because the area around the Fountain was Christian property, the security forces had stayed away from it at first and it belonged, for the moment, to the crowd.

"I tell you," De Kuff informed them in his restrained Louisiana drawl. "That all was once One and will be and has always remained so. That God is One. And faith in Him is One. And all belief is One. And all believers in Him, regardless of sect, are One. Only the human heart divides. So it is written.

"See? Do you see?" De Kuff asked the men who were pulling him down. "Everyone's waiting. And the separateness of things is false."

He went on declaiming, using the images, the reversals, the metaphors everyone knew, expounding the souls, raising their voices, until the great holiness turned to fire and he lost consciousness.

70

ZIMMER WENT to a former kibbutz in the desert for his debriefing, a collection of sand-colored cement rectangles near the nuclear base at Dimona. On the drive down, Fotheringill had asked him, "Who's debriefing who then?"

"Good question," Zimmer said.

The kibbutz had been converted into air force housing, equally divided between civilian technicians and their families and quarters for serving officers. The military sentries at the wire perimeter had been instructed to expect them.

Fotheringill left Zimmer off in front of the largest building and drove on to Dimona for a decent lager. Zimmer braved the fierce afternoon sun in the same shapeless seersucker suit he had worn as a reporter in central Africa, along with a white cotton shirt, a Yucatecan straw hat and dark glasses. He made his way inside the building to a lounge area, air conditioned against the desert heat, a kind of semi-civilian day room that occupants of the building could hire for special occasions, like birthday or promotion parties.

A security man in the hallway outside it asked Zimmer to remove his sunglasses, looked him over in a brusque manner before letting him pass. Two men were sitting on a sun-faded sofa in the dusty, joyless room. They both stood up when Zimmer entered and shook hands.

"Something to drink?" one said. He was a bald, squat man with a hard, pitted face. He wore khaki shorts and a short-sleeved shirt of the same color and sandals with beige socks.

"Water," Zimmer said.

The man who had asked took a tray from the day room's half-sized refrigerator. On it were two liter bottles of still water and a plastic dish of hummus and another of peppers and cucumbers and some Arab bread.

"You have to drink water constantly down here," the man observed. "Four gallons a day, according to Shaviv."

"Six," Shaviv, the second man, said. "Even if you're sedentary like myself."

Naphtali Shaviv was tall and thin, light-haired, with high cheekbones and a prominent nose, which looked as though he had once broken it boxing. The man who had offered the drink was Avram Lind, the former cabinet minister.

Janusz Zimmer accepted his glass of water and sat down.

"So," he asked. "Success?"

Lind started to answer. Shaviv interrupted him. "Survival. Yossi resigned. We'll hear it on the evening news."

"I'm delighted," Zimmer said. "I presume this constitutes your return to public life."

"The PM," Lind said, "has been good enough to ask me to take my former position in the cabinet. He was very sporting, as the English would say. A jolly good sport."

They all laughed quietly.

"The old man was sweating, let me tell you," Naphtali Shaviv said. He was wearing a shirt with a slim blue tie, one that he had bought in the early sixties in Stockholm. Zimmer, taking note of it, could imagine him buying six identical ties then and wearing them for the rest of his life. "You could hear him sweat on the telephone."

"It's possible to hear people sweat," Zimmer said. "Sometimes you can't see any sweat, but you can hear it."

"I like listening to the PM sweat," Lind said. "I'm not so sporting."

"I find it distressing," Shaviv said.

"Yah, well, you're a bureaucrat," Lind told him. "And let me tell you, neither is Yossi Zhidov sporting! He's beside himself, that *paskudnyak*. Slapping his poor Swiss wife. Brutalizing his little Aryan kiddies. Furious, the shmuck."

"I'm not being polite when I say I'm delighted," Shaviv told them.

Zimmer nodded. "No doubt it had to be done. But it was audacious."

"Well," said Shaviv, "*L'audace, toujours*. You did well, Pan Zimmer. Hats off to you."

"Hear, hear!" said Avram Lind.

Both Avram Lind and Naphtali Shaviv had been fighter pilots before taking up their careers in Mossad. Lind's enemies in the cabinet and in his own ministry had forced his resignation the previous spring, but they had not been able to ditch Shaviv, a permanent undersecretary and Avram Lind's wing man in the Yom Kippur War. So Lind had been able to use the resources of the intelligence liaison force in his former ministry to carry out the operation.

Thus they had acquired the services of Janusz Zimmer. Yossi Zhidov, who had replaced Lind for such a surprisingly short time, had been warned by his supporters about a Mossad–air force Mafia in the ministry. But he had not been able to do anything about it.

"The PM is going to practice damage control," Shaviv said. "So we know how this whole thing is going to be presented to the press."

Shaviv, in his understated way, refrained from saying that he himself was handling public relations for the prime minister. In handling the matter, he would be able to control what was said or not said publicly about Lind's organizing of the bomb-plot sting and Zimmer's role in it and all the rest.

"No one believes us anyway," Lind said. "They're all cynical bastards."

"Yes," said Shaviv, "so they don't deserve too much information. Information corrupts."

"Speaking of which," Zimmer said, "I have an American friend writing a book. The book is about religious mania in the country and cults and so on, but he was very close to some of the people we . . ." He stopped and sought an appropriate term for the individuals who had been manipulated.

"Employed," Shaviv suggested.

"He was close to some of the people we employed. No doubt his book will deal with these events. We can use him to float a few truths, as it were. In time future."

"You don't want to discourage him from writing his book?"

"I respectfully submit," Zimmer said, "that through it we can refer discreetly to our accomplishments. For our friends' benefit. You can tell me which accomplishments, and I'll whisper in his ear."

"Our accomplishments," Lind said reflectively. "*Chaver* Shaviv, what would you say were our accomplishments?"

"Ah," said Shaviv, "well, let us see." He stood up, walked to the window and began counting off on his fingers. His pale eyes reflected the coppery landscape beyond the tinted glass.

"Accomplishment one: you, *Chaver* Lind, are restored to the service of the state."

Lind bowed and interrupted. "Not so important," he said, mocking modesty.

"Accomplishment two: we set the Jewish undergrounds, the Temple bombers, back five years." He thought about it for a moment. "Well, three years."

"Two," Zimmer said.

Shaviv continued enumerating accomplishments.

"We flushed out the most violent elements in the Muslim Brotherhood and Hamas, forced them into a premature move. We provided a reason to legislate against the cults and the Christian missionaries. Which will please certain of the rabbis, whose support we shall need one day.

"We hurt the elements here who were cooperating with the American religious right. We demonstrated, I think, that such a policy has a downside. We penetrated the Colombian connection and we have a clearer understanding of how Yossi was using the dope smugglers. These are all good things."

"And the other side of the ledger?" Lind asked. "The losses?"

"Acceptable," Zimmer said. "We're not responsible for the death of that boy in the Gaza Strip. He was not a casualty of this operation. The terrorists got what they deserved.

"And the Communists — well, they would understand. We sent them a message that they won't be needed, that their day is over and that the lives of our people are extremely important to us. Whereas I'm sure they realize that . . . how does the movie line go? The problems of two little people don't amount to a hill of beans in this crazy world. They were under their own discipline. Died with their boots on. Line of duty. So forth. And that woman had no business here."

"As always," Shaviv said, "the American dimension is sensitive."

"I certainly hope no one holds me responsible for the death of any Americans," Zimmer said. "The police made repeated attempts to get that De Kuff fellow out. We still don't know how he turned up in there. We tried to look out for him."

"How's young Melker?" Shaviv asked.

"Still in a coma," Zimmer said. "But he was using heroin that day. So we have concluded that his coma . . ." He shrugged.

"Is the result of a drug overdose?" Shaviv suggested.

"Exactly," said Zimmer. "We're in touch with the U.S. embassy. The parents may be coming over."

"Sad," said Lind.

"How does he look?" Shaviv asked.

"Like he was beaten," Zimmer told him. "The way users often end up looking."

Shaviv sighed. "It *is* sad. A life."

Zimmer said nothing more. He had not cared for Raziel.

"I suppose," Lind said to him after a while, "you'll want to be getting back to town."

"Yes," said Janusz Zimmer.

They had the security man telephone the café in Dimona where Fotheringill had gone and arrange for him to be readmitted. Eventually, they saw the Scotsman and his jeep outside.

"Where on earth," Shaviv asked, peering through the window, "did you acquire that preposterous person?"

"Mr. Fotheringill?" Zimmer smiled slightly. "Mr. Fotheringill and I met in Africa. We always work together. Especially when the operation is . . . unofficial. The Englishman — you know, Lestrade, the *momzer* — he was sure Fotheringill was going to kill him."

"I don't blame him," Shaviv said.

The route back through the desert lay between two stark reefs of iron-spined mountains. As they drove, Zimmer turned his gaze from one range to the other, from the granite massif in the west to the sandstone hills in the east. The vast fateful landscape, which he had seen only once or twice before, inclined him toward recall.

At sixteen — he might even have been fifteen — he had been a fighter with the Polish Communist irregulars during the time of chaos that followed the war. He could remember arriving in Zielce just after the pogroms of 1947, working with the ex-*résistants* of the Bricah, the Zionist group that organized displaced persons for the journey to Palestine. In those days, the Joint Distribution Committee and the Bricah men and the Communist fighters were close. Ben Gurion's Socialists had not yet purged Communists from the Jewish intelligence services.

In the winter of 1947, he had stood guard at the bridge that the Bricah had built over the Oder to carry DPs into Czechoslovakia, and across it into Austria, bound for what would become Israel. But he had never gone along. Wearing his red and white guerrilla armband, he had looked on as columns of weary survivors passed. They had glanced at him, just another Polack as far as they could see, as they hastened to wipe the dust of Central Europe from their shoes.

He had stayed behind and tried to remake the world, watching his fellow operatives drown their apostasy in vodka. He ended up traveling endlessly, running the kinds of errands the Communists ran for their brutal, corrupt creatures in the Third World, attempting to help them prevail over the corrupt, brutal creatures of the Americans.

If he had gone to Israel then, of course, his life would have been different. He would have cast off ideology sooner. He might have occupied the space where Lind and Shaviv now thrived. Instead of being what he had always been, a secret agent, a striker behind the scenes, a representative of that Israel which the country preferred the world to know little about. To know just enough about to strike a little caution in the anti-Semitic heart.

Before long, he thought, despite his best efforts, the underground would succeed in destroying the mosques, in beginning the war that would remove the Arabs. Out of it would come a different Israel. It would be less American. It might just partake of the purity of purpose that had been lost.

And though it was his job to abort that process, he could not help speculating on what hope such a purifying wind might bring. How it might make the Land the singular place it had been meant to be. And just as he could not keep himself from sympathizing, in a certain way, with the Communists, neither could he keep from feeling a bit the same about Rabbi Miller and the football coach and the others who were ready to subsume their lives in the Cause.

Lind and Shaviv and the other politicians in the papers every day — the prime minister, Sharon, Netanyahu — so many of them were like the men who had run Eastern and Central Europe between the wars. The men around Colonel Beck and King Carol and Admiral Horthy — mediocre opportunists, living for their foxes' portion. How difficult it was not to require something more. But, he thought, I am getting old.

"Everything go all right, squire?" Fotheringill asked. "Did they appreciate us, do ye think?"

"I don't think they appreciate us, Ian. But I'm sure we'll be paid."

They would be paid. Fotheringill in Swiss francs, he himself in various complicated ways of his own devising, ways in which money did not necessarily feature. He had enough, he thought.

He had secreted the hand of Sabazios in the nominal custody of a few museum officials whose fortunes he controlled. In fact, the piece was his to dispose of.

As a part of the national patrimony, Zimmer thought, it might be pressed into service, both in his own and the state's behalf. For Zimmer, there was no serious conflict of interest.

For security purposes, he reasoned, the thing to do would be to coat the original with plaster and paint it so that it would resemble a plaster cast. Then it would be possible to produce several actual casts. Properly weighted, they would be superficially indistinguishable from the original. As trade items and objects of desire, such things might prove infinitely useful. The hand and its imitations might touch off a frenzy among collectors from Cairo to California.

The desert sun began to cast its light aslant the distant mountains. The worst of the day's heat was easing, reluctantly, the glare giving way. Just as the underground would one day destroy the Haram, Zimmer thought, one day the Muslims would assemble a nuclear bomb in America. That particular stork would come home to roost. And who knew what might follow? No doubt, in the long run, the Muslims too might feel their certainty, their sense of purpose, flagging.

Before long it would not matter. He might go and live in Africa. A man might acquire some Italian fascist's former villa in the Ethiopian highlands. Walk in the cool of the morning. Rest under thorn trees hidden from the blaze of noon, watch the sunsets, listen for lions.

"The airport, squire?" Fotheringill asked.

Zimmer's single traveling bag was packed in the back of the jeep. He picked up a plastic bag from under his seat, riffled through the dozen passports he kept there and selected one, Canadian, that listed his place of birth as Vilnius and showed the date of his naturalization. Several men were waiting at different ports of entry to take charge of the jeep and his identity equipment.

"Allenby Bridge," Zimmer said. "Over Jordan."

71

OVERLOOKING THE Valley of Hinnom and the Old City walls was an outdoor restaurant run by secular Jews from Romania. It was where Lucas had often stopped with Tsililla when they went to movies at the Cinematheque down the street. Tsililla especially liked going to movies on Friday nights so she could give the finger to the *haredim* who protested hysterically outside the movie house, howling over the violation of Shabbat.

More than once she had come close to getting them both torn to Orphean shreds by giant bearded berserkers. After they had succeeded in passing unhurt through the ranks of demonstrators, she invariably led him to a table at the Romanian joint, whence the caterwauling pious thugs could follow them. She would choose a table as close to the sidewalk as possible so she could give the *haredim* the finger again.

It was this place, because of its wonted quiet on weekdays and its view of the city, that Lucas chose for his afternoon meeting with Faith Melker, Raziel's mother.

Mrs. Melker was a handsome woman with kind brown eyes that beautifully bespoke her grief. She was superbly coiffed, her hair jet black and silver. She wore a finely cut khaki suit with simple gold jewelry. There was about her and her outfit a self-imposed severity, as though she had restrained her striking good looks out of mourning. Looking at her, Lucas could see the source of Raziel's passion and attractiveness. She also reminded him a bit of his father's wife.

"A very nice young woman at the consulate here suggested I talk to you, Mr. Lucas. I'm afraid I've forgotten her name. Is it Miss Chin?"

"Yes," Lucas said. "Sylvia Chin."

"It was good of you to take the time to see me. With the situation as it is, you must be very busy."

"I'm glad to, Mrs. Melker. And I'm very sorry about Raziel." She looked at him uncomprehending. "About Ralph, I mean." He was at the point of explaining the name thing. Then he thought better of it.

"Sometimes I think he can hear me," she told Lucas. "Sometimes I think he responds. He moves his fingers."

Her pain was hard for him to bear, underlined as it was by her cool courage. Her brilliant, funny, multitalented son was lost to her, walled off within his own darkened brain.

"So many families," Lucas said, "have been hurt by drugs." He immediately regretted the banality.

"I try to remember," she said, in kind, "that we're not alone in this. That among the less fortunate in our country so many others have gone through the same thing."

Well, Lucas thought, she was a politician's wife. But there was no question of her sincerity, her generosity in bereavement. He liked her very much. She made him wish he felt sorrier for Raziel.

"With someone as talented and intelligent," Lucas said, "I mean, the more talented and intelligent someone is, the greater the loss."

As if she needed him to tell her. He could, he thought, hardly blame Sylvia for passing the buck. But Faith Melker was nobody's *freier*, as they said in country, nobody's fool. A Detroit girl, even one so gently reared, would presumably waste little time before sensing a cover-up.

The American Presence, the Israeli government and the unknown conspirators behind the events of the previous days had a mutual interest in keeping Faith Melker from tasting of the apple, maintaining her in a state of grace. Somewhere, in letters of fire, was written a narrative of good and evil it was important to all of them that Mrs. Melker not behold.

No one wanted Mr. Melker — the former ambassador, the congressman — arriving at Lod in a state of outraged curiosity. Moreover, Lucas thought, it was just as well they knew the minimum. For everyone, even themselves. Or at least that was the way many of those involved would see it.

His own relations with her would be somewhat different, at least if he planned to persist with the book. They would be meeting again, inevitably exchanging information. At some point, to gain her goodwill, he would have to offer certain insights. He had reason to believe that more of the nature of the story would be revealed to him in the future. He would come to possess information that would require considerable discretion in handling.

Discretion was not his strong point, not one of his native virtues. He had blown the Grenada story for that reason.

"We knew that Ralph had been having problems with drugs," Mrs. Melker said.

"He was" — Lucas hastened to correct himself — "he's a seeker. After absolutes. Sometimes that will do it."

"You knew him well," she asked, "didn't you?"

A difficult question. Difficult to know the answer to it. Problematic in terms of the answer's effect.

"I only knew him a short time," Lucas said. "But I was impressed with his desire for faith. I think the drugs sidetracked something much greater. A much greater yearning."

"Are you Jewish, Mr. Lucas?"

Lucas began to stammer. "B-by background," he succeeded in saying. "Partly. But I wasn't raised in the Jewish faith."

"I see," she said, and gave him a reassuring smile. Then her face darkened with grief. Years overtook it.

"We thought with him here . . . he might be less tempted. To extreme behavior."

Wrong, Lucas thought. Not tempted to extreme behavior here? Here, in the center of the world, where earth touches heaven? Where the destiny of man was written, where words of fire were made flesh, where prophecy uttered in remote millennia determined the morning? In the place whence all we knew of God absconded, promised return, pretended return, promised messengers, whispered messages? Where the invisible wrote fate on stone? Eternally messages, promises. Next year. In the beginning.

Where what was above met what was below, where that which was before met that which was to come. The garden of marble fountains where death, madness, heresy and salvation were all to be found. Less tempted to extreme behavior here?

"Of course," he said.

72

ON A NIGHT soon after his talk with Mrs. Melker, Lucas held his promised meeting with Basil Thomas. This time they did not patronize Fink's, Lucas's and Thomas's favorite spot in town. Instead, they met at a hole-in-the-wall café along Hebron Road, between the Egged depot and the Ramat Rahel kibbutz. It was too warm even for Thomas to wear his leather coat, and he seemed very nervous.

"I have been asked to tell you," Thomas said, as though reciting from memory, "that if you do not act indiscreetly, interesting information may emerge over time. I have been asked to say that it will be information you may use in a book-length project. I have been asked also to say that it is suggested you make plans to leave the country for a considerable period. You will be advised when a return visit is advisable, if your research requires one."

"Am I correct in assuming," Lucas asked, "that the source of your information is no longer the organization whose proposition you offered me before?"

Thomas looked at him dully. Though he wore only a white sport shirt, the big man was perspiring heavily. Then he nodded in the affirmative. Perhaps, Lucas thought, he was wearing a wire. Lucas found the idea of such elaborate, high-tech precautions unlikely, but the notion was daunting. Moreover, Thomas was damp enough to electrocute himself.

"Am I also correct," Lucas asked, "in thinking that the members of that organization . . ."

Thomas began to shake his head frantically, indicating the inadvisability of such a question.

"That that organization no longer exists?"

Basil Thomas then assumed an attitude of extreme frustration, the frustration of a dealer in information, a dealer-connoisseur, attempting to keep his disclosures within the limit of instructions. He made a slightly equivocal gesture with his hands and then said, "Yes."

"Have there been arrests?"

Basil Thomas nodded slowly.

"Will the arrests be announced?"

Thomas then relaxed and wiped his brow and looked at his watch.

"So late," he said. "Forgive me." He stood up and walked out of the café, saying nothing about being paid for his tale-bearing, only leaving Lucas to pay the check.

The next afternoon, when Lucas had packed everyone's belongings at the bungalow in Ein Kerem, he held a brief afternoon's entertainment for Ernest Gross and Dr. Obermann. He served vodka, mineral water and lemonade, along with crackers and small wedges of wrapped French cheese.

"Did you have your meeting with Thomas?" Ernest asked him.

"I did," Lucas said. "He doesn't seem to be speaking for the underground any longer. He's speaking for elements inside the government."

Ernest looked troubled.

"And are we still in business?" Obermann asked.

"Apparently," Lucas told him, "we're still in business. Whoever they are, they seem to want to use us as a conduit."

"As a control," Ernest Gross said. "Like releasing water from a reservoir into a wadi. Shaping the narrative."

"I admit it's a little humiliating," Lucas said. "But it's all we have. Also, they want me out of the country for now."

"Presumably you have enough to keep you busy," Obermann said. He brightened immediately. "Look what I have here. Pictures from the excavation." He went into his briefcase and removed a box of slides and a hand projector. "Just take a look."

"How did you get them?" Ernest asked.

"Aha!" said Dr. Obermann, blooming with self-satisfaction. "Aha!"

"Never mind aha," Lucas said. "How did you?"

"My comrade in the reserves is with the Israel Museum," Obermann said. "My comrade and patient. While they're sorting it out, they're having some archeologists have a look at Sabazios's chamber. Everyone's in uniform, and the Golani are posted all around, so it just looks like part of the investigation. I got these copies from him."

Lucas held the hand projector so that he and Ernest could both view the slides. They showed a series of frescoes on the walls at the top of the chamber that Lucas had been too preoccupied to notice that night. There were also several slides of the statue of Sabazios and of a disembodied hand, its fingers raised in a gesture of benediction. Obermann stood behind his friends and offered commentary.

"The hand is the palm of the lord Sabazios, and the Jewish syncretists knew him as Theos Hypostasis, or the Almighty, or Sabazios Sabaoth. In his mystery cult, he was united with Zeus and Persephone, or with Hermes Trismegistus and Isis. Alone, he was the Lord of Hosts."

Fascinated, Lucas fed the slides into the viewer.

"At the ceremonies in his honor, bread and wine were consumed. The blessing symbolized the Trinity and became the *Benedicta Latina*. His cult was absorbed either into Gnosticism or into Christianity. Essenes, Theraputae, Sabazians, they were all there at the beginning. He's wearing a Phrygian cap, by the way, because he was once a Phrygian god, and Jews from Phrygia and Armenia probably brought him to Jerusalem."

One of the frescoes showed a charioteer driving a quadriga across the sky. A second chariot followed, that one full of symbols of the *merkabah* of Ezekiel.

"Can this have been part of the Temple?" Lucas asked.

"It would have been a very secret, unofficial part," Obermann said. "But, as in the Bible, people were always grafting their own favorite cults onto the body of the national religion. *Hammot*, the questionable shrines were called. The whole series of rooms leading to the chamber was a classic labyrinth. You could get well and truly lost in it."

"How appropriate," Lucas said, changing slides.

"It looks like something from the early Christian era," Obermann said. "So it was probably built before 70 C.E. by Gnostic *minim*."

"Interesting," Lucas said, "about the bread and wine."

"Suggests something, no?" Obermann asked. "Of course, it's possible it was built in the ruins during the Sassanid occupation, but that's less likely."

The next group of slides portrayed things astronomical.

Obermann reached around Lucas's head to point with his finger. "The sun," he told them, "the greater light. Around it, the constellations of the zodiac with their Hebrew names. Around them *tekuphot*, human figures representing the seasons of the year. Also the Dioscuri. There's a synagogue in Chorazin with the same figures."

The next picture looked to Lucas like a communion feast.

"Is this . . . ?"

"It's a communion feast," Obermann said. "Hermes Trismegistus is there. Also Alcestis and the archangel Gabriel."

"Unbelievable," Lucas said.

"Something for everyone," said Obermann.

"And who were the people who worshiped here?" Lucas asked. "Were they Jews?"

"Some yes, some no. Gentiles in search of monotheism, Jews trying to ease the austerity of the *mitzvot*. Or, if you like, attempting to universalize the Law."

"The dream," Lucas said.

"The New Age dreamers of their time," said Obermann. "People who had lost their confidence, who needed to be saved. And in their labyrinths," he said with a flourish, "Christianity was born."

Lucas saw him as practicing for the television special.

"The believers," he went on, "probably became Christians or Gnostics or both."

"Whose idea was it to plant the fake bomb there?" Ernest asked.

"It's the ideal place," Obermann said. "As a protest against *hammot*, against idolatry. Against religious tourism, you might say. And I'm sure the structural dynamics were favorable. The question is, who found it? The Temple builders and their underground? Or the ones who beat them to it?"

"Did you see the paper?" Ernest Gross asked. "The cabinet change? Zhidov out, Lind back in?"

"I did," said Lucas. "Do you think that's all it was about? That whole con game? Complete with fake explosion?"

"Not entirely," Ernest said. "I think there was probably a real bomb plot — maybe a couple of bomb plots — that was penetrated by Shabak or some ad hoc outfit. Maybe they suddenly couldn't keep track, the way they lost control of Hamas.

"They must have thought unless they preempted it and brought in the major players, a bomb would really go off. So they had to do what they do with the Arabs. Fight fire with fire. And Lind, who is a master operator, could conceivably have used it to his advantage. We'll probably never know. But maybe," Ernest said to Lucas, "someday you'll get to meet Avram Lind."

"I can't wait," Lucas said.

"The problem is," said Ernest, "the Palestinians will be convinced beyond a shadow of a doubt that there really was a bomb. The way they dozed it, it *looks* like a bloody bomb. Presently people will start remembering an explosion they never heard."

"I remember an explosion," Lucas said.

"Was there one?" Ernest asked.

"No," said Lucas. "I don't think so."

"Exactly," Ernest said. "Presently the Europeans will all be sure we did it. With the help of the CIA. The French. The Scandinavians."

"But you didn't," said Lucas. "Obermann and I will say that."

"Good luck," Ernest said. "A couple of Jews."

Dr. Obermann put his slides away.

"You know," he told Lucas, "I met Mrs. Melker the other day."

"I thought she'd look you up. Any change in Razz's condition?"

Obermann shook his head. "But what a beautiful woman," he said. "I'd love to see more of her. Perhaps I will."

Lucas and Ernest looked at each other.

"Sure, Obermann," Lucas said. "Put the moves on her. You're an Israeli — you've got to go for it. Forget the fact that her only son's in a coma. That her husband is a former American ambassador and a congressman. Make her trip to the Holy Land a memorable one. You asshole!"

Ernest stood up to go. "You know," he said, "I understand them. I do. I can sympathize with them."

It was Lucas and Obermann's turn to exchange looks.

"With whom, Ernest?" Lucas asked.

"With the people who want to build the Temple. Because they want the Land to stand for more than just all-night falafel stands in Tel Aviv. I didn't come all the way from Durban for that. I want it to mean something too."

"But it does," Obermann said. "It will."

He looked at Lucas again and began to speak. But then, as though he had been reminded of something, he went back to packing his slides.

73

SONIA HAD BEEN lying on her sofa watching a tennis match on television when Lucas arrived at her apartment in Rehavia. A bowl of fruit was set beside the couch. Her hands were bandaged and she had a gauze dressing over one ear. She was wearing a kerchief to cover the places where her hair was gone.

"They're all first-degree burns," she said. "So I'm coping."

"First degree?" Lucas said. "That sounds bad."

"Actually it's good. Superficial. From the flash. Third degree is bad." She looked at herself in a wall mirror. "Even though I look like a crispy critter." She gave the smile that always quickened his heart a little. "Thanks for coming to the hospital with me. And for waiting around."

"Hey," Lucas said. "Least I could do."

"How's Razz?"

"No better."

"Any hope, do they say?"

"I don't think they know. I don't think he's brain dead. Just comatose. So I guess there's always hope. You know, I met his mother the other day. She might be calling you while she's here."

"What's she like?"

"She's lovely," Lucas said. "Beautiful. Heartbroken. Gets to you."

"I'm sure," Sonia said. "Do you have any more of a line on what happened?"

"A lot we'll probably never know," Lucas said. He gave her a rundown on what he knew about the things that they had seen and been part of. He told her what he knew about the scattered disciples. The Rose had taken a leave home to Canada. Sister John was in Holland.

"I think a lot about Nuala," Sonia said. "Nuala and Rashid. Could have been me, you know."

"I guess so," Lucas said. "One of the last casualties of the Cold War."

"But they'll never name a street after them," Sonia said. "Or a dorm at Lumumba University. I don't even think they call it Lumumba University anymore."

"We'll remember," Lucas said. "Of course, she could be a terrible pain in the ass."

"That was her job, Chris. Bugging complacent bourgeois types like you."

"She was good at it."

They sat in silence while the tennis match ran with the sound off.

"I have to leave the country for a while," he said. "How about coming with me?"

"Oh, gee," she said. His heart sank then because he could see she was about to keep it light, could see how it would end with them. Nothing, though, could keep him from trying for her. He'd beg, if that would help. But he knew that nothing would. "Where would we go?"

"I thought we might get a place on the Upper West Side. Around Columbia, maybe. You know, I grew up there."

"Yes, I know," she said. "Wouldn't that be nice."

Because he had nothing to lose, he told her everything he had hoped for, dreamed about.

"I thought we might even get married, if we wanted to. And I thought . . . we might have these great-looking brown kids like they have in that neighborhood. And I heard they were going to open the Thalia again. And, who knows, the Thalia might play *Enfants du Paradis* again, like it used to. And we could go and see it." He shrugged and stopped.

"No, Chris." She reached over and took his hand in her gauze-covered palm. "No, baby. I'm staying here. I'm home."

"Well," he said, "we wouldn't, like, not come back. I have work here. We'd come back a lot."

"I'm making *aliyah*," she said. "I'm going to practice."

"You mean practice . . ."

"I mean practice my faith. Here. And wherever things take me. And this is where I'll come home to."

"That would be all right," Lucas said. "I could convert. I'm half-way there, right?"

She laughed sadly. "Don't put me on, honey. You'll be a Catholic until your dying day. Regardless of what you say you believe. Or think you believe."

"We've been through so much together," he said. "We know each other so well. And I love you so much. I was hoping so much you'd stay with me."

"I love you too, Christopher. I do. But let me tell you something. When I'm not here trying to be the best Jew I can be, I'm going to be in Liberia. Rwanda. Tanzania. In Sudan. Cambodia. I don't know, man, Chechenya. Every township and barrio and shit town. You don't want that. You want to write your book and then you're going to write another and you want a family. I can't live a family life around cholera and bad water and rage. And that's my life, baby. You like traveling, but you like the Colony Hotel too. You like Fink's. I don't go to those places. They don't let me in."

"You like music."

"Chris, you ever watch people collect corn kernels out of other people's feces?"

"I know the NGO world, Sonia. I'd go for the parties."

"Sweetheart, it is not what you want. Do you think I haven't thought about this? Do you think I don't want you? Don't make it hard for me."

"I should make it easy? Think it's easy for me?"

She got up and sat on the floor beside his chair.

"I love you too. I always will. But in the important ways, brother, our paths diverge here. We'll always be friends."

"I was afraid," Lucas said, "you'd say that. 'She's gonna smile and say,' " he sang, " 'Can't we be friends?' " Old song. It was in her repertory, gender reversed.

"Well, we will. We'll see each other again. But if you have to ask me will you be my wife? I have to say no. I don't want that. I want to be free and I want to be here and Jewish and I want to do my little no-account bit for *tikkun olam*. Even if I use up life that way. I'm sorry, my love. There's no doubt in my mind."

"I guess," Lucas said, "I have to believe you."

"You do," she said. "You have to believe me."

He stood up and helped her back to the sofa.

"So sit," he said. "Get off the floor." Going back to his chair, he looked at the silent television set. "Maybe you want to watch the game. I should really leave."

"Oh, come off it," she said. "I'll tell you what — in three years maybe I'll see you at the Floridita in Havana if they let us in. Don't let me catch you with no hooker."

"I'll tell *you* what," Lucas said. "If I'm not at the Floridita, I'll be in Phnom Penh. Look for me at the Café No Problem. To find the Café No Problem, you turn left at the Genocide Museum."

"Christopher!"

"I'm not kidding. It is! Would I joke about a thing like that?"

"Seriously," she said. "What's next for you?"

"I don't know. I have to leave. But I'm going to keep working with Obermann on the book. I guess the relevant powers didn't tell you to make yourself scarce."

"No," she said. "They told me to keep my mouth shut in public. Which I'll do. This time, anyway. Then, as far as I'm concerned, they'll owe me."

"You'll be working for Mossad next."

"Yeah? I don't think so. I don't think I'll be asked. I'm gonna give them such a hard time they'll wish they'd never seen my funny-colored nose."

"You know," Lucas said, "I was just talking to Ernest. He said he sympathized in a way with the guys who were going to bomb and build the Temple. Because they wanted the country to mean something and so did he."

He felt that he needed to keep talking to her. He did not want to leave her, neither did he want to see her slip away.

"The Temple is inside," she said. "The Temple is the Law."

"A lot of people," Lucas said, "think that's been the way too long. They want the real thing."

"Sure," she said. "And the fulfillment of prophecy. Me, I think they're wrong. Lots of places have temples. Utah has a temple. Amritsar. Kyoto. The Temple has to be in the heart. When everybody builds it there, maybe then they can think about Beautiful Gates and the Holy of Holies."

"You'll have a tough time with that."

"Yeah. Well, I'm here to make trouble. I'm a Third World person. And I'm here and I'm entitled."

"Going back to the Strip?"

"I probably will. Someone should fill in for Nuala. Looking after those kids."

"People will call you a traitor."

"Well, I'm not one. I'm not the traitor." She laughed at him. "Don't forget, I really love you. I have ever since you told me that poem."

"Which poem was that?"

"The one about the children. The ones who'd learn to sing before they learned to speak. The thirsty children."

The call to prayer sounded distantly from Silwan.

"Oh," Lucas said, "those children."

"Right," she said. "Milk all the way."

74

L UCAS TOOK his time about removing. He had little more than books to dispose of, and of these he donated many to the hospices in the Old City. Sadness and anxiety dogged him.

Tracking the English-language press for leaks and significances took up part of his day. He held almost daily conferences with Obermann, who was watching the Hebrew press for the same material. The most interesting speculation appeared in the leftist Tel Aviv magazine *Ha'olam Hazeh,* but the forces inside the government tended to employ *Ma'ariv* and the *Jerusalem Post* for leaks.

As if to confirm what Ernest Gross had suggested, Avram Lind began his rise as a political figure of consequence, often profiled and quoted. Lind was plainly a skilled politician. He managed to subtly connect extremist Jewish forces with the recent disorders while concentrating his attacks on the influence of Christian fundamentalist millenarians in the city. The elements within the establishment who had incorporated the fundamentalists into their schemes could only fume silently. Popular opinion was with Lind.

Old British-mandate laws protecting the security of official secrets and criminal prosecutions were invoked, and there was not much hard information to be had about arrests.

Dr. Lestrade had been deposed and kicked out of the country. The public became acquainted with some of his anti-Semitic statements and his taste for the music of Orff and Wagner. A Palestinian youth was discovered to whom Lestrade had made an affectionate present of Alfred Rosenberg's *Myth of the Twentieth Century.*

From time to time, Lucas took walks in the Old City. Sometimes it seemed the place still smelled of burning rubber and tear gas.

There was a reinforced, though discreetly deployed, IDF presence. He strolled in the Bab al-Hadid and had a cup of pomegranate juice at the place where the proprietor's handicapped son swept floors. He was kept waiting a long time for his juice and was served grimly. But the retarded youth smiled and shook hands with Lucas, causing his father and brothers to speak sharply to him.

Lucas often passed the former madrasah where the Palestinians of African descent had lived and where Berger kept his apartment. How clearly he could remember his first glimpse of Sonia, in her henna tattoos and mysterious Eritrean burnoose. The black children had returned, and played soccer in the long shadows of the court-yard.

Sally Conners had a translator who rendered the Arabic-language press into English, and she passed copies of her summaries on to Lucas. He went out with her a few times and heard the story of her life, which, given her youth, was brief, though not uneventful. She had gone to York University and worked as an editorial assistant in Toronto and Boston. She liked to go rock climbing in the Lake District and in northern Wales.

A week or two before he left the country, he went with Sally to the Sinai and they dived the Red Sea. To make the wall dive, they had to crawl in their wet suits over a field of bleached coral that was mined with spiny sea urchins. At the end of the bleached field, the great wall began; they slid off the coral heads and into the bottomless turquoise depths, through clouds of wrasse and tangs in columns of cooling sunlight.

As they descended the face of the wall, the violent desert light sparkled on the creatures that inhabited it. There were sea fans and elkhorn and sea pens, bright grouper audibly crunching the coral and giant golden anemones. Lucas suddenly imagined it as some counterpart of the Kotel, the wall of a temple to the Lord of Creation. Occasionally, the plunging shafts of light awoke the dun colors of the hammerheads prowling far, far below. All the creatures were of the Indo-Pacific, to remind you that out across that blue infinity lay the Indian Ocean, the Indies.

After their dive, out of sheer animal spirits, or at least out of Sally's, they made love and became friends. The Sinai town was full of Italians and places that catered to them, so they drank sangiovese.

"Umm," she said, "spaghetti Bolognese!"

They went to St. Catherine's Monastery and climbed Jebel Musa, the putative Mount Sinai. Lucas picked up a handful of the red stones and put them in his pocket.

Sally was a lovely, fearless child, well read and with a vast, untroubled confidence in her own education. She had black hair and eyes as blue as the Indian Ocean. He tried to fall in love with her, but it was Sonia he wanted. Still, when in the last days before his departure Obermann made a pass at her at the Bixx, Lucas was secretly relieved that she shot him down.

One day, outside the Russian Compound, Lucas encountered Mr. Majoub, the lawyer from Gaza.

"Can I buy you a cup of coffee?" Lucas asked.

"Why not?" said Majoub. They went to the Atara.

Lucas ventured the prospect of his consulting Mr. Majoub on a regular basis in the course of writing his book. He felt, he told Mr. Majoub, that there should be a Palestinian perspective. Majoub agreed.

"No doubt you heard," Majoub said, "that during the disturbances the rumor spread that Salman Rushdie was in the city?"

Lucas flushed. "Yes," he said, "I heard something to that effect."

Majoub smiled very slightly.

"The foreign press were amused," he said. "I'm sure the security forces were also."

"Well," Lucas said, "no one on the spot was in a position to be *too* amused. By anything."

"You were present? At the disturbances?"

"Yes, I was."

"Of course the talk about Rushdie was absurd. There is little hatred for Rushdie here. He is not the enemy."

"I understand that," Lucas said. "I was once told that Woody Allen had come to Jerusalem. It was not," Lucas explained, "a hostile story."

Majoub laughed. "I also have heard this. It was a while ago, no?"

"Yes, a while back."

"When people are powerless," Majoub told him, "when they are very far from power and enraged that their lives are controlled by others — they hang on rumor. The most unlikely stories gain credence among the powerless. We see this every day. Our people in their wretchedness are cut off from the world. For the most part, neither education nor information is available to them. So they become credulous."

"I understand," Lucas said. By now he had claimed to understand anything anyone offered.

The night before he left the country, Lucas had a dream. It began in the Church of the Holy Sepulchre, but the venue kept changing. Pinchas Obermann was in it.

"Sonia was only a singer in Tel Aviv," Obermann was explaining. "You never knew her. You imagined the things that happened, out of guilt."

He also said, "Your mother was never your mother."

"What about my father?" Lucas asked. He and Obermann seemed to have been transported to the top of Mount Sinai, where they could see the sparkling ocean in three directions.

Obermann said, "Your father had nothing to do with you. You are the individual. It's a serious wound. Your mother promised God you would die."

He woke up thinking: Lilith. Lilith bore thousands. He was terrified. His first coherent, conscious thought concerned his age. He was getting older and was still alone. The individual. The two-for-a-farthing sparrow, on the roof of the house.

His departing flight left in the morning, and the *sherut* taking him to Lod passed the tracks of the Tel Aviv train. He saw the field where the old man had been watering kale at Eastertime. The sight stirred his memory and made him recall the dream and this was what he thought about on the way to the airport. The dream and Sonia.

At the airport there was the usual endless, apparently pointless questioning by the young security person. Lucas's examination took longer than most, so long that he was moved out of line in order not to inconvenience the people behind him.

He wondered if he would be taken to a room and questioned directly by Shabak, whether they would ask to see his notes. But no one did. The young woman examining him excused herself for long periods, obviously checking various points with her superiors, but no one else engaged him.

He was walking toward the gate when the young woman he had spoken with called to him.

"Just a moment, sir!"

Security guards, in uniform and in plain clothes, seemed to materialize from every quarter.

"May I ask you what you have in your pocket?"

In no time at all he was being patted down by a person or persons he could not see. He reached into his pocket and came up with the handful of red stones he had picked up on Sinai.

The security woman looked at him questioningly.

"From Sinai," he told her. "To keep."

"Stones?"

"Because they're from here," he said.

She stared at him for a moment and then gave him a smile of such radiance that all the angular suspicion of her features passed away. It made him think again of the *Zohar:* "The light is the light of the eye."

She passed him again later and he gave her a little thumbs-up sign.

He was flying out business class; he had gotten an upgrade on mileage. He took his aisle seat in the cabin and ordered champagne. Moments after takeoff, the plane was over hazy blue ocean. The brown land fell away aft.

The stones were still in his hand, and when his champagne came he spilled them out onto the tray table. When the flight attendant brought him the drink she asked about them.

"Just rocks," he said. "From Sinai. Or what's supposed to be Sinai."

"Oh," she said, "were you there?"

He began to stammer. Perhaps it was the prospect of champagne in the morning. Had he stood on Sinai?

"Yes," he said. "I guess so."

When they approached Frankfurt, where he would be changing planes, he had a moment's panic. New York? But he had no life in New York. No one there. Yet that was a ridiculous notion. One always had a life. Whatever you lived, wherever you lived it, was life.

Yet he kept thinking of life lost. A woman lost, a faith, a father lost, all lost. So he had to remind himself of something an American painter whose work he had once seen at the Whitney had offered as a credo, which had been fixed to the wall beside his work, and which Lucas had never forgotten:

"Losing it is as good as having it."

It was a hard text, one of great subtlety. One needed the *pilpul,* the analytical skills, of a Raziel to interpret it.

It meant, he thought, that a thing is never truly perceived, appreciated or defined except in longing. A land in exile, a God in His absconding, a love in its loss. And that everyone loses everything in the end. But that certain things of their nature cannot be taken away while life lasts. Some things can never be lost utterly that were loved in a certain way.

At Frankfurt airport, between planes, it was a different world.

DAMASCUS GATE

A NOTE FROM THE AUTHOR

The idea of writing a book set in Jerusalem came to me when I first saw the city in 1985 after doing a travel article set in Egypt. I returned, and in 1992 visited Gaza and the West Bank and witnessed some of the disorders attendant on the *intifada,* the struggle that had been in progress for five years against the Israeli military administration. As a result of that trip, I set the action of the book in the spring and summer of 1992, with most events taking place in Jerusalem, as well as Tel Aviv, the Gaza Strip and Galilee.

In *Damascus Gate* I've tried to use a highly charged setting as a background for a story that juxtaposes personal and national dilemmas and conflicts. Jerusalem, with its mystery, timelessness and sacred warren of shrines, relics and commemorative sites, is impinged on by the modern world. Ancient conflicts are carried on with late-twentieth-century weapons and techniques. Pilgrims of all sorts continue to descend on the city as the millennium approaches, obsessed with hopes and illusions that for some are deeply intimate and others hope to project on a vast scale. Frequently the pilgrims become caught up in the ongoing quarrels of the city, sometimes as opportunists, enthusiasts or mere pawns.

Jerusalem is a city in which past, present and future seem to coexist in a way that has no parallel elsewhere. Unlike those of the ancient Greek cities or Rome, its crumbling stones, like Herod's ruined temple built on the site of Solomon's, do not represent a time that has vanished from relevance, but ongoing history, which is the stuff of present struggle and of future prophecy.

At the same time, the city and its environs are a low-grade war zone, where different factions and the security agencies of several countries maneuver for control and advantage. It seemed to me that Jerusalem was an ideal setting for the sort of book I wanted to make *Damascus Gate* and the only one in which I could present characters who represented my reflections.

—Robert Stone

1. Discuss whether and how this book changed your feelings about the situation in the Middle East. Do you believe you understand the many sides of the issues better after reading *Damascus Gate*? How did your own knowledge of this complex place affect your perception of the book? Do you wish you had known more about the religious groups depicted in this book before reading it?

2. How do you feel about Lucas's alternately concealing and revealing his Jewish heritage, depending on the situation he finds himself in? Is he being duplicitous or savvy? Is this strategy any different from Sonia's decision to choose her clothing based on which neighborhood she will be in? How?

3. Is De Kuff a visionary prophet or merely delusional? Is there a fine line between the two? If his preaching helps people, does it matter if he is crazy?

4. At what point is Lucas's role as a journalist eclipsed by his personal quest? What is Lucas questing for? Has he, in fact, been seeking spiritual fulfillment all along? If so, does he consciously decide that he is ready to begin this search? What, in the end, does he discover and does he find it satisfying? How does his background affect his approach to writing about Jerusalem Syndrome—and how does writing about Jerusalem Syndrome affect his quest?

5. *Damascus Gate* has been called "a millennial thriller" (*Booklist*), and a "millennial novel of the millennial place" (Annie Dillard). But aren't the issues explored in this novel—who we are, where we are going, what ultimately matters—questions that have always existed for us in one form or another? What particularly gives this book such strongly millennial overtones?

6. Discuss the nature of the thriller as a genre and how it applies to *Damascus Gate*. How does this book adhere to the conventions of the genre? How does its style and substance differ from more traditional thrillers, like those by Grisham or Turow?

7. Compare the character, motivations, and goals of Raziel and De Kuff. Who is the stronger person and in what way? What does each have to offer the other? Who is really being manipulated and who is really pulling the strings?

8. What is the significance of the title *Damascus Gate*? What is the Damascus Gate and how does it figure in the novel? Given the biblical story of what happens to St. Paul on the

road to Damascus, what metaphorical suggestion might the title have? How does the literal representation of the Gate tie in with its spiritual implications?

9. Ericksen claims that "[Satan's] power has never been greater than it is today" (page 90). What does he mean by this statement? How might it be influenced by the greater availability of information and technology in our world? Is it too easy for us to think we have all the answers? Is it too easy for God to be lost in such a world?

10. Compare Sonia and Linda. How are they different from each other, but how are they also similar? Do they have more in common with each other than they realize? Can they both be described as followers? If so, what is different about the way each one "follows" her leader? Who is more dangerous to herself and/or to others?

11. The House of Galilean is ultimately exposed as a scam. Does this revelation make the sincere devotion of its followers any less legitimate? How much difference is there between the House of Galilean and other mainstream organizations that promote a religious doctrine while also making money? Where do we draw the line?

12. Nuala gets Sonia entangled in transporting both drugs and weapons, even though Sonia's Sufism prohibits any involvement with illegal substances or violence. Do Nuala's passionate beliefs excuse her for putting her friends in danger and for disregarding Sonia's strongest convictions? To what extent is Sonia responsible for her actions? Should one be willing to do *anything*—even break the law—in the name of religion or of personal belief? How might those situations differ? Do strong religious beliefs ever justify violence or deception?

13. What is it about Nuala that Lucas finds so compelling? What drives her to put her life on the line? In the end, is she a martyr who dies for her cause? Or does she simply get what is coming to her? What does Nuala ultimately accomplish?

14. Most of the main characters in *Damascus Gate* are foreign to Israel. What is the significance of being a "foreigner" in Jerusalem? Do you think the author is suggesting that most people in Israel are foreigners of one kind or another? Discuss how the story might be different if it were told from a native's point of view, and how that point of view would be affected by the quarter in which the native lived.

15. How does Berger's death affect Sonia's beliefs? Her behavior? Her need for someone or something to follow? Who is Berger's replacement in Sonia's life? Lucas? De Kuff? No one? Has she become permanently unmoored? What do you think will happen to her after the novel's conclusion?

16. Despite their differences and conflicting belief systems, some of the characters in this book become close friends and confidants. How is this possible? Are these true friendships or fleeting alliances of convenience? How do their personal differences affect their relationships? How do they influence on one another's beliefs? Do any of them truly change their beliefs during the course of the novel? How and why does this happen?

17. Discuss the morality of characters like Zimmer and Fotheringill. Are they villains willing to do anything or side with anyone simply for financial gain? Or does their admitting their true motivations make them honest, if also offensive? What are their roles in the plot to bomb the Temple Mount? What do these roles show us about their characters? Did you think better or worse of them after discovering their true intent?

18. Discuss the fallout of the bomb plot. How did you react to the ending? Were you surprised? How did it affect your perception of the characters? Discuss how knowing the outcome would have affected your reading of the novel.

19. Whether or not Lucas has discovered what he was looking for, he has come to the end of a journey. Where do you think he will go from here? How do you think his experiences in Jerusalem will affect him in the future? What might he be seeking now, that he was not seeking before?